Tales of the Dying Earth

By Jack Vance from Tom Doherty Associates

Alastor
Araminta Station
Big Planet
The Demon Princes, Vols. One and Two
The Dragon Masters
Ecce and Old Earth
The Gray Prince
Green Magic
The Language of Pao
The Last Castle
Night Lamp
Planet of Adventure
Ports of Call
Showboat World
Tales of the Dying Earth
To Live Forever
Throy

Tales of the Dying Earth

The Dying Earth
The Eyes of the Overworld
Cugel's Saga
Rhialto the Marvellous

Jack Vance

A Tom Doherty Associates Book
New York

This is a work of fiction. All the characters and events portrayed in these novels are either fictitious or are used fictitiously.

TALES OF THE DYING EARTH

These novels were originally published together under the title *The Compleat Dying Earth* by the Science Fiction Book Club in December 1998.

An Orb Edition
Published by Tom Doherty Associates, LLC
175 Fifth Avenue
New York, NY 10010

www.tor.com

ISBN 0-312-87456-1

Printed in the United States of America

0 9 8 7

Contents

The Dying Earth

1

Turjan of Miir

Turjan sat in his workroom, legs sprawled out from the stool, back against and elbows on the bench. Across the room was a cage; into this Turjan gazed with rueful vexation. The creature in the cage returned the scrutiny with emotions beyond conjecture.

It was a thing to arouse pity—a great head on a small spindly body, with weak rheumy eyes and a flabby button of a nose. The mouth hung slackly wet, the skin glistened waxy pink. In spite of its manifest imperfection, it was to date the most successful product of Turjan's vats.

Turjan stood up, found a bowl of pap. With a long-handled spoon he held food to the creature's mouth. But the mouth refused the spoon and mush trickled down the glazed skin to fall on the rickety frame.

Turjan put down the bowl, stood back and slowly returned to his stool. For a week now it had refused to eat. Did the idiotic visage conceal perception, a will to extinction? As Turjan watched, the white-blue eyes closed, the great head slumped and bumped to the floor of the cage. The limbs relaxed: the creature was dead.

Turjan sighed and left the room. He mounted winding stone stairs and at last came out on the roof of his castle Miir, high above the river Derna. In the west the sun hung close to old earth; ruby shafts, heavy and rich as wine, slanted past the gnarled boles of the archaic forest to lay on the turfed forest floor. The sun sank in accordance with the old ritual; latter-day night fell across the forest, a soft, warm darkness came swiftly, and Turjan stood pondering the death of his latest creature.

He considered its many precursors: the thing all eyes, the boneless creature with the pulsing surface of its brain exposed, the beautiful female body whose intestines trailed out into the nutrient solution like seeking fibrils, the inverted inside-out creatures . . . Turjan sighed bleakly. His methods were at fault; a fundamental element was lacking from his synthesis, a matrix ordering the components of the pattern.

As he sat gazing across the darkening land, memory took Turjan to a night of years before, when the Sage had stood beside him.

"In ages gone," the Sage had said, his eyes fixed on a low star, "a thousand spells were known to sorcery and the wizards effected their wills. Today, as Earth dies, a hundred spells remain to man's knowledge, and these have come to us through the ancient books . . . But there is one called Pandelume, who knows all the spells, all the incantations, cantraps, runes, and thaumaturgies that have ever wrenched and molded space . . ." He had fallen silent, lost in his thoughts.

"Where is this Pandelume?" Turjan had asked presently.

"He dwells in the land of Embelyon," the Sage had replied, "but where this land lies, no one knows."

"How does one find Pandelume, then?"

The Sage had smiled faintly. "If it were ever necessary, a spell exists to take one there."

Both had been silent a moment; then the Sage had spoken, staring out over the forest.

"One may ask anything of Pandelume, and Pandelume will answer—provided that the seeker performs the service Pandelume requires. And Pandelume drives a hard bargain."

Then the Sage had shown Turjan the spell in question, which he had discovered in an ancient portfolio, and kept secret from all the world.

Turjan, remembering this conversation, descended to his study, a long low hall with stone walls and a stone floor deadened by a thick russet rug. The tomes which held Turjan's sorcery lay on the long table of black steel or were thrust helter-skelter into shelves. These were volumes compiled by many wizards of the past, untidy folios collected by the Sage, leather-bound librams setting forth the syllables of a hundred powerful spells, so cogent that Turjan's brain could know but four at a time.

Turjan found a musty portfolio, turned the heavy pages to the spell the Sage had shown him, the Call to the Violent Cloud. He stared down at the characters and they burned with an urgent power, pressing off the page as if frantic to leave the dark solitude of the book.

Turjan closed the book, forcing the spell back into oblivion. He robed himself with a short blue cape, tucked a blade into his belt, fitted the amulet holding Laccodel's Rune to his wrist. Then he sat down and from a journal chose the spells he would take with him. What dangers he might meet he could not know, so he selected three spells of general application: the Excellent Prismatic Spray, Phandaal's Mantle of Stealth, and the Spell of the Slow Hour.

He climbed the parapets of his castle and stood under the far stars, breathing the air of ancient Earth . . . How many times had this air been breathed before him? What cries of pain had this air experienced, what sighs, laughs, war shouts, cries of exultation, gasps . . .

The night was wearing on. A blue light wavered in the forest. Turjan watched a moment, then at last squared himself and uttered the Call to the Violent Cloud.

All was quiet; then came a whisper of movement swelling to the roar of great winds. A wisp of white appeared and waxed to a pillar of boiling black smoke. A voice deep and harsh issued from the turbulence.

"At your disturbing power is this instrument come; whence will you go?"

"Four Directions, then One," said Turjan. "Alive must I be brought to Embelyon."

The cloud whirled down; far up and away he was snatched, flung head over heels into incalculable distance. Four directions was he thrust, then one, and at last a great blow hurled him from the cloud, sprawled him into Embelyon.

Turjan gained his feet and tottered a moment, half-dazed. His senses steadied; he looked about him.

He stood on the bank of a limpid pool. Blue flowers grew about his ankles and at his back reared a grove of tall blue-green trees, the leaves blurring on high into mist. Was Embelyon of Earth? The trees were Earth-like, the flowers were of familiar form, the air was of the same texture . . . But there was an odd lack to this land and it was difficult to determine. Perhaps it came of the horizon's curious vagueness, perhaps from the blurring quality of the air, lucent and uncertain as water. Most strange, however, was the sky, a mesh of vast ripples and cross-ripples, and these refracted a thousand shafts of colored light, rays which in mid-air wove wondrous laces, rainbow nets, in all the jewel hues. So as Turjan watched, there swept over him beams of claret, topaz, rich violet, radiant green. He now perceived that the colors of the flowers and the trees were but fleeting functions of the sky, for now the flowers were of salmon tint, and the trees a dreaming purple. The flowers deepened to copper, then with a suffusion of crimson, warmed through maroon to scarlet, and the trees had become sea-blue.

"The Land None Knows Where," said Turjan to himself. "Have I been brought high, low, into a pre-existence or into the after-world?" He looked toward the horizon and thought to see a black curtain rising high into the murk, and this curtain encircled the land in all directions.

The sound of galloping hooves approached; he turned to find a black horse lunging break-neck along the bank of the pool. The rider was a young woman with black hair streaming wildly. She wore loose white breeches to the knee and a yellow cape flapping in the wind. One hand clutched the reins, the other flourished a sword.

Turjan warily stepped aside, for her mouth was tight and white as if in anger, and her eyes glowed with a peculiar frenzy. The woman hauled back on the reins, wheeled her horse high around, charged Turjan, and struck out at him with her sword.

Turjan jumped back and whipped free his own blade. When she lunged at him again, he fended off the blow and leaning forward, touched the point to her arm and brought a drop of blood. She drew back startled; then up from her saddle she snatched a bow and flicked an arrow to the string. Turjan sprang forward, dodging the wild sweep of her sword, seized her around the waist, and dragged her to the ground.

She fought with a crazy violence. He had no wish to kill her, and so struggled in a manner not entirely dignified. Finally he held her helpless, her arms pinioned behind her back.

"Quiet, vixen!" said Turjan, "lest I lose patience and stun you!"

"Do as you please," the girl gasped. "Life and death are brothers."

"Why do you seek to harm me?" demanded Turjan. "I have given you no offense."

"You are evil, like all existence." Emotion ground the delicate fibers of her throat. "If power were mine, I would crush the universe to bloody gravel, and stamp it into the ultimate muck."

Turjan in surprise relaxed his grip, and she nearly broke loose. But he caught her again.

"Tell me, where may I find Pandelume?"

The girl stilled her exertion, twisted her head to stare at Turjan. Then: "Search all Embelyon. I will assist you not at all."

If she were more amiable, thought Turjan, she would be a creature of remarkable beauty.

"Tell me where I may find Pandelume," said Turjan, "else I find other uses for you."

She was silent for a moment, her eyes blazing with madness. Then she spoke in a vibrant voice.

"Pandelume dwells beside the stream only a few paces distant."

Turjan released her, but he took her sword and bow.

"If I return these to you, will you go your way in peace?"

For a moment she glared; then without words she mounted her horse and rode off through the trees.

Turjan watched her disappear through the shafts of jewel colors, then went in the direction she had indicated. Soon he came to a long low manse of red stone backed by dark trees. As he approached the door swung open. Turjan halted in mid-stride.

"Enter!" came a voice. "Enter, Turjan of Miir!"

So Turjan wonderingly entered the manse of Pandelume. He found himself in a tapestried chamber, bare of furnishing save a single settee. No one came to greet him. A closed door stood at the opposite wall, and Turjan went to pass through, thinking perhaps it was expected of him.

"Halt, Turjan," spoke the voice. "No one may gaze on Pandelume. It is the law."

Turjan, standing in the middle of the room, spoke to his unseen host.

"This is my mission, Pandelume," he said. "For some time I have been striving to create humanity in my vats. Yet always I fail, from ignorance of the agent that binds and orders the patterns. This master-matrix must be known to you; therefore I come to you for guidance."

"Willingly will I aid you," said Pandelume. "There is, however, another aspect involved. The universe is methodized by symmetry and balance; in every aspect of existence is this equipoise observed. Consequently, even in the trivial scope of our dealings, this equivalence must be maintained, thus and thus. I agree to assist you; in return, you perform a service of equal value for me. When you have completed this small work, I will instruct and guide you to your complete satisfaction."

"What may this service be?" inquired Turjan.

"A man lives in the land of Ascolais, not far from your Castle Miir. About his neck hangs an amulet of carved blue stone. This you must take from him and bring to me."

Turjan considered a moment.

"Very well," he said. "I will do what I can. Who is the man?"

Pandelume answered in a soft voice.

"Prince Kandive the Golden."

"Ah," exclaimed Turjan ruefully, "you have gone to no pains to make my task a pleasant one . . . But I will fulfill your requirement as best I can.''

''Good,'' said Pandelume. ''Now I must instruct you. Kandive wears this amulet hidden below his singlet. When an enemy appears, he takes it out to display on his chest, such is the potency of the charm. No matter what else, do not gaze on this amulet, either before or after you take it, on pain of most hideous consequence.''

''I understand,'' said Turjan. ''I will obey. Now there is a question I would ask—providing the answer will not involve me in an undertaking to bring the Moon back to Earth, or recover an elixir you inadvertently spilled in the sea.''

Pandelume laughed loud. ''Ask on,'' he responded, ''and I will answer.''

Turjan put his question.

''As I approached your dwelling, a woman of insane fury wished to kill me. This I would not permit and she departed in rage. Who is this woman and why is she thus?''

Pandelume's voice was amused. ''I, too,'' he replied, ''have vats where I mold life into varied forms. This girl T'sais I created, but I wrought carelessly, with a flaw in the synthesis. So she climbed from the vat with a warp in her brain, in this manner: what we hold to be beautiful seems to her loathsome and ugly, and what we find ugly is to her intolerably vile, in a degree that you and I cannot understand. She finds the world a bitter place, people with shapes of direst malevolence.''

''So this is the answer,'' Turjan murmured. ''Pitiable wretch!''

''Now,'' said Pandelume, ''you must be on your way to Kaiin; the auspices are good . . . In a moment open this door, enter, and move to the pattern of runes on the floor.''

Turjan performed as he was bid. He found the next room to be circular and high-domed, with the varying lights of Embelyon pouring down through sky-transparencies. When he stood upon the pattern in the floor, Pandelume spoke again.

''Now close your eyes, for I must enter and touch you. Heed well, do not try to glimpse me!''

Turjan closed his eyes. Presently a step sounded behind him. ''Extend your hand,'' said the voice. Turjan did so, and felt a hard object placed therein. ''When your mission is accomplished, crush this crystal and at once you will find yourself in this room.'' A cold hand was laid on his shoulder.

''An instant you will sleep,'' said Pandelume. ''When you awake you will be in the city Kaiin.''

The hand departed. A dimness came over Turjan as he stood awaiting the passage. The air had suddenly become full of sound: clattering, a tinkling of many small bells, music, voices. Turjan frowned, pursed his lips: A strange tumult for the austere home of Pandelume!

A woman's voice sounded close by.

''Look, O Santanil, see the man-owl who closes his eyes to merriment!''

There was a man's laughter, suddenly hushed. ''Come. The fellow is bereft and possibly violent. Come.''

Turjan hesitated, then opened his eyes. It was night in white-walled Kaiin, and festival time. Orange lanterns floated in the air, moving as the breeze took them. From the balconies dangled flower chains and cages of blue fire-flies. The streets surged with the wine-flushed populace, costumed in a multitude of bizarre modes. Here was a Melantine bargeman, here a warrior of Valdaran's Green Legion, here another of ancient times wearing one of the old helmets. In a little cleared space a garlanded courtesan of the Kauchique littoral danced the Dance of the Fourteen Silken Movements to the music of flutes. In the shadow of a balcony a girl barbarian of East Almery embraced a man blackened and in leather harness as a Deodand of the forest. They were gay, these people of waning Earth, feverishly merry, for infinite night was close at hand, when the red sun should finally flicker and go black.

Turjan melted into the throng. At a tavern he refreshed himself with biscuits and wine; then he made for the palace of Kandive the Golden.

The palace loomed before him, every window and balcony aglow with light. Among the lords of the city there was feasting and revelry. If Prince Kandive were flushed with drink and unwary, reflected Turjan, the task should not be too difficult. Yet, entering boldly, he might be recognized, for he was known to many in Kaiin. So, uttering Phandaal's Mantle of Stealth, he faded from the sight of all men.

Through the arcade he slipped, into the grand salon, where the lords of Kaiin made merry like the throngs of the street. Turjan threaded the rainbow of silk, velour, sateen, watching the play with amusement. On a terrace some stood looking into a sunken pool where a pair of captured Deodands, their skins like oiled jet, paddled and glared; others tossed darts at the spread-eagled body of a young Cobalt Mountain witch. In alcoves beflowered girls offered synthetic love to wheezing old men, and elsewhere others lay stupefied by dream-powders. Nowhere did Turjan find Prince Kandive. Through the palace he wandered, room after room, until at last in an upper chamber he came upon the tall golden-bearded prince, lolling on a couch with a masked girl-child who had green eyes and hair dyed pale green.

Some intuition or perhaps a charm warned Kandive when Turjan slipped through the purple hangings. Kandive leapt to his feet.

"Go!" he ordered the girl. "Out of the room quickly! Mischief moves somewhere near and I must blast it with magic!"

The girl ran hastily from the chamber. Kandive's hand stole to his throat and pulled forth the hidden amulet. But Turjan shielded his gaze with his hand.

Kandive uttered a powerful charm which loosened space free of all warp. So Turjan's spell was void and he became visible.

"Turjan of Miir skulks through my palace!" snarled Kandive.

"With ready death on my lips," spoke Turjan. "Turn your back, Kandive, or I speak a spell and run you through with my sword."

Kandive made as if to obey, but instead shouted the syllables bringing the Omnipotent Sphere about him.

"Now I call my guards, Turjan," announced Kandive contemptuously, "and you shall be cast to the Deodands in the tank."

Kandive did not know the engraved band Turjan wore on his wrist, a most powerful rune, maintaining a field solvent of all magic. Still guarding his vision against the amulet, Turjan stepped through the Sphere. Kandive's great blue eyes bulged.

"Call the guards," said Turjan. "They will find your body riddled by lines of fire."

"*Your* body, Turjan!" cried the prince, babbling the spell. Instantly the blazing wires of the Excellent Prismatic Spray lashed from all directions at Turjan. Kandive watched the furious rain with a wolfish grin, but his expression changed quickly to consternation. A finger's breath from Turjan's skin the fire-darts dissolved into a thousand gray puffs of smoke.

"Turn your back, Kandive," Turjan ordered. "Your magic is useless against Laccodel's Rune." But Kandive took a step toward a spring in the wall.

"Halt!" cried Turjan. "One more step and the Spray splits you thousandfold!"

Kandive stopped short. In helpless rage he turned his back and Turjan, stepping forward quickly, reached over Kandive's neck, seized the amulet and raised it free. It crawled in his hand and through the fingers there passed a glimpse of blue. A daze shook his brain, and for an instant he heard a murmur of avid voices . . . His vision cleared. He backed away from Kandive, stuffing the amulet in his pouch. Kandive asked, "May I now turn about in safety?"

"When you wish," responded Turjan, clasping his pouch. Kandive, seeing Turjan occupied, negligently stepped to the wall and placed his hand on a spring.

"Turjan," he said, "you are lost. Before you may utter a syllable, I will open the floor and drop you a great dark distance. Can your charms avail against this?"

Turjan halted in mid-motion, fixed his eyes upon Kandive's red and gold face. Then he dropped his eyes sheepishly. "Ah, Kandive," he fretted, "you have outwitted me. If I return you the amulet, may I go free?"

"Toss the amulet at my feet," said Kandive, gloating. "Also Laccodel's Rune. Then I shall decide what mercy to grant you."

"Even the Rune?" Turjan asked, forcing a piteous note to his voice.

"Or your life."

Turjan reached into his pouch and grasped the crystal Pandelume had given him. He pulled it forth and held it against the pommel of his sword.

"Ho, Kandive," he said, "I have discerned your trick. You merely wish to frighten me into surrender. I defy you!"

Kandive shrugged. "Die then." He pushed the spring. The floor jerked open, and Turjan disappeared into the gulf. But when Kandive raced below to claim Turjan's body, he found no trace, and he spent the rest of the night in temper, brooding over wine.

Turjan found himself in the circular room of Pandelume's manse. Embelyon's many-colored lights streamed through the sky-windows upon his shoulder—sapphire blue, the yellow of marigolds, blood red. There was silence through the house. Turjan moved away from the rune in the floor, glancing uneasily to the door, fearful lest Pandelume, unaware of his presence, enter the room.

"Pandelume!" he called. "I have returned!"

There was no response. Deep quiet held the house. Turjan wished he were in the open air where the odor of sorcery was less strong. He looked at the doors; one led to the entrance hall, the other he knew not where. The door on the right hand must lead outside; he laid his hand on the latch to pull it open. But he paused. Suppose he were mistaken, and Pandelume's form were revealed? Would it be wiser to wait here?

A solution occurred to him. His back to the door, he swung it open.

"Pandelume!" he called.

A soft intermittent sound came to his ears from behind, and he seemed to hear a labored breath. Suddenly frightened, Turjan stepped back into the circular room and closed the door.

He resigned himself to patience and sat on the floor.

A gasping cry came from the next room. Turjan leapt to his feet.

"Turjan? You are there?"

"Yes; I have returned with the amulet."

"Do this quickly," panted the voice. "Guarding your sight, hand the amulet over your neck and enter."

Turjan, spurred by the urgency of the voice, closed his eyes and arranged the amulet on his chest. He groped to the door and flung it wide.

Silence of a shocked intensity held an instant; then came an appalling screech, so wild and demoniac that Turjan's brain sang. Mighty pinions buffeted the air, there was a hiss and the scrape of metal. Then, amidst muffled roaring, an icy wind bit Turjan's face. Another hiss—and all was quiet.

"My gratitude is yours," said the calm voice of Pandelume. "Few times have I experienced such dire stress, and without your aid might not have repulsed that creature of hell."

A hand lifted the amulet from Turjan's neck. After a moment of silence Pandelume's voice sounded again from a distance.

"You may open your eyes."

Turjan did so. He was in Pandelume's workroom; amidst much else, he saw vats like his own.

"I will not thank you," said Pandelume. "But in order that a fitting symmetry be maintained, I perform a service for a service. I will not only guide your hands as you work among the vats, but also will I teach you other matters of value."

In this fashion did Turjan enter his apprenticeship to Pandelume. Day and far into the opalescent Embelyon night he worked under Pandelume's unseen tutelage. He learned the secret of renewed youth, many spells of the ancients, and a strange abstract lore that Pandelume termed "Mathematics."

"Within this instrument," said Pandelume, "resides the Universe. Passive in itself and not of sorcery, it elucidates every problem, each phase of existence, all the secrets of time and space. Your spells and runes are built upon its power and codified according to a great underlying mosaic of magic. The design of this mosaic we cannot surmise; our knowledge is didactic, empirical, arbitrary. Phandaal glimpsed the pattern and so was able to formulate many of the spells which bear his name. I have endeavored through the ages to break the clouded glass, but so far my research has failed. He who discovers the pattern will know all of sorcery and be a man powerful beyond comprehension.''

So Turjan applied himself to the study and learned many of the simpler routines.

''I find herein a wonderful beauty,'' he told Pandelume. ''This is no science, this is art, where equations fall away to elements like resolving chords, and where always prevails a symmetry either explicit or multiplex, but always of a crystalline serenity.''

In spite of these other studies, Turjan spent most of his time at the vats, and under Pandelume's guidance achieved the mastery he sought. As a recreation he formed a girl of exotic design, whom he named Floriel. The hair of the girl he had found with Kandive on the night of the festival had fixed in his mind; and he gave his creature pale green hair. She had skin of creamy tan and wide emerald eyes. Turjan was intoxicated with delight when he brought her wet and perfect from the vat. She learned quickly and soon knew how to speak with Turjan. She was one of dreamy and wistful habit, caring for little but wandering among the flowers of the meadow, or sitting silently by the river; yet she was a pleasant creature and her gentle manners amused Turjan.

But one day the black-haired T'sais came riding past on her horse, steely-eyed, slashing at flowers with her sword. The innocent Floriel wandered by and T'sais, exclaiming ''Green-eyed woman—your aspect horrifies me, it is death for you!'' cut her down as she had the flowers in her path.

Turjan, hearing the hooves, came from the workroom in time to witness the sword-play. He paled in rage and a spell of twisting torment rose to his lips. Then T'sais looked at him and cursed him, and in the pale face and dark eyes he saw her misery and the spirit that caused her to defy her fate and hold to her life. Many emotions fought in him, but at last he permitted T'sais to ride on. He buried Floriel by the river-bank and tried to forget her in intense study.

A few days later he raised his head from his work.

''Pandelume! Are you near?''

''What do you wish, Turjan?''

''You mentioned that when you made T'sais, a flaw warped her brain. Now I would create one like her, of the same intensity, yet sound of mind and spirit.''

''As you will,'' replied Pandelume indifferently, and gave Turjan the pattern.

So Turjan built a sister to T'sais, and day by day watched the same slender body, the same proud features take form.

When her time came, and she sat up in her vat, eyes glowing with joyful life, Turjan was breathless in haste to help her forth.

She stood before him wet and naked, a twin to T'sais, but where the face of T'sais was racked by hate, here dwelt peace and merriment; where the eyes of T'sais glowed with fury, here shone the stars of imagination.

Turjan stood wondering at the perfection of his own creation. "Your name shall be T'sain," said he, "and already I know that you will be part of my life."

He abandoned all else to teach T'sain, and she learned with marvelous speed.

"Presently we return to Earth," he told her, "to my home beside a great river in the green land of Ascolais."

"Is the sky of Earth filled with colors?" she inquired.

"No," he replied. "The sky of Earth is a fathomless dark blue, and an ancient red sun rides across the sky. When night falls the stars appear in patterns that I will teach you. Embelyon is beautiful, but Earth is wide, and the horizons extend far off into mystery. As soon as Pandelume wills, we return to Earth."

T'sain loved to swim in the river, and sometimes Turjan came down to splash her and toss rocks in the water while he dreamed. Against T'sais he had warned her, and she had promised to be wary.

But one day, as Turjan made preparations for departure, she wandered far afield through the meadows, mindful only of the colors at play in the sky, the majesty of the tall blurred trees, the changing flowers at her feet; she looked on the world with a wonder that is only for those new from the vats. Across several low hills she wandered, and through a dark forest where she found a cold brook. She drank and sauntered along the bank, and presently came upon a small dwelling.

The door being open, T'sain looked to see who might live here. But the house was vacant, and the only furnishings were a neat pallet of grass, a table with a basket of nuts, a shelf with a few articles of wood and pewter.

T'sain turned to go on her way, but at this moment she heard the ominous thud of hooves, sweeping close like fate. The black horse slid to a stop before her. T'sain shrank back in the doorway, all Turjan's warnings returning to her mind. But T'sais had dismounted and came forward with her sword ready. As she raised to strike, their eyes met, and T'sais halted in wonder.

It was a sight to excite the brain, the beautiful twins wearing the same white waist-high breeches, with the same intense eyes and careless hair, the same slim pale bodies, the one wearing on her face hate for every atom of the universe, the other a gay exuberance.

T'sais found her voice.

"How is this, witch? You bear my semblance, yet you are not me. Or has the boon of madness come at last to dim my sight of the world?"

T'sain shook her head. "I am T'sain. You are my twin, T'sais, my sister. For this I must love you and you must love me."

"Love? I love nothing! I will kill you and so make the world better by one less evil." She raised her sword again.

"No!" cried T'sain in anguish. "Why do you wish to harm me? I have done no wrong!"

"You do wrong by existing, and you offend me by coming to mock my own hideous mold."

T'sain laughed. "Hideous? No. I am beautiful, for Turjan says so. Therefore you are beautiful, too."

T'sais' face was like marble.

"You make sport of me."

"Never. You are indeed very beautiful."

T'sais dropped the point of her sword to the ground. Her face relaxed into thought.

"Beauty! What is beauty? Can it be that I am blind, that a fiend distorts my vision? Tell me, how does one see beauty?"

"I don't know," said T'sain. "It seems very plain to me. Is not the play of colors across the sky beautiful?"

T'sais looked up in astonishment. "The harsh glarings? They are either angry or dreary, in either case detestable."

"See how delicate are the flowers, fragile and charming."

"They are parasites, they smell vilely."

T'sain was puzzled. "I do not know how to explain beauty. You seem to find joy in nothing. Does nothing give you satisfaction?"

"Only killing and destruction. So then these must be beautiful."

T'sain frowned. "I would term these evil concepts."

"Do you believe so?"

"I am sure of it."

T'sais considered. "How can I know how to act? I have been certain, and now you tell me that I do evil!"

T'sain shrugged. "I have lived little, and I am not wise. Yet I know that everyone is entitled to life. Turjan could explain to you easily."

"Who is Turjan?" inquired T'sais.

"He is a very good man," replied T'sain, "and I love him greatly.

Soon we go to Earth, where the sky is vast and deep and of dark blue.''

''Earth. . . . If I went to Earth, could I also find beauty and love?''

''That may be, for you have a brain to understand beauty, and beauty of your own to attract love.''

''Then I kill no more, regardless of what wickedness I see. I will ask Pandelume to send me to Earth.''

T'sain stepped forward, put her arms around T'sais, and kissed her.

''You are my sister and I will love you.''

T'sais' face froze. Rend, stab, bite, said her brain, but a deeper surge welled up from her flowing blood, from every cell of her body, to suffuse her with a sudden flush of pleasure. She smiled.

''Then—I love you, my sister. I kill no more, and I will find and know beauty on Earth or die.''

T'sais mounted her horse and set out for Earth, seeking love and beauty.

T'sain stood in the doorway, watching her sister ride off through the colors. Behind her came a shout, and Turjan approached.

''T'sain! Has that frenzied witch harmed you?'' He did not wait for a reply. ''Enough! I kill her with a spell, that she may wreak no more pain.''

He turned to voice a terrible charm of fire, but T'sain put her hand to his mouth.

''No, Turjan, you must not. She has promised to kill no more. She goes to Earth seeking what she may not find in Embelyon.''

So Turjan and T'sain watched T'sais disappear across the many-colored meadow.

''Turjan,'' spoke T'sain.

''What is your wish?''

''When we come to Earth, will you find me a black horse like that of T'sais?''

''Indeed,'' said Turjan, laughing, as they started back to the house of Pandelume.

2

Mazirian the Magician

Deep in thought, Mazirian the Magician walked his garden. Trees fruited with many intoxications overhung his path, and flowers bowed obsequiously as he passed. An inch above the ground, dull as agates, the eyes of mandrakes followed the tread of his black-slippered feet. Such was Mazirian's garden—three terraces growing with strange and wonderful vegetations. Certain plants swam with changing iridescences; others held up blooms pulsing like sea-anemones, purple, green, lilac, pink, yellow. Here grew trees like feather parasols, trees with transparent trunks threaded with red and yellow veins, trees with foliage like metal foil, each leaf a different metal—copper, silver, blue tantalum, bronze, green iridium. Here blooms like bubbles tugged gently upward from glazed green leaves, there a shrub bore a thousand pipe-shaped blossoms, each whistling softly to make music of the ancient Earth, of the ruby-red sunlight, water seeping through black soil, the languid winds. And beyond the roqual hedge the trees of the forest made a tall wall of mystery. In this waning hour of Earth's life no man could count himself familiar with the glens, the glades, the dells and deeps, the secluded clearings, the ruined pavilions, the sun-dappled pleasaunces, the gullys and heights, the various brooks, freshets, ponds, the meadows, thickets, brakes and rocky outcrops.

Mazirian paced his garden with a brow frowning in thought. His step was slow and his arms were clenched behind his back. There was one who had brought him puzzlement, doubt, and a great desire: a delightful woman-creature who dwelt in the woods. She came to his garden half-laughing and always wary, riding a black horse with eyes like golden crystals. Many times had Mazirian tried to take her; always her horse had borne her from his varied enticements, threats, and subterfuges.

Agonized screaming jarred the garden. Mazirian, hastening his step, found a mole chewing the stalk of a plant-animal hybrid. He killed the marauder, and the screams subsided to a dull gasping. Mazirian stroked a furry leaf and the red mouth hissed in pleasure.

Then: "K-k-k-k-k-k-k," spoke the plant. Mazirian stooped, held the rodent to the red mouth. The mouth sucked, the small body slid into the stomach-bladder underground. The plant gurgled, eructated, and Mazirian watched with satisfaction.

The sun had swung low in the sky, so dim and red that the stars could be seen. And now Mazirian felt a watching presence. It would be the woman of the forest, for thus had she disturbed him before. He paused in his stride, feeling for the direction of the gaze.

He shouted a spell of immobilization. Behind him the plant-animal froze to rigidity and a great green moth wafted to the ground. He whirled around. There she was, at the edge of the forest, closer than ever she had approached before. Nor did she move as he advanced. Mazirian's young-old eyes shone. He would take her to his manse and keep her in a prison of green glass. He would test her brain with fire, with cold, with pain and with joy. She should serve him with wine and make the eighteen motions of allurement by yellow lamp-light. Perhaps she was spying on him; if so, the Magician would discover immediately, for he could call no man friend and had forever to guard his garden.

She was but twenty paces distant—then there was a thud and pound of black hooves as she wheeled her mount and fled into the forest.

The Magician flung down his cloak in rage. She held a guard—a counter-spell, a rune of protection—and always she came when he was ill-prepared to follow. He peered into the murky depths, glimpsed the wanness of her body flitting through a shaft of red light, then black shade and she was gone . . . Was she a witch? Did she come of her own volition, or—more likely—had an enemy sent her to deal him inquietude? If so, who might be guiding her? There was Prince Kandive the Golden, of Kaiin, whom Mazirian had bilked of his secret of renewed youth. There was Azvan the Astronomer, there was Turjan—hardly Turjan, and here Mazirian's face lit in a pleasing recollection . . . He put the thought aside. Azvan, at least, he could test. He turned his steps to his workshop, went to a table where rested a cube of clear crystal, shimmering with a red and blue aureole. From a cabinet he brought a bronze gong and a silver hammer. He tapped on the gong and the mellow tone sang through the room and out, away and beyond. He tapped again and again. Suddenly Azvan's face shone from the crystal, beaded with pain and great terror.

"Stay the strokes, Mazirian!" cried Azvan. "Strike no more on the gong of my life!"

Mazirian paused, his hand poised over the gong.

"Do you spy on me, Azvan? Do you send a woman to regain the gong?"

"Not I, Master, not I. I fear you too well."

"You must deliver me the woman, Azvan; I insist."

"Impossible, Master! I know not who or what she is!"

Mazirian made as if to strike. Azvan poured forth such a torrent of supplication that Mazirian with a gesture of disgust threw down the hammer and restored the gong to its place. Azvan's face drifted slowly away, and the fine cube of crystal shone blank as before.

Mazirian stroked his chin. Apparently he must capture the girl himself. Later, when black night lay across the forest, he would seek through his books for spells to guard him through the unpredictable glades. They would be poignant corrosive spells, of such a nature that one would daunt the brain of an ordinary man and two render him mad. Mazirian, by dint of stringent exercise, could encompass four of the most formidable, or six of the lesser spells.

He put the project from his mind and went to a long vat bathed in a flood of green light. Under a wash of clear fluid lay the body of a man, ghastly below the green glare, but of great physical beauty. His torso tappered from wide shoulders through lean flanks to long strong legs and arched feet; his face was clean and cold with hard flat features. Dusty golden hair clung about his head.

Mazirian stared at the thing, which he had cultivated from a single cell. It needed only intelligence, and this he knew not how to provide. Turjan of Miir held the knowledge, and Turjan—Mazirian glanced with a grim narrowing of the eyes at a trap in the floor—refused to part with his secret.

Mazirian pondered the creature in the vat. It was a perfect body; therefore might not the brain be ordered and pliant? He would discover. He set in motion a device to draw off the liquid and presently the body lay stark to the direct rays. Mazirian injected a minim of drug into the neck. The body twitched. The eyes opened, winced in the glare. Mazirian turned away the projector.

Feebly the creature in the vat moved its arms and feet, as if unaware of their use. Mazirian watched intently; perhaps he had stumbled on the right synthesis for the brain.

"Sit up!" commanded the Magician.

The creature fixed its eyes upon him, and reflexes joined muscle to muscle. It gave a throaty roar and sprang from the vat at Mazirian's throat. In spite of Mazirian's strength it caught him and shook him like a doll.

For all Mazirian's magic he was helpless. The mesmeric spell had been expended, and he had none other in his brain. In any event he could not have uttered the space-twisting syllables with that mindless clutch at his throat.

His hand closed on the neck of a leaden carboy. He swung and struck the head of his creature, which slumped to the floor.

Mazirian, not entirely dissatisfied, studied the glistening body at his feet. The spinal coordination had functioned well. At his table he mixed a white potion, and, lifting the golden head, poured the fluid into the lax mouth. The creature stirred, opened its eyes, propped itself on its elbows. The madness had left its face—but Mazirian sought in vain for the glimmer of intelligence. The eyes were as vacant as those of a lizard.

The Magician shook his head in annoyance. He went to the window and his brooding profile was cut black against the oval panes . . . Turjan once more? Under the most dire inquiry Turjan had kept his secret close. Mazirian's thin mouth curved wryly. Perhaps if he inserted another angle in the passage . . .

The sun had gone from the sky and there was dimness in Mazirian's garden. His white night-blossoms opened and their captive gray moths fluttered from bloom to bloom. Mazirian pulled open the trap in the floor and descended stone stairs. Down, down, down . . . At last a passage intercepted at right angles, lit with the yellow light of eternal lamps. To the left were his fungus beds, to the right a stout oak and iron door, locked with three locks. Down and ahead the stone steps continued, dropping into blackness.

Mazirian unlocked the three locks, flung wide the door. The room within was bare except for a stone pedestal supporting a glass-topped box. The box measured a yard on a side and was four or five inches high. Within the box—actually a squared passageway, a run with four right angles—moved two small creatures, one seeking, the other evading. The predator was a small dragon with furious red eyes and a monstrous fanged mouth. It waddled along the passage on six splayed legs, twitching its tail as it went. The other stood only half the size of the dragon—a strong-featured man, stark naked, with a copper fillet binding his long black hair. He moved slightly faster than his pursuer, which still kept relentless chase, using a measure of craft, speeding, doubling back, lurking at the angle in case the man should unwarily step around. By holding himself continually alert, the man was able to stay beyond the reach of the fangs. The man was Turjan, whom Mazirian by trickery had captured several weeks before, reduced in size and thus imprisoned.

Mazirian watched with pleasure as the reptile sprang upon the momentarily relaxing man, who jerked himself clear by the thickness of his skin. It was time, Mazirian thought, to give both rest and nourishment. He dropped panels across the passage, separating it into halves, isolating man from beast. To both he gave meat and pannikins of water.

Turjan slumped in the passage.

"Ah," said Mazirian, "you are fatigued. You desire rest?"

Turjan remained silent, his eyes closed. Time and the world had lost meaning for him. The only realities were the gray passage and the interminable flight. At unknown intervals came food and a few hours rest.

"Think of the blue sky," said Mazirian, "the white stars, your castle Miir by the river Derna; think of wandering free in the meadows."

The muscles at Turjan's mouth twitched.

"Consider, you might crush the little dragon under your heel."

Turjan looked up. "I would prefer to crush your neck, Mazirian."

Mazirian was unperturbed. "Tell me, how do you invest your vat creatures with intelligence? Speak, and you go free."

Turjan laughed, and there was madness in his laughter.

"Tell you? And then? You would kill me with hot oil in a moment."

Mazirian's thin mouth drooped petulantly.

"Wretched man, I know how to make you speak. If your mouth were stuffed, waxed and sealed, you would speak! Tomorrow I take a nerve from your arm and draw coarse cloth along its length."

The small Turjan, sitting with his legs across the passageway, drank his water and said nothing.

"Tonight," said Mazirian with studied malevolence, "I add an angle and change your run to a pentagon."

Turjan paused and looked up through the glass cover at his enemy. Then he slowly sipped his water. With five angles there would be less time to evade the charge of the monster, less of the hall in view from one angle.

"Tomorrow," said Mazirian, "you will need all your agility."

But another matter occurred to him. He eyed Turjan speculatively. "Yet even this I spare you if you assist me with another problem."

"What is your difficulty, febrile Magician?"

"The image of a woman-creature haunts my brain, and I would capture her." Mazirian's eyes went misty at the thought. "Late afternoon she comes to the edge of my garden riding a great black horse—you know her, Turjan?"

"Not I, Mazirian." Turjan sipped his water.

Mazirian continued. "She has sorcery enough to ward away Felojun's Second Hypnotic Spell—or perhaps she has some protective rune. When I approach, she flees into the forest."

"So then?" asked Turjan; nibbling the meat Mazirian had provided.

"Who may this woman be?" demanded Mazirian, peering down his long nose at the tiny captive.

"How can I say?"

"I must capture her," said Mazirian abstractedly: "What spells, what spells?"

Turjan looked up, although he could see the Magician only indistinctly through the cover of glass.

"Release me, Mazirian, and on my word as a Chosen Hierarch of the Maram-Or, I will deliver you this girl."

"How would you do this?" asked the suspicious Mazirian.

"Pursue her into the forest with my best Live Boots and a headful of spells."

"You would fare no better than I," retorted the Magician. "I give you freedom when I know the synthesis of your vat-things. I myself will pursue the woman."

Turjan lowered his head that the Magician might not read his eyes.

"And as for me, Mazirian?" he inquired after a moment.

"I will treat with you when I return."

"And if you do not return?"

Mazirian stroked his chin and smiled, revealing fine white teeth. "The dragon could devour you now, if it were not for your cursed secret."

The Magician climbed the stairs. Midnight found him in his study, poring through leather-bound tomes and untidy portfolios . . . At one time a thousand or more runes, spells, incantations, curses and sorceries had been known. The reach of Grand Motholam—Ascolais, the Ide of Kauchique, Almery to the South, the Land of the Falling Wall to the East—swarmed with sorcerers of every description, of whom the chief was the Arch-Necromancer Phandaal. A hundred spells Phandaal personally had formulated—though rumor said that demons whispered at his ear when he wrought magic. Pontecilla the Pious, then ruler of Grand Motholam, put Phandaal to torment, and after a terrible night, he killed Phandaal and outlawed sorcery throughout the land. The wizards of Grand Motholam fled like beetles under a strong light; the lore was dispersed and forgotten, until now, at this dim time, with the sun dark, wilderness obscuring Ascolais, and the white city Kaiin half in ruins, only a few more than a hundred spells remained to the knowledge of man. Of these, Mazirian had access to seventy-three, and gradually, by strategem and negotiation, was securing the others.

Mazirian made a selection from his books and with great effort forced five spells upon his brain: Phandaal's Gyrator, Felojun's Second Hypnotic Spell, The Excellent Prismatic Spray, The Charm of Untiring Nourishment, and the Spell of the Omnipotent Sphere. This accomplished, Mazirian drank wine and retired to his couch.

The following day, when the sun hung low, Mazirian went to walk in his garden. He had but short time to wait. As he loosened the earth at the roots of his moon-geraniums a soft rustle and stamp told that the object of his desire had appeared.

She sat upright in the saddle, a young woman of exquisite configuration. Mazirian slowly stooped, as not to startle her, put his feet into the Live Boots and secured them above the knee.

He stood up. "Ho, girl," he cried, "you have come again. Why are you here of evenings? Do you admire the roses? They are vividly red because live red blood flows in their petals. If today you do not flee, I will make you the gift of one."

Mazirian plucked a rose from the shuddering bush and advanced toward her, fighting the surge of the Live Boots. He had taken but four steps when the woman dug her knees into the ribs of her mount and so plunged off through the trees.

Mazirian allowed full scope to the life in his boots. They gave a great bound, and another, and another, and he was off in full chase.

So Mazirian entered the forest of fable. On all sides mossy boles twisted up to support the high panoply of leaves. At intervals shafts of sunshine drifted through to lay carmine blots on the turf. In the shade long-stemmed flowers and fragile fungi sprang from the humus; in this ebbing hour of Earth nature was mild and relaxed.

Mazirian in his Live Boots bounded with great speed through the forest, yet the black horse, running with no strain, stayed easily ahead.

For several leagues the woman rode, her hair flying behind like a pennon. She looked back and Mazirian saw the face over her shoulder as a face in a dream. Then she bent forward; the golden-eyed horse thundered ahead and soon was lost to sight. Mazirian followed by tracing the trail in the sod.

The spring and drive began to leave the Live Boots, for they had come far and at great speed. The monstrous leaps became shorter and heavier, but the strides of the horse, shown by the tracks, were also shorter and slower. Presently Mazirian entered a meadow and saw the horse, riderless, cropping grass. He stopped short. The entire expanse of tender herbiage lay before him. The trail of the horse leading into the glade was clear, but there was no trail leaving. The woman therefore had dismounted somewhere behind—how far he had no means of knowing. He walked toward the horse, but the creature shied and bolted through the trees. Mazirian made one effort to follow, and discovered that his Boots hung lax and flaccid—dead.

He kicked them away, cursing the day and his ill-fortune. Shaking the cloak free behind him, a baleful tension shining on his face, he started back along the trail.

In this section of the forest, outcroppings of black and green rock, basalt and serpentine, were frequent—forerunners of the crags over the River Derna. On one of these rocks Mazirian saw a tiny man-thing mounted on a dragon-fly. He had skin of a greenish cast; he wore a gauzy smock and carried a lance twice his own length.

Mazirian stopped. The Twk-man looked down stolidly.

"Have you seen a woman of my race passing by, Twk-man?"

"I have seen such a woman," responded the Twk-man after a moment of deliberation.

"Where may she be found?"

"What may I expect for the information?"

"Salt—as much as you can bear away."

The Twk-man flourished his lance. "Salt? No. Liane the Wayfarer provides the chieftain Dandanflores salt for all the tribe."

Mazirian could surmise the services for which the bandit-troubadour paid salt. The Twk-men, flying fast on their dragon-flies, saw all that happened in the forest.

"A vial of oil from my telanxis blooms?"

"Good," said the Twk-man. "Show me the vial."

Mazirian did so.

"She left the trail at the lightning-blasted oak lying a little before you. She made directly for the river valley, the shortest route to the lake."

Mazirian laid the vial beside the dragon-fly and went off toward the river oak. The Twk-man watched him go, then dismounted and lashed the vial to the underside of the dragon-fly, next to the skein of fine haft the woman had given him thus to direct Mazirian.

The Magician turned at the oak and soon discovered the trail over the dead leaves. A long open glade lay before him, sloping gently to the river. Trees towered to either side and the long sundown rays steeped one side in blood, left the other deep in black shadow. So deep was the shade that Mazirian did not see the creature seated on a fallen tree; and he sensed it only as it prepared to leap on his back.

Mazirian sprang about to face the thing, which subsided again to sitting posture. It was a Deodand, formed and featured like a handsome man, finely muscled, but with a dead black lusterless skin and long slit eyes.

"Ah, Mazirian, you roam the woods far from home," the black thing's soft voice rose through the glade.

The Deodand, Mazirian knew, craved his body for meat. How had the girl escaped? Her trail led directly past.

"I come seeking, Deodand. Answer my questions, and I undertake to feed you much flesh."

The Deodand's eyes glinted, flitting over Mazirian's body. "You may in any event, Mazirian. Are you with powerful spells today?"

"I am. Tell me, how long has it been since the girl passed? Went she fast, slow, alone or in company? Answer, and I give you meat at such time as you desire."

The Deodand's lips curled mockingly. "Blind Magician! She has not left the glade." He pointed, and Mazirian followed the direction of the dead black arm. But he jumped back as the Deodand sprang. From his mouth gushed the syllables of Phandaal's Gyrator Spell. The Deodand was jerked off his feet and flung high in the air, where he hung whirling, high and low, faster and slower, up to the treetops, low to the ground. Mazirian watched with a half-smile. After a moment he brought the Deodand low and caused the rotations to slacken.

"Will you die quickly or slow?" asked Mazirian. "Help me and I kill you at once. Otherwise you shall rise high where the pelgrane fly."

Fury and fear choked the Deodand.

"May dark Thial spike your eyes! May Kraan hold your living brain in acid!" And it added such charges that Mazirian felt forced to mutter countercurses.

"Up then," said Mazirian at last, with a wave of his hand. The black sprawling body jerked high above the tree-tops to revolve slowly in the crimson bask of setting sun. In a moment a mottled bat-shaped thing with hooked snout swept close and its beak tore the black leg before the crying Deodand could kick it away. Another and another of the shapes flitted across the sun.

"Down, Mazirian!" came the faint call. "I tell what I know."

Mazirian brought him close to earth.

"She passed alone before you came. I made to attack her but she repelled me with a handful of thyle-dust. She went to the end of the glade and took the trail to the river. This trail leads also past the lair of Thrang. So is she lost, for he will sate himself on her till she dies."

Mazirian rubbed his chin. "Had she spells with her?"

"I know not. She will need strong magic to escape the demon Thrang."

"Is there anything else to tell?"

"Nothing."

"Then you may die." And Mazirian caused the creature to revolve at ever greater speed, faster and faster, until there was only a blur. A strangled wailing came and presently the Deodand's frame parted. The head shot like a bullet far down the glade; arms, legs, viscera flew in all directions.

Mazirian went his way. At the end of the glade the trail led steeply down ledges of dark green serpentine to the River Derna. The sun had set and shade filled the valley. Mazirian gained the riverside and set off downstream toward a far shimmer known as Sanra Water, the Lake of Dreams.

An evil odor came to the air, a stink of putrescence and filth. Mazirian went ahead more cautiously, for the lair of Thrang the ghoul-bear was near, and in the air was the feel of magic—strong brutal sorcery his own more subtle spells might not contain.

The sound of voices reached him, the throaty tones of Thrang and gasping cries of terror. Mazirian stepped around a shoulder of rock, inspected the origin of the sounds.

Thrang's lair was an alcove in the rock, where a fetid pile of grass and skins served him for a couch. He had built a rude pen to cage three women, these wearing many bruises on their bodies and the effects of much horror on their faces. Thrang had taken them from the tribe that dwelt in silk-hung barges along the lake-shore. Now they watched as he struggled to subdue the woman he had just captured. His round gray man's face was contorted and he tore away her jerkin with his human hands. But she held away the great sweating body with an amazing dexterity. Mazirian's eyes narrowed. Magic, magic!

So he stood watching, considering how to destroy Thrang with no harm to the woman. But she spied him over Thrang's shoulder.

"See," she panted, "Mazirian has come to kill you."

Thrang twisted about. He saw Mazirian and came charging on all fours, venting roars of wild passion. Mazirian later wondered if the ghoul had cast some sort of spell, for a strange paralysis strove to bind his brain. Perhaps the spell lay in the sight of Thrang's raging gray-white face, the great arms thrust out to grasp.

Mazirian shook off the spell, if such it were, and uttered a spell of his own, and all the valley was lit by streaming darts of fire, lashing in from all directions to split Thrang's blundering body in a thousand places. This was the Excellent Prismatic Spray—many-colored stabbing lines. Thrang was dead almost at once, purple blood flowing from countless holes where the radiant rain had pierced him.

But Mazirian heeded little. The girl had fled. Mazirian saw her white form running along the river toward the lake, and took up the chase, heedless of the piteous cries of the three women in the pen.

The lake presently lay before him, a great sheet of water whose further rim was but dimly visible. Mazirian came down to the sandy shore and stood seeking across the dark face of Sanra Water, the Lake of Dreams. Deep night with only a verge of afterglow ruled the sky, and stars glistened on the smooth surface. The water lay cool and still, tideless as all Earth's waters had been since the moon had departed the sky.

Where was the woman? There, a pale white form, quiet in the shadow across the river. Mazirian stood on the riverbank, tall and commanding, a light breeze ruffling the cloak around his legs.

"Ho, girl," he called. "It is I, Mazirian, who saved you from Thrang. Come close, that I may speak to you."

"At this distance I hear you well, Magician," she replied. "The closer I approach the farther I must flee."

"Why then do you flee? Return with me and you shall be mistress of many secrets and hold much power."

She laughed. "If I wanted these, Mazirian, would I have fled so far?"

"Who are you then that you desire not the secrets of magic?"

"To you, Mazirian, I am nameless, lest you curse me. Now I go where you may not come." She ran down the shore, waded slowly out till the water circled her waist, then sank out of sight. She was gone.

Mazirian paused indecisively. It was not good to use so many spells and thus shear himself of power. What might exist below the lake? The sense of quiet magic was there, and though he was not at enmity with the Lake Lord, other beings might resent a trespass. However, when the figure of the girl did not break the surface, he uttered the Charm of Untiring Nourishment and entered the cool waters.

He plunged deep through the Lake of Dreams, and as he stood on the bottom, his lungs at ease by virtue of the charm, he marveled at the fey place he had come upon. Instead of blackness a green light glowed everywhere and the water was but little less clear than air. Plants undulated to the current and with them moved the lake flowers, soft with blossoms of red, blue and yellow. In and out swam large-eyed fish of many shapes.

The bottom dropped by rocky steps to a wide plain where trees of the underlake floated up from slender stalks to elaborate fronds and purple water-fruits, and so till the misty wet distance veiled all. He saw the woman, a white water nymph now, her hair like dark fog. She half-swam, half-ran across the sandy floor of the water-world, occasionally looking back over her shoulder. Mazirian came after, his cloak streaming out behind.

He drew nearer to her, exulting. He must punish her for leading him so far . . . The ancient stone stairs below his work-room led deep and at last opened into chambers that grew ever vaster as one went deeper. Mazirian had found a rusted cage in one of these chambers. A week or two locked in the blackness would curb her willfulness. And once he had dwindled a woman small as his thumb and kept her in a little glass bottle with two buzzing flies . . .

A ruined white temple showed through the green. There were many columns, some toppled, some still upholding the pediment. The woman entered the great portico under the shadow of the architrave. Perhaps she was attempting to elude him; he must follow closely. The white body glimmered at the far end of the nave, swimming now over the rostrum and into a semi-circular alcove behind.

Mazirian followed as fast as he was able, half-swimming, half-walking through the solemn dimness. He peered across the murk. Smaller columns here precariously upheld a dome from which the keystone had dropped. A sudden fear smote him, then realization as he saw the flash of movement from above. On all sides the columns toppled in, and an avalanche of marble blocks tumbled at his head. He jumped frantically back.

The commotion ceased, the white dust of the ancient mortar drifted away. On the pediment of the main temple the woman kneeled on slender knees, staring down to see how well she had killed Mazirian.

She had failed. Two columns, by sheerest luck, had crashed to either side of him, and a slab had protected his body from the blocks. He moved his head painfully. Through a chink in the tumbled marble he could see the woman, leaning to discern his body. So she would kill him? He, Mazirian, who had already lived more years than he could easily reckon? So much more would she hate and fear him later. He called his charm, the Spell of the Omnipotent Sphere. A film of force formed around his body, expanding to push aside all that resisted. When the marble ruins had been thrust back, he destroyed the sphere, regained his feet, and glared about for the woman. She was almost out of sight, behind a brake of long purple kelp, climbing the slope to the shore. With all his power he set out in pursuit.

T'sain dragged herself up on the beach. Still behind her came Mazirian the Magician, whose power had defeated each of her plans. The memory of his face passed before her and she shivered. He must not take her now.

Fatigue and despair slowed her feet. She had set out with but two spells, the Charm of Untiring Nourishment and a spell affording strength to her arms—the last permitting her to hold off Thrang and tumble the temple upon Mazirian. These were exhausted; she was bare of protection; but, on the other hand, Mazirian could have nothing left.

Perhaps he was ignorant of the vampire-weed. She ran up the slope and stood behind a patch of pale, wind-beaten grass. And now Mazirian came from the lake, a spare form visible against the shimmer of the water.

She retreated, keeping the innocent patch of grass between them. If the grass failed—her mind quailed at the thought of what she must do.

Mazirian strode into the grass. The sickly blades became sinewy fingers. They twined about his ankles, holding him in an unbreakable grip, while others sought to find his skin.

So Mazirian chanted his last spell—the incantation of paralysis, and the vampire grass grew lax and slid limply to earth. T'sain watched with dead hope. He was now close upon her, his cloak flapping behind. Had he no weakness? Did not his fibers ache, did not his breath come short? She whirled and fled across the meadow, toward a grove of black trees. Her skin chilled at the deep shadows, the somber frames. But the thud of the Magician's feet was loud. She plunged into the dread shade. Before all in the grove awoke she must go as far as possible.

Snap! A thong lashed at her. She continued to run. Another and another—she fell. Another great whip and another beat at her. She staggered up, and on, holding her arms before her face. Snap! The flails whistled through the air, and the last blow twisted her around. So she saw Mazirian.

He fought. As the blows rained on him, he tried to seize the whips and break them. But they were supple and springy beyond his powers, and jerked away to beat at him again. Infuriated by his resistance, they concentrated on the unfortunate Magician, who foamed and fought with transcendent fury, and T'sain was permitted to crawl to the edge of the grove with her life.

She looked back in awe at the expression of Mazirian's lust for life. He staggered about in a cloud of whips, his furious obstinate figure dimly silhouetted. He weakened and tried to flee, and then he fell. The blows pelted at him—on his head, shoulders, the long legs. He tried to rise but fell back.

T'sain closed her eyes in lassitude. She felt the blood oozing from her broken flesh. But the most vital mission yet remained. She reached her feet, and reelingly set forth. For a long time the thunder of many blows reached her ears.

Mazirian's garden was surpassingly beautiful by night. The star-blossoms spread wide, each of magic perfection, and the captive half-vegetable moths flew back and forth. Phosphorescent water-lillies floated like charming faces on the pond and the bush which Mazirian had brought from far Almery in the south tinctured the air with sweet fruity perfume.

T'sain, weaving and gasping, now came groping through the garden. Certain of the flowers awoke and regarded her curiously. The half-animal hybrid sleepily chittered at her, thinking to recognize Mazirian's step. Faintly to be heard was the wistful music of the blue-cupped flowers singing of ancient nights when a white moon swam the sky, and great storms and clouds and thunder ruled the seasons.

T'sain passed unheeding. She entered Mazirian's house, found the workroom where glowed the eternal yellow lamps. Mazirian's golden-haired vat-thing sat up suddenly and stared at her with his beautiful vacant eyes.

She found Mazirian's keys in the cabinet, and managed to claw open the trap door. Here she slumped to rest and let the pink gloom pass from her eyes. Visions began to come—Mazirian, tall and arrogant, stepping out to kill Thrang; the strange-hued flowers under the lake; Mazirian, his magic lost, fighting the whips . . . She was brought from the half-trance by the vat-thing timidly fumbling with her hair.

She shook herself awake, and half-walked, half-fell down the stairs. She unlocked the thrice-bound door, thrust it open with almost the last desperate urge of her body. She wandered in to clutch at the pedestal where the glass-topped box stood and Turjan and the dragon were playing their desperate game. She flung the glass crashing to the floor, gently lifted Turjan out and set him down.

The spell was disrupted by the touch of the rune at her wrist, and Turjan became a man again. He looked aghast at the nearly unrecognizable T'sain.

She tried to smile up at him.

"Turjan—you are free—"

"And Mazirian?"

"He is dead." She slumped wearily to the stone floor and lay limp. Turjan surveyed her with an odd emotion in his eyes.

"T'sain, dear creature of my mind," he whispered, "more noble are you than I, who used the only life you knew for my freedom."

He lifted her body in his arms.

"But I shall restore you to the vats. With your brain I build another T'sain, as lovely as you. We go."

He bore her up the stone stairs.

3

T'sais

T'sais came riding from the grove. She checked her horse at the verge as if in indecision, and sat looking across the shimmering pastel meadow toward the river . . . She stirred her knees and the horse proceeded across the turf.

She rode deep in thought, and overhead the sky rippled and cross-rippled, like a vast expanse of windy water, in tremendous shadows from horizon to horizon. Light from above, worked and refracted, flooded the land with a thousand colors, and thus, as T'sais rode, first a green beam flashed on her, then ultramarine, and topaz and ruby red, and the landscape changed in similar tintings and subtlety.

T'sais closed her eyes to the shifting lights. They rasped her nerves, confused her vision. The red glared, the green stifled, the blues and purples hinted at mysteries beyond knowledge. It was as if the entire universe had been expressly designed with an eye to jarring her, provoking her to fury. . . . A butterfly with wings patterned like a precious rug flitted by, and T'sais made to strike at it with her rapier. She restrained herself with great effort; for T'sais was of a passionate nature and not given to restraint. She looked down at the flowers below her horse's feet—pale daisies, blue-bells, Judas-creeper, orange sunbursts. No more would she stamp them to pulp, rend them from their roots. It had been suggested to her that the flaw lay not in the universe but in herself. Swallowing her vast enmity toward the butterfly and the flowers and the changing lights of the sky, she continued across the meadow.

A bank of dark trees rose above her, and beyond were clumps of rushes and the gleam of water, all changing in hue as the light changed in the sky. She turned and followed the river bank to the long low manse.

She dismounted, walked slowly to the door of black smoky wood, which bore the image of a sardonic face. She pulled at the tongue and inside a bell tolled.

There was no reply.

"Pandelume!" she called.

Presently there was a muffled answer: "Enter."

She pushed open the door and came into a high-ceilinged room, bare except for a padded settee, a dim tapestry.

"What is your wish?" The voice, mellow and of an illimitable melancholy, came from beyond the wall.

"Pandelume, today I have learned that killing is evil, and further that my eyes trick me, and that beauty is where I see only harsh light and evil forms."

For a period Pandelume maintained a silence; then the muffled voice came, replying to the implicit plea for knowledge.

"That is, for the most part, true. Living creatures, if nothing else, have the right to life. It is their only truly precious possession, and the stealing of life is a wicked theft. . . . As for the other, the fault is not with you. Beauty lies everywhere free to be seen by all—by all except you. For this I feel sorrow, for I created you. I built your primal cell; I stamped the strings of life with the pattern of your body and brain. And in spite of my craft I erred, so that when you climbed from the vat, I found that I had molded a flaw into your brain; that you saw ugliness in beauty, evil in good. True ugliness, true evil you have never seen, for in Embelyon there is nothing wicked or foul . . . Should you be so unfortunate to encounter these, I fear for your brain."

"Cannot you change me?" cried T'sais. "You are a magician. Must I live my life out blind to joy?"

The shadow of a sigh penetrated the wall.

"I am a magician indeed, with knowledge of every spell yet devised, the sleight of runes, incantations, designs, exorcisms, talismans. I am Master Mathematician, the first since Phandaal, yet I can do nothing to your brain without destroying your intelligence, your personality, your soul—for I am no god. A god may will things to existence; I must rely on magic, the spells which vibrate and twist space."

Hope faded from T'sais' eyes. "I wish to go to Earth," she said presently. "The sky of Earth is a steady blue, and a red sun moves over the horizons. I tire of Embelyon where there is no voice but yours."

"Earth," mused Pandelume. "A dim place, ancient beyond

knowledge. Once it was a tall world of cloudy mountains and bright rivers, and the sun was a white blazing ball. Ages of rain and wind have beaten and rounded the granite, and the sun is feeble and red. The continents have sunk and risen. A million cities have lifted towers, have fallen to dust. In place of the old peoples a few thousand strange souls live. There is evil on Earth, evil distilled by time. . . . Earth is dying and in its twilight . . ." he paused.

T'sais said doubtfully: "Yet I have heard Earth is a place of beauty, and I would know beauty, even though I die."

"How will you know beauty when you see it?"

"All human beings know beauty . . . Am I not human?"

"Of course."

"Then I will find beauty, and perhaps even—" T'sais faltered over the word, so alien was it to her mind, yet so full of disturbing implication.

Pandelume was silent. At last:

"You shall go if you wish. I will aid you as I may. I will give you runes to ward you from magic; I will strike life into your sword; and I will give you advice, which is this: Beware of men, for men loot beauty to sate their lust. Permit intimacy to none . . . I will give you a bag of jewels, which are riches on Earth. With these you may attain much. Yet, again, show them nowhere, for certain men will slay for a copper bit."

A heavy silence came, a weight was gone from the air.

"Pandelume," called T'sais softly. There was no reply.

After a moment Pandelume returned, and the sense of his presence reached to her mind.

"In a moment," he said, "you may enter this room."

T'sais waited a period; then, as she was bid, entered the next room.

"On the bench to the left," came Pandelume's voice, "you will find an amulet and a little sack of gems. Clasp this amulet upon your wrist; it will reflect magic intended evilly against him who utters the spell. This is a most powerful rune; guard it well."

T'sais obeyed, and tied the jewels inside her sash.

"Lay your sword upon this bench, stand upon the rune in the floor and close your eyes tightly. I must enter the room. I charge you, do not attempt to see me—for there are terrible consequences."

T'sais discarded her sword, stood upon the metal rune, locked her eyes. She heard a slow step, heard the clink of metal, then a high intense shrilling, dying slowly.

"Your sword lives," said Pandelume, and his voice sounded

strangely loud, coming from so near. "It will kill your enemies with intelligence. Reach your hand and take it."

T'sais sheathed her slim rapier, now warm and quivering.

"Where on Earth will you go?" asked Pandelume. "To the land of men, or to the great ruined wildernesses?"

"To Ascolais," said T'sais, for the one who had told her of beauty had spoken of this land.

"As you wish," said Pandelume. "Now hark! If you ever seek to return to Embelyon—"

"No," said T'sais. "I would rather die."

"Please yourself in that regard."

T'sais remained silent.

"Now I will touch you. You will be dizzy a moment—and then you will open your eyes on Earth. It is almost night, and terrible things rove the dark. So seek shelter quickly."

In high excitement T'sais felt the touch of Pandelume. There was a wavering in her brain, a swift unthinkable flight . . . Strange soil was under her feet, strange air at her face with a sharper tang. She opened her eyes.

The landscape was strange and new. There was a dark blue sky, an ancient sun. She stood in a meadow, encircled by tall gloomy trees. These trees were unlike the calm giants of Embelyon; these were dense and brooding, and the shadows were enigmatic. Nothing in sight, nothing of Earth was raw or harsh—the ground, the trees, the rock ledge protruding from the meadow; all these had been worked upon, smoothed, aged, mellowed. The light from the sun, though dim, was rich, and invested every object of the land, the rocks, the trees, the quiet grasses and flowers, with a sense of lore and ancient recollection.

A hundred paces distant rose the mossy ruins of a long-tumbled castelry. The stones were blackened now by lichens, by smoke, by age; grass grew rank through the rubble—the whole a weird picture in the long light of sunset.

T'sais slowly approached. Some of the walls yet were standing, stone on weathered stone, the mortar long since dissolved. She moved wonderingly around a great effigy, mouldered, chipped, cracked, almost entirely buried; puzzled a moment at the characters carved in the base. Wide-eyed she stared at what remained of the visage—cruel eyes, sneering mouth, a nose broken off. T'sais shuddered faintly. There was nothing here for her; she turned to go.

A laugh, high-pitched, gleeful, rang across the clearing. T'sais, mindful of Pandelume's warnings, waited in a dark recess. Movement flickered between the trees; a man and woman lurched into the failing sunlight; then came a young man treading light as air, singing and whistling. He held a light sword, which he used to prod the two, who were bound.

They halted before the ruins, close by T'sais, and she could see the faces. The bound man was a thin-faced wretch with a ragged red beard and eyes darting and desperate; the woman was short and plump. Their captor was Liane the Wayfarer. His brown hair waved softly, his features moved in charm and flexibility. He had golden-hazel eyes, large and beautiful, never still. He wore red leather shoes with curled tops, a suit of red and green, a green cloak, and a peaked hat with a red feather.

T'sais watched without comprehension. The three were equally vile, of sticky blood, red pulp, inner filth. Liane seemed slightly less ignoble—he was the most agile, the most elegant. And T'sais watched with little interest.

Liane deftly threw loops around the ankles of man and woman and pushed them so that they fell among the flints. The man groaned softly, the woman fell to whimpering.

Liane made a gay flourish of his hat and sprang away to the ruins. Not twenty feet from T'sais he slid aside a stone in the ancient flags, came forth with tinder and flint, and kindled a fire. From his pouch he took a bit of meat, which he toasted and ate daintily, sucking his fingers.

No word had yet passed. Liane at last stood up, stretched, and glanced at the sky. The sun was dropping below the dark wall of trees, and already blue shadows filled the glade.

"To business," cried Liane. His voice was shrill and clear as the call of a flute. "First," and he made a solemnly waggish gesture, "I must assure that our revelations are weighted with soberness and truth."

He ducked into his lair under the flags and brought forth four stout staffs. He laid one of these across the thighs of the man, passed the second across this, through the crotch of his captive's legs, so that with slight effort he could crush down at the thighs and up at the small of the back. He tested his device and crowed as the man cried out. He adjusted a similar arrangement upon the woman.

T'sais watched in perplexity. Evidently the young man was preparing to cause his captives pain. Was this a custom of Earth? But how was she to judge, she who knew nothing of good or evil?

"Liane! Liane!" cried the man, "Spare my wife! She knows nothing! Spare her, and you may have all I possess, and I serve you my lifetime!"

"Ho!" laughed Liane, and the feather of his cap quivered. "Thank you, thank you for your offer—but Liane wants no faggots of wood, no turnips. Liane likes silk and gold, the gleam of daggers, the sounds a girl makes in love. So thank you—but I seek the brother of your wife, and when your wife chokes and screams, you will tell where he hides.

To T'sais the scene began to assume meaning. The two captives were concealing information the young man desired; hence he would hurt them until in desperation they did as he asked. A clever artifice, one which she would hardly have thought of herself.

"Now," said Liane, "I must ensure that lies are not artfully mingled into the truth. You see," he confided, "when one is under torment, he is too distraught to invent, to fabricate—and hence speaks naught but exactness." He snatched a brand from the fire, wedged it between the man's bound ankles, and instantly leapt to ply the torture lever upon the woman.

"I know nothing, Liane!" babbled the man. "I know nothing—oh, indeed!"

Liane stood away with dissatisfaction. The woman had fainted. He snatched the brand away from the man and flung it pettishly into the blaze.

"What a nuisance!" he said, but presently his good spirits reasserted themselves. "Ah well, we have much time." He stroked his pointed chin.

"Perhaps you speak truth," he mused. "Perhaps your good wife shall be the informant after all." He revived her with slaps and an aromatic which he held under her nose. She stared at him numbly, her face twisted and bloated.

"Attend," said Liane. "I enter the second phase of the question. I reason, I think, I theorize. I say, perhaps the husband does not know where he whom I seek has fled, perhaps the wife alone knows."

The woman's mouth opened slightly. "He is my brother—please—"

"Ah! So you know!" cried Liane in delight, and strode back and forth before the fire. "Ah, you know! We renew the trial. Now attend. With this staff I make jelly of your man's legs, and bring his spine up through his stomach—unless you speak."

He set about his task.

"Say nothing—" gasped the man, and lapsed into pain. The woman cursed, sobbed, pleaded. At last: "I tell, I tell you all!" she cried. "Dellare has gone to Efred!"

Liane relaxed his efforts. "Efred. So. In the Land of the Falling

Wall.'' He pursed his lips. ''It might be true. But I disbelieve. You must tell me once more, under the influence of the truth-evoker.'' And he brought a brand from the fire and adjusted it at her ankles—and set to work on the man once more. The woman spoke not.

''Speak, woman,'' snarled Liane, panting. ''I am in perspiration with this work.'' The woman spoke not. Her eyes were wide, and stared glassily upwards.

''She is dead!'' cried her husband. ''Dead! My wife is dead! Ah—Liane, you demon, you foulness!'' he screamed. ''I curse you! by Thial, by Kraan—'' His voice quavered into high-pitched hysteria.

T'sais was disturbed. The woman was dead. Was not killing wicked? So Pandelume had said. If the woman were good, as the bearded man had said, then Liane was evil. Things of blood and filth all, of course. Still, it was vile, hurting a live thing till it died.

Knowing nothing of fear, she stepped out from her hiding place and advanced into the fire-light. Liane looked up and sprang back. But the intruder was a slender girl of passionate beauty. He caroled, he danced.

''Welcome, welcome!'' He glared in distaste at the bodies on the ground. ''Unpleasant; we must ignore them.'' He flung his cloak back, ogled her with his luminous hazel eyes, strutted toward her like a plumed cock.

''You are lovely, my dear, and I—I am the perfect man; so you shall see.''

T'sais laid her hand on her rapier, and it sprang out by itself. Liane leapt back, alarmed by the blade and likewise by the blaze which glowed deep from the warped brain.

''What means this? Come, come,'' he fretted. ''Put away your steel. It is sharp and hard. You must lay it away. I am a kind man, but I brook no annoyance.''

T'sais stood over the prone bodies. The man looked up at her feverishly. The woman stared at the dark sky.

Liane sprang forward, planning to clasp her while her attention was distracted. The rapier sprang up by itself, darted forward, pierced the agile body.

Liane the Wayfarer sank to his knees coughing blood. T'sais pulled away the rapier, wiped the blood on the gay green cloak, and sheathed it with difficulty. It wished to stab, to pierce, to kill.

Liane lay unconscious. T'sais turned away, sick. A thin voice reached her. ''Release me—''

T'sais considered, then she cut the bonds. The man stumbled to his wife, stroked her, flung off the bonds, called to her uplifted face.

There was no answer. He sprang erect in madness and howled into the night. Raising the limp form in his arms he stumbled off into the darkness, lurching, falling, cursing . . .

T'sais shivered. She glanced from the prone Liane to the black forest where the flickering circle of the firelight failed to reach. Slowly, with many backward glances, she left the tumbled ruins, the meadow. The bleeding figure of Liane remained by the dying fire.

The glimmer of flame waned, was lost in the darkness. T'sais groped her way between the looming trunks; and the murk was magnified by the twist in her brain. There never had been night in Embelyon, only an opalescent dimming. So T'sais continued down the sighing forest courses, stifled, weighed, yet oblivious to the things she might have met—the Deodands, the pelgrane, the prowling erbs (creatures mixed of beasts, man and demon) the gids, who leaps twenty feet across the turf and clasped themselves to their victims.

T'sais went unmolested, and presently reached the edge of the forest. The ground rose, the trees thinned, and T'sais come out on an illimitable dark expanse. This was Modavna Moor, a place of history, a tract which had borne the tread of many feet and absorbed much blood. At one famous slaughtering, Golickan Kodek the Conqueror had herded here the populations of two great cities, G'Vasan and Bautiku, constricted them in a circle three miles across, gradually pushed them tighter, tighter, tighter, panicked them toward the center within his flapping-armed sub-human cavalry, until at last he had achieved a gigantic squirming mound, half a thousand feet high, a pyramid of screaming flesh. It is said that Golickan Kodek mused ten minutes at his monument, then turned and rode his bounding mount back to the land of Laidenur from whence he had come.

The ghosts of the ancient populations had paled and dissolved and Modavna Moor was less stifling than the forest. Bushes grew like blots from the ground. A line of rocky crags at the horizon jutted sharp against a faint violet afterglow. T'sais picked her way across the turf, relieved that the sky was open above. A few minutes later she came to an ancient road of stone slab, cracked and broken, bordered by a ditch where luminous star-shaped flowers grew. A wind came sighing off the moor to dampen her face with mist. She went wearily down the road. No shelter was visible, and the wind whipped coldly at her cloak.

A rush of feet, a tumble of shapes, and T'sais was struggling against hard grasping hands. She fought for her rapier, but her arms were pinioned.

One struck a light, fired a torch, to examine his prize. T'sais saw three bearded, scarred rogues of the moor; they wore gray pandy-suits, stained and fouled by mud and filth.

"Why, it's a handsome maid!" said one, leering.

"I'll seek about her for silver," said another and slid his hands with evil intimacy over T'sais' body. He found the sack of jewels, and turned them into his palm, a trickle of hundred-colored fire. "Mark these! The wealth of princes!"

"Or sorcerers!" said another. And in sudden doubt they relaxed their holds. But still she could not reach her rapier.

"Who are you, woman of the night?" asked one with some respect. "A witch, to have such jewels, and walk Modavna Moor alone?"

T'sais had neither wit nor experience to improvise falsehood.

"I am no witch! Release me, you stinking animals!"

"No witch? Then what manner of woman are you? Whence do you come?"

"I am T'sais, of Embelyon," she cried angrily. "Pandelume created me, and I seek love and beauty on Earth. Now drop your hands, for I would go my way!"

The first rogue chortled. "Ho, ho! Seeking love and beauty! You have achieved somehing of your quest, girl—for while we lads are no beauties, to be sure, Tagman being covered with scab and Lasard lacking his teeth and ears—still we have much love, hey, lads? We will show you as much love as you desire! Hey, lads?"

And in spite of T'sais horrified outcries, they dragged her across the moor to a stone cabin.

They entered, and one kindled a roaring fire, while two stripped T'sais of her rapier and flung it in a corner. They locked the door with a great iron key, and released her. She sprang for her sword, but a buffet sent her to the foul floor.

"May that quiet you, fiend-cat!" panted Tagman. "You should be happy," and they renewed their banter. "Admitted we are not beauties, yet we will show you all the love you may wish."

T'sais crouched in a corner. "I know not what love is," she panted. "In any event I want none of yours!"

"Is it possible?" they crowed. "You are yet innocent?" And T'sais listened with eyes glazing as they proceeded to describe in evil detail their concept of love.

T'sais sprang from her corner in a frenzy, kicking, beating her fists at the moor-men. And when she had been flung into her corner, bruised and half-dead, the men brought out a great cask of mead, to fortify themselves for their pleasure.

Now they cast lots as to who should be the first to enjoy the girl. The issue was declared, and here an altercation arose, two claiming that he who won had cheated. Angry words evolved, and as T'sais watched, dazed in horror beyond the concept of a normal mind, they fought like bulls in a rut, with great curses, mighty blows. T'sais crept to her rapier, and as it felt her touch, it lofted into the air like a bird. It lunged itself into the fight, dragging T'sais behind. The three shouted hoarsely, the steel flickered—in, out, faster than the eye. Cries, groans—and three sprawled on the earthen floor, gaping-mouthed corpses. T'sais found the key, unlocked the door, fled madly through the night.

She ran over the dark and windy moor, across the road, stumbled into the ditch, dragged herself up the cold muddy bank and sank on her knees . . . This was Earth! She remembered Embelyon, where the most evil things were flowers and butterflies. She remembered how these had aroused her hate.

Embelyon was lost, renounced. And T'sais wept.

A rustling in the heather aroused her. Aghast she lifted her head, listened. What new outrage to her mind? The sinister sounds again, as of cautious footfalls. She searched the darkness in terror.

A black figure stole into her sight, creeping along the ditch. In the light of the fireflies she saw him—a Deodand, wandered from the forest, a hairless man-thing with charcoal-black skin, a handsome face, marred and made demoniac by two fangs gleaming long, sharp and white down his lip. It was clad in a leather harness, and its long slit eyes were fastened hungrily on T'sais. He sprang at her with an exulting cry.

T'sais stumbled clear, fell, snatched herself up. Wailing, she fled across the moor, insensible to scratching furze, tearing thorn. The Deodand bounded after, venting eerie moans.

Over moor, turf, hummock, briar and brook, across the dark wastes went the chase, the girl fleeing with eyes starting and staring into nothing, the pursuer uttering his wistful moans.

A loom, a light ahead—a cottage. T'sais, breath coming in sobs, lurched to the threshold. The door mercifully gave. She fell in, slammed the door, dropped the bar. The weight of the Deodand thudded against the barrier.

The door was stout, the windows small and crossed by iron. She was safe. She sank to her knees, the breath rasping in her throat, and slowly lapsed into unconsciousness . . .

The man who dwelt in the cottage rose from his deep seat at the fire, tall, broad of shoulder, moving with a curiously slow step. He was perhaps a young man, but no one could know, for face and head were draped in a black hood. Behind the eye-slits were steady blue eyes.

The man came to stand over T'sais, who lay flung like a doll on the red brick floor. He stooped, lifted the limp form, and carried her to a wide padded bench beside the fire. He removed her sandals, her quivering rapier, her sodden cloak. He brought unguent and applied it to her scratches and bruises. He wrapped her in soft flannel blanketing, pillowed her head, and, assured that she was comfortable, once more sat himself by the fire.

The Deodand outside had lingered, and had been watching through the iron-barred window. Now it knocked at the door.

"Who's there?" called the man in the black hood, twisting about.

"I desire the one who has entered. I hunger for her flesh," said the soft voice of the Deodand.

The man in the hood spoke sharply.

"Go, before I speak a spell to burn you with fire. Never return!"

"I go," said the Deodand, for he greatly feared magic, and departed into the night.

And the man turned and sat staring into the fire.

T'sais felt warm pungent liquid in her mouth and opened her eyes. Kneeling beside her was a tall man, hooded in black. One arm supported her shoulders and head, another held a silver spoon to her mouth.

T'sais shrank away. "Quietly," said the man. "Nothing will harm you." Slowly, doubtfully, she relaxed and lay still.

Red sunlight poured in through the windows, and the cottage was warm. It was paneled in golden wood, with a fretwork painted in red and blue and brown circling the ceiling. Now the man brought more broth from the fire, bread from a locker, and placed them before her. After a moment's hesitation, T'sais ate.

Recollection suddenly came to her; she shuddered, looked wildly around the room. The man noted her taut face. He stooped and laid a hand on her head. T'sais lay quiet, half in dread.

"You are safe here," said the man. "Fear nothing."

A vagueness came over T'sais. Her eyes grew heavy. She slept.

When she woke the cottage was empty, and the maroon sunlight slanted in from an opposite window. She stretched her arms, tucked her hands behind her head, and lay thinking. This man of the black hood, who was he? Was he evil? Everything else of Earth had been past thought. Still, he had done nothing to harm her . . . She spied her garments upon the floor. She rose from the couch and dressed herself. She went to the door and pushed it open. Before her stretched the moor, fading far off beyond the under-slant of the horizon. To her left jutted a break of rocky crags, black shadow and lurid red stones. To the right extended the black margin of the forest.

Was this beautiful? T'sais pondered. Her warped brain saw bleakness in the line of the moor, cutting harshness in the crags, and in the forest—terror.

Was this beauty? At a loss, she twisted her head, squinted. She heard footsteps, jerked about, wide-eyed, expecting anything. It was he of the black hood, and T'sais leaned back against the door-jamb.

She watched him approach, tall and strong, slow of step. Why did he wear the hood? Was he ashamed of his face? She could understand something of this, for she herself found the human face repellent—an object of watery eye, wet unpleasant apertures, spongy outgrowths.

He halted before her. "Are you hungry?"

T'sais considered. "Yes."

"Then we will eat."

He entered the cottage, stirred up the fire, and spitted meat. T'sais stood uncertainly in the background. She had always served herself. She felt an uneasiness: cooperation was an idea she had not yet encoutered.

Presently the man arose, and they sat to eat at his table.

"Tell me of yourself," he said after a few moments. So T'sais, who had never learned to be other than artless, told him her story, thus;

"I am T'sais. I came to Earth from Embelyon; where the wizard Pandelume created me."

"Embelyon? Where is Embelyon? And who is Pandelume?"

"Where is Embelyon?" she repeated in puzzlement. "I don't know. It is in a place that is not Earth. It is not very large, and lights of many colors come from the sky. Pandelume lives in Embelyon. He is the greatest wizard alive—so he tells me."

"Ah," the man said. "Perhaps I see . . ."

"Pandelume created me," continued T'sais, "but there was a flaw in the pattern." And T'sais stared into the fire. "I see the world as a dismal place of horror; all sounds to me are harsh, all living creatures vile, in varying degrees—things of sluggish movement and inward filth. During the first of my life I thought only to trample, crush, destroy. I knew nothing but hate. Then I met my sister T'sain, who is as I without the flaw. She told me of love and beauty and happiness—and I came to Earth seeking these."

The grave blue eyes studied her.

"Have you found them?"

"So far," said T'sais in a faraway voice. "I have found only such evil as I never even encountered in my nightmares." Slowly she told him her adventures.

"Poor creature," he said and fell to studying her once again.

"I think I shall kill myself," said T'sais, in the same distant voice, "for what I want is infinitely lost." And the man, watching, saw how the red afternoon sun coppered her skin, noted the loose black hair, the long thoughtful eyes. He shuddered at the thought of this creature being lost into the dust of Earth's forgotten trillions.

"No!" he said sharply. T'sais stared at him in surprise. Surely one's life was one's own, to do with as one pleased.

"Have you found nothing on Earth," he asked, "that you would regret leaving?"

T'sais knit her brows. "I can think of nothing—unless it be the peace of this cottage."

The man laughed. "Then this shall be your home, for as long as you wish, and I will try to show you that the world is sometimes good—though in truth—" his voice changed "—I have not found it so."

"Tell me," said T'sais, "what is your name? Why do you wear the hood?"

"My name? Etarr," he said in a voice subtly harsh. "Etarr is enough of it. I wear the mask because of the most wicked woman of Ascolais—Ascolais, Almery, Kauchique—the entire world. She made my face such that I cannot abide my own sight."

He relaxed, and gave a weary laugh. "No need for anger any more."

"Is she alive still?"

"Yes, she lives, and no doubt still works evil on all she meets." He sat looking into the fire. "One time I knew nothing of this. She was young, beautiful, laden with a thousand fragrances and charming playfulnesses. I lived beside the ocean—in a white villa among poplar trees. Across Tenebrosa Bay the Cape of Sad Remembrance reached into the ocean, and when sunset made the sky red and the mountains black, the cape seemed to sleep on the water like one of the ancient earth-gods . . . All my life I spent here, and was as content as one may be while dying Earth spins out its last few courses.

"One morning I looked up from my star-charts and saw Javanne walking through the portal. She was as young and slender as yourself.

Her hair was a wonderful red, and strands fell before her shoulders. She was very beautiful, and—in her white gown—pure and innocent.

"I loved her, and she said she loved me. And she gave me a band of black metal to wear. In my blindness I clasped it to my wrist, never recognizing it for the evil rune it was. And weeks of great delight passed. But presently I found that Javanne was one of dark urges that the love of man could never quell. And one midnight I found her in the embrace of a black naked demon, and the sight twisted my mind.

"I stood back aghast. I was not seen, and I went slowly away. In the morning she came running across the terrace, smiling and happy, like a child. 'Leave me,' I told her. 'You are vile beyond calculation.' She uttered a word and the rune on my arm enslaved me. My mind was my own, but my body was hers, forced to obey her words.

"And she made me tell what I had seen, and she revelled and jeered. And she put me through foul degradations, and called up things from Kalu, from Fauvune, from Jeldred, to mock and defile my body. She made me witness her play with these things, and when I pointed out the creature that sickened me the most, by magic she gave me its face, the face I wear now."

"Can such women exist?" marvelled T'sais.

"Indeed." The grave blue eyes studied her attentively. "At last one night while the demons tumbled me across the crags behind the hills, a flint tore the rune from my arm. I was free; I chanted a spell which sent the shapes shrieking off through the sky, and returned to the villa. "And I met Javanne of the red hair in the great hall, and her eyes were cool and innocent. I drew my knife to stab her throat, but she said 'Hold! Kill me and you wear your demon-face forever, for only I know how to change it.' So she ran blithely away from the villa, and I, unable to bear the sight of the place, came to the moors. And always I seek her, to regain my face."

"Where is she now?" asked T'sais, whose troubles seemed small compared to those of Etarr the Masked.

"Tomorrow night, I know where to find her. It is the night of the Black Sabbath—the night dedicated to evil since the dawn of Earth."

"And you will attend this festival?"

"Not as a celebrant—though in truth," said Etarr ruefully, "without my hood I would be one of the things who are there, and would pass unnoticed."

T'sais shuddered and pressed back against the wall. Etarr saw the gesture and sighed.

Another idea occurred to her. "With all the evil you have suffered, do you still find beauty in the world?"

''To be sure,'' said Etarr. ''See how these moors stretch, sheer and clean, of marvellous subtle color. See how the crags rise in grandeur, like the spine of the world. And you,'' he gazed into her face, ''you are of a beauty surpassing all.''

''Surpassing Javanne?'' asked T'sais, and looked in puzzlement as Etarr laughed.

''Indeed surpassing Javanne,'' he assured her.

T'sais' brain went off at another angle.

''And Javanne, do you wish to revenge yourself against her?''

''No,'' answered Etarr, eyes far away across the moors. ''What is revenge? I care nothing for it. Soon, when the sun goes out, men will stare into the eternal night, and all will die, and Earth will bear its history, its ruins, the mountains worn to knolls—all into infinite dark. Why revenge?''

Presently they left the cottage and wandered across the moor, Etarr trying to show her beauty—the slow river Scaum flowing through green rushes, clouds basking in the wan sunlight over the crags, a bird wheeling on spread wings, the wide smoky sweep of Modavna Moor. And T'sais strove always to make her brain see this beauty, and always did she fail. But she had learned to check the wild anger that the sights of the world had once aroused. And her craving to kill diminished, and her face relaxed from its tense set.

So they wandered on, each to his own thoughts. And they watched the sad glory of the sunset, and they saw the slow white stars raise in the heavens.

''Are not the stars beautiful?'' whispered Etarr through his black hood. ''They have names older than man.''

And T'sais, finding only mournfulness in the sunset, and thinking the stars but small sparks in meaningless patterns, could not answer.

''Surely two more unfortunate people do not exist,'' she sighed.

Etarr said nothing. They walked on in silence. Suddenly he grasped her arm and pulled her low in the furze. Three great shapes went flapping across the afterglow. ''The pelgrane!''

They flew close overhead—gargoyle creatures, with wings creaking like rusty hinges. T'sais caught a glimpse of hard leathern body, great hatchet beak, leering eyes in a wizened face. She shrank against Etarr. The pelgrane flapped across the forest.

Etarr laughed harshly. ''You shrink from the visage of the pelgrane. The countenance I wear would put the pelgrane themselves to flight.''

The next morning he took her into the woods, and she found the trees mindful of Embelyon. They returned to the cottage in the early afternoon, and Etarr retired to his books.

"I am no sorcerer," he told her regretfully. "I am acquainted with but a few simple spells. Yet I make occasional use of magic, which may ward me from danger tonight."

"Tonight?" T'sais inquired vaguely, for she had forgotten.

"Tonight is the Black Sabbath, and I must go to find Javanne."

"I would go with you," said T'sais. "I would see the Black Sabbath, and Javanne also."

Etarr assured her that the sights and sounds would horrify her and torment her brain. T'sais persisted, and Etarr finally allowed her to follow him, when two hours after sunset he set off in the direction of the crags.

Over the heath, up scaly outcroppings, Etarr picked a way through the dark, with T'sais a slender shadow behind. A great scarp lay across their path. Into a black fissure, up a flight of stone steps, cut in the immemorial past, and out on top of the cliff, with Modavna Moor a black sea below.

Now Etarr gestured T'sais to great caution. They stole through a gap between two towering rocks; concealed in the shadow, they surveyed the congress below.

They were overlooking an amphitheater lit by two blazing fires. In the center rose a dais of stone, as high as a man. About the fire, about the dais, two-score figures, robed in gray monks-cloth, reeled sweatingly, their faces unseen.

T'sais felt a premonitory chill. She looked at Etarr doubtfully.

"Even here is beauty," he whispered. "Weird and grotesque, but a sight to enchant the mind." T'sais looked again in dim comprehension.

More of the robed and cowled figures now were weaving before the fires; whence they came T'sais had not observed. It was evident that the festival had just begun, that the celebrants were only marshalling their passions. They pranced, shuffled, wove in and out, and presently began a muffled chant.

The weaving and gesticulation became feverish, and the caped figures crowded more closely around the dais. And now one leapt up on the dais and doffed her robe—a middleaged witch of squat naked body with a great broad face. She had ecstatic glittering eyes, large features pumping in ceaseless idiotic motion. Mouth open, tongue protruding, stiff black hair like a furze bush, falling from side to side over her face as she shook her head, she danced a libidinous sidelong dance in the light of the fires, looking slyly over the gathering. The chant of the cavorting figures below swelled to a vile chorus, and overhead dark shapes appeared, settling with an evil sureness.

The crowd began to slip from their robes, to reveal all manner of men and women, old and young—orange-haired witches of the Cobalt Mountain; forest sorcerers of Ascolais; white-bearded wizards of the Forlorn Land, with babbling small succubi. And one clad in splendid silk was the Prince Datul Omaet of Cansapara, the city of fallen pylons across the Melantine Gulf. And another creature of scales and staring eyes came of the lizardmen in the barren hills of South Almery. And these two girls, never apart, were Saponids, the near-extinct race from the northern tundras. The slender dark-eyed ones were necrophages from the Land of the Falling Wall. And the dreamy-eyed witch of the blue hair—she dwelt on the Cape of Sad Remembrance and waited at night on the beach for that which came in from the sea.

And as the squat witch with the black ruff and swinging breasts danced, the communicants became exalted, raised their arms, contorted their bodies, pantomimed all the evil and perversion they could set mind to.

Except one—a quiet figure still wrapped in her robe, moving slowly through the saturnalia with a wonderful grace. She stepped up on the dias now, let the robe slip from her body, and Javanne stood revealed in a clinging white gown of mist-stuff, gathered at the waist, fresh and chaste as salt spray. Shining red hair fell over her shoulders like a stream, and curling strands hung over her breasts. Her great gray eyes demure, strawberry mouth a little parted, she gazed back and forth across the crowd. They called and crowed, and Javanne, with tantalizing deliberation, moved her body.

Javanne danced. She raised her arms, wove them down, twisting her body on slender white legs . . . Javanne danced, her face shining with the most reckless passions. A dim shape dropped from above, a beautiful half-creature, and he joined his body to Javanne's in a fantastic embrace. And the crowd below cried, leapt, rolled, tossed, joined together in a swift culmination of their previous antics.

From the rocks T'sais watched, mind under an intensity no normal brain could understand. But—in strange paradox—the sight and sound fascinated her, reached below the warp, touched the dark chords latent to humanity. Etarr looked down at her, eyes glowing blue fire, and she stared back in a tumult of contradictory emotions. He winced and turned away; at last she looked back to the orgy below—a drug-dream, a heaving of wild flesh in the darting firelight. A palpable aura was cast up, a weft in space meshed of varying depravities. And the demons swooped like birds alighting and joined the delirium. Foul face after face T'sais saw, and each burnt her brain until she thought she must scream and die—visages of leering eye, bulbed cheek, lunatic body, black faces of spiked nose, expressions outraging thought, writhing, hopping, crawling, the spew of the demon-lands. And one had a nose like a three-fold white worm, a mouth that was a putrefying blotch, a mottled jowl and black malformed forehead; the whole a thing of retch and horror. To this Etarr directed T'sais' gaze. She saw and her muscles knotted. "There," said Etarr in a muffled voice, "there is a face twin to the one below this hood." And T'sais, staring at Etarr's black concealment, shrank back.

He chuckled weakly, bitterly . . . After a moment T'sais reached out and touched his arm. "Etarr."

He turned back to her. "Yes?"

"My brain is flawed. I hate all I see. I cannot control my fears. Nevertheless that which underlies my brain—my blood, my body, my spirit—that which is me loves you, the you underneath the mask."

Etarr studied the white face with a fierce intentness. "How can you love when you hate?"

"I hate you with the hate that I give to all the world; I love you with a feeling nothing else arouses."

Etarr turned away. "We make a strange pair . . ."

The turmoil, the whimpering joinings of flesh and half-flesh, quieted. A tall man in a conical black hat appeared on the dais. He flung back his head, shouted spells to the sky, wove runes in the air with his arms. And as he chanted, high above a gigantic wavering figure began to form, tall, taller than the highest trees, taller then the sky. It shaped slowly, green mists folding and unfolding, and presently the outline was clear—the wavering shape of a woman, beautiful, grave, stately. The figure slowly became steady, glowing with an unearthly green light. She seemed to have golden hair, coiffed in the manner of a dim past, and her clothes were those of the ancients.

The magician who had called her forth screamed, exulted, shouted vast windy taunts that rang past the crags.

"She lives!" murmured T'sais aghast. "She moves! Who is she?"

"It is Ethodea, goddess of mercy, from a time while the sun was still yellow," said Etarr.

The magician flung out his arm and a great bolt of purple fire soared up through the sky and spattered against the dim green form. The calm face twisted in anguish, and the watching demons, witches and necrophages called out in glee. The magician on the dias flung out his arm again, and bolt after bolt of purple fire darted up to smite the captive goddess. The whoops and cries of those by the fire were terrible to hear.

Then there came the clear thin call of a bugle, cutting brilliantly through the exaultation. The revel jerked breathlessly alert.

The bugle, musical and bright, rang again, louder, a sound alien to the place. And now, breasting over the crags like spume, charged a company of green-clad men, moving with fanatic resolve.

"Valdaran!" cried the magician on the dais, and the green figure of Ethodea wavered and disappeared.

Panic spread through the amphitheater. There were hoarse cries, a milling of lethargic bodies, a cloud of rising shapes as the demons sought flight. A few of the sorcerers stood boldly forth to chant spells of fire, dissolution, and paralysis against the assault, but there was strong counter-magic, and the invaders leapt unscathed into the amphitheater, vaulting the dais. Their swords rose and fell, hacking, slashing, stabbing without mercy or restraint.

"The Green Legion of Valdaran the Just," whispered Etarr. "See, there he stands!" He pointed to a brooding black-clad figure on the crest of the ridge, watching all with a savage satisfaction.

Nor did the demons escape. As they flapped through the night, great birds bestrode by men in green swooped down from the darkness. And these bore tubes which sprayed fans of galling light, and the demons who came within range gave terrible screams and toppled to earth, where they exploded in black dust.

A few sorcerers had escaped to the crags, to dodge and hide among the shadows. T'sais and Etarr heard a scrabbling and panting below. Frantically clambering up the rocks was she whom Etarr had come seeking—Javanne, her red hair streaming back from her clear young face. Etarr made a leap, caught her, clamped her with strong arms.

"Come," he said to T'sais, and bearing down the struggling figure, he strode off through the shadows.

At length as they passed down upon the moor, the tumult faded in the distance. Etarr set the woman upon her feet, unclamped her mouth. She caught sight for the first time of him who had seized her. The flame died from her face and through the night a slight smile could be seen. And she combed her long red hair with her fingers, arranging the locks over her shoulders, eyeing Etarr the while. T'sais wandered close, and Javanne turned her a slow apprasising glance.

She laughed. "So, Etarr, you have been unfaithful to me; you have found a new lover."

"She is no concern of yours," said Etarr.

"Send her away," said Javanne, "and I will love you again. Remember how you first kissed me beneath the poplars, on the terrace of your villa?''

Etarr gave a short sharp laugh. ''There is a single thing I require of you, and that is my face.''

And Javanne mocked him. ''Your face? What is amiss with the one you wear? You are better suited to it; and in any event, your former face is lost.''

''Lost? How so?''

''He who wore it was blasted this night by the Green Legion, may Kraan preserve their living brains in acid!''

Etarr turned his blue eyes off toward the crags.

''So now is your countenance dust, black dust,'' murmured Javanne. Etarr, in blind rage, stepped forward and struck at the sweetly impudent face. But Javanne took a quick step back.

''Careful, Etarr, lest I mischief you with magic. You may go limping, hopping hence with a body to suit your face. And your beautiful dark-haired child shall be play for demons.''

Etarr recovered himself and stood back, eyes smouldering.

''I have magic as well, and even without I would smite you silent with my fist ere you worded the first frame of your spell.''

''Ha, that we shall see,'' cried Javanne, skipping away. ''For I have a charm of wonderful brevity.'' As Etarr lunged at her she spoke a charm. Etarr stopped in mid-stride, his arms fell listless to his side, and he became a creature without volition, all his will drained by the leaching magic.

But Javanne stood in precisely the same posture, and her gray eyes stared dumbly forth. Only T'sais was free—for T'sais wore Pandelume's rune which reflected magic back against him who launched it.

She stood bewildered in the dark night, the two inanimate figures standing like sleep-walkers before her. She ran to Etarr, tugged at his arm. He looked at her with dull eyes.

''Etarr! What is wrong with you?'' And Etarr, because his will was paralyzed, forced to answer all questions and obey all orders, replied to her.

''The witch has spoken a spell which leaves me without volition. Therefore I cannot move or speak without command.''

''What shall I do. How can I save you?'' inquired the distressed girl. And, though Etarr was without volition, he retained his thought and passion. He could give her what information she asked, and nothing more.

''You must order me to a course which will defeat the witch.''

''But how will I know this course?''

"You will ask and I will tell you."

"Then would it not be better to order you to act as your brain directs?"

"Yes."

"Then do so; act under all circumstances as Etarr would act."

Thus in the dark of night the spell of Javanne the witch was circumvented and nullified. Etarr was recovered and conducted himself according to his normal promptings. He approached the immobile Javanne.

"Now do you fear me, witch?"

"Yes," said Javanne. "I fear you indeed."

"Is in truth the face you stole from me black dust?"

"Your face is in the black dust of an exploded demon."

The blue eyes looked steadily at her through the slits of the hood.

"How can I recover it?"

"It is mighty magic, a reaching into the past; and now your face is of the past. Magic stronger than mine is required, magic stronger than the wizards of Earth and the demon-worlds possess. I know of two only who are strong enough to make a mold of the past. The one is named Pandelume, who lives in a many-colored land—"

"Embelyon," murmured T'sais.

"—but the spell to journey to this land has been forgotten. Then there is another, who is no wizard, who knows no magic. To get your face, you must seek it of one of these," and Javanne stopped, the question of Etarr answered.

"Who is this latter one?" he asked.

"I know not his name. Far in the past, far beyond thought, so the legend runs, a race of just people lived in a land east of the Maurenron Mountains, past the Land of the Falling Wall, by the shores of a great sea. They built a city of spires and low glass domes, and dwelt in great content. These people had no god, and presently they felt the need of one whom they might worship. So they built a lustrous temple of gold, glass and granite, wide as the Scaum River where it flows through the Valley of Graven Tombs, as long again, and higher than the trees of the north. And this race of honest men assembled in the temple, and all flung a mighty prayer, a worshipful invocation, and, so legend has it, a god molded by the will of this people was brought into being, and he was of their attributes, a divinity of utter justice.

"The city at last crumbled, the temple became shards and splinters, the people vanished. But the god still remains, rooted forever to the place where his people worshipped him. And this god has power beyond magic. To each who faces him, the god wills and justice is done.

And let the evil beware, for those who face the god find no whit of mercy. Therefore few dare to bring their faces before this god.''

''And to this god we go,'' said Etarr with grim pleasure. ''The three of us, and the three of us shall face justice.''

They returned across the moors to Etarr's cabin, and he searched his books for means to transport them to the ancient site. In vain; he had no such magic at his command. He turned to Javanne.

''Do you know of magic to take us to this ancient god?''

''Yes.''

''What is this magic?''

''I will call three winged creatures from the Iron Mountains, and they will carry us.''

Etarr gazed at Javanne's white face sharply.

''What reward do they demand?''

''They kill those whom they transport.''

''Ah, witch,'' exclaimed Etarr, ''even with your will drugged and your answer willy-nilly honest, you contrive to harm us.'' He stood towering over the beautiful evil of red hair and wet lips. ''How may we get to the god unharmed and unmolested?''

''You must put the winged creatures under a charge.''

''Summon the things,'' Etarr ordered, ''and place them under the charge; and bind them with all the sorcery you know.''

Javanne called the creatures; they settled flapping on great leather wings. She placed them under a pact of safety, and they whined and stamped with disappointment.

And the three mounted, and the creatures took them swiftly through the night air, which already smelled of morning.

East, ever east. Dawn came, and the dim red sun ballooned slowly upward into the dark sky. The black Maurenron Range passed under; and the misty Land of the Falling Wall was left behind. To the south were the deserts of Almery, and an ancient sea-bed filled with jungle; to the north, the wild forests.

All during the day they flew, over dusty waste, dry cliffs, another great range of mountains, and as sunset came they slowly sloped downward over a green parkland.

Ahead shone a glimmering sea. The winged things landed on the wide strand, and Javanne bound them to immobility for their return.

The beach, the woodland behind, both were bare of any trace of the wondrous city of the past. But a half-mile out to sea rose a few broken columns.

''The sea has come,'' Etarr muttered. ''The city has foundered.''

He waded out. The sea was calm and shallow. T'sais and Javanne followed. With the water around their waists, and dusk coming from the sky, they came through the broken columns of the ancient temple.

A brooding presence pervaded the place, dispassionate, supernal, of illimitable will and power.

Etarr stood in the center of the old temple.

"God of the past!" he cried. "I know not how you were called, or I would invoke you by name. We three come from a far land to the west to seek justice of you. If you hear and will administer us each our due, give me a sign!"

A low sibilant voice from the air: "I hear and will give each his due." And each saw a vision of a golden six-armed figure with a round, calm face, sitting impassive in the nave of a monstrous temple.

"I have been bereft of my face," said Etarr. "If you deem me fit, restore me the face I once wore."

The god of the vision extended its six arms.

"I have searched your mind. Justice shall be meted. You may remove your hood." Slowly Etarr doffed his mask. He put his hand to his face. It was his own.

T'sais looked numbly at him. "Etarr!" she gasped. "My brain is whole! I see—*I see the world!*"

"To each who comes, justice is done," said the sibilant voice.

They heard a moan. They turned and looked at Javanne. Where was the lovely face, the strawberry mouth, the fair skin?

Her nose was a three-fold white squirming thing, her mouth a putrefying blotch. She had dangling mottled jowls and a peaked black forehead. The only thing left of Javanne was the long red hair dangling over her shoulders.

"To each who comes, justice is done," said the voice, and the vision of the temple faded, and once more the cool water of the twilight sea lapped at their waists, and the broken columns leaned black on the sky.

They returned slowly to the winged creatures.

Etarr turned to Javanne. "Go," he commanded. "Fly back to your lair. When the sun sets tomorrow, release yourself from the spell. Never bother us henceforth, for I have magic which will warn me and blast you if you approach."

And Javanne wordlessly bestrode her dark creature and winged off through the night.

Etarr turned to T'sais, and took her hand. He gazed down at her tilted white face, into the eyes glowing with such feverish joy that they seemed afire. He bent and kissed her forehead; then, together, hand in hand, they went to their fretting winged creatures, and so flew back to Ascolais.

4

Liane the Wayfarer

Through the dim forest came Liane the Wayfarer, passing along the shadowed glades with a prancing light-footed gait. He whistled, he caroled, he was plainly in high spirits. Around his finger he twirled a bit of wrought bronze—a circlet graved with angular crabbed characters, now stained black.

By excellent chance he had found it, banded around the root of an ancient yew. Hacking it free, he had seen the characters on the inner surface—rude forceful symbols, doubtless the cast of a powerful antique rune . . . Best take it to a magician and have it tested for sorcery.

Liane made a wry mouth. There were objections to the course. Sometimes it seemed as if all living creatures conspired to exasperate him. Only this morning, the spice merchant—what a tumult he had made dying! How carelessly he had spewed blood on Liane's cock comb sandals! Still, thought Liane, every unpleasantness carried with it compensation. While digging the grave he had found the bronze ring.

And Liane's spirits soared; he laughed in pure joy. He bounded, he leapt. His green cape flapped behind him, the red feather in his cap winked and blinked . . . But still—Liane slowed his step—he was no whit closer to the mystery of the magic, if magic the ring possessed.

Experiment, that was the word!

He stopped where the ruby sunlight slanted down without hindrance from the high foliage, examined the ring, traced the glyphs with his fingernail. He peered through. A faint film, a flicker? He held it at arm's length. It was clearly a coronet. He whipped off his cap, set the band on his brow, rolled his great golden eyes, preened himself . . .

Odd. It slipped down on his ears. It tipped across his eyes. Darkness. Frantically Liane clawed it off . . . A bronze ring, a hand's-breadth in diameter. Queer.

He tried again. It slipped down over his head, his shoulders. His head was in the darkness of a strange separate space. Looking down, he saw the level of the outside light dropping as he dropped the ring.

Slowly down . . . Now it was around his ankles—and in sudden panic, Liane snatched the ring up over his body, emerged blinking into the maroon light of the forest.

He saw a blue-white, green-white flicker against the foliage. It was a Twk-man, mounted on a dragon-fly, and light glinted from the dragon-fly's wings.

Liane called sharply, "Here, sir! Here, sir!"

The Twk-man perched his mount on a twig. "Well, Liane, what do you wish?"

"Watch now, and remember what you see." Liane pulled the ring over his head, dropped it to his feet, lifted it back. He looked up to the Twk-man, who was chewing a leaf. "And what did you see?"

"I saw Liane vanish from mortal sight—except for the red curled toes of his sandals. All else was as air."

"Ha!" cried Liane. "Think of it! Have you ever seen the like?"

The Twk-man asked carelessly, "Do you have salt? I would have salt."

Liane cut his exultations short, eyed the Twk-man closely.

"What news do you bring me?"

"Three erbs killed Florejin the Dream-builder, and burst all his bubbles. The air above the manse was colored for many minutes with the flitting fragments."

"A gram."

"Lord Kandive the Golden has built a barge of carven mo-wood ten lengths high, and it floats on the River Scaum for the Regatta, full of treasure."

"Two grams."

"A golden witch named Lith has come to live on Thamber Meadow. She is quiet and very beautiful."

"Three grams."

"Enough," said the Twk-man, and leaned forward to watch while Liane weighed out the salt in a tiny balance. He packed it in small panniers hanging on each side of the ribbed thorax, then twitched the insect into the air and flicked off through the forest vaults.

Once more Liane tried his bronze ring, and this time brought it entirely past his feet, stepped out of it and brought the ring up into the darkness beside him. What a wonderful sanctuary! A hole whose opening could be hidden inside the hole itself! Down with the ring to his feet, step through, bring it up his slender frame and over his shoulders, out into the forest with a small bronze ring in his hand.

Ho! and off to Thamber Meadow to see the beautiful golden witch.

Her hut was a simple affair of woven reeds—a low dome with two round windows and a low door. He saw Lith at the pond barelegged among the water shoots, catching frogs for her supper. A white kirtle was gathered up tight around her thighs; stock-still she stood and the dark water rippled rings away from her slender knees.

She was more beautiful than Liane could have imagined, as if one of Florejin's wasted bubbles had burst here on the water. Her skin was pale creamed stirred gold, her hair a denser, wetter gold. Her eyes were like Liane's own, great golden orbs, and hers were wide apart, tilted slightly.

Liane strode forward and planted himself on the bank. She looked up startled, her ripe mouth half-open.

"Behold, golden witch, here is Liane. He has come to welcome you to Thamber; and he offers you his friendship, his love . . ."

Lith bent, scooped a handful of slime from the bank and flung it into his face.

Shouting the most violent curses, Liane wiped his eyes free, but the door to the hut had slammed shut.

Liane strode to the door and pounded it with his fist.

"Open and show your witch's face, or I burn the hut!"

The door opened, and the girl looked forth, smiling. "What now?"

Liane entered the hut and lunged for the girl, but twenty thin shafts darted out, twenty points pricking his chest. He halted, eyebrows raised, mouth twitching.

"Down, steel," said Lith. The blades snapped from view. "So easily could I seek your vitality," said Lith, "had I willed."

Liane frowned and rubbed his chin as if pondering. "You understand," he said earnestly, "what a witless thing you do. Liane is feared by those who fear fear, loved by those who love love. And you—" his eyes swam the golden glory of her body—"you are ripe as a sweet fruit, you are eager, you glisten and tremble with love. You please Liane, and he will spend much warmness on you."

"No, no," said Lith, with a slow smile. "You are too hasty."

Liane looked at her in surprise. "Indeed?"

"I am Lith," said she. "I am what you say I am. I ferment, I burn, I seethe. Yet I may have no lover but him who has served me. He must be brave, swift, cunning."

"I am he," said Liane. He chewed at his lip. "It is not usually thus. I detest this indecision." He took a step forward. "Come, let us—"

She backed away. "No, no. You forget. How have you served me, how have you gained the right to my love?"

"Absurdity!" stormed Liane. "Look at me! Note my perfect grace, the beauty of my form and feature, my great eyes, as golden as your own, my manifest will and power . . . It is you who should serve me. That is how I will have it." He sank upon a low divan. "Woman, give me wine."

She shook her head. "In my small domed hut I cannot be forced. Perhaps outside on Thamber Meadow—but in here, among my blue and red tassels, with twenty blades of steel at my call, you must obey me. . . . So choose. Either arise and go, never to return, or else agree to serve me on one small mission, and then have me and all my ardor."

Liane sat straight and stiff. An odd creature, the golden witch. But, indeed, she was worth some exertion, and he would make her pay for her impudence.

"Very well, then," he said blandly. "I will serve you. What do you wish? Jewels? I can suffocate you in pearls, blind you with diamonds. I have two emeralds the size of your fist, and they are green oceans, where the gaze is trapped and wanders forever among vertical green prisms . . ."

"No, no jewels—"

"An enemy, perhaps. Ah, so simple. Liane will kill you ten men. Two steps forward, thrust—*thus!*" He lunged. "And souls go thrilling up like bubbles in a beaker of mead."

"No. I want no killing."

He sat back, frowning. "What, then?"

She stepped to the back of the room and pulled at a drape. It swung aside, displaying a golden tapestry. The scene was a valley bounded by two steep mountains, a broad valley where a placid river ran, past a quiet village and so into a grove of trees. Golden was the river, golden the mountains, golden the trees—golds so various, so rich, so subtle that the effect was like a many-colored landscape. But the tapestry had been rudely hacked in half.

Liane was entranced. "Exquisite, exquisite . . ."

Lith said, "It is the Magic Valley of Ariventa so depicted. The other half has been stolen from me, and its recovery is the service I wish of you."

"Where is the other half?" demanded Liane. "Who is the dastard?"

Now she watched him closely. "Have you ever heard of Chun? Chun the Unavoidable?"

Liane considered. "No."

"He stole the half to my tapestry, and hung it in a marble hall, and this hall is in the ruins to the north of Kaiin."

"Ha!" muttered Liane.

"The hall is by the Place of Whispers, and is marked by a leaning column with a black medallion of a phoenix and a two-headed lizard."

"I go," said Liane. He rose. "One day to Kaiin, one day to steal, one day to return. Three days."

Lith followed him to the door. "Beware of Chun the Unavoidable," she whispered.

And Liane strode away whistling, the red feather bobbing in his green cap. Lith watched him, then turned and slowly approached the golden tapestry. "Golden Ariventa," she whispered, "my heart cries and hurts with longing for you . . ."

The Derna is a swifter, thinner river than the Scaum, its bosomy sister to the south. And where the Scaum wallows through a broad dale, purple with horse-blossom, pocked white and gray with crumbling castles, the Derna has sheered a steep canyon, overhung by forested bluffs.

An ancient flint road long ago followed the course of the Derna, but now the exaggeration of the meandering has cut into the pavement, so that Liane, treading the road to Kaiin, was occasionally forced to leave the road and make a detour through banks of thorn and the tube-grass which whistled in the breeze.

The red sun, drifting across the universe like an old man creeping to his death-bed, hung low to the horizon when Liane breasted Porphiron Scar, looked across white-walled Kaiin and the blue bay of Sanreale beyond.

Directly below was the market-place, a medley of stalls selling fruits, slabs of pale meat, molluscs from the slime banks, dull flagons of wine. And the quiet people of Kaiin moved among the stalls, buying their sustenance, carrying it loosely to their stone chambers.

Beyond the market-place rose a bank of ruined columns, like broken teeth—legs to the arena built two hundred feet from the ground by Mad King Shin; beyond, in a grove of bay trees, the glossy dome of the palace was visible, where Kandive the Golden ruled Kaiin and as much of Ascolais as one could see from a vantage on Porphiron Scar.

The Derna, no longer a flow of clear water, poured through a network of dank canals and subterranean tubes, and finally seeped past rotting wharves into the Bay of Sanreale.

A bed for the night, thought Liane; then to his business in the morning.

He leapt down the zig-zag steps—back, forth, back, forth—and came out into the market-place. And now he put on a grave demeanor. Liane the Wayfarer was not unknown in Kaiin, and many were ill-minded enough to work him harm.

He moved sedately in the shade of the Pannone Wall, turned through a narrow cobbled street, bordered by old wooden houses glowing the rich brown of old stump-water in the rays of the setting sun, and so came to a small square and the high stone face of the Magician's Inn.

The host, a small fat man, sad of eye, with a small fat nose the identical shape of his body, was scraping ashes from the hearth. He straightened his back and hurried behind the counter of his little alcove.

Liane said, "A chamber, well-aired, and a supper of mushrooms, wine and oysters."

The innkeeper bowed humbly.

"Indeed, sir—and how will you pay?"

Liane flung down a leather sack, taken this very morning. The innkeeper raised his eyebrows in pleasure at the fragrance.

"The ground buds of the spase-bush, brought from a far land," said Liane.

"Excellent, excellent . . . Your chamber, sir, and your supper at once."

As Liane ate, several other guests of the house appeared and sat before the fire with wine, and the talk grew large, and dwelt on wizards of the past and the great days of magic.

"Great Phandaal knew a lore now forgot," said one old man with hair dyed orange. "He tied white and black strings to the legs of sparrows and sent them veering to his direction. And where they wove their magic woof, great trees appeared, laden with flowers, fruits, nuts, or bulbs of rare liqueurs. It is said that thus he wove Great Da Forest on the shores of Sanra Water."

"Ha," said a dour man in a garment of dark blue, brown and black, "this I can do." He brought forth a bit of string, flicked it, whirled it, spoke a quiet word, and the vitality of the pattern fused the string into a tongue of red and yellow fire, which danced, curled, darted back and forth along the table till the dour man killed it with a gesture.

"And this I can do," said a hooded figure in a black cape sprinkled with silver circles. He brought forth a small tray, laid it on the table and sprinkled therein a pinch of ashes from the hearth. He brought forth a whistle and blew a clear tone, and up from the tray came glittering motes, flashing the prismatic colors red, blue, green, yellow. They floated up a foot and bust in coruscations of brilliant colors, each a beautiful star-shaped pattern, and each burst sounded a tiny repetition of the original tone—the clearest, purest sound in the world. The motes became fewer, the magician blew a different tone, and again the motes floated up to burst in glorious ornamental spangles. Another time—another swarm of motes. At last the magician replaced his whistle, wiped off the tray, tucked it inside his cloak and lapsed back to silence.

Now the other wizards surged forward, and soon the air above the table swarmed with visions, quivered with spells. One showed the group nine new colors of ineffable charm and radiance; another caused a mouth to form on the landlord's forehead and revile the crowd, much to the landlord's discomfiture, since it was his own voice. Another displayed a green glass bottle from which the face of a demon peered and grimaced; another a ball of pure crystal which rolled back and forward to the command of the sorcerer who owned it, and who claimed it to be an earring of the fabled master Sankaferrin.

Liane had attentively watched all, crowing in delight at the bottled imp, and trying to cozen the obedient crystal from its owner, without success.

And Liane became pettish, complaining that the world was full of rock-hearted men, but the sorcerer with the crystal earring remained indifferent, and even when Liane spread out twelve packets of rare spice he refused to part with his toy.

Liane pleaded, "I wish only to please the witch Lith."

"Please her with the spice, then."

Liane said ingenuously, "Indeed, she has but one wish, a bit of tapestry which I must steal from Chun the Unavoidable."

And he looked from face to suddenly silent face.

"What causes such immediate sobriety? Ho, Landlord, more wine!"

The sorcerer with the earring said, "If the floor swam ankle-deep with wine—the rich red wine of Tanvilkat—the leaden print of that name would still ride the air."

"Ha," laughed Liane, "let only a taste of that wine pass your lips, and the fumes would erase all memory."

"See his eyes," came a whisper. "Great and golden."

"And quick to see," spoke Liane. "And these legs—quick to run, fleet as starlight on the waves. And this arm—quick to stab with steel.

And my magic—which will set me to a refuge that is out of all cognizance.'' He gulped wine from a beaker. ''Now behold. This is magic from antique days.'' He set the bronze band over his head, stepped through, brought it up inside the darkness. When he deemed that sufficient time had elapsed, he stepped through once more.

The fire glowed, the landlord stood in his alcove, Liane's wine was at hand. But of the assembled magicians, there was no trace.

Liane looked about in puzzlement. ''And where are my wizardly friends?''

The landlord turned his head: ''They took to their chambers; the name you spoke weighed on their souls.''

And Liane drank his wine in frowning silence.

Next morning he left the inn and picked a roundabout way to the Old Town—a gray wilderness of tumbled pillars, weathered blocks of sandstone, slumped pediments with crumbled inscriptions, flagged terraces overgrown with rusty moss. Lizards, snakes, insects crawled the ruins; no other life did he see.

Threading a way through the rubble, he almost stumbled on a corpse—the body of a youth, one who stared at the sky with empty eye-sockets.

Liane felt a presence. He leapt back, rapier half-bared. A stooped old man stood watching him. He spoke in a feeble, quavering voice: ''And what will you have in the Old Town?''

Liane replaced his rapier. ''I seek the Place of Whispers. Perhaps you will direct me.''

The old man made a croaking sound at the back of his throat. ''Another? Another? When will it cease? . . .'' He motioned to the corpse. ''This one came yesterday seeking the Place of Whispers. He would steal from Chun the Unavoidable. See him now.'' He turned away. ''Come with me.'' He disappeared over a tumble of rock.

Liane followed. The old man stood by another corpse with eye-sockets bereft and bloody. ''This one came four days ago, and he met Chun the Unavoidable . . . And over there behind the arch is still, a great warrior in cloison armor. And there—and there—'' he pointed, pointed. ''And there—and there—like crushed flies.''

He turned his watery blue gaze back to Liane. ''Return, young man, return—lest your body lie here in its green cloak to rot on the flagstones.''

Liane drew his rapier and flourished it. ''I am Liane the Wayfarer; let them who offend me have fear. And where is the Place of Whispers?''

"If you must know," said the old man, "it is beyond that broken obelisk. But you go to your peril."

"I am Liane the Wayfarer. Peril goes with me."

The old man stood like a piece of weathered statuary as Liane strode off.

And Liane asked himself, suppose this old man were an agent of Chun, and at this minute were on his way to warn him? . . . Best to take all precautions. He leapt up on a high entablature and ran crouching back to where he had left the ancient.

Here he came, muttering to himself, leaning on his staff. Liane dropped a block of granite as large as his head. A thud, a croak, a gasp—and Liane went his way.

He strode past the broken obelisk, into a wide court—the Place of Whispers. Directly opposite was a long wide hall, marked by a leaning column with a big black medallion, the sign of a phoenix and a two-headed lizard.

Liane merged himself with the shadow of a wall, and stood watching like a wolf, alert for any flicker of motion.

All was quiet. The sunlight invested the ruins with dreary splendor. To all sides, as far as the eye could reach, was broken stone, a wasteland leached by a thousand rains, until now the sense of man had departed and the stone was one with the natural earth.

The sun moved across the dark-blue sky. Liane presently stole from his vantage-point and circled the hall. No sight nor sign did he see.

He approached the building from the rear and pressed his ear to the stone. It was dead, without vibration. Around the side—watching up, down, to all sides; a breach in the wall. Liane peered inside. At the back hung half a golden tapestry. Otherwise the hall was empty.

Liane looked up, down, this side, that. There was nothing in sight. He continued around the hall.

He came to another broken place. He looked within. To the rear hung the golden tapestry. Nothing else, to right or left, no sight or sound.

Liane continued to the front of the hall and sought into the eaves; dead as dust.

He had a clear view of the room. Bare, barren, except for the bit of golden tapestry.

Liane entered, striding with long soft steps. He halted in the middle of the floor. Light came to him from all sides except the rear wall. There were a dozen openings from which to flee and no sound except the dull thudding of his heart.

He took two steps forward. The tapestry was almost at his fingertips.

He stepped forward and swiftly jerked the tapestry down from the wall.

And behind was Chun the Unavoidable.

Liane screamed. He turned on paralyzed legs and they were leaden, like legs in a dream which refused to run.

Chun dropped out of the wall and advanced. Over his shiny black back he wore a robe of eyeballs threaded on silk.

Liane was running, fleetly now. He sprang, he soared. The tips of his toes scarcely touched the ground. Out the hall, across the square, into the wilderness of broken statues and fallen columns. And behind came Chun, running like a dog.

Liane sped along the crest of a wall and sprang a great gap to a shattered fountain. Behind came Chun.

Liane darted up a narrow alley, climbed over a pile of refuse, over a roof, down into a court. Behind came Chun.

Liane sped down a wide avenue lined with a few stunted old cypress trees, and he heard Chun close at his heels. He turned into an archway, pulled his bronze ring over his head, down to his feet. He stepped through, brought the ring up inside the darkness. Sanctuary. He was alone in a dark magic space, vanished from earthly gaze and knowledge. Brooding silence, dead space . . .

He felt a stir behind him, a breath of air. At his elbow a voice said, "I am Chun the Unavoidable."

Lith sat on her couch near the candles, weaving a cap from frogskins. The door to her hut was barred, the windows shuttered. Outside, Thamber Meadow dwelled in darkness.

A scrape at her door, a creak as the lock was tested. Lith became rigid and stared at the door.

A voice said, "Tonight, O Lith, tonight it is two long bright threads for you. Two because the eyes were so great, so large, so golden . . .

Lith sat quiet. She waited an hour; then, creeping to the door, she listened. The sense of presence was absent. A frog croaked nearby.

She eased the door ajar, found the threads and closed the door. She ran to her golden tapestry and fitted the threads into the ravelled warp.

And she stared at the golden valley, sick with longing for Ariventa, and tears blurred out the peaceful river, the quiet golden forest. "The cloth slowly grows wider . . . One day it will be done, and I will come home. . ."

5

Ulan Dhor

Prince Kandive the Golden spoke earnestly to his nephew Ulan Dhor. "It must be understood that the expansion of craft and the new lore will be shared between us."

Ulan Dhor, a slender young man, pale of skin, with the blackest of hair, eyes, and eyebrows, smiled ruefully. "But it is I who journey the forgotten water, I who must beat down the sea-demons with my oar."

Kandive leaned back into his cushions and tapped his nose with a ferrule of carved jade.

"And it is I who make the venture possible. Further, I am already an accomplished wizard; the increment of lore will merely enhance my craft. You, not even a novice, will gain such knowledge as to rank you among the magicians of Ascolais. This is a far cry from your present ineffectual status. Seen in this light, my gain is small, yours is great."

Ulan Dhor grimaced. "True enough, though I dispute the word 'ineffectual'. I know Phandaal's Critique of the Chill, I am reckoned a master of the sword, ranked among the Eight Delaphasians as a . . ."

"Pah!" sneered Kandive. "The vapid mannerisms of pale people, using up their lives. Mincing murder, extravagant debauchery, while Earth passes its last hours, and none of you have ventured a mile from Kaiin."

Ulan Dhor held his tongue, reflecting that Prince Kandive the Golden was not known to scorn the pleasures of wine, couch, or table; and that his farthest known sally from the domed palace had taken him to his carven barge on the River Scaum.

Kandive, appeased by Ulan Dhor's silence, brought forward an ivory box. "Thus and so. If we are agreed, I will invest you with knowledge."

Ulan Dhor nodded. "We are agreed."

Kandive said, "The mission will take you to the lost city Ampridatvir." He watched Ulan Dhor's face from sidelong eyes; Ulan Dhor maintained an even expression.

"I have never seen it," continued Kandive. "Porrina the Ninth lists it as the last of the Olek'hnit cities, situated on an island in the North Melantine." He opened the box. "This tale I found in an ancient bundle of scrolls—the testament of a poet who fled Ampridatvir after the death of Rogol Domedonfors, their last great leader, a magician of great force, mentioned forty-three times in the Cyclopedia . . ."

Kandive brought forth a crackling scroll, and, whipping it open, read:

" 'Ampridatvir now is lost. My people have forsaken the doctrine of strength and discipline and concern themselves only with superstition and theology. Unending is the bicker: Is Pansiu the excellent principle and Cazdal depraved, or is Cazdal the virtuous god, and Pansiu the essential evil?

" 'These questions are debated with fire and steel, and the memory sickens me; now I leave Ampridatvir to the decline which must surely come, and remove to the kind valley of Mel-Palusas, where I will end this firefly life of mine.

" 'I have known the Ampridatvir of old; I have seen the towers glowing with marvellous light, thrusting beams through the night to challenge the sun itself. Then Ampridatvir was beautiful—ah my heart pains when I think of the olden city. Semir vines cascaded from a thousand hanging gardens, water ran blue as vaulstone in the three canals. Metal cars rolled the streets, metal hulls swarmed the air as thick as bees around a hive—for marvel of marvels, we had devised wefts of spitting fire to spurn the weighty power of Earth . . . But even in my life I saw the leaching of spirit. A surfeit of honey cloys the tongue; a surfeit of wine addles the brain; so a surfeit of ease guts a man of strength. Light, warmth, food, water, were free to all men, and gained by a minimum of effort. So the people of Ampridatvir, released from toil, gave increasing attention to faddishness, perversity, and the occult.

" 'To the furthest reach of my memory, Rogol Domedonfors ruled the city. He knew lore of all ages, secrets of fire and light, gravity and counter-gravity, the knowledge of superphysic numeration, metathasm, corolopsis. In spite of his profundity, he was impractical in his rule, and blind to the softening of Ampridatvirian spirit. Such weakness and lethargy as he saw he ascribed to a lack of education, and in his last years he evolved a tremendous machine to release men from all labor, and thus permit full leisure for meditation and ascetic discipline.

" 'While Rogol Domedonfors completed his great work, the city dissolved into turbulence—the result of a freak religious hysteria.

" 'The rival sects of Pansiu and Cazdal had long existed, but few other than the priests heeded the dispute. Suddenly the cults became fashionable; the population flocked to worship one or the other of the dieties. The priests, long-jealous rivals, were delighted with their new power, and exhorted the converts to a crusading zeal. Friction arose, emotion waxed, there was rioting and violence. And on one evil day a stone struck Rogol Domedonfors, toppled him from a balcony.

" 'Crippled and wasting but refusing to die, Rogol Domedonfors completed his underground mechanism, installed vestibules throughout the city, and then took to his death-bed. He issued one directive to his new machine, and when Ampridatvir awoke the next morning, the people found their city without power or light, the food factories quiet, the canals diverted.

" 'In terror they rushed to Rogol Domedonfors, who said: "I have long been blind to your decadence and eccentricities; now I despise you; you have been the death of me."

" ' "But the city dies! The race perishes!" they cried.

" ' "You must save yourselves," Rogol Domedonfors told them. "You have ignored the ancient wisdom, you have been too indolent to learn, you have sought easy complacence from religion, rather than facing manfully to the world. I have resolved to impose a bitter experience upon you, which I hope will be salutary."

" 'He called the rival priests of Pansiu and Cazdal, and handed to each a tablet of transparent metal.

" 'These tablets singly are useless; laid together a message may be read. He who reads the message will have the key to the ancient knowledge, and will wield the power I had planned for my own use. Now go, and I will die."

" 'The priests, glaring at each other, departed, called their followers, and so began a great war.

" 'The body of Rogol Domedonfors was never found, and some say his skeleton still lies in the passages below the city. The tablets are housed in the rival temples. By night there is murder, by day there is starvation in the streets. Many have fled to the mainland, and now I follow, leaving Ampridatvir, the last home of the race. I will build a wooden hut on the slope of Mount Liu and live out my days in the valley of Mel-Palusas.' "

Kandive twisted the scroll and replaced it in the box. "Your task," he told Ulan Dhor, "is to journey to Ampridatvir and recover the magic of Rogol Domedonfors."

Ulan Dhor said thoughtfully, "It was a long time ago... Thousands of years..."

"Correct," said Kandive. "However, none of the histories of indices make further mention of Rogol Domedonfors, and herefore I believe that the wisdom of Rogol Domedonfors still remains to be found in ancient Ampridatvir."

Three weeks Ulan Dhor sailed the nerveless ocean. The sun rose bright as blood from the horizon and belled across the sky, and the water was calm, save for the ruffle of the breeze and the twin widening marks of Ulan Dhor's wake.

Then came the setting, the last sad glance across the world; then purple twilight and the night. The old stars spanned the sky and the wake behind Ulan Dhor shone ghastly white. Then did he watch for heavings of the surface, for he felt greatly alone on the dark face of the ocean.

Three weeks Ulan Dhor sailed the Melantine Gulf, to the north and west, and one morning he saw to the right the dark shadow of coastland and to the left the loom of an island, almost lost in the haze.

Close off his bow goated an ungainly barge, moving sluggishly under a square sail of plaited reeds.

Ulan Dhor laid a course so as to draw alongside, and saw on the barge two men in coarse green smocks trolling for fish. They had oat-yellow hair and blue eyes, and they wore expressions of stupefaction.

Ulan Dhor dropped his sail and laid hold of the barge. The fishermen neither moved nor spoke.

Ulan Dhor said, "You seem unfamiliar with the sight of man."

The older man broke into a nervous chant which Ulan Dhor understood to be an invocation against demons and frits.

Ulan Dhor laughed. "Why do you inveigh against me? I am a man like yourself."

The younger man said in a broad dialect: "We reason you to be a demon. First, there are none of our race with night-black hair and eyes. Second, the Word of Pansiu denies the existence of all other men. Therefore you can be no man, and must be a demon."

The older man said under his hand, "Hold your tongue; speak no word. He will curse the tones of your voice..."

"You are wrong, I assure you," replied Ulan Dhor politely. "Have either of you ever seen a demon?"

"None but the Gauns."

"Do I resemble the Gauns?"

"Not at all," admitted the older man. His companion indicated Ulan Dhor's dull scarlet coat and green trousers. "He is evidently a Raider; note the color of his garb."

Ulan Dhor said, "No, I am neither Raider nor demon. I am merely a man . . ."

"No men exist except the Greens—so says Pansiu."

Ulan Dhor threw back his head and laughed. "Earth is but wilderness and ruins, true enough, but many men yet walk abroad . . . Tell me, is the city Ampridatvir to be found on that island ahead?"

The younger man nodded.

"And you live there?"

Again the young man assented.

Ulan Dhor said uncomfortably, "I understood that Ampridatvir was a deserted ruin—forlorn, desolate."

The young man asked with a shrewd expression, "And what do you seek at Ampridatvir?"

Ulan Dhor thought, I will mention the tablets and observe their reaction. It is well to learn if these tablets are known, and if so, how they are regarded. He said, "I have sailed three weeks to find Ampridatvir and investigate some legendary tablets."

"Ah," said the older man. "The tablets! He is a Raider, then. I see it clearly. Note his green trousers. A Raider for the Greens . . ."

Ulan Dhor, expecting hostility as a result of this identification, was surprised to find a more pleasant expression on the faces of the men, as if now they had resolved a troublesome parodox. Very well, he thought, if that is how they will have it, let it be.

The younger man wished total clarity. "Is that your claim then, dark man? Do you wear red as a Raider for the Greens?"

Ulan Dhor said cautiously, "My plans are not settled."

"But you wear red! That is the color the Raiders wear!"

Here is a peculiarly disrupted way of thinking, reflected Ulan Dhor. It is almost as if a rock blocked the stream of their thought and diverted the current in a splash and a spray. He said, "Where I come from, a man wears such colors as he chooses."

The older man said eagerly, "But you wear Green, so evidently you have chosen to raid for the Greens."

Ulan Dhor shrugged, sensing the block across a mental channel. "If you wish . . . What others are there?"

"None, no other," replied the older man. "We are the Greens of Ampridatvir."

"Then—whom does a Raider raid?"

The younger man moved uneasily and pulled in his line. "He raids a ruined temple to the demon Cazdal, for the lost tablet of Rogol Domedonfors."

"In that case," said Ulan Dhor, "I might become a Raider."

"For the Greens," said the old man, peering at him side-wise.

"Enough, enough," said the other. "The sun is past the zenith. We had best be homeward."

"Aye, aye," said the older man, with sudden energy. "The sun drops."

The younger man looked at Ulan Dhor. "If you propose to raid, you had best come with us."

Ulan Dhor passed a line to the barge, adding his fabric sail to the plaited reeds, and they turned their bows toward shore.

It was very beautiful, crossing the sunny afternoon swells toward the forested island, and as they rounded the eastern cape, Ampridatvir came into view.

A line of low buildings faced the harbor, and beyond rose such towers as Ulan Dhor had never imagined to exist—metal spires soaring past the central height of the island to glisten in the light of the setting sun. Such cities were legends of the past, dreams of the time when the Earth was young.

Ulan Dhor stared speculatively at the barge, at the coarse green cloaks of the fishermen. Were they peasants? Would he become a butt for ridicule, thus arriving at the glistening city? He turned uncomfortably back to the island, chewing his lips. According to Kandive, Ampridatvir would be toppled columns and rubble, like the Old Town above Kaiin . . .

The sun dropped against the water, and now Ulan Dhor, with a sudden shock, noticed the crumble at the base of the towers; here was his expectation, as much desolation as Kandive had predicted. Strangely the fact gave Ampridatvir an added majesty, the dignity of a lost monument.

The wind had slackened, the progress of boat and barge was slow indeed. The fishermen betrayed anxiety, muttering to each other, adjusting their sail to draw its best, tightening their stays. But before they drifted inside the breakwater, purple twilight had dropped across the city, and the towers became tremendous black monoliths. In near-darkness they tied to a landing of logs, among other barges, some painted green, others gray.

Ulan Dhor jumped up to the dock. "A moment," said the younger fisherman, eyeing Ulan Dhor's red coat. "It would be unwise to dress thus, even at night." He rummaged through a box and brought forth a green cape, ragged and smelling of fish. "Wear this, and hold the hood over your black hair . . ."

Ulan Dhor obeyed with a private grimace of distaste. He asked, "Where may I sup and bed tonight? Are there inns or hostels in Ampridatvir?"

The younger man said without enthusiasm, "You may pass the night at my hall."

The fishermen slung the day's catch over their shoulders, climbed to the dock, and peered anxiously through the rubble.

"You are ill at ease," observed Ulan Dhor.

"Aye," said the younger man. "At night the Gauns roam the streets."

"What are the Gauns?"

"Demons."

"There are many varieties of demons," Ulan Dhor said lightly. "What be these?"

"They are like horrible men. They have great long arms that clutch and rend . . ."

"Ho!" muttered Ulan Dhor, feeling for his sword hilt. "Why do you permit them abroad?"

"We cannot harm them. They are fierce and strong—but fortunately not too agile. With luck and watchfulness . . ."

Ulan Dhor now searched the rubble with an expression as careful as the fishermen's. These people were familiar with the dangers of the place; he would obey their counsel until he knew better.

They threaded the first tumble of ruins, entered a canyon shadowed from the afterglow by the pinnacles to either side, brimming with gloom.

Deadness! thought Ulan Dhor. The place was under the pall of dusty death. Where were the active millions of long ago Ampridatvir? Dead dust, their moisture mingled in the ocean, beside that of every other man and woman who had lived on Earth.

Ulan Dhor and the two fishermen moved down the avenue, pygmy figures wandering a dream-city, and Ulan Dhor looked coldly from side to side . . . Prince Kandive the Golden had spoken truth. Ampridatvir was the very definition of antiquity. The windows gaped black, concrete had cracked, balconies hung crazily, terraces were mounded with dust. Debris filled the streets—blocks of stone from fallen columns, crushed and battered metal.

But Ampridatvir still moved with a weird unending life where the builders had used ageless substance, eternal energies. Strips of a dark glistening material flowed like water at each side of the street—slowly at the edges, rapidly at the center.

The fishermen matter-of-factly stepped on this strip, and Ulan Dhor gingerly followed them to the swift center. "I see roads flowing like rivers in Ampridatvir," he said. "You call me demon; truly I think the glove is on the other hand."

"It is no magic," said the younger man shortly. "It is the way of Ampridatvir."

At regular intervals along the street stood stone vestibules about ten feet high that had the appearance of sheltering ramps leading below the street.

"What lies below?" inquired Ulan Dhor.

The fishermen shrugged. "The doors are tight. No man has ever gone through. Legend says it was the last work of Rogol Domedonfors."

Ulan Dhor withheld further questions, observing a growing nervousness in the fishermen. Infected by their apprehension he kept his hand at his sword.

"None live in this part of Ampridatvir," said the old fisherman in a hoarse whisper. "It is ancient beyond imagining, ridden with ghosts."

The streets broke into a central square, the towers fell away before them. The sliding strip coasted to a stop, like water flowing into a pool. Here glowed the first artificial light Ulan Dhor had seen—a bright globe hung on a looping metal stanchion.

In this light Ulan Dhor saw a youth in a gray cloak hurrying across the square . . . A movement among the ruins; the fishermen gasped, crouched. A corpse-pale creature sprang out into the light. Its arms hung knotted and long; dirty fur covered its legs. Great eyes glared from a peaked, fungus-white skull; two fangs hung over the undershot mouth. It leapt upon the wretch in the gray robe and tucked him under his arm; then, turning, gave Ulan Dhor and the fishermen a look of baleful triumph. And now they saw that the victim was a woman . . .

Ulan Dhor drew his sword. "No, no!" whispered the older man. "The Gaun will go its way!"

"But the woman it has taken! We can save her!"

"The Gaun has seized no one." The old man clutched at his shoulder.

"Are you blind, man?" cried Ulan Dhor.

"There are none in Ampridatvir but the Greens," said the younger man. "Stay by us."

Ulan Dhor hesitated. Was the woman in gray, then, a ghost? If so, why did not the fishermen say as much? . . .

The Gaun, with insolent leisure, stalked toward a long edifice of dark tumbled arches.

Ulan Dhor ran across the white square of ancient Ampridatvir.

The monster twisted to face him and flung out a great knotted arm, as long as a man was tall, ending in a white-furred clump of fingers. Ulan Dhor hewed a tremendous blow with his sword; the Gaun's forearm dangled by a shred of flesh and bone-splinter.

Jumping back to avoid the spray of blood, Ulan Dhor ducked the grasp of the other arm as it swung past. He hacked again, another great blow, and the second forearm dangled loosely. He sprang close, plunged his blade at the creature's eye and struck up into the beast's skull-case.

The creature died in a series of wild capers, maniac throes that took it dancing around the square.

Ulan Dhor, panting, fighting nausea, looked down to the wide-eyed woman. She was rising weakly to her feet. He reached an arm to steady her, noticing that she was slim and young, with blonde hair hanging loosely to the level of her jaw. She had a pleasant, pretty face, thought Ulan Dhor—candid, clear-eyed, innocent.

She appeared not to notice him, but stood half-turned away, wrapping herself in her gray cloak. Ulan Dhor began to fear that the shock had affected her mind. He moved forward and peered into her face.

"Are you well? Did the beast harm you?"

Surprise came over her face, almost as if Ulan Dhor were another Gaun. Her gaze brushed his green cloak, quickly moved back to his face, his black hair.

"Who . . . are you?" she whispered.

"A stranger," said Ulan Dhor, "and much puzzled by the ways of Ampridatvir." He looked around for the fishermen; they were nowhere in sight.

"A stranger?" the girl asked. "But Cazdal's Tract tells us that the Gauns have destroyed all men but the Grays of Ampridatvir."

"Cazdal is as incorrect as Pansiu," remarked Ulan Dhor. "There are still many men in the world."

"I must believe," said the girl. "You speak, you exist—so much is clear."

Ulan Dhor noticed that she kept her eyes averted from the green cloak. It stank of fish; without further ado he cast it aside.

Her glance went to his red coat. "A Raider . . ."

"No, no, no!" exclaimed Ulan Dhor. "In truth, I find this talk of color tiresome. I am Ulan Dhor of Kaiin, nephew to Prince Kandive the Golden, and my mission is to seek the tablets of Rogol Domedonfors."

The girl smiled wanly. "Thus do the Raiders, and thus they dress in red, and then every man's hand is turned against them, for when they are in red, who knows whether they be Grays or . . ."

"Or what?"

She appeared confused, as if this facet to the question had not occurred to her. "Ghosts? Demons? There are strange manifestations in Ampridatvir."

"Beyond argument," agreed Ulan Dhor. He glanced across the square. "If you wish, I will guard you to your home; and perhaps there will be a corner where I may sleep tonight."

She said, "I owe you my life, and I will help you as best I can. But I dare not take you to my hall." Her eyes drifted down his body as far as his green trousers and veered away. "There would be confusion and unending explanations . . ."

Ulan Dhor said obliquely, "You have a mate, then?"

She glanced at him swiftly—a strange coquetry, strange flirtation there in the shadows of ancient Ampridatvir, the girl in the coarse gray cloak, her head tilted sideways and the yellow hair falling clear to her shoulder; Ulan Dhor elegant, darkly aquiline, in full command of his soul.

"No," she said. "There have been none, so far." A slight sound disturbed her; she jerked, looked fearfully across the square.

"There may be more Gauns. I can take you to a safe place; then tomorrow we will talk . . ."

She led him through an arched portico into one of the towers, up to a mezzanine floor. "You'll be safe here till morning." She squeezed his arm. "I'll bring you food, if you'll wait for me . . ."

"I'll wait."

Her gaze fell with the strange half-averted wavering of the eyes to his red coat, just brushed his green trousers. "And I'll bring you a cloak." She departed. Ulan Dhor saw her flit down the stair and out of the tower like a wraith. She was gone.

He settled himself on the floor. It was a soft elastic substance, warm to the touch . . . A strange city, thought Ulan Dhor, a strange people, reacting to unguessed compulsions. Or were they ghosts, in truth?

He fell into a series of spasmodic dozes, and awoke at last to find the wan pink of the latter-day dawn seeping through the arched portico.

He rose to his feet, rubbed his face, and, after a moment's hesitation, descended from the mezzanine to the floor of the tower and walked out into the street. A child in a gray smock saw his red coat, flicked his eyes away from the green trousers, screamed in terror, and ran across the square.

Ulan Dhor retreated into the shadows with a curse. He had expected desolation. Hostility he could have countered or fled, but this bewildered fright left him helpless.

A shape appeared at the entrance—the girl. She peered through the shadows; her face was drawn, anxious. Ulan Dhor appeared. She smiled suddenly and her face changed.

"I brought your breakfast," she said, "also a decent garment."

She lay bread and smoked fish before him, and poured warm herb tea from an earthenware jar.

As he ate he watched her, and she watched him. There was a tension in their relations; she felt incompletely secure, and he could sense the pressures on her mind.

"What is your name?" she asked.

"I am Ulan Dhor. And you?"

"Elai."

"Elai . . . Is that all?"

"Do I need more? It is sufficient, is it not?"

"Oh, indeed."

She seated herself cross-legged before him.

"Tell me about the land from which you come."

Ulan Dhor said, "Ascolais now is mostly a great forest, where few care to venture. I live in Kaiin, a very old city, perhaps as old as Ampridatvir, but we have no such towers and floating roads. We live in the old-time palaces of marble and wood, even the poorest and most menial. Indeed, some beautiful manses fall to ruins for lack of tenants."

"And what is your color?" she asked in a tentative voice.

Ulan Dhor said impatiently, "Such nonsense. We wear all colors; no one thinks one way or the other about it . . . Why do you worry about color so? For instance, why do you wear gray and not green?"

Her gaze wavered and broke from his; she clenched her hands restlessly. "Green? That is the color of the demon Pansiu. No one in Ampridatvir wears green."

"Certainly people wear green," said Ulan Dhor. "I met two fishermen yesterday at sea wearing green, and they guided me into the city."

She shook her head, smiling sadly. "You are mistaken."

Ulan Dhor sat back. He said presently. ''A child saw me this morning and ran off screaming.''

''Because of your red cloak,'' said Elai. ''When a man wishes to win honor for himself, he dons a red coat and sets forth across the city to the ancient deserted temple of Pansiu, to seek the lost half of Rogol Domedonfors' tablet. Legend says that when the Grays recover the lost tablet, then will their power be strong once more.''

''If the temple is deserted,'' asked Ulan Dhor dryly, ''why has not some man taken the tablet?''

She shrugged and looked vaguely into space. ''We believe that it is guarded by ghosts . . . At any rate, sometimes a man in red is found raiding Cazdal's temple also, whereupon he is killed. A man in red is therefore everybody's enemy, and every hand is turned against him.''

Ulan Dhor rose to his feet and wrapped himself in the gray robe the girl had brought.

''What are your plans?'' she asked, rising quickly.

''I wish to look upon the tablets of Rogol Domedonfors, both in Cazdal's Temple and in Pansiu's.''

She shook her head. ''Impossible. Cazdal's Temple is forbidden to all but the venerable priests, and Pansiu's Temple is guarded by ghosts.''

Ulan Dhor grinned. ''If you'll show me where the temples are situated . . .''

She said, ''I'll go with you . . . But you must remain wrapped in the cloak, or it will go badly for both of us.''

They stepped out into the sunlight. The square was dotted with slow-moving groups of men and women. Some wore green, others wore gray, and Ulan Dhor saw that there was no intercourse between the two. Greens paused by little green-painted booths selling fish, leather, fruit, meal, pottery, baskets. Grays bought from identical shops which were painted gray. He saw two groups of children, one in green rags, the other in gray, playing ten feet apart, acknowledging each other by not so much as a glance. A ball of tied rags rolled from the Gray children into the scuffling group of Greens. A Gray child ran over, picked up the ball from under the feet of a Green child, and neither took the slightest notice of the other.

''Strange,'' muttered Ulan Dhor. ''Strange.''

''What's strange?'' inquired Elai. ''I see nothing strange . . .''

''Look,'' said Ulan Dhor, ''by that pillar. Do you see that man in the green cloak?''

She glanced at him in puzzlement. ''There is no man there.''

''There is a man there,'' said Ulan Dhor. ''Look again.''

She laughed. "You are joking . . . or can you see ghosts?"

Ulan Dhor shook his head in defeat. "You are the victims of some powerful magic."

She led him to one of the flowing roadways; as they were carried through the city he noticed a boat-shaped hull built of bright metal with four wheels and a transparent-domed compartment.

He pointed. "What is that?"

"It is a magic car. When a certain lever is pressed the wizardry of the older times gives it great speed. Rash young men ride them along the streets . . . See there," and she pointed to a somewhat similar hull toppled into the basin of a long, dry fountain. "That is another one of the ancient wonders—a craft with the power to fly through the air. There are many of them scattered through the city—on the towers, on high terraces, and sometimes, like this one, fallen into the streets."

"And no one flies them?" asked Ulan Dhor curiously.

"We are all afraid."

Ulan Dhor thought, what a marvel to own one of these air-cars! He stepped off the flowing road.

"Where are you going?" asked Elai anxiously, coming after him.

"I wish to examine one of these air-cars."

"Be careful, Ulan Dhor. They are said to be dangerous . . ."

Ulan Dhor peered through the transparent dome, saw a cushioned seat, a series of little levers inscribed with characters strange to him and a large knurled ball mounted on a metal rod.

He said to the girl, "Those are evidently the guides to the mechanism . . . How does one enter such a car?"

She said doubtfully, "This button will perhaps release the dome." She pressed a knob; the dome snapped back, releasing a puff of stagnant air.

"Now," said Ulan Dhor, "I will experiment." He reached within, turned down a switch. Nothing happened.

"Be careful, Ulan Dhor!" breathed the girl. "Beware of magic!"

Ulan Dhor twisted a knob. The car quivered. He touched another lever. The boat made a curious whining sound, jerked. The dome began to settle. Ulan Dhor snatched back his arm. The dome snapped into place over a fold of his gray cloak. The boat jerked again, made a sudden movement, and Ulan Dhor was dragged willy-nilly after.

Elai cried out, seized his ankles. Cursing, Ulan Dhor dropped out of his cloak, watched while the air-boat took a wild uncontrolled curvet, crashed against the side of a tower. It fell with another clang of colliding metal and stone.

"Next time," said Ulan Dhor, "I will . . ."

He became aware of a strange pressure in the air. He turned. Elai was staring at him, hand against her mouth, eyes screwed up as if she were repressing a scream.

Ulan Dhor glanced around the streets. The slowly moving people, Grays and Greens, had vanished. The streets were empty.

"Elai," said Ulan Dhor, "why do you look at me like that?"

"The red, in daylight—and the color of Pansiu on your legs—it is our death, our death!"

"By no means," said Ulan Dhor cheerfully. "Not while I wear my sword and . . ."

A stone, coming from nowhere, crashed into the ground at his feet. He looked right and left for his assailant, nostrils flaring in anger.

In vain. The doorways, the arcades, the porticos were bare and empty.

Another stone, large as his fist, struck him between the shoulder-blades. He sprang around and saw only the crumble facade of ancient Ampridatvir, the empty street, the glistening gliding strip.

A stone hissed six inches from Elai's head, and at the same instant another struck his thigh.

Ulan Dhor recognized defeat. He could not fight stones with his sword. "We had better retreat . . ." He ducked a great paving block that would have split his skull.

"Back to the strip," the girl said in a dull and helpless voice. "We can take refuge across the square." A stone, looping idly down, struck her cheek; she cried in pain and fell to her knees.

Ulan Dhor snarled like an animal and sought men to kill. But no living person, man, woman, or child, was visible, though the stones continued to hurtle at his head.

He stooped, picked up Elai and ran to the swift central flow of the strip.

The rain of stones presently halted. The girl opened her eyes, winced, and shut them again. "Everything whirls," she whispered. "I have gone mad. Almost I might think—"

Ulan Dhor thought to recognize the tower where he had spent the night. He stepped off the strip and approached the portico. He was wrong; a crystal plane barred him the tower. As he hesitated, it melted at a spot directly in front of him and formed a doorway. Ulan Dhor stared wonderingly. Further magic of the ancient builders . . .

It was impersonal magic, and harmless. Ulan Dhor stepped through. The doorway dwindled, fused, and became clear crystal behind him.

The hall was bare and cold, though the walls were rich with colored metals and gorgeous enamel. A mural decorated one wall—men and women in flowing clothes were depicted tending flowers in gardens curiously bright and sunny, playing airy games, dancing.

Very beautiful, thought Ulan Dhor, but no place to defend himself against attack. Passageways to either side were echoing and empty; ahead was a small chamber with a floor of glimmering floss, which seemed to radiate light. He stepped within. His feet rose from the floor; he floated, lighter than thistle-down. Elai no longer weighed in his arms. He gave an involuntary hoarse call, struggled to return to his feet to ground, without success.

He floated upward like a leaf wafted in the wind. Ulan Dhor prepared himself for the sickening plunge when the magic quieted. But the floors fell past, and the ground level became ever more distant. A marvellous spell, thought Ulan Dhor grimly, thus to rob a man of his footing; how soon would the force relax and dash them to their deaths?

"Reach out," said Elai faintly. "Take hold of the bar."

He leaned far over, seized the railing, drew them to a landing, and, disbelieving his own safety, stepped into an apartment of several rooms. Crumbled heaps of dust were all that remained of the furniture.

He lay Elai on the soft floor; she raised her hand to her face and smiled wanly. "Ooh—it hurts."

Ulan Dhor watched with a strange sense of weakness and lassitude.

Elai said, "I don't know what we will do now. There is no longer a home for me; so shall we starve, for no one will give us food."

Ulan Dhor laughed sourly. "We will never lack for food—not while the keeper of a Green booth can not see a man in a gray cloak . . . But there are other things more important—the tablets of Rogol Domedonfors—and they seem completely inaccessible."

She said earnestly, "You would be killed. The men in red must fight everyone—as you saw today. And even if you reached the Temple of Pansiu, there are pitfalls, traps, poison stakes, and the ghosts on guard."

"Ghosts? Nonsense. They are men, exactly like the Grays, except that they wear green. Your brain refuses to see men in green . . . I have heard of such things, such obstructions of the mind . . ."

She said in a injured tone, "No other Grays see them. Perhaps it is you who suffers the hallucinations."

"Perhaps," agreed Ulan Dhor with a wry grin. They sat for a space in the dusty stillness of the old tower, then Ulan Dhor sat forward, clasped his knees, frowning. Lethargy was the precursor of defeat. "We must consider this Temple of Pansiu."

"We shall be killed," she said simply.

Ulan Dhor, already in better spirits, said, "You should practice optimism . . . Where can I find another air-car?

She stared at him. "Surely you are a madman!"

Ulan Dhor rose to his feet. "Where may one be found?"

She shook her head. "You are resolved on death, one way or another." She rose also. "We will ascend the Shaft of No-weight to the tower's highest level."

Without hesitation she stepped into the void, and Ulan Dhor gingerly followed. To the dizziest height they floated, and the walls of the shaft converged to a point far below. At the topmost landing they pulled themselves to solidity, stepped out on a terrace high up in the clean winds. Higher than the central mountains they stood, and the streets of Ampridatvir were gray threads far below. The harbor was a basin, and the sea spread away into the haze at the horizon.

Three air-cars rested on the terrace, and the metal was as bright, the glass as clear, the enamel as vivid as if the cars had just dropped from the sky.

They went to the nearest; Ulan Dhor pressed the entry button, and the dome slid back with a thin dry hiss of friction.

The interior was like that of the other car—a long cushioned seat, a globe mounted on a rod, a number of switches. The cloth of the seat crackled with age as Ulan Dhor prodded it with his hand, and the trapped air smelt very stale. He stepped inside, and Elai followed. "I will accompany you; death by falling is faster than starvation, and less painful than the rocks . . ."

"I hope we will neither fall nor starve," replied Ulan Dhor. Cautiously he touched the switches, ready to throw them back at any dangerous manifestation.

The dome snapped over their heads; relays thousands of years old meshed, cams twisted, shafts plunged home. The air-car jerked, lofted up into the red and dark blue sky. Ulan Dhor grasped the globe, found how to turn the boat, how to twist the nose up or down. This was pure joy, intoxication—wonderful mastery of the air! It was easier than he had imagined. It was easier than walking. He tried all the handles and switches, found how to hover, drop, brake. He found the speed handle and pushed it far over, and the wind sang past the air-boat. Far over the sea they flew, until the island was blue loom at the rim of the world. Low and high—skimming the wave-crests, plunging through the magenta wisps of the upper clouds.

Elai sat relaxed, calm, exalted. She had changed; she seemed closer to Ulan Dhor than to Ampridatvir; some subtle tie had been cut.

"Let's go on," she said. "On and on and on—across the world, past the forests . . ."

Ulan Dhor glanced at her sideways. She was very beautiful now—cleaner, finer, stronger than the women he had known in Kaiin. He said regretfully, "Then we would starve indeed—for neither of us has the craft to survive in the wilderness. And I am bound to seek the tablets . . ."

She sighed. "Very well. We will be killed. What does it matter? All Earth dies . . ."

Evening came, and they returned to Ampridatvir. "There," said Elai, "there is the Temple of Cazdal and there the Temple of Pansiu."

Ulan Dhor dropped the boat low over the Temple of Pansiu. "Where is the entrance?"

"Through the arch—and every place holds a different danger."

"But we fly," Ulan Dhor reminded her.

He lowered the boat ten feet above the ground and slid it through the arch.

Guided by a dim light ahead, Ulan Dhor manoeuvered the boat down the dark passage, through another arch; and they were in the nave.

The podium where the tablet sat was like the citadel of a walled city. The first obstacle was a wide pit, backed by a glassy wall. Then there was a moat of sulfur-colored liquid, and beyond, in an open space, five men kept a torpid watch. Undetected, Ulan Dhor moved the boat through the upper shadows and halted directly over the podium.

"Ready now," he muttered, and grounded the boat. The glistening tablet was almost within reach. He raised the dome; Elai leaned out, seized the tablet. The five guards gave an anguished roar, rushed forward.

"Back!" cried Ulan Dhor. He warded off a flying spear with his sword. She drew back with the tablet, Ulan Dhor slammed the dome. The guards leapt on the ship, clawing at the smooth metal, beating at it with their fists. The ship rose high; one by one they lost their grip, fell screaming to the floor.

Back through the arch, down the back passageway, through the entrance and out into the dark sky. Behind them a great horn set up a crazy clangor.

Ulan Dhor examined his prize—an oval sheet of transparent substance bearing a dozen lines of meaningless marks.

"We have won!" said Elai raptly. "You are the Lord of Ampridatvir!"

"Half yet remains," said Ulan Dhor. "There is still the tablet in the Temple of Cazdal."

"But—it is madness! Already you have—"

"One is useless without the other."

Her wild arguments subsided only as they hovered over the arch into Cazdal's Temple.

As the boat glided through the dark gap it struck a thread which dropped a great load of stones from a chute. The first of these, striking the sloping side of the air-car, buffeted it away. Ulan Dhor cursed. The guards would be alert and watchful.

He drifted along at the very top of the passage, hidden in the murk. Presently two guards, bearing torches and careful of their steps, came to investigate the sound. They passed directly below the boat, and Ulan Dhor hastened forward, through the arch into the nave. As in the Temple of Pansiu, the tablet gleamed in the middle of a fortress.

The guards were wide awake, nervously watching the opening.

"Boldness, now!" said Ulan Dhor. He sent the boat darting across the walls and pits and seething moat, settled beside the podium, snapped the dome back, sprang out. He seized the tablet as the guards came roaring forward, spears extended. The foremost flung his spear; Ulan Dhor struck it down and tossed the tablet into the boat.

But they were upon him; he would be impaled if he sought to climb within the boat. He sprang forward, hewed off the shaft of one spear, chopped at one man's shoulder on the back-sweep, seized the shaft of the third spear, and pulled the man into range of his sword point. The third guard fell back, shouting for help. Ulan Dhor turned, leapt into the boat. The guard rushed forward, Ulan Dhor whirled and met him with the point of his sword in his cheek. Spouting blood and wailing hysterically, the guard fell back. Ulan Dhor threw the lift lever; the boat rose high and moved toward the opening.

And presently the alarm horn at Cazdal's Temple was adding its harsh yell to the sound from across the city.

The boat drifted slowly through the sky.

"Look!" said Elai, grasping his arm. By torchlight men and women crowded and milled in the streets—Greens and Grays, panicked by the message of the horns.

Elai gasped. "Ulan Dhor! I see! I see! The men in Green! It is possible . . . Have they always been . . ."

"The brain-spell has broken," said Ulan Dhor, "and not only for you. Below they see each other, too . . ."

For the first time in memory, Greens and Grays looked at each other. Their faces twisted, contorted. In the flicker of torches Ulan

Dhor saw them drawing back in revulsion from each other, and heard the tumult of their cries: ''Demon! . . . Demon! . . . Gray ghost! . . . Vile Green Demon! . . .''

Thousands of obsessed torch-bearers sidled past each other, glowering, reviling each other, screaming in hate and fear. They were all mad, he thought—tangled, constricted of brain . . .

As by a secret signal, the crowd seethed into battle, and the hateful yells curdled Ulan Dhor's blood. Elai turned sobbing away. Terrible work was done, on men, women, children—no matter who the victim, if he wore the opposite color.

A louder snarling arose at the edge of the mob—a joyful sound, and a dozen shambling Gauns appeared, towering above the Greens and Grays. They rended, tore, ripped, and insane hate melted before fear. Greens and Grays separated, and ran to their homes, and the Guans roamed the streets alone.

Ulan Dhor tore his glance away and held his forehead. ''Was this my doing? . . . Was this a deed of mine?''

''Sooner or later it would have happened,'' said Elai dully. ''Unless Earth waned and died first . . .''

Ulan Dhor picked up the two tablets. ''And here is what I sought to attain—the tablets of Rogol Domedonfors. They pulled me a thousand leagues across the Melantine; I have them in my hands now, and they are like worthless shards of glass . . .''

The boat floated high, and Ampridatvir became a setting of pale crystals in the starlight. In the luminescence of the instrument panel, Ulan Dhor fitted the two tablets together. The marks merged, became characters, and the characters bore the words of the ancient magician:

> ''Faithless children—Rogol Domedonfors dies, and so lives forever in the Ampridatvir he has loved and served! When intelligence and good will restore order to the city; or when blood and steel teaches the folly of bridled credulity and passion, and all but the toughest dead:—then shall these tablets be read. And I say to him who reads it, go to the Tower of Fate with the yellow dome, ascend to the topmost floor, show red to the left eye of Rogol Domedonfors, yellow to the right eye, and then blue to both; do this, I say, and share the power of Rogol Domedonfors.''

Ulan Dhor asked, ''Where is the Tower of Fate?''

Elai shook her head. ''There is Rodeil's Tower, and the Red Tower the Tower of the Screaming Ghost, and the Tower of Trumpets and the Bird's Tower and the Tower of Guans—but I know of no Tower of Fate.''

''Which tower has a yellow dome?''

''I don't know.''

''We will search in the morning.''

''In the morning,'' she said leaning against him drowsily.

''The morning . . .'' said Ulan Dhor, fondling her yellow hair.

When the old red sun rose, they drifted back over the city and found the people of Ampridatvir awake before them, intent on murder.

The fighting and the killing was not so wild as the night before. It was a craftier slaughter. Stealthy groups of men waylaid stragglers, or broke into houses to strangle women and children.

Ulan Dhor muttered, ''Soon there will be none left in Ampridatvir upon whom to work. Rogol Domedonfors' power.'' He turned to Elai. ''Have you no father, no mother, for whom you fear?''

She shook her head. ''I have lived my life with a dull and tyrannical uncle.''

Ulan Dhor turned away. He saw a yellow dome; no other was visible: The Tower of Fate.

''There.'' He pointed, turned down the nose of the air-car.

Parking on a high level, they entered the dusty corridors, found an anti-gravity shaft, and rose to the top-most floor. Here they found a small chamber, decorated with vivid murals. The scene was a court of ancient Ampridatvir. Men and women in colored silks conversed and banqueted and, in the central plaque, paid homage to a patriarchal ruler with a rugged chin, burning eyes, and a white beard. He was clad in a purple and black gown and sat on a carved chair.

''Rogol Domedonfors!'' murmured Elai, and the room held its breath, grew still. They felt the stir their living breath made in the long-quiet air, and the depicted eyes stared deep into their brains . . .

Ulan Dhor said, '' 'Red to the left eye, yellow to the right; then blue to both.' Well—there are blue tiles in the hall, and I wear a red coat.''

They found blue and yellow tiles, and Ulan Dhor cut a strip from the hem of his tunic.

Red to the left eye, yellow to the right. Blue to both. A click, a screech, a whirring like a hundred bee-hives.

The wall opened on a flight of steps. Ulan Dhor entered, and, with Elai breathing hard at his back, mounted the steps.

They came out in a flood of daylight, under the dome itself. In the center on a pedestal sat a glistening round-topped cylinder, black and vitreous.

The whirring rose to a shrill whine. The cylinder quivered, softened, became barely transparent, slumped a trifle. In the center hung a pulpy white mass—a brain?

The cylinder was alive.

It sprouted pseudopods which poised wavering in the air. Ulan Dhor and Elai watched frozen, close together. One black finger shaped itself to an eye, another formed a mouth. The eye inspected them carefully.

The mouth said cheerfully, "Greetings across time, greetings. So you have come at last to rouse old Rogol Domedonfors from his dreams? I have dreamed long and well—but it seems for an unconscionable period. How long? Twenty years? Fifty years? Let me look."

The eye swung to a tube on the wall, a quarter full of gray powder.

The mouth gave a cry of wonder. "The energy has nearly dissipated! How long have I slept? With a half-life of 1,200 years—over five thousand years!" The eye swung back to Ulan Dhor and Elai. "Who are you then? Where are my bickering subjects, the adherents of Pansiu and Cazdal? Did they kill themselves then, so long ago?"

"No," said Ulan Dhor with a sick grin. "They are still fighting in the streets."

The eye-tentacle extended swiftly, thrust through a window, and looked down over the city. The central jelly twitched, became suffused with an orange glow. The voice spoke again, and it held a terrible harshness. Ulan Dhor's neck tingled and he felt Elai's hand clenching deep into his arm.

"Five thousand years!" cried the voice. "Five thousand years and the wretches still quarrel? Time has taught them no wisdom? Then stronger agencies must be used. Rogol Domedonfors will show them wisdom. Behold!"

A vast sound came from below, a hundred sharp reports. Ulan Dhor and Elai hastened to the window and looked down. A mind-filling sight occupied the streets.

The ten-foot vestibules leading below the city had snapped open. From each of these licked a great tentacle of black transparent jelly like the substance of the fluid roads.

The tentacles reached into the air, sprouted a hundred branches which pursued the madly fleeing Ampridatvians, caught them, stripped away their robes of gray and green, then whipping them high through the air, dropped them into the great central square. In the chill morning air the populace of Ampridatvir stood mingled naked together and no man could distinguish Green from Gray.

"Rogol Domedonfors has great long arms now," cried a vast voice, "strong as the moon, all-seeing as the air."

The voice came from everywhere, nowhere.

"I'm Rogol Domedonfors, the last ruler of Ampridatvir. And to this state have you descended? Dwellers in hovels, eaters of filth? Watch—in a moment I repair the neglect of five thousand years!"

The tentacles sprouted a thousand appendages—hard horny cutters, nozzles that spouted blue flame, tremendous scoops, and each appendage sprouted an eye-stalk. These ranged the city, and wherever there was crumbling or mark of age the tentacles dug, tore, blasted, burnt; then spewed new materials into place and when they passed new and gleaming structure remained behind.

Many-armed tentacles gathered the litter of ages; when loaded they snapped high through the air, a monstrous catapult, flinging the rubbish far out over the sea. And wherever was gray paint or green paint a tentacle ground off the color, sprayed new various pigments.

Down every street ran the tremendous root-things and offshoots plunged into every tower, every dwelling, every park and square—demolishing, stripping, building, clearing, repairing. Ampridatvir was gripped and permeated by Rogol Domedonfors as a tree's roots clench the ground.

In a time measured by breaths, a new Ampridatvir had replaced the ruins, a gleaming, glistening city—proud, intrepid, challenging the red sun.

Ulan Dhor and Elai had watched in a half-conscious, uncomprehending daze. Was it possibly reality; was there such a being which could demolish a city and build it anew while a man watched?

Arms of black jelly darted over the hills of the island, threaded the caves where the Gauns lay gorged and torpid. It seized, snatched them through the air, and dangled them above the huddled Ampridatvians—a hundred Gauns on a hundred tentacles, horrible fruits on a weird tree.

"Look!" boomed a voice, boastful and wild. "These whom you have feared! See how Rogol Domedonfors deals with these!"

The tentacles flicked, and a hundred Gauns hurtled—sprawling, wheeling shapes—high over Ampridatvir; and they fell far out in the sea.

"The creature is mad," whispered Ulan Dhor to Elai. "The long dreaming has addled its brain."

"Behold the new Ampridatvir!" boomed the mighty voice. "See it for the first and last time. For now you die! You have proved unworthy of the past—unworthy to worship the new god Rogol Domedonfors. There are two here beside me who shall found the new race—''

Ulan Dhor started in alarm. What? He to live in Ampridatvir under the thumb of the mad super-being?

No.

And perhaps he would never be so close to the brain again.

With a single motion he drew his sword and hurled it point-first into the translucent cylinder of jelly—transfixed the brain, skewered it on the shaft of steel.

The most awful sound yet heard on Earth shattered the air. Men and women went mad in the square.

Rogol Domedonfors' city-girding tentacles beat up and down in frantic agony, as an injured insect lashes his legs. The gorgeous towers toppled, the Ampridatvians fled shrieking through cataclysm.

Ulan Dhor and Elai ran for the terrace where they had left the air-car. Behind they heard a hoarse whisper—a broken voice.

''I—am not—dead—yet! If all else, if all dreams are broken—I will kill you two . . .''

They tumbled into the air-car. Ulan Dhor threw it into the air. By a terrible effort a tentacle stopped its mad thrashing and jerked up to intercept them. Ulan Dhor swerved, plunged off through the sky. The tentacle darted to cut them off.

Ulan Dhor pressed hard down on the speed lever, and air whined and sang behind the craft. And directly behind came the wavering black arm of the dying god, straining to touch the fleeting midge that had so hurt it.

''More! More!'' prayed Ulan Dhor to the air-car.

''Go higher,'' whispered the girl. ''Higher—faster—''

Ulan Dhor tilted the nose; up on a slant flashed the car, and the straining arm followed behind—a tremendous member stretching rigid through the sky, a black rainbow footed in distant Ampridatvir.

Rogol Domedonfors died. The arm snapped into a wisp of smoke and slowly sank toward the sea.

Ulan Dhor held his boat at full speed until the island disappeared across the horizon. He slowed, sighed, relaxed.

Elai suddenly flung herself against his shoulder and burst into hysteria.

''Quiet, girl, quiet,'' admonished Ulan Dhor. ''We are safe; we are forever done of the cursed city.''

She quieted; presently: ''Where do we go now?''

Ulan Dhor's eyes roved about the air-car with doubt and calculation. ''There will be no magic for Kandive. However, I will have a great tale to tell him, and he may be satisfied . . . He will surely want the air-car. But I will contrive, I will contrive . . .''

She whispered, ''Cannot we fly to the east, and fly and fly and fly, till we find where the sun rises, and perhaps a quiet meadow where there are fruit trees . . .''

Ulan Dhor looked to the south and thought of Kaiin with its quiet nights and wine-colored days, the wide palace where he made his home, and the couch from which he could look out over Sanreale Bay, the ancient olive trees, the harlequinade festival-times.

He said, ''Elai, you will like Kaiin.''

6

Guyal of Sfere

Guyal of Sfere had been born one apart from his fellows and early proved a source of vexation for his sire. Normal in outward configuration, there existed within his mind a void which ached for nourishment. It was as if a spell had been cast upon his birth, a harrassment visited on the child in a spirit of sardonic mockery, so that every occurrence, no matter how trifling, became a source of wonder and amazement. Even as young as four seasons he was expounding such inquiries as:

"Why do squares have more sides than triangles?"

"How will we see when the sun goes dark?"

"Do flowers grow under the ocean?"

"Do stars hiss and sizzle when rain comes by night?"

To which his impatient sire gave such answers as:

"So it was ordained by the Pragmatica; squares and triangles must obey the rote."

"We will be forced to grope and feel our way."

"I have never verified this matter; only the Curator would know."

"By no means, since the stars are high above the rain, higher even than the highest clouds, and swim in rarified air where rain will never breed."

As Guyal grew to youth, this void in his mind, instead of becoming limp and waxy, seemed to throb with a more violent ache. And so he asked:

"Why do people die when they are killed?"

"Where does beauty vanish when it goes?"

"How long have men lived on Earth?"

"What is beyond the sky?"

To which his sire, biting acerbity back from his lips, would respond:

"Death is the heritage of life; a man's vitality is like air in a bladder. Poinct this bubble and away, away, away, flees life, like the color of fading dream."

"Beauty is a luster which love bestows to guile the eye. Therefore it may be said that only when the brain is without love will the eye look and see no beauty."

"Some say men rose from the earth like grubs in a corpse; others aver that the first men desired residence and so created Earth by sorcery. The question is shrouded in technicality; only the Curator may answer with exactness."

"An endless waste."

And Guyal pondered and postulated, proposed and expounded, until he found himself the subject of surreptitious humor. The demesne was visited by a rumor that a gleft, coming upon Guyal's mother in labor, had stolen part of Guyal's brain, which deficiency he now industriously sought to restore.

Guyal therefore drew himself apart and roamed the grassy hills of Sfere in solitude. But ever was his mind acquisitive, ever did he seek to exhaust the lore of all around him, until at last his father in vexation refused to hear further inquiries, declaring that all knowledge had been known, that the trivial and useless had been discarded, leaving a residue which was all that was necessary to a sound man.

At this time Guyal was in his first manhood, a slight but well-knit youth with wide clear eyes, a penchant for severely elegant dress, and a hidden trouble which showed itself in the clamps at the corner of his mouth.

Hearing his father's angry statement Guyal said, "One more question, then I ask no more."

"Speak," declared his father. "One more question I grant you."

"You have often referred me to the Curator; who is he, and where may I find him, so as to allay my ache for knowledge?"

A moment the father scrutinized the son, whom he now considered past the verge of madness. Then he responded in a quiet voice, "The Curator guards the Museum of Man, which antique legend places in the Land of the Falling Wall—beyond the mountains of Fer Aquila and north of Ascolais. It is not certain that either Curator or Museum still exist; still it would seem that if the Curator knows all things, as is the legend, then surely he would know the wizardly foil to death."

Guyal said, "I would seek the Curator and the Museum of Man, that I likewise may know all things."

The father said with patience, "I will bestow on you my fine white horse, my Expansible Egg for your shelter, my Scintillant Dagger to illuminate the night. In addition, I lay a blessing along the trail, and danger will slide you by so long as you never wander from the trail."

Guyal quelled the hundred new questions at his tongue, including an inquisition as to where his father had learned these manifestations of sorcery, and accepted the gifts: the horse, the magic shelter, the dagger with the luminous pommel, and the blessing to guard him from the disadvantageous circumstances which plagued travellers along the dim trails of Ascolais.

He caparisoned the horse, honed the dagger, cast a last glance around the old manse at Sfere, and set forth to the north, with the void in his mind athrob for the soothing pressure of knowledge.

He ferried the River Scaum on an old barge. Aboard the barge and so off the trail, the blessing lost its puissance and the barge-tender, who coveted Guyal's rich accoutrements, sought to cudgel him with a knoblolly. Guyal fended off the blow and kicked the man into the murky deep, where he drowned.

Mounting the north bank of the Scaum he saw ahead the Porphiron Scar, the dark poplars and white columns of Kaiin, the dull gleam of Sanreale Bay.

Wandering the crumbled streets, he put the languid inhabitants such a spate of questions that one in wry jocularity commended him to a professional augur.

This one dwelled in a booth painted with the Signs of the Aumoklopelastianic Cabal. He was a lank brownman with red-rimmed eyes and a stained white beard.

"What are your fees?" inquired Guyal cautiously.

"I respond to three questions," stated the augur. "For twenty terces I phrase the answer in clear and actionable language; for ten I use the language of cant, which occasionally admits of ambiguity; for five, I speak a parable which you must interpret as you will; and for one terce, I babble in an unknown tongue."

"First I must inquire, how profound is your knowledge?"

"I know all," responded the augur. "The secrets of red and the secrets of black, the lost spells of Grand Motholam, the way of the fish and the voice of the bird."

"And where have you learned all these things?"

"By pure induction," explained the augur. "I retire into my booth, I closet myself with never a glint of light, and, so sequestered, I resolve the profundities of the world."

"With all this precious knowledge at hand," ventured Guyal,

"why do you live so meagerly, with not an ounce of fat to your frame and these miserable rags to your back?"

The augur stood back in fury. "Go along, go along! Already I have wasted fifty terces of wisdom on you, who have never a copper to your pouch. If you desire free enlightenment," and he cackled in mirth, "seek out the Curator." And he sheltered himself in his booth.

Guyal took lodging for the night, and in the morning continued north. The ravaged acres of the Old Town passed to his left, and the trail took to the fabulous forest.

For many a day Guyal rode north, and, heedful of danger, held to the trail. By night he surrounded himself and his horse in his magical habiliment, the Expansible Egg—a membrane impermeable to thew, claw, ensorcelment, pressure, sound and chill—and so rested at ease despite the efforts of the avid creatures of the dark.

The great dull globe of the sun fell behind him; the days became wan and the nights bitter, and at last the crags of Fer Aquila showed as a tracing on the north horizon.

The forest had become lower and less dense, and the characteristic tree was the daobado, a rounded massy construction of heavy gnarled branches, these a burnished russet bronze, clumped with dark balls of foliage. Beside a giant of the species Guyal came upon a village of turf huts. A gaggle of surly louts appeared and surrounded him with expressions of curiosity. Guyal, no less than the villagers, had questions to ask, but none would speak till the hetman strode up—a burly man who wore a shaggy fur hat, a cloak of brown fur and a bristling beard, so that it was hard to see where one ended and the other began. He exuded a rancid odor which displeased Guyal, who, from motives of courtesy, kept his distaste concealed.

"Where go you?" asked the hetman.

"I wish to cross the mountains to the Museum of Man," said Guyal. "Which way does the trail lead?"

The hetman pointed out a notch on the silhouette of the mountains. "There is Omona Gap, which is the shortest and best route, though there is no trail. None comes and none goes, since when you pass the Gap, you walk an unknown land. And with no traffic there manifestly need be no trail."

The news did not cheer Guyal.

"How then is it known that Omona Gap is on the way to the Museum?"

The hetman shrugged. "Such is our tradition."

Guyal turned his head at a hoarse snuffling and saw a pen of woven wattles. In a litter of filth and matted straw stood a number of hulking men eight or nine feet tall. They were naked, with shocks of dirty yellow hair and watery blue eyes. They had waxy faces and expressions of crass stupidity. As Guyal watched, one of them ambled to a trough and noisily began gulping gray mash.

Guyal said, "What manner of things are these?"

The hetman blinked in amusement to Guyal's naivete. "Those are our oasts, naturally." And he gestured in disapprobation at Guyal's white horse. "Never have I seen a stranger oast than the one you bestride. Ours carry us easier and appear to be less vicious; in addition no flesh is more delicious than oast properly braised and kettled."

Standing close, he fondled the metal of Guyal's saddle and the red and yellow embroidered quilt. "Your deckings however are rich and of superb quality. I will therefore bestow you my large and weighty oast in return for this creature with its accoutrements."

Guyal politely declared himself satisfied with his present mount, and the hetman shrugged his shoulders.

A horn sounded. The hetman looked about, then turned back to Guyal. "Food is prepared; will you eat?"

Guyal glanced toward the oast-pen. "I am not presently hungry, and I must hasten forward. However, I am grateful for your kindness."

He departed; as he passed under the arch of the great daobado, he turned a glance back toward the village. There seemed an unwonted activity among the huts. Remembering the hetman's covetous touch at his saddle, and aware that no longer did he ride the protected trail, Guyal urged his horse forward and pounded fast under the trees.

As he neared the foothills the forest dwindled to a savannah, floored with a dull, joined grass that creaked under the horse's hooves. Guyal glanced up and down the plain. The sun, old and red as an autumn pomegranate, wallowed in the south-west; the light across the plain was dim and watery; the mountains presented a curiously artificial aspect, like a tableau planned for the effect of eery desolation.

Guyal glanced once again at the sun. Another hour of light, then the dark night of the latter-day Earth. Guyal twisted in the saddle, looked behind him, feeling lone, solitary, vulnerable. Four oasts, carrying men on their shoulders, came trotting from the forest. Sighting Guyal, they broke into a lumbering run. With a crawling skin Guyal wheeled his horse and eased the reins, and the white horse loped across the plain toward Omona Gap. Behind came the oasts, bestraddled by the fur-cloaked villagers.

As the sun touched the horizon, another forest ahead showed as an indistinct line of murk. Guyal looked back to his pursuers, bounding now a mile behind, turned his gaze back to the forest. An ill place to ride by night . . .

The darkling foliage loomed above him; he passed under the first gnarled boughs. If the oasts were unable to sniff out a trail, they might now be eluded. He changed directions, turned once, twice, a third time, then stood his horse to listen. Far away a crashing in the brake reached his ears. Guyal dismounted, led the horse into a deep hollow where a bank of foliage made a screen. Presently the four men on their hulking oasts passed in the afterglow above him, black double-shapes in attitudes suggestive of ill-temper and disappointment.

The thud and pad of feet dwindled and died.

The horse moved restlessly; the foliage rustled.

A damp air passed down the hollow and chilled the back of Guyal's neck. Darkness rose from old Earth like ink in a basin.

Guyal shivered: best to ride away through the forest, away from the dour villagers and their numb mounts. Away . . .

He turned his horse up to the height where the four had passed and sat listening. Far down the wind he heard a hoarse call. Turning in the opposite direction he let the horse choose its own path.

Branches and boughs knit patterns on the fading purple over him; the air smelt of moss and dank mold. The horse stopped short. Guyal, tensing in every muscle, leaned a little forward, head twisted, listening. There was a feel of danger on his cheek. The air was still, uncanny; his eyes could plumb not ten feet into the black. Somewhere near was death—grinding, roaring death, to come as a sudden shock.

Sweating cold, afraid to stir a muscle, he forced himself to dismount. Stiffly he slid from the saddle, brought forth the Expansible Egg, and flung it around his horse and himself. Ah, now . . . Guyal released the pressure of his breath. Safety.

Wan red light slanted through the branches from the east. Guyal's breath steamed in the air when he emerged from the Egg. After a handful of dried fruit for himself and a sack of meal for the horse, he mounted and set out toward the mountains.

The forest passed, and Guyal rode out on an upland. He scanned the line of mountains. Suffused with rose sunlight, the gray, sage green, dark green range rambled far to the west toward the Melantine, far to the east into the Falling Wall country. Where was Omona Gap?

Guyal of Sfere searched in vain for the notch which had been visible from the village of the fur-cloaked murderers.

He frowned and turned his eyes up the height of the mountains. Weathered by the rains of earth's duration, the slopes were easy and the crags rose like the stumps of rotten teeth. Guyal turned his horse uphill and rode the trackless slope into the mountains of Fer Aquila.

Guyal of Sfere had lost his way in a land of wind and naked crags. As night came he slouched numbly in the saddle while his horse took him where it would. Somewhere the ancient way through Omona Gap led to the northern tundra, but now, under a chilly overcast, north, east, south, and west were alike under the lavender-metal sky. Guyal reined his horse and, rising in the saddle, searched the landscape. The crags rose, tall, remote; the ground was barren of all but clumps of dry shrub. He slumped back in the saddle, and his white horse jogged forward.

Head bowed to the wind rode Guyal, and the mountains slanted along the twilight like the skeleton of a fossil god.

The horse halted, and Guyal found himself at the brink of a wide valley. The wind had died; the valley was quiet. Guyal leaned forward, staring. Below spread a dark and lifeless city. Mist blew along the streets and the afterglow fell dull on slate roofs.

The horse snorted and scraped the stony ground.

"A strange town," said Guyal, "with no lights, no sound, no smell of smoke . . . Doubtless an abandoned ruin from ancient times . . ."

He debated descending to the streets. At times the old ruins were haunted by peculiar distillations, but such a ruin might be joined by the tundra by a trail. With this thought in mind he started his horse down the slope.

He entered the town and the hooves rang loud and sharp on the cobbles. The buildings were framed of stone and dark mortar and seemed in uncommonly good preservation. A few lintels had cracked and sagged, a few walls gaped open, but for the most part the stone houses had successfully met the gnaw of time . . . Guyal scented smoke. Did people live here still? He would proceed with caution.

Before a building which seemed to be a hostelry flowers bloomed in an urn. Guyal reined his horse and reflected that flowers were rarely cherished by persons of hostile disposition.

"Hallo!" he called—once, twice.

No heads peered from the doors, no orange flicker brightened the windows. Guyal slowly turned and rode on.

The street widened and twisted toward a large hall, where Guyal saw a light. The building had a high facade, broken by four large windows, each of which had its two blinds of patined bronze filigree, and each overlooked a small balcony. A marble balustrade fronting the terrace shimmered bone-white and, behind, the hall's portal of massive wood stood sightly ajar; from here came the beam of light and also a strain of music.

Guyal of Sfere, halting, gazed not at the house nor at the light through the door. He dismounted and bowed to the young woman who sat pensively along the course of the balustrade. Though it was very cold, she wore but a simple gown, yellow-orange, a daffodil's color. Topaz hair fell loose to her shoulders and gave her face a cast of gravity and thoughtfulness.

As Guyal straightened from his greeting the woman nodded, smiled slightly, and absently fingered the hair by her cheek.

''A bitter night for travelers.''

''A bitter night for musing on the stars,'' responded Guyal.

She smiled again. ''I am not cold. I sit and dream . . . I listen to the music.''

''What place is this?'' inquired Guyal, looking up the street, down the street, and once more to the girl. ''Are there any here but yourself?''

''This is Carchesel,'' said the girl, ''abandoned by all ten thousand years ago. Only I and my aged uncle live here, finding this place a refuge from the Saponids of the tundra.''

Guyal thought: this woman may or may not be a witch.

''You are cold and weary,'' said the girl, ''and I keep you standing in the street.'' She rose to her feet. ''Our hospitality is yours.''

''Which I glady accept,'' said Guyal, ''but first I must stable my horse.''

''He will be content in the house yonder. We have no stable.'' Guyal, following her finger, saw a low stone building with a door opening into blackness.

He took the white horse thither and removed the bridle and saddle; then, standing in the doorway, he listened to the music he had noted before, the piping of a weird and ancient air.

''Strange, strange,'' he muttered, stroking the horse's muzzle. ''The uncle plays music, the girl stares alone at the stars of the night . . .'' He considered a moment. ''I may be over-suspicious. If witch she be, there is naught to be gained from me. If they be simple refugees as she says, and lovers of music, they may enjoy the airs from Ascolais; it will repay, in some measure, their hospitality.'' He reached into his saddle-bag, brought forth his flute, and tucked it inside his jerkin.

He ran back to where the girl awaited him.

''You have not told me your name,'' she reminded him, ''that I may introduce you to my uncle.''

"I am Guyal of Sfere, by the River Scaum in Ascolais. And you?"

She smiled, pushing the portal wider. Warm yellow light fell into the cobbled street.

"I have no name. I need none. There has never been any but my uncle; and when he speaks, there is no one to answer but I."

Guyal stared in astonishment; then, deeming his wonder too apparent for courtesy, he controlled his expression. Perhaps she suspected him of wizardry and feared to pronounce her name lest he make magic with it.

They entered a flagged hall, and the sound of piping grew louder.

"I will call you Ameth, if I may," said Guyal. "That is a flower of the south, as golden and kind and fragrant as you seem to be."

She nodded. "You may call me Ameth."

They entered a tapestry-hung chamber, large and warm. A great fire glowed at one wall, and here stood a table bearing food. On a bench sat the musician—an old man, untidy, unkempt. His white hair hung tangled down his back; his beard, in no better case, was dirty and yellow. He wore a ragged kirtle, by no means clean, and the leather of his sandals had broken into dry cracks. Strangely, he did not take the flute from his mouth, but kept up his piping; and the girl in yellow, so Guyal noted, seemed to move in rhythm to the tones.

"Uncle Ludowik," she cried in a gay voice, "I bring you a guest, Sir Guyal of Sfere."

Guyal looked into the man's face and wondered. The eyes, though somewhat rheumy with age, were gray and bright—feverishly bright and intelligent; and, so Guyal thought, awake with a strange joy. This joy further puzzled Guyal, for the lines of the face indicated nothing other than years of misery.

"Perhaps you play?" inquired Ameth. "My uncle is a great musician, and this is his time for music. He has kept the routine for many years . . ." She turned and smiled at Ludowik the musician. Guyal nodded politely.

Ameth motioned to the bounteous table. "Eat, Guyal, and I will pour you wine. Afterwards perhaps you will play the flute for us."

"Gladly," said Guyal, and he noticed how the joy on Ludowik's face grew more apparent, quivering around the corners of his mouth.

He ate and Ameth poured him golden wine until his head went to reeling. And never did Ludowik cease his piping—now a tender melody of running water, again a grave tune that told of the lost ocean to the west, another time a simple melody such as a child might sing at his games. Guyal noted with wonder how Ameth fitted her mood to the music—grave and gay as the music led her. Strange! thought

Guyal. But then—people thus isolated were apt to develop peculiar mannerisms, and they seemed kindly withal.

He finished his meal and stood erect, steadying himself against the table. Ludowik was playing a lilting tune, a melody of glass birds swinging round and round on a red string in the sunlight. Ameth came dancing over to him and stood close—very close—and he smelled the warm perfume of her loose golden hair. Her face was happy and wild . . . Peculiar how Ludowik watched so grimly, and yet without a word. Perhaps he misdoubted a stranger's intent. Still . . .

''Now,'' breathed Ameth, ''perhaps you will play the flute; you are so strong and young.'' Then she said quickly, as she saw Guyal's eyes widen. ''I mean you will play on the flute for old uncle Ludowik, and he will be happy and go off to bed—and then we will sit and talk far into the night.''

''Gladly will I play the flute,'' said Guyal. Curse the tongue of his, at once so fluent and yet so numb. It was the wine. ''Gladly will I play. I am accounted quite skillfull at my home manse at Sfere.''

He glanced at Ludowik, then stared at the expression of crazy gladness he had surprised. Marvelous that a man should be so fond of music.

''Then—play!'' breathed Ameth, urging him a little toward Ludowik and the flute.

''Perhaps,'' suggested Guyal, ''I had better wait till your uncle pauses. I would seem discourteous—''

''No, as soon as you indicate that you wish to play, he will let off. Merely take the flute. You see,'' she confided, ''he is rather deaf.''

''Very well,'' said Guyal, ''except that I have my own flute.'' And he brought it out from under his jerkin. ''Why—what is the matter?'' For a startling change had come over the girl and the old man. A quick light had risen in her eyes, and Ludowik's strange gladness had gone, and there was but dull hopelessness in his eyes, stupid resignation.

Guyal slowly stood back, bewildered. ''Do you not wish me to play?''

There was a pause. ''Of course,'' said Ameth, young and charming once more. ''But I'm sure that Uncle Ludowik would enjoy hearing you play his flute. He is accustomed to the pitch—another scale might be unfamiliar . . .''

Ludowik nodded, and hope again shone in the rheumy old eyes. It was indeed a fine flute, Guyal saw, a rich piece of white metal, chased and set with gold, and Ludowik clutched this flute as if he would never let go.

''Take the flute,'' suggested Ameth. ''He will not mind in the least.'' Ludowik shook his head, to signify the absence of his objections. But Guyal, noting with distaste the long stained beard, also shook his head. ''I can play any scale, any tone on my flute. There is no need for me to use that of your uncle and possibly distress him. Listen,'' and he raised his instrument. ''Here is a song of Kaiin, called 'The Opal, the Pearl and the Peacock'.''

He put the pipe to his lips and began to play, very skillfully indeed, and Ludowik followed him, filling in gaps, making chords. Ameth, forgetting her vexation, listened with eyes half-closed, and moved her arm to the rhythm.

''Did you enjoy that?'' asked Guyal, when he had finished.

''Very much. Perhaps you would try it on Uncle Ludowik's flute? It is a fine flute to play, very soft and easy to the breath.''

''No,'' said Guyal, with sudden obstinacy. ''I am able to play only my own instrument.'' He blew again, and it was a dance of the festival, a quirking carnival air. Ludowik, playing with supernal skill, ran merry phrases as might fit, and Ameth, carried away by the rhythm, danced a dance of her own, a merry step in time to the music.

Guyal played a wild tarantella of the peasant folk, and Ameth danced wilder and faster, flung her arms, wheeled, jerked her head in a fine display. And Ludowik's flute played a brilliant obbligato, hurtling over, now under, chording, veering, warping little silver strings of sound around Guyal's melody, adding urgent little grace-phrases.

Ludowik's eyes now clung to the whirling figure of the dancing girl. And suddenly he struck up a theme of his own, a tune of wildest abandon, of a frenzied beating rhythm; and Guyal, carried away by the force of the music, blew as he never had blown before, invented trills and runs, gyrating arpeggios, blew high and shrill, loud and fast and clear.

It was as nothing to Ludowik's music. His eyes were starting; sweat streamed from his seamed old forehead; his flute tore the air into quivering ecstatic shreds.

Ameth danced frenzy; she was no longer beautiful, she appeared grotesque and unfamiliar. The music became something more than the senses could bear. Guyal's own vision turned pink and gray; he saw Ameth fall in a faint, in a foaming fit; and Ludowik, fiery-eyed, staggered erect, hobbled to her body and began a terrible intense concord, slow measures of most solemn and frightening meaning.

Ludowik played death.

Guyal of Sfere turned and ran wide-eyed from the hall. Ludowik, never noticing, continued his terrible piping, played as if every note were a skewer through the twitching girl's shoulder-blades.

Guyal ran through the night, and cold air bit at him like sleet. He burst into the shed, and the white horse softly nickered at him. On with the saddle, on with the bridle, away down the streets of old Carchasel, past the gaping black windows, ringing down the starlit cobbles, away from the music of death!

Guyal of Sfere galloped up the mountain with the stars in his face, and not until he came to the shoulder did he turn in the saddle to look back.

The verging of dawn trembled into the stony valley. Where was Carchasel? There was no city—only a crumble of ruins . . .

Hark! A far sound? . . .

No. All was silence.

And yet . . .

No. Only crumbled stones in the floor of the valley.

Guyal, fixed of eye, turned and went his way, along the trail which stretched north before him.

The walls of the defile which led the trail were steep gray granite, stained scarlet and black by lichen, mildewed blue. The horse's hooves made a hollow clop-clop-clop on the stone, loud to Guyal's ears, hypnotic to his brain, and after the sleepless night he found his frame sagging. His eyes grew dim and warm with drowsiness, but the trail ahead led to unseen vistas, and the void in Guyal's brain drove him without surcease.

The lassitude became such that Guyal slipped halfway from his saddle. Rousing himself, he resolved to round one more bend in the trail and then take rest.

The rock beetled above and hid the sky where the sun had passed the zenith. The trail twisted around a shoulder of rock; ahead shone a patch of indigo heaven. One more turning, Guyal told himself. The defile fell open, the mountains were at his back and he looked out across a hundred miles of steppe. It was a land shaded with subtle colors, washed with delicate shadows, fading and melting into the lurid haze at the horizon. He saw a lone eminence cloaked by a dark company of trees, the glisten of a lake at its foot. To the other side a ranked mass of gray-white ruins was barely discernible. The Museum of Man? . . . After a moment of vacillation, Guyal dismounted and sought sleep within the Expansible Egg.

The sun rolled in sad sumptuous majesty behind the mountains; murk fell across the tundra. Guyal awoke and refreshed himself in a rill nearby. Giving meal to his horse, he ate dry fruit and bread; then he mounted and rode down the trail. The plain spread vastly north before him, into desolation; the mountains lowered black above and behind; a slow cold breeze blew in his face. Gloom deepened; the plain sank from sight like a drowned land. Hesitant before the murk, Guyal reined his horse. Better, he thought, to ride in the morning. If he lost the trail in the dark, who could tell what he might encounter?

A mournful sound. Guyal stiffened and turned his face to the sky. A sigh? A moan? A sob? . . . Another sound, closer, the rustle of cloth, a loose garment. Guyal cringed into his saddle. Floating slowly down through the darkness came a shape robed in white. Under the cowl and glowing with eer-light a drawn face with eyes like the holes in a skull.

It breathed its sad sound and drifted away on high . . . There was only the blow of the wind past Guyal's ears.

He drew a shuddering breath and slumped against the pommel. His shoulders felt exposed, naked. He slipped to the ground and established the shelter of the Egg about himself and his horse. Preparing his pallet, he lay himself down; presently, as he lay staring into the dark, sleep came on him and so the night passed.

He awoke before dawn and once more set forth. The trail was a ribbon of white sand between banks of gray furze and the miles passed swiftly.

The trail led toward the three-clothed eminence Guyal had noted from above; now he thought to see roofs through the heavy foliage and smoke on the sharp air. And presently to right and left spread cultivated fields of spikenard, callow and mead-apple. Guyal continued with eyes watchful for men.

To one side appeared a fence of stone and black timber: the stone chiselled and hewn to the semblance of four globes beaded on a central pillar, the black timbers which served as rails fitted in sockets and carved in precise spirals. Behind this fence a region of bare earth lay churned, pitted, cratered, burnt and wrenched, as if visited at once by fire and the blow of a tremendous hammer. In wondering speculation Guyal gazed and so did not notice the three men who came quietly upon him.

The horse started nervously; Guyal, turning, saw the three. They barred his road and one held the bridle of his horse.

They were tall, well-formed men, wearing tight suits of somber leather bordered with black. Their headgear was heavy maroon cloth crumpled in precise creases, and leather flaps extended horizontally over each ear. Their faces were long and solemn, with clear golden-ivory skin, golden eyes and jet-black hair. Clearly they were not savages: they moved with a silky control, they eyed Guyal with critical appraisal, their garb implied the discipline of an ancient convention.

The leader stepped forward. His expression was neither threat nor welcome. "Greetings, stranger; whither bound?"

"Greetings," replied Guyal cautiously. "I go as my star directs . . . You are the Saponids?"

"That is our race, and before you is our town Saponce." He inspected Guyal with frank curiosity. "By the color of your custom I suspect your home to be in the south."

"I am Guyal of Sfere, by the river Scaum in Ascolais."

"The way is long," observed the Saponid. "Terrors beset the traveler. Your impulse must be most intense, and your star must draw with fervant allure."

"I come," said Guyal, "on a pilgrimage for the ease of my spirit; the road seems short when it attains its end."

The Saponid offered polite acquiescence. "Then you have crossed the Fer Aquilas?"

"Indeed; through cold wind and desolate stone." Guyal glance back at the looming mass. "Only yesterday at nightfall did I leave the gap. And then a ghost hovered above till I thought the grave was marking me for its own."

He paused in surprise; his words seemed to have released a powerful emotion in the Saponids. Their features lengthened, their mouths grew white and clenched. The leader, his polite detachment a trifle diminished, searched the sky with ill-concealed apprehension. "A ghost . . . In a white garment, thus and so, floating on high?"

"Yes; is it a known familiar of the region?"

There was a pause.

"In a certain sense," said the Saponid. "It is a signal of woe . . . But I interrupt your tale."

"There is little to tell. I took shelter for the night, and this morning I fared down to the plain."

"Were you not molested further? By Koolbaw the Walking Serpent, who ranges the slopes like fate?"

"I saw neither walking serpent nor crawling lizard; further, a blessing protects my trail and I come to no harm so long as I keep my course."

"Interesting, interesting."

"Now," said Guyal, "permit me to inquire of you, since there is much I would learn; what is this ghost and what evil does he commemorate?"

"You ask beyond my certain knowledge," replied the Saponid cautiously. "Of this ghost it is well not to speak lest our attention reinforce his malignity."

"As you will," replied Guyal. "Perhaps you will instruct me . . ." He caught his tongue. Before inquiring for the Museum of Man, it would be wise to learn in what regard the Saponids held it, lest, learning his interest, they seek to prevent him from knowledge.

"Yes?" inquired the Saponid. "What is your lack?"

Guyal indicated the seared area behind the fence of stone and timber. "What is the portent of this devastation?"

The Saponid stared across the area with a blank expression and shrugged. "It is one of the ancient places; so much is known, no more. Death lingers here, and no creature may venture across the place without succumbing to a most malicious magic which raises virulence and angry sores. Here is where those whom we kill are sent . . . But away. You will desire to rest and refresh yourself at Saponce. Come; we will guide you."

He turned down the trail toward the town, and Guyal, finding neither words nor reasons to reject the idea, urged his horse forward.

As they approached the tree-shrouded hill the trail widened to a road. To the right hand the lake drew close, behind low banks of purple reeds. Here were docks built of heavy black baulks and boats rocked to the wind-feathered ripples. They were built in the shape of sickles, with bow and stern curving high from the water.

Up into the town, and the houses were hewn timber, ranging in tone from golden brown to weathered black. The construction was intricate and ornate, the walls rising three stories to steep gables overhanging front and back. Pillars and piers were carved with complex designs: meshing ribbons, tendrils, leaves, lizards, and the like. The screens which guarded the windows were likewise carved, with foliage patterns, animal faces, radiant stars: rich textures in the mellow wood. It was clear that much expressiveness had been expended on the carving.

Up the steep lane, under the gloom cast by the trees, past the houses half-hidden by the foliage, and the Saponids of Saponce came north to stare. They moved quietly and spoke in low voices, and their garments were of an elegance Guyal had not expected to see on the northern steppe.

His guide halted and turned to Guyal. "Will you oblige me by waiting till I report to the Voyevode, that he may prepare a suitable reception?"

The request was framed in candid words and with guileless eyes. Guyal thought to perceive ambiguity in the phrasing, but since the hooves of his horse were planted in the center of the road, and since he did not propose leaving the road, Guyal assented with an open face.

The Saponid disappeared and Guyal sat musing on the pleasant town perched so high above the plain.

A group of girls approached to glance at Guyal with curious eyes. Guyal returned the inspection, and now found a puzzling lack about their persons, a discrepancy which he could not instantly identify. They wore graceful garments of woven wool, striped and dyed various colors; they were supple and slender, and seemed not lacking in coquetry. And yet . . .

The Saponid returned. "Now, Sir Guyal, may we proceed?"

Guyal, endeavoring to remove any flavor of suspicion from his words, said, "You will understand, Sir Saponid, that by the very nature of my father's blessing I dare not leave the delineated course of the trail; for then, instantly, I would become liable to any curse, which, placed on me along the way, might be seeking just such occasion for leeching close on my soul."

The Saponid made an understanding gesture. "Naturally; you follow a sound principle. Let me reassure you. I but conduct you to a reception by the Voyevode who even now hastens to the plaza to greet a stranger from the far south."

Guyal bowed in gratification, and they continued up the road.

A hundred paces and the road levelled, crossing a common planted with small, fluttering, heart-shaped leaves colored in all shades of purple, red, green and black.

The Saponid turned to Guyal. "As a stranger I must caution you never to set foot on the common. It is one of our sacred places, and tradition requires that a severe penalty be exacted for transgressions and sacrilege."

"I note your warning," said Guyal. "I will respectfully obey your law."

They passed a dense thicket; with hideous clamor a bestial shape sprang from concealment, a creature staring-eyed with tremendous fanged jaws. Guyal's horse shield, bolted, sprang out onto the sacred common and trampled the fluttering leaves.

A number of Saponid men rushed forth, grasped the horse, seized Guyal and dragged him from the saddle.

"Ho!" cried Guyal. "What means this? Release me!"

The Saponid who had been his guide advanced, shaking his head in reproach. "Indeed, and only had I just impressed upon you that gravity of such an offense!"

"But the monster frightened my horse!" said Guyal. "I am no wise responsible for this trespass; release me, let us proceed to the reception."

The Saponid said, "I fear that the penalties prescribed by tradition must come into effect. Your protests, though of superficial plausibility, will not bear serious examination. For instance, the creature you term a monster is in reality a harmless domesticated beast. Secondly, I observe the animal you bestride; he will not make a turn or twist without the twitch of the reins. Thirdly, even if your postulates were conceded, you thereby admit to guilt by virtue of negligence and omission. You should have secured a mount less apt to unpredictable action, or upon learning of the sanctitude of the common, you should have considered such a contingency as even now occurred, and therefore dismounted, leading your beast. Therefore, Sir Guyal, though loath, I am forced to believe you guilty of impertinence, impiety, disregard and impudicity. Therefore, as Castellan and Sergeant-Reader of the Litany, so responsible for the detention of lawbreakers, I must order you secured, contained, pent, incarcerated and confined until such time as the penalties will be exacted."

"The entire episode is mockery!" raged Guyal. "Are you savages, then, thus to mistreat a lone wayfarer?"

"By no means," replied the Castellan. "We are a highly civilized people, with customs bequeathed us by the past. Since the past was more glorious than the present, what presumption we would show by questioning these laws!"

Guyal fell quiet. "And what are the usual penalties for my act?"

The Castellan made a reassuring motion. "The rote prescribes three acts of penance, which in your case, I am sure will be nominal. But—the forms must be observed, and it is necessary that you be constrained in the Felon's Caseboard." He motioned to the men who held Guyal's arm. "Away with him; cross neither track nor trail, for then your grasp will be nerveless and he will be delivered from justice."

Guyal was pent in a well-aired but poorly lighted cellar of stone. The floor he found dry, the ceiling free of crawling insects. He had not been searched, nor had his Scintillant Dagger been removed from his sash. With suspicious crowding his brain he lay on the rush bed and, after a period, slept.

Now ensued the passing of a day. He was given food and drink; and at last the Castellan came to visit him.

"You are indeed fortunate," said the Saponid, "in that, as a witness, I was able to suggest your delinquencies to be more the result of negligence than malice. The last penalties exacted for the crime were stringent; the felon was ordered to perform the following three acts: first, to cut off his toes and sew the severed members into the skin at his neck; second, to revile his forbears for three hours, commencing with a Common Bill of Anathema, including feigned madness and hereditary disease, and at last defiling the hearth of his clan with ordure; and third, walking a mile under the lake with leaded shoes in search of the Lost Book of Kells.'' And the Castellan regarded Guyal with complacency.

''What deeds must I perform?'' inquired Guyal drily.

The Castellan joined the tips of his fingers together. ''As I say, the penances are nominal, by decree of the Voyevode. First you must swear never again to repeat your crime.''

''That I gladly do,'' said Guyal, and so bound himself.

''Second,'' said the Castellan with a slight smile, ''you must adjudicate at a Grand Pageant of Pulchritude among the maids of the village and select her whom you deem the most beautiful.''

''Scarcely an arduous task,'' commented Guyal. ''Why does it fall to my lot?''

The Castellan looked vaguely to the ceiling. ''There are a number of concomitants to victory in this contest . . . Every person in the town would find relations among the participant—a daughter, a sister, a niece—and so would hardly be considered unprejudiced. The charge of favoritism could never be levelled against you; therefore you make an ideal selection for this important post.''

Guyal seemed to hear the ring of sincerity in the Saponid's voice; still he wondered why the selection of the town's loveliest was a matter of such import.

''And third?'' he inquired.

''That will be revealed after the contest, which occurs this afternoon.''

The Saponid departed the cell.

Guyal, who was not without vanity, spent several hours restoring himself and his costume from the ravages of travel. He bathed, trimmed his hair, shaved his face, and, when the Castellan came to unlock the door, he felt that he made no discreditable picture.

He was led out upon the road and directed up the hill toward the summit of the terraced town of Saponce. Turning to the Castellan he said, ''How is it that you permit me to walk the trail once more? You must know that now I am safe from molestation . . .''

The Castellan shrugged. ''True. But you would gain little by insisting upon your temporary immunity. Ahead the trail crosses a bridge, which we could demolish; behind we need but breach the dam to Peilvemchal Torrent; then, should you walk the trail, you would be swept to the side and so rendered vulnerable. No, sir Guyal of Sfere, once the secret of your immunity is abroad then you are liable to a variety of stratagems. For instance, a large wall might be placed athwart the way, before and behind you. No doubt the spell would preserve you from thirst and hunger, but what then? So would you sit till the sun went out.''

Guyal said no word. Across the lake he noticed a trio of the crescent boats approaching the docks, prows and sterns rocking and dipping into the shaded water with a graceful motion. The void in his mind made itself known. ''Why are boats constructed in such fashion?''

The Castellan looked blankly at him. ''It is the only practicable method. Do not the oe-pods grow thusly to the south?''

''Never have I seen oe-pods.''

''They are the fruit of a great vine, and grow in scimitar-shape. When sufficiently large, we cut and clean them, slit the inner edge, grapple end to end with strong line and constrict till the pod opens as is desirable. Then when cured, dried, varnished, carved, burnished, and lacquered; fitted with deck, thwarts and gussets—then have we our boats.''

They entered the plaza, a flat area at the summit surrounded on three sides by tall houses of carved dark wood. The fourth side was open to a vista across the lake and beyond to the loom of the mountains. Trees overhung all and the sun shining through made a scarlet pattern on the sandy floor.

To Guyal's surprise there seemed to be no preliminary ceremonies or formalities to the contest, and small spirit of festivity was manifest among the townspeople. Indeed they seemed beset by subdued despondency and eyed him without enthusiasm.

A hundred girls stood gathered in a disconsolate group in the center of the plaza. It seemed to Guyal that they had gone to few pains to embellish themselves for beauty. To the contrary, they wore shapeless rags, their hair seemed deliberately misarranged, their faces dirty and scowling.

Guyal stared and turned to his guide. ''These girls seem not to relish the garland of pulchritude.''

The Castellan nodded wryly. ''As you see, they are by no means jealous for distinction; modesty has always been a Saponid trait.''

Guyal hesitated. ''What is the form of procedure? I do not desire in my ignorance to violate another of your arcane apochrypha.''

The Castellan said with a blank face, ''There are no formalities. We conduct these pageants with expedition and the least possible ceremony. You need but pass among these maidens and point out her whom you deem the most attractive.''

Guyal advanced to his task, feeling more than half-foolish. Then he reflected: this is a penalty for contravening an absurd tradition; I will conduct myself with efficiency and so the quicker rid myself of the obligation.

He stood before the hundred girls, who eyed him with hostility and anxiety, and Guyal saw that his task would not be simple, since, on the whole, they were of a comeliness which even the dirt, grimacing and rags could not disguise.

''Range yourselves, if you please, into a line,'' said Guyal. ''In this way, none will be at disadvantage.''

Sullenly the girls formed a line.

Guyal surveyed the group. He saw at once that a number could be eliminated: the squat, the obese, the lean, the pocked and coarse-featured—perhaps a quarter of the group. He said suavely, ''Never have I seen such unanimous loveliness; each of you might legitimately claim the cordon. My task is arduous; I must weigh fine imponderables; in the end my choice will undoubtedly be based on subjectivity and those of real charm will no doubt be the first discharged from the competition.'' He stepped forward. ''Those whom I indicate may retire.''

He walked down the line, pointed, and the ugliest, with expressions of unmistakable relief, hastened to the sidelines.

A second time Guyal made his inspection, and now, somewhat more familiar with those he judged, he was able to discharge those who, while suffering no whit from ugliness, were merely plain.

Roughly a third of the original group remained. These stared at Guyal with varying degrees of apprehension and truculence as he passed before them, studying each in turn . . . All at once his mind was determined, and his choice definite. Somehow the girls felt the change in him, and in their anxiety and tension left off the expressions they had been wearing to daunt and bemuse him.

Guyal made one last survey down the line. No, he had been accurate in his choice. There were girls here as comely as the senses could desire, girls with opal-glowing eyes and hyacinth features, girls as lissome as reeds, with hair silky and fine despite the dust which they seemed to have rubbed upon themselves.

The girl whom Guyal had selected was slighter than the others and possessed of a beauty not at once obvious. She had a small triangular face, great wistful eyes and thick black hair cut raggedly short at the ears. Her skin was of a transparent paleness, like the finest ivory;

her form slender, graceful, and of a compelling magnetism, urgent of intimacy. She seemed to have sensed his decision and her eyes widened.

Guyal took her hand, led her forward, and turned to the Voyevode—an old man sitting stolidly in a heavy chair.

''This is she whom I find the loveliest among your maidens.''

There was silence through the square. Then there came a hoarse sound, a cry of sadness from the Castellan and Sergeant-Reader. He came forward, sagging of face, limp of body. ''Guyal of Sfere, you have wrought a great revenge for my tricking you. This is my beloved daughter, Shierl, whom you have designated for dread.''

Guyal turned in wonderment from the Castellan to the girl Shierl, in whose eyes he now recognized a film of numbness, a gazing into a great depth.

Returning to the Castellan, Guyal stammered, ''I meant but complete impersonality. This your daughter Shierl I find one of the loveliest creatures of my experience; I cannot understand where I have offended.''

''No, Guyal,'' said the Castellan, ''you have chosen fairly, for such indeed is my own thought.''

''Well, then,'' said Guyal, ''reveal to me now my third task that I may have done and continue my pilgrimage.''

The Castellan said, ''Three leagues to the north lies the ruin which tradition tells us to be the olden Museum of Man.

''Ah,'' said Guyal, ''go on, I attend.''

''You must, as your third charge, conduct this my daughter Shierl to the Museum of Man. At the portal you will strike on a copper gong and announce to whomever responds: 'We are those summoned from Saponce'.''

Guyal started, frowned. ''How is this? 'We'?''

''Such is your charge,'' said the Castellan in a voice like thunder.

Guyal looked to left, right, forward and behind. But he stood in the center of the plaza surrounded by the hardy men of Saponce.

''When must this charge be executed?'' he inquired in a controlled voice.

The Castellan said in a voice bitter as oak-wort: ''Even now Shierl goes to clothe herself in yellow. In one hour shall she appear, in one hour shall you set forth for the Museum of Man.''

''And then?''

''And then—for good or for evil, it is not known. You fare as thirteen thousand have fared before you.''

* * *

Down from the plaza, down the leafy lanes of Saponce came Guyal, indignant and clamped of mouth, though the pit of his stomach felt tender and heavy with trepidation. The ritual carried distastful overtones: execution or sacrifice. Guyal's step faltered.

The Castellan seized his elbow with a hard hand. "Forward."

Execution or sacrifice . . . The faces along the lane swam with morbid curiosity, inner excitement; gloating eyes searched him deep to relish his fear and horror, and the mouths half-drooped, half-smiled in the inner hugging for joy not to be the one walking down the foliage streets, and forth to the Museum of Man.

The eminence, with the tall trees and carved dark houses, was at his back; they walked out into the claret sunlight of the tundra. Here were eighty women in white chlamys with ceremonial buckets of woven straw over their heads; around a tall tent of yellow silk they stood.

The Castellan halted Guyal and beckoned to the Ritual Matron. She flung back the hangings at the door of the tent; the girl within, Shierl, came slowly forth, eyes wide and dark with fright.

She wore a stiff gown of yellow brocade, and the wan of her body seemed pent and constrained within. The gown came snug under her chin, left her arms bare and raised past the back of her head in a stiff spear-headed cowl. She was frightened as a small animal trapped is frightened; she stared at Guyal, at her father, as if she had never seen them before.

The Ritual Matron put a gentle hand on her waist, propelled her forward. Shierl stepped once, twice, irresolutely halted. The Castellan brought Guyal forward and placed him at the girl's side; now two children, a boy and a girl, came hastening up with cups which they proffered to Guyal and Shierl. Dully she accepted the cup. Guyal took his and glanced suspiciously at the murky brew. He looked up to the Castellan. "What is the nature of this potion?"

"Drink," said the Castellan. "So will your way seem the shorter; so will terror leave you behind, and you will march to the Museum with a steadier step."

"No," said Guyal. "I will not drink. My senses must be my own when I meet the Curator. I have come far for the privilege; I would not stultify the occasion stumbling and staggering." And he handed the cup back to the boy.

Shierl stared dully at the cup she held. Said Guyal: "I advise you likewise to avoid the drug; so will we come to the Museum of Man with our dignity to us."

Hesitantly she returned the cup. The Castellan's brow clouded, but he made no protest.

An old man in a black costume brought forward a satin pillow on which rested a whip with a handle of carved steel. The Castellan now lifted this whip, and advancing, laid three light strokes across the shoulders of both Shierl and Guyal.

"Now, I charge thee, get hence and go from Saponce, outlawed forever; thou art waifs forlorn. Seek succor at the Museum of Man. I charge thee, never look back, leave all thoughts of past and future here at North Garden. Now and forever are you sundered from all bonds, claims, relations, and kinships, together with all pretenses to amity, love, fellowship and brotherhood with the Saponids of Saponce. Go, I exhort; go, I command; go, go, go,!"

Shierl sunk her teeth into her lower lip; tears freely coursed her cheek though she made no sound. With hanging head she started across the lichen of the tundra, and Guyal, with a swift stride, joined her.

Now there was no looking back. For a space the murmurs, the nervous sounds followed their ears; then they were alone on the plain. The limitless north lay across the horizon; the tundra filled the foreground and background, an expanse dreary, dun and moribund. Alone marring the region, the white ruins—once the Museum of Man—rose a league before them, and along the faint trail they walked without words.

Guyal said in a tentative tone, "There is much I would understand."

"Speak," said Shierl. Her voice was low but composed.

"Why are we forced and exhorted to this mission?"

"It is thus because it has always been thus. Is not this reason enough?"

"Sufficient possibly for you," said Guyal, "but for me the causality is unconvincing. I must acquaint you with the avoid in my mind, which lusts for knowledge as a lecher yearns for carnality; so pray be patient if my inquisition seems unnecessarily thorough."

She glanced at him in astonishment. "Are all to the south so strong for knowing as you?"

"In no degree," said Guyal. "Everywhere normality of the mind may be observed. The habitants adroitly perform the motions which fed them yesterday, last week, a year ago. I have been informed of my aberration well and full. 'Why strive for a pedant's accumulation?' I have been told. 'Why seek and search? Earth grows cold; man gasps his last; why forego merriment, music, and revelry for the abstract and abstruse?' "

"Indeed," said Shierl. "Well do they counsel; such is the consensus at Saponce."

Guyal shrugged. "The rumor goes that I am demon-bereft of my senses. Such may be. In any event the effect remains, and the obsession haunts me."

Shierl indicated understanding and acquiescence. "Ask on then; I will endeavor to ease these yearnings."

He glanced at her sidelong, studied the charming triangle of her face, the heavy black hair, the great lustrous eyes, dark as yu-sapphires. "In happier circumstances, there would be other yearnings I would beseech you likewise to ease."

"Ask," replied Shierl of Saponce. "The Museum of Man is close; there is occasion for naught but words."

"Why are we thus dismissed and charged, with tacit acceptance of our doom?"

"The immediate cause is the ghost you saw on the hill. When the ghost appears, then we of Saponce know that the most beautiful maiden and the most handsome youth of the town must be despatched to the Museum. The prime behind the custom I do not know. So it is; so it has been; so it will be till the sun gutters like a coal in the rain and darkens Earth, and the winds blow snow over Saponce."

"But what is our mission? Who greets us, what is our fate?"

"Such details are unknown."

Guyal mused, "The likelihood of pleasure seems small . . . There are discordants in the episode. You are beyond doubt the loveliest creature of the Saponids, the loveliest creature of Earth—but I, I am a casual stranger, and hardly the most well-favored youth of the town."

She smiled a trifle. "You are not uncomely."

Guyal said somberly, "Over-riding the condition of my person is the fact that I am a stranger and so bring little loss to the town of Saponce."

"That aspect has no doubt been considered," the girl said.

Guyal searched the horizon. "Let us then avoid the Museum of Man, let us circumvent this unknown fate and take to the mountains, and so south to Ascolais. Lust for enlightenment will never fly me in the face of destruction so clearly implicit."

She shook her head. "Do you suppose that we would gain by the ruse? The eyes of a hundred warriors follow us till we pass through the portals of the Museum; should we attempt to scamp our duty we should be bound to stakes, stripped of our skins by the inch, and at last be placed in bags with a thousand scorpions poured around our heads. Such is the traditional penalty; twelve times in history has it been invoked."

Guyal threw back his shoulders and spoke in a nervous voice. "Ah, well—the Museum of Man has been my goal for many years. On this motive I set forth from Sfere, so now I would seek the Curator and satisfy my obsession for brain-filling."

"You are blessed with great fortune," said Shierl, "for you are being granted your heart's desire."

Guyal could find nothing to say, so for a space they walked in silence. Then he spoke. "Shierl."

"Yes, Guyal of Sfere?"

"Do they separate us and take us apart?"

"I do not know."

"Shierl."

"Yes?"

"Had we met under a happier star . . ." He paused.

Shierl walked in silence.

He looked at her coolly. "You speak not."

"But you ask nothing," she said in surprise.

Guyal turned his face ahead, to the Museum of Man.

Presently she touched his arm. "Guyal, I am greatly frightened."

Guyal gazed at the ground beneath his feet, and a blossom of fire sprang alive in his brain. "See the marking through the licken?"

"Yes; what then?"

"Is it a trail?"

Dubiously she responded, "It is a way worn by the passage of many feet. So then—it is a trail."

Guyal said in restrained jubilation, "Here is safety, if I never permit myself to be cozened from the way. But you—ah, I must guard you; you must never leave my side, you must swim in the charm which protects me; perhaps then we will survive."

Shierl said sadly, "Let us not delude our reason, Guyal of Sfere."

But as they walked, the trail grew plainer, and Guyal became correspondingly sanguine. And ever larger bluked the crumble which marked the Museum of Man, presently to occupy all their vision.

If a storehouse of knowledge had existed here, little sign of it remained. There was a great flat floor, flagged in white stone, now chalky, broken and inter-thrust by weeds. Around this floor rose a series of monoliths, pocked and worn, and toppled off at various heights. These at one time had supported a vast roof; now of roof there was none and the walls were but dreams of the far past.

So here was the flat floor bounded by the broken stumps of pillars, bare to the winds of time and the glare of cool red sun. The rains had washed the marble, the dust from the mountains had been laid on and swept off, laid on and swept off, and those who had built the Museum were less than a mote of this dust, so far and forgotten were they.

"Think," said Guyal, "think of the vastness of knowledge which once was gathered here and which is now one with the soil—unless, of course, the Curator has salvaged and preserved."

Shierl looked about apprehensively. "I think rather of the portal, and that which awaits us . . . Guyal," she whispered, "I fear, I fear greatly . . . Suppose they tear us apart? Suppose there is torture and death for us? I fear a tremendous impingement, the shock of horror . . ."

Guyal's own throat was hot and full. He looked about with challenge. "While I still breathe and hold power in my arms to fight, there will be none to harm us."

Shierl groaned softly. "Guyal, Guyal, Guyal of Sfere—why did you choose me?"

"Because," said Guyal, "my eyes went to you like the nectar moth flits to the jacynth; because you were the loveliest and I thought nothing but good in store for you."

With a shuddering breath Shierl said, "I must be courageous; after all, if it were not I it would be some other maid equally fearful . . . And there is the portal."

Guyal inhaled deeply, inclined his head, and strode forward. "Let us be to it, and know . . ."

The portal opened into a nearby monolith, a door of flat black metal. Guyal followed the trail to the door, and rapped staunchly with his fist on the small copper gong to the side.

The door groaned wide on its hinges, and cool air, smelling of the under-earth, billowed forth. In the black gape their eyes could find nothing.

"Hola within!" cried Guyal.

A soft voice, full of catches and quavers, as if just after weeping, said, "Come ye, come ye forward. You are desired and awaited."

Guyal leaned his head forward, straining to see. "Give us light, that we may not wander from the trail and bottom ourselves."

The breathless quaver of a voice said, "Light is not needed; anywhere you step, that will be your trail, by an arrangement so agreed with the Way-Maker."

"No," said Guyal, "we would see the visage of our host. We come at his invitation; the minimum of his guest-offering is light; light there must be before we set foot inside the dungeon. Know we come as seekers after knowledge; we are visitors to be honored."

"Ah, knowledge, knowledge," came the sad breathlessness. "That shall be yours, in full plentitude—knowledge of many strange affairs; oh, you shall swim in a tide of knowledge—''

Guyal interrupted the sad, sighing voice. ''Are you the Curator? Hundreds of leagues have I come to bespeak the Curator and put him my inquiries. Are you he?''

''By no means. I revile the name of the Curator as a trecherous non-essential.''

''Who then may you be?''

''I am no one, nothing. I am an abstraction, an emotion, the ooze of terror, the sweat of horror, the shake in the air when a scream has departed.''

''You speak the voice of man.''

''Why not? Such things as I speak lie in the closest and dearest center of the human brain.''

Guyal said in a subdued voice, ''You do not make your invitation as enticing as might be hoped.''

''No matter, no matter; enter you must, into the dark and on the instant, as my lord, who is myself, waxes warm and languorous.''

''If light there be, we enter.''

''No light, no insolent scorch is ever found in the Museum.''

''In this case,'' said Guyal, drawing forth his Scintillant Dagger, ''I innovate a welcome reform. For see, now there is light!''

From the under-pommel issued a searching glare; the ghost tall before them screeched and fell into twinkling ribbons like pulverized tinsel. There were a few vagrant motes in the air; he was gone.

Shierl, who had stood stark and stiff as one mesmerized, gasped a soft warm gasp and fell against Guyal. ''How can you be so defiant?''

Guyal said in a voice half-laugh, half-quaver, ''In truth I do not know . . . Perhaps I find it incredible that the Norns would direct me from pleasant Sfere, through forest and crag, into the northern waste, merely to play the role of cringing victim. Disbelieving so inconclusive a destiny, I am bold.''

He moved the dagger to right and left, and they saw themselves to be at the portal of a keep, cut from concreted rock. At the back opened a black depth. Crossing the floor swiftly, Guyal kneeled and listened.

He heard no sound. Shierl, at his back, stared with eyes as balck and deep as the pit itself, and Guyal, turning, received a sudden irrational impression of a sprite of the olden times—a creature small and delicate, heavy with the weight of her charm, pale, sweet, clean.

Leaning with his glowing dagger, he saw a crazy rack of stairs voyaging down into the dark, and his light showed them and their shadows in so confusing a guise that he blinked and drew back.

Shierl said, "What do you fear?"

Guyal rose, turned to her. "We are momentarily untended here in the Museum of Man, and we are impelled forward by various forces; you by the will of your people; I by that which has driven me since I first tasted air . . . If we stay here we shall be once more arranged in harmony with the hostile pattern. If we go forward boldly, we may so come to a position of strategy and advantage. I propose that we set forth in all courage, descend these stairs and seek the Curator."

"But does he exist?"

"The ghost spoke fervently against him."

"Let us go then," said Shierl. "I am resigned."

Guyal said gravely, "We go in the mental frame of adventure, aggressiveness, zeal. Thus does fear vanish and the ghosts become creatures of mind-weft; thus does our elan burst the under-earth terror."

"We go."

They started down the stairs.

Back, forth, back, forth, down flights at varying angles, stages of varying heights, treads at varying widths, so that each step was a matter for concentration. Back, forth, down, down, down, and the black-barred shadows moved and jerked in bizarre modes on the walls.

The flight ended, they stood in a room similar to the entry above. Before them was another black portal, polished at one spot by use; on the walls to either side were inset brass plaques bearing messages in unfamiliar characters.

Guyal pushed the door open against a slight pressure of cold air, which, blowing through the aperture, made a slight rush, ceasing when Guyal opened the door farther.

"Listen."

It was a far sound, an intermittent clacking, and it held enough fell significance to raise the hairs at Guyal's neck. He felt Shierl's hand gripping his with clammy pressure.

Dimming the dagger's glow to a glimmer, Guyal passed through the door, with Shierl coming after. From afar came the evil sound, and by the echoes they knew they stood in a great hall.

Guyal directed the light to the floor: it was of a black resilient material. Next the wall: polished stone. He permitted the light to glow in the direction opposite to the sound, and a few paces distant they saw a bulky black case, studded with copper bosses, topped by a shallow glass tray in which could be seen an intricate concourse of metal devices.

With the purpose of the black cases not apparent, they followed the wall, and as they walked similar cases appeared, looming heavy and dull, at regular intervals. The clacking receded as they walked; then they came at a right angle, and turning the corner, they seemed to approach the sound. Black case after black case passed; slowly, tense as foxes, they walked, eyes groping for sight through the darkness.

The wall made another angle, and here there was a door.

Guyal hesitated. To follow the new direction of the wall would mean approaching the source of the sound. Would it be better to discover the worst quickly or to reconnoitre as they went?

He propounded the dilemma to Shierl, who shrugged, "It is all one; sooner or later the ghosts will flit down to pluck at us; then we are lost."

"Not while I possess light to stare them away to wisps and shreds," said Guyal. "Now I would find the Curator, and possibly he is to be found behind this door. We will so discover."

He laid his shoulder to the door; it eased ajar with a crack of golden light. Guyal peered through. He sighed, a muffled sound of wonder.

Now he opened the door further; Shierl clutched at his arm.

"This is the Museum," said Guyal in rapt tone. "Here there is no danger . . . He who dwells in beauty of this sort may never be other than beneficient . . ." He flung wide the door.

The light came from an unknown source, from the air itself, as if leaking from the discrete atoms; every breath was luminous, the room floated full of invigorating glow. A great rug pelted the floor, a monster tabard woven of gold, brown, bronze, two tones of green, fuscous red and smalt blue. Beautiful works of human fashioning ranked the walls. In glorious array hung panels of rich woods, carved, chased, enameled; scenes of olden times painted on woven fiber; formulas of color, designed to convey emotion rather than reality. To one side hung plats of wood laid on with slabs of soapstone, malachite and jade in rectangular patterns, richly varied and subtle, with miniature flecks of cinnabar, rhodocrosite and coral for warmth. Beside was a section given to disks of luminous green, flickering and flourescent with varying blue films and moving dots of scarlet and black. Here were representations of three hundred marvelous flowers, blooms of a forgotten age, no longer extant on waning Earth; there were as many star-burst patterns, rigidly conventionalized in form, but each of subtle distinction. All these and a multitude of other creations, selected from the best of human fervor.

The door thudded softly behind them; staring, every inch of skin a-tingle, the two from Earth's final time moved forward through the hall.

"Somewhere near must be the Curator," whispered Guyal. "There is a sense of careful tending and great effort here in the gallery."

"Look."

Opposite were two doors, laden with the sense of much use. Guyal strode quickly across the room but was unable to discern the means for opening the door, for it bore no latch, key, handle, knob or bar. He rapped with his knuckles and waited; no sound returned.

Shierl tugged at his arm. "These are private regions. It is best not to venture too rudely."

Guyal turned away and they continued down the gallery. Past the real expression of man's brightest dreamings they walked, until the concentration of so much fire and spirit and creativity put them into awe. "What great minds lie in the dust," said Guyal in a low voice "What gorgeous souls have vanished into the buried ages; what marvelous creatures are lost past the remotest memory . . . Nevermore will there be the like; now, in the last fleeting moments, humanity festers rich as rotten fruit. Rather than master and overpower our world, our highest aim is to cheat it through sorcery."

Shierl said, "But you, Guyal—you are apart. You are not like this . . ."

"I would know," declared Guyal with fierce emphasis. "In all my youth this ache has driven me, and I have journeyed from the old manse at Sfere to learn from the Curator . . . I am dissatisfied with the mindless accomplishments of the magicians, who have all their lore by rote."

Shierl gazed at him with a marveling expression, and Guyal's soul throbbed with love. She felt him quiver and whispered recklessly, "Guyal of Sfere, I am yours, I melt for you . . ."

"When we win to peace," said Guyal, "then our world will be of gladness . . ."

The room turned a corner, widened. And now the clacking sound they had noticed in the dark outer hall returned, louder, more suggestive of unpleasantness. It seemed to enter the gallery through an arched doorway opposite.

Guyal moved quietly to this door, with Shierl at his heels, and so they peered into the next chamber.

A great face looked from the wall, a face taller than Guyal, as tall as Guyal might reach with hands on high. The chin rested on the floor, the scalp slanted back into the panel.

Guyal stared, taken aback. In this pagent of beautiful objects the grotesque visage was the disparity and dissonance a lunatic might have created. Ugly and vile was the face, of a gut-wrenching silly obscenity. The skin shone a gun-metal sheen, the eyes gazed dully from slanting folds of greenish tissue. The nose was a small lump, the mouth a gross pulpy slash.

In sudden uncertainty Guyal turned to Shierl. "Does this not seem an odd work so to be honored here in the Museum of Man?"

Shierl was staring with eyes agonized and wide. Her mouth opened, quivered, wetness streaked her chin. With hands jerking, shaking, she grabbed his arm, staggered back into the gallery.

"Guyal," she cried, "Guyal, come away!" Her voice rose to a pitch. "Come away, come away!"

He faced her in surprise. "What are you saying?"

"That horrible thing in there—"

"It is but the diseased effort of an elder artist."

"It lives."

"How is this!"

"It lives!" she babbled. "It looked at me, then turned and looked at you. And it moved—and then I pulled you away . . ."

Guyal shrugged off her hand; in stark disbelief he faced through the doorway.

"Ahhhh . . ." breathed Guyal.

The face had changed. The torpor had evaporated; the glaze had departed the eye. The mouth squirmed; a hiss of escaping gas sounded. The mouth opened; a great gray tongue lolled forth. And from this tongue darted a tendril slimed with mucus. It terminated in a grasping hand, which groped for Guyal's ankle. He jumped aside; the hand missed its clutch, the tendril coiled.

Guyal, in an extremity, with his bowels clenched by sick fear, sprang back into the gallery. The hand seized Shierl, grasped her ankle. The eyes glistened; and now the flabby tongue swelled another wen, sprouted a new member . . . Shierl stumbled, fell limp, her eyes staring, foam at her lips. Guyal, shouting in a voice he could not hear, shouting high and crazy, ran forward slashing with his dagger. He cut at the gray wrist, but his knife sprang away as if the steel itself were horrified. His gorge at his teeth, he seized the tendril; with a mighty effort he broke it against his knee.

The face winced, the tendril jerked back. Guyal leapt forward, dragged Shierl into the gallery, lifted her, carried her back, out of reach.

Through the doorway now, Guyal glared in hate and fear. The mouth had closed; it sneered disappointment and frustrated lust. And now Guyal saw a strange thing: from the dank nostril oozed a wisp of white which swirled, writhed, formed a tall thing in a white robe—a thing with a draw face and eyes like holes in a skull. Whimpering and mewing in distaste for the light, it wavered forward into the gallery, moving with curious little pauses and hesitancies.

Guyal stood still. Fear had exceeded its power; fear no longer had meaning. A brain could react only to the maximum of its intensity; how could this thing harm him now? He would smash it with his hands, beat it into sighing fog.

"Hold, hold, hold!" came a new voice. "Hold, hold, hold. My charms and tokens, an ill day for Thorsingol . . . But then, avaunt, you ghost, back to the orifice, back and avaunt, avaunt, I say! Go, else I loose the actinics; trespass is not allowed, by supreme command from the Lycurgat; aye, the Lycurgat of Thorsingol. Avaunt, so then."

The ghost wavered, paused, staring in fell passivity at the old man who had hobbled into the gallery.

Back to the snoring face wandered the ghost, and let itself be sucked up into the nostril.

The face rumbled behind its lips, then opened the great gray gape and belched a white fiery lick that was like flame but not flame. It sheeted, flapped at the old man, who moved not an inch. From a rod fixed high on the door frame came a whirling disk of golden sparks. It cut and dismembered the white sheet, destroyed it back to the mouth of the face, whence now issued a black bar. This bar edged into the whirling disk and absorbed the sparks. There was an instant of dead silence.

Then the old man crowed, "Ah, you evil episode; you seek to interrupt my tenure. But no, there is no validity in you purpose; my clever baton holds your unnatural sorcery in abeyance; you are as naught; why do you not disengage and retreat into Jeldred?"

The rumble behind the large lips continued. The mouth opened wide: a gray viscous cavern was so displayed. The eyes glittered in titantic emotion. The mouth yelled, a roaring wave of violence, a sound to buffet the head and drive shock like a nail into the mind.

The baton sprayed a mist of silver. The sound curved and centralized and sucked into the metal fog; the sound was captured and consumed; it was never heard. The fog balled, lengthened to an arrow, plunged with intense speed at the nose, and buried itself in the pulp.

There was a heavy sound, an explosion; the face seethed in pain and the nose was a blasted clutter of shredded gray plasms. They waved like starfish arms and grew together once more, and now the nose was pointed like a cone.

The old man said, "You are captious today, my demoniac visitant—a vicious trait. You would disturb poor old Kerlin in his duties? So. You are ingenuous and neglectful. So ho, Baton," and he turned and peered at the rod, "you have tasted that sound? Spew out a fitting penalty, smear the odious face with your infallible retort."

A flat sound, a black flail which curled, slapped the air and smote home to the face. A glowing weal sprang into being. The face sighed and the eyes twisted up into their folds of greenish tissue.

Kerlin the Curator laughed, a shrill yammer on a single tone. He stopped short and the laugh vanished as if it had never begun. He turned to Guyal and Shierl, who stood pressed together in the doorframe.

"How now, how now? You are after the gong; the study hours are long ended. Why do you linger?" He shook a stern finger. "The Museum is not the site for roguery; this I admonish. So now be off, home to Thorsingol; be more prompt the next time; you disturb the established order . . ." He paused and threw a fretful glance over his shoulder. "The day has gone ill; the Nocturnal Keykeeper is inexcusably late . . . Surely I have waited an hour on the sluggard; the Lycurgat shall be so informed. I would be home to couch and hearth; here is ill use for old Kerlin, thus to detain him for the careless retard of the night-watch . . . And, further, the encroachment of you two laggards; away now, and be off; out into the twilight!" And he advanced, making directive motions with his hands.

Guyal said, "My lord Curator, I must speak words with you."

The old man halted, peered. "Eh? What now? At the end of a long day's effort? No, no, you are out of order; regulation must be observed. Attend my audiarium at the fourth circuit tomorrow morning; then we shall hear you. So go now, go."

Guyal fell back nonplussed. Shierl fell on her knees. "Sir Curator, we beg you for help; we have no place to go."

Kerlin the Curator looked at her blankly. "No place to go! What folly you utter! Go to your domicile, or to the Pub-escentarium, or to the Temple, or to the Outward Inn. For-sooth, Thorsingol is free with lodging; the Museum is no casual tavern."

"My lord," cried Guyal desperately, "will you hear me? We speak from emergency."

"Say on then."

''Some malignancy has bewitched your brain. Will you credit this?''

''Ah, indeed?'' ruminated the Curator.

''There is no Thorsingol. There is naught but dark waste. Your city is an eon gone.''

The Curator smiled benevolently. ''Ah, sad . . . A sad case. So it is with these younger minds. The frantic drive of life is the Prime Unhinger.'' He shook his head. ''My duty is clear. Tired bones, you must wait your well-deserved rest. Fatigue—begone; duty and simple humanity make demands; here is madness to be countered and cleared. And in any event the Nocturnal Keykeeper is not here to relieve me of my tedium.'' He beckoned. ''Come.''

Hesitantly Guyal and Shierl followed him. He opened one of his doors, passed through muttering and expostulating with doubt and watchfulness, Guyal and Shierl came after.

The room was cubical, floored with dull black stuff, walled with myriad golden knobs on all sides. A hooded chair occupied the center of the room, and beside it was a chest-high lectern whose face displayed a number of toggles and knurled wheels.

''This is the Curator's own Chair of Knowledge,'' explained Kerlin. ''As such it will, upon proper adjustment, impost the Pattern of Hynomeneural Clarity. So—I demand the correct sometsyndic arrangement—'' he manipulated the manuals ''—and now, if you will compose yourself, I will repair your hallucination. It is beyond my normal call of duty, but I am humane and would not be spoken of as mean or unwilling.''

Guyal inquired anxiously, ''Lord Curator, this Chair of Clarity, how will it affect me?''

Kerlin the Curator said grandly, ''The fibers of your brain are twisted, snarled, frayed, and so make contact with unintentional areas. By the marvelous craft of our modern cerebrologists, this hood will compose your synapses with the correct readings from the library—those of normality, you must understand—and so repair the skein, and make you once more a whole man.''

''Once I sit in the chair,'' Guyal inquired, ''what will you do?''

''Merely close this contact, engage this arm, throw in this toggle—then you daze. In thirty seconds, this bulb glows, signaling the success and completion of the treatment. Then I reverse the manipulation, and you arise a creature of renewed sanity.''

Guyal looked at Shierl. ''Did you hear and comprehend?''

''Yes, Guyal,'' in a small voice.

"Remember." Then to the Curator: "Marvelous. But how must I sit?"

"Merely relax in the seat. Then I pull the hood slightly forward, to shield the eyes from distraction."

Guyal leaned forward, peered gingerly into the hood. "I fear I do not understand."

The Curator hopped forward impatiently. "It is an act of the utmost facility. Like this." He sat in the chair.

"And how will the hood be applied?"

"In this wise." Kerlin seized a handle, pulled the shield over his face.

"Quick," said Guyal to Shierl. She sprang to the lectern; Kerlin the Curator made a motion to release the hood; Guyal seized the spindly frame, held it. Shierl flung the switches; the Curator relaxed, sighed.

Shierl gazed at Guyal, dark eyes wide and liquid as the great water-flamerian of South Almery. "Is he—dead?"

"I hope not."

They gazed uncertainly at the relaxed form. Seconds passed.

A clanging noise sounded from afar—a crush, a wrench, an exultant bellow, lesser halloos of wild triumph.

Guyal rushed to the door. Prancing, wavering, sidling into the gallery came a multitude of ghosts; through the open door behind, Guyal could see the great head. It was shoving out, pushing into the room. Great ears appeared, part of a bull-neck, wreathed with purple wattles. The wall cracked, sagged, crumbled. A great hand thrust through, a forearm . . .

Shierl screamed. Guyal, pale and quivering, slammed the door in the face of the nearest ghost. It seeped in around the jamb, slowly, wisp by wisp.

Guyal sprang to the lectern. The bulb showed dullness. Guyal's hands twitched along the controls. "Only Kerlin's awareness controls the magic of the baton," he panted. "So much is clear." He stared into the bulb with agonized urgency. "Glow, bulb, glow . . ."

By the door the ghost seeped and billowed.

"Glow, bulb, glow . . ."

The bulb glowed. With a sharp cry Guyal returned the switches to neutrality, jumped down, flung up the hood.

Kerlin the Curator sat looking at him.

Behind the ghost formed itself—a tall white thing in white robes, and the dark eye-holes stared like outlets into non-imagination.

Kerlin the Curator sat looking.

The ghost moved under the robes. A hand like a bird's foot appeared, holding a clod of dingy matter. The ghost cast the matter to the floor; it exploded into a puff of black dust. The motes of the cloud grew, became a myriad of wriggling insects. With one accord they darted across the floor, growing as they spread, and became scuttling creatures with monkey-heads.

Kerlin the Curator moved. "Baton," he said. He held up his hand. It held his baton. The baton spat an orange gout—red dust. It puffed before the rushing horde and each mote became a red scorpion. So ensued a ferocious battle, and little shrieks, and chittering sounds rose from the floor.

The monkey-headed things were killed, routed. The ghost sighed, moved his claw-hand once more. But the baton spat forth a ray of purest light and the ghost sloughed into nothingness.

"Kerlin!" cried Guyal. "The demon is breaking into the gallery."

Kerlin flung open the door, stepped forth.

"Baton," said Kerlin, "perform thy utmost intent."

The demon said, "No, Kerlin, hold the magic; I thought you dazed. Now I retreat."

With a vast quaking and heaving he pulled back until once more only his face showed through the hole.

"Baton," said Kerlin, "be you on guard."

The baton disappeared from his hand.

Kerlin turned and faced Guyal and Shierl.

"There is need for many words, for now I die. I die, and the Museum shall lie alone. So let us speak quickly, quickly, quickly . . ."

Kerlin moved with feeble steps to a portal which snapped aside as he approached. Guyal and Shierl, speculating on the probable trends of Kerlin's disposition, stood hesitantly to the rear.

"Come, come," said Kerlin in sharp impatience. "My strength flags, I die. You have been my death."

Guyal moved slowly forward, with Shierl half a pace behind. Suitable response to the accusation escaped him; words seemed without conviction.

Kerlin surveyed them with a thin grin. "Halt your misgivings and hasten; the necessities to be accomplished in the time available there to make the task like trying to write the Tomes of Kae in a minim of ink. I wane; my pulsing comes in shallow tides, my sight flickers . . ."

He waved a despairing hand, then, turning, led them into the inner chamber, where he slumped into a great chair. With many uneasy glances at the door, Guyal and Shierl settled upon a padded couch.

Kerlin jeered in a feeble voice, "You fear the white phantasms?

Poh, they are pent from the gallery by the baton, which contains their every effort. Only when I am smitten out of mind—or dead—will the baton cease its function. You must know," he added with somewhat more vigor, "that the energies and dynamics do not channel from my rain but from the central potentium of the Museum, which is perpetual; I merely direct and order the rod."

"But this demon—who or what is he? Why does he come to look through the walls?"

Kerlin's face settled into a bleak mask. "He is Blikdak, Ruler-Divinity of the demon-world Jeldred. He wrenched the hole intent on gulfing the knowledge of the Museum into his mind, but I forestalled him; so he sits waiting in the hole till I die. Then he will glut himself with erudition to the great disadvantage of men."

"Why cannot this demon be exhorted hence and the hole abolished?"

Kerlin the Curator shook his head. "The fires and furious powers I control are not valid in the air of the demon-world, where substance and form are of different entity. So far as you see him, he has brought his environment with him; so far he is safe. When he ventures further into the Museum, the power of Earth dissolves the Jeldred mode; then may I spray him with prismatic fervor from the potentium . . . But stay, enough of Blikdak for the nonce; tell me, who are you, why are you ventured here, and what is the news of Thorsingol?"

Guyal said in a halting voice, "Thorsingol is passed beyond memory. There is naught above but arid tundra and the old town of the Saponids. I am of the southland; I have coursed many leagues so that I might speak to you and fill my mind with knowledge. This girl Shierl is of the Saponids, and victim of an ancient custom which sends beauty into the Museum at the behest of Blikdak's ghosts."

"Ah," breathed Kerlin, "have I been so aimless? I recall these youthful shapes which Blikdak employed to relieve the tedium of his vigil . . . They flit down my memory like may-flies along a panel of glass . . . I put them aside as creatures of his own conception, postulated by his own imagery . . ."

Shierl shrugged in bewilderment. "But why? What use to him are human creatures?"

Kerlin said dully, "Girl, you are all charm and freshness; the monstrous urges of the demon-lord Blikdak are past your conceiving. These youths, of both sexes, are his play, on whom he practices various junctures, joinings, coiti, perversions, sadisms, nauseas, antics and at last struggles to the death. Then he sends forth a ghost demanding further youth and beauty."

Shierl whispered, "This was to have been I . . ."

Guyal said in puzzlement, "I cannot understand. Such acts, in my understanding, are the characteristic derangements of humanity. They are anthropoid by the very nature of the functioning sacs, glands and organs. Since Blikdak is a demon . . ."

"Consider him!" spoke Kerlin. "His lineaments, his apparatus. He is nothing else but anthropoid, and such is his origin, together with all the demons, frits and winged glowing-eyed creatures that infest latter-day Earth. Blikdak, like the others, is from the mind of man. The sweaty condensation, the stench and vileness, the cloacal humors, the brutal delights, the rapes and sodomies, the scatophilac whims, the manifold tittering lubricities that have drained through humanity formed a vast tumor; so Blikdak assumed his being, so now this is he. You have seen how he molds his being, so he performs his enjoyments. But of Blikdak, enough. I die, I die!" He sank into the chair with heaving chest.

"See me! My eyes vary and waver. My breath is shallow as a bird's, my bones are the pith of an old vine. I have lived beyond knowledge; in my madness I knew no passage of time. Where there is no knowledge there are no somatic consequences. Now I remember the years and centuries, the millennia, the epochs—they are like quick glimpses through a shutter. So, curing my madness, you have killed me."

Shierl blinked, drew back. "But when you die? What then? Blikdak . . ."

Guyal asked, "In the Museum of Man is there no knowledge of the exorcisms necessary to dissolve this demon? He is clearly our first antagonist, our immediacy."

"Blikdak must be eradicated," said Kerlin. "Then will I die in ease; then must you assume the care of the Museum." He licked his white lips. "An ancient principle specifies that, in order to destroy a substance, the nature of the substance must be determined. In short, before Blikdak may be dissolved, we must discover his elemental nature." And his eyes moved glassily to Guyal.

"Your pronouncement is sound beyond argument," admitted Guyal, but how may this be accomplished? Blikdak will never allow such an investigation."

"No; there must be subterfuge, some instrumentality . . ."

"The ghost are part of Blikdak's stuff?"

"Indeed."

"Can the ghosts be stayed and prevented?"

"Indeed; in a box of light, the which I can effect by a thought.

Yes, a ghost we must have." Kerlin raised his head. "Baton! one ghost; admit a ghost!"

A moment passed; Kerlin held up his hand. There was a faint scratch at the door, and a soft whine could be heard without. "Open," said a voice, full of sobs and catches and quavers. "Open and let forth the youthful creatures to Blikdak. He finds boredom and lassitude in his vigil; so let the two come forth to negate his unease."

Kerlin laboriously rose to his feet. "It is done."

From behind the door came a sad voice, "I am pent, I am snared in scorching brilliance!"

"Now we discover," said Guyal. "What dissolves the ghost dissolves Blikdak."

"True indeed," assented Kerlin.

"Why not light?" inquired Shierl. "Light parts the fabric of the ghosts like a gust of wind tatters the fog."

"But merely for their fragility; Blikdak is harsh and solid, and can withstand the fiercest radiance safe in his demon-land alcove." And Kerlin mused. After a moment he gestured to the door. "We go to the image-expander; there we will explode the ghost to macroid dimension; so shall we find his basis. Guyal of Sfere, you must support my frailness; in truth my limbs are weak as wax."

On Guyal's arm he tottered forward, and with Shierl close at their heels they gained the gallery. Here the ghost wept in its cage of light, and searched constantly for a dark aperture to seep his essence through.

Paying him no heed Kerlin hobbled and limped across the gallery. In their wake followed the box of light and perforce the ghost.

"Open the great door," cried Kerlin in a voice beset with cracking and hoarseness. "The great door into the Cognative Repository!"

Shierl ran ahead and thrust her force against the door; it slid aside, and they looked into the great dark hall, and the golden light from the gallery dwindled into the shadows and was lost.

"Call for Lumen," Kerlin said.

"Lumen!" cried Guyal. "Lumen, attend!"

Light came to the great hall, and it proved so tall that the pilasters along the wall dwindled to threads, and so long and wide that a man might be winded to fatigue in running a dimension. Spaced in equal rows were the black cases with the copper bosses that Guyal and Shierl had noted on their entry. And above each hung five similar cases, precisely fixed, floating without support.

"What are these?" asked Guyal in wonder.

"Would my poor brain encompassed a hundredth part of what these banks know," panted Kerlin. "They are great brains crammed with all that known, experienced, achieved, or recorded by man. Here is all the lost lore, early and late, the fabulous imaginings, the history of ten million cities, the beginnings of time and the presumed finalities; the reason for human existence and the reason for the reason. Daily I have labored and toiled in these banks; my achievement has been a synopsis of the most superficial sort: a panorama across a wide and multifarious country.''

Said Shierl, ''Would not the craft to destroy Blikdak be contained here?''

''Indeed, indeed; our task would be merely to find the information. Under which casing would we search? Consider these categories: Demonlands; Killings and Mortefactions; Expositions and Dissolutions of Evil; History of Granvilunde (where such an entity was repelled); Attractive and Detractive Hyperordnets; Therapy for Hallucinants and Ghost-takers; Constructive Journal, item for regeneration of burst walls, sub-division for invasion by demons; Procedural Suggestions in Time of Risk . . . Aye, these and a thousand more. Somewhere is knowledge of how to smite Blikdak's abhorred face back into his quasiplace. But where to look? There is no Index Major; none except the poor synopsis of my compilation. He who seeks specific knowledge must often go on an extended search . . .'' His voice trailed off. Then: ''Forward! Forward through the banks to the Mechanismus.''

So through the banks they went, like roaches in a maze, and behind drifted the cage of light with the wailing ghost. At last they entered a chamber smelling of metal; again Kerlin instructed Guyal and Guyal called, ''Attend us, Lumen, attend!''

Through intricate devices walked the three, Guyal lost and rapt beyond inquiry, even though his brain ached with the want of knowing.

At a tall booth Kerlin halted the cage of light. A pane of vitrean dropped before the ghost. ''Observe now,'' Kerlin said, and manipulated the activants.

They saw the ghost, depicted and projected: the flowing robe, the haggard visage. The face grew large, flattened; a segment under the vacant eye became a scabrous white place. It separated into pustules, and a single pustule swelled to fill the pane. The crater of the pustule was an intricate stippled surface, a mesh as of fabric, knit in a lacy pattern.

''Behold!'' said Shierl. ''He is a thing woven as if by thread.''

Guyal turned eagerly to Kerlin; Kerlin raised a finger for silence. ''Indeed, indeed, a goodly thought, especially since here beside us is a rotor of extreme swiftness, used in reeling the cognitive filaments of the cases . . . Now then observe: I reach to this panel, I select a mesh,

I withdraw a thread, and note! The meshes ravel and loosen and part. And now to the bobbin on the rotor, and I wrap the thread, and now with a twist we have the cincture made . . .''

Shierl said dubiously, ''Does not the ghost observe and note your doing?''

''By no means,'' asserted Kerlin. ''The pane of vitrean shields our actions; he is too exercised to attend. And now I dissolve the cage and he is free.''

The ghost wandered forth, cringing from the light.

''Go!'' cried Kerlin. ''Back to your genetrix; back, return and go!''

The ghost departed. Kerlin said to Guyal, ''Follow; find when Blikdak snuffs him up.''

Guyal at a cautious distance watched the ghost seep up into the black nostril, and returned to where Kerlin waited by the rotor. ''The ghost has once more become part of Blikdak.''

''Now then,'' said Kerlin, ''we cause the rotor to twist, the bobbin to whirl, and we shall observe.''

The rotor whirled to a blur; the bobbin (as long as Guyal's arm) became spun with ghost-thread, at first glowing pastel polychrome, then nacre, then fine milk-ivory.

The rotor spun, a million times a minute, and the thread drawn unseen and unknown from Blikdak thickened on the bobbin.

The rotor spun; the bobbin was full—a cylinder shining with glossy silken sheen. Kerlin slowed the rotor; Guyal snapped a new bobbin into place, and the unraveling of Blikdak continued.

Three bobbins—four—five—and Guyal, observing Blikdak from afar, found the giant face quiescent, the mouth working and sucking, creating the clacking sound which had first caused them apprehension.

Eight bobbins. Blikdak opened his eyes, stared in puzzlement around the chamber.

Twelve bobbins: a discolored spot appeared on the sagging cheek, and Blikdak quivered in uneasiness.

Twenty bobbins: the spot spread across Blikdak's visage, across the slanted fore-dome, and his mouth hung lax; he hissed and fretted.

Thirty bobbins: Blikdak's head seemed stale and putrid; the gun-metal sheen had become an angry maroon, the eyes bulged, the mouth hung open, the tongue lolled limp.

Fifty bobbins: Blikdak collapsed. His dome lowered against the febrile mouth; his eyes shone like feverish coals.

Sixty bobbins: Blikdak was no more.

And with the dissolution of Blikdak so dissolved Jeldred, the demonland created for the housing of evil. The breach in the wall gave on barren rock, unbroken and rigid.

And in the Mechanismus sixty shining bobbins lay stacked neat; the evil so disorganized glowed with purity and irridescence.

Kerlin fell back against the wall. "I expire; my time has come. I have guarded well the Museum; together we have won it away from Blikdak . . . Attend me now. Into your hands I pass the curacy; now the Museum is your charge to guard and preserve."

"For what end?" asked Shierl. "Earth expires, almost as you . . . Wherefore knowledge?"

"More now than ever," gasped Kerlin. "Attend: the stars are bright, the stars are fair; the banks know blessed magic to fleet you to youthful climes. Now—I go. I die."

"Wait!" cried Guyal. Wait, I beseech!"

"Why wait?" whispered Kerlin. "The way to peace is on me; you call me back?"

"How do I extract from the banks?"

"The key to the index is in my chambers, the index of my life . . ." And Kerlin died.

Guyal and Shierl climbed to the upper ways and stood outside the portal on the ancient flagged floor. It was night; the marble shone faintly underfoot, the broken columns loomed on the sky.

Across the plain the yellow lights of Saponce shone warm through the trees; above in the sky shone the stars.

Guyal said to Shierl, "There is your home; there is Saponce. Do you wish to return?"

She shook her head. "Together we have looked through the eyes of knowledge. We have seen old Thorsingol, and the Sherit Empire before it, and Golwan Andra before that and the Forty Kades even before. We have seen the warlike green-men, and the knowledgeable Pharials and the Clambs who departed Earth for the stars, as did the Merioneth before them and the Gray Sorcerers still earlier. We have seen oceans rise and fall, the mountains crust up, peak and melt in the beat of rain; we have looked on the sun when it glowed hot and full and yellow . . . No, Guyal, there is no place for me at Saponce . . ."

Guyal, leaning back on the weathered pillar, looked up to the stars. "Knowledge is ours, Shierl—all of knowing to our call. And what shall we do?"

Together they looked up to the white stars.

"What shall we do . . ."

The Eyes of the Overworld

1

The Overworld

On the heights above the river Xzan, at the site of certain ancient ruins, Iucounu the Laughing Magician had built a manse to his private taste: an eccentric structure of steep gables, balconies, sky-walks, cupolas, together with three spiral green glass towers through which the red sunlight shone in twisted glints and peculiar colors.

Behind the manse and across the valley, low hills rolled away like dunes to the limit of vision. The sun projected shifting crescents of black shadow; otherwise the hills were unmarked, empty, solitary. The Xzan, rising in the Old Forest to the east of Almery, passed below, then three leagues to the west made junction with the Scaum. Here was Azenomei, a town old beyond memory, notable now only for its fair, which attracted folk from all the region. At Azenomei Fair Cugel had established a booth for the sale of talismans.

Cugel was a man of many capabilities, with a disposition at once flexible and pertinacious. He was long of leg, deft of hand, light of finger, soft of tongue. His hair was the blackest of black fur, growing low down his forehead, coving sharply back above his eyebrows. His darting eye, long inquisitive nose and droll mouth gave his somewhat lean and bony face an expression of vivacity, candor, and affability. He had known many vicissitudes, gaining therefrom a suppleness, a fine discretion, a mastery of both bravado and stealth. Coming into the possession of an ancient lead coffin—after discarding the contents—he had formed a number of leaden lozenges. These, stamped with appropriate seals and runes, he offered for sale at the Azenomei Fair.

Unfortunately for Cugel, not twenty paces from his booth a certain Fianosther had established a larger booth with articles of greater variety and more obvious efficacy, so that whenever Cugel halted a passerby to enlarge upon the merits of his merchandise, the passerby would like as not display an article purchased from Fianosther and go his way.

On the third day of the fair Cugel had disposed of only four periapts, at prices barely above the cost of the lead itself, while Fianosther was hard put to serve all his customers. Hoarse from bawling futile inducements, Cugel closed down his booth and approached Fianosther's place of trade in order to inspect the mode of construction and the fastenings at the door.

Fianosther, observing, beckoned him to approach. "Enter, my friend, enter. How goes your trade?"

"In all candor, not too well," said Cugel. "I am both perplexed and disappointed, for my talismans are not obviously useless."

"I can resolve your perplexity," said Fianosther. "Your booth occupies the site of the old gibbet, and has absorbed unlucky essences. But I thought to notice you examining the manner in which the timbers of my booth are joined. You will obtain a better view from within, but first I must shorten the chain of the captive erb which roams the premises during the night."

"No need," said Cugel. "My interest was cursory."

"As to the disappointment you suffer," Fianosther went on, "it need not persist. Observe these shelves. You will note that my stock is seriously depleted."

Cugel acknowledged as much. "How does this concern me?"

Fianosther pointed across the way to a man wearing garments of black. This man was small, yellow of skin, bald as a stone. His eyes resembled knots in a plank; his mouth was wide and curved in a grin of chronic mirth. "There stands Iucounu the Laughing Magician," said Fianosther. "In a short time he will come into my booth and attempt to buy a particular red libram, the casebook of Dibarcas Maior, who studied under Great Phandaal. My price is higher than he will pay, but he is a patient man, and will remonstrate for at least three hours. During this time his manse stands untenanted. It contains a vast collection of thaumaturgical artifacts, instruments, and activants, as well as curiosa, talismans, amulets and librams. I'm anxious to purchase such items. Need I say more?"

"This is all very well," said Cugel, "but would Iucounu leave his manse without guard or attendant?"

Fianosther held wide his hands. "Why not? Who would dare steal from Iucounu the Laughing Magician?"

"Precisely this thought deters me," Cugel replied. "I am a man of resource, but not insensate recklessness."

"There is wealth to be gained," stated Fianosther. "Dazzles and displays, marvels beyond worth, as well as charms, puissances, and elixirs. But remember, I urge nothing, I counsel nothing; if you are apprehended, you have only heard me exclaiming at the wealth of Iucounu the Laughing Magician! But here he comes. Quick: turn your back so that he may not see your face. Three hours he will be here, so much I guarantee!"

Iucounu entered the booth, and Cugel bent to examine a bottle containing a pickled homunculus.

"Greetings, Iucounu!" called Fianosther. "Why have you delayed? I have refused munificent offers for a certain red libram, all on your account! And here—note this casket! It was found in a crypt near the site of old Karkod. It is yet sealed and who knows what wonder it may contain? My price is a modest twelve thousand terces."

"Interesting," murmured Iucounu. "The inscription—let me see. . . . Hmm. Yes, it is authentic. The casket contains calcined fish-bone, which was used throughout Grand Motholam as a purgative. It is worth perhaps ten or twelve terces as a curio. I own caskets eons older, dating back to the Age of Glow."

Cugel sauntered to the door, gained the street, where he paced back and forth, considering every detail of the proposal as explicated by Fianosther. Superficially the matter seemed reasonable: here was Iucounu; there was the manse, bulging with encompassed wealth. Certainly no harm could result from simple reconnaissance. Cugel set off eastward along the banks of the Xzan.

The twisted turrets of green glass rose against the dark blue sky, scarlet sunlight engaging itself in the volutes. Cugel paused, made a careful appraisal of the countryside. The Xzan flowed past without a sound. Nearby, half-concealed among black poplars, pale green larch, drooping pall-willow, was a village—a dozen stone huts inhabited by bargemen and tillers of the river terraces: folk engrossed in their own concerns.

Cugel studied the approach to the manse: a winding way paved with dark brown tile. Finally he decided that the more frank his approach the less complex need be his explanations, if such were demanded. He began the climb up the hillside, and Iucounu's manse reared above him. Gaining the courtyard, he paused to search the landscape. Across the river hills rolled away into the dimness, as far as the eye could reach.

Cugel marched briskly to the door, rapped, but evoked no response. He considered. If Iucounu, like Fianosther, maintained a guardian beast, it might be tempted to utter a sound if provoked. Cugel called out in various tones: growling, mewing, yammering.

Silence within.

He walked gingerly to a window and peered into a hall draped in pale gray, containing only a tabouret on which, under a glass bell jar, lay a dead rodent. Cugel circled the manse, investigating each window as he came to it, and finally reached the great hall of the ancient castle. Nimbly he climbed the rough stones, leapt across to one of Iucounu's fanciful parapets and in a trice had gained access to the manse.

He stood in a bed chamber. On a dais six gargoyles supporting a couch turned heads to glare at the intrusion. With two stealthy strides Cugel gained the arch which opened into an outer chamber. Here the walls were green and the furnishings black and pink. He left the room for a balcony circling a central chamber, light streaming through oriels high in the walls. Below were cases, chests, shelves and racks containing all manner of objects: Iucounu's marvelous collection.

Cugel stood poised, tense as a bird, but the quality of the silence reassured him: the silence of an empty place. Still, he trespassed upon the property of Iucounu the Laughing Magician, and vigilance was appropriate.

Cugel strode down a sweep of circular stairs into a great hall. He stood enthralled, paying Iucounu the tribute of unstinted wonder. But his time was limited; he must rob swiftly and be on his way. Out came his sack; he roved the hall, fastidiously selecting those objects of small bulk and great value: a small pot with antlers, which emitted clouds of remarkable gasses when the prongs were tweaked; an ivory horn through which sounded voices from the past; a small stage where costumed imps stood ready to perform comic antics; an object like a cluster of crystal grapes, each affording a blurred view into one of the demon-worlds; a baton sprouting sweetmeats of assorted flavor; an ancient ring engraved with runes; a black stone surrounded by nine zones of impalpable color. He passed by hundreds of jars of powders and liquids, likewise forebore from the vessels containing preserved heads. Now he came to shelves stacked with volumes, folios and librams, where he selected with care, taking for preference those bound in purple velvet, Phandaal's characteristic color. He likewise selected folios of drawings and ancient maps, and the disturbed leather exuded a musty odor.

He circled back to the front of the hall past a case displaying a score of small metal chests, sealed with corroded bands of great age. Cugel selected three at random; they were unwontedly heavy. He passed by several massive engines whose purpose he would have liked to explore, but time was advancing, and best he should be on his way, back to Azenomei and the booth of Fianosther. . . .

Cugel frowned. In many respects the prospect seemed impractical. Fianosther would hardly choose to pay full value for his goods, or, more accurately, Iucounu's goods. It might be well to bury a certain proportion of the loot in an isolated place. . . . Here was an alcove Cugel had not previously noted. A soft light welled like water against the crystal pane, which separated alcove from hall. A niche to the rear displayed a complicated object of great charm. As best Cugel could distinguish, it seemed a miniature carousel on which rode a dozen beautiful dolls of seeming vitality. The object was clearly of great value, and Cugel was pleased to find an aperture in the crystal pane.

He stepped through, but two feet before him a second pane blocked his way, establishing an avenue which evidently led to the magic whirligig. Cugel proceeded confidently, only to be stopped by another pane which he had not seen until he bumped into it. Cugel retraced his steps and to his gratification found the doubtlessly correct entrance a few feet back. But this new avenue led him by several right angles to another blank pane. Cugel decided to forego acquisition of the carousel and depart the castle. He turned, but discovered himself to be a trifle confused. He had come from his left—or was it his right?

. . . Cugel was still seeking egress when in due course Iucounu returned to his manse.

Pausing by the alcove, Iucounu gave Cugel a stare of humorous astonishment. "What have we here? A visitor? And I have been so remiss as to keep you waiting! Still, I see you have amused yourself, and I need feel no mortification." Iucounu permitted a chuckle to escape his lips. He then pretended to notice Cugel's bag. "What is this? You have brought objects for my examination? Excellent! I am always anxious to enhance my collection, in order to keep pace with the attrition of the years. You would be astounded to learn of the rogues who seek to despoil me! That merchant of claptrap in his tawdry little booth, for instance—you could not conceive his frantic efforts in this regard! I tolerate him because to date he has not been bold enough to venture himself into my manse. But come, step out here into the hall, and we will examine the contents of your bag."

Cugel bowed graciously. "Gladly. As you assume, I have indeed been waiting for your return. If I recall correctly, the exit is by this passage . . ." He stepped forward, but again was halted. He made a gesture of rueful amusement. "I seem to have taken a wrong turning."

"Apparently so," said Iucounu. "Glancing upward, you will notice a decorative motif upon the ceiling. If you heed the flexion of the lunules you will be guided to the hall."

"Of course!" And Cugel briskly stepped forward in accordance with the directions.

"One moment!" called Iucounu. "You have forgotten your sack!"

Cugel reluctantly returned for the sack, once more set forth, and presently emerged into the hall.

Iucounu made a suave gesture. "If you will step this way I will be glad to examine your merchandise."

Cugel glanced reflectively along the corridor toward the front entrance. "It would be a presumption upon your patience. My little knickknacks are below notice. With your permission I will take my leave."

"By no means!" declared Iucounu heartily. "I have few visitors, most of whom are rogues and thieves. I handle them severely, I assure you! I insist that you at least take some refreshment. Place your bag on the floor."

Cugel carefully set down the bag. "Recently I was instructed in a small competence by a sea-hag of White Alster. I believe you will be interested. I require several ells of stout cord."

"You excite my curiosity!" Iucounu extended his arm; a panel in the wainscoting slid back; a coil of rope was tossed to his hand. Rubbing his face as if to conceal a smile, Iucounu handed the rope to Cugel, who shook it out with great care.

"I will ask your cooperation," said Cugel. "A small matter of extending one arm and one leg."

"Yes, of course." Iucounu held out his hand, pointed a finger. The rope coiled around Cugel's arms and legs, pinning him so that he was unable to move. Iucounu's grin nearly split his great soft head. "This is a surprising development! By error I called forth Thief-taker! For your own comfort, do not strain, as Thief-taker is woven of wasp-legs. Now then, I will examine the contents of your bag." He peered into Cugal's sack and emitted a soft cry of dismay. "You have rifled my collection! I note certain of my most treasured valuables!"

Cugel grimaced. "Naturally! But I am no thief; Fianosther sent me here to collect certain objects, and therefore—"

Iucounu held up his hand. "The offense is far too serious for flippant disclaimers. I have stated my abhorrence for plunderers and thieves, and now I must visit upon you justice in its most unmitigated rigor—unless, of course, you can suggest an adequate requital."

"Some such requital surely exists," Cugel averred. "This cord however rasps upon my skin, so that I find cogitation impossible."

"No matter. I have decided to apply the Charm of Forlorn Encystment, which constricts the subject in a pore some forty-five miles below the surface of the earth."

Cugel blinked in dismay. "Under these conditions, requital could never be made."

"True," mused Iucounu. "I wonder if after all there is some small service which you can perform for me."

"The villain is as good as dead!" declared Cugel. "Now remove these abominable bonds!"

"I had no specific assassination in mind," said Iucounu. "Come."

The rope relaxed, allowing Cugel to hobble after Iucounu into a side chamber hung with intricately embroidered tapestry. From a cabinet Iucounu brought a small case and laid it on a floating disk of glass. He opened the case and gestured to Cugel, who perceived that the box showed two indentations lined with scarlet fur, where reposed a single small hemisphere of filmed violet glass.

"As a knowledgeable and traveled man," suggested Iucounu, "you doubtless recognize this object. No? You are familiar of course, with the Cutz Wars of the Eighteenth Aeon? No?" Iucounu hunched up his shoulders in astonishment. "During these ferocious events the demon Unda-Hrada—he is listed as 16-04 Green in Thrump's Almanac—thought to assist his principals, and to this end thrust certain agencies up from the sub-world La-Er. In order that they might perceive, they were tipped with cusps similar to the one you see before you. When events went amiss, the demon snatched himself back to La-Er. The hemispheres were dislodged and broadcast across Cutz. One of these, as you see, I own. You must procure its mate and bring it to me, whereupon your trespass shall be overlooked."

Cugel reflected. "The choice, if it lies between a sortie into the demon-world La-Er and the Spell of Forlorn Encystment, is moot. Frankly, I am at a loss for decision."

Iucounu's laugh almost split the big yellow bladder of his head. "A visit to La-Er perhaps will prove unnecessary. You may secure the article in that land once known as Cutz."

"If I must, I must," growled Cugel, thoroughly displeased by the manner in which the day's work had ended. "Who guards this violet hemisphere? What is its function? How do I go and how return? With what necessary weapons, talismans and other magical adjuncts do you undertake to fit me out?"

"All in good time," said Iucounu. "First I must ensure that, once at liberty, you conduct yourself with unremitting loyalty, zeal and singleness of purpose.''

''Have no fear,'' declared Cugel. ''My word is my bond.''

''Excellent!'' cried Iucounu. ''This knowledge represents a basic security which I do not in the least take lightly. The act now to be performed is doubtless supererogatory.''

He departed the chamber and after a moment returned with a covered glass bowl containing a small white creature, all claws, prongs, barbs and hooks, squirming angrily. ''This,'' said Iucounu, ''is my friend Firx, from the star Achernar, who is far wiser than he seems. Firx is annoyed at being separated from his comrade with whom he shares a vat in my work-room. He will assist you in the expeditious discharge of your duties.'' Iucounu stepped close, deftly thrust the creature against Cugel's abdomen. It merged into his viscera and took up a vigilant post clasped around Cugel's liver.

Iucounu stood back, laughing in that immoderate glee which had earned him his cognomen. Cugel's eyes bulged from his head. He opened his mouth to utter an objurgation, but instead clenched his jaw and rolled up his eyes.

The rope uncoiled itself. Cugel stood quivering, every muscle knotted.

Iucounu's mirth dwindled to a thoughtful grin. ''You spoke of magical adjuncts. What of those talismans whose efficacy you proclaimed from your booth in Azenomei? Will they not immobilize enemies, dissolve iron, impassion virgins, confer immortality?''

''These talismans are not uniformly dependable,'' said Cugel. ''I will require further competences.''

''You have them,'' said Iucounu, ''in your sword, your crafty persuasiveness and the agility of your feet. Still, you have aroused my concern and I will help you to this extent.'' He hung a small square tablet about Cugel's neck. ''You now may put aside all fear of starvation. A touch of this potent object will induce nutriment into wood, bark, grass, even discarded clothing. It will also sound a chime in the presence of poison. So then—there is nothing to delay us! Come, we will go. Rope? Where is Rope?''

Obediently the rope looped around Cugel's neck, and Cugel was forced to march along behind Iucounu.

They came out upon the roof of the antique castle. Darkness had long since fallen over the land. Up and down the valley of the Xzan faint lights glimmered, while the Xzan itself was an irregular width darker than dark.

Iucounu pointed to a cage. "This will be your conveyance. Inside."

Cugel hesitated. "It might be preferable to dine well, to sleep and rest, to set forth tomorrow refreshed."

"What?" spoke Iucounu in a voice like a horn. "You dare stand before me and state preferences? You, who came skulking into my house, pillaged my valuables and left all in disarray? Do you understand your luck? Perhaps you prefer the Forlorn Encystment?"

"By no means!" protested Cugel nervously. "I am anxious only for the success of the venture!"

"Into the cage, then."

Cugel turned despairing eyes around the castle roof, then slowly went to the cage and stepped within.

"I trust you suffer no deficiency of memory," said Iucounu. "But even if this becomes the case, and if you neglect your prime responsibility, which is to say, the procuring of the violet cusp, Firx is on hand to remind you."

Cugel said, "Since I am now committed to this enterprise, and unlikely to return, you may care to learn my appraisal of yourself and your character. In the first place—"

But Iucounu held up his hand. "I do not care to listen; obloquy injures my self-esteem and I am skeptical of praise. So now—be off!" He drew back, stared up into the darkness, then shouted that invocation known as Thasdrubal's Laganetic Transfer. From high came a thud and a buffet, a muffled bellow of rage.

Iucounu retreated a few steps, shouting up words in an archaic language; and the cage with Cugel crouching within was snatched aloft and hurled through the air.

Cold wind bit Cugel's face. From above came a flapping and creaking of vast wings and dismal lamentation; the cage swung back and forth. Below all was dark, a blackness like a pit. By the disposition of the stars Cugel perceived that the course was to the north, and presently he sensed the thrust of the Maurenron Mountains below; and then they flew over that wilderness known as the Land of the Falling Wall. Once or twice Cugel glimpsed the lights of an isolated castle, and once he noted a great bonfire. For a period a winged sprite came to fly alongside the cage and peer within. It seemed to find Cugel's plight amusing, and when Cugel sought information as to the land below, it merely uttered raucous cries of mirth. It became fatigued and sought to cling to the cage, but Cugel kicked it away, and it fell off into the wind with a scream of envy.

The east flushed the red of old blood, and presently the sun appeared, trembling like an old man with a chill. The ground was shrouded by mist; Cugel was barely able to see that they crossed a land of black mountains and dark chasms. Presently the mist parted once more to reveal a leaden sea. Once or twice he peered up, but the roof of the cage concealed the demon except for the tips of the leathern wings.

At last the demon reached the north shore of the ocean. Swooping to the beach, it vented a vindictive croak, and allowed the cage to fall from a height of fifteen feet.

Cugel crawled from the broken cage. Nursing his bruises, he called a curse after the departing demon, then plodded back through sand and dank yellow spinifex, and climbed the slope of the foreshore. To the north were marshy barrens and a far huddle of low hills, to east and west ocean and dreary beach. Cugel shook his fist to the south. Somehow, at some time, in some manner, he would visit revenge upon the Laughing Magician! So much he vowed.

A few hundred yards to the west was the trace of an ancient seawall. Cugel thought to inspect it, but hardly moved three steps before Firx clamped prongs into his liver. Cugel, rolling up his eyes in agony, reversed his direction and set out along the shore to the east.

Presently he hungered, and bethought himself of the charm furnished by Iucounu. He picked up a piece of driftwood and rubbed it with the tablet, hoping to see a transformation into a tray of sweetmeats or a roast fowl. But the driftwood merely softened to the texture of cheese, retaining the flavor of driftwood. Cugel ate with snaps and gulps. Another score against Iucounu! How the Laughing Magician would pay!

The scarlet globe of the sun slid across the southern sky. Night approached, and at last Cugel came upon human habitation: a rude village beside a small river. The huts were like birds'-nests of mud and sticks, and smelled vilely of ordure and filth. Among them wandered a people as unlovely and graceless as the huts. They were squat, brutish and obese; their hair was a coarse yellow tangle; their features were lumps. Their single noteworthy attribute—one in which Cugel took an instant and keen interest—was their eyes: blind-seeming violet hemispheres, similar in every respect to that object required by Iucounu.

Cugel approached the village cautiously but the inhabitants took small interest in him. If the hemisphere coveted by Iucounu were identical to the violet eyes of these folk, then a basic uncertainty of the mission was resolved, and procuring the violet cusp became merely a matter of tactics.

Cugel paused to observe the villagers, and found much to puzzle him. In the first place, they carried themselves not as the ill-smelling loons they were, but with a remarkable loftiness and a dignity which verged at times upon hauteur. Cugel watched in puzzlement: were they a tribe of dotards? In any event, they seemed to pose no threat, and he advanced into the main avenue of the village, walking gingerly to avoid the more noxious heaps of refuse. One of the villagers now deigned to notice him, and addressed him in grunting guttural voice. "Well, sirrah: what is your wish? Why do you prowl the outskirts of our city Smolod?"

"I am a wayfarer," said Cugel. "I ask only to be directed to the inn, where I may find food and lodging."

"We have no inn; travelers and wayfarers are unknown to us. Still, you are welcome to share our plenty. Yonder is a manse with appointments sufficient for your comfort." The man pointed to a dilapidated hut. "You may eat as you will; merely enter the refectory yonder and select what you wish; there is no stinting at Smolod."

"I thank you gratefully," said Cugel, and would have spoken further except that his host had strolled away.

Cugel gingerly looked into the shed, and after some exertion cleaned out the most inconvenient debris, and arranged a trestle on which to sleep. The sun was now at the horizon and Cugel went to that storeroom which had been identified as the refectory. The villager's description of the bounty available, as Cugel had suspected, was in the nature of hyperbole. To one side of the storeroom was a heap of smoked fish, to the other a bin containing lentils mingled with various seeds and cereals. Cugel took a portion to his hut, where he made a glum supper.

The sun had set; Cugel went forth to see what the village offered in the way of entertainment, but found the streets deserted. In certain of the huts lamps burned, and Cugel peering through the cracks saw the residents dining upon smoked fish or engaged in discourse. He returned to his shed, built a small fire against the chill and composed himself for sleep.

The following day Cugel renewed his observation of the village Smolod and its violet-eyed folk. None, he noticed, went forth to work, nor did there seem to be fields near at hand. The discovery caused Cugel dissatisfaction. In order to secure one of the violet eyes, he would be obliged to kill its owner, and for this purpose freedom from officious interference was essential.

He made tentative attempts at conversation among the villagers, but they looked at him in a manner which presently began to jar at Cugel's equanimity: it was almost as if they were gracious lords and he the ill-smelling lout!

During the afternoon he strolled south, and about a mile along the shore came upon another village. The people were much like the inhabitants of Smolod, but with ordinary-seeming eyes. They were likewise industrious; Cugel watched them till fields and fish the ocean.

He approached a pair of fishermen on their way back to the village, their catch slung over their shoulders. They stopped, eyeing Cugel with no great friendliness. Cugel introduced himself as a wayfarer and asked concerning the lands to the east, but the fishermen professed ignorance other than the fact that the land was barren, dreary and dangerous.

"I am currently guest at the village Smolod," said Cugel. "I find the folk pleasant enough, but somewhat odd. For instance, why are their eyes as they are? What is the nature of their affliction? Why do they conduct themselves with such aristocratic self-assurance and suavity of manner?"

"The eyes are magic cusps," stated the older of the fishermen in a grudging voice. "They afford a view of the Overworld; why should not the owners behave as lords? So will I when Radkuth Vomin dies, for I inherit his eyes."

"Indeed!" exclaimed Cugel, marveling. "Can these magic cusps be detached at will and transferred as the owner sees fit?"

"They can, but who would exchange the Overworld for this?" The fisherman swung his arm around the dreary landscape. "I have toiled long and at last it is my turn to taste the delights of the Overworld. After this there is nothing and the only peril is death through a surfeit of bliss."

"Vastly interesting!" remarked Cugel. "How might I qualify for a pair of these magic cusps?"

"Strive as do all the others of Grodz: place your name on the list, then toil to supply the lords of Smolod with sustenance. Thirty-one years have I sown and reaped lentils and emmer and netted fish and dried them over slow fires, and now the name of Bubach Angh is at the head of the list, and you must do the same."

"Thirty-one years," mused Cugel. "A period of not negligible duration." And Firx squirmed restlessly, causing Cugel's liver no small discomfort.

The fishermen proceeded to their village Grodz; Cugel returned to Smolod. Here he sought out that man to whom he had spoken upon his arrival at the village. "My lord," said Cugel, "as you know, I am a traveler from a far land, attracted here by the magnificence of the city Smolod."

"Understandable," grunted the other. "Our splendor cannot help but inspire emulation."

"What then is the source of the magic cusps?"

The elder turned the violet hemispheres upon Cugel as if seeing him for the first time. He spoke in a surly voice. "It is a matter we do not care to dwell upon, but there is no harm in it, now that the subject has been broached. At a remote time the demon Underherd sent up tentacles to look across Earth, each tipped with a cusp. Simbilis the Sixteenth pained the monster, which jerked back to his subworld and the cusps became dislodged. Four hundred and twelve of the cusps were gathered and brought to Smolod, then as splendid as now it appears to me. Yes, I realize that I see but a semblance, but so do you, and who is to say which is real?"

"I do not look through magic cusps," said Cugel.

"True." The elder shrugged. "It is a matter I prefer to overlook. I dimly recall that I inhabit a sty and devour the coarsest of food—but the subjective reality is that I inhabit a glorious palace and dine on splendid viands among the princes and princesses who are my peers. It is explained thus: the demon Underherd looked from the subworld to this one; we look from this to the Overworld, which is the quintessence of human hope, visionary longing, and beatific dream. We who inhabit this world—how can we think of ourselves as other than splendid lords? This is how we are."

"It is inspiring!" exclaimed Cugel. "How may I obtain a pair of these magic cusps?"

"There are two methods. Underherd lost four hundred and fourteen cusps; we control four hundred and twelve. Two were never found, and evidently lie on the floor of the ocean's deep. You are at liberty to secure these. The second means is to become a citizen of Grodz, and furnish the lords of Smolod with sustenance till one of us dies, as we do infrequently."

"I understand that a certain Lord Radkuth Vomin is ailing."

"Yes, that is he." The elder indicated a potbellied old man with a slack, drooling mouth, sitting in filth before his hut. "You see him at his ease in the pleasaunce of his palace. Lord Radkuth strained himself with a surfeit of lust, for our princesses are the most ravishing creations of human inspiration, just as I am the noblest of princes. But Lord Radkuth indulged himself too copiously, and thereby suffered a mortification. It is a lesson for us all."

"Perhaps I might make special arrangements to secure his cusps?" ventured Cugel.

"I fear not. You must go to Grodz and toil as do the others. As did I, in a former existence which now seems dim and inchoate. . . . To think I suffered so long! But you are young; thirty or forty or fifty years is not too long a time to wait."

Cugel put his hand to his abdomen to quiet the fretful stirring of Firx. "In the space of so much time, the sun may well have waned. Look!" He pointed as a black flicker crossed the face of the sun and seemed to leave a momentary crust. "Even now it ebbs!"

"You are over-apprehensive," stated the elder. "To us who are lords of Smolod, the sun puts forth a radiance of exquisite colors."

"This may well be true at the moment," said Cugel, "but when the sun goes dark, what then? Will you take an equal delight in the gloom and the chill?"

But the elder no longer attended him. Radkuth Vomin had fallen sideways into the mud, and appeared to be dead.

Toying indecisively with his knife, Cugel went to look down at the corpse. A deft cut or two—no more than the work of a moment—and he would have achieved his goal. He swayed forward, but already the fugitive moment had passed. Other lords of the village had approached to jostle Cugel aside; Radkuth Vomin was lifted and carried with the most solemn nicety into the ill-smelling precincts of his hut.

Cugel stared wistfully through the doorway, calculating the chances of this ruse and that.

"Let lamps be brought!" intoned the elder. "Let a final effulgence surround Lord Radkuth on his gem-encrusted bier! Let the golden clarion sound from the towers; let the princesses don robes of samite; let their tresses obscure the faces of delight Lord Radkuth loved so well! And now we must keep vigil! Who will guard the bier?"

Cugel stepped forward. "I would deem it honor indeed."

The elder shook his head. "This is a privilege reserved for his peers. Lord Maulfag, Lord Glus: perhaps you will act in this capacity." Two of the villagers approached the bench on which Lord Radkuth Vomin lay.

"Next," declared the elder, "the obsequies must be proclaimed, and the magic cusps transferred to Bubach Angh, that most deserving squire of Grodz. Who, again, will go to notify this squire?"

"Again," said Cugel, "I offer my services, if only to requite in some small manner the hospitality I have enjoyed at Smolod."

"Well spoken!" intoned the elder. "So, then, at speed to Grodz;

return with that squire who by his faith and dutiful toil deserves advancement.''

Cugel bowed, and ran off across the barrens toward Grodz. As he approached the outermost fields he moved cautiously, skulking from tussock to copse, and presently found that which he sought: a peasant turning the dank soil with a mattock.

Cugel crept quietly forward and struck down the loon with a gnarled root. He stripped off the bast garments, the leather hat, the leggings and foot-gear; with his knife he hacked off the stiff straw-colored beard. Taking all and leaving the peasant lying dazed and naked in the mud, he fled on long strides back toward Smolod. In a secluded spot he dressed himself in the stolen garments. He examined the hacked-off beard with some perplexity, and finally, by tying up tufts of the coarse yellow hair and tying tuft to tuft, contrived to bind enough together to make a straggling false beard for himself. That hair which remained he tucked up under the brim of the flapping leather hat.

Now the sun had set; plum-colored gloom obscured the land. Cugel returned to Smolod. Oil lamps flickered before the hut of Radkuth Vomin, where the obese and misshapen village women wailed and groaned.

Cugel stepped cautiously forward, wondering what might be expected of him. As for his disguise it would either prove effective or it would not. To what extent the violet cusps befuddled perception was a matter of doubt; he could only hazard a trial.

Cugel marched boldly up to the door of the hut. Pitching his voice as low as possible, he called, ''I am here, revered princes of Smolod: Squire Bubach Angh of Grodz, who for thirty-one years has heaped the choicest of delicacies into the Smolod larders. Now I appear, beseeching elevation to the estate of nobility.''

''As is your right,'' said the Chief Elder. ''But you seem a man different from that Bubach Angh who so long has served the princes of Smolod.''

''I have been transfigured—through grief at the passing of Prince Radkuth Vomin and through rapture at the prospect of elevation.''

''This is clear and understandable. Come, then—prepare yourself for the rites.''

''I am ready as of this instant,'' said Cugel. ''Indeed, if you will but tender me the magic cusps I will take them quietly aside and rejoice.''

The Chief Elder shook his head indulgently. ''This is not in accord with the rites. To begin with you must stand naked here on the pavilion of this mighty castle, and the fairest of the fair will anoint you in aromatics. Then comes the invocation to Eddith Bran Maur. And then—''

''Revered,'' stated Cugel, ''allow me one boon. Before the ceremonies begin, fit me with the magic cusps so that I may understand the full portent of the ceremony.''

The Chief Elder considered. ''The request is unorthodox, but reasonable. Bring forth the cusps!''

There was a wait, during which Cugel stood first on one foot then the other. The minutes dragged; the garments and the false beard itched intolerably. And now at the outskirts of the village he saw the approach of several new figures, coming from the direction of Grodz. One was almost certainly Bubach Angh, while another seemed to have been shorn of his beard.

The Chief Elder appeared, holding in each hand a violet cusp. ''Step forward!''

Cugel called loudly, ''I am here, sir.''

''I now apply the potion which sanctifies the junction of magic cusp to right eye.''

At the back of the crowd Bubach Angh raised his voice. ''Hold! What transpires?''

Cugel turned, pointed. ''What jackal is this that interrupts solemnities? Remove him: hence!''

''Indeed!'' called the Chief Elder peremptorily. ''You demean yourself and the dignity of the ceremony.''

Bubach Angh crouched back, momentarily cowed.

''In view of the interruption,'' said Cugel, ''I had as lief merely taken custody of the magic cusps until these louts can properly be chastened.''

''No,'' said the Chief Elder. ''Such a procedure is impossible.'' He shook drops of rancid fat in Cugel's right eye. But now the peasant of the shorn beard set up an outcry: ''My hat! My blouse! My beard! Is there no justice?''

''Silence!'' hissed the crowd. ''This is a solemn occasion!''

''But I am Bu—''

Cugel called, ''Insert the magic cusp, lord; let us ignore these louts.''

''A lout, you call me?'' roared Bubach Angh. ''I recognize you now, you rogue. Hold up proceedings!''

The Chief Elder said inexorably, ''I now invest you with the right cusp. You must temporarily hold this eye closed to prevent a discord which would strain the brain, and cause stupor. Now the left eye.'' He stepped forward with the ointment, but Bubach Angh and the beardless peasant no longer would be denied.

"Hold up proceedings! You ennoble an impostor! I am Bubach Angh, the worthy squire! He who stands before you is a vagabond!"

The Chief Elder inspected Bubach Angh with puzzlement. "For a fact you resemble that peasant who for thirty-one years has carted supplies to Smolod. But if you are Bubach Angh, who is this?"

The beardless peasant lumbered forward. "It is the soulless wretch who stole the clothes from my back and the beard from my face."

"He is a criminal, a bandit, a vagabond—"

"Hold!" called the Chief Elder. "The words are ill-chosen. Remember that he has been exalted to the rank of prince of Smolod."

"Not altogether!" cried Bubach Angh. "He has one of my eyes. I demand the other!"

"An awkward situation," muttered the Chief Elder. He spoke to Cugel: "Though formerly a vagabond and cut-throat, you are now a prince, and a man of responsibility. What is your opinion?"

"I suggest a hiding for these obstreperous louts. Then—"

Bubach Angh and the beardless peasant, uttering shouts of rage, sprang forward. Cugel, leaping away, could not control his right eye. The lid flew open; into his brain crashed such a wonder of exaltation that his breath caught in his throat and his heart almost stopped from astonishment. But concurrently his left eye showed the reality of Smolod. The dissonance was too wild to be tolerated; he stumbled and fell against a hut. Bubach Angh stood over him with mattock raised high, but now the Chief Elder stepped between.

"Do you take leave of your senses? This man is a prince of Smolod!"

"A man I will kill, for he has my eye! Do I toil thirty-one years for the benefit of a vagabond?"

"Calm yourself, Bubach Angh, if that be your name, and remember the issue is not yet entirely clear. Possibly an error has been made—undoubtedly an honest error, for this man is now a prince of Smolod, which is to say, justice and sagacity personified."

"He was not that before he received the cusp," argued Bubach Angh, "which is when the offense was committed."

"I cannot occupy myself with casuistic distinctions," replied the elder. "In any event, your name heads the list and on the next fatality—"

"Ten or twelve years hence?" cried Bubach Angh. "Must I toil yet longer, and receive my reward just as the sun goes dark? No, no, this cannot be!"

The beardless peasant made a suggestion: "Take the other cusp. In this way you will at least have half of your rights, and so prevent the interloper from cheating you totally."

Bubach Angh agreed. "I will start with my one magic cusp; I will then kill that knave and take the other, and all will be well."

"Now then," said the Chief Elder haughtily. "This is hardly the tone to take in reference to a prince of Smolod!"

"Bah!" snorted Bubach Angh. "Remember the source of your viands! We of Grodz will not toil to no avail."

"Very well," said the Chief Elder. "I deplore your uncouth bluster, but I cannot deny that you have a measure of reason on your side. Here is the left cusp of Radkuth Vomin. I will dispense with the invocation, anointment and the congratulatory paean. If you will be good enough to step forward and open your left eye—so."

As Cugel had done, Bubach Angh looked through both eyes together and staggered back in a daze. But clapping his hand to his left eye he recovered himself, and advanced upon Cugel. "You now must see the futility of your trick. Extend me that cusp and go your way, for you will never have the use of the two."

"It matters very little," said Cugel. "Thanks to my friend Firx I am well content with the one."

Bubach Angh ground his teeth. "Do you think to trick me again? Your life has approached its end: not just I but all Grodz goes warrant for this!"

"Not in the precincts of Smolod!" warned the Chief Elder. "There must be no quarrels among the princes: I decree amity! You who have shared the cusps of Radkuth Vomin must also share his palace, his robes, appurtenances, jewels and retinue, until that hopefully remote occasion when one or the other dies, whereupon the survivor shall take all. This is my judgment; there is no more to be said."

"The moment of the interloper's death is hopefully near at hand," rumbled Bubach Angh. "The instant he sets foot from Smolod will be his last! The citizens of Grodz will maintain a vigil of a hundred years, if necessary!"

Firx squirmed at the news and Cugel winced at the discomfort. In a conciliatory voice he addressed Bubach Angh. "A compromise might be arranged: to you shall go the entirety of Radkuth Vomin's estate: his palace, appurtenances, retinue. To me shall devolve only the magic cusps."

But Bubach Angh would have none of it. "If you value your life, deliver that cusp to me this moment."

"This cannot be done," said Cugel.

Bubach Angh turned away and spoke to the beardless peasant, who nodded and departed. Bubach Angh glowered at Cugel, then went to Radkuth Vomin's hut and sat on the heap of rubble before the door. Here he experimented with his new cusp, cautiously closing his right eye, opening the left to stare in wonder at the Overworld. Cugel thought to take advantage of his absorption and sauntered off toward the edge of town. Bubach Angh appeared not to notice. Ha! thought Cugel. It was to be so easy, then! Two more strides and he would be lost into the darkness!

Jauntily he stretched his long legs to take those two strides. A slight sound—a grunt, a scrape, a rustle of clothes—caused him to jerk aside; down swung a mattock blade, cutting the air where his head had been. In the faint glow cast by the Smolod lamps Cugel glimpsed the beardless peasant's vindictive countenance. Behind him Bubach Angh came loping, heavy head thrust forward like a bull. Cugel dodged, and ran with agility back into the heart of Smolod.

Slowly and in vast disappointment Bubach Angh returned to seat himself once more. "You will never escape," he told Cugel. "Give over the cusp and preserve your life!"

"By no means," replied Cugel with spirit. "Rather fear for your own sodden vitality, which goes in even greater peril!"

From the hut of the Chief Elder came an admonitory call. "Cease the bickering! I am indulging the exotic whims of a beautiful princess and must not be distracted."

Cugel, recalling the oleaginous wads of flesh, the leering slab-sided visages, the matted verminous hair, the wattles and wens and evil odors which characterized the women of Smolod, marveled anew at the power of the cusps. Bubach Angh was once more testing the vision of his left eye. Cugel composed himself on a bench and attempted the use of his right eye, first holding his hand before his left. . . .

Cugel wore a shirt of supple silver scales, tight scarlet trousers, a dark blue cloak. He sat on a marble bench before a row of spiral marble columns overgrown with dark foliage and white flowers. To either side the palaces of Smolod towered into the night, one behind the other, with soft lights accenting the arches and windows. The sky was a soft dark blue, hung with great glowing stars: among the palaces were gardens of cypress, myrtle, jasmine, sphade, thyssam; the air was pervaded with the perfume of flowers and flowing water. From somewhere came a wisp of music: a murmur of soft chords, a sigh of melody. Cugel took a deep breath and rose to his feet. He stepped forward, moving across the terrace. Palaces and gardens shifted perspective; on a dim lawn three girls in gowns of white gauze watched him over their shoulders.

Cugel took an involuntary step forward, then, recalling the malice of Bubach Angh paused to check on his whereabouts. Across the plaza rose a palace of seven stories, each level with its terrace garden, with vines and flowers trailing down the walls. Through the windows Cugel glimpsed rich furnishings, lustrous chandeliers, the soft movement of liveried chamberlains. On the pavilion before the palace stood a hawk-featured man with a cropped golden beard in robes of ocher and black, with gold epaulettes and black buskins. He stood with one foot on a stone griffin, arms on bent knee, gazing toward Cugel with an expression of brooding dislike. Cugel marveled: could this be the pig-faced Bubach Angh? Could the magnificent seven-tiered palace be the hovel of Radkuth Vomin?

Cugel moved slowly off across the plaza, and now came upon a pavilion lit by candelabra. Tables supported meats, jellies and pastries of every description; and Cugel's belly, nourished only by driftwood and smoked fish, urged him forward. He passed from table to table, sampling morsels from every dish, and found all to be of the highest quality.

"Smoked fish and lentils I may still be devouring," Cugel told himself, "but there is much to be said for the enchantment by which they become such exquiste delicacies. Indeed, a man might do far worse than spend the rest of his life here in Smolod."

Almost as if Firx had been anticipating the thought, he instantly inflicted upon Cugel's liver a series of agonizing pangs, and Cugel bitterly reviled Iucounu the Laughing Magician and repeated his vows of vengeance.

Recovering his composure, he sauntered to that area where the formal gardens surrounding the palaces gave way to parkland. He looked over his shoulder, to find the hawk-faced prince in ocher and black approaching, with manifestly hostile intent. In the dimness of the park Cugel noted other movement and thought to spy a number of armored warriors.

Cugel returned to the plaza and Bubach Angh followed once more to stand glowering at Cugel in front of Radkuth Vomin's palace.

"Clearly," said Cugel aloud, for the benefit of Firx, "there will be no departure from Smolod tonight. Naturally I am anxious to convey the cusp to Iucounu, but if I am killed then neither the cusp nor the admirable Firx will ever return to Almery."

Firx made no further demonstration. Now, thought Cugel, where to pass the night? The seven-tiered palace of Radkuth Vomin manifestly offered ample and spacious accommodation for both himself and Bubach Angh. In essence, however, the two would be crammed together in a one-roomed hut, with a single heap of damp reeds for a couch. Thoughtfully, regretfully, Cugel closed his right eye, opened his left.

Smolod was as before. The surly Bubach Angh crouched before the door to Radkuth Vomin's hut. Cugel stepped forward and kicked Bubach Angh smartly. In surprise and shock, both Bubach Angh's eyes opened, and the rival impulses colliding in his brain induced paralysis. Back in the darkness the beardless peasant roared and came charging forward, mattock on high, and Cugel relinquished his plan to cut Bubach Angh's throat. He skipped inside the hut, closed and barred the door.

He now closed his left eye and opened his right. He found himself in the magnificent entry hall of Radkuth Vomin's palace, the portico of which was secured by a portcullis of forged iron. Without, the golden-haired prince in ocher and black, holding his hand over one eye, was lifting himself in cold dignity from the pavement of the plaza. Raising one arm in noble defiance, Bubach Angh swung his cloak over his shoulder and marched off to join his warriors.

Cugel sauntered through the palace, inspecting the appointments with pleasure. If it had not been for the importunities of Firx, there would have been no haste in trying the perilous journey back to the Valley of the Xzan.

Cugel selected a luxurious chamber facing to the south, doffed his rich garments for satin nightwear, settled upon a couch with sheets of pale blue silk, and instantly fell asleep.

In the morning there was a degree of difficulty remembering which eye to open, and Cugel thought it might be well to fashion a patch to wear over that eye not currently in use.

By day the palaces of Smolod were more grand than ever, and now the plaza was thronged with princes and princesses, all of utmost beauty.

Cugel dressed himself in handsome garments of black with a jaunty green cap and green sandals. He descended to the entry hall, raised the portcullis with a gesture of command, and went forth into the plaza.

There was no sign of Bubach Angh. The other inhabitants of Smolod greeted him with courtesy and the princesses displayed noticeable warmth, as if they found him of good address. Cugel responded politely, but without fervor: not even the magic cusp could persuade him against the sour wads of fat, flesh, grime and hair which were the Smolod women.

He breakfasted on delightful viands at the pavilion, then returned to the plaza to consider his next course of action. A cursory inspection of the parklands revealed Grodz warriors on guard. There was no immediate prospect of escape.

The nobility of Smolod applied themselves to their diversions. Some wandered the meadows; others went boating upon the delightful waterways to the north. The Chief Elder, a prince of sagacious and noble visage, sat alone on an onyx bench, deep in reverie.

Cugel approached; the Chief Elder aroused himself and gave Cugel a salute of measured cordiality. "I am not easy in my mind," he declared. "In spite of all judiciousness, and allowing for your unavoidable ignorance of our customs, I feel a certain inequity has been done, and I am at a loss as how to repair it."

"It seems to me," said Cugel, "that Squire Bubach Angh, though doubtless a worthy man, exhibits a lack of discipline unfitting the dignity of Smolod. In my opinion he would be all the better for a few years more seasoning at Grodz."

"There is something in what you say," replied the elder. "Small personal sacrifices are sometimes essential to the welfare of the group. I feel certain that you, if the issue arose, would gladly offer up your cusp and enroll anew at Grodz. What are a few years? They flutter past like butterflies."

Cugel made a suave gesture. "Or a trial by lot might be arranged, in which all who see with two cusps participate, the loser of the trial donating one of his cusps to Bubach Angh. I myself will make do with one."

The elder frowned. "Well—the contingency is remote. Meanwhile you must participate in our merrymaking. If I may say so, you cut a personable figure and certain of the princesses have been casting sheep's eyes in your direction. There, for instance, the lovely Udela Narshag—and there, Zokoxa of the Rose-Petals, and beyond the vivacious Ilviu Lasmal. You must not be backward; here in Smolod we live an uncircumscribed life."

"The charm of these ladies has not escaped me," said Cugel. "Unluckily I am bound by a vow of continence."

"Unfortunate man!" exclaimed the Chief Elder. "The princesses of Smolod are nonpareil! And notice—yet another soliciting your attention!"

"Surely it is you she summons," said Cugel, and the elder went to confer with the young woman in question, who had come riding into the plaza in a magnificent boat-shaped car which walked on six swan-feet. The princess reclined on a couch of pink down and was beautiful enough to make Cugel rue the fastidiousness of his recollection, which projected every matted hair, mole, dangling underlip, sweating seam and wrinkle of the Smolod women to the front of his memory. This princess was indeed the essence of a daydream: slender and supple, with skin like still cream, a delicate nose, lucent brooding eyes, a mouth of delightful flexibility. Her expression intrigued Cugel, for it was more complex than that of the other princesses: pensive, yet willful; ardent yet dissatisfied.

Into the plaza came Bubach Angh, accoutered in military wise, with corselet, morion and sword. The Chief Elder went to speak to him; and now to Cugel's irritation the princess in the walking boat signaled to him.

He went forward. ''Yes, princess; you saluted me, I believe?''

The princess nodded. ''I speculate on your presence up here in these northern lands.'' She spoke in a soft clear voice like music.

Cugel said, ''I am here on a mission; I stay but a short while at Smolod, and then must continue east and south.''

''Indeed!'' said the princess. ''What is the nature of your mission?''

''To be candid, I was brought here by the malice of a magician. It was by no means a yearning of my own.''

The princess laughed softly. ''I see few strangers. I long for new faces and new talk. Perhaps you will come to my palace and we will talk of magic and the strange circumstances which throng the dying earth.''

Cugel bowed stiffly. ''Your offer is kind. But you must seek elsewhere; I am bound by a vow of continence. Control your displeasure, for it applies not only to you but to Udela Narshag yonder, to Zorkoxa, and to Ilviu Lasmal.''

The princess raised her eyebrows, sank back on her down-covered couch. She smiled faintly. ''Indeed, indeed. You are a harsh man, a stern relentless man, thus to refuse yourself to so many imploring women.''

''This is the case, and so it must be.'' Cugel turned away to face the Chief Elder, who approached with Bubach Angh at his back.

''Sorry circumstances,'' announced the Chief Elder in a troubled voice. ''Bubach Angh speaks for the village of Grodz. He declares that no more victuals will be furnished until justice is done, and this they define as the surrender of your cusp to Bubach Angh, and your person to a punitive committee who waits in the parkland yonder.''

Cugel laughed uneasily. "What a distorted view! You assured them of course that we of Smolod would eat grass and destroy the cusps before agreeing to such detestable provisions?"

"I fear that I temporized," stated the Chief Elder. "I feel that the others of Smolod favor a more flexible course of action."

The implication was clear, and Firx began to stir in exasperation. In order to appraise circumstances in the most forthright manner possible, Cugel shifted the patch to look from his left eye.

Certain citizens of Grodz, armed with scythes, mattocks and clubs, waited at a distance of fifty yards: evidently the punitive committee to which Bubach Angh had referred. To one side were the huts of Smolod; to the other the walking boat and the princess of such—Cugel stared in astonishment. The boat was as before, walking on six bird-legs, and sitting in the pink down was the princess—if possible, more beautiful than ever. But now her expression, rather than faintly smiling, was cool and still.

Cugel drew a deep breath and took to his heels. Bubach Angh shouted an order to halt, but Cugel paid no heed. Across the barrens he raced, with the punitive committee in pursuit.

Cugel laughed gleefully. He was long of limb, sound of wind; the peasants were stumpy, knot-muscled, phlegmatic. He could easily run two miles to their one. He paused, and turned to wave farewell. To his dismay two legs from the walking boat detached themselves and leapt after him. Cugel ran for his life. In vain. The legs came bounding past, one on either side. They swung around and kicked him to a halt.

Cugel sullenly walked back, the legs hopping behind. Just before he reached the outskirts of Smolod he reached under the patch and pulled loose the magic cusp. As the punitive committee bore down on him, he held it aloft. "Stand back—or I break the cusp to fragments!"

"Hold! Hold!" called Bubach Angh. "This must not be! Come, give me the cusp and accept your just deserts."

"Nothing has yet been decided," Cugel reminded him. "The Chief Elder has ruled for no one."

The girl rose from her seat in the boat. "I will rule; I am Derwe Coreme, of the House of Domber. Give me the violet glass, whatever it is."

"By no means," said Cugel. "Take the cusp from Bubach Angh."

"Never!" exclaimed the squire from Grodz.

"What? You both have a cusp and both want two? What are these precious objects? You wear them as eyes? Give them to me."

Cugel drew his sword. "I prefer to run, but I will fight if I must."

"I cannot run," said Bubach Angh. "I prefer to fight." He pulled the cusp from his own eye. "Now then, vagabond, prepare to die."

"A moment," said Derwe Coreme. From one of the legs of the boat thin arms reached to seize the wrists of both Cugel and Bubach Angh. The cusps fell to earth; that of Bubach Angh struck a stone and shivered to fragments. He howled in anguish and leapt upon Cugel, who gave ground before the attack.

Bubach Angh knew nothing of swordplay; he hacked and slashed as if he were cleaning fish. The fury of his attack, however was unsettling and Cugel was hard put to defend himself. In addition to Bubach Angh's sallies and slashes, Firx was deploring the loss of the cusp.

Derwe Coreme had lost interest in the affair. The boat started off across the barrens, moving faster and ever faster. Cugel slashed out with his sword, leapt back, leapt back once more, and for the second time fled across the barrens, and the folk of Smolod and Grodz shouted curses after him.

The boat-car jogged along at a leisurely rate. Lungs throbbing, Cugel gained upon it, and with a great bound leapt up, caught the downy gunwhale and pulled himself astride.

It was as he expected. Derwe Coreme had looked through the cusp and lay back in a daze. The violet cusp reposed in her lap.

Cugel seized it, then for a moment stared down into the exquisite face and wondered if he dared more. Firx thought not. Already Derwe Coreme was sighing and moving her head.

Cugel leapt from the boat, and only just in time. Had she seen him? He ran to a clump of reeds which grew by a pond, and flung himself into the water. From here he saw the walking-boat halt while Derwe Coreme rose to her feet. She felt through the pink down for the cusp, then she looked all around the countryside. But the blood-red light of the low sun was in her eyes when she looked toward Cugel, and she saw only the reeds and the reflection of sun on water.

Angry and sullen as never before, she set the boat into motion. It walked, then cantered, then loped to the south.

Cugel emerged from the water, inspected the magic cusp, tucked it into his pouch, and looked back toward Smolod. He started to walk south, then paused. He took the cusp from his pocket, closed his left eye, and held the cusp to his right. There rose the palaces, tier on tier, tower above tower, the gardens hanging down the terraces. . . . Cugel would have stared a long time, but Firx became restive.

Cugel returned the cusp to his pouch, and once again set his face to the south, for the long journey back to Almery.

2

CIL

Sunset across the northern wastelands was a mournful process, languid as the bleeding of a dead animal; twilight came to find Cugel toiling across a salt-marsh. The dark red light of afternoon had deceived him; starting across a low-lying barrens, he first found dankness underfoot, then a soggy softness, and now on all sides were mud, bog-grass, a few larches and willows, puddles and sloughs reflecting the leaden purple of the sky.

To the east were low hills; toward these Cugel proceeded, jumping from tussock to tussock, running delicately over the crusted slime. At times he missed his footing, to sprawl into mud or rotting reeds, whereupon his threats and imprecations in regard to Iucounu the Laughing Magician reached a maximum of rancor.

Dusk held until, tottering with fatigue, he reached the slope of the eastern hills, where his condition was worsened rather than improved. Certain half-human bandits had noted his approach, and now they set upon him. A vile reek reached Cugel even before the sound of their footsteps; fatigue forgotten, he sprang away, and was pursued up the slope.

A shattered tower rose against the sky. Cugel clambered over moldering stones, drew his sword and stepped into the gap which once had served as door-way. Within was silence, the odor of dust and damp stone; Cugel dropped to his knee and against the skyline saw the three grotesque shapes come to a halt at the edge of the ruins.

Odd, thought Cugel, though gratifying—if coincidentally somewhat ominous. The creatures apparently feared the tower.

The last vestige of twilight departed; by various portents Cugel came to understand that the tower was haunted. Near the middle of night a ghost appeared, wearing pale robes and a silver fillet supporting twenty moonstones on long silver stalks. It swirled close to Cugel, staring down with vacant eye-sockets into which a man might lose his thoughts. Cugel pressed back against the wall so that his bones creaked, unable to move a muscle.

The ghost spoke: "Demolish this fort. While stone joins stone I must stay, even while Earth grows cold and swings through darkness."

"Willingly," croaked Cugel, "if it were not for those outside who seek my life."

"To the back of the hall is a passage. Use stealth and strength, then do my behest."

"The fort is as good as razed," declared Cugel fervently. "But what circumstances bound you to so unremitting a post?"

"They are forgotten; I remain. Perform my charge, or I curse you with an everlasting tedium like my own!"

Cugel awoke in the dark, aching with cold and cramp. The ghost had vanished: how long had he slept? He looked through the door to find the eastern sky colored by the approach of dawn.

After an interminable wait the sun appeared, sending a flaming ray through the door and to the back of the hall. Here Cugel found a stone stairway descending to a dusty passage, which after five minutes of slow groping returned him to the surface. From concealment he surveyed the ground and saw the three bandits, at separate points each hidden behind a tumbled pillar.

Cugel unsheathed his sword and with great caution stole forth. He reached the first prone figure, and thrust steel into the corded neck. The creature flung out its arms, groped at the ground and died.

Cugel wrenched free his blade and wiped it on the leather of the corpse. With the deftest and most facile stealth he came up behind the second bandit, which in its dying made a sound of distress. The third bandit came to investigate.

Springing from concealment, Cugel ran it through. The bandit screamed, drew its own dagger and lunged, but Cugel leapt back and hurled a heavy stone which felled it to the ground. Here it lay, grimacing in hate.

Cugel came cautiously forward. "Since you face death, tell me what you know of hidden treasure."

"I know of none," said the bandit. "Were there such you would be the last to learn, for you have killed me."

"This is no fault of mine," said Cugel. "You pursued me, not I you. Why did you do so?"

"To eat, to survive, though life and death are equally barren and I despise both equally."

Cugel reflected. "In this case you need not resent my part in the transition which you now face. The question regarding hidden valuables again becomes relevant. Perhaps you have a final word on this matter?"

"I have a final word. I display my single treasure." The creature groped in its pouch and withdrew a round white pebble. "This is the skull-stone of a grue, and at this moment trembles with force. I use this force to curse you, to bring upon you the immediate onset of cankerous death."

Cugel hastily killed the bandit, then heaved a dismal sigh. The night had brought only difficulty. "Iucounu, if I survive, there shall be a reckoning indeed!"

Cugel turned to examine the fort. Certain of the stones would fall at a touch; others would require much more effort. He might well not survive to perform the task. What were the terms of the bandit's curse? "—immediate onset of cankerous death." Sheer viciousness. The ghost-king's curse was no less oppressive: how had it gone? "—everlasting tedium."

Cugel rubbed his chin and nodded gravely. Raising his voice, he called, "Lord ghost, I may not stay to do your bidding: I have killed the bandits and now I depart. Farewell and may the eons pass with dispatch."

From the depths of the fort came a moan, and Cugel felt the pressure of the unknown. "I activate my curse!" came a whisper to Cugel's brain.

Cugel strode quickly away to the southeast. "Excellent; all is well. The 'everlasting tedium' exactly countervenes the 'immediate onset of death' and I am left only with the 'canker' which, in the person of Firx, already afflicts me. One must use his wits in dealing with maledictions."

He proceeded over the barrens until the fort was beyond vision, and presently came once more to the sea. Mounting the foreshore, he looked up and down the beach, to see a dark headland to east and another to west. He descended to the beach, and set off to the east. The sea, sluggish and gray, sent listless surf against the sand, which was smooth, unmarked by footprint.

Ahead Cugel spied a dark blot, which a moment later proved to be an aged man on his knees, passing the sand of the beach through a sieve.

Cugel halted to watch. The old man gave him a dignified nod and proceeded with his work.

Cugel's curiosity at last prompted him to speak. "What do you seek so assiduously?"

The old man put down his sieve and rubbed his arms. "Somewhere along the beach an amulet was lost by the father of my great-grandfather. During his entire life he sifted sand, hoping to find that which he had lost. His son, and after him my grandfather, then my father and now I, the last of my line, have done likewise. All the way from Cil we have sifted sand, but there is yet six leagues to Benbadge Stull."

"These names are unknown to me," said Cugel. "What place is Benbadge Stull?"

The old man indicated the headland to the west. "An ancient port, though now you will find only a crumbled breakwater, an old jetty, a hut or two. Yet barques from Benbadge Stull once plied the sea to Falgunto and Mell."

"Again, regions beyond my knowledge," said Cugel. "What lies beyond Benbadge Stull?"

"The land dwindles into the north. The sun hangs low over marsh and bog; there are none to be found here but a few forlorn outcasts."

Cugel turned his attention to the east. "And what place is Cil?"

"This entire domain is Cil, which my ancestor forfeited to the House of Domber. All grandeur is gone; there remains the ancient palace and a village. Beyond, the land becomes a dark and dangerous forest, so much has our realm dwindled." The old man shook his head and returned to his sieving.

Cugel stood watching a moment, then, kicking idly in the sand, uncovered a glint of metal. Stooping, he picked up a bracelet of black metal shining with a purple luster. Around the circumference were thirty studs in the form of carbuncles, each circled by a set of engraved runes. "Ha!" exclaimed Cugel, displaying the bracelet. "Notice this fine object: a treasure indeed!"

The old man put down scoop and sieve, rose slowly to his knees, then to his feet. He lurched forward, blue eyes round and staring. He held forth his hand. "You have uncovered the amulet of my ancestors, the House of Slaye! Give it to me!"

Cugel stepped back. "Come, come, you make a flagrantly unreasonable request!"

"No no! The amulet is mine; you do wrong by withholding it. Do you wish to vitiate the work of my lifetime and of four lifetimes before mine?"

"Why do you not rejoice that the amulet has been found?" demanded Cugel peevishly. "You are now relieved from further search. Explain, if you will, the potency of this amulet. It exhales a heavy magic. How does it profit the owner?"

"The owner is myself," groaned the old man. "I implore you, be generous!"

"You put me in an uncomfortable position," said Cugel. "My property is too small to admit of largesse but I cannot consider this a failure of generosity. If you had found the amulet, would you have given it to me?"

"No, since it is mine!"

"Here we disagree. Assume, if you will, that your conviction is incorrect. Your eyesight will attest that the amulet is in my hands, under my control, and, in short, my property. I would appreciate, therefore, any information upon its capabilities and mode of employment."

The old man threw his arms in the air, kicked his sieve with such wild emotion he burst out the mesh, and the sieve went trundling down the beach to the water's edge. A wave swept in and floated the sieve; the old man made an involuntary motion to retrieve it, then once more threw up his hands and tottered up the foreshore. Cugel gave his head a shake of grave disapproval, and turned to continue east along the beach.

Now occurred an unpleasant altercation with Firx, who was convinced that the most expeditious return to Almery lay west through the port of Benbadge Stull. Cugel clasped his hands to his belly in distress. "There is but one feasible route! By means of the lands which lie to the south and east. What if the ocean offers a more direct route? There are no boats to hand; it is not possible to swim so great a distance!"

Firx administered a few dubious pangs, but finally permitted Cugel to continue eastward along the shore. Behind, on the ridge of the foreshore, sat the old man, scoop dangling between his legs, staring out to sea.

Cugel proceeded along the beach, well pleased with the events of the morning. He examined the amulet at length: it exuded a rich sense of magic, and in addition was an object of no small beauty. The runes, incised with great skill and delicacy, unfortunately were beyond his capacity to decipher. He gingerly slipped the bracelet on his wrist, and in so doing pressed one of the carbuncles. From somewhere came an abysmal groan, a sound of the deepest anguish. Cugel stopped short, and looked up and down the beach. Gray sea, pallid beach, foreshore with clumps of spinifex. Benbadge Stull to west, Cil to east, gray sky above. He was alone. Whence had come the great groan?

Cautiously Cugel touched the carbuncle again, and again evoked the stricken protest.

In fascination Cugel pressed another of the carbuncles, this time bringing forth a wail of piteous despair in a different voice. Cugel was puzzled. Who along this sullen shore manifested so frivolous a disposition? Each carbuncle in turn he pressed and caused to be produced a whole concert of outcries, ranging the gamut of anguish and pain. Cugel examined the amulet critically. Beyond the evocation of groans and sobs it displayed no obvious power and Cugel presently tired of the occupation.

The sun reached its zenith. Cugel appeased his hunger with seaweed, which he rendered nutritious by rubbing it with the charm Iucounu had provided for this purpose. As he ate he seemed to hear voices and careless prattling laughter, so indistinct that it might have been the sound of the surf. A tongue of rock protruded into the ocean nearby; listening carefully, Cugel discovered the voices to be coming from this direction. They were clear and childlike, and rang with innocent gaiety.

He went cautiously out upon the rock. At the far end, where the ocean surged and dark water heaved, four large shells had attached themselves. These now were open; heads looked forth, attached to naked shoulders and arms. The heads were round and fair, with soft cheeks, blue-gray eyes, tufts of pale hair. The creatures dipped their fingers in the water, and from the drops they pulled thread which they deftly wove into fine soft fabric. Cugel's shadow fell on the water; instantly the creatures clamped themselves into their shells.

"How so?" exclaimed Cugel jocularly. "Do you always lock yourselves apart at the sight of a strange face? Are you so timorous then? Or merely surly?"

The shells remained closed. Dark water swirled over the fluted surfaces.

Cugel came a step closer, squatted on his haunches and cocked his head askew. "Or perhaps you are proud? So that you withdraw yourselves in disdain? Or is it that you lack grace?"

Still no response. Cugel remained as before, and began to whistle, trilling a tune he had heard at the Azenomei Fair.

Presently the shell at the far edge of the rock opened a crack, and eyes peered at him. Cugel whistled another bar or two, then spoke once more. "Open your shells! Here waits a stranger, anxious to learn the road to Cil, and others matters of import!"

Another shell opened a crack; another set of eyes glistened from the dark within.

''Perhaps you are ignorant,'' scoffed Cugel. ''Perhaps you know nothing save the color of fish and the wetness of water.''

The shell of the farthest opened further, enough to show the indignant face within. ''We are by no means ignorant!''

''Nor indolent, nor lacking in grace, nor disdainful,'' shouted the second.

''Nor timorous!'' added a third.

Cugel nodded sagely. ''This well may be. But why do you withdraw so abruptly at my mere approach?''

''Such is our nature,'' said the first shell-creature. ''Certain creatures of the sea would be happy to catch us unaware, and it is wise to retreat first and investigate second.''

All four of the shells were now ajar, though none stood as fully wide as when Cugel had approached.

''Well then,'' he said, ''what can you tell me of Cil? Are strangers greeted with cordiality, or driven off? Are inns to be found, or must the wayfarer sleep in a ditch?''

''Such matters lie beyond our specific knowledge,'' said the first shell-creature. It fully opened its shell, and extruded pale arms and shoulders. ''The folk of Cil, if rumor of the sea goes correctly, are withdrawn and suspicious, even to their ruler, who is a girl, no more, of the ancient House of Domber.''

''There walks old Slaye now,'' said another. ''He returns early to his cabin.''

Another tittered. ''Slaye is old; never will he find his amulet, and thus the House of Domber will rule Cil till the sun goes out.''

''What is all this?'' asked Cugel ingenuously. ''Of what amulet do you speak?''

''As far as memory can return,'' one of the shell-creatures explained, ''old Slaye has sifted sand, and his father before him, and yet other Slayes across the years. They seek a metal band, by which they hope to regain their ancient privileges.''

''A fascinating legend!'' said Cugel with enthusiasm. ''What are the powers of the amulet, and how are they activated?''

''Slaye possibly would provide this information,'' said one dubiously.

''No, for he is dour and crabbed,'' declared another. ''Consider his petulant manner when he sieves a scoop of sand to no avail!''

''Is there no information elsewhere?'' Cugel demanded anxiously. ''No rumor of the sea? No ancient tablet or set of glyphs?''

The shell-creatures laughed in merriment. "You ask so earnestly that you might be Slaye himself. Such lore is unknown to us."

Concealing his dissatisfaction, Cugel asked further questions, but the creatures were artless and unable to maintain their attention upon any single matter. As Cugel listened they discussed the flow of the ocean, the flavor of pearl, the elusive disposition of a certain sea-creature they had noted the day previously. After a few minutes Cugel once more turned the conversation to Slaye and the amulet, but again the shell-creatures were vague, almost childlike in the inconsequence of their talk. They seemed to forget Cugel, and, dipping their fingers in the water, drew pallid threads from the drops. Certain conches and whelks had aroused their disapproval through impudence, and they discussed a great urn lying on the off-shore seabottom.

Cugel finally tired of the conversation and rose to his feet, at which the shell-creatures once more gave him their attention. "Must you fare forth so soon? Just when we were about to inquire the reason for your presence; passers-by are few along Great Sandy Beach, and you seem a man who has journeyed far."

"This is correct," said Cugel, "and I must journey yet farther. Notice the sun: it starts down the western curve, and tonight I wish to house myself at Cil."

One of the shell-creatures lifted up its arms and displayed a fine garment it had woven from water-threads. "This garment we offer as a gift. You seem a sensitive man and so may require protection from wind and cold." It tossed the garment to Cugel. He examined it, marveling at the suppleness of the cloth and its lucent shimmer.

"I thank you indeed," said Cugel. "This is generosity beyond my expectation." He wrapped himself in the garment, but at once it reverted to water and Cugel was drenched. The four in the shells shouted loud in mischievous glee, and as Cugel stepped wrathfully forward they snapped their shells shut.

Cugel kicked the shell of the creature which had tossed him the garment, bruising his foot and exacerbating his rage. He seized a heavy rock and dashed it down upon the shell, crushing it. Snatching forth the squealing creature, Cugel hurled it far up the beach, where it lay staring at him, head and small arms joined to pale entrails.

In a faint voice it asked, "Why did you treat me so? For a prank you have taken my life from me, and I have no other."

"And thereby you will be prevented from further pranks," declared Cugel. "Notice you have drenched me to the skin!"

"It was merely an act of mischief; a small matter surely." The shell-creature spoke in a fading voice. "We of the rocks know little magic, yet I am given the power to curse, and this I now pronounce: may you lose your heart's-desire, whatever its nature; you shall be bereft before a single day is gone.''

''Another curse?'' Cugel shook his head in displeasure. ''Two curses already I have voided this day; am I now inflicted with another?''

''This curse you shall not void,'' whispered the shell-creature. ''I make it the final act of my life.''

''Malice is a quality to be deplored,'' said Cugel fretfully. ''I doubt the efficacy of your curse; nevertheless, you would be well-advised to clear the air of its odium and so regain my good opinion.''

But the shell-creature said no more. Presently it collapsed into a cloudy slime which was absorbed into the sand.

Cugel set off down the beach, considering how best to avert the consequences of the shell-creature's curse. ''One must use his wits in dealing with maledictions,'' Cugel said for the second time. ''Am I known as Cugel the Clever for nothing?'' No stratagem came to mind, and he proceeded along the beach pondering the matter in all its aspects.

The headland to the east grew distinct. Cugel saw it to be cloaked in tall dark trees, through which appeared glimpses of white buildings.

Slaye showed himself once more, running back and forth across the beach like one departed of his senses. He approached Cugel and fell on his knees. ''The amulet, I beg of you! It belongs to the House of Slaye; it conferred upon us the rule of Cill! Give it to me and I will fulfill your heart's-desire!''

Cugel stopped short. Here was a pretty paradox! If he surrendered the amulet, Slaye evidently would betray him, or at the very least fail to make good his promise—assuming the potency of the curse. On the other hand, if Cugel retained the amulet, he would lose his heart's-desire to no less a degree—assuming the potency of the curse—but the amulet would yet be his.

Slaye misinterpreted the hesitation as a sign of pliancy. ''I will make you grandee of the realm!'' he cried in a fervent voice. ''You shall have a barge of carved ivory, and two hundred maidens shall serve your wants; your enemies shall be clamped into a rotating cauldron—only give me the amulet!''

''The amulet confers so much power?'' inquired Cugel. ''It is possible to achieve all this?''

''Indeed, indeed!'' cried Slaye, ''when one can read the runes!''

''Well then,'' said Cugel, ''what is their import?''

Slaye gazed at him in woeful injury. ''That I cannot say; I must have the amulet!''

Cugel flourished his hand in a contemptuous gesture. "You refuse to gratify my curiosity; in my turn I denounce your arrogant ambitions!"

Slaye turned to look toward the headland, where white walls gleamed among the trees. "I understand all. You intend to rule Cil in your own right!"

There were less desirable prospects, thought Cugel, and Firx, appreciating something of this, performed a small monitory constriction. Regretfully Cugel put aside the scheme; nevertheless, it suggested a means to nullify the shell-creature's curse. "If I am to be deprived of my heart's-desire," Cugel told himself, "I would be wise to fix upon a new goal, a fervent new enthusiasm, for at least the space of a day. I shall therefore aspire to the rule of Cil, which now becomes my heart's-desire." So as not to arouse the vigilance of Firx, he said aloud, "I intend to use this amulet to achieve highly important ends. Among them may well be the lordship of Cil, to which I believe I am entitled by virtue of my amulet."

Slaye gave a wild sardonic laugh. "First you must convince Derwe Coreme of your authority. She is of the House of Domber, gloomy and fitful; she looks little more than a girl, but she manifests the brooding carelessness of a forest grue. Beware of Derwe Coreme; she will order you and my amulet plunged into the ocean's deep!"

"If you fear to this extent," said Cugel with asperity, "instruct me in the use of the amulet, and I will prevent that calamity."

But Slaye mulishly shook his head. "The deficiencies of Derwe Coreme are known; why exchange them for the outlandish excesses of a vagabond?"

For his outspokenness Slaye received a buffet which sent him staggering. Cugel then proceeded along the shore. The sun wallowed low upon the sea; he hastened his steps, anxious to find shelter before dark.

He came at last to the end of the beach. The headland loomed above, with the tall dark trees standing still higher. A balustrade surrounding the gardens showed intermittently through the foliage; somewhat below, a colonnaded rotunda overlooked the ocean to the south. Grandeur indeed! thought Cugel, and he examined the amulet with a new attentiveness. His temporary heart's-desire, sovereignty over Cil, had become no longer felicitious. And Cugel wondered if he should not fix upon a new heart's-desire—an aspiration to master the lore of animal husbandry, for instance, or a compelling urge to excel at acrobatic feats . . . Reluctantly Cugel dismissed the scheme. In any event, the cogency of the shell-creature's curse was not yet certain.

A path left the beach, to wind up among bushes and odorous

shrubs: dymphian, heliotrope, black quince, olus, beds of long-stemmed stardrops, shade ververica, flowering amanita. The beach became a ribbon fading into the maroon blur of sunset, and the headland at Benbadge Stull could no longer be seen. The path became level, traversed a dense grove of bay trees, and issued upon a weed-grown oval, at one time a parade ground or exercise field.

Along the left boundary was a tall stone wall, broken by a great ceremonial portico which held aloft a heraldic device of great age. The gates stood wide upon a marble-flagged promenade a mile in length leading to the palace: this a richly detailed structure of many tiers, with a green bronze roof. A terrace extended along the front of the palace; promenade and terrace were joined by a flight of broad steps. The sun had now disappeared; gloom descended from the sky. With no better shelter in prospect, Cugel set off toward the palace.

The promenade at one time had been a work of monumental elegance, but now all was in a state of dilapidation which the twilight invested with a melancholy beauty. To right and left were elaborate gardens now untended and overgrown. Marble urns festooned with garlands of carnelian and jade flanked the promenade; down the center extended a line of pedestals somewhat taller than the height of a man. Each of these supported a bust, identified by an inscription in runes which Cugel recognized as similar to those carved on the amulet. The pedestals were five paces apart, and proceeded the entire mile to the terrace. The carving of the first was softened by wind and rain until the faces were barely discernible; as Cugel proceeded the features became more keen. Pedestal after pedestal, bust after bust; each face stared briefly at Cugel as he marched toward the palace. The last of the series, obscure in the fading light, depicted a young woman. Cugel stopped short: this was the girl of the walking boat, whom he had encountered in the land to the north: Derwe Coreme, of the House of Domber, ruler of Çil!

Beset by misgivings, Cugel paused to consider the massive portal. He had not departed from Derwe Coreme in amity; indeed she might be expected to harbor resentment. On the other hand, at their first encounter she had invited him to her palace, using language of unmistakable warmth; possibly her resentment had disappeared, leaving only the warmth. And Cugel, recalling her remarkable beauty, found the prospect of a second meeting stimulating.

But what if she were still resentful? She must be impressed by the amulet, provided she did not insist that Cugel demonstrate its use. If only he knew how to read the runes, all would be simplicity itself. But since the knowledge was not to be derived from Slaye, he must seek it elsewhere which in practicality meant within the palace.

He stood before a reach of shallow steps leading up to the terrace. The marble treads were cracked; the balustrade along the terrace was stained by moss and lichen: a condition which the murk of twilight invested with a mournful grandeur. The palace behind seemed in somewhat better repair. An extremely tall arcade rose from the terrace, with slender fluted columns and an elaborately carved entablature, the pattern of which Cugel could not discern through the gloom. At the back of the arcade were tall arched windows, showing dim lights, and the great portal.

Cugel mounted the steps, beset by renewed doubts. What if Derwe Coreme laughed at his pretensions, defied him to do his worst? What then? Groans and outcries might not be enough. He crossed the terrace on lagging steps, optimism waning as he went, and halted under the arcade; perhaps after all, it might be wise to seek shelter elsewhere. But looking back over his shoulder, he thought to see a tall still shape standing among the pedestals. Cugel thought no more of seeking shelter elsewhere, and walked quickly to the tall door: if he presented himself in humble guise he might escape the notice of Derwe Coreme. There was a stealthy sound on the steps. With great urgency Cugel plied the knocker. The sound reverberated inside the palace.

A minute passed, and Cugel thought to hear further sounds behind him. He rapped again, and again the sound echoed within. A peephole opened and an eye inspected Cugel with care. The eye moved up; a mouth appeared. "Who are you?" spoke the mouth. "What do you wish?" The mouth slid away, to reveal an ear.

"I am a wayfarer, I wish shelter for the night, and with haste for a creature of dread approaches."

The eye reappeared, looked carefully across the terrace, then returned to focus on Cugel. "What are your qualities, where are your certifications?"

"I have none," said Cugel. He glanced over his shoulder. "I much prefer to discuss the matter within, since the creature step by step mounts to the terrace."

The peephole slammed shut. Cugel stared at the blank door. He banged on the knocker, peering back into the gloom. With a scrape and creak the portal opened. A small stocky man wearing purple livery motioned to him. "Inside, with haste."

Cugel slipped smartly through the door, which the footman at once heaved shut and bolted with three iron pegs. Even as he did so there came a creak and a pressure upon the door.

The footman struck the door smartly with his fist. "I have thwarted the creature again," he said with satisfaction. "Had I been less swift, it would have been upon you, to my distress as well as yours. This is now my chief amusement, depriving the creature of its pleasures."

"Indeed," said Cugel, breathing heavily. "What manner of being is it?"

The footman signified his ignorance. "Nothing definite is known. It has only appeared of late, to lurk by night among the statues. Its behavior is both vampirish and unnaturally lustful, and several of my associates have had cause to complain; in fact, all are dead by its odious acts. So now, to divert myself, I taunt the creature and cause it dissatisfaction." The footman stood back, to survey Cugel with attention. "What of yourself? Your manner, the tilt of your head, the swing of your eyes from side to side denotes recklessness and unpredictability. I trust you will hold this quality in abeyance, if indeed it exists."

"At this moment," said Cugel, "my wants are simple: an alcove, a couch, a morsel of food for my supper. If I am provided these, you will find me benevolence personified; indeed I will assist you in your pleasures; together we will contrive stratagems to bait the ghoul."

The footman bowed. "Your needs can be fulfilled. Since you are a traveler from afar, our ruler will wish to speak to you, and indeed may extend a bounty far more splendid than your minimal requirements."

Cugel hurriedly disavowed any such ambition. "I am of low quality; my garments are soiled, my person reeks; my conversation consists of insipid platitudes. Best not to disturb the ruler of Cil."

"We will repair what deficiencies we may," said the footman. "Follow, if you will."

He took Cugel along corridors lit by cressets, finally turning into a set of apartments. "Here you may wash; I will brush your garments and find fresh linen."

Cugel reluctantly divested himself of his clothes. He bathed, trimmed the soft black mat of his hair, shaved his beard, rubbed his body with pungent oil. The footman brought fresh garments, and Cugel, much refreshed, dressed himself. Donning his jacket he chanced to touch the amulet at his wrist, pressing one of the carbuncles. From deep under the floor came a groan of the most profound anguish.

The footman sprang about in terror, and his eye fell upon the amulet. He stared in gape-mouthed astonishment, then became obsequious. "My dear sir, had I realized your identity, I would have conducted you to apartments of state, and brought forth the finest robes."

"I make no complaints," said Cugel, "though for a fact the linens were a trifle stale." In jocular emphasis he tapped a carbuncle at his wrist, and the responsive groan caused the servitor's knees to knock together.

"I beseech your understanding," he quavered.

"Say no more," said Cugel. "Indeed it was my hope to visit the palace incognito, so to speak, that I might see how affairs were conducted."

"This is judicious," agreed the servitor. "Undoubtedly you will wish to discharge both Sarman the chamberlain and Bilbab the undercook when their peccancies come to light. As for myself, when your lordship restores Cil to its ancient grandeur, perhaps there will be a modest sinecure for Yodo, the most loyal and cooperative of your servants."

Cugel made a gracious gesture. "If such an event comes to pass—and it is my heart's-desire—you shall not be neglected. For the present I shall remain quietly in this apartment. You may bring hither a suitable repast, with a variety of choice wines."

Yodo performed a sweeping bow. "As your lordship desires." He departed. Cugel relaxed upon the most comfortable couch of the chamber and fell to studying the amulet which had so promptly aroused Yodo's fidelity. The runes, as before, were inscrutable; the carbuncles produced only groans, which, while diverting, were of small practical utility. Cugel attempted every exhortation, compulsion, rigor and enjoinment his smattering of wizardry provided, to no avail.

Yodo returned to the apartment, but without the repast Cugel had ordered.

"Your lordship," stated Yodo, "I have the honor to convey to you an invitation from Derwe Coreme, erstwhile ruler of Cil, to attend her at the evening banquet."

"How is this possible?" demanded Cugel. "She has had no information of my presence; as I recall, I gave you specific instructions in this regard."

Yodo performed another sweeping bow. "Naturally I obeyed your lordship. The wiles of Derwe Coreme exceed my understanding. By some device she learned of your presence and so has issued the invitation which you have just heard."

"Very well," said Cugel glumly. "Be so good as to lead the way. You mentioned my amulet to her?"

"Derwe Coreme knows all," was Yodo's ambiguous reply. "This way, your lordship, if you please."

He led Cugel along the old corridors, finally through a tall narrow arch into a great hall. To either side stood a row of what appeared to be men-at-arms in brass armor with helmets of checkered bone and jet; there were forty in all, but only six suits of armor were occupied by living men, the others being supported on racks. Telamons of exaggerated elongation and grotesquely distorted visage supported the smoky beams; a rich rug of green concentric circles on a black ground covered the floor.

Derwe Coreme sat at the end of a circular table, this so massive as to give her the seeming of a girl, a sullen brooding girl of the most delicate beauty. Cugel approached with a confident mien, halted and bowed curtly. Derwe Coreme inspected him with gloomy resignation, her eyes dwelling upon the amulet. She drew a deep breath. "Whom do I have the privilege to address?"

"My name is of no consequence," said Cugel. "You may address me as 'Exalted.' "

Derwe Coreme shrugged indifferently. "As you will. I seem to recall your face. You resemble a vagabond whom lately I ordered whipped."

"I am that vagabond," said Cugel. "I cannot say that your conduct has failed to leave a residue of resentment and I am now here to demand an explanation." And Cugel touched a carbuncle, evoking so desolate and heartfelt a groan that the crystalware rattled on the table.

Derwe Coreme blinked and her mouth sagged. She spoke ungraciously. "It appears that my actions were poorly conceived. I failed to perceive your exalted condition, and thought you only the ill-conditioned scapegrace your appearance suggests."

Cugel stepped forward, put his hand under the small pointed chin and turned up the exquisite face. "Yet you besought me to visit you at your palace. Do you recall this?"

Derwe Coreme gave a grudging nod.

"Just so," said Cugel. "I am here."

Derwe Coreme smiled, and for a brief period became winsome. "So you are, and knave, vagabond, or whatever your nature, you wear the amulet by which the House of Slaye ruled across two hundred generations. You are of this house?"

"In due course you will know me well," said Cugel. "I am a generous man, though given to caprice, and were it not for a certain Firx . . . Be that as it may, I hunger, and now I invite you to share the banquet which I have ordered the excellent Yodo to set before me. Kindly be good enough to move a place or two aside, and I will be seated."

Derwe Coreme hesitated, whereupon Cugel's hand went suggestively toward the amulet. She moved with alacrity and Cugel settled himself into the seat she had vacated. He rapped on the table: "Yodo? Where is Yodo?"

"I am here, Exalted!"

"Bring forth the banquet: the finest fare the palace offers!"

Yodo bowed, scuttled away, and presently a line of footmen appeared bearing trays and flagons, and a banquet more than meeting Cugel's specifications was arranged on the table.

Cugel brought forth the periapt provided by Iucounu the Laughing Magician, which not only converted organic waste to nourishment, but also chimed warning in the presence of noxious substances. The first few courses were salubrious and Cugel ate with gusto. The old wines of Cil were as beneficial, and Cugel drank freely, from goblets of black glass, carved cinnabar and ivory inlaid with turquoise and mother-of-pearl.

Derwe Coreme toyed with her food and sipped her wine, watching Cugel thoughtfully all the while. Further delicacies were brought and now Derwe Coreme leaned forward. "You truly plan to rule Cil?"

"Such is my heart's-desire!" declared Cugel with fervor.

Derwe Coreme moved close to him. "Do you then take me as your consort? Say yes; you will be more than content."

"We will see, we will see," said Cugel expansively. "Tonight is tonight, tomorrow is tomorrow. Many changes will be made, this is certain."

Derwe Coreme smiled faintly, and nodded to Yodo. "Bring the most ancient of our vintages—we will drink the health of the new Lord of Cil."

Yodo bowed, and brought a dull flagon webbed and dusty, which he decanted with utmost solicitude, and poured into crystal goblets. Cugel raised his goblet, and the charm purred warning. Cugel abruptly set down the goblet, and watched as Derwe Coreme raised hers to her lips. He reached forth, took the goblet, and again the charm purred. Poison in both? Strange. Perhaps she had not intended to drink. Perhaps she had already ingested an antidote.

Cugel signaled Yodo. "Another goblet, if you please . . . and the decanter." Cugel poured a third measure and again the charm signified direness. Cugel said, "Though my acquaintance with the excellent Yodo is of short duration, I hereby elevate him to the post of Major-Domo of the Palace!"

"Exalted," stammered Yodo, "this is a signal honor indeed."

"Drink then of the ancient vintage, to solemnize this new dignity!"

Yodo bowed low. "With the most heartfelt gratitude, Exalted." He raised the goblet and drank. Derwe Coreme watched indifferently. Yodo put down the goblet, frowned, gave a convulsive jerk, turned a startled glance at Cugel, fell to the rug, cried out, twitched and lay still.

Cugel frowningly inspected Derwe Coreme. She appeared as startled as had Yodo. Now she turned to look at him. "Why did you poison Yodo?"

"It was your doing," said Cugel. "Did you not order poison in the wine?"

"No."

"You must say 'No Exalted.' "

"No, Exalted."

"If you did not—who?"

"I am perplexed. The poison perhaps was meant for me."

"Or both of us." Cugel signaled one of the footmen. "Remove the corpse of Yodo."

The footman signaled a pair of hooded underservants, who carried off the unfortunate major-domo.

Cugel took the crystal goblets and stared down into the amber liquid, but did not communicate his thoughts. Derwe Coreme leaned back in her chair, and contemplated him at length. "I am puzzled," she said presently. "You are a man past the teaching of my experience. I cannot decide upon the color of your soul."

Cugel was charmed by the quaint turn of phrase. "You see souls in color, then?"

"Indeed. It was the birth-gift of a lady sorceress, who also provided me my walking boat. She is dead and I am alone, with no friend nor any who thinks of me with love. And so I have ruled Cil with little joy. And now you are here, with a soul which flickers through many colors, like that of no human man to come before me."

Cugel forebore to mention Firx, whose own spiritual exhalation, mingling with that of Cugel's, undoubtedly caused the variegation Derwe Coreme had noted. "There is a reason for this effect," said Cugel, "which in due course will be voided, or so I hope. Until then, you may regard my soul as one shining with the purest ray imaginable."

"I will try to keep this in mind, Exalted."

Cugel frowned. In Derwe Coreme's remarks and the poise of her head he noted barely concealed insolence, which he found exasperating. Still, there was ample time to correct the matter after learning the use of the amulet, a business of prime urgency. Cugel leaned back into the cushion, and spoke as one who muses idly: "Everywhere at this time of Earth's dying exceptional circumstances are to be noted. Recently, at the manse of Iucounu the Laughing Magician, I saw a great libram which indexed all the writings of magic, and all styles of thaumaturgical rune. Perhaps you have similiar volumes in your library?"

"It well may be," said Derwe Coreme. "The Fourteenth Garth Haxt of Slaye was a diligent collator, and compiled a voluminous pandect on the subject."

Cugel clapped his hands together. "I wish to see this important work at once!"

Derwe Coreme looked at him in wonder. "Are you then such a bibliophile? A pity, because The Eighth Rubel Zaff ordered this particular compendium submerged off Cape Horizon."

Cugel made a sour face. "Are no other treatises at hand?"

"Doubtless," said Derwe Coreme. "The library occupies the whole of the north wing. But will not tomorrow suffice for your research?" "And, stretching in languid warmth, she contrived to twist her body into first one luxurious position, then another.

Cugel drank deep from a black glass goblet. "Yes, there is no haste in this matter. And now—" He was interrupted by a woman of middle age in voluminous brown garments, evidently one of the underservants, who at this moment rushed into the hall. She was shouting hysterically and several footmen sprang forward to support her. Between racking sobs she made clear the source of her anguish: an abominable act only just now committed by the ghoul upon her daughter.

Derwe Coreme gracefully indicated Cugel. "Here is the new Lord of Cil; he has vast powers of magic and will order the ghoul destroyed. Will you not, Exalted?"

Cugel thoughtfully rubbed his chin. A dilemma indeed. The woman and all the servitors fell down upon their knees. "Exalted, if you control this corrosive magic, employ it instantly to destroy the vile ghoul!"

Cugel winced, and turning his head met Derwe Coreme's thoughtful gaze. He jumped to his feet. "What need I of magic when I can wield a sword? I will hack the creature organ from organ!" He signaled the six men-at-arms who stood by in their brass armor. "Come! Bring torches! We fare forth to dismember the ghoul!"

The men-at-arms obeyed without enthusiasm. Cugel herded them toward the great portal. "When I fling wide the doors, rush forth with the torches, to create a blaze which will illuminate the evil being! Have swords drawn so that when I send him reeling you may strike the coup de grace!"

The men-at-arms each with torch and drawn sword stood before the portal. Cugel slid back the bolts and flung wide of the portals. "Out! Shine upon the ghoul the last light of his existence!"

The men-at-arms raced desperately forth, with Cugel swaggering after, flourishing his sword. The men-at-arms paused at the head of the steps, to look uncertainly out over the promenade, from which a quite horrid sound could be heard.

Cugel looked over his shoulder to see Derwe Coreme watching attentively from the doorway. "Forward!" he shouted. "Surround this wretched creature, whose death is now upon him."

The men-at-arms gingerly descended the steps, with Cugel marching to the rear. "Hack with a will!" he called. "There is ample glory for all! The man who fails to deal a stroke I blast by magic!"

The flickering lights shone on the pedestals, ranging in a long line to merge at last with the darkness. "Forward!" cried Cugel. "Where is the bestial being? Why does he not appear to receive his deserts?" And Cugel peered through the wavering shadows, hoping the ghoul by now would have taken alarm and fled.

At his side came a small sound. Turning, Cugel saw a tall pale shape standing quietly. The men-at-arms gasped, and fled incontinently up the broad stones. "Slay the beast by magic, Exalted!" called the sergeant. "The most expeditious method is often the best!"

The ghoul came forward; Cugel stumbled back. The ghoul took a quick step forward. Cugel sprang behind a pedestal. The ghoul swung out its arm; Cugel hacked with his sword, sprang to the protection of another pedestal, then raced with great ability back across the terrace. The door was already closing; Cugel flung himself through the dwindling aperture. He heaved the door shut, and thrust home the bolts. The ghoul's weight slammed against the timbers and the bolts creaked in protest.

Cugel turned to meet the bright-eyed appraisal of Derwe Coreme. "What ensued?" she asked. "Why did you not slay the ghoul?"

"The warriors decamped with the torches," said Cugel. "I could see neither where to hack nor where to hew."

"Strange," mused Derwe Coreme. "There seemed ample illumination for so negligible an exercise. Why did you not employ the power of the amulet or rend the ghoul limb from limb?"

"So simple and quick a death is unsuitable," stated Cugel with dignity. "I must cogitate at length, and decide how he may best expiate his crimes."

"Indeed," said Derwe Coreme. "Indeed."

Cugel stode back into the great hall. "Back to the banquet! Let the wine flow! Everyone must drink to the accession of the new Lord of Cil!''

Derwe Coreme said in a silky voice, ''If you please, Exalted, make some display of the power of the amulet, to gratify our curiosity!''

''Certainly!'' And Cugel touched carbuncle after carbuncle, producing rumbles and groans of grievous woe, with occasionally a wail or scream.

''Can you do more?'' inquired Derwe Coreme, smiling the soft smile of an impish child.

''Indeed, should I so choose. But enough! Drink one and all!''

Derwe Coreme signaled the sergeant of the guard. ''Take sword and strike off the fool's arm; bring me the amulet.''

''With pleasure, Great Lady.'' The sergeant advanced with bared blade.

Cugel shouted, ''Stay! One more step and magic will turn each of your bones at right angles!''

The sergeant looked at Derwe Coreme who laughed. ''As I bade you, or fear my revenge, which is as you know.''

The sergeant winced, and marched forward again. But now an under-servitor rushed to Cugel, and under his hood Cugel saw the seamed face of old Slaye. ''I will save you. Show me the amulet!''

Cugel allowed the eager fingers to grope among the carbuncles. Slaye pressed one of these, and called something in a voice so exultant and shrill that the syllables were lost. There was a great fluttering, and an enormous black shape stood at the back of the hall. ''Who torments me?'' it moaned. ''Who will give me surcease?''

''I!'' cried Slaye. ''Advance through the hall, kill all but myself!''

''No!'' cried Cugel. ''It is I who possess the amulet! I whom you must obey! Kill all but me!''

Derwe Coreme clutched at Cugel's arm, striving to see the amulet. ''It avails nothing unless you call him by name. We are all lost!''

''What is his name?'' cried Cugel. ''Counsel me!''

''Hold back!'' declared Slaye. ''I have considered—''

Cugel dealt him a blow and sprang behind the table. The demon was approaching, pausing to pluck up the men-at-arms and dash them against the walls. Derwe Coreme ran to Cugel. ''Let me see the amulet; do you know nothing whatever? I will order him!''

''By no means!'' said Cugel. ''Am I Cugel the Clever for nothing? Show me which carbuncle, recite me the name.''

Derwe Coreme bent her head, read the rune, thrust out to press carbuncle, but Cugel knocked her arm aside. ''What name? Or we all die!''

"Call on Vanille! Press here, call on Vanille!"

Cugel pressed the carbuncle. "Vanille! Halt this strife."

The black demon heeded not at all. There was a second great sound, and a second demon appeared. Derwe Coreme cried out in terror. "It was not Vanille; show me the amulet once more!"

But there was insufficient time; the black demon was upon them.

"Vanille!" bellowed Cugel. "Destroy this black monster!"

Vanille was low and broad, and of a swimming green color, with eyes like scarlet lights. It flung itself upon the first demon, and the terrible bellow of the encounter stunned the ears, and eyes could not follow the frenzy of the fight. The walls shuddered as the great forces struck and rebounded. The table splintered under great splayed feet; Derwe Coreme was flung into a corner. Cugel crawled after, to find her crumpled and staring, half-conscious but bereft of will. Cugel thrust the amulet before her eyes. "Read the runes! Call forth the names; each I will try in turn! Quick, to save our lives!"

But Derwe Coreme merely made a soft motion with her lips. Behind, the black demon, mounted astride Vanille, was methodically clawing up handfuls of his substance and casting it aside, while Vanille bellowed and screamed and turned his ferocious head this way and that, snapping and snarling, striking with great green arms. The black demon plunged its arms deep, seized some central node and Vanille became a sparking green slime of a myriad of parts, each gleam and sparkle flitting and quivering and dissolving into the stone.

Slaye stood grinning above Cugel. "Do you wish your life? Hand here the amulet and I spare you. Delay one instant and you are dead!"

Cugel divested himself of the amulet, but could not bring himself to relinquish it. He said with sudden cunning, "I can give the amulet to the demon."

Slaye glared down at him. "And then we all are dead. To me it does not matter. Do so. I defy you. If you want life—the amulet."

Cugel looked down at Derwe Coreme. "What of her?"

"Together you shall be banished. The amulet, for here is the demon."

The black demon towered above; Cugel hastily handed the amulet to Slaye, who uttered a sharp cry and touched a carbuncle. The demon whimpered, involuted and disappeared.

Slaye stood back, grinning in triumph. "Now away with you and the girl. I keep my word to you, no more. You have your miserable lives: depart,"

"Grant me one desire!" pled Cugel. "Transport us to Almery, to the Vally of the Xzan, where I may rid myself of a canker called Firx!"

"No," said Slaye. "I deny your heart's-desire. Go at once."

Cugel lifted Derwe Coreme to her feet. Still dazed, she stared at the wreckage of the hall. Cugel turned to Slaye. "The ghoul waits in the promenade."

Slaye nodded. "This may well be true. Tomorrow I shall chastise him. Tonight I call sub-world artisans to repair the hall and restore the glory of Cil. Hence! Do you think I care how you fare with the ghoul?" His face became suffused and his hand strayed toward the carbuncles of the amulet. "Hence, at once!"

Cugel took Derwe Coreme's arm and led her from the hall to the great front portal. Slaye stood with feet apart, shoulders hunched, head bent forward, eyes following Cugel's every move. Cugel eased back the bolts, opened the door and stepped out upon the terrace.

There was silence along the promenade. Cugel led Derwe Coreme down the steps and off to the side, into the rank growth of the old garden. Here he paused to listen. From the palace came sounds of activity: rasping and scraping, hoarse shouts and bellows, the flash of many-colored lights. Down the center of the promenade came a tall white shape, stepping from the shadow of one pedestal to the next. It paused to listen to the sounds and watch the flaring lights in wonder. While it was so absorbed Cugel led Derwe Coreme away, behind the dark banks of foliage, and so off into the night.

3

The Mountains of Magnatz

Shortly after sunrise Cugel and Derwe Coreme emerged from the hillside byre where they had huddled the night. The air was chill and the sun, a wine-colored bubble behind high mist, produced no warmth. Cugel clapped his arms and jigged back and forth, while Derwe Coreme stood pinch-faced and limp beside the old byre.

Cugel presently became irritated by her posture, which implied a subtle disparagement of himself. "Fetch wood," he told her curtly. "I will strike a fire; we will breakfast in comfort."

Without a word the erstwhile princess of Cil went to gather furze. Cugel turned to inspect the dim expanse to the east, voicing an automatic curse upon Iucounu the Laughing Magician, whose rancor had flung him into this northern wasteland.

Derwe Coreme returned with an armful of twigs; Cugel gave a nod of approval. For a brief period after their expulsion from Cil she had carried herself with an inappropriate hauteur, which Cugel had tolerated with a quiet smile for himself. Their first couching had been both eventful and taxing; thereafter Derwe Coreme had modified at least her overt behavior. Her face, delicate and clear of feature, had lost little of its brooding melancholy, but the arrogance had altered, as milk becomes cheese, to a new and wakeful appreciation of reality.

The fire crackled cheerfully; they ate a breakfast of rampion and pulpy black gallberries, while Cugel put questions regarding the lands to the east and south. Derwe Coreme could return only small information, none of which was optimistic. "The forest is said to be endless. I have heard it called several names: the Great Erm, the Forest of the East, the Lig Thig. To the south you see the Mountains of Magnatz, which are reputedly dreadful."

"In what respect?" demanded Cugel. "The knowledge is of importance; we must cross these mountains on our way to Almery."

Derwe Coreme shook her head. "I have heard only hints, and paid no great heed, as never did I expect to visit the region."

"Nor I," grumbled Cugel. "Were it not for Iucounu I would be elsewhere."

A spark of interest animated the listless face. "Who is this Iucounu?"

"A detestable wizard of Almery. He has a boiled squash for a head, and flaunts a mindless grin. In every way he is odious, and displays the spite of a scalded eunuch."

Derwe Coreme's mouth moved in a small cool smile. "And you antagonized this wizard."

"Bah! It was nothing. For a trivial slight he flung me north on an impossible mission. I am not Cugel the Clever for nothing! The mission is achieved and now I return to Almery."

"And what of Almery—is this a pleasant land?"

"Pleasant enough, compared to this desolation of forest and mist. Still, imperfections exist. Wizardry is rife, and justice is not invariable, as I have intimated.

"Tell me more of Almery. Are there cities? Are there folk other than rogues and wizards?"

Cugel frowned. "Certain cities exist, sad shadows of bygone glory. There is Azenomei, where the Xzan joins Scaum Flow, and Kaiin in Ascolais, and others along the shore opposite Kauchique, where the folk are of great subtlety."

Derwe Coreme nodded thoughtfully. "I will go to Almery. In your company, from which I can soon recover."

Cugel glanced at her sidewise, not liking the flavor of the remark, but before he could particularize, she asked, "What lands lie between us and Almery?"

"They are wide and dangerous and peopled by gids, erbs, and deodands, as well as leucomorphs, ghouls and grues. Otherwise I am ignorant. If we survive the journey, it will be a miracle indeed."

Derwe Coreme looked wistfully back toward Cil, then shrugged and became silent.

The frugal meal was at its end. Cugel leaned back against the byre, to enjoy the warmth of the fire, but Firx would allow no respite, and Cugel, grimacing, jumped to his feet. "Come; we must set forth. The spite of Iucounu permits no less."

Down the slope they walked, following what appeared to be an old road. The landscape changed. Heath gave way to a damp bottomland; presently they came to the forest. Cugel eyed the gloomy shadows with distrust. "We must go quietly, and hope to arouse nothing baneful. I will watch ahead, and you behind, to ensure that nothing follows to leap on our backs."

"We will lose our way."

"The sun hangs in the south: this is our guide."

Derwe Coreme shrugged once more; they plunged forward into the shade. The trees stood tall overhead and the sunlight, filtered through the foliage, only exaggerated the gloom. Coming upon a stream, they walked along its banks and presently entered a glade where flowed a brimming river.

On the bank near a moored raft sat four men in ragged garments. Cugel looked Derwe Coreme over critically, and took the jeweled buttons from her garments. "These by all odds are bandits and we must lull their cupidity, even though they seem a poor lot."

"Better that we avoid them," said Derwe Coreme. "They are animals, no better."

Cugel demurred. "We need their raft and their guidance, which we must command; if we supplicate, they will believe themselves to have a choice, and become captious." He strode forward and Derwe Coreme willy-nilly was forced to follow.

The rogues did not improve upon closer view. Their hair was long and matted, their faces gnarled, with eyes like beetles and mouths showing foul yellow teeth. Withal, their expressions were mild enough, and they watched Cugel and Derwe Coreme approach with wariness rather than belligerence. One of them, it so appeared, was a woman, though this was hardly evident from garments, face or refinement of manner. Cugel gave them a salute of lordly condescension, at which they blinked in puzzlement.

"What people are you?" asked Cugel.

"We call ourselves Busiacos," responded the oldest of the men. "It is both our race and our family; we make no differentiation, being somewhat polyandrous by habit."

"You are denizens of the forest, familiar with its routes and trails?"

"Such is a fair description," admitted the man, "though our knowledge is local. Remember, this is the Great Erm, which sweeps on league after league without termination."

"No matter," said Cugel. "We require only transfer across the river, then guidance upon a secure route to the lands of the south."

The man consulted the others of his group; all shook their heads. "There is no such route; the Mountains of Magnatz lie in the way."

''Indeed,'' said Cugel.

''If I were to ferry you across the river,'' continued the old Busiaco, ''you would be as good as dead, for the region is haunted by erbs and grues. Your sword would be useless, and you carry only the weakest magic—this I know for we Busiacos smell magic as an erb sniffs out meat.''

''How then may we achieve our destination?'' demanded Cugel.

The Busiacos showed little interest in the question. But the man next in age to the eldest, glancing at Derwe Coreme, had a sudden idea, and looked across the river as if pondering. The effort presently overwhelmed him, and he shook his head in defeat.

Cugel, observing carefully, asked, ''What baffles you?''

''A problem of no great complexity,'' replied the Busiaco. ''We have small practice in logic and any difficulty thwarts us. I only speculated as to which of your belongings you would exchange for guidance through the forest.''

Cugel laughed heartily. ''A good question. But I own only what you see: namely garments, shoes, cape and sword, all of which are necessary to me. Though, for a fact, I know an incantation which can produce a jeweled button or two.''

''These would be small inducement. In a nearby crypt jewels are heaped as high as my head.''

Cugel rubbed his jaw reflectively. ''The generosity of the Busiacos is everywhere known; perhaps you will lead us past this crypt.''

The Busiaco made a gesture of indifference. ''If you wish, although it is adjacent to the den of a great mother gid, now in oestrus.''

''We will proceed directly toward the south,'' said Cugel. ''Come, let us depart at once.''

The Busiaco maintained his stubborn crouch. ''You have no inducement to offer?''

''Only my gratitude, which is no small matter.''

''What of the woman? She is somewhat gaunt, but not unappealing. Since you must die in the Mountains of Magnatz, why waste the woman?''

''True.'' Cugel turned to look at Derwe Coreme. ''Perhaps we can come to terms.''

''What?'' she gasped in outrage. ''Do you dare suggest such a thing? I will drown myself in the river!''

Cugel took her aside. ''I am not called Cugel the Clever for nothing,'' he hissed in her ear. ''Trust me to outwit this moon-calf!''

Derwe Coreme surveyed him with distrust, then turned away, tears of bitter anger streaming down her cheeks. Cugel addressed the Busiaco. "Your proposal is clearly the better part of wisdom; so now, let us be off."

"The woman may remain here," said the Busiaco, rising to his feet. "We walk an enchanted path and rigid discipline is necessary."

Derwe Coreme took a determined stride toward the river. "No!" cried Cugel hastily. "She is of sentimental temperament, and wishes to see me safely on my way to the Mountains of Magnatz, even though it means my certain death."

The Busiaco shrugged. "It is all one." He led them aboard the raft, cast off the rope, and poled across the river. The water seemed shallow, the pole never descending more than a foot or two. It seemed to Cugel that wading across would have been simplicity itself.

The Busiaco, observing, said, "The river swarms with glass reptiles, and an unwary man, stepping forth, is instantly attacked."

"Indeed!" said Cugel, eying the river dubiously.

"Indeed. And now I must caution you as to the path. We will meet all manner of persuasions, but as you value your life, do not step aside from where I lead."

The raft reached the opposite bank; the Busiaco stepped ashore and made it fast to a tree. "Come now, after me." He plunged confidently off among the trees. Derwe Coreme followed, with Cugel coming in the rear. The trail was so faint Cugel could not distinguish it from the untrodden forest, but the Busiaco never faltered. The sun, hanging low behind the trees, could be glimpsed only infrequently, and Cugel was never certain of the direction they traveled. So they proceeded, through sylvan solitudes where not so much as a bird-call could be heard.

The sun, passing its zenith, began to descend, and the trail became no more distinct. Cugel at last called ahead, "You are certain of the trail? It seems that we veer left and right at random."

The Busiaco stopped to explain. "We of the forest are ingenuous folk, but we have this peculiar facility." He tapped his splayed nose significantly. "We can smell out magic. The trail we follow was ordained at a time too remote to be recalled, and yields its direction only to such as ourselves."

"Possibly so," said Cugel petulantly. "But it seems overly circuitous, and where are the fearsome creatures you mentioned? I have seen only a vole, and nowhere have I sensed the distinctive odor of the erb."

The Busiaco shook his head in perplexity. "Unaccountably they have taken themselves elsewhere. Surely you do not complain? Let us proceed, before they return.'' And he set forth once again, by a track no less indistinguishable than before.

The sun sank low. The forest thinned somewhat; scarlet rays slanted along the aisles, burnishing gnarled roots, gilding fallen leaves. The Busiaco stepped into a clearing, where he swung about with an air of triumph. ''I have successfully achieved our goal!''

''How so?'' demanded Cugel. ''We are still deep in the forest.''

The Busiaco pointed across the clearing. ''Notice the four well-marked and distinct trails?''

''This seems to be the case,'' Cugel admitted grudgingly.

''One of these leads to the southern verge. The others plunge into the forest depths, branching variously along the way.''

Derwe Coreme, peering through the branches, uttered a sharp ejaculation. ''There, fifty paces yonder, is the river and the raft!''

Cugel turned the Busiaco a dire look. ''What of all this?''

The Busiaco nodded solemnly. ''Those fifty paces lack the protection of magic. I would have been scamping my responsibility to convey us here by the direct route. And now—'' He advanced to Derwe Coreme, took her arm, then turned back to Cugel. ''You may cross the glade, whereupon I will instruct you as to which trail leads to the southern verge.'' And he busied himself fixing a cord about Derwe Coreme's waist. She resisted with fervor and was only subdued by a blow and a curse. ''This is to prevent any sudden leaps or excursions,'' the Busiaco told Cugel with a sly wink. ''I am not too fleet of foot and when I wish the woman I do not care to pursue her here and there. But are you not in haste? The sun declines, and after dark the leucomorphs appear.''

''Well then, which of the trails leads to the southern verge?'' Cugel asked in a frank manner.

''Cross the clearing and I will so inform you. Of course, if you distrust my instructions, you may make your own choice. But remember, I have vigorously exerted myself for a waspish, gaunt and anemic woman. As of now we are at quits.''

Cugel looked dubiously across the clearing, then to Derwe Coreme, who watched in sick dismay. Cugel spoke cheerfully. ''Well, it seems to be for the best. The Mountains of Magnatz are notoriously dangerous. You are at least secure with this uncouth rogue.''

''No!'' she screamed. ''Let me free of this rope! He is a cheat; you have been duped! Cugel the Clever? Cugel the Fool!''

''Such language is vulgar,'' stated Cugel. ''The Busiaco and I struck a bargain, which is to say, a sacred covenant, which must be discharged.''

"Kill the brute!" cried Derwe Coreme. "Employ your sword! The edge of the forest cannot be far away!"

"An incorrect trail might lead into the heart of the Great Erm," argued Cugel. He raised his arm in farewell. "Far better to drudge for this hirsute ruffian than risk death in the Mountains of Magnatz!"

The Busiaco grinned in agreement, and gave the line a proprietary jerk. Cugel hurried across the clearing with Derwe Coreme's imprecations ringing in his ears, until she was silenced by some means Cugel did not observe. The Busiaco called, "By chance you are approaching the correct path. Follow and you shall presently come to an inhabited place."

Cugel returned a final salute and set forth. Derwe Coreme gave a scream of hysterical mirth: "Cugel the Clever he calls himself! What an extravagant joke!"

Cugel proceeded quickly along the trail, somewhat troubled. "The woman is a monomaniac!" he told himself. "She lacks clarity and perceptiveness; how could I have done else, for her welfare and my own? I am rationality personified; it is unthinking to insist otherwise!"

Scarcely a hundred paces from the clearing the trail emerged from the forest. Cugel stopped short. Only a hundred paces? He pursed his lips. By some curious coincidence three other trails likewise left the forest nearby, all converging to one near where he stood. "Interesting," said Cugel. "It is almost tempting to return to seek out the Busiaco and exact some sort of explanation. . . ."

He fingered his sword thoughtfully, and even took a step or two back toward the forest. But the sun was low and shadows filled the gaps between the gnarled trunks. As Cugel hesitated, Firx impatiently drew several of his prongs and barbs across Cugel's liver, and Cugel abandoned the project of returning into the forest.

The trail led across a region of open land, with mountains riding across the southern sky. Cugel strode along at a smart pace, conscious of the dark shadow of the forest behind, and not completely settled in his mind. From time to time, at some particularly unsettling thought, he slapped his thigh sharply. But what folly! He had obviously managed affairs to their optimum! The Busiaco was gross and stupid; how could he have hoped to trick Cugel? The concept was untenable. As for Derwe Coreme, no doubt she would soon come to terms with her new life. . . .

As the sun dropped behind the Mountains of Magnatz he came upon a rude settlement and a tavern beside the crossroads. This was a staunch structure of stone and timber, with round windows each formed of a hundred blue bull's eyes. Cugel paused at the door and took stock of his resources, which were scant. Then he remembered the jeweled buttons he had taken from Derwe Coreme, and congratulated himself on his forethought.

He pushed through the door, into a long room hung with old bronze lamps. The publican presided at a short buffet where he poured grogs and punches to the three men who were his present customers. All turned to stare as Cugel entered the room.

The publican spoke politely enough. "Welcome, wanderer; what is your pleasure?"

"First a cup of wine, then supper and a night's lodging, and finally such knowledge regarding the road south as you can provide."

The publican set forth a cup of wine. "Supper and lodging in due course. As to the road south, it leads into the realm of Magnatz, which is enough to know."

"Magnatz then is a creature of dread?"

The publican gave his head a dour shake. "Men have fared south never to return. No man in memory has come north. I can vouch for only so much."

The three men who sat drinking nodded in solemn corroboration. Two were peasants of the region, while the third wore the tall black boots of a professional witch-chaser. The first peasant signaled the publican: "Pour this unfortunate a cup of wine, at my expense."

Cugel accepted the cup with mixed feelings. "I drink with thanks, though I specifically disavow the appellation 'unfortunate' lest the virtue of the word project upon my destiny."

"As you will," responded the peasant indifferently, "though in these melancholy times, who is otherwise?" And for a space the peasants argued the repair of the stone fence which separated their lands.

"The work is arduous, but the advantages great," declared one.

"Agreed," stated the other, "but my luck is such that no sooner would we complete the task than the sun would go black, with all the toil for naught."

The first flourished his arms in derisive rejection of the argument. "This is a risk we must assume. Notice: I drink wine, though I may not live to become drunk. Does this deter me? No! I reject the future; I drink now, I become drunk as circumstances dictate."

The publican laughed and pounded the buffet with his fist. "You are as crafty as a Busiaco, of whom I hear there is an encampment nearby. Perhaps the wanderer met them?" And he looked questioningly at Cugel, who nodded grudgingly.

"I encountered such a group: crass rather than crafty, in my opinion. In reference once more to the road south, can anyone here supply specific advice?''

The witch-chaser said gruffly, ''I can: avoid it. You will first encounter deodands avid for your flesh. Beyond is the realm of Magnatz, beside whom the deodands appear as angels of mercy, if a tenth of the rumors are true.''

''This is discouraging news,'' said Cugel. ''Is there no other route to the lands of the south?''

''Indeed there is,'' said the witch-chaser, ''and I recommend it. Return north along the trail to the Great Erm, and proceed eastward across the extent of the forest, which becomes even denser and more dread. Needless to say, you will need a stout arm and feet with wings to escape the vampires, grues, erbs and leucomorphs. After penetrating to the remote edge of the forest you must swing south to the Vale of Dharad, where according to rumor an army of basilisks besieges the ancient city Mar. Should you win past the raging battle, the Great Central Steppe lies beyond, where is neither food nor water and which is the haunt of the pelgrane. Crossing the steppe, you turn your face back to the west, and now you wade a series of poisonous swamps. Beyond lies an area of which I know nothing except that it is named the Land of Evil Recollection. After crossing this region you will find yourself at a point to the south of the Mountains of Magnatz.''

Cugel mused a moment or two. ''The route which you delineate, while it may be safer and less taxing than the direct way south, seems of inordinate length. I am disposed to risk the Mountains of Magnatz.''

The first peasant inspected him with awe. ''I surmise you to be a noted wizard, seething with spells.''

Cugel gave his head a smiling shake. ''I am Cugel the Clever; no more, no less. And now—wine!''

The landlord presently brought forth supper: a stew of lentils and land-crabs garnished with wild ramp and bilberries.

After the meal the two peasants drank a final cup of wine and departed, while Cugel, the host and the witch-chaser sat before the fire discussing various aspects of existence. The witch-chaser finally arose to retire to his chamber. Before departing he approached Cugel, and spoke in a frank manner. ''I have noticed your cloak, which is of quality rarely seen in this backward region. Since you are as good as dead, why do you not bestow this cloak upon me, who has need of it?''

Cugel tersely rejected the proposal and went to his own chamber.

During the night he was aroused by a scraping sound near the foot of his bed. Leaping to his feet, he captured a person of no great stature.

When hauled out into the light, the intruder proved to be the pot-boy, still clutching Cugel's shoes, which he evidently had intended to purloin. "What is the meaning of this outrage?" demanded Cugel, cuffing the lad. "Speak! How dare you attempt such an act!"

The pot-boy begged Cugel to desist. "What difference does it make? A doomed man needs no such elegant footwear!"

"I will be the judge of that," said Cugel. "Do you expect me to walk barefoot to my death in the Mountains of Magnatz? Be off with you!" And he sent the wretched lad sprawling down the hall.

In the morning at breakfast he spoke of the incident to the landlord, who showed no great interest. When it came time to settle his score, Cugel tossed one of the jeweled buttons upon the counter. "Fix, if you will, a fair value upon this gem, subtract the score and give me my change in gold coins."

The landlord examined the ornament, pursed his lips and cocked his head to the side. "The total of the charges to your account exactly equals the worth of this trinket—there is no change forthcoming."

"What?" stormed Cugel. "This clear aquamarine flanked by four emeralds? For a cup or two of poor wine, a porridge and sleep disturbed by the villainy of your pot-boy? Is this a tavern or a bandit lair?"

The landlord shrugged. "The charges are somewhat in excess of the usual fee, but money moldering in the pockets of a corpse serves no one."

Cugel at last extracted several gold coins from the landlord together with a parcel of bread, cheese, and wine. The landlord came to the door and pointed. "There is but a single trail, that leading south. The Mountains of Magnatz rise before you. Farewell."

Not without foreboding, Cugel set off to the south. For a space the trail led past the tillage of local peasants; then as the foothills bulked to either side the trail became first a track, then a trace winding along a dry riverbed beside thickets of prickle-bush, spurge, yarrow, asphodel. Along the crest of the hill paralleling the trail grew a tangle of stunted oak, and Cugel, thinking to improve his chances for going unobserved, climbed to the ridge and continued in the shelter of the foliage.

The air was clear, the sky a brilliant dark blue. The sun wallowed up to the zenith and Cugel bethought himself of the food he carried in his pouch. He seated himself, but as he did so the motion of a skipping dark shadow caught his eye. His blood chilled. The creature surely meant to leap upon his back.

Cugel pretended not to notice, and presently the shadow moved forward again: a deodand, taller and heavier than himself, black as midnight except for shining white eyes, white teeth and claws, wearing straps of leather to support a green velvet skirt.

Cugel debated his best course of action. Face to face, chest to chest, the deodand would tear him to pieces. With his sword ready, Cugel might hack and stab and hold the creature at bay until its frenzy for blood overcame its fear of pain and it flung itself forward regardless of hurt. Possibly Cugel was more fleet, and might out-distance the creature, but only after a long and dogged pursuit. . . . It slipped forward again, to stand behind a crumbling outcrop twenty paces downslope from where Cugal sat. As soon as it had disappeared, Cugel ran to the outcrop and jumped to the top. Here he lifted a heavy stone and, as the deodand came skulking below, threw it down upon the creature's back. It toppled and lay kicking, and Cugel jumped down to deliver the death-stroke.

The deodand had pulled himself against the rock and hissed in horror at the sight of Cugel's naked blade. ''Hold your stroke,'' it said. ''You gain nothing by my death.''

''Only the satisfaction of killing one who planned to devour me.''

''A sterile pleasure!''

''Few pleasures are otherwise,'' said Cugel. ''But while you live, inform me regarding the Mountains of Magnatz.''

''They are as you see: stern mountains of ancient black rock.''

''And what of Magnatz?''

''I have no knowledge of any such entity.''

''What? The men to the north shudder at the very word!''

The deodand pulled himself slightly more erect. ''This well may be. I have heard the name, and consider it no more than a legend of old.''

''Why do travelers go south and none go north?''

''Why should anyone seek to travel north? As for those coming south, they have provided food for myself and my fellows.'' And the deodand inched himself up. Cugel picked up a great stone, held it aloft and dashed it down upon the black creature, which fell back, kicking feebly. Cugel picked up another stone.

''Hold!'' called the deodand in a faint voice. ''Spare me, and I will aid you to life.''

''How is this?'' asked Cugel.

''You seek to travel south; others like me inhabit caves along the way: how can you escape them unless I guide you by ways they do not frequent?''

''You can do this?''

"If you undertake to spare my life."

"Excellent. But I must take safeguards; in your lust for blood you might ignore the agreement."

"You have maimed me; what further security do you need?" cried the deodand. Cugel nevertheless bound the creature's arms and arranged a halter around the thick black neck.

In such fashion they proceeded, the deodand limping and hopping, and directing Cugel by a circuitous route above certain caves.

The mountains lifted higher; winds boomed and echoed down the stone canyons. Cugel continued to question the deodand regarding Magnatz, but elicited only the opinion that Magnatz was a creature of fable.

At last they came to a sandy flat high above the low-lands, which the deodand declared beyond the zone of his particular sept.

"What lies beyond?" asked Cugel.

"I have no knowledge; this is the limit of my wandering. Now release me and go your way, and I will return to my people."

Cugel shook his head. "Night is not too far distant. What is to prevent you from following to attack me once again? Best that I kill you."

The deodand laughed sadly. "Three others follow us. They have kept their distance only because I waved them back. Kill me and you will never wake to see the morning sun."

"We will travel further together," said Cugel.

"As you wish."

Cugel led the way south, the deodand limping to the rear. The valley became a chasm floored with giant boulders, and looking back Cugel saw black shapes moving among the shadows. The deodand grinned meaningfully at Cugel. "You would do well to halt at once; why wait until dark? Death comes with less horror while the light shines."

Cugel made no response, but pressed forward with all speed. The trail left the valley, climbing to a high meadow where the air blew cool. Larch, kaobab and balm-cedar grew to either side, and a stream ran among grasses and herbs. The deodand began to evince uneasiness, jerking at its halter, limping with exaggerated debility. Cugel could see no reason for the display: the countryside, except for the presence of the deodands, seemed without threat. Cugel became impatient. "Why do you delay? I hope to find a mountain hospice before the coming of dark. Your lagging and limping discommode me."

"You should have considered this before you mained me with a rock,'' said the deodand. ''After all, I do not accompany you of my own choice.''

Cugel looked behind. The three deodands who previously had skulked among the rocks now followed quite casually. ''You have no control over the grisly appetites of your fellows?'' Cugel demanded.

''I have no control over my own,'' responded the deodand. ''Only the fact of my broken limbs prevents me from leaping at your throat.''

''Do you wish to live?'' asked Cugel, putting his hand significantly to sword-hilt.

''To a certain extent, though with not so fervent a yearning as do true men.''

''If you value life even an iota, order your fellows to turn back, to give over their sinister pursuit.''

''It would be a futile exercise. And in any event what is life to you? Look, before you tower the Mountains of Magnatz!''

''Ha!'' muttered Cugel. ''Did you not claim the repute of the region to be purely fabulous?''

''Exactly; but I did not enlarge upon the nature of the fable.''

As they spoke there came a swift sigh in the air; looking about, Cugel saw that the three deodands had fallen, transfixed by arrows. From a nearby grove stepped four young men in brown hunting costumes. They were of a fair, fresh complexion, brown hair, good stature, and seemed of good disposition.

The foremost called out, ''How is it that you come from the uninhabited north? And why do you walk with this dire creature of the night?''

''There is no mystery to either of your questions,'' said Cugel. ''First, the north is not uninhabited; some hundreds of men yet remain alive. As to this black hybrid of demon and cannibal, I employed it to lead me safely through the mountains, but I am dissatisfied with its services.''

''I did all expected of me,'' declared the deodand. ''Release me in accordance with our pact.''

''As you will,'' said Cugel He released the halter which secured the creature's throat, and it limped away glaring over its shoulder. Cugel made a sign to the leader of the huntsmen; he spoke a word to his fellows; they raised their bows and shot the deodand with arrows.

Cugel gave a curt nod of approval. ''What of yourselves? And what of Magnatz who reputedly makes the mountains unsafe for travel?''

The huntsmen laughed. ''A legend merely. At one time a terrible creature named Magnatz did indeed exist, and in deference to the tradition we of Vull Village still appoint one of our number to serve as Watchman. But this is all the credit to be given the tale.''

''Strange,'' said Cugel, ''that the tradition wields so wide an influence.''

The huntsmen shrugged indifferently. ''Night approaches; it is time to turn back. You are welcome to join us, and at Vull there is a tavern where you may rest the night.''

''I gladly avail myself of your company.''

The group set off up the trail. As they marched Cugel made inquiry regarding the road to the south, but the huntsmen were of little assistance. ''Vull Village is situated on the shores of Lake Vull, which is unnavigable for its whirlpools, and a few of us have explored the mountains to the south. It is said that they are barren and drop off into an inhospitable gray waste.''

''Possibly Magnatz roams the mountains across the lake?'' inquired Cugel delicately.

''Tradition is silent on this score,'' replied the huntsman.

After an hour's march the group reached Vull, a village of an affluence surprising to Cugel. The dwellings were solidly constructed of stone and timber, the streets neatly laid-out and well-drained; there was a public market, a granary, a hall, a repository, several taverns, a number of modestly luxurious mansions. As the huntsmen marched up the main street, a man called out to them. ''Important news! The Watchman has perished!''

''Indeed?'' inquired the leader of the huntsmen with keen interest. ''Who serves in the interim?''

''It is Lafel, son to the hetman—who else?''

''Who else indeed?'' remarked the huntsman, and the group passed on.

''Is the post of Watchman held in such high esteem then?'' asked Cugel.

The huntsman shrugged. ''It is best described as a ceremonial sinecure. A permanent functionary will no doubt be chosen tomorrow. But notice in the door of the hall!'' And he pointed to a stocky broad-shouldered man wearing brown fur-trimmed robes and black bifold hat. ''That is Hylam Wiskode, the hetman himself. Ho, Wiskode! We have encountered a traveler from the north!''

Hylam Wiskode approached, and saluted Cugel with courtesy. ''Welcome! Strangers are a novelty; our hospitality is yours!''

''I thank you indeed,'' said Cugel. ''I had expected no such affability in the Mountains of Magnatz, which all the world holds in dread.''

The hetman chuckled. "Misapprehensions are common everywhere; you may well find certain of our notions quaint and archaic, like our Watch for Magnatz. But come! here is our best tavern. After you have established yourself we will sup."

Cugel was taken to a comfortable chamber, furnished various conveniences and presently, clean and refreshed, he rejoined Hylam Wiskode in the common room. An appetizing supper was set before him, together with a flagon of wine.

After the meal the hetman conducted Cugel on a tour of the town, which enjoyed a pleasant aspect above the lake.

Tonight seemed to be a special occasion: everywhere cressets threw up plumes of flame, while the folk of Vull walked the streets, pausing to confer in small knots and groups. Cugel inquired the reason for the obvious perturbation. "Is it because your watchman has died?"

"This is the case," said the hetman. "We treat our traditions with all earnestness, and the selection of a new Watchman is a matter for public debate. But observe: here is the public repository, where the common wealth is collected. Do you care to look within?"

"I abide your pleasure," said Cugel. "If you wish to inspect the communal gold, I will be glad to join you."

The hetman threw back the door. "Here is much more than gold! In this bin are jewels; that rack holds antique coins. Those bales contain fine silks and embroidered damask; to the side are cases of precious spice, even more precious liquors, and subtle pastes without value. But I should not use these terms on you, a traveler and man of experience, who has looked upon real wealth."

Cugel insisted that the riches of Vull were by no means to be deprecated. The hetman bowed appreciatively and they proceeded to an esplanade beside the lake, now a great dark expanse illuminated by feeble starlight.

The hetman indicated a cupola supported five hundred feet in the air by a slender pillar. "Can you guess the function of that structure?"

"It would seem to be the post of the Watchman," said Cugel.

"Correct! You are man of discernment. A pity you are in such haste and can not linger in Vull!"

Cugel, considering his empty wallet and the riches of the storehouse, made a suave gesture. "I would not be averse to such a sojourn, but in all candor, I travel in penury, and would be forced to seek some sort of gainful employment. I wonder regarding the office of Watchman, which I understand to be a post of some prestige."

"Indeed it is," said the hetman. "My own son stands watch tonight. Still, there is no reason why you should not be a suitable candidate for the position. The duties are by no means arduous; indeed the post is something of a sinecure.''

Cugel became conscious of Firx's fretful stirrings. ''And as to the emoluments?''

''They are excellent. The Watchman enjoys great prestige here in Vull, since, in a purely formal sense, he protects us all from danger.''

''They are, specifically, what?''

The hetman paused to reflect, and ticked off the points on his fingers. ''First, he is provided a comfortable watch-tower, complete with cushions, an optical device whereby distant objects are made to seem close at hand, a brazier to provide heat and an ingenious communications system. Next, his food and drink are of the highest quality and provided free of charge, at his pleasure and to his order. Next, he is generally granted the subsidiary title 'Guardian of the Public Repository,' and to simplify matters he is invested with full title to, and powers of dispensation over, the total wealth of Vull. Fourth, he may select as his spouse that maiden who seems to him the most attractive. Fifthly, he is accorded the title of 'Baron' and must be saluted with profound respect.''

''Indeed, indeed,'' said Cugel. ''The position appears worthy of consideration. What responsibilities are entailed?''

''They are as the nomenclature implies. The Watchman must keep watch, for this is one of the old-fashioned customs we observe. The duties are hardly onerous, but they must not be scamped, because that would signify farce, and we are serious folk, even in connection with our quaint traditions.''

Cugel nodded judiciously. ''The conditions are straight forward. The Watchman watches; nothing could be more clearly expressed. But who is Magnatz, in what direction should he be apprehended, and how may he be recognized?''

''These questions are of no great application,'' said the hetman, ''since the creature, in theory, has no existence.''

Cugel glanced up at the tower, across the lake, back toward the public repository. ''I hereby make application for the position, providing all is as you state.''

Firx instantly impinged a series of racking pangs upon Cugel's vitals. Cugel bent double, clasped his abdomen, straightened, and making excuses to the perplexed hetman, moved to the side. ''Patience!'' he implored Firx. ''Temperance! Have you no concept of realities? My purse is empty; there are long leagues ahead! To travel with any degree of expedition, I must restore my strength and replenish my wallet. I plan to work at this office only long enough to do both, then it is post-haste to Almery!"

Firx reluctantly diminished the demonstrations, and Cugel returned to where the hetman waited.

"All is as before," said Cugel. "I have taken counsel with myself and believe I can adequately fulfill the obligations of the job."

The hetman nodded. "I am pleased to hear this. You will find my presentation of the facts to be accurate in every essential aspect. I likewise have been reflecting, and I can safely say that no other person of the town aspires to so august a position, and I hereby pronounce you Watchman of the Town!" Ceremoniously the hetman brought forth a golden collar, which he draped around Cugel's neck.

They returned toward the tavern, and as they went, the folk of Vull, noting the golden collar, pressed upon the hetman with eager questions. "Yes," was his answer. "This gentleman has demonstrated his capabilities, and I have pronounced him Watchman of the Town!"

At the news the folk of Vull became generously expansive, and congratulated Cugel as if he had been a resident the whole of his life.

All repaired to the tavern; wine and spiced meat were set out; pipers appeared and there was decorous dancing and merrymaking.

During the course of the evening Cugel spied an extremely beautiful girl dancing with a young man who had been part of the hunting party. Cugel nudged the hetman, directed his attention to the girl.

"Ah yes: the delightful Marlinka! She dances with the lad whom I believe she plans to espouse."

"Her plans possibly are subject to alteration?" inquired Cugel meaningfully.

The hetman winked slyly. "You find her attractive?"

"Indeed, and since this is a prerequisite of my office, I hereby declare this delightful creature my bride-elect. Let the ceremonies be performed at once!"

"So swiftly?" inquired the hetman. "Ah, well, the hot blood of youth brooks no delay." He signaled the girl and she danced merrily over to the table. Cugel arose and performed a deep bow. The hetman spoke. "Marlinka, the Watchman of the Town finds you desirable and wishes you for his spouse."

Marlinka seemed first surprised, then amused. She glanced roguishly at Cugel, and performed an arch curtsy. "The watchman does me great honor."

"Further," intoned the hetman, "he requires that the marital ceremonies be performed on the instant."

Marlinka looked dubiously at Cugel, then over her shoulder at the young man with whom she had been dancing. "Very well," she said. "As you will."

The ceremony was performed, and Cugel found himself espoused to Marlinka, whom, on closer examination, he saw to be a creature of delightful animation, charming manners and exquisite appearance. He put his arm around her waist. "Come," he whispered, "let us slip away for a period and solemnize the connubiality."

"Not so soon," whispered Marlinka. "I must have time to order myself; I am overexcited!" She released herself, and danced away.

There was further feasting and merrymaking, and to his vast displeasure Cugel noted Marlinka again dancing with the youth to whom she formerly had been betrothed. As he watched she embraced this young man with every evidence of ardor. Cugel marched forward, halted the dance, and took his bride aside. "Such an act is hardly appropriate; you have only been married an hour!"

Marlinka, both surprised and nonplused, laughed, then frowned, then laughed again and promised to behave with greater decorum. Cugel attempted to lead her to his chamber, but she once again declared the moment unsuitable.

Cugel drew a deep sigh of vexation, but was consoled by the recollection of his other perquisites: the freedom of the repository, for instance. He leaned over to the hetman. "Since now I am titular guardian to the public repository, it is only prudent that I acquaint myself in detail with the treasure I am charged with guarding. If you will be so good as to turn over the keys, I will go to make a quick inventory."

"Even better," said the hetman, "I will accompany you, and do what I can in the way of assistance."

They crossed to the repository. The hetman unlocked the door and held a light. Cugel entered and examined the valuables. "I see that all is in order, and perhaps it is advisable to wait till my head is settled before undertaking a detailed inventory. But in the meantime—" Cugel went to the jewel bin, selected several gems, and began to tuck them into his pouch.

"A moment," said the hetman. "I fear you inconvenience yourself. Shortly you will be fitted with garments of rich cloth deserving of your rank. The wealth is most conveniently kept here in the treasury; why trouble yourself with the weight, or incur the possibility of loss?"

"There is something in what you say," remarked Cugel, "but I wish to order the construction of a mansion overlooking the lake and I will need wealth to pay the costs of construction."

"In due time, in due time. The actual work can hardly commence until you have examined the countryside and chosen the most felicitous site."

"True," agreed Cugel. "I can see that there are busy times ahead. But now—back to the tavern! My spouse is overmodest and now I will brook no further delay!"

But upon their return Marlinka was nowhere to be found. "Doubtless she has gone to array herself in seductive garments," suggested the hetman. "Have patience!"

Cugel compressed his lips in displeasure, and was further annoyed to find that the young huntsman had likewise departed.

The merrymaking waxed apace, and after many toasts, Cugel became a trifle fuddled, and was carried up to his chamber.

Early in the morning the hetman rapped at the door, and entered at Cugel's summons. "We must now visit the watchtower," said the hetman. "My own son guarded Vull this last night, since our tradition demands incessant vigilance."

With poor grace Cugel dressed himself and followed the hetman out into the cool air of morning. They walked to the watchtower, and Cugel was astounded both by its height and by the elegant simplicity of its construction, the slender stem rearing five hundred feet into the air to support the cupola.

A rope ladder was the only means of ascent. The hetman started up and Cugel came below, the ladder swaying and jiggling in such a fashion as to cause Cugel vertigo.

They gained the cupola in safety and the hetman's weary son descended. The cupola was furnished in rather less luxury than Cugel had expected, and indeed seemed almost austere. He pointed out this fact to the hetman, who stated that the deficiencies were readily repaired. "Merely state your requirements: they shall be met!"

"Well then: I will want a heavy rug for the floor—tones of green and gold might be the most felicitous. I require a more elegant couch, of greater scope than that disreputable pallet I see against the wall, as my spouse Marlinka will be spending much of her time here. A cabinet for gems and valuables there, a compartment for sweetmeats there, a tray for perfume essences there. At this location I will require a taboret with provision for chilling wines."

The hetman assented readily to all. "It shall be as you say. But now we must discuss your duties, which are so simple as almost to require no elaboration: you must keep watch for Magnatz."

"This I understand, but as before a corollary thought occurs to me: in order to work at optimum efficiency I should know what or whom I am to watch for. Magnatz might stalk unhindered along the esplanade were I unable to recognize him. What then is his semblance?''

The hetman shook his head. ''I cannot say; the information is lost in the fog of ages. The legend reports only that he was tricked and baffled by a sorcerer, and taken away.'' The hetman went to the observation post. ''Notice: here is an optical device. Working by an ingenious principle, it bloats and augments those scenes toward which you direct it. From time to time you may choose to inspect landmarks of the area. Yonder is Mount Temus; below is Lake Vull, where no one can sail for vortices and whirlpools. In this direction is Padagar Pass, leading eastward into the land of Merce. You can barely discern that commemorative cairn decreed by Guzpah the Great when he brought eight armies to attack Magnatz. Magnatz erected another cairn—see that great mound to the north?—in order to cover their mangled corpses. And there is the notch Magnatz broke through the mountains so that cooling air might circulate through the valley. Across the lake lie certain titanic ruins, where Magnatz had his palace.''

Cugel inspected the various landmarks through the optical device. ''Magnatz was by all accounts a creature of vast potency.''

''So the legends assert. Now, a final matter. If Magnatz appears—a laughable whimsy, of course—you must pull this rod, which rings the great gong. Our laws stringently forbid ringing the gong, except at the sight of Magnatz. The penalty for such a crime is intensely severe; in fact, the last Watchman betrayed his high office by wantonly ringing the gong. Needless to say, he was judged harshly, and after he had been torn to bits by a criss-cross of chains his fragments were cast into a whirlpool.''

''What an idiotic fellow!'' remarked Cugel. ''Why forfeit so much wealth, good cheer and honor for a footling amusement?''

''We are all of like opinion,'' stated the hetman.

Cugel frowned. ''I am puzzled by his act. Was he a young man, to yield so readily to a frivolous whim?''

''Not even this plea can be made in his behalf. He was a sage of four-score years, three-score of which he had served the town as Watchman.''

''His conduct becomes all the more incredible,'' was Cugel's wondering comment.

''All of Vull feel the same.'' The hetman rubbed his hands briskly. ''I believe that we have discussed all the essentials; I will now depart and leave you to the enjoyment of your duties.''

"One moment," said Cugel. "I insist upon certain alterations and improvements: the rug, the cabinet, the cushions, the tray, the couch."

"Of course," said the hetman. He bent his head over the rail, shouted instructions to those below. There was no instant response and the hetman became exasperated. "What a nuisance!" he exclaimed. "It appears I must see to the matter myself." He began to climb down the rope ladder.

Cugel called after him, "Be good enough to send up my spouse Marlinka, as there are certain matters I wish to take up with her."

"I shall seek her out at once," called the hetman over his shoulder.

Several minutes later there was a creaking of the great pulley; the ladder was lowered at the end of the rope which supported it. Looking over the side, Cugel saw that the cushions were about to be raised. The heavy rope supporting the ladder rattled through the pulley, bringing up a light line—hardly more than a stout cord—and on this cord the cushions were raised. Cugel inspected them with disapproval; they were old and dusty, and not at all of the quality he had envisioned. Most certainly he would insist upon furnishings superior to this! Possibly the hetman intended these merely as a stop-gap until cushions of the requisite elegance could be provided. Cugel nodded: this was obviously the situation.

He looked around the horizon. Magnatz was nowhere to be seen. He swung his arms once or twice, paced back and forth, and went to look down at the plaza, where he expected to find artisans assembling the appurtenances he had ordered. But there was no such activity; the townspeople appeared to be going about their usual affairs. Cugel shrugged, and went to make another inspection of the horizon. As before, Magnatz was invisible.

Once more he surveyed the plaza. He frowned, squinted: was that his spouse Marlinka walking past in the company of a young man? He focused the optical device upon the supple shape: it was Marlinka indeed, and the young man who clasped her elbow with insolent intimacy was the huntsman to whom she had at one time been affianced. Cugel clamped his jaw in outrage. This sort of behavior could not continue! When Marlinka presented herself, he would speak emphatically upon the subject.

The sun reached zenith; the cord quivered. Looking over the side Cugel saw that his noon repast was being hoisted in a basket, and he clapped his hands in anticipation. But the basket, when he lifted the cloth, contained only a half-loaf of bread, a chunk of tough meat and a flask of thin wine. Cugel stared at the sorry fare in shock, and decided to descend on the moment to set matters straight. He cleared his throat and called down for the ladder. No one appeared to hear him. He called more loudly. One or two of the folk looked up in mild curiosity, and passed on about their business. Cugel jerked angrily at the cord and hauled it over the pulley, but no heavy rope appeared nor a rope ladder. The light line was an endless loop, capable of supporting approximately the weight of a basket of food.

Thoughtfully Cugel sat back, and assessed the situation. Then, directing the optical device once more upon the plaza, he searched for the hetman, the one man to whom he might turn for satisfaction.

Late in the afternoon, Cugel chanced to observe the door to the tavern, just as the hetman came staggering forth, obviously much elevated by wine. Cugel called peremptorily down; the hetman stopped short, looked about for the source of the voice, shook his head in perplexity and continued across the plaza.

The sun slanted across Lake Vull; the whirlpools were spirals of maroon and black. Cugel's supper arrived: a dish of boiled leeks and a bowl of porridge. He inspected it with small interest, then went to the side of the cupola. "Send up the ladder!" he called. "Darkness comes! In the absence of light, it is futile to watch for Magnatz or anyone else!"

As before, his remarks passed unheeded. Firx suddenly seemed to take cognizance of the situation and visited several sharp twinges upon Cugel's vitals.

Cugal passed a fitful night. As merrymakers left the tavern Cugel called to them and made representations regarding his plight, but he might as well have saved his breath.

The sun appeared over the mountains. Cugel's morning meal was of fair quality, but by no means up to the standard described by Hylam Wiskode, the double-tongued hetman of Vull. In a rage, Cugel bellowed orders to those below, but was ignored. He drew a deep breath: it seemed then that he was cast upon his own resources. But what of this? Was he Cugel the Clever for nothing? And he considered various means for descending the tower.

The line by which his food ascended was far too light. If doubled and redoubled so that it bore his weight, it would yield, at most, a quarter of the distance to the ground. His clothes and leathers, if torn and knotted, might provide another twenty feet, leaving him dangling in mid-air. The stem of the tower provided no foothold. With appropriate tools and sufficient time he might be able to chisel a staircase down the outside of the tower, or even chip away the tower in its entirety, eventually reducing it to a short stump from which he might leap to earth. . . . The project was not feasible. Cugel slumped on the cushions in despair. Everything was now clear. He had been fooled. He was a prisoner. How long had the previous Watchman remained at his post? Sixty years? The prospect was by no means cheerful.

Firx, of like opinion, jabbed furiously with barb and prong, adding to Cugel's woes.

So passed days and nights. Cugel brooded long and darkly, and contemplated the folk of Vull with great revulsion. On occasion he considered ringing the great gong, as his predecessor had been driven to do—but, recalling the penalty, he restrained himself.

Cugel became familiar with every aspect of town, lake and landscape. In the morning heavy mists covered the lake; after two hours a breeze thrust them aside. The whirlpools sucked and groaned, swinging here and there, and the fishermen of Vull ventured hardly more than the length of their boats off shore. Cugel grew to recognize all the villagers, and learned the personal habits of each. Marlinka, his perfidious spouse, crossed the plaza often, but seldom if ever thought to turn her glance upward. Cugel marked well the cottage where she lived and gave it constant surveillance through the optical device. If she dallied with the young huntsman, her discretion was remarkable, and Cugel's dark suspicions were never documented.

The food failed to improve in quality and not infrequently was forgotten altogether. Firx was persistently acrimonious, and Cugel paced the confines of the cupola with ever more frantic strides. Shortly after sundown, after a particularly agonizing admonishment by Firx, Cugel stopped short in his tracks. To descend the tower was a matter of simplicity! Why had he delayed so long? Cugel the Clever indeed!

He ripped into strips every fragment of cloth the cupola provided, and from the yield plaited a rope twenty feet long. Now he must wait till the town grew quiet: yet an hour or two.

Firx assailed him once more, and Cugel cried out. "Peace, scorpion, tonight we escape this turret! Your acts are redundant!"

Firx gave over his demonstration, and Cugel went to investigate the plaza. The night was cool and misty: ideal for his purposes, and the folk of Vull were early to bed.

Cugel cautiously raised the line on which his food was hoisted; doubled, redoubled and redoubled it again and so produced a cable amply strong to support him. He tied a loop on one end, and made the other fast to the pulley. After one last look around the horizon, he lowered himself over the side. He descended to the end of the cable, thrust himself into the loop and sat swaying some four hundred feet above the plaza. To one end of his twenty-foot rope he tied his shoe for a weight, and after several casts, flung a loop around the stem of the column, and pulled himself close. With infinite caution he slipped himself free and, using the loop around the column as a brake, slid slowly to the ground. He took himself quickly into the shadows and donned his shoes. Just as he rose to his feet the door to the tavern swung open and out reeled Hylam Wiskode, much the worse for drink. Cugel grinned unpleasantly and followed the staggering hetman into a side-street.

A single blow on the back of the head was enough; the hetman toppled into a ditch. Cugel was instantly upon him, and with deft fingers took his keys. Going now to the public repository, he opened the door, slipped inside and filled a sack with gems, coins, flasks of costly essences, relics, and the like.

Returning to the street, Cugel carried the sack to a dock beside the lake, where he hid it under a net. Now he proceeded to the cottage of his spouse Marlinka. Prowling beside the wall, he came to an open window, and stepping through found himself in her chamber.

She was awakened by his hands at her throat. When she tried to scream he cut off her wind. "It is I," he hissed, "Cugel, your spouse! Arise and come with me. Your first sound will be your last!"

In great terror, the girl obeyed. At Cugel's order she threw a cloak about her shoulders and clasped sandals upon her feet. "Where are we going?" she whispered in a tremulous voice.

"No matter. Come now—through the window. Make not a sound!"

Standing outside in the dark, Marlinka cast a horror-stricken glance toward the tower. "Who is on watch? Who guards Vull from Magnatz?"

"No one is on watch," said Cugel. "The tower is empty!"

Her knees gave way; she sagged to the ground. "Up!" said Cugel. "Up! We must proceed!"

"But no one is on watch! This voids the spell the sorcerer cast upon Magnatz, who swore to return when vigilance ceased!"

Cugel lifted the girl to her feet. "This is no concern of mine; I disclaim responsibility. Did you not seek to fool and victimize me? Where were my cushions? Where was the fine food? And my spouse—where were you?"

The girl wept into her hands, and Cugel led her to the dock. He pulled close a fisherman's boat, ordered her aboard, threw in his loot.

Untying the boat he shipped oars and rowed out upon the lake. Marlinka was aghast. "The whirlpools will drown us! Have you lost your reason?"

"Not at all! I have studied the whirlpools with care and know precisely the range of each."

Out upon the face of the lake moved Cugel, counting each stroke of his oars, and watching the stars. "Two hundred paces east . . . a hundred paces north . . . two hundred paces east . . . fifty paces south . . ."

So Cugel rowed while to right and left of them sounded the suck of whirling water. But the mist had gathered to blot out the stars and Cugel was forced to throw out the anchor. "This is well enough," he said. "We are safe now, and there is much that lies between us."

The girl shrank to her end of the boat. Cugel stepped astern and joined her. "Here I am, your spouse! Are you not overjoyed that finally we are alone? My chamber at the inn was far more comfortable, but this boat will suffice."

"No," she whimpered. "Do not touch me! The ceremony was meaningless, a trick to persuade you to serve as Watchman."

"For three-score years perhaps, until I rang the gong from utter desperation?"

"It is not my doing! I am guilty only of merriment! But what will become of Vull? No one watches, and the spell is broken!"

"So much the worse for the faithless folk of Vull! They have lost their treasure, their most beautiful maiden, and when day breaks Magnatz will march upon them."

Marlinka uttered a poignant cry, which was muffled in the mist. "Never speak the cursed name!"

"Why not? I shall shout it across the water! I will inform Magnatz that the spell is gone, that now he may come for his revenge!"

"No, no indeed not!"

"Then you must behave toward me as I expect."

Weeping, the girl obeyed, and at last a wan red light filtering through the mist signaled dawn. Cugel stood up in the boat, but all landmarks were yet concealed.

Another hour passed; the sun was now aloft. The folk of Vull would discover that their Watchman was gone, and with him their treasure. Cugel chuckled, and now a breeze lifted the mists, revealing the landmarks he had memorized. He leapt to the bow and hauled on the anchor line, but to his annoyance the anchor had fouled itself.

He jerked, strained, and the line gave a trifle. Cugel pulled with all his strength. From below came a great bubbling. "A whirlpool!" cried Marlinka in terror.

"No whirlpool here," panted Cugel, and jerked once more. The line seemed to relax and Cugel hauled in the rope. Looking over the side, he found himself staring into an enormous pale face. The anchor had caught in a nostril. As he looked the eyes blinked open.

Cugel threw away the line, leapt for the oars and frantically rowed for the southern shore.

A hand as large as a house raised from the water, groping. Marlinka screamed. There was a great turbulence, a prodigious surge of water which flung the boat toward the shore like a chip, and Magnatz sat up in the center of Lake Vull.

From the village came the sound of the warning gong, a frenzied clanging.

Magnatz heaved himself to his knees, water and muck draining from his vast body. The anchor which had pierced his nostril still hung in place, and a thick black fluid issued from the wound. He raised a great arm and slapped petulantly at the boat. The impact threw up a wall of foam which engulfed the boat, spilled treasure, Cugel and the girl toppling through the dark depths of the lake.

Cugel kicked and thrust, and propelled himself to the seething surface. Magnatz had gained his feet and was looking toward Vull.

Cugel swam to the beach and staggered ashore. Marlinka had drowned, and was nowhere to be seen. Across the lake Magnatz was wading slowly toward the village.

Cugel waited no longer. He turned and ran with all speed up the mountainside.

4

The Sorcerer Pharesm

The mountains were behind: the dark defiles, the tarns, the echoing stone heights—all now a sooty bulk to the north. For a time Cugel wandered a region of low rounded hills the color and texture of old wood, with groves of blue-black trees dense along the ridges, then came upon a faint trail which took him south by long swings and slants, and at last broke out over a vast dim plain. A half-mile to the right rose a line of tall cliffs, which instantly attracted his attention, bringing him a haunting pang of *déja-vu.* He stared mystified. At some time in the past he had known these cliffs: how? when? His memory provided no response.

He settled himself upon a low lichen-covered rock to rest, but now Firx became impatient and inflicted a stimulating pang. Cugel leapt to his feet, groaning with weariness and shaking his fist to the southwest, the presumable direction of Almery. "Iucounu, Iucounu! If I could repay a tenth of your offenses, the world would think me harsh!"

He set off down the trail, under the cliffs which had affected him with such poignant but impossible recollections. Far below spread the plain, filling three-quarters of the horizon with colors much like those of the lichened rock Cugel had just departed: black patches of woodland: a gray crumble where ruins filled an entire valley; nondescript streaks of gray-green, lavender, gray-brown; the leaden glint of two great rivers disappearing into the haze of distance.

Cugel's brief rest had only served to stiffen his joints; he limped, and the pouch chafed his hip. Even more distressing was the hunger gripping his belly. Another tally against Iucounu! True, the Laughing Magician had furnished an amulet converting such normally inedible substances as grass, wood, horn, hair, humus and the like into a nutritious paste. Unfortunately—and this was a measure of Iucounu's mordant humor—the paste retained the flavor of the native substance, and during his passage of the mountains Cugel had tasted little better than spurge, cullion, blackwort, oak-twigs and galls, and on one occasion, when all else had failed, certain refuse discovered in the cave of a bearded thawn. Cugel had eaten only minimally; his long spare frame had become gaunt; his cheekbones protruded like sponsons; the black eyebrows which once had crooked so jauntily now lay flat and dispirited. Truly, truly, Iucounu had much to answer for! And Cugel, as he proceeded, debated the exact quality of revenge he would take if ever he found his way back to Almery.

The trail swung down upon a wide stony flat where the wind had carved a thousand grotesque figures. Surveying the area, Cugel thought to perceive regularity among the eroded shapes, and halted to rub his long chin in appraisal. The pattern displayed an extreme subtlety—so subtle indeed that Cugel wondered if it had not been projected by his own mind. Moving closer, he discerned further complexities, and elaborations upon complexities: twists, spires, volutes; disks, saddles, wrenched spheres; torsons and flexions; spindles, cardioids, lanciform pinnacles: the most laborious, painstaking and intricate rock-carving conceivable, manifestly no random effort of the elements. Cugel frowned in perplexity, unable to imagine a motive for so complex an undertaking.

He went on and a moment later heard voices together with the clank of tools. He stopped short, listened cautiously, then proceeded to come upon a gang of about fifty men ranging in stature from three inches to well over twelve feet. Cugel approached on tentative feet, but after a glance the workers paid him no heed, continuing to chisel, grind, scrape, probe and polish with dedicated zeal.

Cugel watched for several minutes, then approached the overseer, a man three feet in height who stood at a lectern consulting the plans spread before him, comparing them to the work in progress by means of an ingenious optical device. He appeared to note everything at once, calling instructions, chiding, exhorting against error, instructing the least deft in the use of their tools. To exemplify his remarks he used a wonderfully extensible forefinger, which reached forth thirty feet to tap at a section of rock, to scratch a quick diagram, then as swiftly retract.

The foreman drew back a pace or two, temporarily satisfied with the work in progress, and Cugel came forward. "What intricate effort is this and what is its object?"

"The works is as you see," replied the foreman in a voice of penetrating compass. "From natural rock we produce specified shapes, at the behest of the sorcerer Pharesm. . . . Now then! Now then!" The cry was addressed to a man three feet taller than Cugel, who had been striking the stone with a pointed maul. "I detect overconfidence!" The forefinger shot forth. "Use great care at this juncture; note how the rock tends to cleave? Strike here a blow of the sixth intensity at the vertical, using a semi-clenched grip; at this point a fourth-intensity blow groin-wise; then employ a quarter-gauge bant-iron to remove the swange."

With the work once more going correctly, he fell to studying his plans, shaking his head with a frown of dissatisfaction. "Much too slow! The craftsmen toil as if in a drugged torpor, or else display a mulish stupidity. Only yesterday Dadio Fessadil, he of three ells with the green kerchief yonder, used a ninteen-gauge freezing-bar to groove the bead of a small inverted quatrefoil."

Cugel shook his head in surprise, as if never had he heard of so egregious a blunder. And he asked: "What prompts this inordinate rock-hewing?"

"I cannot say," replied the foreman. "The work has been in progress three hundred and eighteen years, but during this time Pharesm has never clarified his motives. They must be pointed and definite, for he makes a daily inspection and is quick to indicate errors." Here he turned aside to consult with a man as tall as Cugel's knee, who voiced uncertainty as to the pitch of a certain volute. The foreman, consulting an index, resolved the matter; then he turned back to Cugel, this time with an air of frank appraisal.

"You appear both astute and deft; would you care to take employment? We lack several craftsmen of the half-ell category, or, if you prefer more forceful manifestations, we can nicely use an apprentice stone-breaker of sixteen ells. Your stature is adjusted in either direction, and there is identical scope for advancement. As you see, I am a man of four ells. I reached the position of Stirker in one year, Molder of Forms in three, Assistant Chade in ten, and I have now served as Chief Chade for nineteen years. My predecessor was two ells, and the Chief Chade before him was a ten-ell man." He went on to enumerate advantages of the work, which included sustenance, shelter, narcotics of choice, nympharium privileges, a stipend starting at ten terces a day, various other benefits including Pharesm's services as diviner and exorciser. "Additionally, Pharesm maintains a conservatory where all may enrich their intellects. I myself take instruction in Insect Identification, the Heraldry of the Kings of Old Gomaz, Unison Chanting, Practical Catalepsy and Orthodox Doctrine. You will never find master more generous than Pharesm the Sorcerer!''

Cugel restrained a smile for the Chief Chade's enthusiasm; still, his stomach was roiling with hunger and he did not reject the proffer out of hand. ''I had never before considered such a career,'' he said. ''You cite advantages of which I was unaware.''

''True; they are not generally known.''

''I cannot immediately say yes or no. It is a decision of consequence which I feel I should consider in all its aspects.''

The Chief Chade gave a nod of profound agreement. ''We encourage deliberation in our craftsmen, when every stroke must achieve the desired effect. To repair an inaccuracy of as much as a fingernail's width the entire block must be removed, a new block fitted into the socket of the old, whereupon all begins anew. Until the work has reached its previous stage nympharium privileges are denied to all. Hence, we wish no opportunistic or impulsive newcomers to the group.''

Firx, suddenly apprehending that Cugel proposed a delay, made representations of a most agonizing nature. Clasping his abdomen, Cugel took himself aside and, while the Chief Chade watched in perplexity, argued heatedly with Firx. ''How may I proceed without sustenance?'' Firx's response was an incisive motion of the barbs. ''Impossible!'' exclaimed Cugel. ''The amulet of Iucounu theoretically suffices, but I can stomach no more spurge; remember, if I fall dead in the trail, you will never rejoin your comrade in Iucounu's vats!''

Firx saw the justice of the argument and reluctantly became quiet. Cugel returned to the lectern, where the Chief Chade had been distracted by the discovery of a large tourmaline opposing the flow of a certain complicated helix. Finally Cugel was able to engage his attention. ''While I weigh the proffer of employment and the conflicting advantages of diminution versus elongation, I will need a couch on which to recline. I also wish to test the perquisites you describe, perhaps for the period of a day or more.''

''Your prudence is commendable,'' declared the Chief Chade. ''The folk of today tend to commit themselves rashly to courses they later regret. It was not so in my youth, when sobriety and discretion prevailed. I will arrange for your admission into the compound, where you may verify each of my assertions. You will find Pharesm stern but just, and only the man who hacks the rock willy-nilly has cause to complain. But observe! here is Pharesm the Sorcerer on his daily inspection!''

Up the trail came a man of imposing stature wearing a voluminous white robe. His countenance was benign; his hair was like yellow down; his eyes were turned upward as if rapt in the contemplation of an ineffable sublimity. His arms were sedately folded, and he moved without motion of his legs. The workers, doffing their caps and bowing in unison, chanted a respectful salute, to which Pharesm returned an inclination of the head. Spying Cugel, he paused, made a swift survey of the work so far accomplished, then glided without haste to the lectern.

"All appears resonably exact," he told the Chief Chade. "I believe the polish on the underside of Epi-projection 56-16 is uneven and I detect a minute chip on the secondary cinctor of the nineteenth spire. Neither circumstance seems of major import and I recommend no disciplinary action."

"The deficiencies shall be repaired and the careless artisans reprimanded: this at the very least!" exclaimed the Chief Chade in an angry passion. "Now I wish to introduce a possible recruit to our workforce. He claims no experience at the trade, and will deliberate before deciding to join our group. If he so elects, I envision the usual period as rubble-gatherer, before he is entrusted with tool-sharpening and preliminary excavation."

"Yes; this would accord with our usual practice. However . . ." Pharesm glided effortlessly forward, took Cugel's left hand and performed a swift divination upon the fingernails. His bland countenance became sober. "I see contradictions of four varieties. Still it is clear that your optimum bent lies elsewhere than in the hewing and shaping of rock. I advise that you seek another and more compatible employment."

"Well spoken!" cried Chief Chade. "Pharesm the Sorcerer demonstrates his infallible altruism! In order that I do not fall short of the mark I hereby withdraw my proffer of employment! Since no purpose can now be served by reclining upon a couch or testing the perquisites, you need waste no more irreplaceable time."

Cugel made a sour face. "So casual a divination might well be inaccurate."

The Chief Chade extended his forefinger thirty feet vertically in outraged remonstrance, but Pharesm gave a placid nod. "This is quite correct, and I will gladly perform a more comprehensive divination, though the process requires six to eight hours."

"So long?" asked Cugel in astonishment.

"This is the barest minimum. First you are swathed head to foot in the intestines of fresh-killed owls, then immersed in a warm bath containing a number of secret organic substances. I must, of course, char the small toe of your left foot, and dilate your nose sufficiently to admit an explorer beetle, that he may study the conduits leading to and from your sensorium. But let us return to my divinatory, that we may commence the process in good time."

Cugel pulled at his chin, torn this way and that. Finally he said, "I am a cautious man, and must ponder even the advisability of undertaking such a divination; hence, I will require several days of calm and meditative somnolence. Your compound and the adjacent nympharium appear to afford the conditions requisite to such a state; hence—"

Pharesm indulgently shook his head. "Caution, like any other virtue, can be carried to an extreme. The divination must proceed at once."

Cugel attempted to argue further but Pharesm was adamant, and presently glided off down the trail.

Cugel, disconsolately went to the side, considering first this stratagem, then that. The sun neared the zenith, and the workmen began to speculate as to the nature of the viands to be served for their midday meal. At last the Chief Chade signaled; all put down their tools and gathered about the cart which contained the repast.

Cugel jocularly called out that he might be persuaded to share the meal, but the Chief Chade would not hear of it. "As in all of Pharesm's activities, an exactitude of consequence must prevail. It is an unthinkable discrepancy that fifty-four men should consume the food intended for fifty-three."

Cugel could contrive no apposite reply, and sat in silence while the rock-hewers munched at meat pies, cheeses and salt fish. All ignored him save for one, a quarter-ell man whose generosity far exceeded his stature, and who undertook to reserve for Cugel a certain portion of his food. Cugel replied that he was not at all hungry, and rising to his feet wandered off through the project, hoping to discover some forgotten cache of food.

He prowled here and there, but the rubble-gatherers had removed every trace of substance extraneous to the pattern. With appetite unassuaged Cugel arrived at the center of the work where, sprawled on a carved disk, he spied a most peculiar creature: essentially a gelatinous globe swimming with luminous particles from which a number of transparent tubes or tentacles dwindled away to nothing. Cugel bent to examine the creature, which pulsed with a slow internal rhythm. He prodded it with his finger, and bright little flickers rippled away from the point of contact. Interesting: a creature of unique capabilities!

Removing a pin from his garments, he prodded a tentacle, which emitted a peevish pulse of light, while the golden flecks in its substance surged back and forth. More intrigued than ever, Cugel hitched himself close, and gave himself to experimentation, probing here and there, watching the angry flickers and sparkles with great amusement.

A new thought occurred to Cugel. The creature displayed qualities reminiscent of both coelenterate and echinoderm. A terrene nudibranch? A mollusc deprived of its shell? More importantly, was the creature edible?

Cugel brought forth his amulet and applied it to the central globe and to each of the tentacles. He heard neither chime nor buzz: the creature was nonpoisonous. He unsheathed his knife and sought to excise one of the tentacles, but found the substance too resilient and tough to be cut. There was a brazier nearby, kept aglow for forging and sharpening the workers' tools. He lifted the creature by two of its tentacles, carried it to the brazier and arranged it over the fire. He toasted it carefully and, when he deemed it sufficiently cooked, sought to eat it. Finally, after various undignified efforts, he crammed the entire creature down his throat, finding it without taste or sensible nutritive volume.

The stone-carvers were returning to their work. With a significant glance for the foreman Cugel set off down the trail.

Not far distant was the dwelling of Pharesm the Sorcerer: a long low building of melted rock surmounted by eight oddly shaped domes of copper, mica and bright blue glass. Pharesm himself sat at leisure before the dwelling, surveying the valley with a serene and all-inclusive magnanimity. He held up a hand in calm salute. "I wish you pleasant travels and success in all future endeavors."

"The sentiment is naturally valued," said Cugel with some bitterness. "You might however have rendered a more meaningful service by extending a share of your noon meal."

Pharesm's placid benevolence was as before. "This would have been an act of mistaken altruism. Too fulsome a generosity corrupts the recipient and stultifies his resource."

Cugel gave a bitter laugh. "I am a man of iron principle, and I will not complain, even though, lacking any better fare, I was forced to devour a great transparent insect which I found at the heart of your rock-carving."

Pharesm swung about with a suddenly intent expression. "A great transparent insect, you say?"

"Insect, epiphyte, mollusc—who knows? It resembled no creature I have yet seen, and its flavor even after carefully grilling at the brazier, was not distinctive."

Pharesm floated seven feet into the air, to turn the full power of his gaze down at Cugel. He spoke in a low harsh voice: "Describe this creature in detail!"

Wondering at Pharesm's severity, Cugel obeyed. "It was thus and thus as to dimension." He indicated with his hands. "In color it was a gelatinous transparency shot with numberless golden specks. These flickered and pulsed when the creature was disturbed. The tentacles seemed to grow flimsy and disappear rather than terminate. The creature evinced a certain sullen determination, and ingestion proved difficult."

Pharesm clutched at his head, hooking his fingers into the yellow down of his hair. He rolled his eyes upward and uttered a tragic cry. "Ah! Five hundred years I have toiled to entice this creature, despairing, doubting, brooding by night, yet never abandoning hope that my calculations were accurate and my great talisman cogent. Then, when finally it appears, you fall upon it for no other reason than to sate your repulsive gluttony!"

Cugel, somewhat daunted by Pharesm's wrath, asserted his absence of malicious intent. Pharesm would not be mollified. He pointed out that Cugel had committed trespass and hence had forfeited the option of pleading innocence. "Your very existence is a mischief, compounded by bringing the unpleasant fact to my notice. Benevolence prompted me to forebearance, which now I perceive for a grave mistake."

"In this case," stated Cugel with dignity, "I will depart your presence at once. I wish you good fortune for the balance of the day, and now, farewell."

"Not so fast," said Pharesm in the coldest of voices. "Exactitude has been disturbed; the wrong which has been committed demands a counter-act to validate the Law of Equipoise. I can define the gravity of your act in this manner: should I explode you on this instant into the most minute of your parts the atonement would measure one ten-millionth of your offense. A more stringent retribution becomes necessary."

Cugel spoke in great distress. "I understand that an act of consequence was performed, but remember! my participation was basically casual. I categorically declare first my absolute innocence, second my lack of criminal intent, and third my effusive apologies. And now, since I have many leagues to travel, I will—"

Pharesm made a peremptory gesture. Cugel fell silent. Pharesm drew a deep breath. "You fail to understand the calamity you have visited upon me. I will explain, so that you may not be astounded by the rigors which await you. As I have adumbrated, the arrival of the creature was the culmination of my great effort. I determined its nature through a perusal of forty-two thousand librams, all written in cryptic language: a task requiring a hundred years. During a second hundred years I evolved a pattern to draw it in upon itself and prepared exact specification. Next I assembled stone-cutters, and across a period of three hundred years gave solid form to my pattern. Since like subsumes like, the variates and intercongeles create a suprapullulation of all areas, qualities and intervals into a crystorrhoid, whorl, eventually exciting the ponentiation of a pro-ubietal chute. Today occurred the concatenation; the 'creature,' as you call it, pervolved upon itself; in your idiotic malice you devoured it.''

Cugel, with a trace of haughtiness, pointed out that the ''idiotic malice'' to which the distraught sorcerer referred was in actuality simple hunger. ''In any event, what is so extraordinary about the 'creature?' Others equally ugly may be found in the net of any fisherman.''

Pharesm drew himself to his full height, glared down at Cugel. ''The 'creature,' '' he said in a grating voice, ''is TOTALITY. The central globe is all of space, viewed from the inverse. The tubes are vortices into various eras, and what terrible acts you have accomplished with your prodding and poking, your boiling and chewing, are impossible to imagine!''

''What of the effects of digestion?'' inquired Cugel delicately. ''Will the various components of space, time and existence retain their identity after passing the length of my inner tract?''

''Bah. The concept is jejune. Enough to say that you have wreaked damage and created a serious tension in the ontological fabric. Inexorably you are required to restore equilibrium.''

Cugel held out his hands. ''Is it not possible a mistake has been made? That the 'creature' was no more than pseudo-TOTALITY? Or is it conceivable that the 'creature' may by some means be lured forth once more?''

''The first two theories are untenable. As to the last, I must confess that certain frantic expedients have been forming in my mind.'' Pharesm made a sign, and Cugel's feet became attached to the soil. ''I must go to my divinatory and learn the full significance of the distressing events. In due course I will return.''

''At which time I will be feeble with hunger,'' said Cugel fretfully. ''Indeed, a crust of bread and a bite of cheese would have averted all the events for which I am now reproached.''

''Silence!'' thundered Pharesm. ''Do not forget that your penalty remains to be fixed; it is the height of impudent recklessness to hector a person already struggling to maintain his judicious calm!"

"Allow me to say this much," replied Cugel. "If you return from your divining to find me dead and desiccated here on the path, you will have wasted much time fixing upon a penalty."

"The restoration of vitality is a small task," said Pharesm. "A variety of deaths by contrasting processes may well enter into your judgement." He started toward his divinatory, then turned back and made an impatient gesture. "Come, it is easier to feed you than return to the road."

Cugel's feet were once more free and he followed Pharesm through a wide arch into the divinatory. In a broad room with splayed gray walls, illuminated by three-colored polyhedra, Cugel devoured the food Pharesm caused to appear. Meanwhile Pharesm secluded himself in his work-room, where he occupied himself with his divinations. As time passed Cugel grew restless, and on three occasions approached the arched entrance. On each occasion, a Presentment came to deter him, first in the shape of a leaping ghoul, next as a zig-zag blaze of energy, and finally as a score of glittering purple wasps.

Discouraged, Cugel went to a bench and sat waiting with elbows on long legs, hands under his chin.

Pharesm at last reappeared, his robe wrinkled, the fine yellow down of his hair disordered into a multitude of small spikes. Cugel slowly rose to his feet.

"I have learned the whereabouts of TOTALITY," said Pharesm, in a voice like the strokes of a great gong. "In indignation, removing itself from your stomach, it has recoiled a million years into the past."

Cugel gave his head a solemn shake. "Allow me to offer my sympathy, and my counsel, which is: never despair! Perhaps the 'creature' will choose to pass this way again."

"An end to your chatter! TOTALITY must be recovered. Come."

Cugel reluctantly followed Pharesm into a small room walled with blue tile, roofed with a tall cupola of blue and orange glass. Pharesm pointed to a black disk at the center of the floor. "Stand there."

Cugel glumly obeyed. "In a certain sense, I feel that—"

"Silence!" Pharesm came forward. "Notice this object!" He displayed an ivory sphere the size of two fists, carved in exceedingly fine detail. "Here you see the pattern from which my great work is derived. It expresses the symbolic significance of NULLITY to which TOTALITY must necessarily attach itself, by Kratinjae's Second Law of Cryptorrhoid Affinities, with which you are possibly familiar."

"Not in every aspect," said Cugel. "But may I ask your intentions?"

Pharesm's mouth moved in a cool smile. "I am about to attempt one of the most cogent spells ever evolved: a spell so fractious, harsh, and coactive, that Phandaal, Ranking Sorcerer of Grand Motholam, barred its use. If I am able to control it, you will be propelled one million years into the past. There you will reside until you have accomplished your mission, then you may return."

Cugel stepped quickly from the black disk. "I am not the man for this mission, whatever it may be. I fervently urge the use of someone else!"

Pharesm ignored the expostulation. "The mission, of course, is to bring the symbol into contact with TOTALITY." He brought forth a wad of tangled gray tissue. "In order to facilitate your search I endow you with this instrument which relates all possible vocables to every conceivable system of meaning." He thrust the net into Cugel's ear, where it swiftly engaged itself with the nerve of consonant expression. "Now," said Pharesm, "You need listen to a strange language for but three minutes when you become proficient in its use. And now, another article to enhance the prospect of success: this ring. Notice the jewel: should you approach to within a league of TOTALITY, darting lights within the gem will guide you. Is all clear?"

Cugel gave a reluctant nod. "There is another matter to be considered. Assume that your calculations are incorrect and that TOTALITY has returned only nine hundred thousand years into the past: what then? Must I dwell out my life in this possibly barbarous era?"

Pharesm frowned in displeasure. "Such a situation involves an error of ten percent. My system of reckoning seldom admits of deviation greater than one percent."

Cugel began to make calculations, but now Pharesm signaled to the black disk. "Back! And do not again move hence, or you will be the worse for it!"

Sweat oozing from his glands, knees quivering and sagging, Cugel returned to the place designated.

Pharesm retreated to the far end of the room, where he stepped into a coil of gold tubing, which sprang spiraling up to clasp his body. From a desk he took four black disks, which he began to shuffle and juggle with such fantastic dexterity that they blurred in Cugel's sight. Pharesm at last flung the disks away; spinning and wheeling, they hung in the air, gradually drifting toward Cugel.

Pharesm next took up a white tube, pressed it tight against his lips and spoke an incantation. The tube swelled and bulged into a great globe. Pharesm twisted the end shut and, shouting a thunderous spell, hurled the globe at the spinning disks, and all exploded. Cugel was surrounded, seized, jerked in all directions outward, compressed with equal vehemence: the net result, a thrust in a direction contrary to all, with an impetus equivalent to the tide of a million years. Among dazzling lights and distorted visions Cugel was transported beyond his consciousness.

Cugel awoke in a glare of orange-gold sunlight, of a radiance he had never known before. He lay on his back looking up into a sky of warm blue, of lighter tone and softer texture than the indigo sky of his own time.

He tested arms and legs and, finding no damage, sat upright, then slowly rose to his feet, blinking in the unfamiliar radiance.

The topography had changed only slightly. The mountains to the north were taller and of harsher texture, and Cugel could not identify the way he had come (or, more properly, the way he would come). The site of Pharesm's project was now a low forest of feather-light green trees, on which hung clusters of red berries. The valley was as before, though the rivers flowed by different courses and three great cities were visible at varying distances. The air drifting up from the valley carried a strange tart fragrance mingled with an antique exhalation of molder and must, and it seemed to Cugel that a peculiar melancholy hung in the air; in fact, he thought to hear music: a slow plaintive melody, so sad as to bring tears to his eyes. He searched for the source of the music, but it faded and disappeared even as he sought it, and only when he ceased to listen did it return.

For the first time Cugel looked toward the cliffs which rose to the west, and now the sense of *déja-vu* was stronger than ever. Cugel pulled at his chin in puzzlement. The time was a million years previous to that other occasion on which he had seen the cliffs, and hence, by definition, must be the first. But it was also the second time, for he well remembered his initial experience of the cliffs. On the other hand, the logic of time could not be contravened, and by such reckoning this view preceded the other. A paradox, thought Cugel: a puzzle indeed! Which experience had provided the background to the poignant sense of familiarity he had felt on both occasions?

. . . Cugel dismissed the subject as unprofitable and was starting to turn away when movement caught his eye. He looked back up the face of the cliffs, and the air was suddenly full and rich with the music he had heard before, music of anguish and exalted despair. Cugel stared in wonder. A great winged creature wearing white robes flapped on high along the face of the cliff. The wings were long, ribbed with black chitin, sheathed with gray membrane. Cugel watched in awe as it swooped into a cave high up in the face of the cliff.

A gong tolled, from a direction Cugel could not determine. Overtones shuddered across the air, and when they died the unheard music became almost audible. From far over the valley came one of the Winged Beings, carrying a human form, of what age and sex Cugel could not determine. It hovered beside the cliff and dropped its burden. Cugel thought to hear a faint cry and the music was sad, stately, sonorous. The body seemed to fall slowly down the great height and struck at last at the base of the cliff. The Winged Being, after dropping the body, glided to a high ledge, where it folded its wings and stood like a man, staring over the valley.

Cugel shrank back behind a rock. Had he been seen? He could not be sure. He heaved a deep sigh. This sad golden world of the past was not to his liking; the sooner he could leave the better. He examined the ring which Pharesm had furnished, but the gem shone like dull glass, with none of the darting glitters which would point the direction to TOTALITY. It was as Cugel feared. Pharesm had erred in his calculations and Cugel could never return to his own time.

The sound of flapping wings caused him to look into the sky. He shrank back into such concealment as the rock offered. The music of woe swelled and sighed away, as in the light of the setting sun the winged creature hovered beside the cliff and dropped its victim. Then it landed on a ledge with a great flapping of wings and entered a cave.

Cugel rose to his feet and ran crouching down the path through the amber dusk

The path presently entered a grove of trees, and here Cugel paused to catch his breath, after which he proceeded more circumspectly. He crossed a path of cultivated ground on which stood a vacant hut. Cugel considered it as shelter for the night, but thought to see a dark shape watching from the interior and passed it by.

The trail led away from the cliffs; across rolling downs, and just before the twilight gave way to night Cugel came to a village standing on the banks of a pond.

Cugel approached warily, but was encouraged by the signs of tidiness and good husbandry. In a park beside the pond stood a pavilion possibly intended for music, miming or declamation; surrounding the park were small narrow houses with high gables, the ridges of which were raised in decorative scallops. Opposite the pond was a larger building, with an ornate front of woven wood and enameled plaques of red, blue and yellow. Three tall gables served as its roof, the central ridge supporting an intricate carved panel, while those to either side bore a series of small spherical blue lamps. At the front was a wide pergola sheltering benches, tables and an open space, all illuminated by red and green fire-fans. Here townsfolk took their ease, inhaling incense and drinking wine, while youths and maidens cavorted in an eccentric high-kicking dance, to the music of pipers and a concertina.

Emboldened by the placidity of the scene, Cugel approached. The villagers were of a type he had never before encountered, of no great stature, with generally large heads and long restless arms. Their skin was a rich pumpkin orange; their eyes and teeth were black; their hair, likewise black, hung smoothly down beside the faces of the men to terminate in a fringe of blue beads, while the women wound their hair around white rings and pegs, to arrive at a coiffure of no small complexity. The features were heavy at jaw and cheek-bone; the long wide-spaced eyes drooped in a droll manner at the outer corners. The noses and ears were long and were under considerable muscular control, endowing the faces with great vivacity. The men wore flounced black kirtles, brown surcoats, headgear consisting of a wide black disk, a black cylinder, another lesser disk, surmounted by a gilded ball. The women wore black trousers, brown jackets with enameled disks at the navel, and at each buttock a simulated tail of green or red plumes, possibly an indication as to marital status.

Cugel stepped into the light of the fire-fans; instantly all talk ceased. Noses became rigid, eyes stared, ears twisted about in curiosity. Cugel smiled to left and right, waved his hands in a debonair all-inclusive greeting, and took a seat at an empty table.

There were mutters of astonishment at the various tables, too quiet to reach Cugel's ears. Presently one of the elders arose and approaching Cugel's table spoke a sentence, which Cugel found unintelligible, for with insufficient scope, Pharesm's mesh as yet failed to yield meaning. Cugel smiled politely, held wide his hands in a gesture of well-meaning helplessness. The elder spoke once more, in a rather sharper voice, and again Cugel indicated his inability to understand. The elder gave his ears a sharp disapproving jerk and turned away. Cugel signaled to the proprietor, pointed to the bread and wine on a nearby table and signified his desire that the same be brought to him.

The proprietor voiced a query which, for all its unintelligibility, Cugel was able to interpret. He brought forth a gold coin, and, satisfied, the proprietor turned away.

Conversation recommenced at the various tables and before long the vocables conveyed meaning to Cugel. When he had eaten and drunk, he rose to his feet and walked to the table of the elder who had first spoken to him, where he bowed respectfully. "Do I have permission to join you at your table?"

"Certainly; if you are so inclined. Sit." The elder indicated a seat. "From your behavior I assumed that you were not only deaf and dumb, but also guilty of mental retardation. It is now clear, at least, that you hear and speak."

"I profess rationality as well," said Cugel. "As a traveler from afar, ignorant of your customs, I thought it best to watch quietly a few moments, lest in error I commit solecism."

"Ingenious but peculiar," was the elder's comment. "Still, your conduct offers no explicit contradiction to orthodoxy. May I inquire the urgency which brings you to Farwan?"

Cugel glanced at his ring; the crystal was dull and lifeless: TOTALITY was clearly elsewhere. "My homeland is uncultured; I travel that I may learn the modes and styles of more civilized folk."

"Indeed!" The elder mulled the matter over for a moment, nodded in qualified approval. "Your garments and physiognomy are of a type unfamiliar to me; where is this homeland of yours?"

"It lies in a region so remote," said Cugel, "that never till this instant had I knowledge of the land of Farwan!"

The elder flattened his ears in surprise. "What? Glorious Farwan, unknown? The great cities Impergos, Tharuwe, Rhaverjand—all unheard of? What of the illustrious Sembers? Surely the fame of the Sembers has reached you? They expelled the star-pirates; they brought the sea to the Land of Platforms; the splendor of Padara Palace is beyond description!"

Cugel sadly shook his head. "No rumor of this extraordinary magnificence has come to my ears."

The elder gave his nose a saturnine twitch. Cugel was clearly a dolt. He said shortly, "Matters are as I state."

"I doubt nothing," said Cugel. "In fact I admit to ignorance. But tell me more, for I may be forced to abide long in this region. For instance, what of the Winged Beings that reside in the cliff? What manner of creature are they?"

The elder pointed toward the sky. "If you had the eyes of a nocturnal titvit you might note a dark moon which reels around the earth, and which cannot be seen except when it casts its shadow upon the sun. The Winged Beings are denizens of this dark world and their ultimate nature is unknown. They serve the Great God Yelisea in this fashion: whenever comes the time for man or woman to die, the Winged Beings are informed by a despairing signal from the dying person's norn. They thereupon descend upon the unfortunate and convey him to their caves, which in actuality constitute a magic opening into the blessed land Byssom."

Cugel leaned back, black eyebrows raised in a somewhat quizzical arch. "Indeed, indeed," he said, in a voice which the elder found insufficiently earnest.

"There can be no doubt as to the truth of the facts as I have stated them. Orthodoxy derives from this axiomatic foundation, and the two systems are mutually reinforcing: hence each is doubly validated."

Cugel frowned. "The matter undoubtedly goes as you aver—but are the Winged Beings consistently accurate in their choice of victim?"

The elder rapped the table in annoyance. "The doctrine is irrefutable, for those whom the Winged Beings take never survive, even when they appear in the best of health. Admittedly the fall upon the rocks conduces toward death, but it is the mercy of Yelisea which sees fit to grant a speedy extinction, rather than the duration of a possibly agonizing canker. The system is wholly beneficent. The Winged Beings summon only the moribund, which are then thrust through the cliff into the blessed land Byssom. Occasionally a heretic argues otherwise and in this case—but I am sure that you share the orthodox view?"

"Wholeheartedly," Cugel asserted. "The tenets of your belief are demonstrably accurate." And he drank deep of his wine. Even as he set down the goblet a murmur of music whispered through the air: a concord infinitely sweet, infinitely melancholy. All sitting under the pergola became silent—though Cugel was unsure that he in fact had heard music.

The elder huddled forward a trifle, and drank from his own goblet. Only then did he glance up. "The Winged Beings are passing over even now."

Cugel pulled thoughtfully at his chin. "How does one protect himself from the Winged Beings?"

The question was ill-put; the elder glared, an act which included the curling forward of his ears. "If a person is about to die, the Winged Beings appear. If not, he need have no fear."

Cugel nodded several times. "You have clarified my perplexity. Tomorrow—since you and I are manifestly in the best of health—let us walk up the hill and saunter back and forth near the cliff."

"No," said the elder, "and for this reason: the atmosphere at such an elevation is insalubrious; a person is likely to inhale a noxious fume, which entails damage to the health."

"I comprehend perfectly," said Cugel. "Shall we abandon this dismal topic? For the nonce we are alive and concealed to some extent by the vines which shroud the pergola. Let us eat and drink and watch the merrymaking. The youths of the village dance with great agility."

The elder drained his goblet and rose to his feet. "You may do as you please; as for me, it is time for my Ritual Abasement, this act being an integral part of our belief."

"I will perform something of a like nature by and by," said Cugel. "I wish you the enjoyment of your rite."

The elder departed the pergola and Cugel was left by himself. Presently certain youths, attracted by curiosity, joined him, and Cugel explained his presence once again, though with less emphasis upon the barbaric crudity of his native land, for several girls had joined the group, and Cugel was stimulated by their exotic coloring and the vivacity of their attitudes. Much wine was served and Cugel was persuaded to attempt the kicking, jumping local dance, which he performed without discredit.

The exercise brought him into close proximity with an especially beguiling girl, who announced her name to be Zhiaml Vraz. At the conclusion of the dance, she put her arm around his waist, conducted him back to the table, and settled herself upon his lap. This act of familiarity excited no apparent disapproval among the others of the group, and Cugel was emboldened further. "I have not yet arranged for a bed-chamber; perhaps I should do so before the hour grows late."

The girl signaled the innkeeper. "Perhaps you have reserved a chamber for this chisel-faced stranger?"

"Indeed; I will display it for his approval."

He took Cugel to a pleasant chamber on the ground floor, furnished with couch, commode, rug and lamp. On one wall hung a tapestry woven in purple and black; on another was a representation of a peculiarly ugly baby which seemed trapped or compressed in a transparent globe. The room suited Cugel; he announced as much to the innkeeper and returned to the pergola, where now the merrymakers were commencing to disperse. The girl Zhiaml Vraz yet remained, and she welcomed Cugel with a warmth which undid the last vestige of his caution. After another goblet of wine; he leaned close to her ear. "Perhaps I am over-prompt; perhaps I overindulge my vanity; perhaps I contravene the normal decorum of the village—but is there reason why we should not repair to my chamber, and there amuse ourselves?"

"None whatever," the girl said. "I am unwed and until this time may conduct myself as I wish, for this is our custom."

"Excellent," said Cugel. "Do you care to precede me, or walk discreetly to the rear?"

''We shall go together; there is no need for furtiveness!''

Together they went to the chamber and performed a number of erotic exercises, after which Cugel collapsed into a sleep of utter exhaustion, for his day had been taxing.

During the middle hours he awoke to find Zhiaml Vraz departed from the chamber, a fact which in his drowsiness caused him no distress and he once more returned to sleep.

The sound of the door angrily flung ajar aroused him; he sat up on the couch to find the sun not yet arisen, and a deputation led by the elder regarding him with horror and disgust.

The elder pointed a long quivering finger through the gloom. ''I thought to detect heretical opinion; now the fact is known! Notice: he sleeps with neither head-covering nor devotional salve on his chin. The girl Zhiaml Vraz reports that at no time in their congress did the villain call out for the approval of Yelisea!''

''Heresy beyond a doubt!'' declared the others of the deputation.

''What else could be expected of an outlander?'' asked the elder contemptuously. ''Look! even now he refuses to make the sacred sign.''

''I do not know the sacred sign!'' Cugel expostulated. ''I know nothing of your rites! This is not heresy, it is simple ignorance!''

''I cannot believe this,'' said the elder. ''Only last night I outlined the nature of orthodoxy.''

''The situation is grievous,'' said another in a voice of portentous melancholy. ''Heresy exists only through putrefaction of the Lobe of Correctitude.''

''This is an incurable and fatal mortification,'' stated another, no less dolefully.

''True! Alas, too true!'' sighed one who stood by the door. ''Unfortunate man!''

''Come!'' called the elder. ''We must deal with the matter at once.''

''Do not trouble yourself,'' said Cugel. ''Allow me to dress myself and I will depart the village never to return.''

''To spread your detestable doctrine elsewhere? By no means!''

And now Cugel was seized and hauled naked from the chamber. Out across the park he was marched, and to the pavilion at the center. Several of the group erected an enclosure formed of wooden posts on the platform of the pavilion and into this enclosure Cugel was thrust. ''What do you do?'' he cried out. ''I wish no part of your rites!''

He was ignored, and stood peering between the interstices of the enclosure while certain of the villagers sent aloft a large balloon of green paper buoyed by hot air, carrying three green fire-fans below.

Dawn showed sallow in the west. The villagers, with all arranged to their satisfaction, withdrew to the edge of the park. Cugel attempted to climb from the enclosure, but the wooden rods were of such dimension and spacing as to allow him no grip.

The sky lightened; high above burnt the green fire-fans. Cugel, hunched and in goose-flesh from the morning chill, walked back and forth the length of the enclosure. He stopped short, as from afar came the haunting music. It grew louder, seeming to reach the very threshold of audibility. High in the sky appeared a Winged Being, white robes trailing and flapping. Down it settled, and Cugel's joints became limp and loose.

The Winged Being hovered over the enclosure, dropped, enfolded Cugel in its white robe and endeavored to bear him aloft. But Cugel had seized a bar of the enclosure and the Winged Being flapped in vain. The bar creaked, groaned, cracked. Cugel fought free of the stifling cloak and tore at the bar with hysterical strength; it snapped and splintered. Cugel seized a fragment and stabbed at the Winged Being. The sharp stick punctured the white cloak, and the Winged Being buffeted Cugel with a wing. Cugel seized one of the chitin ribs and with a mighty effort twisted it around backward, so that the substance cracked and broke and the wing hung torn. The Winged Being, aghast, gave a great bound which carried both it and Cugel out upon the pavilion, and now it hopped through the village trailing its broken wing.

Cugel ran behind belaboring it with a cudgel he had seized up. He glimpsed the villagers staring in awe; their mouths were wide and wet, and they might have been screaming but he heard nothing. The Winged Being hopped faster, up the trail toward the cliff, with Cugel wielding the cudgel with all his strength. The golden sun rose over the far mountains; the Winged Being suddenly turned to face Cugel, and Cugel felt the glare of its eyes, though the visage, if such there was, was concealed beneath the hood of the cloak. Abashed and panting, Cugel stood back, and now it occurred to him that he stood almost defenseless should others drop on him from on high. So now he shouted an imprecation at the creature and turned back to the village.

All had fled. The village was deserted. Cugel laughed aloud. He went to the inn, dressed himself in his garments and buckled on his sword. He went out into the taproom and looking into the till found a number of coins, which he transferred to his pouch, alongside the ivory representation of NULLITY. He returned outdoors: best to depart while none were on hand to detain him.

A flicker of light attracted his attention: the ring on his finger glinted with dozens of streaming sparks, and all pointed up the trail, toward the cliffs.

Cugel shook his head wearily, then checked the darting lights once again. Without ambiguity they directed him back the way he had come. Pharesm's calculations, after all, had been accurate. He had best act with decision, lest TOTALITY once more drift beyond his reach.

He delayed only long enough to find an axe, and hastened up the trail, following the glittering sparks of the ring.

Not far from where he had left it, he came upon the maimed Winged Being, now sitting on a rock beside the road, the hood drawn over its head. Cugel picked up a stone and heaved it at the creature, which collapsed into sudden dust, leaving only a tumble of white cloth to signal the fact of its existence.

Cugel continued up the road, keeping to such cover as offered itself, but to no avail. Overhead hovered Winged Beings, flapping and swooping. Cugel made play with the axe, striking at the wings, and the creatures flew high, circling above.

Cugel consulted the ring and was led on up the trail, with the Winged Beings hovering just above. The ring coruscated with the intensity of its message: there was TOTALITY, resting blandly on a rock!

Cugel restrained the cry of exultation which rose in his throat. He brought forth the ivory symbol of NULLITY, ran forward and applied it to the gelatinous central globe.

As Pharesm had asserted, adherence was instant. With the contact Cugel could feel the spell which bound him to the olden time dissolving.

A swoop, a buffet of great wings! Cugel was knocked to the ground. White cloth enveloped him, and with one hand holding NULLITY he was unable to swing his axe. This was now wrenched from his grasp. He released NULLITY, gripped a rock, kicked, somehow freed himself, and sprang for his axe. The Winged Being seized NULLITY, to which TOTALITY was attached, and bore both aloft and toward a cave high in the cliffs.

Great forces were pulling at Cugel, whirling in all directions at once. There was a roaring in his ears, a flutter of violet lights, and Cugel fell a million years into the future.

* * *

He recovered consciousness in the blue-tiled room with the sting of an aromatic liquor at his lips. Pharesm, bending over him, patted his face and poured more of the liquor into his mouth. ''Awake! Where is TOTALITY? How are you returned?''

Cugel pushed him aside, and sat up on the couch.

''TOTALITY!'' roared Pharesm. ''Where is it? Where is my talisman?''

''I will explain,'' said Cugel in a thick voice. ''I had it in my grasp, and it was wrenched away by winged creatures in the service of Great God Yelisea.''

''Tell me, tell me!''

Cugel recounted the circumstances which had led first to gaining and then losing that which Pharesm sought. As he talked, Pharesm's face became damp with grief, and his shoulders sagged. At last he marched Cugel outside, into the dim red light of late afternoon. Together they scrutinized the cliffs which now towered desolate and lifeless above them. ''To which cave did the creature fly?'' asked Pharesm. ''Point it out, if you are able!''

Cugel pointed. ''There, or so it would seem. All was confusion, all a tumble of wings and white robes . . .''

''Remain here.'' Pharesm went inside the workroom and presently returned. ''I give you light,'' he said, and handed Cugel a cold white flame tied into a silver chain. ''Prepare yourself.''

At Cugel's feet he cast a pellet which broke into a vortex, and Cugel was carried dizzily aloft to that crumbling ledge which he had indicated to Pharesm. Nearby was the dark opening into a cave. Cugel turned the flame within. He saw a dusty passage, three strides wide and higher than he could reach. It led back into the cliff, twisting slightly to the side. It seemed barren of all life.

Holding the lamp before him, Cugel slowly moved along the passage, his heart thumping for dread of something he could not define. He stopped short: music? The memory of music? He listened and could hear nothing; but when he tried to step forward fear clamped his legs. He held high the lantern and peered down the dusty passage. Where did it lead? What lay beyond? Dusty cave? Demonland? The blessed land Byssom? Cugel slowly proceeded, every sense alert. On a ledge he spied a shriveled brown spheroid: the talisman he had carried into the past. TOTALITY had long since disengaged itself and departed.

Cugel carefully lifted the object, which was brittle with the age of a million years, and returned to the ledge. The vortex, at a command from Pharesm, conveyed Cugel back to the ground.

Dreading the wrath of Pharesm, Cugel tendered the withered talisman.

Pharesm took it and held it between thumb and forefinger. "This was all?"

"There was nothing more."

Pharesm let the object fall. It struck and instantly became dust. Pharesm looked at Cugel, took a deep breath, then turned with a gesture of unspeakable frustration and marched back to his divinatory.

Cugel gratefully moved off down the trail, past the workmen standing in an anxious group waiting for orders. They eyed Cugel sullenly and a two-ell man hurled a rock. Cugel shrugged and continued south along the trail. Presently he passed the site of the village, now a waste overgrown with gnarled old trees. The pond had disappeared and the ground was hard and dry. In the valley below were ruins, but none of these marked the sites of the ancient cities Impergos, Tharuwe and Rhaverjand, now gone beyond memory.

Cugel walked south. Behind him the cliffs merged with haze and presently were lost to view.

5

The Pilgrims

1: At the Inn

For the better part of a day Cugel had traveled a dreary waste where nothing grew but salt-grass; then, only a few minutes before sunset, he arrived at the bank of a broad slow river, beside which ran a road. A half-mile to his right stood a tall structure of timber and dark brown stucco, evidently an inn. The sight gave Cugel vast satisfaction, for he had eaten nothing the whole of the day, and had spent the previous night in a tree. Ten minutes later he pushed open the heavy iron-bound door, and entered the inn.

He stood in a vestibule. To either side were diamond-paned casements, burnt lavender with age, where the setting sun scattered a thousand refractions. From the common room came the cheerful hum of voices, the clank of pottery and glass, the smell of ancient wood, waxed tile, leather and simmering cauldrons. Cugel stepped forward to find a score of men gathered about the fire, drinking wine and exchanging the large talk of travelers.

The landlord stood behind a counter: a stocky man hardly as tall as Cugel's shoulder, with a high-domed bald head and a black beard hanging a foot below his chin. His eyes were protuberant and heavy-lidded; his expression was as placid and calm as the flow of the river. At Cugel's request for accommodation he dubiously pulled at his nose. ''Already I am overextended, with pilgrims upon the route to Erze Damath. Those you see upon the benches are not even half of all I must lodge this night. I will put down a pallet in the hall, if such will content you; I can do no more.''

Cugel gave a sigh of fretful dissatisfaction. ''This fails to meet my expectations. I strongly desire a private chamber with a couch of good quality, a window overlooking the river, a heavy carpet to muffle the songs and slogans of the pot-room."

"I fear that you will be disappointed," said the landlord without emotion. "The single chamber of this description is already occupied, by that man with the yellow beard sitting yonder: a certain Lodermulch, also traveling to Erze Damath."

"Perhaps, on the plea of emergency, you might persuade him to vacate the chamber and occupy the pallet in my stead," suggested Cugel.

"I doubt if he is capable of such abnegation," the innkeeper replied. "But why not put the inquiry yourself? I, frankly, do not wish to broach the matter."

Cugel, surveying Lodermulch's strongly-marked features, his muscular arms and the somewhat disdainful manner in which he listened to the talk of the pilgrims, was inclined to join the innkeeper in his assessment of Lodermulch's character, and made no move to press the request. "It seems that I must occupy the pallet. Now, as to my supper: I require a fowl, suitably stuffed, trussed, roasted and garnished, accompanied by whatever side-dishes your kitchen affords."

"My kitchen is overtaxed and you must eat lentils with the pilgrims," said the landlord. "A single fowl is on hand, and this again has been reserved to the order of Lodermulch, for his evening repast."

Cugel shrugged in vexation. "No matter. I will wash the dust of travel from my face, and then take a goblet of wine."

"To the rear is flowing water and a trough occasionally used for this purpose. I furnish unguents, pungent oils and hot cloths at extra charge."

"The water will suffice." Cugel walked to the rear of the inn, where he found a basin. After washing he looked about and noticed at some small distance a shed, stoutly constructed of timber. He started back into the inn, then halted and once more examined the shed. He crossed the intervening area, opened the door and looked within; then, engrossed in thought, he returned to the common room. The landlord served him a mug of mulled wine, which he took to an inconspicuous bench.

Lodermulch had been asked his opinion of the so-called Funambulous Evangels, who, refusing to place their feet upon the ground, went about their tasks by tightrope. In a curt voice Lodermulch exposed the fallacies of this particular doctrine. "They reckon the age of the earth at twenty-nine eons, rather than the customary twenty-three. They stipulate that for every square ell of soil two and one quarter million men have died and laid down their dust, thus creating a dank and ubiquitous mantle of lich-mold, upon which it is sacrilege to walk. The argument has a superficial plausibility, but consider: the dust of one desiccated corpse, spread over a square ell, affords a layer one thirty-third of an inch in depth. The total therefore represents almost one mile of compacted corpse-dust mantling the earth's surface, which is manifestly false."

A member of the sect, who, without access to his customary ropes, walked in cumbersome ceremonial shoes, made an excited expostulation. "You speak with neither logic nor comprehension! How can you be so absolute?"

Lodermulch raised his tufted eyebrows in surly displeasure. "Must I really expatiate? At the ocean's shore, does a cliff one mile in altitude follow the demarcation between land and sea? No. Everywhere is inequality. Headlands extend into the water; more often beaches of pure white sand are found. Nowhere are the massive buttresses of gray-white tuff upon which the doctrines of your sect depend."

"Inconsequential claptrap!" sputtered the Funambule.

"What is this?" demanded Lodermulch, expanding his massive chest. "I am not accustomed to derision!"

"No derision, but hard and cold refutal of your dogmatism! We claim that a proportion of the dust is blown into the ocean, a portion hangs suspended in the air, a portion seeps through crevices into underground caverns, and another portion is absorbed by trees, grasses and certain insects, so that little more than a half-mile of ancestral sediment covers the earth upon which it is sacrilege to tread. Why are not the cliffs you mention everywhere visible? Because of that moistness exhaled and expelled by innumerable men of the past! This has raised the ocean an exact equivalence, so that no brink or precipice can be noted; and herein lies your fallacy."

"Bah," muttered Lodermulch, turning away. "Somewhere there is a flaw in your concepts."

"By no means!" asserted the evangel, with that fervor which distinguished his kind. "Therefore, from respect to the dead, we walk aloft, on ropes and edges, and when we must travel, we use specially sanctified footgear."

During the conversation Cugel had departed the room. Now a moon-faced stripling wearing the smock of a porter approached the group. "You are the worthy Lodermulch?" he asked the person so designated.

Lodermulch squared about in his chair. "I am he."

"I bear a message, from one who has brought certain sums of money due you. He waits in a small shed behind the inn."

Lodermulch frowned increduously. "You are certain that this person required Lodermulch, Provost of Barlig Township?"

"Indeed, sir, the name was specifically so."

"And what man bore the message?"

"He was a tall man, wearing a voluminous hood, and described himself as one of your intimates."

"Indeed," ruminated Lodermulch. "Tyzog, perhaps? Or conceivably Krednip. . . . Why would they not approach me directly? No doubt there is some good reason." He heaved his bulk erect. "I suppose I must investigate."

He stalked from the common room, circled the inn, and looked through the dim light toward the shed. "Ho there!" he called. "Tyzog? Krednip? Come forth!"

There was no response. Lodermulch went to peer into the shed. As soon as he had stepped within, Cugel came around from the rear, slammed shut the door, and threw bar and bolts.

Ignoring the muffled pounding and angry calls, Cugel returned into the inn. He sought out the innkeeper. "An alteration in arrangements: Lodermulch has been called away. He will require neither his chamber nor his roast fowl and has kindly urged both upon me!"

The innkeeper pulled at his beard, went to the door, and looked up and down the road. Slowly he returned. "Extraordinary! He has paid for both chamber and fowl, and made no representations regarding rebate."

"We arranged a settlement to our mutual satisfaction. To recompense you for extra effort, I now pay an additional three terces."

The innkeeper shrugged and took the coins. "It is all the same to me. Come, I will lead you to the chamber."

Cugel inspected the chamber and was well satisfied. Presently his supper was served. The roast fowl was beyond reproach, as were the additional dishes Lodermulch had ordered and which the landlord included with the meal.

Before retiring Cugel strolled behind the inn and satisfied himself that the bar at the door of the shed was in good order and that Lodermulch's hoarse calls were unlikely to attract attention. He rapped sharply on the door. "Peace, Lodermulch!" he called out sternly. "This is I, the innkeeper! Do not bellow so loudly; you will disturb my guests at their slumber."

Without waiting for reply, Cugel returned to the common room, where he fell into conversation with the leader of the pilgrim band.

This was Garstang, a man spare and taut, with a waxen skin, a fragile skull, hooded eyes and a meticulous nose so thin as to be translucent when impinged across a light. Addressing him as a man of experience and erudition, Cugel inquired the route to Almery, but Garstang tended to believe the region sheerly imaginary.

Cugel asserted otherwise. "Almery is a region distinct; I vouch for this personally."

"Your knowledge, then, is more profound than my own," stated Garstang. "This river is the Asc; the land to this side is Sudun, across is Lelias. To the south lies Erze Damath, where you would be wise to travel, thence perhaps, west across the Silver Desert and the Songan Sea, where you might make new inquiry."

"I will do as you suggest," said Cugel.

"We, devout Gilfigites all, are bound for Erze Damath and the Lustral Rite at the Black Obelisk," said Garstang. "Since the route lies through wastes, we are banded together against the erbs and the gids. If you wish to join the group, to share both privileges and restrictions, you are welcome."

"The privileges are self-evident," said Cugel. "As to the restrictions?"

"Merely to obey the commands of the leader, which is to say, myself, and contribute a share of the expenses."

"I agree, without qualification," said Cugel.

"Excellent! We march on the morrow at dawn." Garstang pointed out certain other members of the group, which numbered fifty-seven. "There is Vitz, locutor to our little band, and there sits Casmyre, the theoretician. The man with iron teeth is Arlo, and he of the blue hat and silver buckle is Voynod, a wizard of no small repute. Absent from the room is the estimable though agnostic Lodermulch, as well as the unequivocally devout Subucule. Perhaps they seek to sway each other's convictions. The two who game with dice are Parso and Sayanase. There is Hant, there Cray." Garstang named several others, citing their attributes. At last Cugel, pleading fatigue, repaired to his chamber. He relaxed upon the couch and at once fell asleep.

During the small hours he was subjected to a disturbance. Lodermulch, digging into the floor of the shed, then burrowing under the wall, had secured his freedom and went at once to the inn. First he tried the door to Cugel's chamber, which Cugel had been at pains to lock.

"Who is there?" called Cugel.

"Open! It is I, Lodermulch. This is the chamber where I wish to sleep!"

"By no means," declared Cugel. "I paid a princely sum to secure a bed, and was even forced to wait while the landlord evicted a previous tenant. Be off with you now; I suspect that you are drunk; if you wish further revelry, rouse the wine-steward."

Lodermulch stamped away. Cugel lay back once more.

Presently he heard the thud of blows, and the landlord's cry as Lodermulch seized his beard. Lodermulch was eventually thrust from the inn, by the joint efforts of the innkeeper, his spouse, the porter, the pot-boy and others; whereupon Cugel gratefully returned to sleep.

Before dawn the pilgrims, together with Cugel, arose and took their breakfast. The innkeeper seemed somewhat sullen of mood, and displayed bruises, but he put no questions to Cugel, who in his turn initiated no conversation.

After breakfast the pilgrims assembled in the road, where they were joined by Lodermulch, who had spent the night pacing up and down the road.

Garstang made a count of the group, then blew a great blast on his whistle. The pilgrims marched forward, across the bridge, and set off along the south bank of the Asc toward Erze Damath.

2: The Raft on the River

For three days the pilgrims proceeded beside the Asc, at night sleeping behind a barricade evoked by the wizard Voynod from a circlet of ivory slivers: a precaution of necessity, for beyond the bars, barely visible by the rays of the fire, were creatures anxious to join the company: deodands softly pleading, erbs shifting posture back and forth from four feet to two, comfortable in neither style. Once a gid attempted to leap the barricade; on another occasion three hoons joined to thrust against the posts—backing off, racing forward, to strike with grunts of effort, while from within the pilgrims watched in fascination.

Cugel stepped close, to touch a flaming brand to one of the heaving shapes, and elicited a scream of fury. A great gray arm snatched through the gap; Cugel jumped back for his life. The barricade held and presently the creatures fell to quarreling and departed.

On the evening of the third day the party came to the confluence of the Asc with a great slow river which Garstang indentified as the Scamander. Nearby stood a forest of tall baldamas, pines and spinth oaks. With the help of local woodcutters trees were felled, trimmed and conveyed to the water's edge, where a raft was fabricated. With all the pilgrims aboard, the raft was poled out into the current, where it drifted downstream in ease and silence.

For five days the raft moved on the broad Scamander, sometimes almost out of sight of the banks, sometimes gliding close beside the reeds which lined the shore. With nothing better to do, the pilgrims engaged in lengthy disputations, and the diversity of opinion upon every issue was remarkable. As often as not the talk explored metaphysical arcana, or the subtleties of Gilfigite principle.

Subucule, the most devout of the pilgrims, stated his credo in detail. Essentially he professed the orthodox Gilfigite theosophy, in which Zo Zam, the eight-headed deity, after creating cosmos, struck off his toe, which then became Gilfig, while the drops of blood dispersed to form the eight races of mankind. Roremaund, a skeptic, attacked the doctrine: "Who created this hypothetical 'creator' of yours? Another 'creator?' Far simpler merely to presuppose the end product: in this case, a blinking sun and a dying earth!" To which Subucule cited the Gilfigite Text in crushing refutal.

One named Bluner staunchly propounded his own creed. He believed the sun to be a cell in the corpus of a great deity, who had created the cosmos in a process analogous to the growth of a lichen along a rock.

Subucule considered the thesis over-elaborate: "If the sun were a cell, what then becomes the nature of the earth?"

"An animalcule deriving nutriment," replied Bluner. "Such dependencies are known elsewhere and need not evoke astonishment."

"What then attacks the sun?" demanded Vitz in scorn. "Another animalcule similar to earth?"

Bluner began a detailed exposition of his organon, but before long was interrupted by Pralixus, a tall thin man with piercing green eyes. "Listen to me; I know all; my doctrine is simplicity itself. A vast number of conditions are possible, and there are an even greater number of impossibilities. Our cosmos is a possible condition: it exists. Why? Time is infinite, which is to say that every possible condition must come to pass. Since we reside in this particular possibility and know of no other, we arrogate to ourselves the quality of singleness. In truth, any universe which is possible sooner or later, not once but many times, will exist."

"I tend to a similar doctrine, though a devout Gilfigite," stated Casmyre the theoretician. "My philosophy presupposes a succession of creators, each absolute in his own right. To paraphrase the learned Pralixus, if a deity is possible, it must exist! Only impossible deities will not exist! The eight-headed Zo Zam who struck off his Divine Toe is possible, and hence exists, as is attested by the Gilfigite Texts!"

Subucule blinked, opened his mouth to speak, then closed it once more. Roremaund, the skeptic, turned away to inspect the waters of the Scamander.

Garstang, sitting to the side, smiled thoughtfully. "And you, Cugel the Clever, for once you are reticent. What is your belief?"

"It is somewhat inchoate," Cugel admitted. "I have assimilated a variety of viewpoints, each authoritative in its own right: from the priests at the Temple of Teleologues; from a bewitched bird who plucked messages from a box; from a fasting anchorite who drank a bottle of pink elixir which I offered him in jest. The resulting visions were contradictory but of great profundity. My world-scheme, hence, is syncretic."

"Interesting," said Garstang. "Lodermulch, what of you?"

"Ha," growled Lodermulch. "Notice this rent in my garment; I am at a loss to explain its presence! I am even more puzzled by the existence of the universe."

Others spoke. Voynod the wizard defined the known cosmos as the shadow of a region ruled by ghosts, themselves dependent for existence upon the psychic energies of men. The devout Subucule denounced this scheme as contrary to the Protocols of Gilfig.

The argument continued at length. Cugel and one or two others including Lodermulch became bored and instituted a game of chance, using dice and cards and counters. The stakes, originally nominal, began to grow. Lodermulch at first won scantily, then lost ever greater sums, while Cugel won stake after stake. Lodermulch presently flung down the dice and seizing Cugel's elbow shook it, to dislodge several additional dice from the cuff of his jacket. "Well then!" bawled Lodermulch, "what have we here? I thought to detect knavery, and here is justification! Return my money on the instant!"

"How can you say so?" demanded Cugel. "Where have you demonstrated chicanery? I carry dice—what of that? Am I required to throw my property into the Scamander, before engaging in a game? You demean my reputation!"

"I care nothing for this," retorted Lodermulch. "I merely wish the return of my money."

"Impossible," said Cugel. "For all your bluster you have proved no malfeasance."

"Proof?" roared Lodermulch. "Need there be further? Notice these dice, all askew, some with identical markings on three sides, others rolling only with great effort, so heavy are they at one edge."

"Curios only," explained Cugel. He indicated Voynod the wizard, who had been watching. "Here is a man as keen of eye as he is agile of brain; ask if any illicit transaction was evident."

''None was evident,'' stated Voynod. ''In my estimation Lodermulch has made an over-hasty accusation.''

Garstang came forward, and heard the controversy. He spoke in a voice both judicious and conciliatory: ''Trust is essential in a company such as ours, comrades and devout Gilfigites all. There can be no question of malice or deceit! Surely, Lodermulch, you have misjudged our friend, Cugel!''

Lodermulch laughed harshly. ''If this is conduct characteristic of the devout, I am fortunate not to have fallen in with ordinary folk!'' With this remark, he took himself to a corner of the raft, where he seated himself and fixed Cugel with a glance of menace and loathing.

Garstang shook his head in distress. ''I fear Lodermulch has been offended. Perhaps, Cugel, if in a spirit of amity you were to return his gold—''

Cugel made a firm refusal. ''It is a matter of principle. Lodermulch has assailed my most valuable possession, which is to say, my honor.''

''Your nicety is commendable,'' said Garstang, ''and Lodermulch has behaved tactlessly. Still, for the sake of good-fellowship—no? Well, I cannot argue the point. Ha hum. Always small troubles to fret us.'' Shaking his head, he departed.

Cugel gathered his winnings, together with the dice which Lodermulch had dislodged from his sleeve. ''An unsettling incident,'' he told Voynod. ''A boor, this Lodermulch! He has offended everyone; all have quit the game.''

''Perhaps because all the money is in your possession,'' Voynod suggested.

Cugel examined his winnings with an air of surprise. ''I never suspected that they were so substantial! Perhaps you will accept this sum to spare me the effort of carrying it?''

Voynod acquiesced and a share of the winnings changed hands.

Not long after, while the raft floated placidly along the river, the sun gave an alarming pulse. A purple film formed upon the surface like tarnish, then dissolved. Certain of the pilgrims ran back and forth in alarm, crying, ''The sun goes dark! Prepare for the chill!''

Garstang, however, held up his hands in reassurance. ''Calm, all! The quaver has departed, the sun is as before!''

''Think!'' urged Subucule with great earnestness. ''Would Gilfig allow this cataclysm, even while we travel to worship at the Black Obelisk?''

The group became quiet, though each had his personal interpretation of the event. Vitz, the locutor, saw an analogy to the blurring of vision, which might be cured by vigorous blinking. Voynod declared, "If all goes well at Erze Damath, I plan to dedicate the next four years of life to a scheme for replenishing the vigor of the sun!" Lodermulch merely made an offensive statement to the effect that for all of him the sun could go dark, with the pilgrims forced to grope their way to the Lustral Rites.

But the sun shone on as before. The raft drifted along the great Scamander, where the banks were now so low and devoid of vegetation as to seem distant dark lines. The day passed and the sun seemed to settle into the river itself, projecting a great maroon glare which gradually went dull and dark as the sun vanished.

In the twilight a fire was built around which the pilgrims gathered to eat their supper. There was discussion of the sun's alarming flicker, and much speculation along eschatological lines. Subucule relinquished all responsibility for life, death, the future and past to Gilfig. Haxt, however, declared that he would feel easier if Gilfig had heretofore displayed a more expert control over the affairs of the world. For a period the talk became intense. Subucule accused Haxt of superficiality, while Haxt used such words as "credulity" and "blind abasement." Garstang intervened to point out that as yet all facts were not known, and that the Lustral Rites at the Black Obelisk might clarify the situation.

The next morning a great weir was noted ahead: a line of stout poles obstructing navigation of the river. At one area only was passage possible, and even this gap was closed by a heavy iron chain. The pilgrims allowed the raft to float close to this gap, then dropped the stone which served as an anchor. From a nearby hut appeared a zealot, long of hair and gaunt of limb, wearing tattered black robes and flourishing an iron staff. He sprang out along the weir to gaze threateningly down at those aboard the raft. "Go back, go back!" he shouted. "The passage of the river is under my control; I permit none to go by!"

Garstang stepped forward. "I beg your indulgence! We are a group of pilgrims, bound for the Lustral Rites at Erze Damath. If necessary we will pay a fee to pass the weir, though we trust that in your generosity you will remit the toll."

The zealot gave a cry of harsh laughter and waved his iron staff. "My fee may not be remitted! I demand the life of the most evil in your company—unless one among you can to my satisfaction demonstrate his virtue!" And legs astraddle, black robe flapping in the wind, he stood glaring down at the raft.

Among the pilgrims was a stir of uneasiness, and all looked furtively at one another. There was a mutter, which presently became a confusion of assertions and claims. Casmyre's strident tones at last rang forth. "It cannot be I who am most evil! My life has been clement and austere and during the gambling I ignored an ignoble advantage."

Another called out, "I am even more virtuous, who eat only dry pulses for fear of taking life."

Another: "I am even of greater nicety, for I subsist solely upon the discarded husks of these same pulses, and bark which has fallen from trees, for fear of destroying even vegetative vitality."

Another: "My stomach refuses vegetable matter, but I uphold the same exalted ideals and allow only carrion to pass my lips."

Another: "I once swam on a lake of fire to notify an old woman that the calamity she dreaded was unlikely to occur."

Cugel declared: "My life is incessant humility, and I am unswerving in my dedication to justice and equivalence, even though I fare the worse for my pains."

Voynod was no less staunch: "I am a wizard, true, but I devote my skill only to the amelioration of public woe."

Now it was Garstang's turn: "My virtue is of the quintessential sort, being distilled from the erudition of the ages. How can I be other than virtuous? I am dispassionate to the ordinary motives of mankind."

Finally all had spoken save Lodermulch, who stood to the side, a sour grin on his face. Voynod pointed a finger. "Speak, Lodermulch! Prove your virtue, or else be judged most evil, with the consequent forfeit of your life!"

Lodermulch laughed. He turned and made a great jump which carried him to an outlying member of the weir. He scrampled to the parapet, drew his sword and threatened the zealot. "We are all evil together, you as well as we, for enforcing this absurd condition. Relax the chain, or prepare to face my sword."

The zealot flung high his arms. "My condition is fulfilled; you, Lodermulch, have demonstrated your virtue. The raft may proceed. In addition, since you employ your sword in the defense of honor, I now bestow upon you this salve which when applied to your blade enables it to slice steel or rock as easily as butter. Away, then, and may all profit by the lustral devotions!"

Lodermulch accepted the salve and returned to the raft. The chain was relaxed and the raft slid without hindrance past the weir.

Garstang approached Lodermulch to voice measured approval for his act. He added a caution: "In this case an impulsive, indeed almost insubordinate, act redounded to the general benefit. If a similar circumstance arises in the future, it would be well to take counsel with others to proved sagacity: myself, Casmyre, Voynod or Subucule."

Lodermulch grunted indifferently. "As you wish, so long as the delay involves me in no personal inconvenience.'' And Garstang was forced to be content with this.

The other pilgrims eyed Lodermulch with dissatisfaction, and drew themselves apart, so that Lodermulch sat by himself at the forward part of the raft.

Afternoon came, then sunset, evening and night; when morning arrived it was seen that Lodermulch had disappeared.

There was general puzzlement. Garstang made inquiries, but none could throw light upon the mystery, and there was no general consensus as to what in fact had occasioned the disappearance.

Strangely enough, the departure of the unpopular Lodermulch failed to restore the original cheer and fellowship to the group. Thereafter each of the pilgrims sat dourly silent, casting glances to left and right; there were no further games, nor philosophical discussions, and Garstang's announcement that Erze Damath lay a single day's journey ahead aroused no great enthusiasm.

3: Erze Damath

On the last night aboard the raft a semblance of the old camaraderie returned. Vitz the locutor performed a number of vocal exercises and Cugel demonstrated a high-kneed capering dance typical of the lobster fishermen of Kauchique, where he had passed his youth. Voynod in his turn performed a few simple metamorphoses, and then displayed a small silver ring. He signaled Haxt, ''Touch this with your tongue, press it to your forehead, then look through.''

''I see a procession!'' exclaimed Haxt. ''Men and women by the hundreds, and thousands, marching past. My mother and my father walk before, then my grandparents—but who are the others?''

''Your ancestors,'' declared Voynod, ''each in his characteristic costume, back to the primordial homuncule from which all of us are derived.'' He retrieved the ring, and reaching into his pouch brought forth a dull blue and green gem.

''Watch now, as I fling this jewel into the Scamander!'' And he tossed the gem off to the side. It flickered through the air and splashed into the dark water. ''Now, I merely hold forth my palm, and the gem returns!'' And indeed, as the company watched there was a wet sparkle across the firelight and upon Voynod's palm rested the gem. ''With this gem a man need never fear penury. True, it is of no great value, but he can sell it repeatedly. . . .

''What else shall I show you? This small amulet perhaps. Frankly an erotic appurtenance, it arouses intense emotion in that person toward whom the potency is directed. One must be cautious in its use; and indeed, I have here an indispensable ancillary: a periapt in the shape of a ram's head, fashioned to the order of Emperor Dalmasmius the Tender, that he might not injure the sensibilities of any of his ten thousand concubines. . . . What else can I display? Here: my wand, which instantly affixes any object to any other. I keep it carefully sheathed so that I do not inadvertently weld trouser to buttock or pouch to fingertip. The object has many uses. What else? Let us see. . . . Ah, here! A horn of singular quality. When thrust into the mouth of a corpse, it stimulates the utterance of twenty final words. Inserted into the cadaver's ear it allows the transmission of information into the lifeless brain. . . . What have we here? Yes, indeed: a small device which has brought much pleasure!'' And Voynod displayed a doll which performed a heroic declamation, sang a somewhat raffish song and engaged in repartee with Cugel, who squatted close in front, watching all with great attentiveness.

At last Voynod tired of his display, and the pilgrims one by one reposed themselves to sleep.

Cugel lay awake, hands behind his head, staring up at the stars thinking of Voynod's unexpectedly large collection of thaumaturgical instruments and devices.

When satisfied that all were asleep, he arose to his feet and inspected the sleeping form of Voynod. The pouch was securely locked and tucked under Voynod's arm, much as Cugel had expected. Going to the little pantry where stores were kept, he secured a quantity of lard, which he mixed with flour to produce a white salve. From a fragment of heavy paper he folded a small box, which he filled with the salve. He then returned to his couch.

On the following morning he contrived that Voynod, as if by accident, should see him anointing his sword blade with the salve.

Voynod became instantly horrified. ''It cannot be! I am astounded! Alas, poor Lodermulch!''

Cugel signaled him to silence. ''What are you saying?'' he muttered. ''I merely protect my sword against rust.''

Voynod shook his head with inexorable determination. ''All is clear! For the sake of gain you have murdered Lodermulch! I have no choice but to lodge an information with the thief-takers at Erze Damath!''

Cugel made an imploring gesture. ''Do not be hasty! You have mistaken all; I am innocent!''

Voynod, a tall saturnine man with purple flush under his eyes, a long chin and a tall pinched forehead, held up his hand. ''I have never been one to tolerate homicide. The principle of equivalence must in this case apply, and a rigorous requital is necessary. At minimum, the evildoer may never profit by his act!''

"You refer to the salve?'' inquired Cugel delicately.

"Precisely,'' said Voynod. "Justice demands no less.''

"You are a stern man,'' exclaimed Cugel in distress. "I have no choice but to submit to your judgement.''

Voynod extended his hand. "The salve, then, and since you are obviously overcome by remorse I will say no more of the matter.''

Cugel pursed his lips reflectively. "So be it. I have already anointed my sword. Therefore I will sacrifice the remainder of the salve in exchange for your erotic appurtenance and its ancillary, together with several lesser talismans.''

"Do I hear correctly?'' stormed Voynod. "Your arrogance transcends all! Such effectuants are beyond value!''

Cugel shrugged. "This salve is by no means an ordinary article of commerce.''

After dispute Cugel relinquished the salve in return for a tube which projected blue concentrate to a distance of fifty paces, together with a scroll listing eighteen phases of the Laganetic Cycle; and with these items he was forced to be content.

Not long afterward the outlying ruins of Erze Damath appeared upon the western banks: ancient villas now toppled and forlorn among overgrown gardens.

The pilgrims plied poles to urge the raft toward the shore. In the distance appeared the tip of the Black Obelisk, at which all emitted a glad cry. The raft moved slantwise across the Scamander and was presently docked at one of the crumbling old jetties.

The pilgrims scrambled ashore, to gather around Garstang, who addressed the group: "It is with vast satisfaction that I find myself discharged of responsibility. Behold! The holy city where Gilfig issued the Gneustic Dogma! where he scourged Kazue and denounced Enxis the Witch! Not impossibly the sacred feet have trod this very soil!'' Garstang made a dramatic gesture toward the ground, and the pilgrims, looking downward, shuffled their feet uneasily. "Be that as it may, we are here and each of us must feel relief. The way was tedious and not without peril. Fifty-nine set forth from Pholgus Valley. Bamish and Randol were taken by grues at Sagma Field; by the bridge across the Asc Cugel joined us; upon the Scamander we lost Lodermulch. Now we muster fifty-seven, comrades all, tried and true, and it is a sad thing to dissolve our association, which we all will remember forever!

"Two days hence the Lustral Rites begin. We are in good time.

Those who have not disbursed all their funds gaming''—here Garstang turned a sharp glance toward Cugel—''may seek comfortable inns at which to house themselves. The impoverished must fare as best they can. Now our journey is at its end; we herewith disband and go our own ways, though all will necessarily meet two days hence at the Black Obelisk. Farewell until this time!''

The pilgrims now dispersed, some walking along the banks of the Scamander toward a nearby inn, others turning aside and proceeding into the city proper.

Cugel approached Voynod. ''I am strange to this region, as you are aware; perhaps you can recommend an inn of large comfort at small cost.''

''Indeed,'' said Voynod. ''I am bound for just such an inn: the Old Dastric Empire Hostelry, which occupies the precincts of a former palace. Unless conditions have changed, sumptuous luxury and exquisite viands are offered at no great cost.''

The prospect met with Cugel's approval; the two set out through the avenues of old Erze Damath, past clusters of stucco huts, then across a region where no buildings stood and the avenues created a vacant checkerboard, then into a district of great mansions still currently in use: these set back among intricate gardens. The folk of Erze Damath were handsome enough, if somewhat swarthier than the folk of Almery. The men wore only black: tight trousers and vests with black pompoms; the women were splendid in gowns of yellow, red, orange and magenta, and their slippers gleamed with orange and black sequins. Blue and green were rare, being unlucky colors, and purple signified death.

The women displayed tall plumes in their hair, while the men wore jaunty black disks, their scalps protruding through a central hole. A resinous balsam seemed very much the fashion, and everyone Cugel met exuded a waft of aloes or myrrh or carcynth. All in all the folk of Erze Damath seemed no less cultivated than those of Kauchique, and rather more vital than the listless citizens of Azenomei.

Ahead appeared the Old Dastric Empire Hostelry, not far from the Black Obelisk itself. To the dissatisfaction of both Cugel and Voynod, the premises were completely occupied, and the attendant refused them admittance. ''The Lustral Rites have attracted all manner of devout folk,'' he explained. ''You will be fortunate to secure lodging of any kind.''

So it proved: from inn to inn went Cugel and Voynod, to be turned away in every case. Finally, on the western outskirts of the city, at the very edge of the Silver Desert, they were received by a large tavern of somewhat disreputable appearance: the Inn of the Green Lamp.

"Until ten minutes ago I could not have housed you," stated the landlord, "but the thief-takers apprehended two persons who lodged here, naming them footpads and congenital rogues."

"I trust this is not the general tendency of your clientele?" inquired Voynod.

"Who is to say?" replied the innkeeper. "It is my business to provide food and drink and lodging, no more. Ruffians and deviants must eat, drink, and sleep, no less than savants and zealots. All have passed on occasion through my doors, and, after all, what do I know of you?"

Dusk was falling and without further ado Cugel and Voynod housed themselves at the Inn of the Green Lamp. After refreshing themselves they repaired to the common room for their evening meal. This was a hall of considerable extent, with age-blackened beams, a floor of dark brown tile, and various posts and columns of scarred wood, each supporting a lamp. The clientele was various, as the landlord had intimated, displaying a dozen costumes and complexions. Desert-men lean as snakes, wearing leather smocks, sat on one hand; on the other were four with white faces and silky red top-knots who uttered never a word. Along a counter to the back sat a group of bravos in brown trousers, black capes and leather berets, each with a spherical jewel dangling by a gold chain from his ear.

Cugel and Voynod consumed a meal of fair quality, though somewhat rudely served, then sat drinking wine and considering how to pass the evening. Voynod decided to rehearse cries of passion and devotion frenzies to be exhibited at the Lustral Rites. Cugel thereupon besought him to lend his talisman of erotic stimulation. "The women of Erze Damath show to good advantage, and with the help of the talisman I will extend my knowledge of their capabilities."

"By no means," said Voynod, hugging his pouch close to his side. "My reasons need no amplification."

Cugel put on a sullen scowl. Voynod was a man whose grandiose personal conceptions seemed particularly far-fetched and distasteful, by reason of his unhealthy, gaunt and saturnine appearance.

Voynod drained his mug, with a meticulous frugality Cugel found additionally irritating, and rose to his feet. "I will now retire to my chamber."

As he turned away a bravo swaggering across the room jostled him. Voynod snapped an acrimonious instruction, which the bravo did not choose to ignore. "How dare you use such words to me! Draw and defend yourself, or I cut your nose from your face!'' And the bravo snatched forth his blade.

''As you will,'' said Voynod. ''One moment until I find my sword.'' With a wink at Cugel he anointed his blade with the salve, then turned to the bravo. ''Prepare for death, my good fellow!'' He leapt grandly forward. The bravo, noting Voynod's preparations, and understanding that he faced magic, stood numb with terror. With a flourish Voynod ran him through, and wiped his blade on the bravo's hat.

The dead man's companions at the counter started to their feet, but halted as Voynod with great aplomb turned to face them. ''Take care, you dunghill cocks! Notice the fate of your fellow! He died by the power of my magic blade, which is of inexorable metal and cuts rock and steel like butter. Behold!'' And Voynod struck out at a pillar. The blade, striking an iron bracket, broke into a dozen pieces. Voynod stood non-plussed, but the bravo's companions surged forward.

''What then of your magic blade? Our blades are ordinary steel but bite deep!'' And in a moment Voynod was cut to bits.

The bravos now turned upon Cugel. ''What of you? Do you wish to share the fate of your comrade?''

''By no means!'' stated Cugel. ''This man was but my servant, carrying my pouch. I am a magician; observe this tube! I will project blue concentrate at the first man to threaten me!''

The bravos shrugged and turned away. Cugel secured Voynod's pouch, then gestured to the landlord. ''Be so good as to remove these corpses; then bring a further mug of spiced wine.''

''What of your comrade's account?'' demanded the landlord testily.

''I will settle it in full, have no fear.''

The corpses were carried to the rear compound: Cugel consumed a last mug of wine, then retired to his chamber, where he spread the contents of Voynod's pouch upon the table. The money went into his purse; the talismans, amulets and instruments he packed into his own pouch; the salve he tossed aside. Content with the day's work, he reclined upon the couch, and was soon asleep.

On the following day Cugel roamed the city, climbing the tallest of the eight hills. The vista which spread before him was both bleak and magnificent. To right and left rolled the great Scamander. The avenues of the city marked off square blocks of ruins, empty wastes, the stucco huts of the poor and the palaces of the rich. Erze Damath was the largest city of Cugel's experience, far vaster than any of Almery or Ascolais, though now the greater part lay tumbled in moldering ruin.

Returning to the central section, Cugel sought out the booth of a professional geographer, and after paying a fee inquired the most secure and expeditious route to Almery.

The sage gave no hasty nor ill-considered answer, but brought forth several charts and directories. After profound deliberation he turned to Cugel. "This is my counsel. Follow the Scamander north to the Asc, proceed along the Asc until you encounter a bridge of six piers. Here turn your face to the north, proceed across the Mountains of Magnatz, whereupon you will find before you that forest known as the Great Erm. Fare westward through this forest and approach the shore of the Northern Sea. Here you must build a coracle and entrust yourself to the force of the wind and current. If by chance you should reach the Land of the Falling Wall, then it is a comparatively easy journey south to Almery."

Cugel made an impatient gesture. "In essence this is the way I came. Is there no other route?"

"Indeed there is. A rash man might choose to risk the Silver Desert, whereupon he would find the Songan Sea, across which lie the impassable wastes of a region contiguous to East Almery."

"Well then, this seems feasible. How may I cross the Silver Desert? Are there caravans?"

"To what purpose? There are none to buy the goods thus conveyed—only bandits who prefer to preempt the merchandise. A minimum force of forty men is necessary to intimidate the bandits."

Cugel departed the booth. At a nearby tavern he drank a flask of wine and considered how best to raise a force of forty men. The pilgrims, of course, numbered fifty-six—no, fifty-five, what with the death of Voynod. Still, such a band would serve very well. . . .

Cugel drank more wine and considered further.

At last he paid his score and turned his steps to the Black Obelisk. "Obelisk" perhaps was a misnomer, the object being a great fang of solid black stone rearing a hundred feet above the city. At the base five statues had been carved, each facing a different direction, each the Prime Adept of some particular creed. Gilfig faced to the south, his four hands presenting symbols, his feet resting upon the necks of ecstatic supplicants, with toes elongated and curled upward, to indicate elegance and delicacy.

Cugel sought information of a nearby attendant. "Who, in regard to the Black Obelisk, is Chief Hierarch, and where may he be found?"

"Precursor Hulm is that individual," said the attendant and indicated a splendid structure nearby. "Within that gem-encrusted structure his sanctum may be found."

Cugel proceeded to the building indicated and after many vehement declarations was ushered into the presence of Precursor Hulm: a man of middle years, somewhat stocky and round of face. Cugel gestured to the under-hierophant who so reluctantly had brought him hither. "Go; my message is for the Precursor alone."

The Precursor gave a signal; the hierophant departed. Cugel hitched himself forward. "I may talk without fear of being overheard?"

"Such is the case."

"First of all," said Cugel, "know that I am a powerful wizard. Behold: a tube which projects blue concentrate! And here, a screed listing eighteen phases of the Laganetic Cycle! And this instrument: a horn which allows information to be conveyed into the dead brain! I possess other marvels galore!"

"Interesting indeed," murmured the Precursor.

"My second disclosure is this: at one time I served as incense-blender at the Temple of Teleologues in a far land, where I learned that each of the sacred images was constructed so that the priests, in case of urgency, might perform acts purporting to be those of the divinity itself."

"Why should this not be the case?" inquired the Precursor benignly. "The divinity, controlling every aspect of existence, persuades the priests to perform such acts."

Cugel assented to the proposition. "I therefore assume that the images carved into the Black Obelisk are somewhat similar?"

The Precursor smiled. "To which of the five do you specifically refer?"

"Specifically to the representation of Gilfig."

The Precursor's eyes went vague; he seemed to reflect.

Cugel indicated the various talismans and instruments. "In return for a service I will donate certain of these contrivances to the care of this office."

"What is the service?"

Cugel explained in detail, and the Precursor nodded thoughtfully. "Once more, if you will demonstrate your magic goods."

Cugel did so.

"These are all of your devices?"

Cugel reluctantly displayed the erotic stimulator and explained the function of the ancillary talisman. The Precursor nodded his head briskly this time. "I believe that we can reach agreement; all is as omnipotent Gilfig desires."

"We are agreed, then?"

"We are agreed!"

The following morning the group of fifty-five pilgrims assembled at the Black Obelisk. They prostrated themselves before the image of Gilfig, and prepared to proceed with their devotions. Suddenly the eyes of the image flashed fire and the mouth opened. "Pilgrims!" came a brazen voice. "Go forth to do my bidding! Across the Silver Desert you must travel, to the shore of the Songan Sea! Here you will find a fane, before which you must abase yourselves. Go! Across the Silver Desert, with all despatch!"

The voice quieted. Garstang spoke in a trembling voice. "We hear, O Gilfig! We obey!"

At this moment Cugel leapt forward. "I also have heard this marvel! I, too, will make the journey! Come, let us set forth!"

"Not so fast," said Garstang. "We cannot run skipping and bounding like dervishes. Supplies will be needed, as well as beasts of burden. To this end funds are required. Who then will subscribe?"

"I offer two hundred terces!" "And I, sixty terces, the sum of my wealth!" "I, who lost ninety terces gaming with Cugel, possess only forty terces, which I hereby contribute." So it went, and even Cugel turned sixty-five terces into the common fund.

"Good," said Garstang. "Tomorrow then I will make arrangements, and the following day, if all goes well, we depart Erze Damath by the Old West Gate!"

4: The Silver Desert and the Songan Sea

In the morning Garstang, with the assistance of Cugel and Casmyre, went forth to procure the necessary equipage. They were directed to an outfitting yard, situated on one of the now-vacant areas bounded by the boulevards of the old city. A wall of mud brick mingled with fragments of carved stone surrounded a compound, whence issued sounds: crying, calls, deep bellows, throaty growls, barks, screams and roars, and a strong multiphase odor, combined of ammonia, ensilage, a dozen sorts of dung, the taint of old meat, general acridity.

Passing through a portal, the travelers entered an office overlooking the central yard, where pens, cages and stockades held beasts of so great a variety as to astound Cugel.

The yard-keeper came forward: a tall, yellow-skinned man, much scarred, lacking his nose and one ear. He wore a gown of gray leather belted at the waist and a tall conical black hat with flaring ear-flaps.

Garstang stated the purpose of the visit. "We are pilgrims who must journey across the Silver Desert, and wish to hire pack-beasts. We number fifty or more, and anticipate a journey of twenty days in each direction with perhaps five days spent at our devotions: let this information be a guide in your thinking. Naturally we expect only the staunchest, most industrious and amenable beasts at your disposal."

"All this is very well," stated the keeper, "but my price for hire is identical to my price for sale, so you might as well have the full benefit of your money, in the form of title to the beasts concerned in the transaction."

"And the price?" inquired Casmyre.

"This depends upon your choice; each beast commands a different value."

Garstang, who had been surveying the compound, shook his head ruefully. "I confess to puzzlement. Each beast is of a different sort, and none seem to fit any well-defined categories."

The keeper admitted that such was the case. "If you care to listen, I can explain all. The tale is of a continuing fascination, and will assist you in the management of your beasts."

"We will doubly profit to hear you, then," said Garstang gracefully, though Cugel was making motions of impatience.

The keeper went to a shelf and took forth a leather-bound folio. "In a past eon Mad King Kutt ordained a menagerie like none before, for his private amazement and the stupefaction of the world. His wizard, Follinense, therefore produced a group of beasts and teratoids unique, combining the wildest variety of plasms; to the result that you see."

"The menagerie has persisted so long?" asked Garstang in wonder.

"Indeed not. Nothing of Mad King Kutt is extant save the legend, and a casebook of the wizard Follinense"—here he tapped the leather folio—"which describes his bizarre systemology. For instance—" He opened the folio. "Well . . . hmmm. Here is a statement, somewhat less explicit than others, in which he analyzes the half-men, little more than a brief set of notes:

'Gid: hybrid of man, gargoyle, whorl, leaping insect.
Deodand: wolverine, basilisk, man.
Erb: bear, man, lank-lizard, demon.
Grue: man, ocular bat, the unusual hoon.

Leucomorph: unknown
Bazil: felinodore, man, (wasp?).' ''

Casmyre clapped his hands in astonishment. ''Did Follinense then create these creatures, to the subsequent disadvantage of humanity?''

''Surely not,'' said Garstang. ''It seems more an exercise in idle musing. Twice he admits to wonder.''

''Such is my opinion, in this present case,'' stated the keeper, ''though elsewhere he is less dubious.''

''How are the creatures before us then connected with the menagerie?'' inquired Casmyre.

The keeper shrugged. ''Another of the Mad King's jocularities. He loosed the entire assemblage upon the countryside, to the general disturbance. The creatures, endowed with an eclectic fecundity, became more rather than less bizarre, and now they roam the Plain of Oparona and Blanwalt Forest in great numbers.''

''So then, what of us?'' demanded Cugel. ''We wish pack-animals, docile and frugal of habit, rather than freaks and curiosities, no matter how edifying.''

''Certain of my ample stock are capable of this function,'' said the keeper with dignity. ''These command the highest prices. On the other hand, for a single terce you may own a long-necked big-bellied creature of astounding voracity.''

''The price is attractive,'' said Garstang with regret. ''Unfortunately, we need beasts to carry food and water across the Silver Desert.''

''In this case we must be more pointed.'' The keeper fell to studying his charges. ''The tall beast on two legs is perhaps less ferocious than he appears. . . .''

Eventually a selection of beasts numbering fifteen was made, and a price agreed upon. The keeper brought them to the gate; Garstang, Cugel and Casmyre took possession and led the fifteen ill-matched creatures at a sedate pace through the streets of Erze Damath, to the West Gate. Here Cugel was left in charge, while Garstang and Casmyre went to purchase stores and other necessaries.

By nightfall all preparations were made, and on the following morning, when the first maroon ray of sunlight struck the Black Obelisk, the pilgrims set forth. The beasts carried panniers of food and bladders of water; the pilgrims all wore new shoes and broad-brimmed hats. Garstang had been unable to hire a guide, but had secured a chart from the geographer, though it indicated no more than a small circle labeled ''Erze Damath'' and a larger area marked ''Songan Sea.''

Cugel was given one of the beasts to lead, a twelve-legged creature twenty feet in length, with a small foolishly grinning child's head and tawny fur covering all. Cugel found the task irking, for the beast blew a reeking breath upon his neck, and several times pressed so close as to tread on his heels.

Of the fifty-seven pilgrims who had disembarked from the raft, forty-nine departed for the fane on the shores of the Songan Sea, and the number was almost at once reduced to forty-eight. A certain Tokharin, stepping off the trail to answer a call of nature, was stung by a monster scorpion, and ran northward in great leaps, screaming hoarsely, until presently he disappeared from view.

The day passed with no further incident. The land was a dry gray waste, scattered with flints, supporting only ironweed. To the south was a range of low hills, and Cugel thought to perceive one or two shapes standing motionless along the crest. At sunset the caravan halted; and Cugel, recalling the bandits who reputedly inhabited the area, persuaded Garstang to post two sentries: Lippelt and Mirch-Masen.

In the morning they were gone, leaving no trace, and the pilgrims were alarmed and oppressed. They stood in a nervous cluster looking in all directions. The desert lay flat and dim in the dark low light of dawn. To the south were a few hills, only their smooth top surfaces illuminated; elsewhere the land lay flat to the horizon.

Presently the caravan started off, and now there were but forty-six. Cugel, as before, was put in charge of the long many-legged beast, who now engaged in the practice of butting its grinning face into Cugel's shoulder blades.

The day passed without incident; miles ahead became miles behind. First marched Garstang, with a staff, then came Vitz and Casmyre, followed by several others. Then came the packbeasts, each with its particular silhouette: one low and sinuous; another tall and bifurcate, almost of human conformation, except for its head, which was small and squat like the shell of a horseshoe crab. Another, convex of back, seemed to bounce or prance on its six stiff legs; another was like a horse sheathed in white feathers. Behind the packbeasts straggled the remaining pilgrims, with Bluner characteristically walking to the rear, in accordance with the exaggerated humility to which he was prone. At the camp that evening Cugel brought forth the expansible fence, once the property of Voynod, and enclosed the group in a stout stockade.

The following day the pilgrims crossed a range of low mountains, and here they suffered an attack by bandits, but it seemed no more than an exploratory skirmish, and the sole casualty was Haxt, who suffered a wound in the heel. But a more serious affair occurred two hours later. As they passed below a slope a boulder became dislodged, to roll through the caravan, killing a pack-beast, as well as Andle the Funambulous Evangel and Roremaund the Skeptic. During the night Haxt died also, evidently poisoned by the weapon which had wounded him.

With grave faces the pilgrims set forth, and almost at once were attacked from ambush by the bandits. Luckily the pilgrims were alert, and the bandits were routed with a dozen dead, while the pilgrims lost only Cray and Magasthen.

Now there was grumbling and long looks turned eastward toward Erze Damath. Garstang rallied the flagging spirits: "We are Gilfigites; Gilfig spoke! On the shores of the Songan Sea we will seek the sacred fane! Gilfig is all-wise and all-merciful; those who fall in his service are instantly transported to paradaisical Gamamere! Pilgrims! To the west!"

Taking heart, the caravan once more set forth, and the day passed without further incident. During the night, however, three of the pack-beasts slipped their tethers and decamped, and Garstang was forced to announce short rations for all.

During the seventh day's march, Thilfox ate a handful of poison berries and died in spasms, whereupon his brother Vitz, the locutor, went raving mad and ran up the line of pack-beasts, blaspheming Gilfig and slashing water bladders with his knife, until Cugel finally killed him.

Two days later the haggard band came upon a spring. In spite of Garstang's warning, Sayanave and Arlo flung themselves down and drank in great gulps. Almost at once they clutched their bellies, gagged and choked, their lips the color of sand, and presently they were dead.

A week later fifteen men and four beasts came over the rise to look out across the placid waters of the Songan Sea. Cugel had survived, as well as Garstang, Casmyre and Subucule. Before them lay a marsh, fed by a small stream. Cugel tested the water with that amulet bestowed upon him by Iucounu, and pronounced it safe. All drank to repletion, ate reeds converted to nutritious if insipid substance by the same amulet, then slept.

Cugel, aroused by a sense of peril, jumped up, to note a sinister stir among the reeds. He roused his fellows, and all readied their weapons; but whatever had caused the motion took alarm and retired. The time was middle afternoon; the pilgrims walked down to the bleak shore to take stock of the situation. They looked north and south but found no trace of the fane. Tempers flared; there was a quarrel which Garstang was able to quell only by dint of the utmost persuasiveness.

Then Balch, who had wandered up the beach, returned in great excitement: "A village!"

All set forth in hope and eagerness, but the village, when the pilgrims approached, proved a poor thing indeed, a huddle of reed huts inhabited by lizard people who bared their teeth and lashed sinewy blue tails in defiance. The pilgrims moved off down the beach and sat on hummocks watching the low surf of the Songan Sea.

Garstang, frail and bent with the privations he had suffered, was the first to speak. He attempted to infuse his voice with cheer. "We have arrived, we have triumphed over the terrible Silver Desert! Now we need only locate the fane and perform our devotions; we may then return to Erze Damath and a future of assured bliss!"

"All very well," grumbled Balch, "but where may the fane be found? To right and left is the same bleak beach!"

"We must put our trust in the guidance of Gilfig!" declared Subucule. He scratched an arrow upon a bit of wood, and touched it with his holy ribbon. He called, "Gilfig, O Gilfig! Guide us to the fane! I hereby toss high a marked pointer!" And he flung the chip high into the air. When it alighted, the arrow pointed south. "South we must fare!" cried Garstang. "South to the fane!"

But Balch and certain others refused to respond. "Do you not see that we are fatigued to the point of death? In my opinion Gilfig should have guided our steps to the fane, instead of abandoning us to uncertainty!"

"Gilfig has guided us indeed!" responded Subucule. "Did you not notice the direction of the arrow?"

Balch gave a croak of sardonic laughter. "Any stick thrown high must come down, and it will point south as easily as north."

Subucule drew back in horror. "You blaspheme Gilfig!"

"Not at all; I am not sure that Gilfig heard your instruction, or perhaps you gave him insufficient time to react. Toss up the stick one hundred times; if it points south on each occasion, I will march south in haste."

"Very well," said Subucule. He once again called upon Gilfig and threw up the chip, but when it struck the ground the arrow pointed north.

Balch said nothing. Subucule blinked, then grew red in the face. "Gilfig has no time for games. He directed us once, and deemed it sufficient."

"I am unconvinced," said Balch.

"And I."

"And I."

Garstang held up his arms imploringly. "We have come far; we have toiled together, rejoiced together, fought and suffered together—let us not now fall in dissidence!"

Balch and the others only shrugged. "We will not plunge blindly south."

"What will you do, then? Go north? Or return to Erze Damath?"

"Erze Damath? Without food and only four pack-beasts? Bah!"

"Then let us fare south in search of the fane."

Balch gave another mulish shrug, at which Subucule became angry. "So be it! Those who fare south to this side, those who cast in with Balch to that!"

Garstang, Cugel and Casmyre joined Subucule; the others stayed with Balch, a group numbering eleven, and now they fell to whispering among themselves, while the four faithful pilgrims watched in apprehension.

The eleven jumped to their feet. "Farewell."

"Where do you go?" asked Garstang.

"No matter. Seek your fane if you must; we go about our own affairs." With the briefest of farewells they marched to the village of the lizard folk, where they slaughtered the males, filed the teeth of females, dressed them in garments of reeds, and installed themselves as lords of the village.

Garstang, Subucule, Casmyre and Cugel meanwhile traveled south along the shore. At nightfall they pitched camp and dined upon molluscs and crabs. In the morning they found that the four remaining pack-beasts had departed, and now they were alone.

"It is the will of Gilfig," said Subucule. "We need only find the fane and die!"

"Courage!" muttered Garstang. "Let us not give way to despair!"

"What else is left? Will we ever see Pholgus Valley again?"

"Who knows? Let us first perform our devotions at the fane."

With that they proceeded, and marched the remainder of the day. By nightfall they were too tired to do more than slump to the sand of the beach.

The sea spread before them, flat as a table, so calm that the setting sun cast only its exact image rather than a trail. Clams and crabs once more provided a meager supper, after which they composed themselves to sleep on the beach.

Somewhat after the first hours of night Cugel was awakened by a sound of music. Starting up, he looked across the water to find that a ghostly city had come into existence. Slender towers reared into the sky, lit by glittering motes of white light which drifted slowly up and down, back and forth. On the promenades sauntered the gayest of crowds, wearing pale luminous garments and blowing horns of delicate sound. A barge piled with silken cushions, moved by an enormous sail of cornflower silk, drifted past. Lamps at the bow and stern-post illuminated a deck thronged with merrymakers: some singing and playing lutes, others drinking from goblets.

Cugel ached to share their joy. He struggled to his knees, and called out. The merrymakers put down their instruments and stared at him, but now the barge had drifted past, tugged by the great blue sail. Presently the city flickered and vanished, leaving only the dark night sky.

Cugel stared into the night, his throat aching with a sorrow he had never known before. To his surprise he found himself standing at the edge of the water. Nearby were Subucule, Garstang and Casmyre. All gazed at each other through the dark, but exchanged no words. All returned up the beach, where presently they fell asleep on the sand.

Throughout the next day, there was little conversation, and even a mutual avoidance, as if each of the four wished to be alone with his thoughts. From time to time one or the other looked half-heartedly toward the south, but no one seemed in a mood to leave the spot, and no one spoke of departure.

The day passed while the pilgrims rested in a half-torpor. Sunset came, and night; but none of the group sought to sleep.

During the middle evening the ghost city reappeared, and tonight a fête was in progress. Fireworks of a wonderful intricacy bloomed in the sky: laces, nets, starbursts of red and green and blue and silver. Along the promenade came a parade, with ghost-maidens dressed in iridescent garments, ghost-musicians in voluminous garments of red and orange and capering ghost-harlequins. For hours the sound of revelry drifted across the water, and Cugel went out to stand knee-deep, and here he watched until the fête quieted and the city dimmed. As he turned away, the others followed him back up the shore.

On the following day all were weak from hunger and thirst. In a croaking voice Cugel muttered that they must proceed. Garstang nodded and said huskily, "To the fane, the fane of Gilfig!"

Subucule nodded. The cheeks of his once plump face were haggard; his eyes were filmed and clouded. "Yes," he wheezed. "We have rested; we must go on."

Casmyre nodded dully. "To the fane!"

But none set forth to the south. Cugel wandered up the fore-shore and seated himself to wait for nightfall. Looking to his right, he saw a human skeleton resting in a posture not dissimilar to his own. Shuddering, Cugel turned to the left, and here was a second skeleton, this one broken by time and the seasons, and beyond yet another, this a mere heap of bones.

Cugel rose to his feet and ran tottering to the others. "Quick!" he called. "While strength yet remains to us! To the south! Come, before we die, like those others whose bones rest above!"

"Yes, yes," mumbled Garstang. "To the fane." And he heaved himself to his feet. "Come!" he called to the others. "We fare south!"

Subucule raised himself erect, but Casmyre, after a listless attempt, fell back. "Here I stay," he said. "When you reach the fane, intercede for me with Gilfig; explain that the entrancement overcame the strength of my body."

Garstang wished to remain and plead, but Cugel pointed to the setting sun. "If we wait till darkness, we are lost! Tomorrow our strength will be gone!"

Subucule took Garstang's arm. "We must be away, before nightfall."

Garstang made a final plea to Casmyre. "My friend and fellow, gather your strength. Together we have come, from far Pholgus Valley, by raft down the Scamander, and across the dreadful desert! Must we part before attaining the fane?"

"Come to the fane!" croaked Cugel.

But Casmyre turned his face away. Cugel and Subucule led Garstang away, with tears coursing down his withered cheeks; and they staggered south along the beach, averting their eyes from the clear smooth face of the sea.

The old sun set and cast up a fan of color. A high scatter of cloudflakes glowed halcyon yellow on a strange bronze-brown sky. The city now appeared, and never had it seemed more magnificent, with spires catching the light of sunset. Along the promenade walked youths and maidens with flowers in their hair, and sometimes they paused to stare at the three who walked along the beach. Sunset faded; white lights shone from the city, and music wafted across the water. For a long time it followed the three pilgrims, at last fading into the distance and dying. The sea lay blank to the west, reflecting a few last amber and orange glimmers.

About this time the pilgrims found a stream of fresh water, with berries and wild plums growing nearby, and here they rested the night. In the morning Cugel trapped a fish and caught crabs along the beach. Strengthened, the three continued south, always seeking ahead for the fane, which now Cugel had almost come to expect, so intense was the feeling of Garstang and Subucule. Indeed, as the days passed, it was the devout Subucule who began to despair, to question the sincerity of Gilfig's command, to doubt the essential virtue of Gilfig himself. "What is gained by this agonizing pilgrimage? Does Gilfig doubt our devotion? Surely we proved ourselves by attendance at the Lustral Rite; why has he sent us so far?"

"The ways of Gilfig are inscrutable," said Garstang.

"We have come so far; we must seek on and on and on!"

Subucule stopped short, to look back the way they had come. "Here is my proposal. At this spot let us erect an altar of stones, which becomes our fane; let us then perform a rite. With Gilfig's requirement satisfied, we may turn our faces to the north, to the village where our fellows reside. Here, happily, we may recapture the pack-beasts, replenish our stores, and set forth across the desert, perhaps to arrive once more at Erze Damath."

Garstang hesitated. "There is much to recommend your proposal. And yet—"

"A boat!" cried Cugel. He pointed to the sea where a half-mile offshore floated a fishing boat propelled by a square sail hanging from a long limber yard. It passed behind a headland which rose a mile south of where the pilgrims stood, and now Cugel indicated a village along the shore.

"Excellent!" declared Garstang. "These folk may be fellow Gilfigites, and this village the site of the fane! Let us proceed!"

Subucule still was reluctant. "Could knowledge of the sacred texts have penetrated so far?"

"Caution is the watchword," said Cugel. "We must reconnoiter with great care." And he led the way through a forest of tamarisk and larch, to where they could look down into the village. The huts were rudely constructed of black stone and housed a folk of ferocious aspect. Black hair in spikes surrounded the round clay-colored faces; coarse black bristles grew off the burly shoulders like epaulettes. Fangs protruded from the mouths of male and female alike and all spoke in harsh growling shouts. Cugel, Garstang and Subucule drew back with the utmost caution, and, hidden among the trees, conferred in low voices.

Garstang at last was discouraged and found nothing more to hope for. "I am exhausted, spiritually as well as physically; perhaps here is where I die."

Subucule looked to the north. "I return to take my chances on the

Silver Desert. If all goes well, I will arrive once more at Erze Damath, or even Pholgus Valley."

Garstang turned to Cugel. "And what of you, since the fane of Gilfig is nowhere to be found?"

Cugel pointed to a dock at which a number of boats were moored. "My destination is Almery, across the Songan Sea. I propose to commandeer a boat and sail to the west."

"I then bid you farewell," said Subucule. "Garstang, will you come?"

Garstang shook his head. "It is too far. I would surely die on the desert. I will cross the sea with Cugel and take the Word of Gilfig to the folk of Almery."

"Farewell, then, to you as well," said Subucule. Then he turned swiftly, to hide the emotion in his face, and started north.

Cugel and Garstang watched the sturdy form recede into the distance and disappear. Then they turned to a consideration of the dock. Garstang was dubious. "The boats seem seaworthy enough, but to 'commandeer' is to 'steal': an act specifically discountenanced by Gilfig."

"No difficulty exists," said Cugel. "I will place gold coins upon the dock, to a fair valuation of the boat."

Garstang gave a dubious assent. "What then of food and water?"

"After securing the boat, we will proceed along the coast until we are able to secure supplies, after which we sail due west."

To this Garstang assented and the two fell to examining the boats, comparing one against the other. The final selection was a staunch craft some ten or twelve paces long, of ample beam, with a small cabin.

At dusk they stole down to the dock. All was quiet: the fishermen had returned to the village. Garstang boarded the craft and reported all in good order. Cugel began casting off the lines, when from the end of the dock came a savage outcry and a dozen of the burly villagers came lumbering forth.

"We are lost!" cried Cugel. "Run for your life, or better, swim!"

"Impossible," declared Garstang. "If this is death, I will meet it with what dignity I am able!" And he climbed up on the dock.

In short order they were surrounded by folk of all ages, attracted by the commotion. One, an elder of the village, inquired in a stern voice, "What do you here, skulking on our dock, and preparing to steal a boat?"

"Our motive is simplicity itself," said Cugel. "We wish to cross the sea."

"What?" roared the elder. "How is that possible? The boat carries neither food nor water, and is poorly equipped. Why did you not approach us and make your needs known?''

Cugel blinked and exchanged a glance with Garstang. He shrugged. ''I will be candid. Your appearance caused us such alarm that we did not dare.''

The remark evoked mingled amusement and surprise in the crowd. The spokesman said, ''All of us are puzzled; explain if you will.''

''Very well,'' said Cugel. ''May I be absolutely frank?''

''By all means!''

''Certain aspects of your appearance impress us as feral and barbarous: your protruding fangs, the black mane which surrounds your faces, the cacophony of your speech—to name only a few items.''

The villagers laughed incredulously. ''What nonsense!'' they cried. ''Our teeth are long that we may tear the coarse fish on which we subsist. We wear our hair thus to repel a certain noxious insect, and since we are all rather deaf, we possibly tend to shout. Essentially we are a gentle and kindly folk.''

''Exactly,'' said the elder, ''and in order to demonstrate this, tomorrow we shall provision our best boat and send you forth with hopes and good wishes. Tonight there shall be a feast in your honor!''

''Here is a village of true saintliness,'' declared Garstang. ''Are you by chance worshippers of Gilfig?''

''No; we prostrate ourselves before the fish-god Yob, who seems as efficacious as any. But come, let us ascend to the village. We must make preparations for the feast.''

They climbed steps hewn in the rock of the cliff, which gave upon an area illuminated by a dozen flaring torches. The elder indicated a hut more commodious than the others: ''This is where you shall rest the night; I will sleep elsewhere.''

Garstang again was moved to comment upon the benevolence of the fisher-folk, at which the elder bowed his head. ''We try to achieve a spiritual unity. Indeed, we symbolize this ideal in the main dish of our ceremonial feasts.'' He turned, clapping his hands. ''Let us prepare!''

A great cauldron was hung over a tripod; a block and a cleaver were arranged, and now each of the villagers, marching past the block, chopped off a finger and cast it into the pot.

The elder explained, ''By this simple rite, which naturally you are expected to join, we demonstrate our common heritage and our mutual dependence. Come, let us step into the line.'' And Cugel and Garstang had no choice but to excise fingers and cast them into the pot with others.

The feast continued long into the night. In the morning the villagers were as good as their word. An especially seaworthy boat was provided and loaded with stores, including food left over from the previous night's feast.

The villagers gathered on the dock. Cugel and Garstang voiced their gratitude, then Cugel hoisted the sail and Garstang threw off the mooring lines. A wind filled the sail and the boat moved out on the face of the Songan Sea. Gradually the shore became one with the murk of distance, and the two were alone, with only the black metallic shimmer of the water to all sides.

Noon came, and the boat moved in an elemental emptiness: water below, air above; silence in all directions. The afternoon was long and torpid, unreal as a dream; and the melancholy grandeur of sunset was followed by a dusk the color of watered wine.

The wind seemed to freshen and all night they steered west. At dawn the wind died and with sails flapping idly both Cugel and Garstang slept.

Eight times the cycle was repeated. On the morning of the ninth day a low coastline was sighted ahead. During the middle afternoon they drove the prow of their boat through gentle surf up on a wide white beach. "This then is Almery?" asked Garstang.

"So I believe," said Cugel, "but which quarter I am uncertain. Azenomei may lie to north, west or south. If the forest yonder is that which shrouds East Almery, we would do well to pass to the side, as it bears an evil reputation."

Garstang pointed down the shore. "Notice: another village. If the folk here are like those across the sea, they will help us on our way. Come, let us make our wants known."

Cugel hung back. "It might be wise to reconnoiter, as before."

"To what end?" asked Garstang. "On that occasion we were only misled and confused." He led the way down the beach toward the village. As they approached they could see folk moving across the central plaza: a graceful golden-haired people, who spoke to each other in voices like music.

Garstang advanced joyfully, expecting a welcome even more expansive than that they had received on the other shore; but the villagers ran forward and caught them under nets. "Why do you do this?" called Garstang. "We are strangers and intend no harm!"

"You are strangers; just so," spoke the tallest of the golden-haired villagers. "We worship that inexorable god known as Dangott. Strangers are automatically heretics, and so are fed to the sacred apes." With that they began to drag Cugel and Garstang over the sharp stones of the fore-shore while the beautiful children of the village danced joyously to either side.

Cugel managed to bring forth the tube he had secured from Voynod and expelled blue concentrate at the villagers. Aghast, they toppled to the ground and Cugel was able to extricate himself from the net. Drawing his sword, he leapt forward to cut Garstang free, but now the villagers rallied. Cugel once more employed his tube, and the villagers fled in dismal agony.

"Go, Cugel," spoke Garstang. "I am an old man, of little vitality. Take to your heels; seek safety, with all my good wishes."

"This normally would be my impulse," Cugel conceded. "But these people have stimulated me to quixotic folly; so clamber from the net; we retreat together." Once more he wrought dismay with the blue projection, while Garstang freed himself, and the two fled along the beach.

The villagers pursued with harpoons. Their first cast pierced Garstang through the back. He fell without a sound. Cugel swung about and aimed the tube, but the spell was exhausted and only a limpid exudation appeared. The villagers drew back their arms to hurl a second volley; Cugel shouted a curse, dodged and ducked, and the harpoons plunged past him into the sand of the beach.

Cugel shook his fist a final time, then took to his heels and fled into the forest.

6

The Cave in the Forest

Through the old forest came Cugel, step by furtive step, pausing often to listen for breaking twig or quiet footfall or even the exhalation of a breath. His caution, though it made for slow progress, was neither theoretical nor impractical; others wandered the forest with anxieties and yearnings greatly at odds with his own. All one terrible dusk he had fled and finally outdistanced a pair of deodands; on another occasion he had stopped short at the very brink of a glade where a leucomorph had stood musing: whereupon Cugel had become more diffident and furtive than ever, skulking from tree to tree, peering and listening, darting across open spaces with an extravagantly delicate gait, as if contact with the ground pained his feet.

During a middle afternoon he came upon a small dank glade surrounded by black mandouars, tall and portentuous as hooded monks. A few red rays slanting into the glade, illumined a single twisted quince tree, where hung a strip of parchment. Standing back in the shadows Cugel studied the glade at length, then stepping forward took the parchment. In crabbed characters a message was indicated:

Zaraides the Sage makes a generous offer! He who finds this message may request and obtain an hour of judicious counsel at no charge. Into a nearby hillock opens a cave; the Sage will be found within.

Cugel studied the parchment with puzzlement. A large question hung in the air: why should Zaraides give forth his lore with such casual largesse? The purportedly free was seldom as represented; in one guise or another the Law of Equivalence must prevail. If Zaraides offered counsel—dismissing the premise of absolute altruism—he expected some commodity in return: at minimum an inflation of self-esteem, or knowledge regarding distant events, or polite attention at a recitation of odes, or some such service. And Cugel re-read the message, his skepticism, if anything augmented. He would have flung the parchment aside had not he felt a real and urgent need for information: specifically knowledge regarding the most secure route to the manse of Iucounu, together with a method for rendering the Laughing Magician helpless.

Cugel looked all about, seeking the hillock to which Zaraides referred. Across the glade the ground seemed to rise, and lifting his eyes Cugel noticed gnarled limbs and clotted foliage on high, as if a number of daobados grew on lofty ground.

With maximum vigilance Cugel proceeded through the forest, and presently was halted by a sudden upthrust of gray rock crowned with trees and vines: undoubtedly the hillock in question.

Cugel stood pulling at his chin, showing his teeth in a grimace of doubt. He listened: quiet, utter and complete. Keeping to the shadows, he continued around the hillock, and presently came upon the cave: an arched opening into the rock as high as a man, as wide as his outstretched arms. Above hung a placard printed in untidy characters:

ENTER: ALL ARE WELCOME!

Cugel looked this way and that. No sight nor sound in the forest. He took a few careful steps forward, peered into the cave, and found only darkness.

Cugel drew back. In spite of the genial urgency of the sign, he felt no inclination to thrust himself forward, and squatting on his haunches he watched the cave intently.

Fifteen minutes passed. Cugel shifted his position; and now, to the right, he spied a man approaching, using a caution hardly less elaborate than his own. The newcomer was of medium stature and wore the rude garments of a peasant: gray trousers, a rust-colored blouse, a cocked brown hat with bill thrust forward. He had a round, somewhat coarse face, with a stub of a nose, small eyes set far apart, a heavy chin bestubbled with a fuscous growth. Clutched in his hand was a parchment like that which Cugel had found.

Cugel rose to his feet. The newcomer halted, then came forward. "You are Zaraides? If so, know me for Fabeln the herbalist; I seek a rich growth of wild leeks. Further, my daughter moons and languishes, and will no longer carry panniers; therefore—"

Cugel held up his hand. "You err; Zaraides keeps to his cave."

Fabeln narrowed his eyes craftily. "Who then are you?"

"I am Cugel: like yourself, a seeker after enlightenment."

Fabeln nodded in full comprehension. "You have consulted Zaraides? He is accurate and trustworthy? He demands no fee as his prospectus purports?"

"Correct in every detail," said Cugel. "Zaraides, who is apparently omniscient, speaks from the sheer joy of transmitting information. My perplexities are resolved."

Fabeln inspected him sidelong. "Why then do you wait beside the cave?"

"I also am a herbalist, and I formulate new questions, specifically in regard to a nearby glade profuse with wild leeks."

"Indeed!" ejaculated Fabeln, snapping his fingers in agitation. "Formulate with care, and while you arrange your phrases, I will step within and inquire regarding the lassitude of my daughter."

"As you will," said Cugel. "Still, if you care to delay, I will be only a short time composing my question."

Fabeln made a jovial gesture. "In this short period, I will be into the cave, out and away, for I am a man swift to the point of brusqueness."

Cugel bowed. "In that case, proceed."

"I will be brief." And Fabeln strode into the cave. "Zaraides?" he called. "Where is Zaraides the Sage? I am Fabeln; I wish to make certain inquiries. Zaraides? Be so good as to come forth!" His voice became muffled. Cugel, listening intently, heard the opening and closing of a door, and then there was silence. Thoughtfully he composed himself to wait.

Minutes passed . . . and an hour. The red sun moved down the afternoon sky and passed behind the hillock. Cugel became restive. Where was Fabeln? He cocked his head: once more the opening and closing of a door? Indeed, and here was Fabeln: all then was well!

Fabeln looked forth from the cave. "Where is Cugel the herbalist?" He spoke in a harsh brusque voice. "Zaraides will not sit down to the banquet nor will he discuss leeks, except in the most general terms, until you present yourself."

"A banquet?" asked Cugel with interest. "Does the bounty of Zaraides extend so far?"

"Indeed: did you not notice the tapestried hall, the carved goblets, the silver tureen?" Fabeln spoke with a certain saturnine emphasis which puzzled Cugel. "But come; I am in haste, and do not care to wait. If you already have dined, I will so inform Zaraides."

"By no means," said Cugel, with dignity. "I would burn with humiliation thus to slight Zaraides. Lead on; I follow."

"Come, then." Fabeln turned; Cugel followed him into the cave, where his nostrils were assailed by a revolting odor. He paused. "I seem to notice a stench—one which affects me unpleasantly."

"I noticed the same," said Fabeln. "But through the door and the foul odor is no more!"

"I trust as much," said Cugel peevishly. "It would destroy my appetite. Where then—"

As he spoke he was swarmed upon by small quick bodies, clammy of skin and tainted with the odor he found so detestable. There was a clamor of high-pitched voices; his sword and pouch were snatched; a door was opened; Cugel was pitched into a low burrow. In the light of a flickering yellow flame he saw his captors: creatures half his height, pallid of skin, pointed of face, with ears on the tops of their heads. They walked with a slight forward hunch, and their knees seemed pointed opposite to those of true men, and their feet, in sandals, seemed very soft and supple.

Cugel looked about in bewilderment. Nearby crouched Fabeln, regarding him with loathing mingled with malicious satisfaction. Cugel saw now that a metal band encircled Fabeln's neck, to which was connected a long metal chain. At the far end of the burrow huddled an old man with long white hair, likewise fitted with collar and chain. Even as Cugel looked about him, the rat-people clamped a collar to his own neck. "Hold off!" exclaimed Cugel in consternation. "What does this mean? I deplore such treatment!"

The rat-folk gave him a shove and ran away. Cugel saw that long squamous tails depended from their pointed rumps, which protruded peculiarly from the black smocks which they wore.

The door closed; the three men were alone.

Cugel turned angrily upon Fabeln. "You tricked me; you led me to capture! This is a serious offense!"

Fabeln gave a bitter laugh. "No less serious than the deceit you practiced upon me! By your knavish trick, I was taken; I therefore ensured that you should not escape."

"This in inhuman malice!" roared Cugel. "I shall see to it that you receive your just desserts!"

"Bah," said Fabeln. "Do not annoy me with your complaints. In any event, I did not lure you into the cave from malice alone."

"No? You have a further perverse motive?"

"It is simple: the rat-folk are nothing if not clever! Whoever entices two others into the cave wins his own freedom. You represent one item to my account; I need furnish a second and I go free. Is this not correct, Zaraides?''

''Only in a broad sense,'' replied the old man. ''You may not tally this man to your account; if justice were absolute you and he would fulfill my score; did not my parchments bring you to the cave?''

''But not within!'' declared Fabeln. ''Here lies the careful distinction which must be made! The rat-folk concur, and hence you have not been released.''

''In this case,'' said Cugel, ''I hereby claim you as an item upon my score, since I sent you into the cave to test the circumstances to be encountered.''

Fabeln shrugged. ''This is a matter you must take up with the rat-folk.'' He frowned and blinked his small eyes. ''Why should I not claim myself as a credit to my own account? It is a point worth asserting.''

''Not so, not so,'' came a shrill voice from behind a grate. ''We tally only those items provided after impoundment. Fabeln is tallied to no one's account. He however is adjudged one item: namely, the person of Cugel. Zaraides has a score of null.''

Cugel felt the collar at his neck. ''What if we fail to provide two items?''

''A month is your time; no more. If you fail in this month, you are devoured.''

Fabeln spoke in a voice of sober calculation. ''I believe that I am as good as free. At no great distance my daughter waits. She is suddenly impatient with wild leeks and hence redundant to my household. It is fitting that by her agency I am released.'' And Fabeln nodded with ponderous satisfaction.

''It will be interesting to watch your methods,'' Cugel remarked. ''Precisely where is she to be found and how will she be summoned?''

Fabeln's expression became both cunning and rancorous. ''I tell you nothing! If you wish to tally items, devise the means yourself!''

Zaraides gestured to a board where lay strips of parchment. ''I tie persuasive messages to winged seeds, which are then liberated into the forest. The method is of questionable utility, luring passersby to the mouth of the cave, but enticing them no further. I fear that I have only five days to live. If only I had my librams, my folios, my work-books! What spells, what spells! I would rive this warren end to end; I would convert each of these man-rodents into a blaze of green fire. I would punish Fabeln for cheating me . . . Hmmm. The Gyrator? Lugwiler's Dismal Itch?''

"The Spell of Forlorn Encystment has its advocates," Cugel suggested.

Zaraides nodded. "The idea has much to recommend it . . . But this is an idle dream: my spells were snatched away and conveyed to some secret place."

Fabeln snorted and turned aside. From behind the grate came a shrill admonition: "Regrets and excuses are poor substitutes for items upon your score. Emulate Fabeln! Already he boasts one item and plans a second on the morrow! This is the sort we capture by choice!"

"I captured him!" asserted Cugel. "Have you no probity? I sent him into the cave; he should be credited to my account!"

Zaraides cried out in vehement protest. "By no means! Cugel distorts the case! If pure justice were done, both Cugel and Fabeln should be tallied to my score!"

"All is as before!" called out the shrill voice.

Zaraides threw up his hands and went to writing parchments with furious zeal. Fabeln hunched himself on a stool and sat in placid reflection. Cugel, in crawling past, kicked a leg from the stool and Fabeln fell to the floor. He rose and sprang at Cugel, who threw the stool at him.

"Order!" called the shrill voice. "Order or penalties will be inflicted!"

"Cugel dislodged the stool, to send me sprawling," complained Fabeln. "Why is he not punished?"

"The sheerest mischance," stated Cugel. "In my opinion the irascible Fabeln should be placed incommunicado, for at least two, or more properly, three weeks."

Fabeln began to sputter, but the shrill voice behind the grate enjoined an impartial silence upon all.

Food was presently brought, a coarse porridge of offensive odor. After the meal all were forced to crawl to a constricted burrow on a somewhat lower level, where they were chained to the wall. Cugel fell into a troubled sleep, to be awakened by a call through the door to Fabeln: "The message has been delivered—it was read with great attention."

"Good news!" came Fabeln's voice. "Tomorrow I shall walk the forest a free man!"

"Silence," croaked Zaraides from the dark. "Must I daily write parchments for everyone's benefit but my own, only to lie awake by night to your vile gloating?"

"Ha ha!" chortled Fabeln. "Hear the voice of the ineffectual wizard!"

"Alas for my lost librams!" groaned Zaraides. "You would sing a vastly different tune!"

"In what quarter are they to be found?" inquired Cugel cautiously.

"As to that, you must ask these foul murids; they seized me unawares."

Fabeln raised his head to complain. "Do you intend to exchange reminiscences the whole night through? I wish to sleep."

Zaraides, infuriated, began to upbraid Fabeln in so violent a manner that the rat-folk ran into the burrow and dragged him away, leaving Cugel and Fabeln alone.

In the morning Fabeln ate his porridge with great rapidity. "Now then," he called to the grating, "detach this collar, that I may go forth to summon the second of my tallies, Cugel being the first."

"Bah," muttered Cugel. "Infamous!"

The rat-folk, paying no heed to Fabeln's protests, adjusted the collar even more tightly around his neck, affixed the chain and pulled him forth on hands and knees, and Cugel was left alone.

He tried to sit erect, but the damp dirt pressed on his neck, and he slumped back down on his elbows. "Cursed rat-creatures! Somehow I must evade them! Unlike Fabeln, I have no household to draw from, and the efficacy of Zaraides' parchments is questionable. . . . Conceivably, however, others may wander close, in the fashion of Fabeln and myself." He turned to the gate, behind which sat the sharp-eyed monitor. "In order to recruit the required two items, I wish to wait outside the cave."

"This is permitted," announced the monitor. "Supervision must of course be rigid."

"Supervision is understandable," agreed Cugel. "I request however that the chain and collar be removed from my neck. With a constraint so evident, even the most credulous will turn away."

"There is something in what you say," admitted the monitor. "But what is there to prevent you from taking to your heels?"

Cugel gave a somewhat labored laugh. "Do I seem one to betray a trust? Further, why should I do so, when I can easily procure tally after tally for my score?"

"We shall make certain adjustments." A moment later a number of the rat-folk swarmed into the burrow. The collar was loosened from Cugel's neck, his right leg was seized and a silver pin driven through his ankle, to which, while Cugel called out in anguish, a chain was secured.

"The chain is now inconspicuous," stated one of his captors.

''You may now stand before the cave and attract passers-by as best you may.''

Still groaning in pain, Cugel crawled up through the burrow and into the cave-mouth, where Fabeln sat, a chain about his neck, awaiting the arrival of his daughter. ''Where do you go?'' he asked suspiciously.

''I go to pace before the cave, to attract passers-by and direct them within!''

Fabeln gave a sour grunt, and peered off through the trees.

Cugel went to stand before the cave-mouth. He looked in all directions, then gave a melodious call. ''Does anyone walk near?''

He received no reply, and began to pace back and forth, the chain jingling along the ground.

Movement through the trees: the flutter of yellow and green cloth, and here came Fabeln's daughter, carrying a basket and an axe. At the sight of Cugel she paused, then hesitantly approached. ''I see Fabeln, who has requested certain articles.''

''I will take them,'' said Cugel, reaching for the axe, but the rat-folk were alert and hauled him quickly back into the cave. ''She must place the axe on that far rock,'' they hissed into Cugel's ear. ''Go forth and so inform her.''

Cugel limped forth once more. The girl looked at him in puzzlement. ''Why did you leap back in that fashion?''

''I will tell you,'' said Cugel, ''and it is an odd matter, but first you must place your basket and axe on that rock yonder, where the true Fabeln will presently arrive.''

From within the cave came a mutter of angry protest, quickly stifled.

''What was that sound?'' inquired the girl.

''Do with the axe as I require, and I will make all known.''

The girl, puzzled, took axe and basket to the designated spot, then returned. ''Now, where is Fabeln?''

''Fabeln is dead,'' said Cugel. ''His body is currently possessed by a malicious spirit; do not on any grounds heed it: this is my warning.''

At this Fabeln gave a great groan, and called from the cave. ''He lies, he lies. Come hither, into the cave!''

Cugel held up a hand in restraint. ''By no means. Be cautious!''

The girl peered in wonder and fear toward the cave, where now Fabeln appeared, making the most earnest gesticulations. The girl drew back. ''Come, come!'' cried Fabeln. ''Enter the cave!''

The girl shook her head, and Fabeln in a fury attempted to tear loose his chain. The rat-folk dragged him hastily back into the shadows, where Fabeln fought so vigorously the rat-folk were obliged to kill him and drag his body back into the burrow.

Cugel listened attentively, then turned to the girl and nodded. "All is now well. Fabeln left certain valuables in my care; if you will step within the cave, I will relinquish them to you."

The girl shook her head in bewilderment. "Fabeln owned nothing of value!"

"Be good enough to inspect the objects." Cugel courteously motioned her to the cave. She stepped forward, peered within, and instantly the rat-folk seized her and dragged her down into the burrow.

"This is item one on my score," called Cugel within. "Do not neglect to record it!"

"The tally is duly noted," came a voice from within. "One more such and you go free."

The remainder of the day Cugel paced back and forth before the cave, looking this way and that through the trees, but saw no one. At nightfall he was drawn back into the cave and pent in the low-level burrow where he had passed the previous night. Now it was occupied by Fabeln's daughter. Naked, bruised, vacant-eyed, she stared at him fixedly. Cugel attempted an exchange of conversation, but she seemed bereft of speech.

The evening porridge was served. While Cugel ate, he watched the girl surreptitiously. She was by no means uncomely, though now bedraggled and soiled. Cugel crawled closer, but the odor of the rat-folk was so strong that his lust diminished, and he drew back.

During the night there was furtive sound in the burrow: a scraping, scratching, grating sound. Cugel, blinking sleepily, raised on an elbow to see a section of the floor tilt stealthily ajar, allowing a seep of smoky yellow light to play on the girl. Cugel cried out; into the burrow rushed rat-folk carrying tridents, but it was too late: the girl had been stolen.

The rat-folk were intensely angry. They raised the stone, screamed curses and abuse into the gap. Others poured into the hole, with further vituperation. One aggreivedly explained the situation to Cugel. "Other beings live below; they cheat us at every turn. Someday we will exact revenge; our patience is not inexhaustible! This night you must sleep elsewhere lest they make another sortie." He loosened Cugel's chain, but now was called by those who cemented the hole in the floor.

Cugel moved quietly to the entrance, and when the attention of all were distracted he slipped out into the passage. Gathering up the chain, he crawled in that direction which he thought led to the surface, but encountering a side-passage became confused. The tunnel turned downward and, becoming narrow, constricted his shoulders; then it diminished in height, pressing down on him from above, so that he was forced to writhe forward, jerking himself by his elbows.

His absence was discovered; from behind came squeals of rage, as the rat-folk rushed this way and that.

The passage made a sharp twist, at an angle into which Cugel found it impossible to twist his body. Writhing and jerking, he squeezed himself into a new posture, and now could no longer move. He exhaled and with eyes starting from his head, lunged about and up, and drew himself into a passage more open. In a niche he came upon a fire-ball, which he carried with him.

The rat-folk were approaching, screaming injunctions. Cugel thrust himself into a side-passage which opened into a store-room. The first objects to meet his eye were his sword and pouch.

The rat-folk rushed into the room with tridents. Cugel hacked and slashed and drove them squealing back into the corridor. Here they gathered, darting back and forth, calling shrill threats in at Cugel. Occasionally one would rush forward to gnash its teeth and flourish its trident, but when Cugel killed two of these, they drew back to confer in low tones.

Cugel took occasion to thrust certain heavy cases against the entrance, thus affording himself a moment's respite.

The rat-folk pressed forward, kicking and shoving. Cugel thrust his blade through a chink, eliciting a wail of intense distress.

One spoke: "Cugel, come forth! We are a kindly folk and bear no malice. You have one item upon your score, and shortly no doubt will secure another, and thus go free. Why discommode us all? There is no reason why, in an essentially inconvenient relationship, we should not adopt an attitude of camaraderie. Come forth, then, and we will provide meat for your morning porridge."

Cugel spoke politely. "At the moment I am too distraught to think clearly. Did I hear you say that you planned to set me free without further charge or difficulty?"

There was a whispered conversation in the corridor, then came the response. "There was indeed a statement to that effect. You are hereby declared free, to come and go as you wish. Unblock the entrance, cast down your sword, and come forth!"

"What guarantee can you offer me?" asked Cugel, listening intently at the blocked entrance.

There were shrill chattering whispers, then the reply: "No guarantee is necessary. We now retire. Come forth, walk along the corridor to your freedom."

Cugel made no response. Holding aloft the fireball, he turned to inspect the store-room, which contained a great store of articles of clothing, weapons and tools. In that bin which he had pushed against the entrance he noticed a group of leather-bound librams. On the face of the first was printed:

ZARAIDES THE WIZARD
His Work-book: Beware!

The rat-folk called once more, in gentle voices: ''Cugel, dear Cugel, why have you not come forth?''

''I rest; I recover my strength,'' said Cugel. He extracted the libram from the bin, turned the pages, and found an index.

''Come out, Cugel!'' came a command, somewhat sterner. ''We have here a pot of noxious vapor which we propose to discharge into the chamber where you so obdurately seclude yourself. Come out, or it shall be the worse for you!''

''Patience,'' called Cugel. ''Allow me time to collect my wits!''

''While you collect your wits we ready the pot of acid in which we plan to immerse your head.''

''Just so, just so,'' said Cugel absently, engrossed in the workbook. There was a scraping sound and a tube was thrust into the chamber. Cugel took hold of the tube and twisted it so that it pointed back into the corridor.

''Speak, Cugel!'' came the portentous order. ''Will you come hence or shall we send a great gust of vile gas into the chamber?''

''You lack that capability,'' said Cugel. ''I refuse to enter the corridor.''

''We shall see! Let the gas exude!''

The tube pulsed and hissed; from the passage came a cry of vast dismay. The hissing ceased.

Cugel, not finding what he sought in the workbook, drew forth a tome. This bore the title:

ZARAIDES THE WIZARD
His Compendium of Spells Beware!

Cugel opened and read; finding an appropriate spell, he held the fire-ball close the better to encompass the activating syllables. There were four lines of words, thirty-one syllables in all. Cugel forced them into his brain, where they lay like stones.

A sound behind him? Into the chamber from another portal came the rat-folk. Crouching low, white faces twitching, ears down, they crept forward, tridents leveled.

Cugel menaced them with his sword, then chanted that spell known as the Inside Out and Over, while the rat-folk stared aghast. There came a great tearing sound: a convulsive lift and twist as the passages everted, spewing all through the forest. Rat-folk ran squealing back and forth, and there were also running white things whose nature Cugel could not distinguish by starlight. Rat-folk and the white creatures grappled and tore ferociously at each other, and the forest was filled with snarling and gnashing, shrill screams and small voices raised in outcry.

Cugel moved quietly away, and in a bilberry thicket waited out the night.

When dawn arrived he returned cautiously to the hillock, hoping to possess himself of Zaraides' compendium and work-book. There was a great litter, and many small corpses, but the articles he sought were not to be found. Regretfully Cugel turned away and presently came upon Fabeln's daughter sitting among the ferns. When he approached, she squeaked at him. Cugel pursed his lips and shook his head in disapproval. He led her to a nearby stream and attempted to wash her, but at the first opportunity she disengaged herself and hid under a rock.

7

The Manse of Iucounu

The spell known as the Inside Out and Over was of derivation so remote as to be forgotten. An unknown Cloud-rider of the Twenty-first Eon had construed an archaic version; the half-legendary Basile Blackweb had refined its contours, a process continued by Veronifer the Bland, who had added a reinforcing resonance. Archemand of Glaere had annotated fourteen of its pervulsions: Phandaal had listed it in the 'A,' or 'Perfected,' category of his monumental catalogue. In this fashion it had reached the workbook of Zaraides the Sage, where Cugel, immured under a hillock, had found it and spoken it.

Now, once more searching through the multifarious litter of the spell's aftermath, Cugel found articles of every description: garments new and old; jerkins, vests and cloaks; antique tabards; breeches flared after the new taste of Kauchique, or fringed and tasseled in the style of Old Romarth, or pied and gored in the extravagant Andromach mode. There were boots and sandals and hats of every description; plumes, panaches, emblems and crests; old tools and broken weapons; bangles and trinkets; tarnished filigrees, crusted cameos; gemstones which Cugel could not refrain from gathering and which perhaps delayed him from finding that which he sought: the work-books of Zaraides, which had been scattered with the rest.

Cugel searched at length. He found silver bowls, ivory spoons, porcelain vases, gnawed bones and shining teeth of many sorts, these glittering like pearls among the leaves—but nowhere the tomes and folios which might have helped him overcome Iucounu the Laughing Magician. Even now Iucounu's creature of coercion, Firx, clamped serrated members upon Cugel's liver. Cugel finally called out: "I merely seek the most direct route to Azenomei; you will soon rejoin your comrade in Iucounu's vat! Meanwhile take your ease; are you in such an agony of haste?'' At which Firx sullenly relaxed his pressure.

Cugel wandered disconsolately back and forth, looking among branches and under roots, squinting up the forest aisles, kicking among the ferns and mosses. Then at the base of a stump he saw that which he sought: a number of folios and librams, gathered into a neat stack. Upon the stump sat Zaraides.

Cugel stepped forward, pinch-mouthed with disappointment. Zaraides surveyed him with a serene countenance. ''You appear to seek some misplaced object. The loss, I trust, is not serious?''

Cugel gave his head a terse shake. ''A few trifles have gone astray. Let them molder among the leaves.''

''By no means!'' declared Zaraides. ''Describe the loss; I will send forth a searching oscillation. You will have your property within moments!''

Cugel demurred. ''I would not impose such a trivial business upon you. Let us consider other matters.'' He indicated the stack of tomes, upon which Zaraides had now placed his feet. ''Happily your own property is secure.''

Zaraides nodded with placid satisfaction. ''All is now well; I am concerned only with that imbalance which distorts our relationship.'' He held up his hand as Cugel stood back. ''There is no cause for alarm: in fact, quite the reverse. Your acts averted my death; the Law of Equivalences has been disturbed and I must contrive a reciprocity.'' He combed his beard with his fingers. ''The requital unfortunately must be largely symbolic. I could well fulfill the totality of your desires and still not nudge the scale against the weight of the service you have performed, even if unwittingly, for me.''

Cugel became somewhat more cheerful, but now Firx, once again impatient, made a new demonstration. Clasping his abdomen, Cugel cried out, ''Preliminary to all, be good enough to extract the creature which lacerates my vitals, a certain Firx.''

Zaraides raised his eyebrows. ''What manner of creature is this?''

''A detestable object from a far star. It resembles a tangle, a thicket, a web of white spines, barbs and claws.''

''A matter of no great difficulty,'' said Zaraides. ''These creatures are susceptible to a rather primitive method of extirpation. Come; my dwelling lies at no great distance.''

Zaraides stepped down from the stump, gathered his compendia and flung them into the air; all lofted high to float swiftly over the treetops and out of sight. Cugel watched them go with sadness.

''You marvel?'' inquired Zaraides. ''It is nothing: the simplest of procedures and a curb on the zeal of thieves and foot-pads. Let us set forth; we must expel this creature which causes you such distress.''

He led the way through the trees. Cugel came after, but now Firx, belatedly sensing that all was not to his advantage, made a furious protest. Cugel, bending double, jumping sidewise, forced himself to totter and run after Zaraides, who marched without so much as a backward glance.

In the branches of an enormous daobado Zaraides had his dwelling. Stairs rose to a heavy drooping bough which led to a rustic portico. Cugel crawled up the staircase along the bough, and into a great square room. The furnishings were at once simple and luxurious. Windows looked in all directions over the forest; a thick rug patterned in black, brown and yellow covered the floor.

Zaraides beckoned Cugel into his workroom. ''We will abate this nuisance at once.''

Cugel stumbled after him and at a gesture settled upon a glass pedestal.

Zaraides brought a screen of zinc strips which he placed at Cugel's back. ''This is to inform Firx that a trained wizard is at hand: creatures of his sort are highly antipathetic to zinc. Now then, a simple potion: sulfur, aquastel, tincture of zyche; certain herbs: bournade, hilp, cassas, though these latter are perhaps not essential. Drink, if you will . . . Firx, come hence! you extra-terrestrial pest! Remove! Or I dust Cugel's entire interior with sulfur and pierce him with zinc rods! Come forth! What? Must I flush you out with aquastel? Come; return to Achernar as best you may!''

At this Firx angrily relinquished his grip and issued from Cugel's chest: a tangle of white nerves and tendrils, each with its claw or barb. Zaraides captured the creature in a zinc basin which he covered with a mesh of zinc.

Cugel, who had lost consciousness, awoke to find Zaraides serenely affable, awaiting his recovery. ''You are a lucky man,'' Zaraides told him. ''The treatment was only barely in time. It is the tendency of this maleficent incubus to extend its prongs everywhere through the body, until it clamps upon the brain; then you and Firx are one and the same. How did you become infected with the creature?''

Cugel gave a small grimace of distaste. ''It was at the hands of Iucounu the Laughing Magician. You know him?'' For Zaraides had allowed his eyebrows to arch high.

''Mainly by his reputation for humor and grotesquerie,'' replied the sage.

"He is nothing less than a buffoon!" exclaimed Cugel. "For a fancied slight he threw me to the north of the world, where the sun wheels low and casts no more heat than a lamp. Iucounu must have his joke, but now I will have a joke of my own! You have announced your effusive gratitude, and so, before proceeding to the main body of my desires, we will take a suitable revenge upon Iucounu."

Zaraides nodded thoughtfully and ran his fingers through his beard. "I will advise you. Iucounu is a vain and sensitive man. His most vulnerable spot is his self-esteem. Turn your back on him, take yourself to another quarter! This act of proud disdain will strike a pang more exquisite than any other discomfort you might devise."

Cugel frowned. "The reprisal seems rather too abstract. If you will be good enough to summon a demon, I will give him his instructions in regard to Iucounu. The business will then be at an end, and we can discuss other matters."

Zaraides shook his head. "All is not so simple. Iucounu, himself devious, is not apt to be taken unawares. He would instantly learn who instigated the assault, and the relations of distant cordiality we have enjoyed would be at an end."

"Pah!" scoffed Cugel. "Does Zaraides the Sage fear to identify himself with the cause of justice? Does he blink and draw aside from one so timid and vacillating as Iucounu?"

"In a word—yes," said Zaraides. "At any instant the sun may go dark; I do not care to pass these last hours exchanging jests with Iucounu, whose humor is much more elaborate than my own. So now, attend. In one minute I must concern myself with certain important duties. As a final signal of gratitude I will transfer you to whatever locale you choose. Where shall it be?"

"If this is your best, take me then to Azenomei, at the juncture of the Xzan with the Scaum!"

"As you wish. Be so good as to step upon this stage. Hold out your hands thus. . . . Draw your breath deep, and during the passage neither inhale nor exhale. . . . Are you ready?"

Cugel assented. Zaraides drew back and called a spell. Cugel was jerked up and away. An instant later the ground touched his feet and he found himself walking the main concourse of Azenomei.

He drew a deep breath. "After all the trials, all the vicissitudes, I am once again in Azenomei!" And, shaking his head in wonder, he looked about him. The ancient structures, the terraces overlooking the river, the market: all were as before. Not far distant was the booth of Fianosther. Turning his back to avoid recognition, he sauntered away.

"Now what?" he ruminated. "First, new garments, then the comforts of an inn, where I may weigh every aspect of my present condition. When one wishes to laugh with Iucounu, he should embark upon the project with all caution."

Two hours later, bathed, shorn, refreshed, and wearing new garments of black, green and red, Cugel sat in the common room of the River Inn with a plate of spiced sausages and a flask of green wine.

"This matter of a just settlement poses problems of extreme delicacy," he mused. "I must move with care!"

He poured wine from the flagon, and ate several of the sausages. Then he opened his pouch and withdrew a small object wrapped carefully in soft cloth: the violet cusp which Iucounu wished as a match for the one already in his possession. He raised the cusp to his eye, but stopped short: it would display the surroundings in an illusion so favorable that he might never wish to remove it. And now, as he contemplated the glossy surface, there entered his mind a program so ingenious, so theoretically effective and yet of such small hazard, that he instantly abandoned the search for a better.

Essentially, the scheme was simple. He would present himself to Iucounu and tender the cusp, or more accurately, a cusp of similar appearance. Iucounu would compare it with that which he already owned, in order to test the efficacy of the coupled pair, and inevitably look through both. The discord between the real and the false would jar his brain and render him helpless, whereupon Cugel could take such measures as seemed profitable.

Where was the flaw in the plan? Cugel could see none. If Iucounu discovered the substitution, Cugel need only utter an apology and produce the real cusp, and so lull Iucounu's suspicions. All in all, the probabilities of success seemed excellent.

Cugel finished his sausages in leisure, ordered a second flagon of wine, and observed with pleasure the view across the Xzan. There was no need for haste; indeed, while dealing with Iucounu, impulsiveness was a serious mistake, as he had already learned.

On the following day, still finding no fault in his plan, he visited a glass-blower whose workroom was established on the banks of the Scaum a mile to the east of Azenomei, in a copse of fluttering yellow bilibobs.

The glass-blower examined the cusp. "An exact duplicate, of identical shape and color? No small task, with a violet so pure and rich. Such a color is most difficult to work into glass; there is no specific stain; all must be a matter of guess and hazard. Still—I will prepare a melt. We shall see, we shall see."

After several trials he produced a glass of the requisite hue, from which he fashioned a cusp superficially indistinguishable from the magic lens.

"Excellent!" declared Cugel. "And now, as to your fee?"

"Such a cusp of violet glass I value at a hundred terces," replied the glass-blower in a casual manner.

"What?" cried Cugel in outrage. "Do I appear so gullible? The charge is excessive."

The glass-blower replaced his tools, swages and crucibles, showing no concern for Cugel's indignation. "The universe evinces no true stability. All fluctuates, cycles, ebbs and flows; all is pervaded with mutability. My fees, which are immanent with the cosmos, obey the same laws and vary according to the anxiety of the customer."

Cugel drew back in displeasure, at which the glass-blower reached forth and possessed himself of both cusps. Cugel exclaimed: "What do you intend?"

"I return the glass to the crucible; what else?"

"And what of that cusp which is my property?"

"I retain it as a memento of our conversation."

"Hold!" Cugel drew a deep breath. "I might pay your exorbitant fee if the new cusp were as clear and perfect as the old."

The glass-blower inspected first one, then the other. "To my eye they are identical."

"What of focus?" Cugel challenged. "Hold both to your vision, look through both, then say as much!"

The glass-blower raised both cusps to his eyes. One allowed a view into the Overworld, the other transmitted a view of Reality. Stunned by the discord, the glass-blower swayed and would have fallen had not Cugel, in an effort to protect the cusps, supported him, and guided him to a bench.

Taking the cusps, Cugel tossed three terces to the work-table. "All is mutability, and thus your hundred terces has fluctuated to three."

The glass-blower, too dazed to make sensible reply, mumbled and struggled to raise his hand, but Cugel strode from the studio and away.

He returned to the inn. Here he donned his old garments, stained and torn by much harsh treatment, and set forth along the banks of the Xzan.

As he walked he rehearsed the approaching confrontation, trying to anticipate every possible contingency. Ahead, the sunlight glinted through spiral green glass towers: the manse of Iucounu!

Cugel halted to gaze up at the eccentric structure. How many times during his journey had he envisioned himself standing here, with Iucounu the Laughing Magician close at hand!

He climbed the winding way of dark brown tile, and every step increased the tautness of his nerves. He approached the front door, and saw on the heavy panel an object which he had failed to notice previously: a visage carved in ancient wood, a gaunt face pinched of cheek and jaw, the eyes aghast, the lips drawn back, the mouth wide in a yell of despair or perhaps defiance.

With his hand raised to rap at the door, Cugel felt a chill settle on his soul. He drew back from the haggard wooden countenance, turning to follow the gaze of the blind eyes—across the Xzan and away over the dim bare hills, rolling and heaving as far as vision could reach. He reviewed his plan of operations. Was there a flaw? Danger to himself? None was apparent. If Iucounu discovered the substitution Cugel could always plead error and produce the genuine cusp. Great advantage was to be gained at small risk! Cugel turned back and rapped on the heavy panel.

A minute passed. Slowly the portal swung open. A flow of cool air issued forth, carrying a bitter odor which Cugel could not identify. The sunlight slanting across his shoulder passed through the portal and fell upon the stone floor. Cugel peered uncertainly into the vestibule, reluctant to enter without an express invitation. ''Iucounu!'' he called. ''Come forth, that I may enter your manse! I wish no further unjust accusations!''

Within was a stir, a slow sound of feet. From a room to the side came Iucounu, and Cugel thought to detect a change in his countenance. The great soft yellow head seemed looser than before: the jowls sagged, the nose hung like a stalactite, the chin was little more than a pimple below the great twitching mouth.

Iucounu wore a square brown hat with each of the corners tipped up, a blouse of brown and black diaper, loose pantaloons of a heavy dark brown stuff with black embroidery—a handsome set of garments which Iucounu wore without grace, as if they were strange to him, and uncomfortable; and indeed, he gave Cugel a greeting which Cugel found odd. ''Well, fellow, what is your purpose? You will never learn to walk ceilings standing on your hands.'' And Iucounu hid his mouth with his hands to conceal a snicker.

Cugel raised his eyebrows in surprise and doubt. ''This is not my purpose. I have come on an errand of vast import: namely to report that the mission I undertook on your behalf is satisfactorily terminated.''

''Excellent!'' cried Iucounu. ''You may now tender me the keys to the bread locker.''

''Bread locker?'' Cugel stared in surprise. Was Iucounu mad? ''I am Cugel, whom you sent north on a mission. I have returned with the magic cusp affording a view into the Overworld!''

''Of course, of course!'' cried Iucounu. '' 'Brzmszzst.' I fear I am vague, among so many contrasting situations; nothing is quite as before. But now I welcome you. Cugel, of course! All is clear. You have gone forth, you have returned! How is friend Firx? Well, I trust? I have longed for his companionship. A laudable fellow, Firx!''

Cugel acquiesced with no great fervor. ''Yes, Firx has been a friend indeed, an unflagging source of encouragement.''

''Excellent! Step within! I must provide refreshment! What is your preference: 'sz-mzsm' or 'szk-zsm'?''

Cugel eyed Iucounu askance. His demeanor was more than peculiar. ''I am familiar with neither of the items you mention, and hence will decline both with gratitude. But observe! The magic violet cusp!'' And Cugel displayed the glass fabrication which he had procured only a few hours previously.

''Splendid!'' declared Iucounu. ''You have done well, and your trangressions—now I recall all, having sorted among the various circumstances—are hereby declared nullified. But give me the cusp! I must put it to trial!''

''Of course,'' said Cugel. ''I respectfully suggest, that in order to comprehend the full spendor of the Overworld, you bring forth your own cusp and look through both simultaneously. This is the only appropriate method.''

''True, how true! My cusp; now where did that stubborn rascal conceal it?''

'' 'Stubborn rascal?' '' inquired Cugel. ''Has someone been misarranging your valuables?''

''In a manner of speaking.'' Iucounu gave a wild titter, and kicked up both feet far to the side, falling heavily to the floor, from where he addressed the astounded Cugel. ''It is all one, and no longer of consequence, since all must now transpire in the 'mnz' pattern. Yes. I will shortly consult with Firx.''

''On a previous occasion,'' said Cugel patiently, ''you procured your cusp from a cabinet in that chamber yonder.''

''Silence!'' commanded Iucounu in sudden annoyance. He hauled himself to his feet. '' 'Szsz!' I am well aware as to where the cusp is stored. All is completely coordinated! Follow me. We shall learn the essence of the Overworld at once!'' He emitted a bray of immoderate laughter, at which Cugel stared in new astonishment.

Iucounu shuffled into the side-chamber and returned with the case containing his magic cusp. He made an imperious gesture to Cugel. "Stand exactly at this spot. Do not move, as you value Firx!"

Cugel bowed obediently. Iucounu took forth his cusp. "Now—the new object!"

Cugel tendered the glass cusp. "To your eyes, both together, that you may enjoy the full glory of the Overworld!"

"Yes! This is as it shall be!" Iucounu lifted the two cusps and applied them to his eyes. Cugel, expecting him to fall paralyzed by the discord, reached for the cord he had brought to tie the insensible savant; but Iucounu showed no signs of helplessness. He peered this way and that, chortling in a peculiar fashion. "Splendid! Superb! A vista of pure pleasure!" He removed the cusps and placed them carefully in the case. Cugel watched glumly.

"I am much pleased," said Iucounu, making a sinuous gesture of hands and arms, which further bewildered Cugel. "Yes," Iucounu continued, "you have done well, and the insensate wickedness of your offense is hereby remitted. Now all that remains is the delivery of my indispensable Firx, and to this end I must place you in a vat. You will be submerged in an appropriate liquid for approximately twenty-six hours, which may well suffice to tempt Firx forth."

Cugel grimaced. How was one to reason with a magician not only droll and irascible, but also bereft? "Such an immersion might well affect me adversely," he pointed out cautiously. "Far wiser to allow Firx a period of further perambulation."

Iucounu seemed favorably impressed by the suggestion, and expressed his delight by means of an extremely intricate jig, which he performed with agility remarkable in a man of Iucounu's short limbs and somewhat corpulent body. He concluded the demonstration with a great leap into the air, alighting on his neck and shoulders, arms and legs waving like those of an overturned bettle. Cugel watched in fascination, wondering whether Iucounu was alive or dead.

But Iucounu, blinking somewhat, nimbly gained an upright posture. "I must perfect the exact pressures and thrusts," he ruminated. "Otherwise there is impingement. The eluctance here is of a different order than of 'sszpntz.' " He emitted another great chortle, throwing back his head, and looking into the open mouth Cugel saw, rather than a tongue, a white claw. Instantly he apprehended the reason for Iucounu's bizarre conduct. In some fashion, a creature like Firx had inserted itself into Iucounu's body, and had taken possession of his brain.

Cugel rubbed his chin with interest. A situation of marvel! He applied himself to concentrated thought. Essential to know was whether the creature retained Iucounu's mastery of magic. Cugel said, "Your wisdom astounds me! I am filled with admiration! Have you added to your collection of thaumaturgical curios?"

"No; there is ample at hand," declared the creature, speaking through Iucounu's mouth. "But now I feel the need for relaxation. The evolution I performed a moment or so ago has made quietude necessary."

"A simple matter," said Cugel. "The most effective means to this end is to clamp with extreme intensity upon the Lobe of Directive Volition."

"Indeed?" inquired the creature. "I will attempt as much; let me see: this is the Lobe of Antithesis and here, the Convolvement of Subliminal Configuration. . . . 'Szzm.' Much here puzzles me; it was never thus on Achernar." The creature gave Cugel a sharp look to see if the slip had been noticed. But Cugel put on an attitude of lackadaisical boredom; and the creature continued to sort through the various elements of Iucounu's brain. "Ah yes, here: the Lobe of Directive Volition. Now, a sudden vigorous pressure."

Iucounu's face became taut, the muscles sagged, and the corpulent body crumpled to the floor. Cugel leapt forward and in a trice bound Iucounu's arms and legs and affixed an adhesive pad across the big mouth.

Now Cugel performed a joyful caper of his own. All was well! Iucounu, his manse and his great collection of magical adjuncts were at his disposal! Cugel considered the helpless hulk and started to drag it outside where he might conveniently strike off the great yellow head, but the recollection of the numerous indignities, discomforts and humiliations he had suffered at Iucounu's hands gave him pause. Should Iucounu attain oblivion so swiftly, with neither cognition nor remorse? By no means!

Cugel pulled the still body out into the hall, and sat on a nearby bench to consider.

Presently the body stirred, opened its eyes, made an effort to arise, and, finding this impossible, turned to examine Cugel first in surprise, then outrage. From the mouth came peremptory sounds which Cugel acknowledged with a noncommittal sign.

Presently he arose to his feet, examined the bonds and the mouth-plaster, made all doubly secure, then set about a cautious inspection of the manse, alert for traps, lures or deadfalls which the whimsical Iucounu might have established in order to outwit or beguile intruders. He was especially vigilant during his inspection of Iucounu's work-room, probing everywhere with a long rod, but if Iucounu had set forth snares or beguilements, none were evident.

Looking along Iucounu's shelves, Cugel found sulfur, aquastel, tincture of zyche and herbs from which he prepared a viscous yellow elixir. He dragged the flaccid body into the workroom, administered the potion, called orders and persuasions and finally, with Iucounu an even more intense yellow from ingested sulfur, with aquastel steaming from his ears, with Cugel panting and perspiring from his own exertions, the creature from Achernar clawed free of the heaving body. Cugel caught it in a great stone mortar, crushed it to a paste with an iron pestle, dissolved all with spirits of vitriol, added aromatic mernaunce and poured the resultant slime down a drain.

Iucounu, presently returning to consciousness, fixed Cugel with a glare of disturbing intensity. Cugel administered an exhalation of raptogen and the Laughing Magician, rolling his eyes upward, returned to a state of apathy.

Cugel sat back to rest. A problem existed: how best to restrain Iucounu while he made his representations. Finally, after looking through one or two manuals, he sealed Iucounu's mouth with a daub of juncturing compound, secured his vitality with an uncomplicated spell, then pent him in a tall glass tube, which he suspended from a chain in the vestibule.

This accomplished, and Iucounu once more conscious, Cugel stood back with an affable grin. "At last, Iucounu, matters begin to right themselves. Do you recall the indignities you visited upon me? How gross they were! I vowed that you would regret the circumstance! I now begin to validate the vow. Do I make myself clear?"

The expression distorting Iucounu's face was an adequate response.

Cugel seated himself with a goblet of Iucounu's best yellow wine. "I intend to pursue the matter in this wise: I shall calculate the sum of those hardships I have endured; including such almost incommensurable qualities as chills, cold draughts, insults, pangs of apprehension, uncertainties, bleak despairs, horrors and disgusts, and other indescribable miseries, not the least of which were the ministrations of the unspeakable Firx. From this total I will subtract for my initial indiscretion, and possibly one or two further ameliorations, leaving an imposing balance of retribution. Luckily, you are Iucounu the Laughing Magician: you will certainly derive a wry impersonal amusement from the situation." Cugel turned an inquiring glance up at Iucounu, but the returning gaze was anything but jocular.

"A final question," said Cugel. "Have you arranged any traps or lures in which I might be destroyed or immobilized? One blink will express 'no'; two, 'yes.' "

Iucounu merely gazed contemptuously from the tube.

Cugel sighed. "I see that I must conduct myself warily."

Taking his wine into the great hall, he began to familiarize himself with the collection of magical instruments, artifacts, talismans and curios: now, for all practical purposes, his own property. Iucounu's gaze followed him everywhere with an anxious hope that was by no means reassuring.

Days went by and Iucounu's trap, if such existed, remained unsprung, and Cugel at last came to believe that none existed. During this time he applied himself to Iucounu's tomes and folios, but with disappointing results. Certain of the tomes were written in archaic tongues, indecipherable script or arcane terminology; others described phenomena beyond his comprehension; others exuded a waft of such urgent danger that Cugel instantly clamped shut the covers.

One or two of the workbooks he found susceptible to his understanding. These he studied with great diligence, cramming syllable after wrenching syllable into his mind, where they rolled and pressed and distended his temples. Presently he was able to encompass a few of the most simple and primitive spells, certain of which he tested upon Iucounu: notably Lugwiler's Dismal Itch. But by and large Cugel was disappointed by what seemed a lack of innate competence. Accomplished magicians could encompass three or even four of the most powerful effectuants; for Cugel, attaining even a single spell was a task of extraordinary difficulty. One day, while applying a spatial transposition upon a satin cushion, he inverted certain of the pervulsions and was himself hurled backward into the vestibule. Annoyed by Iucounu's smirk, Cugel carried the tube to the front of the manse and affixed a pair of brackets upon which he hung lamps, which thereafter illuminated the area before the manse during the hours of night.

A month passed, and Cugel became somewhat more confident in his occupancy of the manse. Peasants of a nearby village brought him produce, and in return Cugel performed what small services he was able. On one occasion the father of Jince, the maiden who served as arranger of his bed-chamber, lost a valuable buckle in a deep cistern and implored Cugel to bring it forth. Cugel readily agreed, and lowered the tube containing Iucounu into the cistern. Iucounu finally indicated the location of the buckle, which was then recovered with a grapple.

The episode set Cugel to devising other uses for Iucounu. At the Azenomei Fair a "Contest of Grotesques" had been arranged. Cugel entered Iucounu in the competition, and while he failed to win the prime award, his grimaces were unforgettable and attracted much comment.

At the fair Cugel encountered Fianosther, the dealer in talismans and magical adjuncts who had originally sent Cugel to Iucounu's manse. Fianosther looked in jocular surprise from Cugel to the tube containing Iucounu, which Cugel was transporting back to the manse in a cart. "Cugel! Cugel the Clever!" exclaimed Fianosther. "Rumor then speaks accurately! You are now lord of Iucounu's manse, and of his great collection of instruments and curios!"

Cugel at first pretended not to recognize Fianosther, then spoke in the coolest of voices. "Quite true," he said. "Iucounu has chosen to participate less actively in the affairs of the world, as you see. Nonetheless, the manse is a warren of traps and deadfalls; several famished beasts stalk the grounds by night, and I have established a spell of intense violence to guard each entrance."

Fianosther seemed not to notice Cugel's distant manner. Rubbing his plump hands, he inquired, "Since you now control a vast collection of curios, will you sell certain of the less choice items?"

"I have neither need nor inclination to do so," said Cugel. "Iucounu's coffers contain gold to last till the sun goes dark." And both men, after the habit of time, looked up to gauge the color of the moribund star.

Fianostsher made a gracious sign. "In this case, I wish you a good day, and you as well." The last was addressed to Iucounu, who returned only a surly glare.

Returning to the manse, Cugel brought Iucounu into the vestibule; then, making his way to the roof, he leaned on a parapet and gazed over the expanse of hills which rolled away like swells on a sea. For the hundredth time he pondered Iucounu's peculiar failure of foresight; by no means must he, Cugel, fall into similar error. And he looked about with an eye to defense.

Above rose the spiral green glass towers; below slanted the steep ridges and gables which Iucounu had deemed esthetically correct. Only the face of the ancient keep offered an easy method of access to the manse. Along the slanting outer abutments Cugel arranged sheets of soap-stone in such a manner that anyone climbing to the parapets must step on these and slide to his doom. Had Iucounu taken a similar precaution—so Cugel reflected—instead of arranging the oversubtle crystal maze, he would not now be looking forth from the tall glass tube.

Other defenses must also be perfected: namely those resources to be derived from Iucounu's shelves.

Returning to the great hall, he consumed the repast set forth by Jince and Skivvee, his two comely stewardesses, then immediately applied himself to his studies. Tonight they concerned themselves with the Spell of Forlorn Encystment, a reprisal perhaps more favored in earlier eons than the present, and the Agency of Far Despatch, by which Iucounu had transported him to the northern wastes. Both spells were of no small power; both required a bold and absolutely precise control, which Cugel at first feared he would never be able to supply. Nevertheless he persisted, and at last felt able to encompass either the one or the other, at need.

Two days later it was as Cugel had expected: a rap at the front door which, when Cugel flung wide the portal, indicated the unwelcome presence of Fianosther.

"Good day," said Cugel cheerlessly. "I am indisposed, and must request that you instantly depart."

Fianosther made a bland gesture. "A report of your distressing illness reached me, and such was my concern that I hastened here with an opiate. Allow me to step within"—so saying he thrust his portly figure past Cugel—"and I will decant the specific dose."

"I suffer from a spiritual malaise," said Cugel meaningfully, "which manifests itself in outbursts of vicious rage. I implore you to depart, lest, in an uncontrollable spasm, I cut you in three pieces with my sword, or worse, invoke magic."

Fianosther winced uneasily, but continued in a voice of unquenchable optimism. "I likewise carry a potion against this disorder." He brought forth a black flask. "Take a single swallow and your anxieties will be no more."

Cugel grasped the pommel of his sword. "It seems that I must speak without ambiguity. I command you: depart, and never return! I understand your purpose and I warn you that you will find me a less indulgent enemy than was Iucounu! So now, be off! Or I inflict upon you the Spell of the Macroid Toe, whereupon the signalized member swells to the proportions of a house."

"Thus and so," cried Fianosther in a fury. "The mask is torn aside! Cugel the Clever stands revealed as an ingrate! Ask yourself: who urged you to pillage the manse of Iucounu? It was I, and by every standard of honest conduct I should be entitled to a share of Iucounu's wealth!"

Cugel snatched forth his blade. "I have heard enough; now I act."

"Hold!" And Fianosther raised high the black flask. "I need only hurl this bottle to the floor to unloose a purulence, to which I am immune. Stand back, then!"

But Cugel, infuriated, lunged, to thrust his blade through the upraised arm. Fianosther called out in woe, and flung the black bottle into the air. Cugel leapt to catch it with great dexterity; but meanwhile, Fianosther, jumping forward, struck him a blow, so that Cugel staggered back and collided with the glass tube containing Iucounu. It toppled to the stone and shattered; Iucounu crept painfully away from the fragments.

"Ha ha!" laughed Fianosther. "Matters now move in a different direction!"

"By no means!" called Cugel, bringing forth a tube of blue concentrate which he had found among Iucounu's instruments.

Iucounu strove with a sliver of glass to cut the seal on his lips. Cugel projected a waft of blue concentrate and Iucounu gave a great tight-lipped moan of distress. "Drop the glass!" ordered Cugel. "Turn about to the wall." He threatened Fianosther. "You as well!"

With great care he bound the arms of his enemies, then stepping into the great hall possessed himself of the work-book which he had been studying.

"And now—both outside!" he ordered. "Move with alacrity! Events will now proceed to a definite condition!"

He forced the two to walk to a flat area behind the manse, and stood them somewhat apart. "Fianosther, your doom is well-merited. For your deceit, avarice and odious mannerisms I now visit upon you the Spell of Forlorn Encystment!"

Fianosther wailed piteously, and collapsed to his knees. Cugel took no heed. Consulting the workbook, he encompassed the spell; then, pointing and naming Fianosther, he spoke the dreadful syllables.

But Fianosther, rather than sinking into the earth, crouched as before. Cugel hastily consulted the workbook and saw that in error he had transposed a pair of pervulsions, thereby reversing the quality of the spell. Indeed, even as he understood the mistake, to all sides there were small sounds, and previous victims across the eons were now erupted from a depth of forty-five miles, and discharged upon the surface. Here they lay, blinking in glazed astonishment; though a few lay rigid, too sluggish to react. Their garments had fallen to dust, though the more recently encysted still wore a rag or two. Presently all but the most dazed and rigid made tentative motions, feeling the air, groping at the sky, marveling at the sun.

Cugel uttered a harsh laugh. "I seem to have performed incorrectly. But no matter. I shall not do so a second time. Iucounu, your penalty shall be commensurate with your offense, no more, no less! You flung me willy-nilly to the northern wastes, to a land where the sun slants low across the south. I shall do the same for you. You inflicted me with Firx; I will inflict you with Fianosther. Together you may plod the tundras, penetrate the Great Erm, win past the Mountains of Magnatz. Do not plead; put forward no excuses: in this case I am obdurate. Stand quietly unless you wish a further infliction of blue concentrate!''

So now Cugel applied himself to the Agency of Far Despatch, and established the activating sounds carefully within his mind. ''Prepare yourselves,'' he called, ''and farewell!''

With that he sang forth the spell, hesitating at only one pervulsion where uncertainty overcame him. But all was well. From on high came a thud and a guttural out-cry, as a coursing demon was halted in mid-flight.

''Appear, appear!'' called Cugel. ''The destination is as before: to the shore of the northern sea, where the cargo must be delivered alive and secure! Appear! Seize the designated persons and carry them in accordance with the command!''

A great flapping buffeted the air; a black shape with a hideous visage peered down. It lowered a talon; Cugel was lifted and carried off to the north, betrayed a second time by a misplaced pervulsion.

For a day and a night the demon flew, grumbling and moaning. Somewhat after dawn Cugel was cast down on a beach and the demon thundered off through the sky.

There was silence. To right and left spread the gray beach. Behind rose the foreshore with a few clumps of salt-grass and spinifex. A few yards up the beach lay the splintered cage in which once before Cugel had been delivered to this same spot. With head bowed and arms clasped around his knees, Cugel sat looking out across the sea.

Cugel's Saga

Contents

Chapter 1

FROM SHANGLESTONE STRAND TO SASKERVOY

1

Flutic

Iucounu (known across Almery as 'the Laughing Magician') had worked one of his most mordant jokes upon Cugel. For the second time Cugel had been snatched up, carried north across the Ocean of Sighs, dropped upon that melancholy beach known as Shanglestone Strand.

Rising to his feet, Cugel brushed sand from his cloak and adjusted his hat. He stood not twenty yards from that spot upon which he had been dropped before, also at the behest of Iucounu. He carried no sword and his pouch contained no terces.

The solitude was absolute. No sound could be heard but the sigh of the wind along the dunes. Far to the east a dim headland thrust into the water, as did another, equally remote, to the west. To the south spread the sea, empty except for the reflection of the old red sun.

Cugel's frozen faculties began to thaw, and a whole set of emotions, one after the other, made themselves felt, with fury taking precedence over all.

Iucounu would now be enjoying his joke to the fullest. Cugel raised his fist high and shook it toward the south. "Iucounu, at last you have exceeded yourself! This time you will pay the price! I, Cugel, appoint myself your nemesis!"

For a period Cugel strode back and forth, shouting and cursing: a person long of arm and leg, with lank black hair, gaunt cheeks, and a crooked mouth of great flexibility. The time was middle afternoon, and the sun, already half-way into the west, tottered down the sky like a sick animal. Cugel, who was nothing if not practical, decided to postpone the remainder of his tirade; more urgent was lodging for the night. Cugel called down a final curse of pulsing carbuncles upon

Iucounu, then, picking his way across the shingle, he climbed to the crest of a dune and looked in all directions.

To the north a succession of marshes and huddles of black larch straggled away into the murk.

To the east Cugel gave only a cursory glance. Here were the villages Smolod and Grodz, and memories were long in the Land of Cutz.

To the south, languid and listless, the ocean extended to the horizon and beyond.

To the west, the shore stretched far to meet a line of low hills which, thrusting into the sea, became a headland. . . . A red glitter flashed across the distance, and Cugel's attention was instantly attracted.

Such a red sparkle could only signify sunlight reflecting from glass!

Cugel marked the position of the glitter, which faded from view as the sunlight shifted. He slid down the face of the dune and set off at best speed along the beach.

The sun dropped behind the headland; gray-lavender gloom fell across the beach. An arm of that vast forest known as The Great Erm edged down from the north, suggesting a number of eery possibilities, and Cugel accelerated his pace to a striding bent-kneed lope.

The hills loomed black against the sky, but no sign of habitation appeared. Cugel's spirits sagged low. He proceeded more slowly, searching the landscape with care, and at last, to his great satisfaction, he came upon a large and elaborate manse of archaic design, shrouded behind the trees of an untidy garden. The lower windows glowed with amber light: a cheerful sight for the benighted wanderer.

Cugel turned briskly aside and approached the manse, putting by his usual precautions of surveillance and perhaps peering through the windows, especially in view of two white shapes at the edge of the forest which quietly moved back into the shadows as he turned to stare.

Cugel marched to the door and tugged smartly at the bell-chain. From within came the sound of a far gong.

A moment passed. Cugel looked nervously over his shoulder, and again pulled at the chain. Finally he heard slow steps approaching from within.

The door opened and a pinch-faced old man, thin, pale, and stoop-shouldered, looked through the crack.

Cugel used the suave tones of gentility; "Good evening! What is this handsome old place, may I ask?"

The old man responded without cordiality: "Sir, this is Flutic, where Master Twango keeps residence. What is your business?"

"Nothing out of the ordinary," said Cugel airily. "I am a traveler, and I seem to have lost my way. I will therefore trespass upon Master Twango's hospitality for the night, if I may."

"Quite impossible. From which direction do you come?"

"From the east."

"Then continue along the road, through the forest and over the hill, to Saskervoy. You will find lodging to meet your needs at the Inn of Blue Lamps."

"It is too far, and in any event robbers have stolen my money."

"You will find small comfort here; Master Twango gives short shrift to indigents." The old man started to close the door, but Cugel put his foot into the aperture.

"Wait! I noticed two white shapes at the edge of the forest, and I dare go no farther tonight!"

"In this regard, I can advise you," said the old man. "The creatures are probably rostgoblers, or 'hyperborean sloths', if you prefer the term. Return to the beach and wade ten feet into the water; you will be safe from their lust. Then tomorrow you may proceed to Saskervoy."

The door closed. Cugel looked anxiously over his shoulder. At the entrance to the garden, where heavy yews flanked the walk, he glimpsed a pair of still white forms. Cugel turned back to the door and jerked hard at the bell-chain.

Slow steps padded across the floor, and once again the door opened. The old man looked out. "Sir?"

"The ghouls are now in the garden! They block the way to the beach!"

The old man opened his mouth to speak, then blinked as a new concept entered his mind. He tilted his head and spoke craftily: "You have no funds?"

"I carry not so much as a groat."

"Well then; are you disposed toward employment?"

"Certainly, if I survive the night!"

"In that case, you are in luck! Master Twango can offer employment to a willing worker." The old man threw open the door and Cugel gratefully entered the manse.

With an almost exuberant flourish the old man closed the door. "Come, I will take you to Master Twango, and you can discuss the particulars of your employment. How do you choose to be announced?"

"I am Cugel."

"This way then! You will be pleased with the opportunities! . . . Are you coming? At Flutic we are brisk!"

Despite all, Cugel held back. "Tell me something of the employment! I am, after all, a person of quality, and I do not turn my hand to everything."

"No fear! Master Twango will accord you every distinction. Ah, Cugel, you will be a happy man! If only I were young again! This way, if you please."

Cugel still held back. "First things first! I am tired and somewhat the worse for travel. Before I confer with Master Twango I would like to refresh myself and perhaps take a bite or two of nourishment. In fact, let us wait until tomorrow morning, when I will make a far better impression."

The old man demurred. "At Flutic all is exact, and every jot balances against a corresponding tittle. To whose account would I charge your refreshment? To Gark? To Gookin? To Master Twango himself? Absurd. Inevitably the consumption would fall against the account of Weamish, which is to say, myself. Never! My account at last is clear, and I propose to retire."

"I understand nothing of this," grumbled Cugel.

"Ah, but you will! Come now: to Twango!"

With poor grace Cugel followed Weamish into a chamber of many shelves and cases: a repository of curios, to judge by the articles on display.

"Wait here a single moment!" said Weamish and hopped on spindly legs from the room.

Cugel walked here and there, inspecting the curios and estimating their value. Strange to find such objects in a place so remote! He bent to examine a pair of small quasi-human grotesques rendered in exact detail. Craftsmanship at its most superb! thought Cugel.

Weamish returned. "Twango will see you shortly. Meanwhile he offers for your personal regalement this cup of vervain tea, together with these two nutritious wafers, at no charge."

Cugel drank the tea and devoured the wafers. "Twango's act of hospitality, though largely symbolic, does him credit." He indicated the cabinets. "All this is Twango's personal collection?"

"Just so. Before his present occupation he dealt widely in such goods."

"His tastes are bizarre, even peculiar."

Weamish raised his white eyebrows. "As to that I cannot say. It all seems ordinary enough to me."

"Not really," said Cugel. He indicated the pair of grotesques.

"For instance, I have seldom seen objects so studiously repulsive as this pair of bibelots. Skillfully done, agreed! Notice the detail in these horrid little ears! The snouts, the fangs: the malignance is almost real! Still, they are undeniably the work of a diseased imagination."

The objects reared erect. One of them spoke in a rasping voice: "No doubt Cugel has good reason for his unkind words; still, neither Gark nor I can take them lightly."

The other also spoke: "Such remarks carry a sting! Cugel has a feckless tongue." Both bounded from the room.

Weamish spoke in reproach. "You have offended both Gark and Gookin, who came only to guard Twango's valuables from pilferage. But what is done is done. Come; we will go to Master Twango."

Weamish took Cugel to a large workroom, furnished with a dozen tables piled with ledgers, crates and various oddments. Gark and Gookin, wearing smart long-billed caps of red and blue respectively, glared at Cugel from a bench. At an enormous desk sat Twango, who was short and corpulent, with a small chin, a dainty mouth and a bald pate surrounded by varnished black curls. Under his chin hung a faddish little goatee.

Upon the entrance of Cugel and Weamish, Twango swung around in his chair. "Aha, Weamish! This gentleman, so I am told, is Cugel. Welcome, Cugel, to Flutic!"

Cugel doffed his hat and bowed. "Sir, I am grateful for your hospitality on this dark night."

Twango arranged the papers on his desk and appraised Cugel from the corner of his eye. He indicated a chair. "Be seated, if you will. Weamish tells me that you might be inclined to employment, under certain circumstances."

Cugel nodded graciously. "I will be pleased to consider any post for which I am qualified, and which offers an appropriate compensation."

Weamish called from the side: "Just so! Conditions at Flutic are always optimum and at worst meticulous."

Twango coughed and chuckled. "Dear old Weamish! We have had a long association! But now our accounts are settled and he wishes to retire. Am I correct in this, Weamish?"

"You are, in every last syllable!"

Cugel made a delicate suggestion: "Perhaps you will describe the various levels of employment available and their corresponding perquisites. Then, after analysis, I will be able to indicate how best I can serve you."

Weamish cried out: ''A wise request! Good thinking, Cugel! You will do well at Flutic, or I am much deceived.''

Twango again straightened the papers on his desk. ''My business is simple at its basis. I exhume and refurbish treasures of the past. I then survey, pack, and sell them to a shipping agent of Saskervoy, who delivers them to their ultimate consignee, who, so I understand, is a prominent magician of Almery. If I shape each phase of the operation to its best efficiency—Weamish, in a spirit of jocularity, used the word 'meticulous'—I sometimes turn a small profit.''

''I am acquainted with Almery,'' said Cugel. ''Who is the magician?''

Twango chuckled. ''Soldinck the shipping agent refuses to release this information, so that I will not sell direct at double profit. But from other sources I learn that the consignee is a certain Iucounu of Pergolo. . . . Cugel, did you speak?''

Cugel smilingly touched his abdomen. ''An eructation only. I usually dine at this time. What of your own meal? Should we not continue our discussion over the evening repast?''

''All in good time,'' said Twango. ''Now then, to continue. Weamish has long supervised my archaeological operations, and his position now becomes open. Is the name 'Sadlark' known to you?''

''Candidly, no.''

''Then for a moment I must digress. During the Cutz Wars of the Eighteenth Aeon, the demon Underherd interfered with the overworld, so that Sadlark descended to set matters right. For reasons obscure—I personally suspect simple vertigo—Sadlark plunged into the mire, creating a pit now found in my own back garden. Sadlark's scales persist to this day, and these are the treasures which we recover from the slime.''

''You are fortunate in that the pit is so close to your residence,'' said Cugel. ''Efficiency is thereby augmented.''

Twango tried to follow Cugel's reasoning, then gave up the effort. ''True.'' He pointed to a nearby table. ''There stands a reconstruction of Sadlark in miniature!''

Cugel went to inspect the model, which had been formed by attaching a large number of silver flakes to a matrix of silver wires. The sleek torso stood on a pair of short legs terminating in circular webs. Sadlark lacked a head; the torso rose smoothly to a prow-like turret, fronted by a particularly complex scale with a red node at the center. Four arms hung from the upper torso; neither sense organs nor digestive apparatus were evident, and Cugel pointed out this fact to Twango as a matter of curiosity.

"Yes, no doubt," said Twango. "Things are done differently in the overworld. Like the model, Sadlark was constructed of scales on a matrix not of silver wires but wefts of force. When Sadlark plunged into the mire, the dampness annulled his forces; the scales dispersed and Sadlark became disorganized, which is the overworld equivalent of mortality."

"A pity," said Cugel, returning to his seat. "His conduct from the first would seem to have been quixotic."

"Possibly true," said Twango. "His motives are difficult to assess. Now, as to our own business: Weamish is leaving our little group and his post as 'supervisor of operations' becomes open. Is such a position within your capacity?"

"I should certainly think so," said Cugel. "Buried valuables have long engaged my interest!"

"Then the position should suit you famously!"

"And my stipend?"

"It shall be exactly that of Weamish, even though Weamish is a skilled and able associate of many years. In such cases, I play no favorites."

"In round numbers, then, Weamish earns how many terces?"

"I prefer to keep such matters confidential," said Twango, "but Weamish, so I believe, will allow me to reveal that last week he earned almost three hundred terces, and the week before as much again."

"True, from first to last!" said Weamish.

Cugel rubbed his chin. "Such a stipend would seem adequate to my needs."

"Just so," said Twango. "When can you assume your duties?"

Cugel considered for only a moment. "At once, for purposes of salary computation. However, I will want a few days to study your operation. I assume that you can provide me adequate board and lodging over this period?"

"Such facilities are provided at a nominal cost." Twango rose to his feet. "But I keep you talking when you are surely tired and hungry. Weamish, as his last official duty, will take you to the refectory, where you may dine to your selection. Then you may rest in whatever style of accomodation you find congenial. Cugel, I welcome you into our employ! In the morning we can settle the details of your compensation."

"Come!" cried Weamish. "To the refectory." He ran limping to the doorway, where he paused and beckoned. "Come along, Cugel! At Flutic one seldom loiters!"

Cugel looked at Twango. "Why is Weamish so animated, and why must one never loiter?"

Twango shook his head in fond bemusement. "Weamish is a non-pareil! Do not try to match his performance; I could never hope to find another like him!"

Weamish called again: "Come, Cugel! Must we stand here while the sun goes out?"

"I am coming, but I refuse to run blindly through this long dark corridor!"

"This way, then: after me!"

Cugel followed Weamish to the refectory: a hall with tables to one side and a buffet loaded with viands to the other. Two men sat dining. The first, a person large and thick-necked with a florid complexion, a tumble of blond curls and a surly expression, ate broad beans and bread. The second, who was as lean as a lizard, with a dark leathery skin, a narrow bony face and coarse black hair, consumed a meal no less austere, of steamed kale, with a wedge of raw onion for savor.

Cugel's attention, however, focused on the buffet. He turned to Weamish in wonder. "Does Twango always provide such a bounty of delicacies?"

Weamish responded in a disinterested fashion. "Yes, this is usually the case."

"The two men yonder: who are they?"

"To the left sits Yelleg; the other is Malser. They comprise the work-force which you will supervise."

"Only two? I expected a larger crew."

"You will find that these two suffice."

"For workmen, their appetites are remarkably moderate."

Weamish glanced indifferently across the room. "So it would seem. What of yourself: how will you dine?"

Cugel went to inspect the buffet at closer range. "I will start with a dish of these smoked oil-fish, and a salad of pepper-leaf. Then this roast fowl seems eminently edible, and I will try a cut off the rare end of the joint. . . . The garnishes are nicely turned out. Finally, a few of these pastries and a flask of the Violet Mendolence: this should suffice. No question but what Twango does well by his employees!"

Cugel arranged a tray with viands of quality, while Weamish took only a small dish of boiled burdock leaves. Cugel asked in wonder: "Is that paltry meal adequate to your appetite?"

Weamish frowned down at his dish. "It is admittedly a trifle spare. I find that an over-rich diet reduces my zeal."

Cugel laughed confidently. "I intend to innovate a program of rational operations, and this frantic harum-scarum zeal of yours, with all shirt-tails flying, will become unnecessary.'' Weamish pursed his lips.

''You will find that, at times, you are working as hard as your underlings. That is the nature of the supervisorial position.''

''Never!'' declared Cugel expansively. ''I insist upon a rigid separation of functions. A toiler does not supervise and the supervisor does not toil. But as for your meal tonight, you are retired from work; you may eat and drink as you see fit!''

''My account is closed,'' said Weamish. ''I do not care to reopen the books.''

''A small matter, surely,'' said Cugel. ''Still, if you are concerned, eat and drink as you will, to my account!''

''That is most generous!'' Jumping to his feet, Weamish limped at speed to the buffet. He returned with a selection of choice meats, preserved fruits, pastries, a large cheese and a flask of wine, which he attacked with astonishing gusto.

A sound from above attracted Cugel's attention. He looked up to discover Gark and Gookin crouched on a shelf. Gark held a tablet upon which Gookin made entries, using an absurdly long stylus.

Gark inspected Cugel's plate. ''Item: oil-fish, smoked and served with garlic and one leek, at four terces. Item: one fowl, good quality, large size, served with one cup of sauce and seven garnishes, at eleven terces. Item: three pastries of mince with herbs, at three terces each, to a total of nine terces. A salad of assorted stuffs: six terces. Item: three fardels, at two terces, to a total of six terces. Item: one large order of quince conserve, valued at three terces. Wine, nine terces. A service of napery and utensils: one terce.''

Gookin spoke. ''Noted and calculated. Cugel, place your mark at this point.''

''Not so fast!'' spoke Weamish sharply. ''My supper tonight is at Cugel's expense. Include the charges to his account.''

Gark demanded: ''Cugel, is this correct?''

''I did in fact issue the invitation,'' said Cugel. ''I dine here, however, in my capacity as supervisor. I hereby order that the charges for sustenance be waived. Weamish, as an honoured ex-employee, also eats without charge.''

Gark and Gookin uttered shrill cackles of laughter, and even Weamish showed a painful smile. ''At Flutic,'' said Weamish, ''nothing is left to chance. Twango carefully distinguishes sentiment from business. If Twango owned the air, we would pay over coins for every gasp.''

Cugel spoke with dignity: ''These practises must be revised and at once! Otherwise I will resign my position. I must also point out that the fowl was underdone and the garlic lacked savor.''

Gark and Gookin paid him no heed. Gookin tallied the charges on Weamish's meal. ''Very well, Cugel; once more, we require your mark.''

Cugel inspected the tablet. ''These bird scratchings mean nothing to me!''

''Is that truly the case?'' asked Gookin mildly. He took the tablet. ''Aha, I notice an oversight. Add three terces for Weamish's digestive pastilles.''

''Hold up!'' roared Cugel. ''What is the account at this instant?''

''One hundred and sixteen terces. We are often rendered a gratuity for our services.''

''This is not one of the occasions!'' Cugel snatched the tablet and scribbled his mark. ''Now be off with you! I cannot dine in dignity with a pair of weird little swamp-hoppers peering over my shoulder.''

Gark and Gookin bounded away in a fury. Weamish said: ''That last remark struck somewhat close to the knuckle. Remember, Gark and Gookin prepare the food and whoever irks them sometimes finds noxious substances in his victual.''

Cugel spoke firmly. ''They should rather beware of me! As supervisor, I am a person of importance. If Twango fails to enforce my directives, I will resign my post!''

''That option is of course open to you—as soon as you pay off your account.''

''I see no great problem there. If the supervisor earns three hundred terces a week, I can quickly discharge my account.''

Weamish drank deeply from his goblet. The wine seemed to loosen his tongue. He leaned toward Cugel and spoke in a hoarse whisper. ''Three hundred terces a week, eh? For me that was a fluke! Yelleg and Malser are slime-divers, as we call them. They earn three to twenty terces for each scale found, depending on quality. The 'Clover-leaf Femurials' bring ten terces, as do the 'Dorsal Double Luminants'. An 'Interlocking Sequalion' for either turret or pectorus brings twenty terces. The rare 'Lateral Flashers' are also worth twenty terces. Whoever finds the 'Pectoral Sky-break Spatterlight' will gain one hundred terces.''

Cugel poured more wine into Weamish's goblet. ''I am listening with two ears.''

Weamish drank the wine but otherwise seemed hardly to notice Cugel's presence. ''Yelleg and Malser work from before dawn until dark. They earn ten to fifteen terces a day on the average, from which the costs of board, lodging and incidentals are deducted. As supervisor you will see to their safety and comfort, at a salary of ten terces per day. Additionally, you gain a bonus of one terce for each scale exhumed by Yelleg and Malser, regardless of type. While Yelleg and Malser warm themselves at the fire or take their tea, you yourself are entitled to dive for scales.''

'' 'Dive'?'' asked Cugel in perplexity.

''Precisely so, into the pit created by Sadlark's impact with the mire. The work is tedious and one must dive deep. Recently—'' here Weamish drank an entire goblet of wine at a gulp ''—I scratched into a whole nest of good quality scales, with many 'specials' among them, and the next week, by great good fortune, I did the same. Thus I was able to amortize my account, and I have elected to retire on the instant.''

Cugel's meal had suddenly gone tasteless. ''And your previous earnings?''

''On good days I might earn as much as Yelleg and Malser.''

Cugel turned his eyes to the ceiling. ''With an income of twelve terces a day and expenses ten times as much, how does one profit by working?''

''Your question is to the point. First of all, one learns to dine without reference to subtle distinctions. Also, when one sleeps the sleep of exhaustion, he ignores the decor of his chamber.''

''As supervisor, I will make changes!'' But Cugel spoke with little conviction.

Weamish, now somewhat befuddled, held up a long white finger. ''Still, do not overlook the opportunities! They exist, I assure you, and in unexpected places!'' Leaning forward, Weamish showed Cugel a leer of cryptic significance.

''Speak on!'' said Cugel. ''I am attentive!''

After belching, swallowing another draught of wine, and looking over his shoulder, Weamish said: ''I can only emphasize that, to overcome the wiles of such as Twango, the most superb skills are necessary.''

''Your remarks are interesting,'' said Cugel. ''May I refill your goblet?''

''With pleasure.'' Weamish drank with satisfaction, then leaned once more toward Cugel. ''Would you care to hear a great joke?''

''I would indeed.''

Weamish spoke in a confidential whisper: ''Twango considers me already in my dotage!'' Leaning back in his chair, Weamish showed Cugel a gap-toothed grin.

Cugel waited, but Weamish's joke had been told. Cugel laughed politely. ''What an absurdity!''

''Is it not? When by a most ingenious method I have settled my accounts? Tomorrow I will leave Flutic and spend several years traveling among the fashionable resorts. Then let Twango wonder as to who is in his dotage, he or I.''

''I have no doubt as to his verdict. In fact, all is clear except the details of your 'ingenious method'.''

Weamish gave a wincing grimace and licked his lips, as vanity and bravado struggled against the last reeling elements of his caution. He opened his mouth to speak. . . . A gong sounded, as someone at the door pulled hard on the bell-rope.

Weamish started to rise, then, with a careless laugh, subsided into his chair. ''Cugel, it now becomes your duty to attend to late visitors, and to early visitors as well.''

''I am 'supervisor of operations', not general lackey,'' said Cugel.

''A noble hope,'' said Weamish wistfully. ''First you must cope with Gark and Gookin, who enforce all regulations to the letter.''

''They will learn to walk softly in my presence!''

The shadow of a lumpy head and a dapper long-billed cap fell over the table. A voice spoke. ''Who will learn to walk softly?''

Cugel looked up to find Gookin peering over the edge of the shelf.

Again the gong sounded. Gookin called out: ''Cugel, to your feet! Answer the door! Weamish will instruct you in the routine.''

''As supervisor,'' said Cugel, ''I hereby assign you to this task. Be quick!''

In response Gookin flourished a small three-stranded knout, each thong terminating in a yellow sting.

Cugel thrust up on the shelf with such force that Gookin sprawled head over heels through the air to fall into a platter of assorted cheeses which had been set out upon the buffet. Cugel picked up the knout and held it at the ready. ''Now then: will you go about your duties? Or must I beat you well, then throw both you and your cap into this pot of tripes?''

Into the refectory came Twango on the run, with Gark sitting bulge-eyed on his shoulder. ''What is all this commotion? Gookin, why do you lie among the cheeses?''

Cugel said: ''Since I am supervisor, you should properly address me. The facts of the case are these: I ordered Gookin to answer the door. He attempted a flagrant insolence, and I was about to chastise him.''

Twango's face became pink with annoyance. ''Cugel, this is not our usual routine! Heretofore the supervisor has habitually answered the door.''

''We now make an instant change! The supervisor is relieved of menial duties. He will earn triple the previous salary, with lodging and sustenance included at no charge.''

Once more the gong sounded. Twango muttered a curse. ''Weamish! Answer the door! Weamish? Where are you?''

Weamish had departed the refectory.

Cugel gave a stern order: ''Gark! Respond to the gong!''

Gark gave back a surly hiss. Cugel pointed to the door. ''Gark, you are hereby discharged, on grounds of insubordination! The same applies to Gookin. Both of you will immediately leave the premises and return to your native swamp.''

Gark, now joined by Gookin, responded only with hisses of defiance.

Cugel turned to Twango. ''I fear that unless my authority is affirmed I must resign.''

Twango threw up his arms in vexation. ''Enough of this foolishness! While we stand here the gong rings incessantly!'' He marched off down the corridor toward the door, with Gark and Gookin bounding behind him.

Cugel followed at a more leisurely gait. Twango threw open the door, to admit a sturdy man of middle age wearing a hooded brown cloak. Behind him came two others in similar garments.

Twango greeted the visitor with respectful familiarity. ''Master Soldinck! The time is late! Why, at this hour, do you fare so far?''

Soldinck spoke in a heavy voice: ''I bring serious and urgent news, which could not wait an instant.''

Twango stood back aghast. ''Mercantides is dead?''

''The tragedy is one of deception and theft!''

''What has been stolen?'' asked Twango impatiently. ''Who has been deceived?''

''I will recite the facts. Four days ago, at noon precisely, I arrived here with the strong-wagon. I came in company with Rincz and Jornulk, both, as you know, elders and persons of probity.''

''Their reputations have never been assailed, to my knowledge. Why now do you bring them into question?''

''Patience; you shall hear!''

''Proceed! Cugel, you are a man of experience; stand by and exercise your judgment. This, incidentally, is Master Soldinck of the firm Soldinck and Mercantides, Shipping Agents.''

Cugel stepped forward and Soldinck continued his declaration.

''With Rincz and Jornulk, I entered your workroom. There, in our presence, you counted out and we packed six hundred and eighty scales into four crates.''

''Correct. There were four hundred 'ordinaries', two hundred 'specials' and eighty 'premium specials' of unique character.''

''Just so. Together, and in the presence of Weamish, we packed the crates, sealed them, affixed bands and plaques. I suggest that Weamish be summoned, that he may put his wisdom to the solution of our mystery.''

''Gark! Gookin! Be so good as to summon Weamish. Still, Master Soldinck, you have not defined the mystery itself!''

''I will now do so. With yourself, Weamish, Rincz, Jornulk and myself on hand, the scales were encased as always in your workroom. Weamish then, to our supervision, placed the cases upon the wheeled carrier, and we complimented him both for the nicety in which he had decorated the carrier and his care to ensure that the cases might not fall to the ground. Then, with Rincz and me in the lead, you and Jornulk behind, Weamish carefully rolled the cases down the corridor, pausing, so I recall, only long enough to adjust his shoe and comment to me upon the unseasonable chill.''

''Precisely so. Continue.''

''Weamish rolled the carrier to the wagon and the cases were transferred into the strong-box, which was immediately locked. I wrote a receipt to you, which Rincz and Jornulk counter-signed, and on which Weamish placed his mark as witness. Finally I paid over to you your money, and you gave me the receipted invoice.''

''We drove the wagon directly to Saskervoy, where, with all formality, the cases were transferred into a vault, for dispatch to far Almery.''

''And then?''

''Today, Mercantides thought to verify the quality of the scales. I opened a case, so carefully certified, to find only lumps of mud and gravel. Thereupon all cases were investigated. Each case contained nothing but worthless soil, and there you have the mystery. We hope that either you or Weamish can help us resolve this shocking affair, or, failing that, refund our money.''

''The last possibility is out of the question. I can add nothing to your statement. All went as you have described. Weamish may have noticed some peculiar incident, but surely he would have notified me.''

"Still, his testimony may suggest an area of investigation, if only he would present himself."

Gark bounded into the room, eyes bulging in excitement. He called out in a rasping voice: "Weamish is on the roof. He is behaving in an unusual manner!"

Twango flourished his arms in distress. "Senile, yes, but foolish so soon? He has only just retired!"

"What?" cried Soldinck. "Weamish retired? A great surprise!"

"For us all! He settled his accounts to the last terce, then declared his retirement."

"Most odd!" said Soldinck. "We must bring Weamish down from the roof and at once!"

With Gark bounding ahead, Twango ran out into the garden, with Soldinck, Rincz, Jornulk and Cugel coming after.

The night was dark, illuminated only by a few sickly constellations. Light from within, striking up through the roofpanes, showed Weamish walking a precarious route along the ridge.

Twango called out: "Weamish, why are you walking on high? Come down at once!"

Weamish looked here and there to discover the source of the call. Observing Twango and Soldinck, he uttered a wild cry in which defiance seemed mingled with mirth.

"That is at best an ambiguous response," said Soldinck.

Twango called again: "Weamish, a number of scales are missing, and we wish to ask a question or two."

"Ask away, wherever you like and all night long—anywhere except only here. I am walking the roof and do not care to be disturbed."

"Ah, but Weamish, it is you of whom we wish to ask the question! You must come down at once!"

"My accounts are settled! I walk where I will!"

Twango clenched his fists. "Master Soldinck is puzzled and disturbed! The missing scales are irreplaceable!"

"No less am I, as you will learn!" Again Weamish uttered his strange cacchination.

Soldinck spoke sourly: "Weamish has become addled."

"Work gave his life meaning," explained Twango. "He dived deep into the slime and found a whole nest of scales, so he paid off his account. Ever since he has been acting strangely."

Soldinck asked: "When did he find the scales?"

"Only two days ago." Once more Twango raised his voice. "Weamish! Come down at once! We need your help!"

Soldinck asked: "Weamish found his scales after we had accepted the last shipment?"

"Quite true. One day later, as a matter of fact."

"A curious coincidence."

Twango stared at him blankly. "Surely you cannot suspect Weamish!"

"The facts point in his direction."

Twango turned sharply about. "Gark, Gookin, Cugel! Up to the roof! Help Weamish to the ground!"

Cugel spoke haughtily. "Gark and Gookin are my subordinates. Inform me as to your wishes and I will issue the necessary orders."

"Cugel, your attitudes have become intolerable! You are hereby demoted! Now, up on the roof with you! I want Weamish brought down at once!"

"I have no head for heights," said Cugel. "I resign my position."

"Not until your accounts are settled. They include the fine cheeses into which you flung Gookin."

Cugel protested, but Twango turned his attention back to the roof and refused to listen.

Weamish strolled back and forth along the ridge. Gark and Gookin appeared behind him. Twango called up: "Weamish, take all precautions! Gark and Gookin will lead the way!"

Weamish gave a final wild scream, and running along the ridge, hurled himself off into space, to land head-first upon the pavement below. Gark and Gookin crept to the edge of the roof to peer pop-eyed down at the limp figure.

After a brief inspection, Twango turned to Soldinck. "I fear that Weamish is dead."

"What then of the missing scales?"

"You must look elsewhere," said Twango. "The theft could not have occurred at Flutic."

"I am not so sure," said Soldinck. "In fact, I suspect otherwise."

"You are deceived by coincidences," said Twango. "The night is chill; let us return inside. Cugel, convey the corpse to the gardener's shed in the back garden. Weamish's grave is ready; in the morning you may bury him."

"If you recall," said Cugel, "I have resigned my place. I no longer consider myself employed at Flutic, unless you concede distinctly better terms."

Twango stamped his feet. "Why, at this time of tribulation, must you annoy me with your nonsense? I lack the patience to deal with you! Gark! Gookin! Cugel thinks to shirk his duties!"

Gark and Gookin crept forward. Gookin flung a noose around Cugel's ankles, while Gark threw a net over Cugel's head. Cugel fell heavily to the ground, where Gark and Gookin beat him well with short staves.

After a period Twango came to the door. He cried out: "Stop! The clamor offends our ears! If Cugel has changed his mind, let him go about his work."

Cugel decided to obey Twango's orders. Cursing under his breath, he dragged the corpse to a shed in the back garden. Then he limped to that hut vacated by Weamish, and here he passed a wakeful night, by reason of sprains, bruises, and contusions.

At an early hour Gark and Gookin pounded on the door. "Out and about your work!" called Gookin. "Twango wishes to inspect the interior of this hut."

Cugel, despite his aches, had already made such a search, to no avail. He brushed his clothing, adjusted his hat, sauntered from the hut, and stood aside while Gark and Gookin, under Twango's direction, searched the premises. Soldinck, who apparently had spent the night at Flutic, watched vigilantly from the doorway.

Twango finished the search. "There is nothing here," he told Soldinck. "Weamish is vindicated!"

"He might have secreted the scales elsewhere!"

"Unlikely! The scales were packed while you watched. Under close guard they were taken to the wagon. You yourself, with Rincz and Jornulk, transferred the cases to your wagon. Weamish had no more opportunity to steal the scales than I myself!"

"Then how do you explain Weamish's sudden wealth?"

"He found a nest of scales; is that so bizarre?"

Soldinck had nothing more to say. Departing Flutic, he returned over the hill to Saskervoy.

Twango called a staff meeting in the refectory. The group included Yelleg, Malser, Cugel and Bilberd the feeble-minded gardener. Gark and Gookin crouched on a high shelf, monitoring the conduct of all.

Twango spoke somberly. "I stand here today in sorrow! Poor Weamish, while strolling in the dark, suffered an accident and is no longer with us. Sadly, he did not live to enjoy his retirement. This concept alone must give us all cause for reflection!

"There is other news, no less disturbing. Four cases of scales, representing great value, have somehow been preempted, or stolen. Does anyone here have information, no matter how trivial, concerning this heinous act?" Twango looked from face to face. "No? In that case, I have no more to say. All to their tasks, and let Weamish's lucky find be an inspiration to all!

"One final word! Since Cugel is unfamiliar with the routines of his work, I ask that all extend to him the hand of cheerful good-fellowship and teach him whatever he needs to know. All to work, then, at speed and efficiency!"

Twango called Cugel aside. "Last night we seem to have had a misunderstanding as to the meaning of the word 'supervisor'. At Flutic, this word denotes a person who supervises the comfort and convenience of his fellow workers, including me, but who by no means controls their conduct."

"That distinction has already been made clear," said Cugel shortly.

"Precisely so. Now, as your first duty, you will bury Weamish. His grave is yonder, behind the bilberry bush. At this time you may select a site and excavate a grave for yourself, in the unhappy event that you should die during your tenure at Flutic."

"This is not to be thought of," said Cugel. "I have far to go before I die."

"Weamish spoke in much the same terms," said Twango. "But he is dead! And his comrades are spared a melancholy task, since he dug, tended and decorated a fine grave." Twango chuckled sadly. "Weamish must have felt the flutter of the black bird's wings! Only two days ago I found him cleaning and ordering his grave, and setting all to rights!"

"Two days ago?" Cugel considered. "This was after he had found his scales."

"True! He was a dedicated man! I trust that you, Cugel, as you live and work at Flutic, will be guided by his conduct!"

"I hope to do exactly that," said Cugel.

"Now you may bury Weamish. His carrier is yonder in the shed. He built it himself and it is only fitting that you use it to convey his corpse to the grave."

"That is a kind thought." With no further words Cugel went to the shed and brought out the carrier: a table rolling on four wheels. Impelled, so it would seem, by a desire to beautify his handiwork, Weamish had attached a skirt of dark blue cloth to hang as a fringe below the top surface.

Cugel loaded Weamish's body upon the carrier and rolled it out into the back garden. The carrier functioned well, although the top surface seemed insecurely attached to the frame. Odd, thought Cugel, when the vehicle must carry valuable cases of scales! Making an inspection, Cugel found that a peg secured the top surface to the frame. When he pulled away the peg, the top pivoted and would have spilled the corpse had he not been alert.

Cugel investigated the carrier in some detail, then wheeled the corpse to that secluded area north of the manse which Weamish had selected for his eternal rest.

Cugel took stock of the surroundings. A bank of myrhadion trees dangled long festoons of purple blossoms over the grave. Gaps in the foliage allowed a view along the beach and over the sea. To the left a slope grown over with bitterbush and syrinx descended to the pond of of black slime.

Already Yelleg and Malser were at work. Hunching and shuddering to the chill, they dived from a platform into the slime. Pulling themselves as deep as possible by means of weights and ropes, they groped for scales; and at last emerged panting and gasping and dripping black ooze.

Cugel gave his head a shake of distaste, then uttered a sharp exclamation as something stung his right buttock. Jerking about he discovered Gark watching from under the broad leaf of a madder plant. He carried a small contrivance by which he could launch pebbles, and which he had evidently used upon Cugel. Gark adjusted the bill of his red cap and hopped forward. ''Work at speed, Cugel! There is much to be done!''

Cugel deigned no response. With all dignity he unloaded the corpse, and Gark took his leave.

Weamish indeed had maintained his grave with pride. The hole, five feet deep, had been dug square and true, although at the bottom and to the side the dirt seemed loose and friable. Cugel nodded with quiet satisfaction.

''Quite likely,'' Cugel told himself. ''Not at all unlikely.''

With spade in hand he jumped into the grave and prodded into the dirt. From the corner of his eye he noticed the approach of a small figure in a red cap. Gark had returned, hoping to catch Cugel unaware, and fair game for another skillfully aimed pebble. Cugel loaded the spade with dirt, swung it high, up and over, and heard a gratifying squawk of surprise.

Cugel climbed from the grave. Gark squatted at a little distance, shaking the dirt from his cap. ''You are careless where you throw your dirt!''

Cugel, leaning on his spade, chuckled. ''If you skulk through the bushes, how can I see you?''

''The responsibility is yours. It is my duty to inspect your work.''

"Jump down into the grave, where you may inspect at close range!"

Gark's eyes bulged in outrage, and he gnashed the chitinous parts of his mouth. "Do you take me for a numbskull? Get on with your work! Twango will not pay good terces for idle hours of dreaming!"

"Gark, you are stern!" said Cugel. "Well, if I must, I must." Without further ceremony he rolled Weamish into his grave, covered him over, and tamped down the mold.

So passed the morning. At noon Cugel made an excellent lunch of braised eel with ramp and turnips, a conserve of exotic fruits and a flask of white wine. Yelleg and Malser, lunching upon coarse bread and pickled acorns, watched sidelong in mingled surprise and envy.

During the late afternoon, Cugel went out to the pond to assist the divers as they finished work for the day. First Malser emerged from the pond, hands like claws, then Yelleg. Cugel flushed away the slime with water piped from a stream, then Yelleg and Malser went to a shed to change clothes, their skin shriveled and lavender from the cold. Since Cugel had neglected to build a fire, their complaints were curtailed only by the chattering of their teeth.

Cugel hastened to repair the lack, while the divers discussed the day's work. Yelleg had gleaned three 'ordinary' scales from under a rock, while Malser, exploring a crevice, had discovered four of the same quality.

Yelleg told Cugel: "Now you may dive if you see fit, though the light fails fast."

"This is the time Weamish dived," said Malser. "He often used the hours of early morning, as well. But no matter what his exertions never did he neglect our warming fire."

"It was an oversight on my part," said Cugel. "I am not yet accustomed to the routine."

Yelleg and Malser grumbled somewhat more, then went to the refectory, where they dined on boiled kelp. For his own meal, Cugel took first a tureen of hunter's goulash, with morels and dumplings. For a second course, he selected a fine cut of roast mutton, with a piquant sauce, assorted side dishes, and a rich red wine; then, for dessert, he devoured a large dish of mungberry trifle.

Yelleg and Malser, on their way from the refectory, stopped to advise Cugel. "You are consuming meals of excellent quality, but the prices are inordinate! Your account with Twango will occupy your efforts for the rest of your life."

Cugel only laughed and made an easy gesture. "Sit down, and

allow me to repair my deficiencies of this afternoon. Gark! Two more goblets, another flask of wine and be quick about it!''

Yelleg and Malser willingly seated themselves. Cugel poured wine with a generous hand, and refilled his own goblet as well. He leaned comfortably back in his chair.

''Naturally,'' said Cugel, ''the possibility of exorbitant charges has occurred to me. Since I do not intend to pay, I care not a fig for expense!''

Both Yelleg and Malser murmured in surprise. ''That is a remarkably bold attitude!''

''Not altogether. At any instant the sun may lurch into oblivion. At this time, were I to owe Twango ten thousand terces for a long series of excellent meals, my last thoughts would be happy ones!''

Both Yelleg and Malser were impressed by the logic of the concept, which had not previously occurred to them.

Yelleg mused: ''Your point seems to be that if one's debt to Twango hovers always at thirty or forty terces, it might as well be ten thousand!''

Malser said thoughtfully: ''Twenty thousand, or even thirty thousand, would seem an even more worthy debt.''

''This is an ambition of truly great scope!'' declared Yelleg. ''As of this moment, I believe that I will try a good slice of that roast mutton!''

''And I as well!'' said Malser. ''Let Twango worry about the cost! Cugel, I drink to your health!''

Twango jumped from a nearby booth, where he had sat unseen. ''I have heard the whole of this base conversation! Cugel, your concepts do you no credit! Gark! Gookin! In the future Cugel must be served only the Grade Five cuisine, similar to that formerly enjoyed by Weamish.''

Cugel only shrugged. ''If necessary, I will pay my account.''

''That is good news!'' said Twango. ''And what will you use for terces?''

''I have my little secrets,'' said Cugel. ''I will tell you this much: I intend notable innovations in the scale-gathering process.''

Twango snorted incredulously. ''Please perform these miracles in your spare time. Today you neglected to dust the relics; you neither waxed nor polished the parquetry. You failed to dig your grave, and you neglected to carry out the kitchen wastes.''

''Gark and Gookin must carry out the garbage,'' said Cugel. ''While I was still supervisor, I rearranged the work schedule.''

Gark and Gookin, on the high shelf, set up a protest.

"The schedule is as before," said Twango. "Cugel, you must observe the regular routine." He departed the room, leaving Cugel, Yelleg and Malser to finish their wine.

Before sunrise Cugel was awake and abroad in the back garden, where the air was damp and chill, and heavy with silence. Bottle-yew and larch imposed silhouettes in a ragged fringe around the mulberry-gray sky; must lay in low ribbons across the pond.

Cugel went to the gardener's shed, where he secured a stout spade. Somewhat to the side, under a lush growth of pauncewort, he noticed an iron tub, or trough, ten feet long by three feet wide, built to a purpose not now in evidence. Cugel examined the trough with care, then went to the back of the garden. Under the myrhadion tree he started to dig the grave ordained by Twango.

Despite the melancholy nature of the task, Cugel dug with zest.

The work was interrupted by Twango himself, who came carefully across the garden, wearing his black gown and a bicorn hat of black fur to guard his head against the bite of the morning chill.

Twango paused beside the grave. "I see that you have taken my censure to heart. You have worked to good effect, but why, may I ask, have you dug so close to poor Weamish? You will lie essentially side by side."

"Quite so. I feel that Weamish, were he allowed one last glimmer of perception, would take comfort in the fact."

Twango pursed his lips. "That is a nice sentiment, though perhaps a trifle florid." He glanced up toward the sun. "Time passes us by! In your attention to this particular task, you are neglecting routine. At this moment you should be emptying the kitchen waste bins!"

"Those are chores more properly consigned to Gark and Gookin."

"Not so! The handles are too high."

"Let them use smaller bins! I have more urgent work at hand, such as the efficient and rapid recovery of Sadlark's scales."

Twango peered sharply sidewise. "What do you know about such matters?"

"Like Weamish, I bring a fresh viewpoint to bear. As you know, Weamish made a notable success."

"True. . . . Yes, quite so. Still, we cannot turn Flutic topsy-turvy for the sake of possibly impractical speculation."

"Just as you like," said Cugel. He climbed from the grave and for the rest of the morning worked at menial tasks, laughing and singing with such verve that Gark and Gookin made a report to Twango.

At the end of the afternoon Cugel was allowed an hour to his own devices. He laid a spray of lilies on Weamish's grave, then resumed digging in his own grave. . . . After a few moments he noticed Gookin's blue cap, where that grotesque pastiche of homunculus and frog crouched under a mallow leaf.

Cugel pretended not to notice and dug with energy. Before long he encountered the cases which Weamish had secreted to the side of his own grave.

Pretending to rest, Cugel surveyed the landscape. Gookin crouched as before. Cugel returned to his work.

One of the cases had been broken open, presumably by Weamish, and all its contents removed except for a small parcel of twenty low-value 'specials', left behind perhaps by oversight. Cugel tucked the parcel into his pouch, then covered over the case, just as Gookin came hopping across the sward. "Cugel, you have overstayed your time! You must learn precision!"

Cugel responded with dignity. "You will notice that I am digging my grave."

"No matter! Yelleg and Malser are in need of their tea."

"All in good time," said Cugel. He climbed from the grave and went to the gardener's shed where he found Yelleg and Malser standing hunched and numb. Yelleg cried out: "Tea is one of the few free perquisites rendered by Twango! All day we grope through the freezing slime, anticipating the moment when we may drink tea and warm our shriveled skin at the fire!"

Malser chimed in: "There is neither tea nor fire! Weamish was more assiduous!"

"Be calm!" said Cugel. "I still have not mastered the routine."

Cugel set the fire alight and brewed tea; Yelleg and Malser grumbled further but Cugel promised better service in the future and the divers were appeased. They warmed themselves and drank tea, then once more ran down to the pond and plunged into the slime.

Shortly before sunset Gookin summoned Cugel to the pantry. He indicated a tray upon which rested a silver goblet. "This is Twango's tonic which you must serve to him every day at this time."

"What?" cried Cugel. "Is there no end to my duties?"

Gookin responded only with a croak of indifference. Cugel snatched up the tray and carried it to the workroom. He found Twango sorting scales: inspecting each in turn through a lens, then placing it into one of several boxes, his hands encased in soft leather gloves.

Cugel put down the tray. "Twango, a word with you!"

Twango, with lens to his eye, said: "At the moment, Cugel, I am occupied, as you can see."

''I serve this tonic under protest! Once again I cite the terms of our agreement, by which I became 'supervisor of operations' at Flutic. This post does not include the offices of valet, scullion, porter, dogsbody and general roustabout. Had I known the looseness of your categories—''

Twango made an impatient gesture. ''Silence, Cugel! Your peevishness grates on the nerves.''

''Still, what of our agreement?''

''Your position has been reclassified. The pay remains the same, so you have no cause for dissatisfaction.'' Twango drank the tonic. ''Let us hear no more on the subject. I might also mention that Weamish customarily donned a white coat before serving the tonic. We thought it a nice touch.''

Twango went back to his work, referring on occasion to the pages of a large leather-bound book hinged with brass and reinforced with brass filigree. Cugel watched sourly from the side. Presently he asked: ''What will you do when the scales run out?''

''I need not concern myself for some time to come,'' said Twango primly.

''What is that book?''

''It is a work of scholarship and my basic reference: Haruviot's *Intimate Anatomy of Several Overworld Personages*. I use it to identify the scales; it is invaluable in this regard.''

''Interesting!'' said Cugel. ''How many sorts do you find?''

''I cannot specify exactly.'' Twango indicated a group of unsorted scales. ''These gray-green 'ordinaries' are typical of the dorsal areas; the pinks and vermilions are from under the torso. Each has its distinctive chime.'' Twango held a choice gray-green 'ordinary' to his ear and tapped it with a small metal bar. He listened with eyes half-closed. ''The pitch is perfect! It is a pleasure to handle scales such as this.''

''Then why do you wear gloves?''

''Aha! Much that we do confuses the layman! Remember, we deal with stuff of the overworld! When wet it is mild, but when dry, it often irks the skin.''

Twango looked to his diagram and selected one of the 'specials'. ''Hold out your hand. . . . Come, Cugel, do not cringe! You will not suddenly become an overworld imp, I assure you of this!''

Cugel gingerly extended his hand. Twango touched the 'special' to his palm. Cugel felt a puckering of the skin and a stinging as if at the abrasive suck of a lamprey. With alacrity he jerked back his hand.

Twango chuckled and returned the scale to its position. "For this reason I wear gloves when I handle dry scales."

Cugel frowned down at the table. "Are all so acrid?"

"You were stung by a 'Turret Frontal Lapidative', which is quite active. These 'Juncture Spikes' are somewhat easier. The 'Pectoral Sky-break Spatterlight', so I suspect, will prove to be the most active of all, as it controlled Sadlark's entire web of forces. The 'ordinaries' are mild, except upon long contact."

"Amazing how these forces persist across the aeons!"

"What is 'time' in the overworld? The word may not even enter the parlance. And speaking of time, Weamish customarily devoted this period to diving for scales; often he worked long hours into the night. His example is truly inspiring! Through fortitude, persistence and sheer grit, he paid off his account!"

"My methods are different," said Cugel. "The results may well be the same. Perhaps in times to come you will mention the name 'Cugel' to inspire your staff."

"I suppose that it is not impossible."

Cugel went out into the back garden. The sun had set; in the twilight the pond lay black and lusterless. Cugel went to work with a fervor which might have impressed even Weamish. Down to the shore of the pond he dragged the old iron trough, then brought down several coils of rope.

Daylight had departed, save only for a streak of metallic eggplant along the ocean's horizon. Cugel considered the pond, where at this time of day Weamish was wont to dive, guided by the flicker of a single candle on the shore.

Cugel gave his head a sardonic shake and sauntered back to the manse.

Early in the morning Cugel returned to the pond. He knotted together several coils of rope to create a single length, which he tied from a stunted juniper on one side of the pond to a bull-thorn bush on the other, so that the rope stretched across the center of the pond.

Cugel brought a bucket and a large wooden tub to the shore. He launched the trough upon the pond, loaded tub and bucket into his makeshift scow, climbed aboard, and then, tugging on the rope, pulled himself out to the middle.

Yelleg and Malser, arriving on the scene, stopped short to stare. Cugel also noted the red and blue caps of Gark and Gookin where they lurked behind a bank of heliotrope.

Cugel dropped the bucket deep into the pond, pulled it up and poured the contents into the tub. Six times he filled and emptied the bucket, then pulled the scow back to shore.

He carried a bucket full of slime to the stream and, using a large sieve, screened the stuff in the bucket.

To Cugel's amazement, when the water flushed away the slime, two scales remained in the sieve: an 'ordinary' and a second scale of remarkable size, with elaborate radiating patterns and a dull red node at the center.

A flicker of movement, a darting little arm: Cugel snatched at the fine new scale, but too late! Gookin started to bound away. Cugel jumped out like a great cat and bore Gookin to the ground. He seized the scale, kicked Gookin's meager haunches, to project him ten feet through the air. Alighting, Gookin jumped to his feet, brandished his fist, chattered a set of shrill curses. Cugel retaliated with a heavy clod. Gookin dodged, then turned and ran at full speed toward the manse.

Cugel reflected a moment, then scooped a hole in the mold beside a dark blue mitre-bush and buried his fine new scale. The 'ordinary' he tucked into his pouch, then went to fetch another bucket of slime from the scow.

Five minutes later, with stately tread, Twango came across the garden. He halted to watch as Cugel sieved a bucketful of slime.

"An ingenious arrangement," said Twango. "Quite clever—though you might have asked permission before sequestering my goods to your private use."

Cugel said coldly: "My first concern is to gather scales, for our mutual benefit."

"Hmmf. . . . Gookin tells me that already you have recovered a notable 'special'."

"A 'special'? It is no more than an 'ordinary'." Cugel brought the scale from his pouch.

With pursed lips Twango inspected the scale. "Gookin was quite circumstantial in his report."

"Gookin is that individual for whom the word 'mendacity' was coined. He is simply not to be trusted. Now please excuse me, as I wish to return to work. My time is valuable."

Twango stood dubiously aside and watched as Cugel sieved a third bucket-load of slime. "It is very strange about Gookin. How could he imagine the 'Spatterlight' in such vivid detail?"

"Bah!" said Cugel. "I cannot take time to reflect upon Gookin's fantasies."

"That is quite enough, Cugel! I am not interested in your views. In exactly seven minutes you are scheduled to sanitize the laundry."

* * *

Halfway through the afternoon Master Soldinck, of the firm Soldinck and Mercantides, arrived at Flutic. Cugel conducted him to Twango's work-room, then busied himself nearby while Soldinck and Twango discussed the missing scales.

As before, Soldinck asserted that the scales had never truly been given into his custody, and on these grounds demanded a full refund of his payment.

Twango indignantly rejected the proposal. "It is a perplexing affair," he admitted. "In the future we shall use iron-clad formalities."

"All very well, but at this moment I am concerned not with the future but with the past. Where are my missing scales?"

"I can only reiterate that you signed the receipt, made payment, and took them away in your wagon. This is indisputable! Weamish would so testify were he alive!"

"Weamish is dead and his testimony is worth nothing."

"The facts remain. If you wish to make good your loss, then the classical recourse remains to you: raise the price to your ultimate customer. He must bear the brunt."

"There, at least, is a constructive suggestion," said Soldinck. "I will take it up with Mercandides. In the meantime, we will soon be shipping a mixed cargo south aboard the *Galante*, and we hope to include a parcel of scales. Can you assemble another order of four cases, within a day or so?"

Twango tapped his chin with a plump forefinger. "I will have to work overtime sorting and indexing; still, using all my reserves, I believe that I can put up an order of four cases within a day or two."

"That will be satisfactory, and I will report as much to Mercantides."

Two days later Cugel placed a hundred and ten scales, for the most part 'ordinaries', before Twango where he sat at his oak table.

Twango stared in sheer amazement. "Where did you find these?"

"I seem to have plumbed the pocket from which Weamish took so many scales. These will no doubt balance my account."

Twango frowned down at the scales. "A moment while I look over the records. . . . Cugel, I find that you still owe fifty-three terces. You spent quite heavily in the refectory and I show extra charges upon which you perhaps failed to reckon."

"Let me see the invoices. . . . I can make nothing of these records."

"Some were prepared by Gark and Gookin. They are perhaps a trifle indistinct."

Cugel threw down the invoices in disgust. "I insist upon a careful, exact and legible account!"

Twango spoke through compressed lips. "Your attitude, Cugel, is both brash and cynical. I am not favorably impressed."

"Let us change the subject," said Cugel. "When next do you expect to see Master Soldinck?"

"Sometime in the near future. Why do you ask?"

"I am curious as to his commercial methods. For instance, what would he charge Iucounu for a truly notable 'special', such as the 'Skybreak Spatterlight'?"

Twango said heavily: "I doubt if Master Soldinck would release this information. What, may I ask, is the basis for your interest?"

"No great matter. During one of our discussions, Weamish theorized that Soldinck might well prefer to buy expensive 'specials' direct from the diver, thus relieving you of considerable detail work."

For a moment Twango moved his lips without being able to produce words. At last he said: "The idea is inept, in all its phases. Master Soldinck would reject any and all scales of such dubious antecedents. The single authorized dealer is myself, and my seal alone guarantees authenticity. Each scale must be accurately identified and correctly indexed."

"And the invoices to your staff: they are also accurate and correctly indexed? Or, from sheer idle curiosity, shall I put the question to Master Soldinck?"

Twango angrily took up Cugel's account once again. "Naturally, there may be small errors, in one or another direction. They tend to balance out in the end. . . . Yes, I see an error here, where Gark misplaced a decimal point. I must counsel him to a greater precision. It is time you were serving tea to Yelleg and Malser. You must cure this slack behaviour! At Flutic we are brisk!"

Cugel sauntered out to the pond. The time was the middle afternoon of a day extraordinarily crisp, with peculiar black-purple clouds veiling the bloated red sun. A wind from the north creased the surface of the slime; Cugel shivered and pulled his cloak up around his neck.

The surface of the pond broke; Yelleg emerged and with crooked arms pulled himself ashore, to stand in a crouch, dripping ooze. He examined his gleanings but found only pebbles, which he discarded in disgust. Malser, on his hands and knees, clambered ashore and joined Yelleg; the two of them ran to the rest hut, only to emerge a moment later in a fury. "Cugel! Where is our tea? The fire is cold ashes! Have you no mercy?"

Cugel strolled over to the hut, where both Yelleg and Malser advanced upon him in a threatening manner. Yelleg shook his massive fist in Cugel's face. "You have been remiss for the last time! Today we propose to beat you and throw you into the pond!"

"One moment," said Cugel. "Allow me to build a fire, as I myself am cold. Malser, start the tea, if you will."

Speechless with rage, the two divers stood back while Cugel kindled a fire. "Now then," said Cugel, "you will be happy to learn that I have dredged into a rich pocket of scales. I paid off my account and now Bilberd the gardener must serve the tea and build the fire."

Yelleg asked between clenched teeth: "Are you then resigning your post?"

"Not altogether. I will continue, for at least a brief period, in an advisory capacity."

"I am puzzled," said Malser. "How is it that you find so many scales with such little effort?"

Cugel smiled and shrugged. "Ability, and not a little luck."

"But mostly luck, eh? Just as Weamish had luck?"

"Ah, Weamish, poor fellow! He worked hard and long for his luck! Mine came more quickly. I have been fortunate!"

Yelleg spoke thoughtfully: "A curious succession of events! Four cases of scales disappeared. Then Weamish pays off his account. Then Gark and Gookin come with their hooks and Weamish jumps from the roof. Next, honest hard-working Cugel pays off his account, though he dredges but an hour a day."

"Curious indeed!" said Malser. "I wonder where the missing scales could be!"

"And I, no less!" said Yelleg.

Cugel spoke in mild rebuke: "Perhaps you two have time for wool-gathering, but I must troll for scales."

Cugel went to his scow and sieved several buckets of slime. Yelleg and Malser decided to work no more, each having gleaned three scales. After dressing, they stood by the edge of the pond watching Cugel, muttering together in low voices.

During the evening meal Yelleg and Malser continued their conversation, from time to time darting glances toward Cugel. Presently Yelleg struck his fist into the palm of his hand, as if he had been struck by a novel thought, which he immediately communicated to Malser. Then both nodded wisely and glanced again toward Cugel.

The next morning, while Cugel worked his sieve, Yelleg and Malser marched out into the back garden. Each carried a lily which he laid upon Weamish's grave. Cugel watched intently from the side of his eye. Neither Malser nor Yelleg gave his own grave more than cursory attention: so little, in fact, that Malser, in backing away, fell into the excavation. Yelleg helped him up and the two went off about their work.

Cugel ran to the grave and peered down to the bottom. The dirt had broken away from the side wall and the corner of a case might possibly have been evident to a careful inspection.

Cugel pulled thoughtfully at his chin. The case was not conspicuous. Malser, mortified by his clumsy fall, in all probability had failed to notice it. This, at least, was a reasonable theory. Nevertheless, to move the scales might be judicious; he would do so at the first opportunity.

Taking the scow out upon the slime, Cugel filled the tub; then, returning to the shore, he sieved the muck, to discover a pair of 'ordinaries' in the sieve.

Twango summoned Cugel to the work-room. "Cugel, tomorrow we ship four cases of prime scales at precisely noon. Go to the carpenter shop and build four stout cases to proper specifications. Then clean the carrier, lubricate the wheels, and put it generally into tip-top shape; there must be no mishaps on this occasion."

"Have no fear," said Cugel. "We will do the job properly."

At noon Soldinck, with his companions Rincz and Jornulk, halted their wagon before Flutic. Cugel gave them a polite welcome and ushered them into the work-room.

Twango, somewhat nettled by Soldinck's scrutiny of floor, walls and ceiling, spoke crisply. "Gentlemen, on the table you will observe scales to the number of six hundred and twenty, both 'ordinary' and 'special', as specified on this invoice. We shall first inspect, verify and pack the 'specials'."

Soldinck pointed toward Gark and Gookin. "Not while those two subhuman imps stand by! I believe that in some way they cast a spell to befuddle not only poor Weamish but all the rest of us. Then they made free with the scales."

Cugel stated: "Soldinck's point seems valid. Gark, Gookin: begone! Go out and chase frogs from the garden!"

Twango protested: "That is foolishly and unnecessarily harsh! Still, if you must have it so, Gark and Gookin will oblige us by departing."

With red-eyed glares toward Cugel, Gark and Gookin darted from the room.

Twango now counted out the 'special' scales, while Soldinck checked them against an invoice and Cugel packed them one by one into the case under the vigilant scrutiny of Rincz and Jornulk. Then, in the same manner, the 'ordinaries' were packed. Cugel, watched closely by all, fitted covers to the cases, secured them well, and placed them on the carrier.

"Now," said Cugel, "since from this point to the wagon I will be prime custodian of the scales, I must insist that, while all witness, I seal the cases with wax, into which I inscribe my special mark. By this means I and every one else must be assured that the cases we pack and load here arrive securely at the wagon."

"A wise precaution," said Twango. "We will all witness the process."

Cugel sealed the boxes, made his mark into the hardening wax, then strapped the cases to the carrier. He explained: "We must take care lest a vibration or an unforeseen jar dislodge one of the cases, to the possible damage of the contents."

"Right, Cugel! Are we now prepared?"

"Quite so. Rincz and Jornulk, you will go first, taking care that the way is without hindrance. Soldinck, you will precede the carrier by five paces. I will push the carrier and Twango will follow five paces to the rear. In absolute security we shall thereby bring the scales to the wagon."

"Very good," said Soldinck. "So it shall be. Rincz, Jornulk! You will go first, using all alertness!"

The procession departed the work-room and passed through a dark corridor fifteen yards long, pausing only long enough for Cugel to call ahead to Soldinck: "Is all clear?"

"All is clear," came back Soldinck's reassurance. "You may come forward!"

Without further delay Cugel rolled the carrier out to the wagon. "Notice all! The cases are delivered to the wagon in the number of four, each sealed with my seal. Soldinck, I hereby transfer custody of these valuables to you. I will now apply more wax, upon which you will stamp your own mark. . . . Very good; my part of the business is done."

Twango congratulated Cugel. "And done well, Cugel! All was proper and efficient. The carrier looked neat and orderly with its fine coat of varnish and the neat apron installed by Weamish. Now then,

Soldinck, if you will render me the receipt and my payment in full, the transaction will be complete.''

Soldinck, still in a somewhat surly mood, gave over the receipt and counted out terces to the stipulated amount; then, with Rincz and Jornulk, he drove his wagon back to Saskervoy.

Cugel meanwhile wheeled the carrier to the shop. He inverted the top surface on its secret pivot, to bring the four cases into view. He removed the lids, lifted out the packets, put the broken cases into the fire, and poured the scales into a sack.

A flicker of motion caught his attention. Cugel peered sideways and glimpsed a smart red cap disappearing from view at the window.

Cugel stood motionless for ten seconds, then he moved with haste. He ran outside, but saw neither Gark nor Gookin, nor yet Yelleg nor Malser who presumably were diving in the pond.

Returning into the shop, Cugel took the sack of scales and ran fleet-footed to that hovel inhabited by Bilberd the half-witted gardener. Under a pile of rubbish in the corner of the room he hid the sack, then ran back to the shop. Into another sack he poured an assortment of nails, studs, nuts, bolts and assorted trifles of hardware, and replaced this sack on the shelf. Then, after stirring the fire around the burning cases, he busied himself varnishing the upper surface of the carrier.

Three minutes later Twango arrived with Gark and Gookin at his heels, the latter carrying long-handled man-hooks.

Cugel held up his hand. ''Careful, Twango! The varnish is wet!''

Twango called out in a nasal voice: ''Cugel, let us have no evasion! Where are the scales?''

'' 'Scales'? Why do you want them now?''

''Cugel, the scales, if you please!''

Cugel shrugged. ''As you like.'' He brought down a tray. ''I have had quite a decent morning. Six 'ordinaries' and a fine 'special'! Notice this extraordinary specimen, if you will!''

''Yes, that is a 'Malar Astrangal', which fits over the elbow part of the third arm. It is an exceedingly fine specimen. Where are the others, which, so I understand, are numbered in the hundreds?''

Cugel looked at him in amazement. ''Where have you heard such an extraordinary fantasy?''

''That is a matter of no consequence! Show me the scales or I must ask Gark and Gookin to find them!''

''Do so, by all means,'' said Cugel with dignity. ''But first let me protect my property.'' He placed the six 'ordinaries' and the 'Malar Astrangal' in his pouch. At this moment, Gark, hopping up on the bench, gave a rasping croak of triumph and pulled down the sack

Cugel had so recently placed there. "This is the sack! It is heavy with scales!"

Twango poured out the contents of the sack. "A few minutes ago," said Cugel, "I looked through this sack for a clevis to fit upon the carrier. Gark perhaps mistook these objects for scales." Cugel went to the door. "I will leave you to your search."

The time was now approaching the hour when Yelleg and Malser ordinarily took their tea. Cugel looked into the shed, but the fire was dead and the divers were nowhere to be seen.

Good enough, thought Cugel. Now was the time to remove from his grave those scales originally filched by Weamish.

He went to the back of the garden, where, in the shade of the myrhadian tree he had buried Weamish and dug his own grave.

No unwelcome observers were in evidence. Cugel started to jump down into his grave, but stopped short, deterred by the sight of four broken and empty cases at the bottom of the hole.

Cugel returned to the manse and went to the refectory where he found Bilberd the gardener.

"I am looking for Yelleg and Malser," said Cugel. "Have you seen them recently?"

Bilberd simpered and blinked. "Indeed I have, about two hours ago, when they departed for Saskervoy. They said that they were done diving for scales."

"That is a surprise," said Cugel through a constricted throat.

"True," said Bilberd. "Still, one must make an occasional change, otherwise he risks stagnation. I have gardened at Flutic for twenty-three years and I am starting to lose interest in the job. It is time that I myself considered a new career, perhaps in fashion design, despite the financial risks."

"An excellent idea!" said Cugel. "Were I a wealthy man, I would instantly advance to you the necessary capital!"

"I appreciate the offer!" said Bilberd warmly. "You are a generous man, Cugel!"

The gong sounded, signaling visitors. Cugel started to respond, then settled once more into his seat: let Gark or Gookin or Twango himself answer the door.

The gong sounded, again and again, and finally Cugel, from sheer vexation, went to answer the summons.

At the door stood Soldinck, with Rincz and Jornulk. Soldinck's face was grim. "Where is Twango? I wish to see him at once."

"It might be better if you returned tomorrow," said Cugel. "Twango is taking his afternoon rest."

"No matter! Rouse him out, in double-quick time! The matter is urgent!"

"I doubt if he will wish to see you today. He tells me that his fatigue is extreme."

"What?" roared Soldinck. "He should be dancing for joy! After all, he took my good terces and gave me cases of dried mud in exchange!"

"Impossible," said Cugel. "The precautions were exact."

"Your theories are of no interest to me," declared Soldinck. "Take me to Twango at once!"

"He is unavailable for any but important matters. I wish you a cordial good-day." Cugel started to close the door, but Soldinck set up an outcry, and now Twango himself appeared on the scene. He asked: "What is the reason for this savage uproar? Cugel, you know how sensitive I am to noise!"

"Just so," said Cugel, "but Master Soldinck seems intent upon a demonstration."

Twango turned to Soldinck. "What is the difficulty? We have finished our business for the day."

Cugel did not await Soldinck's reply. As Bilberd had remarked, the time had come for a change. He had lost a goodly number of scales to the dishonesty of Yelleg and Malser, but as many more awaited him in Bilberd's hut, with which he must be content.

Cugel hastened through the manse. He looked into the refectory, where Gark and Gookin worked at the preparation of the evening meal.

Very good, thought Cugel, in fact, excellent! Now he need only avoid Bilberd, take the sack of scales and be away. . . . He went out into the garden, but Bilberd was not at his work.

Cugel went to Bilberd's hut and put his head through the door. "Bilberd?"

There was no response. A shaft of red light slanting through the door illuminated Bilberd's pallet in full detail. By the diffused light, Cugel saw that the hut was empty.

Cugel glanced over his shoulder, entered the hut and went to the corner where he had hidden the sack.

The rubbish had been disarranged. The sack was gone.

From the manse came the sound of voices. Twango called: "Cugel! Where are you? Come at once!"

Quick and silent as a wraith, Cugel slipped from Bilberd's hut and took cover in a nearby juniper copse. Sidling from shadow to shadow, he circled the manse and came out upon the road. He looked right and left, then, discovering no threat, set off on long loping strides to the west. Through the forest and over the hill marched Cugel, and presently arrived at Saskervoy.

Some days later, while strolling the esplanade,* Cugel chanced to approach that ancient tavern known as 'The Iron Cockatrice'. As he drew near, the door opened and two men lurched into the street: one massive, with yellow curls and a heavy jaw; the other lean, with gaunt cheeks, black hair and a hooked nose. Both wore costly garments, with double-tiered hats, red satin sashes and boots of fine leather.

Cugel, looking once, then a second time, recognized Yelleg and Malser. Each had enjoyed at least a bottle of wine and possibly two. Yelleg sang a ballad of the sea and Malser sang "Tirra la lirra, we are off to the land where the daisies grow!" in refrain. Preoccupied with the exact rhythm of their music, they brushed past Cugel, looking neither right nor left, and went off along the esplanade toward another tavern, 'The Star of the North'.

Cugel started to follow, then jumped back at the rumble of approaching wheels. A fine carriage, drawn by a pair of high-stepping perchers, swerved in front of him and rolled off along the esplanade. The driver wore a black velvet suit with silver epaulettes, and a large hat with a curling black plume; beside him sat a buxom lady in an orange gown. Only with difficulty could Cugel identify the driver as Bilberd, former gardener at Flutic. Cugel muttered sourly under his breath: "Bilberd's new career, which I generously offered to finance, has cost me rather more than I expected."

Early the next morning Cugel left Saskervoy by the east road. He crossed over the hills and came down upon upon Shanglestone Strand.

Nearby, the eccentric towers of Flutic rose into the morning sunlight, sharp against the northern murk.

Cugel approached the manse by a devious route, keeping to the cover of shrubs and hedges, pausing often to listen. He heard nothing; a desolate mood hung in the air.

Cautiously Cugel circled the manse. The pond came into view. Out in the middle Twango sat in the iron scow, shoulders hunched and neck pulled down. As Cugel watched, Twango hauled in a rope; up from the depths came Gark with a small bucket of slime, which Twango emptied into the tub.

Twango returned the bucket to Gark who made a chattering sound

*Let it be noted that this particular occasion follows upon events to be chronicled in the next chapter, for reasons of narrative cohesion.

and dived again into the depths. Twango pulled on a second rope to bring up Gookin with another bucket.

Cugel retreated to the dark blue mitre-bush. He dug down and, using a folded cloth to protect his hand, retrieved the 'Pectoral Sky-break Spatterlight'.

Cugel went to take a final survey of the pond. The tub was full. Gark and Gookin, two small figures caked with slime, sat at either end of the scow, while Twango heaved at the overhead rope. Cugel watched a moment, then turned and went his way back to Saskervoy.

2

The Inn of Blue Lamps

When Master Soldinck returned to Flutic in search of his missing scales, Cugel decided not to take part in the inquiry. He imediately departed Flutic by an obscure route and set off to the west toward the town Saskervoy.*

After a period Cugel paused to catch his breath. His mood was bitter. Through the duplicity of underlings he carried, not a valuable parcel of scales, but only a handful of 'ordinaries' and a single 'special' of distinction: the 'Malar Astrangal'. The most precious scale of all, the 'Pectoral Sky-break Spatterlight', remained hidden in the back garden at Flutic, but Cugel hoped to retain this scale, if only because it was coveted by Iucounu the Laughing Magician.

Cugel again set off along the road: through a dank forest of thamber oak, yew, mernache and goblin-tree. Wan red sunlight sifted through the foliage; shadows, by some trick of perception, seemed to be stained dark blue.

Cugel maintained an uneasy watch to either side, as was only prudent during these latter times. He saw much that was strange and sometimes beautiful: white blossoms held high on tall tendrils above spangles of low flat leaves: fairy castles of fungus growing in shelves, terraces and turrets over rotting stumps; patterns of black and orange bracken. Once, indistinct at a distance of a hundred yards, Cugel thought to see a tall man-like shape in a lavender jerkin. Cugel carried no weapon, and he breathed easier when the road, mounting a hillside, broke out into the afternoon daylight.

*This narrative returns in time to Cugel's first departure from Flutic, before the events chronicled in the last few pages.

At this moment Cugel heard the sound of Soldinck's wagon returning from Flutic. He stepped off the road and waited in the shadow of a rock. The wagon passed by, and Soldinck's grim expression was a convincing sign that his talks with Twango had not gone well.

The sound of the wagon receded and Cugel resumed his journey. The road crossed over a windy ridge, descended the slope by a series of traverses, then, rounding a bluff, allowed Cugel a view over Saskervoy.

Cugel had thought to find little more than a village. Saskervoy exceeded his expectations, both in size and in its air of ancient respectability. Tall narrow houses stood side by side along the streets, the stone of their structure weathered by ages of lichen, smoke and sea-fog. Windows glistened and brass-work twinkled in the red sunlight; such was the way at Saskervoy.

Cugel followed the road down into the town and proceeded toward the harbor. Strangers were evidently a novelty for the folk of Saskervoy. At Cugel's approach, all stopped to stare, and not a few hurriedly crossed the street. They seemed, thought Cugel, a people of old-fashioned habit, and perhaps conservative in their views. The men wore black swallow-tail coats with voluminous trousers and black buckled shoes, while the women, in their shapeless gowns and round punch-bowl hats pulled low, were like dumplings.

Cugel arrived at a plaza beside the harbor. Several ships of good proportion lay alongside the dock, any one of which might be sailing south, perhaps as far as Almery.

Cugel went to sit on a bench. He examined the contents of his pouch, discovering sixteen 'ordinaries', two 'specials' of minor value and the 'Malar Astrangal'. Depending upon Soldinck's standards of payment, the scales might or might not cover the costs of a sea voyage.

Almost directly across the plaza, Cugel noticed a sign affixed to the front of an imposing stone building:

SOLDINCK AND MERCANTIDES
EXPORTERS AND IMPORTERS OF QUALITY PRODUCTS
SHIPPING AGENTS

Cugel considered a range of strategies, each more subtle than the next. All grounded against a crude and basic reality: in order to take lodging at an inn, he must sell scales to pay his account.

Afternoon was waning. Cugel rose to his feet. He crossed the plaza and entered the offices of Soldinck and Mercantides.

The premises were heavy with dignity and tradition; along with the odors of varnish and old wood, the sweet-sour scent of decorum hung in the air. Crossing the hush of a high-ceilinged chamber, Cugel approached a polished brown marble counter. On the other side an old clerk sat frowning into a ledger, and failed to acknowledge Cugel's presence.

Cugel gave a peremptory rap on the counter.

"One moment! Patience, if you please!" said the clerk, and went on with his work, despite Cugel's second irritated rap.

Finally, making the best of circumstances, Cugel set himself to wait upon the clerk's convenience.

The outer door opened; into the chamber came a man of Cugel's own age, wearing a tall-crowned hat of brown felt and a rumpled suit of blue velvet. His face was round and placid; tufts of pale hair like wisps of hay protruded from under his hat. His belly pressed forward the front of his coat, and a pair of broad buttocks rode upon two long spindle-shanked legs.

The newcomer advanced to the counter; the clerk jumped to his feet with alacrity. "Sir, how may I be of assistance?"

Cugel stepped forward in annoyance and raised his finger. "One moment! My business remains to be dealt with!"

The others paid him no heed. The newcomer said: "My name is Bunderwal, and I wish to see Soldinck."

"This way, sir! I am happy to say that Soldinck is at liberty."

The two departed the room, while Cugel fumed with impatience.

The clerk returned. He started to go to his ledger, then noticed Cugel. "Did you want something?"

"I also require a few words with Soldinck," said Cugel haughtily. "Your methods are incorrect. Since I entered the chamber first, you should have dealt first with my affairs."

The clerk blinked. "The idea, I must say, has an innocent simplicity in its favor. What is your business with Soldinck?"

"I want to arrange passage by the quickest and most comfortable means to Almery."

The clerk went to study a wall map. "I see no mention of such a place."

"Almery lies below the bottom edge of the map."

The clerk gave Cugel a wondering glance. "That is a far distance. Well, come along; perhaps Soldinck will see you."

'You need merely announce the name 'Cugel'."

The clerk led the way to the end of a hall and pushed his head through a pair of hangings. "A certain 'Cugel' is here to see you."

There was a moment of strained silence, then Soldinck's voice came in response: "Well then, Diffin: what does he want?"

"Transport to a possibly imaginary land, as best I can make out."

"Hmmf. . . . Show him in."

Diffin held aside the hangings for Cugel, then shuffled back the way he had come. Cugel entered an octagonal chamber furnished in austere luxury. Soldinck, gray-haired and stern-faced, stood beside an octagonal table while Bunderwal sat on a couch upholstered in maroon plush. Crimson sunlight, entering through high windows, illuminated a pair of barbaric wall-hangings, woven in the backlands of Far Cutz. A heavy black iron chandelier hung by an iron chain from the ceiling.

Cugel rendered Soldinck a formal greeting, which Soldinck acknowledged without warmth. "What is your business, Cugel? I am consulting Bunderwal on matters of importance and I can spare only a moment or two."

"I will be brief," said Cugel coldly. "Am I correct in assuming that you ship scales to Almery at the command of Iucounu the Magician?"

"Not entirely," said Soldinck. "We convey the scales to our factor at Port Perdusz, who then arranges trans-shipment."

"Why, may I ask, do you not ship directly to Almery?"

"It is not practical to venture so far south."

Cugel frowned in annoyance. "When does your next ship leave for Port Perdusz?"

"The *Galante* sails before the week is out."

"And what are the charges for passage to Port Perdusz?"

"We carry only select passengers. The charges, so I believe, are three hundred terces: a sum—" and here Soldinck's voice became somewhat lofty "—perhaps beyond your competence."

"Not at all. I have here a number of scales which should bring considerably more than that amount."

Soldinck showed a flicker of interest. "I will at least look them over."

Cugel displayed his scales. "Notice especially this very fine 'Malar Astrangal'!"

"It is a decent specimen, despite the greenish tinge to the marathaxus." Soldinck scanned the scales with a practiced eye. "I value the lot generously at approximately one hundred and eighty-three terces."

The sum was twenty terces more than Cugel had dared hope for. He started to make an automatic protest, then thought better of it. "Very well; the scales are yours."

"Take them to Diffin; he will give you your money." Soldinck gestured toward the hangings.

"Another matter. From curiosity, what will you pay for the 'Pectoral Sky-break Spatterlight'?"

Soldinck looked up sharply. "You have custody of this scale?"

"For the moment let us think in hypothetical cases."

Soldinck raised his eyes to the ceiling. "If it were in prime condition, I might well risk as much as two hundred terces."

Cugel nodded. "And why should you not, since Iucounu will pay two thousand terces or even more?"

"I suggest then that you take this hypothetical item directly to Iucounu. I can even suggest a convenient route. If you return eastward along Shanglestone Strand, you will come to Hag Head and the Castle Cil. Veer south to avoid the Great Erm, which you will find to be infested with erbs and leucomorphs. The Mountains of Magnatz lie ahead of you; they are extremely dangerous, but if you try to bypass them you must risk the Desert of Obelisks. Of the lands beyond I know little."

"I have some acquaintance with these lands," said Cugel. "I prefer passage aboard the *Galante*."

"Mercantides insists that we transport only persons in our own employ. We are chary of well-spoken passengers who, at a given signal, become merciless pirates."

"I will be pleased to accept a position with your firm," said Cugel. "I have capabilities of many sorts; I believe that you will find me useful."

Soldinck smiled a cold brief smile. "Unfortunately, a single post is open at the moment, that of supercargo aboard the *Galante*, for which I already have a qualified applicant, namely Bunderwal."

Cugel gave Bunderwal a careful inspection. "He seems to be a modest, decent and unassuming person, but definitely not a sound choice for the position of supercargo."

"And why do you say that?"

"If you will notice," said Cugel, "Bunderwal shows the drooping nostrils which indicate an infallible tendency toward sea-sickness."

"Cugel is a man of discernment!" declared Bunderwal. "I would rate him an applicant of fair to good quality, and I urge you to ignore his long spatulate fingers which I last noticed on Larkin the baby-stealer. There is a significant difference between the two: Larkin has been hanged and Cugel has not been hanged."

Cugel said: "We are posing problems for poor Soldinck, who already has worries enough. Let us be considerate. I suggest that we trust our fortunes to Mandingo the three-eyed Goddess of Luck.'' He brought a packet of playing cards from his pouch.

''The idea has merit,'' said Bunderwal. ''But let us use my cards which are newer and easier for the eyes of Soldinck.''

Cugel frowned. He gave his head a decisive shake and replaced the cards in his pouch. ''As I analyze the situation, I see that despite your inclinations—I am truly sorry to say this, Bunderwal—it is not proper to deal with Soldinck's important affairs in so frivolous a fashion. I suggested it only as a test. A person of the proper qualities would have rejected the idea out of hand!''

Soldinck was favorably impressed. ''On the mark, Cugel!''

''Allow me to suggest a comprehensive program,'' said Cugel. ''By reason of my wide experience and better address, I will accept the post of supercargo. Bunderwal, so I believe, will make an excellent understudy to Diffin the clerk.''

Soldinck turned to Bunderwal: ''What do you say to this?''

''Cugel's qualifications are impressive,'' Bunderwal admitted. ''Against them I can counterpose only honesty, skill, dedication, and tireless industry. Further, I am a dignified citizen of the area, not a fox-faced vagabond in an over-fancy hat.''

Cugel turned to Soldinck: ''At last—and we are lucky in this—Bunderwal's style, which consists of slander and vituperation, can be contrasted with my own dignity and restraint. I still must point out his oily skin and over-large buttocks; they indicate a bent for high-living and even a tendency toward peculation. If indeed you hire Bunderwal as under-clerk, I suggest that all locks be reinforced, for the better protection of your valuables.''

Bunderwal cleared his throat to speak, but Soldinck held up his hands. ''Gentlemen, I have heard enough! I will discuss your qualifications with Mercantides, who may well wish to interview you both. Tomorrow at noon I will have further news for you.''

Cugel bowed. ''Thank you, sir.'' He turned to Bunderwal and indicated the hangings. ''You may go, Bunderwal. I wish a private word with Soldinck.''

Bunderwal started to protest but Cugel said: ''I must discuss the sale of valuable scales.''

Bunderwal reluctantly departed. Cugel turned to Soldinck. ''During our discussion, the 'Spatterlight' was mentioned.''

''True. You never defined the exact state of your control over this scale.''

''Nor will I do so now, except to emphasize that the scale is safely hidden. If I were attacked by footpads, their efforts would fail. I mention this only to save us both inconvenience.''

Soldinck showed a grim smile. ''Your claims as to 'comprehensive experience' would seem to be well-founded.''

Cugel collected the sum of one hundred and eighty-three terces from Diffin, who counted out the coins three times, and passed them only reluctantly across the brown marble counter. Cugel swept the terces into his pouch, then departed the premises.

Recalling the advice of Weamish, Cugel took lodging at The Inn of Blue Lamps. For his supper he consumed a platter of roasted blowfish, with side dishes of carbade, yams and sluteberry mash. Leaning back over wine and cheese, he surveyed the company.

Across the room, at a table beside the fireplace, two men began to play at cards. The first was tall and thin with a cadaverous complexion, bad teeth in a long jaw, lank black hair and drooping eyelids. The second displayed a powerful physique, a heavy nose and jaw, a top-knot of red hair and a fine glinting red beard.

To augment their game, they cast about for other players. The tall man cried out: ''Hoy there, Fursk! What about a round at Skax? No?''

The man with the red beard called: ''There's good Sabtile, who never refuses a game! Sabtile, this way with your full purse and bad luck! Excellent.''

''Who else? What about you there, with the long nose and fancy hat?''

Cugel diffidently approached the table. ''What game do you play? I warn you, at cards I am a hopeless duffer.''

''The game is Skax, and we don't care how you play, so long as you cover your bets.''

Cugel smiled politely. ''If only to be sociable, I will venture a hand or two, but you must teach me the fine points of the game.''

The red-bearded man guffawed. ''No fear! You will learn them as fast as the hands are dealt! I am Wagmund; this is Sabtile and this saturnine cutthroat is Koyman, embalmer to the town Saskervoy and a most reputable citizen. Now then! The rules for Skax are thus and so.'' Wagmund went on to explain the mode of play, emphasizing his points by pounding the table with a blunt forefinger. ''So then, Cugel, is this all clear? Do you think you will be able to cope with the game? Remember, all bets must be made in solid terces. One may not hold his cards beneath the table or move them back and forth in a suspicious manner.''

''I am both inexperienced and cautious,'' said Cugel. ''Still, I think I understand the game and I will risk two, no three, terces, and I hereby bet one discrete, solid and whole terce on the first sally.''

''That's the spirit, Cugel!'' said Wagmund approvingly. ''Koyman, distribute the cards, if you will!''

''First,'' Sabtile pointed out, ''you must place out your own bet!''

''True,'' admitted Wagmund. ''See that you do the same.''

''No fear of that; I am known for my quick and clever style of play.''

''Fewer boasts and more money!'' called Koyman. ''I await your terces!''

''What of your own bet, my good stealer of ornamental gold sphincter-clasps* from the corpses entrusted into your care?''

''An oversight: simply that and no more.''

The play proceeded. Cugel lost eleven terces, and drank two mugs of the local beer: a pungent liquid brewed from acorns, bittermoss and black sausage. Presently Cugel was able to introduce his own cards into the game, whereupon his luck changed and he quickly won thirty-eight terces, with Wagmund, Koyman and Sabtile crying out and smiting their foreheads in disbelief at the unfavorable consequences of their play.

Into the common room ambled Bunderwal. He called for beer and for a space stood watching the game, teetering up and down on his toes and smoking dried herbs in a long-stemmed clay pipe. He seemed a skillful analyst of the game, and from time to time called out his approval of good play, while chaffing the losers for their blunders. ''Ah then, Koyman, why did you not play down your Double-red and sweep the field before Cugel beat you with his Green Varlets?''

Koyman snapped: ''Because the last time I did so, Cugel brought out the Queen of Devils and destroyed my hopes.'' Koyman rose to his feet. ''I am destitute. Cugel, at least tender me a beer from your winnings.''

''With pleasure!'' Cugel called the serving boy. ''Beer for Koyman and also for Bunderwal!''

''Thank you.'' Koyman signaled Bunderwal to his place. ''You may try your luck against Cugel, who plays with uncanny skill.''

''I will try him for a terce or two. Ho boy! Bring fresh cards, and throw away these limp old rags! Some are short, some are long; some are stained; others show strange designs.''

''New cards by all means,'' cried Cugel heartily. ''Still I will take

*An awkward rendering of the more succinct *Anfangel dongobel.*

these old cards and use them for practice. Bunderwal, where is your bet?"

Bunderwal placed out a terce and distributed the new cards with a fluttering agility of the fingers which caused Cugel to blink.

Several sallies were played out, but luck had deserted Cugel. He relinquished his chair to another and went to stand behind Bunderwal, in order to study the manner in which Bunderwal conducted his play.

After winning ten terces, Bunderwal declared that he wanted no more gaming for the evening. He turned to Cugel. "Allow me to invest some of my winnings in a noble purpose: the ingestion of good beer. This way; I see a couple of chairs vacant by the wall. Boy! Two mugs of the best Tatterblass!"

"Right, sir!" The boy saluted and ran down into the still-room.

Bunderwal put away his pipe. "Well, Cugel: what do you think of Saskervoy?"

"It seems a pleasant community, with prospects for the earnest worker."

"Exactly so, and in fact it is to this subject that I address myself. First, I drink to your continued prosperity."

"I will drink to prosperity in the abstract," said Cugel cautiously. "I have had little experience of it."

"What? With your dexterity at Skax? My eyes are crossed from the attempt to follow your flamboyant flourishes."

"A foolish mannerism," said Cugel. "I must learn to play with less display."

"It is no great matter," said Bunderwal. "Of more importance is that employment offered by Soldinck, which already has prompted several regrettable interchanges."

"True," said Cugel. "Let me make a suggestion."

"I am always open to new concepts."

"The supercargo possibly controls other posts aboard the *Galante*. If you will—"

Bunderwal held up his hand. "Let us be realistic. I perceive you to be a man of decision. Let us put our case to the test here and now, and let Mandingo determine who applies for the position and who stands aloof."

Cugel brought out his cards. "Will you play Skax or Rampolio?"

"Neither," said Bunderwal. "We must settle upon a test where the outcome is not fore-ordained. . . . Notice the glass yonder, where Krasnark the landlord keeps his sphigales." Bunderwal indicated a glass-sided box. Within resided a number of crustaceans, which, when broiled, were considered a notable delicacy. The typical sphigale measured eight inches in length, with a pair of powerful pincer-claws and a whip-tail sting.

"These creatures show different temperaments," said Bunderwal. "Some are fast, some slow. Choose one and I will choose another. We will set our racers upon the floor and the first to reach the opposite wall wins the test."

Cugel studied the sphigales. "They are mettlesome beasts, no question as to this." One of the sphigales, a creature striped red, yellow and an unpleasant chalk-blue, caught his eye. "Very well; I have selected my racer."

"Extract him with the tongs, but take care! They use both pincers and sting with a will."

Working discreetly so as to avoid attention, Cugel seized his racer with the tongs and placed it on the line; Bunderwal did likewise.

Bunderwal addressed his beast: "Good sphigale, run your best; my future hangs on your speed! At the ready! Take position! Go!"

Both men lifted their tongs and discreetly departed the vicinity of the tank. The sphigales ran out across the floor. Bunderwal's racer, noticing the open doorway, turned aside and fled into the night. Cugel's sphigale took refuge in the boot removed by Wagmund that he might warm his feet at the fire.

"I declare both contestants disqualified," said Bunderwal. "We must test our destiny by other means."

Cugel and Bunderwal resumed their seats. After a moment Bunderwal conceived a new scheme. "The still-room is beyond this wall and half a level lower. To avoid collisions, the serving-boys descend by the steps on the right, and come up with their trays by the steps to the left. Each passageway is closed outside of working hours by one of those heavy sliding shutters. As you will observe, the shutters are held up by a chain. Notice further. This chain here to hand controls the shutter to the stairs on the left, up which the serving boys come with their beer and other orders. Thirdly, each of the serving boys wears a round pill-box cap, to keep his hair out of the food. The game we play is this. Each man in turn adjusts the chain, and he is obliged to lower the shutter by one or more links. At length one of the boys will brush off his cap on the bottom bar of the shutter. When this occurs the man last to touch the chain loses the wager and must relinquish all claim to the post of supercargo."

Cugel considered the chain, the shutter which slid up and down to close off the passageway, and appraised the serving boys.

"The boys vary somewhat in height," Bunderwal pointed out, "with perhaps three inches separating the shortest from the most tall.

On the other hand, I believe that the tallest boy is inclined to hunch down his head. It makes for an intricate strategy.''

Cugel said: ''I must stipulate that neither of us may signal, call or cause distractions calculated to upset the pure logic of the game.''

''Agreed!'' said Bunderwal. ''We must play the game like gentlemen. Further, to avoid spurious tactics of delay, let us stipulate that the move must be made before the second boy emerges. For instance, you have lowered the shutter and I have calculated that the tallest boy is next to emerge. I may, or may not, as I choose, wait until one boy has emerged, but then I must slip my chain before the second boy appears.''

''A wise regulation, to which I agree, Do you care to go first?''

Bunderwal disclaimed the privilege. ''You, in a sense, are our guest here in Saskervoy, and you shall have the honor of the first play.''

''Thank you.'' Cugel lifted the chain from its peg and lowered the shutter by two links. ''It is now your turn, Bunderwal. You may wait until one boy has emerged, if you choose, and indeed I will expedite the process by ordering more beer for ourselves.''

''Good. Now, I must bend my keenest faculties to the game. I see that one must develop an exquisite sense of timing. I hereby lower the chain two links.''

Cugel waited and the tall boy emerged carrying a tray loaded with four pitchers of beer. By Cugel's estimate, he avoided the shutter by a gap equivalent to thirteen links of the chain. Cugel at once let slip four links.

''Aha!'' said Bunderwal. ''You play with a flair! I will show that I am no less dashing than you! Another four links!''

Cugel appraised the shutter under narrow lids. A slippage of six more links should strike off the tall boy's cap with smartness and authority. If the boys served regularly in turn, the tall boy should be emerging third in line. Cugel waited until the next boy, of medium stature, passed through, then lowered the chain five full links.

Bunderwal sucked in his breath, then gave a chirrup of triumph. ''Clever thinking, Cugel! But now quickly, I lower the chain another two links. So I will avoid the short boy, who even now mounts the stairs.''

The short boy passed below with a link or two to spare, and Cugel must now move or forfeit the game. Glumly he let go another link from the chain, and now up from the still-room came the tallest boy. As luck would have it, while mounting the stairs he bobbed his head in order to wipe his nose on his sleeve and so passed under the shutter with cap still in place, and it was Cugel's turn to chortle in triumph. "Move, Bunderwal, if you will, unless you wish to concede."

Bunderwal disconsolately let slip a link in the chain. "Now I can only pray for a miracle."

Up the steps came Krasnark the landlord: a heavy-featured man taller than the tall boy, with massive arms and lowering black eyebrows. He carried a tray loaded with a tureen of soup, a brace of roast fowl and a great hemisphere of sour-wabble pudding. His head struck the bar; he fell over backward and disappeared from view. From the still-room came the crash of broken crockery and almost at once a great outcry.

Bunderwal and Cugel quickly hauled up the shutter to its original position and moved to new seats. Cugel said, "I feel that I must be declared winner of the game, since yours was the last hand to touch the chain."

"By no means!" Bunderwal protested. "The thrust of the game, as stated, was to dislodge a cap from the head of one of three persons. This was not done, since Krasnark chose to interrupt the play."

"Here he is now," said Cugel. "He is examining the shutter with an air of perplexity."

"I see no point in carrying the matter any further," said Bunderwal. "So far as I am concerned, the game is ended."

"Except for the adjudication," said Cugel. "I am clearly the winner, from almost any point of view."

Bunderwal could not be swayed. "Krasnark wore no cap, and there the matter must rest. Let me suggest another test, in which chance plays a more decisive role."

"Here is the boy with our beer, at last. Boy, you are remarkably slow!"

"Sorry, sir. Krasnark fell into the still-room and caused no end of tumult."

"Very well; no more need be said. Bunderwal, explain your game."

"It is so simple as to be embarrassing. The door yonder leads out to the urinal. Look about the room; select a champion. I will do likewise. Whichever champion is last to patronize the urinal wins the game for his sponsor."

"The contest seems fair," said Cugel. "Have you selected a champion?"

"I have indeed. And you?"

"I selected my man on the instant. I believe him to be invincible in a contest of this sort. He is the somewhat elderly man with the thin nose and the pursy mouth sitting directly to my left. He is not large but I am made confident by the abstemious manner in which he holds his glass.''

''He is a good choice,'' Bunderwal admitted. ''By coincidence I have selected his companion, the gentleman in the gray robe who sips his beer as if with distaste.''

Cugel summoned the serving boy and spoke behind his hand, out of Bunderwal's hearing. ''The two gentlemen to my left—why do they drink so slowly?''

The boy shrugged. ''If you want the truth, they hate to part with their coin, although both command ample funds. Still, they sit by the hour nursing a gill of our most acrid brew.''

''In that case,'' said Cugel, ''bring the gentleman in the gray cloak a double-quart of your best ale, at my expense, but do not identify me.''

''Very good, sir.''

The boy turned at a signal from Bunderwal who also initiated a short muttered conversation. The boy bowed and ran down to the still-room. Presently he returned to serve the two champions large double-quart mugs of ale, which, after explanation from the boy, they accepted with gloomy good grace, though clearly they were mystified by the bounty.

Cugel became dissatisfied at the fervent manner in which his champion now drank beer. ''I fear that I made a poor selection,'' he fretted. ''He drinks as if he had just come in after a day in the desert.''

Bunderwal was equally critical of his own champion. ''He is already nose-deep in the double-quart. That trick of yours, Cugel, if I must say so, was definitely underhanded. I was forced to protect my own interests, at consideral expense.''

Cugel thought, by conversation, to distract his champion from the beer. He leaned over and said: ''Sir, you are a resident of Saskervoy, I take it?''

''I am that,'' said the gentleman. ''We are noted for our reluctance to talk with strangers in outlandish costumes.''

''You are also noted for your sobriety,'' suggested Cugel.

''That is nonsense!'' declared the champion. ''Observe the folk around this room, all gulping beer by the gallon. Excuse me, I wish to follow their example.''

''I must warn you that this local beer is congestive,'' said Cugel. ''With every mouthful you risk a spasmodic disorder.''

''Balderdash! Beer purifies the blood! Put aside your own drink, if you are alarmed, but leave me in peace with mine.'' Raising his mug, the champion drank an impressive draught.

Displeased with Cugel's maneuver, Bunderwal sought to distract his own champion by treading on his toe and causing an altercation, which might have persisted for a goodly period, had not Cugel interceded and pulled Bunderwal back to his chair. ''Play the game by sporting standards or I withdraw from the contest!''

''Your own tactics are somewhat sharp,'' muttered Bunderwal.

''Very well!'' said Cugel. ''Let us have no more interference, of any sort!''

''I agree, but the point becomes moot as your champion is showing signs of uneasiness. He is about to rise to his feet, in which case I win.''

''Not so! The first to use the trough loses the game. Notice! Your own champion is rising to his feet; they are going together.''

''Then the first to leave the common room must be deemed loser, since almost certainly he will be first at the trough!''

''With my champion in the lead? Not so! The first actually to use the trough is the loser.''

''Come then; there can be no exact judgment from this distance.''

Cugel and Bunderwal hastened to follow the two champions: through the yard and out to an illuminated shed where a trough fixed to a masonry wall served the needs of the inn's patrons.

The two champions seemed in no hurry; they paused to comment upon the mildness of the night, then, almost in synchrony, went to the trough. Cugel and Bunderwal followed, one to each side, and made ready to render judgment.

The two champions prepared to relieve themselves. Cugel's champion, glancing to the side, noticed the quality of Cugel's attention, and instantly became indignant. ''What are you looking at? Landlord! Out here at once! Call the night-guards!''

Cugel tried to explain. ''Sir, the situation is not as you think! Bunderwal will verify the case! Bunderwal?''

Bunderwal, however, had returned into the common room. Krasnark the landlord appeared, a bandage across his forehead. ''Please, sirs, a moment of quiet! Master Chernitz, be good enough to compose yourself! What is the difficulty?''

''No difficulty!'' sputtered Chernitz. ''An outrage, rather! I came out here to relieve myself, whereupon this person ranged himself beside me and acted most offensively. I raised the alarm at once!''

His friend, Bunderwal's erstwhile champion, spoke through

clenched lips: ''I stand behind the accusation! This man should be ejected from the premises and warned out of town!''

Krasnark turned to Cugel. ''These are serious charges! How do you answer them?''

''Master Chernitz is mistaken! I also came out here to relieve myself. Glancing along the wall I noticed my friend Bunderwal and signaled to him, whereupon Master Chernitz set up an embarrassing outcry, and made infamous hints! Better that you eject these two old tree-weasels!''

''What?'' cried Chernitz in a passion. ''I am a man of substance!''

Krasnark threw up his arms. ''Gentlemen, be reasonable! The matter is essentially trivial. Agreed: Cugel should not make signals and greet his friends at the urinal. Master Chernitz might be more generous in his assumptions. I suggest that Master Chernitz retract the term 'moral leper' and Cugel his 'tree-weasel', and there let the matter rest.''

''I am not accustomed to such degradations,'' said Cugel. ''Until Master Chernitz apologizes, the term remains in force.''

Cugel returned to the common room and resumed his place beside Bunderwal. ''You left the urinal quite abruptly,'' said Cugel. ''I waited to verify the results of the contest. Your champion was defeated by several seconds.''

''Only after you distracted your own champion. The contest is void.''

Master Chernitz and his friend returned to their seats. After a single cold glance toward Cugel, they turned away and spoke in low voices.

At Cugel's signal the serving boy brought full mugs of Tatterblass beer and both he and Bunderwal refreshed themselves. After a few moments Bunderwal said: ''Despite our best efforts, we still have not settled our little problem.''

''And why? Because contests of this sort abandon all to chance! As such, they are incompatible with my personal temperament. I am not one to crouch passively with my hind-quarters raised, awaiting either the kick or the caress of Destiny! I am Cugel! Fearless and indomitable, I confront every adversity! Through the force of sheer will I—''

Bunderwal made an impatient gesture. ''Silence, Cugel! I have heard enough of your braggadocio. You have taken too much beer, and I believe you to be drunk.''

Cugel stared at Bunderwal in disbelief. ''Drunk? On three draughts of this pallid Tatterblass? I have swallowed rain-water of greater force. Boy! Bring more beer! Bunderwal, what of you?''

''I will join you, with pleasure. Now then, since you reject a further test, are you willing, then, to concede defeat?''

''Never! Let us drink beer, quart for quart, while we dance the double coppola! The first to fall flat is the loser.''

Bunderwal shook his head. ''Our capacities are both noble and the stuff of which myths are made. We might dance all night, to a state of mutual exhaustion and enrich only Krasnark.''

''Well then: do you have a better idea?''

''I do indeed! If you will glance to your left, you will see that both Chernitz and his friend are dozing. Notice how their beards jut out! Here is a swange for cutting kelp. Cut off one beard or the other, and I concede you victory.''

Cugel looked askance toward the dozing men. ''They are not soundly asleep. I challenge Destiny, yes, but I do not leap off cliffs.''

''Very well,'' said Bunderwal. ''Give me the swange. If I cut a beard, then you must allow me the victory.''

The serving-boy brought fresh beer. Cugel drank a deep and thoughtful draught. He said in a subdued voice: ''The feat is not as easy as it might appear. Suppose I decided upon Chernitz. He need only open his eyes and say: 'Cugel, why are you cutting my beard?' Whereupon, I would suffer whatever penalty the law of Saskervoy prescribes for this offense.''

''The same applies to me,'' said Bunderwal. ''But I have carried my thinking a step farther. Consider this: could either Chernitz or the other see your face, or my face, if the lights were out?''

''If the lights were out, the project becomes feasible,'' said Cugel. ''Three steps across the floor, seizure of the beard, a strike of the swange, three steps back and the deed is done, and yonder I see the valve which controls the lucifer.''

''This is my own thinking,'' said Bunderwal. ''Well then: who will make the trial, you or I? The choice is yours.''

The better to order his faculties, Cugel took a long draught of beer. ''Let me feel the swange. . . . It is adequately sharp. Well then, a job of this sort must be done while the mood is on one.''

''I will control the lucifer valve,'' said Bunderwal. ''As soon as the lights go out, leap to the business at hand.''

''Wait,'' said Cugel. ''I must select a beard. That of Chernitz is tempting, but the other projects at a better angle. Ah. . . . Very well; I am ready.''

Bunderwal rose to his feet and sauntered to the valve. He looked toward Cugel and nodded.

Cugel prepared himself.

The lights went out. The room was dark but for the glimmer of firelight. Cugel strode on long legs across the floor, seized his chosen beard and skillfully wielded the swange. . . . For an instant the valve slipped in Bunderwal's grip, or perhaps a bubble of lucifer remained in the tubes. In any event, for a fraction of a second the lights flashed bright and the now beardless gentleman, staring up in startlement, looked for a frozen instant eye to eye with Cugel. Then the lights once more went out, and the gentleman was left with the image of a dark long-nosed visage with lank black hair hanging from under a stylish hat.

The gentleman cried out in confusion: "Ho! Krasnark! Rascals and knaves are on us! Where is my beard?"

One of the serving boys, groping through the dark, turned the valve and light once more emanated from the lamps.

Krasnark, bandage askew, rushed forth to investigate the confusion. The beardless gentleman pointed to Cugel, now leaning back in his chair with mug in hand, as if somnolent. "There sits the rogue! I saw him as he cut my beard, grinning like a wolf!"

Cugel called out: "He is raving; pay no heed! I sat here steadfast as a rock while the beard was being cut. This man is the worse for drink."

"Not so! With both my eyes I saw you!"

Cugel spoke in long-suffering tones. "Why should I take your beard? Does it have value? Search me if you choose! You will find not a hair!"

Krasnark said in a puzzled voice: "Cugel's remarks are logical! Why, after all, should he cut your beard?"

The gentleman, now purple with rage, cried out: "Why should anyone cut my beard? Someone did so; look for yourself!"

Krasnark shook his head and turned away. "It is beyond my imagination! Boy, bring Master Mercantides a mug of good Tatterblass at no charge, to soothe his nerves."

Cugel turned to Bunderwal. "The deed is done."

"The deed has been done, and well," said Bunderwal generously. "The victory is yours! Tomorrow at noon we shall go together to the offices of Soldinck and Mercantides, where I will recommend you for the post of supercargo."

" 'Mercantides'," mused Cugel. "Was not that the name by which Krasnark addressed the gentleman whose beard I just cut?"

''Now that you mention it, I believe that he did so indeed,'' said Bunderwal.

Across the room Wagmund gave a great yawn. ''I have had enough excitement for one evening! I am both tired and torpid. My feet are warm and my boots are dry; it is time I departed. First, my boots.''

At noon Cugel met Bunderwal in the plaza. They proceeded to the offices of Soldinck and Mercantides, and entered the outer office.

Diffin the clerk ushered them into the presence of Soldinck, who indicated a couch of maroon plush. ''Please be seated. Mercantides will be with us shortly and then we will take up our business.''

Five minutes later Mercantides entered the room. Looking neither right nor left he joined Soldinck at the octagonal table. Then, looking up, he noticed Cugel and Buderwal. He spoke sharply: ''What are you two doing here?''

Cugel spoke in a careful voice: ''Yesterday Bunderwal and I applied for the post of supercargo aboard the *Galante*. Bunderwal has withdrawn his application; therefore—''

Mercantides thrust his head forward. ''Cugel, your application is rejected, on several grounds. Bunderwal, can you reconsider your decision?''

''Certainly, if Cugel is no longer under consideration.''

''He is not. You are hereby appointed to the position. Soldinck, do you endorse my decision?''

''I am well-pleased with Bunderwal's credentials.''

''Then that is all there is to it,'' said Mercantides. ''Soldinck, I have a head-ache. If you need me, I will be at home.''

Mercantides departed the room, almost as Wagmund entered, supporting the weight of his right foot on a crutch.

Soldinck looked him up and down. ''Well then, Wagmund? What has happened to you?''

''Sir, I suffered an accident last night. I regret that I cannot make this next voyage aboard the *Galante*.''

Soldinck sat back in his chair. ''That is bad news for all of us! Wormingers are hard to come by, especially Wormingers of quality!''

Bunderwal rose to his feet. ''As newly-appointed supercargo of the *Galante*, allow me to make a recommendation. I propose that Cugel be hired to fill the vacant position.''

Without enthusiasm Soldinck looked toward Cugel: ''You have had experience in this line of work?''

"Not in recent years," said Cugel. "I will, however, consult with Wagmund in regard to modern trends."

"Very well; we cannot be too choosy, since the *Galante* sails in three days. Bunderwal, you will report at once to the ship. Cargo and supplies must be stowed, and properly! Wagmund, perhaps you will show Cugel your worms and explain their little quirks. Are there any questions? If not, all to their duties! The *Galante* sails in three days!"

Chapter II

FROM SASKERVOY TO TUSTVOLD

1

Aboard the *Galante*

Cugel's first impression of the *Galante* was, on the whole, favorable. The hull was generously proportioned and floated in a buoyant and upright manner. The careful joinery and the lavish use of ornamental detail implied an equal concern for luxury and comfort below-decks. A single mast supported a yard to which was attached a sail of dark blue silk. From a swan's-neck stanchion at the bow swung an iron lantern; another even more massive lantern hung from a pedestal on the quarter-deck.

To these appurtenances Cugel gave his approval; they contributed to the forward motion of the ship and served the convenience of the crew. On the other hand, he could not automatically endorse a pair of ungainly outboard walkways, or sponsons, which ran the length of the hull, both port and starboard, only inches above the waterline. What could be their function? Cugel stepped a few paces along the dock, to secure a better view of the odd constructions. Were they promenade decks for the passengers' exercise? They seemed too narrow and too precarious, and too rudely exposed to wave and spray. Might they be platforms from which passengers and crew might conveniently bathe and launder their clothes while the ship lay becalmed? Or [illegible] from which the crew might repair the hull?

Cugel put the problem aside. So long as the *Galante* car [illegible] in comfort to Port Perdusz, why cavil at details? Of more immediate concern were his duties as ''worminger': an occupation of which he knew nothing.

Wagmund, the previous worminger, suffered a sore leg and had refused to help Cugel. In a gruff voice Wagmund said: ''First things first! Go aboard the ship, make sure of your quarters and stow your gear; Captain Baunt is a martinet and will not tolerate clutter. When you are properly squared away, search out Drofo, the Chief Worminger; let him provide you instruction. Luckily for you, the worms are in prime condition.''

Cugel owned only the clothes on his back; this was his 'gear', although in his pouch he carried an article of great value: the 'Pectoral Sky-break Spatterlight' from the turret of the demiurge Sadlark. Now, as Cugel stood on the dock, he conceived a cunning scheme to safeguard 'Spatterlight' from pilferage.

In a secluded area behind a pile of crates, Cugel doffed his fine triple-tiered hat. He removed the rather garish ornament which clipped up the side-brim, then, using great care to avoid 'Spatterlight's' avid bite, he wired the scale to his hat, where now it seemed only a hat-clasp. The erstwhile ornament he tucked into his pouch.

Cugel returned along the dock to the *Galante*. He climbed the gangway and stepped down upon the midship deck. To his right was the after-house, with a companion-way leading up to the quarter-deck. Forward, tucked into the bluff bows, was the forepeak, with the galley and crew's mess-hall; and below, the crew's quarters.

Three persons stood within range of Cugel's vision. The first was the cook, who had stepped out on deck in order to spit over the side. The second, a person tall and gaunt with the long sallow face of a tragic poet, stood by the rail, brooding over the sea. A sparse beard the color of dark mahogany straggled across his chin; his hair, of the same dark roan-russet color, was bound in a black kerchief. With gnarled white hands he gripped the rail and turned not so much as a glance toward Cugel.

The third man carried a bucket whose contents he tossed over the side. His hair was thick, white and close-cropped; his mouth was a thin slash in a ruddy square-jawed face. This would be the cabin steward, thought Cugel: a post for which the man's brisk and even truculent demeanor seemed unsuitable.

Of the three, only the man with the bucket chose to notice Cugel. He called out sharply: ''Hoy, you skew-faced vagabond! Be off with you! We need no salves nor talismans nor prayers nor erotic adjuncts!''

Cugel responded coldly: ''You would do well to moderate your tone. I am Cugel, and I am here at the express solicitation of Soldinck! You may now show me to my quarters, and with a civil tongue in your head!'' The other heaved a heavy sigh, as of infinite patience put to the test. He called down a passageway: ''Bork! On deck!''

A short fat man with a round red face bounded up from below. ''Aye, sir; what needs to be done?''

"Show this fellow to his quarters; he says he is Soldinck's guest. I forget his name: Fugle or Kungle or something of the sort."

Bork scratched his nose in puzzlement. "I have had no notice of him. With Master Soldinck and all his family aboard, where will I find accommodation? Not unless this gentleman uses your own cabin, while you go forward to double up with Drofo."

"That idea is not to my liking!"

Bork spoke plaintively: "Have you a better suggestion?"

The other threw up his arms and stalked off up the deck. Cugel looked after him. "And who is that surly fellow?"

"That is Captain Baunt. He is irritated because you will be occupying his cabin."

Cugel rubbed his chin. "All taken with all, I would prefer to use a cabin ordinarily assigned to single gentlemen."

"Not possible on this voyage, sir. Master Soldinck is accompanied by Madame Soldinck and their three daughters, and space is at a premium."

"I hesitate to inconvenience Captain Baunt," said Cugel. "Perhaps I should—"

"Say no more, sir! Drofo's snores will not trouble Captain Baunt, and I daresay we will all manage very well. This way, sir; I will show you to your cabin."

The steward led Cugel to the commodious chamber formerly occupied by Captain Baunt. Cugel looked approvingly here and there. "This will do quite nicely. I particularly like the view from these windows."

Captain Baunt appeared in the doorway. "I trust that all is to your satisfaction?"

"Eminently so. I will be very comfortable here." To Bork Cugel said: "You may serve me a light collation, if you will, as I breakfasted early."

"Certainly, sir; by all means."

Captain Baunt said gruffly: "I ask only that you do not disarrange the shelves. My collection of water-moth shells is irreplaceable and I do not wish my antique books to be disturbed."

"Have no fear! Your belongings are as secure as if they were my own. And now, if you will excuse me, I wish to rest a few hours before inquiring into my duties."

" 'Duties'?" Captain Baunt frowned in puzzlement. "What might they be?"

Cugel spoke with dignity. "Soldinck has asked me to undertake a few simple tasks during the voyage."

"Odd. He said nothing about this to me. Bunderwal is the new supercargo and I understand that some weird lank-limbed outlander is to serve as under-worminger."

"I have accepted the post of worminger," said Cugel in austere tones.

Captain Baunt stared at Cugel slack-jawed. "You are the under-worminger?"

"That is my understanding," said Cugel.

Cugel's new quarters were located far forward in the bilges, where the stem-piece met the keel. The furnishings were simple: a narrow bunk with a sackful of dried reeds and a case where hung a few rancid garments abandoned by Wagmund.

By the light of a candle Cugel assessed his contusions. None seemed of a dangerous or disfiguring nature, even though Captain Baunt's conduct had exceeded all restraint.

A nasal voice reached his ears: "Cugel, where are you? On deck, at the double!"

Cugel groaned and limped up to the deck. Awaiting him was a tall fleshy young man with a thick cluster of black curls and small close-set black eyes. This person inspected Cugel with frank curiosity. "I am Lankwiler, worminger full and able, and hence your superior, though both of us serve under Chief Worminger Drofo. He now wishes to deliver an inspirational lecture. Listen carefully, if you know what is good for you. Come this way."

Beside the mast stood Drofo: the gaunt man with dark mahogany beard whom Cugel had noticed on his arrival aboard ship.

Drofo pointed toward the hatch. "Sit."

Cugel and Lankwiler seated themselves and waited with polite attention.

With head bent forward and hands clasped behind his back Drofo surveyed his underlings. After a moment he spoke, in a deep and passionless voice. "I can tell you much! Listen, and you will gain wisdom to surpass the scholars at the Institute, with their concords and paradigms! But do not mistake me! The weight of my words is no more than the weight of a single rain-drop! To know, you must do! After a hundred worms and ten thousand leagues, then with justice you may say, 'I am wise!' or, to precisely the same effect: 'I am a worminger!' At this time, because you are wise and because you are a worminger, you will not wish to utter vainglories. You will choose reticence, since your worth will speak for itself!" Drofo looked from face to face. "Am I clear?"

Lankwiler spoke in puzzlement: "Not entirely. The scholars at the Institute routinely calculate the weight of single raindrops. Is this to be considered good or bad?"

Drofo responded politely: "We are not adjudging the research of scholars at the Institute. We are discussing, rather, the work of the worminger."

"Ah! All is now clear!"

"Precisely so!" said Cugel. "Proceed, Drofo, with your interesting remarks!"

With arms behind his back, Drofo took a step to port, then a step to starboard. "Our calling is starkly noble! The dilettante, the weakling, the fool: all reveal themselves in their true colors. When the voyage goes well, then any mooncalf is bright and merry; he dances a jig and plays the concertina, and everyone thinks: 'Oh, for the life of the worminger!' But then hardship attacks! Black pust rages without remorse; impactions come like the gongs of Fate; the worm takes to rearing and plunging: then the popinjay is revealed, or, more likely, is discovered hiding in the darkest corner of the hold!"

Cugel and Lankwiler mulled over the remarks, while Drofo paced to port, then to starboard.

Drofo pointed a long pale fore-finger toward the sea. "Yonder we go, halfway between the sky and the ocean floor, where the secrets of every age are concealed in a darkness which will grow absolute when the sun goes out."

As if to emphasize Drofo's remarks, the face of the sun momentarily glazed over with a dark film, similar to a rheum in an old man's eye. After a flutter and a wink, the light of day returned, to the obvious relief of Lankwiler, although Drofo ignored the incident. He held his finger in the air.

"The worm is a familiar of the sea! It is wise, though it uses six concepts only: sun, wave, wind, horizon, dark deep, faithful direction, hunger, and satiation. . . . Yes, Lankwiler? Why are you counting on your fingers?"

"Sir, it is no great matter."

"The worms are not clever," said Drofo. "They perform no tricks and they know no jokes. The good worminger, like his worms, is a man of simplicity. He cares little for what he eats and is indifferent as to whether he sleeps wet or dry, or even if he sleeps at all. When his worms drive straight, when the wake lies true, when ingestion is sharp and voidure is proper: then the worminger is serene. He craves no more from the world, neither wealth nor ease nor the sensuous caress of languid females nor trinkets like that foppish bedazzlement Cugel wears in his hat. His way is the watery void!"

"Most inspiring!" cried Lankwiler. "I am proud to be a worminger! Cugel, what of you?

"I no less!" declared Cugel. "It is a worthy calling, and the hat ornament, while of no intrinsic value, is an heirloom."

Drofo gave an indifferent nod. "Now I will divulge the first axiom of our trade, which indeed can be expanded to a universal application. Thus: 'A man may show himself to you and say, "I am a Master Worminger!" Or a Master Worminger may stand to the side and speak no word. How is truth to be known? It is told by the worms.'

"I will particularize. Should you see a yellow bilious creature with bloated fausicles, gills crusted with gangue, an impacted clote, who is thereby at fault? The worm, who knows only water and space? Or he who should tend it? Can we call him a worminger? Form your own opinion. But here is another worm, strong, steadfast in direction, pink as the sunrise! This worm testifies to the faith of its worminger, who tirelessly burnishes its linctures, disimpedes its clote, scrapes and combs the gills until they shine like silver! He is in mystical communion with surge and sea, and knows the serenity only the worminger can know!

"I will say little more. Cugel, you have small acquaintance with the trade, but I take it as a good sign that you have come to me for training, since my methods are not soft. You will learn or you will drown, or suffer a blow of the flukes, or worse, incur my displeasure. But you have started well and I will teach you well. Never think me harsh, or over-bearing; you will be in self-defeating error! I am stern, yes, even severe, but in the end, when I acknowledge you a worminger, you will thank me."

"Good news indeed," muttered Cugel.

Drofo paid him no heed. "Lankwiler, you perhaps lack something of Cugel's intensity, but you have the advantage of a voyage beside Wagmund, who suffers a sore leg. I have pointed out to you certain errors and laxities, and my remarks are surely fresh in your mind; am I correct?"

"Absolutely!" said Lankwiler with a bland smile.

"Good. You will show Cugel the bins and sacks, and fit him out with a good reamer and pincts. Cugel, does your equipment include a pair of sound straddlers?"

Cugel made a negative sign. "I neglected them in my haste."

"A pity. . . . Well, you may use Wagmund's excellent equipment, but you must see to its care."

"I shall do so."

"Then make ready your gear. It is almost time to fetch the worms; the *Galante* sails directly upon Soldinck's order."

Lankwiler took Cugel forward to the locker under the forepeak, where he sorted through the gear, putting aside the best articles for his own use and tossing Cugel a casual selection from what remained.

Lankwiler advised Cugel: "Pay no great heed to old Drofo. He has inhaled too much salt-spray and I suspect that he uses the worms' ear-tonic as a tipple, for he is often queer."

Emboldened by Lankwiler's affability Cugel put a cautious question: "If we are dealing only with worms, why do we need such crude and heavy gear?"

Lankwiler looked up blankly, and Cugel hastened to add: "I assume that we work with our worms at a table, or perhaps a bench; therefore I wonder why Drofo glorifies deprivation and exposure to the elements. Are we required to rinse the worms in salt water, or dig them from the mire by night?"

Lankwiler chuckled. "You have never wormed before?"

"Very little, certainly."

"All will be made clear; let us not gossip and theorize, or waste time in idle verbalizing; like Drofo, I am a man of deeds, not rhetoric."

"Just so," said Cugel coldly.

With a twitch of sly mockery on his lips, Lankwiler said: "From the peculiar style of your hat I deduce that you derive from a far and exotic region."

"True," said Cugel.

"And how do you find the Land of Cutz?"

"It has interesting aspects; still I am anxious to return to civilization."

Lankwiler sniffed. "I am from Tugersbir sixty miles to the north, where civilization is also rife. Now then: here are Wagmund's straddles. I think that I will borrow this set with the silver conches; you may choose from among the others. Be careful; Wagmund, like a bald-headed man in a fur hat, is proud and vain, and childishly meticulous with his gear. Briskly now, unless you are ready for another barrage of Drofo's dogma." The two took their gear to the deck. With Drofo in the lead they disembarked from the *Galante* and marched north along the dock to a long pen where a number of enormous tubular creatures, seven to nine feet in diameter and almost as long as the *Galante* itself, lay placidly afloat.

Drofo pointed. "Yonder with the yellow knobs, Lankwiler, are the beasts which were assigned into your care. As you see, they are in need of attention. Cugel, the two beasts at the extreme left, with the blue knobs, are Wagmund's fine worms which now come under your supervision.''

Lankwiler made a thoughtful suggestion. ''Why not let Cugel supervise the worms with the yellow knobs, while I command the Blues? This scheme has the advantage of affording Cugel valuable training in basic procedures at a formative time in his career.''

Drofo ruminated a moment. ''Possibly so, possibly so. But we lack time to analyze the matter in all its aspects; therefore we will abide by the original plan.''

''This is correct thinking,'' said Cugel. ''It conforms with the Second Axiom of our trade: 'If Worminger A despoils his beasts, then Worminger A must restore them to health, not blameless hard-working Worminger B'.

Lankwiler was discomfited. ''Cugel may have learned thirty different axioms from a book, but, as Drofo himself pointed out, these are no substitute for experience.''

''The original plan will hold,'' said Drofo. ''Now then: bring your beasts to the ship and clamp them into their cinctures: Cugel to port, Lankwiler to starboard.''

Lankwiler quickly recovered his composure. ''Aye, aye, sir,'' he cried heartily. ''Come along, Cugel; shake a leg, now! We'll have those worms clamped up in jig-time, Tugersbir-style!''

''So long as you tie none of your peculiar Tugersbir knots,'' said Drofo. ''Last trip Captain Baunt and I pondered the complications of your easy-off hitch for half an hour.''

Lankwiler and Cugel descended to the pens where a dozen worms idled at the surface of the water, or moved slowly to the thrust of their caudal flukes. Some were pink or even scarlet-rose; others were pale ivory or a sour and sulfurous yellow. The head parts were complicated: a short thick proboscis, an optical bump with a single small eye and immediately behind, a pair of knobs on short stalks. These knobs, painted in different colors, denoted ownership, and functioned as directional apparatus.

''Smartly now, Cugel!'' called Lankwiler. ''Use all your theorems! Old Drofo likes to see our coat-tails fluttering in the wind! Get into your straddles and mount one of your worms!''

''In all candour,'' said Cugel nervously, ''I have forgotten many of my skills.''

''Little skill is needed,'' said Lankwiler. ''Watch me! I jump on the beast, I throw the hood over its eye. I seize its knobs and the worm carries me where I wish to go. Watch! You will see!''

Lankwiler jumped out on one of the worms, ran along its length, jumped to another, and then another and at last straddled a worm with yellow knobs. He threw a hood over its eye and seized the knobs. The worm swung its flukes and carried him out the water-gate, which Drofo had opened, and across the water to the *Galante*.

Cugel gingerly sought to achieve the same result, but his worm, when finally he straddled it and grasped its knobs, promptly dived deep. Cugel, in despair, pulled back on the knobs and the worm rushed to the surface, flung itself fifteen feet into the air and sent Cugel flying across the pen.

Cugel struggled ashore. By the gate stood Drofo, his brooding gaze directed toward Cugel.

The worms floated as placidly as before. Cugel heaved a deep sigh, once again jumped down upon the worm, and again straddled it. He hooded the eye and with cautious fingers tweaked the blue knobs. The creature paid no heed. Cugel delicately twisted the organ, which startled the worm so that it moved forward. Cugel continued to experiment, and by spasms and jerks the worm approached the end of the pen, where Drofo waited. Through chance, or perversity, the worm swam for the gate; Drofo pulled it ajar, and the worm slid past, with Cugel, head on high, feigning a confident and easy control.

"Now then!" said Cugel. "To the *Galante*!"

The worm, despite Cugel's wishes, veered toward the open sea. Standing by the gate, Drofo gave a sad nod, as if in verification of some inner conviction. He brought from his waistcoat a silver whistle and blew three shrill tones. The worm swung in a circle and drove up beside the water-gate. Drofo jumped down upon the ridged pink back, and kicked negligently at the knobs. "Observe! The knobs are played thus and so. Right, left. Shallow, deep. Halt, start. Is this clear?"

"Once more, if you will," said Cugel. "I am anxious to learn your technique."

Drofo repeated the procedure, then, urging the worm toward the *Galante*, stood in melancholy reflection while the worm drove through the water and ranged itself beside the ship, and at last Cugel apprehended the purpose of the walkways which had so perplexed him: they allowed swift and ready access to the worms.

"Observe," said Drofo. "I will demonstrate how the beast is clamped. So, and so, and so. Unction is applied here and here, to prevent the formation of galls. Are you clear on this?"

"Absolutely!"

"Then bring the second worm."

Profiting by the instruction, Cugel guided the second worm to its place and clamped it properly. Then, as Drofo had instructed, Cugel applied unction. A few minutes later, to his gratification, he heard Drofo chiding Lankwiler for neglecting the unction. Lankwiler's explanation, that he disliked the odor of the substance, found no favor with Drofo.

A few minutes later, Drofo stood both Lankwiler and Cugel at attention while he again made the two under-wormingers aware of his expectations.

"On the last voyage Wagmund and Lankwiler were the wormingers. I was not aboard; Gieselman was Chief Worminger. I see that he was far too slack. While Wagmund dealt most professionally with his worms, Lankwiler, through ignorance and sloth, allowed his worms to deteriorate. Examine these beasts. They are yellow as quince. Their gills are black with gangue. You may be sure that in the future Lankwiler will deal more faithfully with his worms. As for Cugel, his training has definitely been sub-standard. Aboard the *Galante* his deficiency will almost magically be corrected, as will Lankwiler's turpitude.

"Now heed! We depart Saskervoy for the wide sea in two hour's time. You will now feed your beasts a half-measure of victual, and make ready your baits. Cugel, you will then groom your beasts and inspect for timp. Lankwiler, you will immediately begin to chip gangue. You will also inspect for timp, pust and fluke-mites. Your off-beast shows signs of impaction; you must give it a drench."

"Wormingers, to your beasts!"

With brush, scraper, gouge and reamer, with pots of salve, toner and unction, Cugel groomed his worms to Drofo's instruction. From time to time a wave washed over the worms, and across the walkway. Drofo, leaning over the rail, advised Cugel from above: "Ignore the wet! It is an artificial and factitious sensation. You are constantly wet on the inside of your skin from all manner of fluids, many of a vulgar nature; why shrink from good salt brine on the outside? Ignore wetness of all sorts; it is a worminger's natural state."

Halfway into the afternoon Master Soldinck and his party arrived at the dock. Captain Baunt mustered all hands on the midship deck to welcome the group aboard ship.

First to step from the gangplank was Soldinck, with Madame Soldinck on his arm, followed by Soldinck's daughters Meadhre, Salasser and Tabazinth.

Captain Baunt, taut and immaculate in his dress uniform, delivered a short speech. "Soldinck, we of the *Galante* welcome you and your admirable family aboard! Since we will live in proximity for several weeks, or even months, allow me to perform introductions.

"I am Captain Baunt; this is our supercargo, Bunderwal. Beside him stands Sparvin, our redoubtable boatswain, who commands Tilitz—see him yonder with the blond beard—and Parmele. Our cook is Angshott and the carpenter is Kinnolde.

"Here stand the stewards. They are trusty Bork, who is learned in the identification of sea-birds and water-moths. He is assisted by Claudio and Vilip, and occasionally, when he can be found, and when the mood is on him, by Codniks the deck-boy.

"By the rail, aloof from the society of ordinary mortals, we find our wormingers! Conspicuous in any company is Chief Worminger Drofo, who deals with the profundities of nature as casually as Angshott the cook juggles his broad-beans and garlic. At his back, fierce and ready, stand Lankwiler and Cugel. Agreed, they seem sodden and dispirited, and smell somewhat of worm, but this is as it should be. To quote Drofo's favorite dictum: 'A dry sweet-smelling worminger is a lazy worminger'. So never be deceived; these are hardy men of the sea, and ready for anything!

"And there you have it: a fine ship, a strong crew and now, by some miracle, a bevy of beautiful girls to enhance the seascape! The presages are good, though our voyage is long! Our course is south by east across the Ocean of Sighs. In due course we will raise the estuary of the Great Chaing River which opens into the Land of the Falling Wall, and there, at Port Perdusz, we will make our arrival. So now: the moment of departure is at hand! Master Soldinck, what is your word?"

"I find all in order. Give the command at discretion."

"Very good, sir. Tillitz, Parmele! Cast off the lines, fore and aft! Drofo, ready with your worms! Sparvin, steer slantwise past the old sun's azimuth, until we clear Bracknock Shoal! The sea is calm, the wind is slack. Tonight we shall dine by lantern-light on the quarterdeck, while our great worms, tended by Cugel and Lankwiler, drive us through the dark!"

Three days passed, during which Cugel acquired a sound foundation in the worminger's trade.

Drofo, in his commentaries, provided a number of valuable theoretical insights. "For the worminger," said Drofo, "day and night, water, air and foam are but slightly different aspects of a larger environment, whose parameters are defined by the grandeur of the sea and the tempo of the worm."

"Allow me this question," said Cugel. "When do I sleep?"

" 'Sleep'? When you are dead, then you shall sleep long and sound. Until that mournful event, guard each iota of awareness; it is the only treasure worthy of the name. Who knows when fire will leave the sun? Even the worms, which are ordinarily fatalistic and inscrutable, give uneasy signs. This very morning at dawn I saw the sun falter at the horizon and sag backward as if in debility. Only after a great sick pulse could it swing itself into the sky, One morning we will look to the east and wait, but the sun will fail to appear. Then you may sleep."

Cugel learned the use of sixteen implements and discovered much in regard to the worms' physiology. Timp, fluke-mites, gangue and pust became his hated enemies; impactions of the clote were a major annoyance, requiring the sub-surface use of reamer, drench-bar and hose, in a position which, when the impaction was eased, became subject to the full force of the effluxion.

Drofo spent much of his time at the bow, brooding over the sea. Occasionally Soldinck, or Madame Soldinck, strolled forward to speak with him; at other times Meadhre, Salasser and Tabazinth, alone or in concert, joined Drofo at the bow and listened respectfully to his opinions. At Captain Baunt's sly suggestion, they prevailed upon Drofo to play the flute. "False modesty is not befitting to a worminger," said Drofo. He played and simultaneously danced three hornpipes and a saltarello.

Drofo seemed inattentive to either worms or wormingers, but this negligence was illusory. One afternoon Lankwiler neglected fully to bait the baskets which hung eight inches in front of his worms; as a result they slackened their effort, while Cugel's worms, properly baited, swam with zeal, so that the *Galante* began to swing westward in a great slow curve, despite the helmsman's correction.

Drofo, summoned from the bow, instantly diagnosed the difficulty and, further, discovered Lankwiler asleep in a warm nook beside the galley.

Drofo nudged Lankwiler with his toe. "Be good enough to arouse yourself. You have not baited your worms; as a result the ship is off course."

Lankwiler stared up in confusion, his black curls matted and his eyes looking in different directions. "Ah yes," mumbled Lankwiler. "The bait! It slipped my mind and I fear that I dozed off."

"I am surprised that you could sleep so soundly while your worms went slack!" said Drofo. "A skilled worminger is constantly keen. He learns to sense the least irregularity, and instantly divines its source."

"Yes, yes," muttered Lankwiler. "I now understand my mistake. 'Sense irregularity', 'divine source'. I will make a memorandum."

"Furthermore," said Drofo, "I notice a virulent case of timp on your off-worm, which you must take pains to abate."

"Absolutely, sir! At once, if not sooner!" Lankwiler struggled to his feet, hid a cavernous yawn behind his hand while Drofo watched impassively, then lurched off to his worms.

Later in the day Cugel chanced to overhear a conversation between Drofo and Captain Baunt. "Tomorrow afternoon," said Drofo, "we shall have a taste of wind. It will be good for the worms. They are not yet at full vigor, and I see no reason to push them."

"True, true," said the captain. "How do you fancy your wormingers?"

"At this time neither enjoys a rating of 'excellent,' " said Drofo. "Lankwiler is obtuse and somewhat sluggish. Cugel lacks experience and wastes energy preening in front of the girls. He works to an absolute minimum, and detests water with the fervor of a hydrophobic cat."

"His worms appear sound."

Drofo gave his head a disparaging shake. "Cugel does the right things for the wrong reasons. Through sloth he neither overfeeds nor overbaits; his worms suffer little bloat. He despises the work of dealing with timp and gangue so fiercely that he obliterates its first appearance."

"In that case, his work would seem satisfactory."

"Only to a layman! For a worminger, style and harmony of purpose are everything!"

"You have your problems; I have mine."

"How so? I thought that all went smoothly."

"To a certain extent. As you may be aware, Madame Soldinck is a woman of strong and immutable purposes."

"I divined something along those lines."

"At lunch today I mentioned that our position was two or three days sail north-east of Lausicaa."

"That would be my own reckoning, by the lay of the sea," said Drofo. "It is an interesting island. Pulk the worminger lives at Pompodouros."

"Are you acquainted with the Paphnissian Baths?"

"Not of my own experience. I believe that women bathe in these springs hoping to regain youth and beauty."

"Just so. Madame Soldinck, we will agree, is an estimable woman."

"In every respect. She is stern in her principles, unyielding in her rectitude and she will not submit to injustice."

"Yes. Bork calls her opinionated, obstinate and cantankerous, but this is not quite the same thing."

"Bork's language at least has the merit of economy," said Drofo.

"In any event, Madame Soldinck is neither young nor beautiful. Indeed, she is plump and squat. Her face is prognathous and she wears a faint black mustache. She is definitely genteel and her character is strong, so that Soldinck is guided by her suggestions. So now, since Madame Soldinck wishes to bathe in the Paphnissian Springs, we must perforce put in to Lausicaa."

"The event will serve my own interests very well," said Drofo. "At Pompodouros I will hire the worminger Pulk and discharge either Cugel or Lankwiler, who can then find his own way back to the mainland."

"Not a bad idea, if Pulk still resides at Pompodouros."

"He does indeed and will gladly return to the sea."

"In that case, half your problems are solved. Which will you put ashore: Cugel or Lankwiler?"

"I have not yet decided. It will depend on the worms."

The two men moved away and Cugel was left to ponder the conversation. It seemed that, at least until the *Galante* departed Lausicaa, he must work with vigor, and diminish his attentions to Soldinck's daughters.

Cugel at once found his scrapers and removed all traces of gangue from his worms, then combed gills till they shone silver-pink.

Lankwiler meanwhile had inspected the advanced infestation of timp on his off-worm. During the night he painted the knobs of this worm blue and then, while Cugel drowsed, he drove his off-worm around the vessel and exchanged it for Cugel's excellent off-worm, which he clamped into place on his own side. He painted the knobs yellow and congratulated himself that he had avoided a tedious task.

In the morning Cugel was startled to discover the deterioration of his off-worm.

Drofo came past and called down to Cugel: "That infestation of timp is an abomination. Also, unless I am much mistaken, that swelling indicates a severe impaction which must be relieved at once."

Cugel, recalling the overheard conversation, went to work with a will. While towed underwater he plied reamer, drench-hoses and gant-hook, and after three hours exertion, dislodged the impaction. At once the worm lost something of its bilious color and strained for its bait with renewed zest.

When Cugel finally returned to the deck he heard Drofo call down to Lankwiler: "Your off-worm has improved noticeably! Keep up the good work!"

Cugel went to look down at Lankwiler's off-worm . . . Strange that overnight Lankwiler's impacted yellow beast with its crawling infestation of timp should become so notably sound, while, during the same interval, Cugel's healthy pink worm had suffered so profound a disaster!

Cugel pondered the circumstances with care. He climbed down on the sponson and scraped at the off-worm's knobs, to discover under the blue paint, the gleam of yellow.

Cugel ruminated further, then transferred his worms, placing the healthy worm in the 'off' position.

While Cugel and Lankwiler took their evening meal, Cugel spoke of his trials. "Amazing how quickly they take up a case of timp, or an impaction! All day I worked on the beast, and tonight I moved it inboard where I can tend it more conveniently."

"A sound idea," said Lankwiler. "At last I have cured one of my beasts, and the other shows signs of improvement. Have you heard? We are putting into Lausicaa, so that Madame Soldinck can dive into the Paphnissian waters and emerge a virgin."

"I will tell you something in absolute confidence," said Cugel. "The deck boy tells me that Drofo plans to hire a veteran worminger by the name of Pulk at Pompodouros."

Lankwiler chewed his lips. "Why should he do that? He already has two expert wormingers."

"I can hardly believe that he plans to discharge you or yet me," said Cugel. "Still, that would seem the only possibility."

Lankwiler frowned and finished his meal in silence.

Cugel waited until Lankwiler went off for his evening nap, then stole down to the starboard sponson and cut deeply into the knobs of Lankwiler's sick beast; then, returning to his own sponson, he made a great show of attacking the timp.

From the corner of his eye he saw Drofo come to the rail, pause a moment, then continue on his way.

At midnight the baits were removed so that the worms might rest. The *Galante* floated quietly on the calm sea. The helmsman lashed the wheel; the deck boy drowsed under the great forward lantern where he was supposed to keep sharp lookout. Overhead glimmered those stars yet surviving including Achernar, Algol, Canopus and Cansaspara.

From his cranny crept Lankwiler. He slipped across the deck like a great black rat, and swung down to the starboard sponson. He unclamped the sick worm and urged it from its traces.

The worm floated free. Lankwiler sat in the straddles and pulled at the knobs but the nerves had been severed and the signal caused only pain. The worm beat its flukes and surged away to the northwest, with Lankwiler sitting a-straddle and frantically tugging at the knobs.

In the morning Lankwiler's disappearance dominated all conversations. Chief Worminger Drofo, Captain Baunt and Soldinck met in the grand saloon to discuss the affair, and presently Cugel was called before the group.

Soldinck, sitting on a tall-backed chair of carved skeel, cleared his throat. ''Cugel, as you know, Lankwiler has gone off with a valuable worm. Can you shed any light on the affair?''

''Like everyone else, I can only theorize.''

''We would be pleased to hear your ideas,'' said Soldinck.

Cugel spoke in a judicious voice: ''I believe that Lankwiler despaired of becoming a competent worminger. His worms went sick, and Lankwiler could not face up to the challenge. I tried to help him; I let him take one of my sound worms so that I might bring his sickly creature back to health, as Drofo must surely have noticed, although he was unusually reticent in this regard.''

Soldinck turned to Drofo. ''Is this true? If so, it reflects great credit upon Cugel.''

Drofo spoke in a subdued voice: ''Yesterday morning I counseled Cugel in this regard.''

Soldinck turned back to Cugel. ''Continue, if you will.''

''I can only surmise that dejection urged Lankwiler to perform a final despairing act.''

Captain Baunt cried out: ''That is unreasonable! If he felt dejection, why not simply jump into the sea? Why suborn our valuable worm to his personal and private uses?''

Cugel reflected a moment. ''I suppose that he wanted to make a ceremony of the occasion.''

Soldinck blew out his cheeks. ''All this to the side, Lankwiler's act is a great inconvenience. Drofo, how will we fare with only three worms?''

''We shall have no great difficulty. Cugel can readily manage both sponsons. To ease the helmsman we will use double bait to starboard and half-bait to port, and so without difficulty we will arrive at Lausicaa, and there make adjustments.''

* * *

Captain Baunt had already altered course toward Lausicaa, so that Madame Soldinck might bathe in the Paphnissian Springs. Baunt, who had hoped to make a quick passage, was not happy with the delay, and watched Cugel closely, to make sure that the worms were used to the maximum efficiency. "Cugel!" called Captain Baunt. "Adjust the lead on that off-worm; it is pulling us broadside!"

"Aye, sir."

And presently: "Cugel! Your starboard worm is listless; it merely slaps the water. Freshen its bait!"

"I am already at double-bait," grumbled Cugel. "It was fresh an hour ago."

"Then use half a gill of Heidinger's Allure, and be quick about it! I wish to make Pompodouros before sunset tomorrow!"

During the night the starboard worm, becoming fretful, began to slap at the water with its flukes. Drofo, aroused by the splashing, came up from his cabin. Leaning on the rail he watched as Cugel ran back and forth along the sponson, trying to throw a check-line over the mischievous worm's flukes.

After a few moments observation, Drofo diagnosed the problem. He called out in a nasal voice: "Always lift the bait before throwing a check-line . . . Now then, what is happening down there?"

Cugel responded sullenly: "The worm wants to swim up, down and sideways."

"What did you feed?"

"The usual: half Chalcorex and half Illem's Best."

"You might use a bit less Chalcorex for the next day or so. That lump of tissue behind the turret is usually a dependable signal. How did you bait?"

"Double-bait, as I was instructed. The captain ordered a further half-gill of Heidinger's Allure."

"There is your problem. You have over-baited, which is an act of folly."

"At Captain Baunt's orders!"

"That excuse is worse than none. Who is the worminger, you or Captain Baunt? You know your worms; you must work them by the dictates of your experience and good judgment. If Baunt interferes, ask him to come down and advise you in regard to an infestation of gangue. That is the way of the worminger! Change bait at once and drench the worm with a seep of Blagin's Mulcent."

"Very good, sir," said Cugel between his teeth.

Drofo made a brief survey of sky and horizon, then returned to his cabin and Cugel busied himself with the drench.

Captain Baunt had ordered the sail set, hoping to catch a waft of favorable air. Two hours after midnight a cross-wind arose, causing the sail to flap against the mast, creating a dismal sound which aroused Captain Baunt from his slumber. Baunt lurched out on deck. "Where is the watch? Hoy! Worminger! You there! Is no one about?"

Cugel, clambering up to the deck from the sponson, replied: "Only the lookout, who is asleep under the lantern."

"Well then, what of you? Why have you not silenced that sail? Are you deaf?"

"No sir. I have been under-water, drenching with Blagin's Mulcent."

"Well then, heave aft on the leach-line, and abate that cursed slatting!"

Cugel hastened to obey, while Captain Baunt went to the starboard rail. Here he discovered new cause for dissatisfaction. "Worminger, where is your bait? I ordered double-bait, with aroma of Allure!"

"Sir, one cannot drench while the worm exerts itself for bait."

"Why then did you drench? I ordered no Mulcent!"

Cugel drew himself up. "Sir, I drenched that worm according to the dictates of my best judgment and experience."

Captain Baunt stared blankly, threw his arms in the air, turned and went back to his bed.

2

Lausicaa

The sun, dropping down the sky, passed behind a ledge of low clouds and twilight came early. The air was still; the ocean lay flat, with a surface like heavy satin, exactly reflecting the sky, so that the *Galante* seemed to float through a void of marvellous lavender luminosity. Only the bow waves, spreading away at V-angles in rolling black and lavender ripples, defined the surface of the sea.

An hour before sunset Lausicaa appeared on the horizon: a shadow almost lost in the plum-colored murk.

As darkness fell, a dozen lights flickered from the town Pompodouros, reflecting across the opening into the harbor and easing the approach for Captain Baunt.

A wharf fronting the town showed as a heavy mark, blacker than black, across the reflections. In unfamiliar waters and in the dark, Captain Baunt prudently elected to drop anchor rather than attempt mooring at the dock.

From the quarter-deck Captain Baunt called forward: "Drofo! Bring up your baits!"

"Up baits!" came back Drofo's acknowledgment, then, in a different voice: "Cugel! Debait all worms!"

Cugel snatched bait from the two port worms, scrambled across the deck, jumped down upon the starboard sponson and debaited the starboard worm. The *Galante* barely drifted through the water, to idle motions of the worms' flukes.

Captain Baunt called out again: "Drofo, muffle your worms!"

"Muffle worms!" came Drofo's response, and then: "Cugel, muffles all around! Quick now!"

Cugel muffled the starboard worm, but fell into the water and was slow with the port muffles, prompting a complaint from Captain Baunt. ''Drofo, hurry the muffles! Are you conducting a rite for the dead? Boatswain, ready the anchor!''

''Muffles going on!'' sang out Drofo. ''Look sharp, Cugel!''

''Anchor at the ready, sir.''

The worms were muffled at last, and the *Galante* barely drifted through the water.

''Let go the anchor!'' called Captain Baunt.

''Anchor in the water, sir! Bottom at six fathoms.''

The *Galante* lay placidly to anchor. Cugel eased the worms in their cinctures, applied unguent and fed each worm a measure of victual.

After the evening meal Captain Baunt assembled the ship's company on the midship deck. Standing halfway up the companionway ladder he spoke a few words in regard to Lausicaa and the town Pompodouros.

''Those of you who have visited this place before, I doubt if there are many, will understand why I must issue warnings. In a nut-shell, you will find certain customs which guide the folk of this island to be at variance with our own. They may impress you as strange, grotesque, laughable, disgraceful, picturesque or commendable, depending upon your point of view. Whatever the case, we must take note of these customs and abide by them, since the folk of Lausicaa will definitely not alter their ways in favor of ours.''

Captain Baunt smilingly acknowledged the presence of Madame Soldinck and her three daughters. ''My remarks apply almost exclusively to the gentlemen aboard, and if I touch upon topics which might be considered tasteless, I can only plead necessity; so I beg your indulgence!''

Soldinck cried out bluffly: ''Enough of your breast-beating, Baunt! Speak up! We are all reasonable people aboard, Madame Soldinck included!''

Captain Baunt waited until the laughter had died down. ''Very well then! Look along the dock yonder; you will notice three persons standing under the street-lamp. All are men. The faces of each are hidden behind hoods and veils. For this precaution there is reason: the ebullience of the local females. So vivacious is their nature that men dare not display their faces for fear of provoking ungovernable impulses. Female voyeurs go so far as to peek through windows of the clubhouse where the men gather to drink beer, sometimes with their faces partially exposed.''

At this information Madame Soldinck and her daughters laughed nervously. "Extraordinary!" said Madame Soldinck. "And women of every social class act in this fashion?"

"Absolutely!"

Meadhre asked diffidently: "Do the men propose marriage with their faces concealed?"

Captain Baunt reflected. "So far as I know, the idea never enters anyone's head."

"It does not seem a wholesome atmosphere in which to bring up children," said Madame Soldinck.

"Apparently the children are not seriously affected," said Captain Baunt. "Until the age of ten boys may sometimes be seen bare-faced, but even during these tender years they are protected from adventurous young females. At the age of ten they 'go under the veil', to use the local idiom."

"How tiresome for the girls!" sighed Salasser.

"And also undignified!" said Tabazinth with emphasis. "Suppose I noticed what appeared to be a handsome young man, and ran after him and finally subdued him, and then, when I pulled away his hood, I found protruding yellow teeth, a big nose and a narrow receding forehead. What next? I would feel a fool simply getting up and walking away."

Meadhre suggested: "You could tell the gentleman that you merely wanted directions back to the ship."

"Whatever the case," Captain Baunt went on, "the women of Lausicaa have evolved techniques to restore the equilibrium. After this fashion:

"The men are partial to spraling, which are small delicate bidechtils. They swim at the surface of the sea in the early morning. The women, therefore, arise in the pre-dawn hours, wade out into the sea, where they capture as much spraling as possible, then return to their huts.

"Those women with a good catch set their fires going and hang out signs, such as: FINE SPRALING TODAY, or TASTY SPRALING TO YOUR ORDER.

"The men arise in due course and stroll about the town. When at last they work up an appetite, they stop by a hut where the sign offers refreshment to their taste. Often, if the spraling is fresh and the company good, they may stay for dinner as well."

Madame Soldinck sniffed and murmured aside to her daughters, who merely shrugged and shook their heads.

Soldinck climbed two steps up the companionway ladder. "Captain Baunt's remarks are not be taken lightly! When you go ashore, wear a robe or a loose gown and by some means muffle your face so as to avoid any unseemly or improper incident! Am I clear?''

Captain Baunt said: ''In the morning we will moor at the dock and attend to our various items of business. Drofo, I suggest that you put this interval to good purpose. Anoint your animals well and cure all chafes, galls and cankers. Exercise them daily about the harbor, since idleness brings on impaction. Cure all your infestations; trim all gills. These hours in port are precious; each must be used to the fullest, without regard for day or night.''

''This echoes my own thinking,'' said Drofo. ''I will immediately give the necessary orders to Cugel.''

Soldinck called out: ''A final word! Lankwiler's departure with the starboard off-worm might have caused us enormous inconvenience were it not for the wise tactics of our Chief Worminger. I propose a cheer for the estimable Drofo!''

Drofo acknowledged the acclamation with a curt jerk of the head, then turned away to instuct Cugel, after which he went forward to lean on the rail and brood across the waters of the harbor.

Cugel worked until midnight with his cutters, burnishing irons and reamer, then treated pust, gangue, and timp. Drofo had long since vacated his place on the bow and Captain Baunt had retired early. Cugel stealthily abandoned his work and went below to his bunk.

Almost immediately, or so it seemed, he was aroused by Codnicks the deck-boy. Blinking and yawning Cugel stumbled up to the deck, to find the sun rising and Captain Baunt impatiently pacing back and forth.

At the sight of Cugel Captain Baunt stopped short. ''Hurrah! You have finally decided to honor us with your presence! Naturally our important business ashore can wait until you have drowsed and dozed to your heart's content. Are you finally able to face the day?''

''Aye, sir!''

''Thank you, Cugel. Drofo, here, at long last, is your worminger!''

''Very good, Captain. Cugel, you must learn to be on hand when you are needed. Now return your worms into cincture. We are ready to work our way into the dock. Keep your muffles ready to hand. Use no bait.''

With Captain Baunt on the quarter-deck, Drofo alert at the bow and Cugel tending worms to port and starboard, the *Galante* eased across the harbor to the dock. Longshoremen, wearing long black gowns, tall hats with veils shrouding their faces, took mooring-lines and made the ship fast to bollards. Cugel muffled the worms, eased cinctures and fed victual all around.

Captain Baunt assigned Cugel and the deck-boy to gangplank watch; every one else, suitably dressed and veiled, went ashore. Cugel immediately concealed his features behind a makeshift veil, donned a cloak and likewise went ashore, followed in short order by Codnicks the deck-boy.

Many years before, Cugel had passed through the old city Kaiin in Ascolais, north of Almery. In the decayed grandeur of Pompodouros he discovered haunting recollections of Kaiin, conveyed principally by the fallen and ruined palaces along the hillside, now overgrown with foxglove and stone-weed and a few small pencil cypresses.

Pompodouros occupied a barren hollow surrounded by low hills. The present inhabitants had put the mouldering stones from the ruins to their own purposes: huts, the men's clubhouse, the market-dome, a sick-house for men and another for women, one slaughter-house, two schools, four taverns, six temples, a number of small work-shops and the brewery. In the plaza a dozen white dolomite statues, now more or less dilapidated, cast stark black shadows away from the wan red sunlight.

There seemed no streets to Pompodouros, only open areas and cleared spaces through the rubble which served as avenues. Along these by-ways the men and women of the town moved about their business. The men, by virtue of their long gowns and black veils hanging below their hats, seemed tall and spare. The women wore skirts of furze dyed dark green, dark red, gray or violet-gray, tasseled shawls and beaded caps, into which the more coquettish inserted the plumes of sea-birds.

A number of small carriages, drawn by those squat heavy-legged creatures known as 'droggers', moved through the places of Pompodouros; others, awaiting hire, ranged in a line before the men's club-house.

Bunderwal had been delegated to escort Madame Soldinck and her daughters on a tour of nearby places of interest; they hired a carriage and set off about their sight-seeing. Captain Baunt and Soldinck were met by several local dignitaries and conducted into the men's club-house.

With his face concealed behind the veil, Cugel also entered the club-house. At a counter he bought a pewter jug of beer and took it to a booth close beside that where Captain Baunt, Soldinck, and some others drank beer and discussed business of the voyage.

By pressing his ear against the back of the booth and listening with care, Cugel was able to capture the gist of the conversation.

"—most extraordinary flavor to this beer," came Soldinck's voice. "It tastes of tar."

"I believe that it is brewed from tarweed and other such constituents," replied Captain Baunt. "It is said to be nutritious but it slides down the gullet as if it had claws. . . . Aha! Here is Drofo."

Soldinck lifted his veil to look. "How can you tell, with his face concealed?"

"Easily. He wears the yellow boots of a worminger."

"That is clear enough. Who is the other person?"

"I suspect the gentleman to be his friend Pulk. Hoy, Drofo! Over here!"

The newcomers joined Captain Baunt and Soldinck. Drofo said: "I hereby introduce the worminger Pulk, of whom you have heard me speak. I have hinted of our needs and Pulk has been kind enough to give the matter his attention."

"Good!" said Captain Baunt. "I hope that you also mentioned our need for a worm, preferably a 'Motilator' or a 'Magna-fluke'?"

"Well, Pulk," asked Drofo, "what of it?"

Pulk spoke in a measured voice. "I believe that a worm of the requisite quality might be available from my nephew Fuscule, especially if he were signed aboard the *Galante* as a worminger."

Soldinck looked from one to the other. "Then we would have three wormingers aboard ship, in addition to Drofo. That is impractical."

"Quite so," said Drofo. "Ranked in order of indispensability, the wormingers would be first, myself, then Pulk, then Fuscule, and finally—" Drofo paused.

"Cugel?"

"Just so."

"You are suggesting that we discharge Cugel upon this bleak and miserable island?"

"It is one of our options."

"But how will Cugel return to the mainland?"

"No doubt some means will suggest itself."

Pulk said: "Lausicaa, after all, is not the worst place in the world. The spraling is excellent."

"Ah yes, the spraling!" Soldinck spoke with warmth in his voice. "How does one sample this delicacy?"

"Nothing could be easier," said Pulk. "One merely walks along the streets of the female quarter until he sees a sign which meets his fancy. He thereupon reaches out, detaches the sign and carries it into the house."

"Does he knock?" Soldinck inquired cautiously.

"Sometimes. Knocking is considered a mark of gentility."

"Another matter. How does one discover the attributes of his hostess before he, let us say, commits himself?"

"Several tactics exist. The casual visitor, such as yourself, is well-advised to act upon local advice, since once the door opens and the visitor enters the house, he will find it difficult if not impossible to make a graceful exit. If you like, I will ask Fuscule to advise you."

"Discreetly, of course. Madame Soldinck would not care to learn of my interest in the local cuisine."

"You will find Fuscule accomodating in all respects."

"Another matter: Madame Soldinck wants to visit the Paphnissian Baths, of which she has heard many remarkable reports."

Pulk made a courteous gesture. "I myself would be happy to escort Madame Soldinck; unfortunately I will be more than busy during the next few days. I suggest that we assign Fuscule to this duty as well."

"Madame Soldinck will be happy with this plan. Well, Drofo, shall we hazard another goblet of this phenolic seepage? It is at least not deficient in authority."

"Sir, my tastes are austere."

"Captain, what of you?"

Captain Baunt made a negative indication. "I must now return to the ship and discharge Cugel from his post, since this has been your disposition of the case." He arose to his feet and departed the club-house, followed by Drofo.

Soldinck drank from the pewter goblet and made a wry face. "Conceivably, this brew might be painted upon the ship's bottom, to discourage the growth of marine pests. Still, we must make do." He tilted the goblet on high, and set it down with a thud. "Pulk, perhaps now is as good a time as any to taste the local spraling. Is Fuscule at liberty?"

"He might be resting, or perhaps burnishing his worm, but in any case he will happy to assist you. Boy! Run to Fuscule's house and ask him to meet Master Soldinck here at once. Explain that I, Pulk, sent the message and pronounced it urgent. And now, sir—" Pulk rose to his feet "—I will leave you in the care of Fuscule, who will be along shortly."

Cugel jumped up from the booth, hastened outdoors and waited in the shadow beside the club-house. Pulk and the serving-boy emerged and went off in different directions. Cugel ran after the boy and called him to a halt. "One moment! Soldinck has altered his plans. Here is a florin for your trouble."

"Thank you, sir." The boy turned back toward the clubhouse. Cugel once again engaged his attention. "No doubt you are acquainted with the women of Pompodouros?"

"Only by sight. They will serve me no spraling; in fact they are quite vulgar in their taunts."

"A pity! But no doubt your time will come. Tell me, of all the women, which might be considered the most formidable and awesome?"

The boy reflected. "That is a very hard choice to make. Krislen? Ottleia? Terlulia? In all justice, I must select Terlulia. There is a joke to the effect that when she goes to catch spraling, the sea-birds fly to the other side of the island. She is tall and portly, with red spots on her arms and large teeth. Her manner is commanding and it is said that she insists on a good bargain for her spraling."

"And where does this person make her home?"

The boy pointed. "See yonder the hut with the two windows? That is the place."

"And where will I find Fuscule?"

"Farther along this very avenue, at the worm-pen."

"Good. Here is another florin for you. When you return to the club-house, tell Master Soldinck only that Fuscule will be along shortly."

"As you say, sir."

Cugel proceeded along the road at best speed, and in short order arrived at the house of Fuscule, hard beside a worm-pen built of stones piled out into the sea. At a work-bench, repairing a burnishing tool, stood Fuscule: a tall man, very thin, all elbows, knees and long spare shanks.

Cugel put on a haughty manner and approached. "You, my good fellow, I assume to be Fuscule?"

"What of it?" demanded Fuscule in a sour voice, barely looking up from his work. "Who are you?"

"You may call me Master Soldinck, of the ship *Galante*. I understand that you consider yourself a worminger of sorts."

Fuscule looked briefly up from his work. "Understand as you like."

"Come, fellow! Do not take that tone with me! I am a man of importance! I have come to buy your worm if you are willing to sell cheap."

Fuscule put down his tools and gave Cugel a stony inspection from under his veil. "Certainly I will sell my worm. No doubt you are in dire need, or you would not come to Lausicaa to buy a worm. My price, under the circumstances and in view of your gracious personality, is five thousand terces. Take it or leave it."

Cugel gave a rasping cry of outrage. "Only a villain could make such avaricious demands! I have traveled far across this dying world; never have I encountered such cruel rapacity! Fuscule, you are a larcenous scoundrel, and physically repulsive as well!"

Fuscule's stony grin shifted the fabric of his veil. "This sort of abuse will never persuade me to lower my prices."

"It is tragic, but I have no choice but to submit," lamented Cugel. "Fuscule, you drive a hard bargain!"

Fuscule shrugged. "I am not interested in your opinions. Where is the money? Pay it over, every terce in cold hard coin! Then take the worm and our transaction is complete."

"Patience!" said Cugel sternly. "Do you think I carry such sums on my person? I must fetch the money from the ship. Will you wait here?"

"Be quick! Though in all candour—" Fuscule gave voice to a harsh chuckle "—for five thousand terces I will wait an appreciable time."

Cugel picked up one of Fuscule's tools and carelessly tossed it into the worm-pen. In slack-jawed amazement Fuscule ran to look down after the tool. Stepping forward, Cugel pushed him into the water, then stood watching as Fuscule floundered about the pen. "That is punishment for your insolence," said Cugel. "Remember, I am Master Soldinck and an important person. I will be back in due course with the money."

With long strides Cugel returned to the club-house and went to the booth where Soldinck waited. "I am Fuscule," said Cugel, disguising his voice. "I understand that you have worked up an appetite for some good spraling."

"True!" Soldinck peered up into Cugel's veil and winked in sly camaraderie. "But we must be discreet! That is of the essence!"

"Just so! I understand completely!"

Cugel and Soldinck departed the club-house and stood in the plaza. Soldinck said: "I must admit that I am somewhat fastidious, perhaps to a fault. Pulk has eulogized you as a man of rare discrimination in these matters."

Cugel nodded sagely. "It can justly be said that I know my left foot from my right."

Soldinck spoke on in a pensive voice. "I like to dine in pleasant surroundings, to which the charm of the hostess makes an important contribution. She should be a person of excellent or even exquisite appearance, neither portly nor emaciated. She should be flat in the belly, round in the haunch and fine in the shank like a swift racing animal. She should be reasonably clean and not smell of fish, and if she had a poetic soul and a romantic disposition, it would not come amiss.''

''This is a select category,'' said Cugel. ''It would include Krislen, Ottleia and most certainly Terlulia.''

''Why waste time, then? You may take me to the hut of Terlulia, but by carriage if you please. I am almost foundered under the cargo of beer I have taken aboard.''

''It shall be as you say or my name is not Fuscule.'' Cugel signaled for a carriage. After assisting Soldinck into the passenger space, Cugel went to confer with the driver. ''Do you know the house of Terlulia?''

The driver looked around in evident curiosity, but the veil concealed his expression. ''Certainly, sir.''

''You may take us to a place nearby.'' Cugel climbed to a seat beside Soldinck. The driver kicked down a pedal connected to a lever, which in turn drove a flexible rod smartly against the drogger's rump. The animal trotted across the plaza, the driver steering by a wheel which, when rotated, pulled at cords connected to the drogger's long slender ears.

As they rode, Soldinck spoke of the *Galante* and affairs of the voyage. ''Wormingers are a temperamental lot. This has been made clear to me by Lankwiler who leapt on a worm and rode off to the north, and Cugel, whose conduct is barely less eccentric. Cugel of course will be put ashore here at Pompodouros, and you, so I hope, will assume his duties—especially, my dear fellow, if you will sell me your good worm at a price fair to us both.''

''No difficulty whatever,'' said Cugel. ''What price did you have in mind?''

Under his veil Soldinck frowned thoughtfully. ''At Saskervoy such a worm as yours might well sell for as high as seven hundred or even eight hundred terces. Applying the proper discounts, we arrive at a rough but generous sum of six hundred terces.''

''The figure seems somewhat low,'' said Cugel dubiously. ''I had hoped for at least a hundred terces more.''

Soldinck reached into his pouch and counted forth six golden centums. ''I fear that this is all I am now able to pay.''

Cugel accepted the money. ''The worm is yours.''

''That is the way I like to do business,'' said Soldinck. ''Briskly and with minimal haggling. Fuscule, you are a clever fellow and a hard bargainer! You will go far in this world."

"I am happy to hear your good opinion," said Cugel. "Now see yonder: that is the house of Terlulia. Driver, stop the carriage!"

The driver, pulling back a long lever, constricted brackets against the legs of the drogger, and so brought the beast to a stand-still.

Soldinck alighted and considered the structure which Cugel had pointed out. "That is the house of Terlulia?"

"Exactly so. You will notice her sign."

Soldinck dubiously surveyed the placard which Terlulia had affixed to her door. "With the red paint and flashing orange lights it is hardly demure."

"That is the basic nature of camouflage," said Cugel. "Go to the door, detach the sign and carry it into the hut."

Soldinck drew a deep breath. "So be it! Mind you now, not so much as a hint to Madame Soldinck! In fact, now would be an excellent time to show her the Paphnissian Baths if Bunderwal has brought her back to the ship."

Cugel bowed politely. "I shall see to it at once. Driver, take me to the ship *Galante*."

The carriage returned toward the harbor. Looking over his shoulder, Cugel saw Soldinck approach Terlulia's hut. The door opened to his coming; Soldinck seemed to freeze in his tracks and then to sag somewhat on limp legs. By a means invisible to Cugel, he was snatched forward and into the house.

As the carriage approached the harbor, Cugel spoke to the driver: "Tell me something of the Paphnissian Baths. Do they confer any palpable benefits?"

"I have heard conflicting reports," said the driver. "We are told that Paphnis, then Goddess of Beauty and Gynodyne of the Century, paused on the summit of Mount Dein to rest. Nearby she found a spring where she laved her feet, thus charging the water with virtue. Sometime later the Pandalect Cosmei founded a nympharium on the site and built a splendid balneario of green glass and nacre, and so the legends were proliferated."

"And now?"

"The spring flows as before. On certain nights the ghost of Cosmei wanders among the ruins. At other times one may hear the faint sound of singing, no more than a whisper, apparently echoes of songs sung by the nymphs."

"If there were indeed efficacy to the waters," mused Cugel, "one would think that Krislen and Ottleia and even the redoubtable Terlulia would make use of the magic. Why do they not do so?"

"They claim that they want the men of Pompodouros to love them for their spiritual qualities. It may be sheer obstinacy, or perhaps they have all tested the springs, without effect. It is one of the great female mysteries."

"What of the spraling?"

"Everyone must eat."

The carriage entered the plaza and Cugel called the driver to a halt. "Which of these avenues leads up to the Paphnissian Baths?"

The driver pointed. "Just along there and then five miles up the mountainside."

"And what is your fee for the trip?"

"Ordinarily I charge three terces, but for persons of importance the fee is occasionally somewhat higher."

"Well then, Soldinck has required me to escort Madame Soldinck to the Baths and she prefers that we go alone, to minimize her embarrassment. I will therefore hire the use of your carriage for ten terces, plus an additional five terces to buy your beer during my absence. Soldinck will disburse this sum upon his return from the hut of Terlulia."

"If he has the strength to lift his hand," grumbled the driver. "All fees should be paid in advance."

"Here is your beer money, at least," said Cugel. "The rest must be collected from Soldinck."

"It is irregular, but I suppose it will do. Observe then. This pedal accelerates the vehicle. This lever brings it to a halt. Turn this wheel to direct the vehicle in the way you wish to go. If the drogger squats to the ground this lever drives a spur into its groin and it will leap forward with renewed vigor."

"Clarity itself," said Cugel. "I will return your carriage to the rank in front of the club-house."

Cugel drove the carriage to the wharf and halted beside the *Galante*. Madame Soldinck and her daughters sat in lounging-chairs on the quarter-deck looking across the plaza and commenting upon the curious sights of the tovn.

"Madame Soldinck!" called Cugel. "It is I, Fuscule, who have come to escort you to the Baths of Paphnis. Are you ready? We must make haste, since the day is drawing on!"

"I am quite ready. Is there room for all of us?"

"I am afraid not. The beast could not pull us up the mountain. Your daughters must remain behind."

Madame Soldinck descended the gangplank and Cugel jumped to the ground. " 'Fuscule'?" mused Madame Soldinck. "I have heard your name but I cannot place you."

"I am the nephew of Pulk the worminger. I am selling a worm to Master Soldinck and I hope to become worminger aboard your ship."

"I see. Whatever the case, it is kind of you to take me on this excursion. Will I need special bathing clothes?"

"None are necessary. There is adequate seclusion, and garments diminish the effect of the waters."

"Yes, that seems reasonable."

Cugel assisted Madame Soldinck into the carriage, then climbed into the driver's seat. He thrust down the accelerator pedal and the carriage rolled off across the plaza.

Cugel followed the road up the mountainside. Pompodouros fell below, then disappeared among the stony hills. Thick black sedge to either side gave off a sharp aromatic odor and it became clear to Cugel where the folk of the island derived the raw material for their beer.

The road at last turned off into a dreary little meadow. Cugel halted the carriage to rest the drogger. Madame Soldinck called out in a reedy voice: "Are we almost to the fountain? Where is the temple which shelters the baths?"

"There is still some distance to go," said Cugel.

"Truly? Fuscule, you should have provided a more comfortable carriage. This vehicle bounces and jounces as if I were riding a board being dragged over the rocks, nor is there protection from the dust."

Swinging around in his seat, Cugel spoke severely: "Madame Soldinck, please put aside your complaints, as they grate on the nerves. In fact, there is more to be said, and I will use the even-handed candour of a worminger. For all your estimable qualities, you have been spoiled and pampered by too much luxury, and, of course, over-eating. You are living a decadent dream! In reference to the carriage: enjoy the comfort while it is available to you, since, when the way becomes steep, you will be obliged to walk."

Madame Soldinck stared up speechless.

"Furthermore, this is the place where I customarily collect my fee," said Cugel. "How much money do you carry on your person?"

Madame Soldinck at last found her tongue. She spoke icily: "Surely you can wait until we return to Pompodouros. Master Soldinck will deal justly with you at the proper time."

"I prefer hard terces now to justice then. Here I can maximize my fee. In Pompodouros I must compromise with Soldinck's avarice."

"That is a callous point of view."

"It is the voice of classical logic, as we are taught at wormingers' school. You may pay over at least forty-five terces."

"Absurd! I carry no such sum on my person!"

"Then you may give me that fine opal you wear at your shoulder."

"Never! That is a valuable gem! Here is eighteen terces; it is all I have with me. Now take me at once to the baths and without further insolence."

"You are starting out on the wrong foot, Madame Soldinck! I plan to sign upon the *Galante* as worminger, no matter what the inconvenience to Cugel. He can be marooned here forever, for all I care. In any case you will be seeing much of me, and cordiality will be returned in kind, and you may also introduce me to your toothsome daughters."

Again Madame Soldinck found herself at a loss for words. Finally she said: "Take me to the baths."

"It is time to proceed," said Cugel. "I suspect that the drogger, if consulted, would claim already to have expended eighteen terces worth of effort. On Lausicaa we are not grossly overweight like you outlanders."

Madame Soldinck said with flinty control: "Your remarks, Fuscule, are extraordinary."

"Save your breath, as you may need it when the drogger begins to flag."

Once again Madame Soldinck sat silent.

The hillside indeed became more steep and the road traversed back and forth until, breasting a little ridge, it dipped into a glade shaded under yellow-green gingerberry trees, and a single tall lancelade, with a glossy dark red trunk and feathery black foliage, standing like a king.

Cugel halted the carriage beside a stream which trickled across the glade. "Here we are, Madame Soldinck. You may bathe in the water and I will take note of the results."

Madame Soldinck surveyed the stream without enthusiasm. "Can this be the site of the baths? Where is the temple? And the fallen statue? Where is Cosmei's bower?"

"The baths proper are farther up the mountain," said Cugel in a languid voice. "This is the identical water, which in any event works to small effect, especially in exaggerated cases."

Madame Soldinck grew red in the face. "You may drive me down the hill at once. Master Soldinck will make other arrangements for me."

"As you like. However, I will take my gratuity now, if you please."

"You may refer to Master Soldinck for your gratuity. I am sure that he will have something to say to you."

Cugel turned the carriage about and started back down-hill, saying: "Never will I understand the ways of women."

Madame Soldinck sat in frigid silence and in due course the carriage came down into Pompodouros. Cugel took Madame Soldinck to the *Galante*; without a backward glance she stalked up the gangplank.

Cugel returned the carriage to the rank, then entered the club-house and seated himself in an inconspicuous booth. He rearranged his veil, draping it from inside the brim of his hat, that he might no longer be mistaken for Fuscule.

An hour passed. Captain Baunt and Chief Worminger Drofo, having completed various errands, strolled across the plaza to stand in conversation in front of the club-house, where they were presently joined by Pulk.

"And where is Soldinck?" asked Pulk. "Surely by now he has consumed all the spraling good for him."

"So I would think," said Captain Baunt. "He could hardly have come to any mishap."

"Not with Fuscule in charge," said Pulk. "No doubt they are standing by the pen, discussing Fuscule's worm."

Captain Baunt pointed up the hill. "Here comes Soldinck now! He seems in a bad way, as if he can hardly put one foot in front of another!"

Hunched forward and walking with exaggerated care, Soldinck crossed the plaza by an indirect route and at last joined the group in front of the club-house. Captain Baunt stepped forward to meet him. "Are you well? Has something gone wrong?"

Soldinck spoke in a voice thin and husky: "I have had an awful experience."

"What happened? At least you are alive!"

"Only barely. These last few hours will haunt me forever. I blame Fuscule, in all respects. I name him a demon of perversity! I bought his worm; at least that is ours. Drofo, go fetch it to the ship; we will leave this sink-hole at once."

Pulk put a tentative question: "Will Fuscule still be our worminger?"

"Ha!" declared Soldinck savagely. "He will not tend worms on my ship! Cugel commands the position."

Madame Soldinck, having observed Soldinck as he crossed the plaza, could restrain her rage no longer. She descended to the dock and approached the club-house. As soon as she came within ear-shot of Soldinck she cried out: "So there you are at last! Where were you while I was suffering insolence and ridicule at the hands of that vicious Fuscule? The instant he puts his foot aboard our ship I leave! Compared to Fuscule, Cugel is a blessed angel of light! Cugel must remain the worminger!"

"That, my dear, is exactly my own opinion."

Pulk tried to insert a soothing word. "I cannot believe that Fuscule would act other than correctly! Surely there has been a mistake or a misunderstanding of some sort—"

"A misunderstanding, when he demanded forty-five terces and took eighteen only because I had no more; and wanted my precious opal in the bargain, then visited upon me ignominies I cannot bear to think upon? And he boasted, if you can believe it, of how he intended to worm aboard the *Galante*! That will never be, if I myself must stand guard at the gang-plank!"

Captain Baunt said: "The decision is definite in this regard. Fuscule must be a madman!"

"A madman or worse! It is hard to describe the scope of his evil! And yet, all the while, I sensed familiarity; as if somewhere, in a previous existence, or a nightmare, I had known him!"

"The mind plays strange tricks," observed Captain Baunt. "I am anxious to meet this remarkable individual."

Pulk called out: "Here he comes now, with Drofo! At last we shall have an explanation, and perhaps a suitable apology."

"I want neither!" cried Madame Soldinck. "I want only to see the last of this dismal island!" Turning on her heel, she swept off across the plaza and back aboard the *Galante*.

Marching with vigorous steps, Fuscule approached the group, with Drofo strolling a pace or two behind. Fuscule halted, and raising his veil, surveyed the group. "Where is Soldinck?"

Keeping a tight grip on his temper, Soldinck said coldly: "You know very well who I am! I know you as well, for a scoundrel and a blackguard. I will not comment upon the poor taste of your prank, nor your insufferable conduct toward Madame Soldinck. I prefer that we conclude our business on the basis of absolute formality. Drofo, why are you not taking our worm to the *Galante*?"

"I will respond to that question," said Fuscule. "Drofo will be allowed the worm after you have paid me my five thousand terces, plus eleven terces for my double-cambered fluke-chister which you discarded with such cavalier ease, together with another twenty terces for your attack upon my person. Your account therefore stands at a total of five thousand and thirty-one terces. You may pay me on this instant."

Cugel, mingling with a group of others, came from the club-house and stood watching the altercation from a little distance.

Soldinck advanced two pugnacious steps toward Fuscule. "Are you mad? I bought your worm for a fair sum and paid you cash on the spot. Let us have no more dancing and dodging! Deliver the worm to Drofo at once, or we will take immediate and drastic measures!"

"Needless to say, you have forfeited your post as worminger aboard the *Galante*," Captain Baunt pointed out. "So deliver the worm and let us have an end to the business."

"Pah!" cried Fuscule in a passion. "You shall not have my worm, not for five thousand terces nor yet ten! And as for the other items on the account—" stepping forward he struck Soldinck smartly on the side of the head "—that will pay for the chister and this—" he dealt Soldinck another blow "—must settle for the remainder."

Soldinck rushed forward to settle his own accounts; Captain Baunt attempted to intervene but his intent was misunderstood by Pulk, who with one mighty heave threw him to the ground.

The confusion was eventually controlled by Drofo, who put himself between the opposing parties and held out his arms to induce restraint. "Peace, every one! There are peculiar aspects to this situation which must be analyzed. Fuscule, you claim that Soldinck offered you five thousand terces for your worm, then threw your chister into the water?"

"That indeed is my claim!" cried Fuscule furiously.

"Are those likely events? Soldinck is notorious for his parsimony! Never would he offer five thousand terces for a worm worth at best two thousand! How do you explain such a paradox?"

"I am a worminger, not a student of weird psychological mysteries," grumbled Fuscule. "Still, now that I reflect on it, the man who called himself Soldinck stood a head taller than this little toad. He also wore an unusual hat of several folds, and walked with his legs bent at the knees."

Soldinck spoke excitedly: "The description might well fit the villain who recommended me to the hut of Terlulia! He walked with a stealthy gait, and called himself Fuscule."

"Aha!" said Pulk. "Affairs are starting to sort themselves out. Let us find a booth in the club-house and approach our inquiry properly, over a jug of good black beer!"

"The concept is sound but in this case unnecessary," said Drofo. "I can already put a name to the individual at fault."

Captain Baunt said: ''I also have an intuition in this regard.''

Soldinck looked resentfully from face to face. ''Am I then so dense? Who is this person?''

''Can there be any more doubt?'' asked Drofo. ''His name is Cugel.''

Soldinck blinked, then clapped his hands together. ''That is a reasonable deduction!''

Pulk spoke in gentle admonition: ''Now that the guilty person has been identified, it appears that you owe Fuscule an apology.''

The memory of Fuscule's blows still rankled with Soldinck. ''I will feel more generous when he returns the five hundred terces I paid him for his worm. And never forget: it was he who accused me of throwing away his chister. Apologies are due from the other direction.''

''You are still confused,'' said Pulk. ''The five hundred terces were paid to Cugel.''

''Possibly so. Still, I feel that careful inquiries are in order.''

Captain Baunt turned to look around the bystanders. ''I thought that I saw him a few minutes ago. . . . He seems to have slipped away.''

For a fact, as soon as he had seen which way the wind was blowing, Cugel had taken himself in haste to the *Galante*. Madame Soldinck was in the cabin, acquainting her daughters with the events of the day. No one was on hand to interfere as Cugel ran here and there about the ship. He dropped the gang-plank, threw off the mooring-lines, pulled hoods from the worms and placed triple bait in the hoppers, then ran up to the quarter-deck and threw the wheel hard over.

At the club-house Soldinck was saying: ''I distrusted him from the start! Still, who could imagine such protean depravity?''

Bunderwal, the supercargo, concurred. ''Cugel, while plausible, is nonetheless a bit of a scoundrel.''

''He must now be summoned to an accounting,'' said Captain Baunt. ''It is always an unpleasant task.''

''Not all that unpleasant,'' muttered Fuscule.

''We must give him a fair hearing, and the sooner the better. I fancy the club-house will serve as well as any for our forum.''

''First we must find him,'' said Soldinck. ''I wonder where the rascal has taken cover? Drofo, you and Pulk look aboard the *Galante*. Fuscule, glance inside the club-house. Do or say nothing to alarm him; merely indicate that I want to put a few general questions. . . . Yes, Drofo? Why are you not off about your errand?''

Drofo pointed toward the sea. He spoke in his usual pensive voice: ''Sir, you may look for yourself.''

3

The Ocean of Sighs

The red morning sun reflected from the dark sea in exact replica.

The worms idled effortlessly at half-bait; the *Galante* drifted through the water as softly as a boat sliding through a dream.

Cugel slept somewhat later than usual, in that bed formerly enjoyed by Soldinck.

The crew of the *Galante* worked quietly and efficiently at their appointed tasks.

A tap at the door aroused Cugel from his rest. After stretching and yawning Cugel called out in a melodious voice: "Enter!"

The door opened; into the cabin came Tabazinth, the youngest and perhaps the most winsome of Madame Soldinck's daughters, though Cugel, had he been pressed for judgment, would have stoutly defended the special merits of each.

Tabazinth, who was gifted with a buxom chest and robust little haunches while still retaining a slender and flexible waist, showed to the world a round face, a mop of dark curls and a pink mouth chronically pursed as if in restraint of a smile. She carried a tray which she set on the bedside table. With a demure glance over her shoulder she started to leave the chamber. Cugel called her back.

"Tabazinth, my dear! The morning is fine; I will take my breakfast on the quarter-deck. You may instruct Madame Soldinck to lash the wheel and take her relief."

"As you like, sir." Tabazinth picked up the tray and left the cabin.

Cugel arose from the bed, applied a scented lotion to his face, rinsed his mouth with one of Soldinck's select balsams, then wrapped himself in an easy gown of pale blue silk. He listened. . . . Down the companion-way ladder came the thud of Madame Soldinck's steps.

Through the forward port-hole Cugel watched as she marched forward to that cabin formerly occupied by Chief Worminger Drofo. As soon as she had disappeared from view, Cugel stepped out upon the midship deck. He inhaled and exhaled deep breaths of the cool morning air, then climbed to the quarter-deck.

Before sitting down to his breakfast Cugel went to the taffrail, to survey the state of the sea and assess the progress of the ship. From horizon to horizon the water lay flat, with nothing to be seen but the image of the sun. The wake astern seemed adequately straight—a testimony as to the quality of Madame Soldinck's steering—while the claw of the escalabra pointed due south.

Cugel gave a nod of approval; Madame Soldinck might well become a competent helmswoman. On the other hand, she showed small skill as a worminger, and her daughters here were marginal at best.

Cugel seated himself to his breakfast. One by one he raised the silver covers to peer into the platters. He discovered a compote of spiced fruit, poached sea-bird livers, porridge of drist and raisins, a pickle of lily-bulbs and small black fungus-balls with several different kinds of pastry: a breakfast more than adequate in which he recognized the work of Meadhre, oldest and most conscientious of the daughters. Madame Soldinck, on the single time she had been pressed into service, had prepared a meal so quietly unappetizing that Cugel had refrained from again assigning her to the galley.

Cugel ate at leisure. A most pleasant harmony existed between himself and the world: an interlude to be prolonged, cherished and savored to the utmost. To memorialize this special condition Cugel lifted his exquisitely delicate tea-cup and sipped the limpid nectar brewed from Soldinck's choicest blend of herbs.

"Just so!" said Cugel. The past was gone; the future might end tomorrow, should the sun go dark. Now was now, to be dealt with on its own terms.

"Precisely so!" said Cugel.

And yet. . . . Cugel glanced uneasily over his shoulder. It was right and proper to exploit the excellences of the moment, but still, when conditions reached an apex, there was nowhere to go but down.

Even now, without tangible reason, Cugel felt an eery strain in the atmosphere, as if, just past the edge of his awareness, something had gone askew.

Cugel jumped to his feet and looked over the port rail. The worms, on half-bait, worked without strain. Everything seemed in order. Likewise with the starboard worm. Cugel slowly went back to his breakfast.

Cugel applied the full force of his intellect to the problem: what had aroused his uneasiness? The ship was sound; food and drink were ample; Madame Soldinck and her daughters had apparently come to terms with their new careers; and Cugel congratulated himself upon his wise, kindly but firm administration.

For a period immediately after departure Madame Soldinck produced a furious torrent of abuse, which Cugel finally decided to abate, if only in the interests of ship-board morale. "Madame," said Cugel, "your outcries disturb us all. They must cease."

"I name you an oppressor! A monster of evil! A laharq, or a keak*!"

Cugel replied: "Unless you desist I will order you confined in the hold."

"Bah!" said Madame Soldinck. "Who will carry out your orders?"

"If necessary I will implement them myself! Ship's discipline must be maintained. I am now captain of this vessel, and these are my commands. First, you are to hold your tongue. Second, you will assemble aft on the midship deck to hear the address I am about to deliver."

With poor grace Madame Soldinck and her daughters gathered at the spot which Cugel had designated.

Cugel climbed halfway up the companionway ladder. "Ladies! I will be grateful for your complete attention!" Cugel looked smilingly from face to face. "Now then! I am aware that today has not yielded optimum rewards to us all. Still, now is now, and we must come to terms with circumstance. In this regard I can offer a word or two of advice.

"Our first concern is for marine regulation, which stipulates quick and exact obedience to the captain's orders. Shipboard work will be shared. I have already accepted the duties of command. From you, my crew, I will expect good will, cooperation and zest, whereupon you will find me lenient, understanding and even affectionate."

Madame Soldinck called out sharply: "We want neither you nor your lenience! Take us back to Pompodouros!"

Meadhre the oldest daughter, said in a melancholy voice: "Hush, Mama! Be realistic! Cugel does not dare return to Pompodouros, so let us find where in fact he plans to take us."

"I will now provide that information," said Cugel. "Our port of

*laharq: a creature of vicious habits, native to the tundras north of Saskervoy.
keak: a horrid hybrid of demon and deep-sea fanged eel.

destination is Val Ombrio on the coast of Almery, a goodly sail to the south.''

Madame Soldinck cried out in shock: ''You cannot be serious! In between lie waters of deadly peril! This is common knowledge!''

Cugel said coldly: ''I suggest, Madame, that you place your faith in someone like myself, rather than the housewives of your social circle.''

Salasser advised her mother: ''Cugel will do as he likes in any case; why oppose his wishes? It will only make him angry.''

''Sound thinking!'' declared Cugel. ''Now, as to the work of the ship: each of you must become a competent worminger, at my instruction. Since we have ample time we will drive the worms at half-bait only, which will be to their advantage. We also lack the services of Angshott the cook; still, we have ample stores and I see no reason to stint ourselves. I encourage all of you to give full scope to your culinary skills.''

''Today I will prepare a tentative work-schedule. During the day I will maintain the look-out and supervise ship-board processes. Perhaps here I should mention that Madame Soldinck, by virtue of her years and social position, will not be required to act as 'night-steward'. Now then, in regard to—''

Madame Soldinck took a quick step forward. ''One moment! The 'night-steward'—what are her duties and why should I be disqualified?''

Cugel looked off across the sea. ''The duties of the 'night-steward' are more or less self-explanatory. She is assigned to the aft-cabin, where she looks to the convenience of the captain. There is prestige to the post; it is only fair that it should be shared among Meadhre, Salasser and Tabazinth.''

Again Madame Soldinck became agitated. ''It is as I feared! I, Cugel, will be 'night-steward'! Do not attempt to dissuade me!''

''All very well, madame, but your skills are needed at the helm.''

Meadhre said: ''Come, Mama, we are not so frail and pathetic as you fear.''

Tabazinth said with a laugh: ''Mama, it is you who deserves special consideration and not we. We can cope with Cugel very well.''

Salasser said: ''We must let Cugel make the decisions, since the responsibilities are his.''

Cugel spoke. ''There I suggest we let the matter rest. Now I must deal, once and once only, with a somewhat macabre concept. Let us assume that someone aboard this ship—let us call her Zita, after the Goddess of Unknowable Things—let us assume that Zita has decided to remove Cugel from the realm of the living. She considers poison in his food, a knife in his gullet, a blow and a push so that Cugel falls into the sea.

"Genteel persons are not likely to consider such conduct," said Cugel. "Still, I have evolved a plan to reduce this likelihood to nothing. Deep in the forward hold I will install a destructive device, using a quantity of explosive, a candle, and a fuse. Every day I will unlock an impregnable iron-bound door and replace the candle. If I neglect to do so, the candle will burn down and ignite the wick. The explosive will blow a hole in the hull and the ship will sink like a stone. Madame Soldinck, you appear distrait; did you hear me properly?"

"I heard you all too well."

"Then this completes my remarks for the moment. Madame Soldinck, you may report to the wheel, where I will demonstrate the basic principles of steering. Girls, you will first prepare our lunch, then see to the comfort of our various cabins."

At the wheel Madame Soldinck continued to warn of dangers to the south. "The pirates are blood-thirsty! There are sea-monsters: the blue codorfins, the thryfwyd, the forty-foot water-shadow! Storms strike from all directions; they toss ships about like corks!"

"How do the pirates survive amid such dangers?"

"Who cares how they survive? Our fervent hope is that they perish."

Cugel laughed. "Your warnings fly in the face of facts! We carry goods for Iucounu which must be delivered by way of Val Ombrio, on the coast of Almery."

"It is you who are ignorant of facts! The goods are transshipped through Port Perdusz, where our factors make special arrangements. To Port Perdusz we must go."

Cugel laughed once again. "Do you take me for a fool? On the instant the ship touched dock you would be bawling in all directions for the thief-takers. As before: steer south." Cugel went off to his lunch, leaving Madame Soldinck glowering at the escalabra.

On the morning of the next day Cugel felt the first intimation that something had gone askew at the edges of reality. Try as he might, the exact discrepancy, or slippage, or unconformity evaded his grasp. The ship functioned properly, although the worms, on half-bait, seemed a trifle sluggish, as if after a hard stint, and Cugel made a mental note to dose them with a tonic.

A covey of high clouds in the western sky presaged wind, which, if favorable, would further rest the worms. . . . Cugel frowned in perplexity. Drofo had made him aware as to variations in the ocean's color, texture and clarity. Now it seemed as if this were the identical ocean they had crossed the day before. Ridiculous, Cugel told himself; he must keep a grip upon his imagination.

Late in the afternoon Cugel, looking astern, noticed a portly little cog approaching at its best speed. Cugel took up his lens and studied the ship, which was propelled by four splashing and inefficient worms being driven to their utmost. On the deck Cugel thought to recognize Soldinck, Captain Baunt, Pulk and others, while a tall pensive figure, surely Drofo, stood at the bow contemplating the sea.

Cugel looked around the sky. Night was two hours distant. Without urgency he ordered double-bait for all worms and a half-gill each of Rouse's Tonic. The *Galante* moved easily away from the pursuing ship.

Madame Soldinck had watched all with interest. She asked at last: "Who sailed that ship?"

"They seemed to be Sarpent Island traders," said Cugel. "A rough lot, by all accounts. In the future give such ships a wide berth."

Madame Soldinck made no comment, and Cugel went off to ponder a new mystery: how had Soldinck come at him so swiftly?

With the coming of darkness, Cugel changed course and the pursuing ship was lost astern. Cugel told Madame Soldinck: "In the morning they'll be ten leagues off our course." He turned to go below. . . . A gleam of light, from the black iron stern lantern, caught his eye.

Cugel uttered a cry of vexation and extinguished the light. He turned angrily to Madame Soldinck: "Why did you not tell me that you had lit up the lantern?"

Madame Soldinck gave an indifferent shrug. "In the first place, you never asked."

"And in the second place?"

"It is prudent to show a light while at sea. That is the rule of the cautious mariner."

"Aboard the *Galante* it is unnecessary to light lights except upon my orders."

"Just as you like."

Cugel tapped the escalabra. "Keep to the present course for one hour, then turn south."

"Unwise! Tragically unwise!"

Cugel descended to the midship deck and stood leaning on the rail until the soft chime of silver bells summoned him to his dinner, which tonight was served in the aft cabin on a table spread with white linen.

The meal was adequate to Cugel's expectations and he so informed

Tabazinth who tonight was on duty as 'night-steward'. "There was perhaps a trace too much fennel in the fish sauce," he noted, "and the second service of wine—I refer to the Pale Montrachio—was clearly taken up a year before its fullest bounty. Still, all in all, there was little to be faulted and I hope you will so inform the kitchen."

"Now?" asked Tabazinth demurely.

"Not necessarily," said Cugel. "Why not tomorrow?"

"Soon enough, I should think."

"Exactly so. We have our own business to discuss. But first—" Cugel glanced out the stern window "—as I half-expected, that crafty old woman has again put light to the stern lantern. I cannot imagine what she has in her mind. What good is a great flare of light astern? She is not steering backward."

"She probably wishes to warn off that other ship which was following so close on our heels."

"The chances of collision are small. I want to avoid attention, not attract it."

"All is well, Cugel. You must not fret." Tabazinth approached and placed her hands on his shoulders. "Do you like the way I dress my hair? I have put on a special scent; it is called 'Tanjence', who was a beautiful woman of fable."

"Your hair is charming to the point of distraction; the scent is sublime; but I must go up and set things right with your mother."

With pouts and smiles Tabazinth tried to restrain him. "Ah, Cugel, how can I put faith in your flattery if at the first pretext you run off helter-skelter? Stay with me now; show me the full measure of your interest! Leave the poor old woman to her steering."

Cugel put her aside. "Control your amiability, my bountiful little poppet! I will be gone no more than an instant, and then you shall see!"

Cugel ran from the cabin, climbed to the quarter-deck. As he had feared, the lantern burned with a blatant glare. Without pausing to chide Madame Soldinck, Cugel not only extinguished the light, but removed glow-box, spurts and lumenex, and threw them into the sea.

Cugel addressed Madame Soldinck: "You have seen the last of my kindly forbearance. If lights again show from this ship, you will not enjoy the aftermath."

Madame Soldinck haughtily held her tongue, and after a final inspection of the escalabra, Cugel returned to his cabin. After more wine and several hours of frolicking with Tabazinth, he fell soundly asleep and did not return to the quarter-deck that night.

In the morning, as Cugel sat blinking in the sunlight, he again felt that strange sense of displacement which had troubled him on other occasions. He climbed to the quarter-deck, where Salasser stood at the wheel. Cugel went to look at the escalabra; the claw pointed directly to the south.

Cugel returned to the midship deck and inspected the worms; they eased and lolled through the water on half-bait, apparently healthy save for what seemed to be fatigue and a touch of timp on the port outboard beast.

Today there would be wet work along the sponsons, from which only the 'night-steward' might hope to be excused.

A day passed, and another: for Cugel a halcyon time of ease, zestful refreshment in the sea air, splendid cuisine, and the unstinting attention of his 'night-stewards'. A single source of disturbance were those strange displacements in time and space which he now thought to be no more than episodes of déjà vu.

On the morning that Tabazinth served him breakfast on the quarter-deck, his meal was interrupted by the sighting of a small fishing vessel. Beyond, to the south-west, Cugel made out the dim outline of an island, which he studied in perplexity. Déjà vu, once again?

Cugel took the wheel and steered so as to pass close by the fishing-boat, which was worked by a man and two boys. As he passed abeam, Cugel went to the rail and hailed the fisherman: "Halloo! What island lies yonder?"

The fisherman looked at Cugel as if he lacked intelligence. "It is Lausicaa, as you should well know. If I were in your shoes, I would give this region a wide berth."

Cugel gaped toward the island. Lausicaa? How could it be, unless magic were at work?

Cugel went in confusion to the escalabra; all seemed in order. Amazing! He had departed toward the south; now he returned from the north, and must change course or run aground upon the place from which he had started!

Cugel swung the ship to the east and Lausicaa faded over the horizon. He then changed course again, and steered once more to the south.

Madame Soldinck, standing by, curled her lip in disgust. "South again? Have I not warned of dangers to the south?"

"Steer south! Not an iota east, not the fraction of an iota west! South is our desired direction! Put north astern and steer south!"

"Insanity!" muttered Madame Soldinck.

"Insanity, not at all! I am as sane as yourself! Admittedly this voyage has given me several queasy moments. I am unable to explain our approach to Lausicaa from the north. It is as if we had completed a circumnavigation!''

''Iucounu the Magician has put a spell on the ship to safeguard his shipment. This is the most reasonable hypothesis and yet another reason to make for Port Perdusz.''

''Out of the question,'' said Cugel. ''I am now going below to think. Report all extraordinary circumstances.''

''The wind is coming up,'' said Madame Soldinck. ''We may even have a storm.''

Cugel went to the rail, and indeed cat's-paws from the northwest roughened the glossy black surface of the sea. ''Wind will rest the worms,'' said Cugel. ''I cannot imagine why they are so spiritless! Drofo would insist that they have been over-worked, but I know better.''

Descending to the midship deck, Cugel dropped the blue silk mainsail from its brails and sheeted home the clews. The sail bellied to the breeze and water tinkled under the hull.

Cugel arranged a comfortable chair where he could prop his feet on the rail and, with a bottle of Rozpagnola Amber at his elbow, settled himself to watch Meadhre and Tabazinth as they dealt with an incipient case of gangue on the port inboard worm.

The afternoon passed and Cugel drowsed to the gentle motion of the ship. He awoke to find that the cat's-paws had become a soft breeze, so that there was a surging motion to the ship, a modest bow wave and a gurgle of wake at the stern.

Salasser, the 'night-steward', served tea in a silver pot and a selection of small pastries, which Cugel consumed in an unusually abstracted mood.

Rising from his chair, Cugel climbed to the quarter-deck. He found Madame Soldinck in a testy mood. ''The wind is not good,'' she told him. ''Better that you pull in the sail.''

Cugel rejected her advice. ''The wind blows us nicely along our course and the worms are able to rest.''

''The worms need no rest,'' snapped Madame Soldinck. ''With the sails pulling the ship, I cannot steer where I want to steer.''

Cugel indicated the escalabra. ''Steer south! That is the way you want to steer! The claw shows the way!''

Madame Soldinck had no more to say, and Cugel left the quarter-deck.

The time was sunset. Cugel went forward to the bow and stood under the lantern, as Drofo was wont to do. Tonight the western sky was dramatic with a high array of cirrus wisps scarlet on the dark blue sky. At the horizon the sun lingered and hesitated, as if reluctant to leave the world of daylight. A sour blue-green corona rimmed the edge of the globe: a phenomenon which Cugel had never noticed before. A purple bruise on the sun's surface seemed to pulse, like the orifice of a polyp: a portent? . . . Cugel started to turn away, then, struck by a sudden thought, looked up into the lantern. The glow-box, spurts and lumenex, which Cugel had removed from the stern lantern, were not to be seen here either.

It seemed, thought Cugel, as if fertile minds worked hard aboard the *Galante*. "Nonetheless," Cugel told himself, "it is with me whom they deal, and I am not known as Cugel the Clever for nothing."

For still a few minutes Cugel stood at the bow. On the quarter-deck the three girls and Madame Soldinck drank tea and watched Cugel sidelong. Cugel put an arm to the lantern-post, creating a gallant silhouette against the sky of sunset. The high clouds now showed the color of old blood, and were clearly the precursors of wind. It might be wise to tuck a reef into the sail.

The light of sunset died. Cugel pondered the strange events of the voyage. To sail south all day and wake up the next morning in waters farther north than the starting point of the day before: this was an unnatural sequence. . . . What sensible explanation, other than magic, existed? An ocean swirl? A retrograde escalabra?

One conjecture followed another across Cugel's mind, each more unlikely than the last. At one especially preposterous notion he paused to voice a sardonic chuckle before rejecting it along with other more plausible theories. . . . He stopped short and returned to review the idea, since, oddly enough, the theory fitted precisely to all the facts.

Except in a single crucial aspect.

The theory rested on the premise that Cugel's mental capacity was of a low order. Cugel chuckled once again, but less comfortably, and presently he stopped chuckling.

The mysteries and paradoxes of the voyage were now illuminated. It seemed that Cugel's innate chivalry and sense of decency had been exploited and his easy trustfulness had been turned against him. But now the game would change!

A tinkle of silver bells announced the service of his dinner. Cugel delayed a moment for a last look around the horizon. The breeze was blowing with greater force and piling up small waves which slapped against the *Galante*'s bluff bows.

Cugel walked slowly aft. He climbed to the quarter-deck where Madame Soldinck had only just come on watch. Cugel gave her a crisp nod which she ignored. He looked at the escalabra; the claw indicated 'South'. Cugel went to the taff-rail and casually glanced up into the lantern. The glow-box was not in place, which proved nothing. Cugel said to Madame Soldinck: "A nice breeze will rest the worms."

"That may well be."

"The course is south, fair and true."

Madame Soldinck deigned no response. Cugel descended to a dinner which in all respects met his critical standards. The meal was served by the 'night-steward' Salasser, whom Cugel found no less charming than her sisters. Tonight she had dressed her hair in the style of the Spanssian Corybants, and wore a simple white gown belted at the waist with a golden rope—a costume which nicely set off her slender figure. Of the three girls, Salasser possessed possibly the most refined intelligence, and her conversation, while sometimes quaint, impressed Cugel by reason of its freshness and subtlety.

Salasser served Cugel his dessert: a torte of five flavors, and while Cugel consumed the delicacy, Salasser began to remove his shoes.

Cugel drew his feet back. "For a time I will wear my shoes."

Salasser raised her eyebrows in surprise. Cugel was usually ready enough to seek the comforts of the couch as soon as he had finished his dessert.

Tonight Cugel put aside the torte half-finished. He jumped to his feet, ran from the cabin and climbed to the quarter-deck where he found Madame Soldinck in the act of putting light to the lantern.

Cugel spoke angrily: "I believe that I have made myself clear on this subject!" He reached into the lantern and despite Madame Soldinck's cry of protest removed the functioning parts and threw them far into the dark.

He descended to the cabin. "Now," he told Salasser, "you may remove my shoes."

An hour later Cugel jumped from the couch and wrapped himself in his gown. Salasser raised to her knees. "Where are you going? I have thought of something innovative."

"I will be back at once."

On the quarter-deck Cugel once again discovered Madame Soldinck as she put fire to several candles which she had placed into the lantern. Cugel snatched away the candles and threw them into the sea.

Madame Soldinck protested: "What are you doing? I need the light for steering purposes!"

"You must steer by the glim in the escalabra! You have heard my last warning!"

Madame Soldinck, muttering under her breath, hunched over the wheel. Cugel returned to the cabin. "Now," he told Salasser, "to your innovation! Although I suspect that, after twenty aeons, few stones have been left unturned."

"So it may be," said Salasser with charming simplicity. "But are we then to be deterred from a new trial?"

"Naturally not," said Cugel.

The innovation was tested, and Cugel suggested a variation which also proved successful. Cugel then jumped to his feet and started to run from the room, but Salasser caught him and drew him back to the couch. "You are as restless as a tonquil! What has vexed you so?"

"The wind is rising! Listen how the sail flaps! I must make an inspection."

"Why irk yourself?" coaxed Salasser. "Let Mama deal with such things."

"If she trims the sail, she must leave the wheel. And who is tending the worms?"

"The worms are resting. . . . Cugel! Where are you going?"

Cugel had already run out upon the midship-deck, to find the sail back-winded and furiously flogging at the sheets. He climbed to the quarter-deck, where he discovered that Madame Soldinck, becoming discouraged, had abandoned her post and gone to her quarters.

Cugel checked the escalabra. The claw indicated a northerly direction, with the ship ducking and yawing and sidling astern. Cugel spun the wheel; the bow fell off; the wind caught the sail with a great clap of sound, so that Cugel feared for the sheets. Irritated by the jerking, the worms swung up from the water, plunged, broke their cinctures and swam away.

Cugel called out: "All hands on deck!" but no-one responded. He lashed the wheel and working in the dark brailed up the sail, suffering several sharp blows from the flailing sheets.

The ship now blew directly down-wind, in an easterly direction. Cugel went in search of his crew, to discover that all had locked themselves in their cabins, from which they silently ignored his orders.

Cugel kicked furiously at the doors, but only bruised his foot. He limped back amidships and made all as secure as possible.

The wind howled through the rigging and the ship began to show an inclination to broach. Cugel once more ran forward and roared orders to his crew. He elicited a response only from Madame Soldinck: "Go away, and leave us to die in peace! We are all sick."

Cugel gave a final kick to the door and, limping, made his way to the wheel, where with great exertion he managed to keep the ship tracking steady before the wind.

All night Cugel stood at the wheel while the wind keened and shrieked and the waves reared ever higher, sometimes to break against the transom in surging white foam. On one such occasion Cugel looked over his shoulder, to discover a glare of reflected light.

Light? From where?

The source must be the windows of the aft cabin. Cugel had set no lamps aglow—which implied that someone else had done so, in defiance of his explicit orders.

Cugel dared not leave the wheel to extinguish the light. . . . Small matter, Cugel told himself; tonight he could shine a beacon across the ocean and there would be none to see.

Hours went by and the ship rushed eastward before the gale, with Cugel a barely animate hulk at the wheel. After an interminable period the night came to an end and a dull purple blush entered the sky. At last the sun rose to reveal an ocean of rolling black waves tumbled with white froth.

The wind abated. Cugel found that once again the ship would hold its own course. Painfully he straightened his body, stretched his arms, and worked his numb fingers. He descended to the aft-cabin, and discovered that someone had arranged two lamps in the stern window.

Cugel extinguished the lights and changed from the gown of pale blue silk to his own clothes. He pulled the three-tiered hat clasped with 'Spatterlight' upon his head, adjusted the tilt to best effect and marched forward. He found Madame Soldinck and her daughters in the galley, sitting at the table over a breakfast of tea and sweet-cakes. None displayed the ravages of sea-sickness; indeed all seemed well-rested and serene.

Madame Soldinck, turning her head, looked Cugel up and down. "Well then, what do you want here?"

Cugel spoke with icy formality. "Madame, be advised that all your schemes are known."

"Indeed? You know them all?"

"I know all those I care to know. They add no luster to your reputation."

"Which schemes are these? Inform me, if you please."

"As you wish," said Cugel. "I will agree that your plot, to a certain degree, was ingenious. At your request we sailed south during the day on half-bait, that we might rest the worms. At night, when I had gone to take my rest, you veered course to the north."

"More accurately, north by east."

Cugel made a gesture to indicate that it was all one. "Then, driving the worms on tonics and double-bait, you tried to keep the ship in the neighborhood of Lausicaa. But I caught you out.''

Madame Soldinck gave a scornful chuckle. ''We wanted no more sea-voyage; we were returning to Saskervoy.''

Cugel was momentarily taken aback. The plan had been insolent beyond his suspicions. He feigned easy carelessness of manner. ''No great difference. From the first I sensed that we were not sailing new water, and indeed it caused me a moment or two of bafflement—until I noticed the sorry state of the worms, and all became clear. Still, I tolerated your mischief; such melodramatic efforts amused me! And meanwhile I enjoyed my rest,. the ocean air, meals of fine quality—''

Meadhre interjected a comment. ''I, Tabazinth, Salasser—we spat in every dish. Mama sometimes stepped into the galley. I do not know what she did.''

With an effort Cugel retained his aplomb. ''At night I was entertained by games and antics, and here at least I have no complaint.''

Salasser said: ''The reverse is not true. Your fumbling and groping with cold hands has bored us all.''

Tabazinth said, ''I am not naturally unkind but the truth must be told. Your natural characteristics are really inadequate and, also, your habit of whistling between your teeth should be corrected.''

Meadhre began to giggle. ''Cugel is innocently proud of his innovations, but I have heard small children exchanging theories of more compelling interest.''

Cugel said stiffly: ''Your remarks add nothing to the discussion. On occasions to come, you may be assured that—''

''What occasions?'' asked Madame Soldinck. ''There will be no others. Your foolishness has run its course.''

''The voyage is not over,'' said Cugel haughtily. ''When the wind moderates, we will resume our course to the south.''

Madame Soldinck laughed aloud. ''The wind is not just wind. It is the monsoon. It will shift in three months. When I decided that Saskervoy was impractical, I steered to where the wind will blow us into the estuary of the Great Chaing River. I have signaled Master Soldinck and Captain Baunt that all was in order, and to keep clear until I bring us in to Port Perdusz.''

Cugel laughed airily. ''It is a pity, Madame, that a plot of such intricacy must come to naught.'' He bowed stiffly and departed the galley.

Cugel took himself aft to the chart-room and consulted the portfolio. The estuary of the Great Chaing cut a long cleft into that region known as the Land of the Falling Wall. To the north a blunt peninsula marked 'Gador Porrada' shouldered into the ocean, apparently uninhabited save for the village 'Tustvold'. South of the Chaing, another peninsula: 'The Dragon's Neck', longer and narrower than Gador Porrada, thrust a considerable distance into the ocean, to terminate in a scatter of rocks, reefs and small islands: 'The Dragon-Fangs'. Cugel studied the chart in detail, then closed the portfolio with a fateful thud. "So be it!" said Cugel. "How long, oh how long, must I entertain false hopes and fond dreams? Still, all will be well. . . . Let us see how the land lays."

Cugel climbed to the quarter-deck. At the horizon he noted a ship which under the lens proved to be that lubberly little cog he had evaded several days before. Even without worms, using clever tactics, he could easily evade so clumsy a craft!

Cugel sheeted the sail hard back to the starboard, then jumping up to the quarter-deck, he swung the wheel to bring the ship around on a port tack, steering as close to north as the ship would point.

The crew of the cog, noting his tactic, veered to cut him off and drive him back south into the estuary, but Cugel refused to be intimidated and held his course.

To the right the low coast of Gador Porrada was now visible; to the left, the cog blundered importantly through the water.

Using the lens Cugel discerned the gaunt form of Drofo on the bow, signaling triple-bait for the worms.

Madame Soldinck and the three girls came from the galley to stare across the water at the cog, and Madame Soldinck screamed officious instructions to Cugel which were blown away on the wind.

The *Galante*, with a hull ill-adapted to sailing, made a great deal of leeway. For best speed Cugel fell away several points to the east, in the process veering closer upon the low-lying coast, while the cog pressed relentlessly down upon him. Cugel desperately swung the wheel, thinking to achieve a remarkable down-wind jibe which would totally discomfit those persons aboard the cog, not to mention Madame Soldinck. For best effect he sprang down upon the deck to trim the sheets, but before he could return to the wheel, the ship rushed off downwind.

Cugel climbed back to the quarter-deck and spun the wheel, hoping to bring the ship back on a starboard reach. Glancing toward the near shore of Gador Porrada, Cugel saw a curious sight: a group of sea-birds walking on what appeared to be the surface of the water. Cugel stared in wonder, as the sea-birds walked this way and that, occasionally lowering their heads to peck at the surface.

The *Galante* came to slow sliding halt. Cugel decided that he had run aground on the Tustvold mud-flats.

So much for birds who walked on water.

A quarter-mile to sea the cog dropped anchor and began to lower a boat. Madame Soldinck and the girls waved their arms in excitement. Cugel wasted no time in farewells. He lowered himself over the side and floundered toward the shore.

The mud was deep, viscous, and smelled most unpleasantly. A heavy ribbed stalk terminating in a globular eye reared from the mud to peer at him, and twice he was attacked by pincer-lizards, which luckily he was able to out-distance.

Finally Cugel arrived at the shore. Rising to his feet, he found that a contingent from the cog had already arrived aboard the *Galante*. One of the forms Cugel saw to be Soldinck, who pointed toward Cugel and shook his fist. At this same moment Cugel discovered that he had left the total sum of his terces aboard the *Galante*, including the six golden centums received from Soldinck in the sale of Fuscule's worm.

This was a bitter blow. Soldinck was joined at the rail by Madame Soldinck, who made insulting signals of her own.

Disdaining response, Cugel turned and trudged off along the shore.

Chapter III

FROM TUSTVOLD TO PORT PERDUSZ

1

The Columns

Cugel marched along the foreshore, shivering to the bite of the wind. The landscape was barren and dreary; to the left, black waves broke over the mud-flats; to the right, a line of low hills barred access to inland regions.

Cugel's mood was bleak. He carried neither terces nor so much as a sharp stick to protect himself against footpads. Slime from the mud-flats squelched in his boots and his sodden garments smelled of marine decay.

At a tidal pool Cugel rinsed out his boots and thereafter walked more comfortably, though the slime still made a mockery of style and dignity. Hunching along the shore Cugel resembled a great bedraggled bird.

Where a sluggish river seeped into the sea, Cugel came upon an old road, which might well lead to the village Tustvold, and the possibility of food and shelter. Cugel turned inland, away from the shore.

To keep himself warm Cugel began to trot and jog, with knees jerking high. So passed a mile or two, and the hills gave way to a curious landscape of cultivated fields mingled with areas of wasteland. In the distance steep-sided knolls rose at irregular intervals, like islands in a sea of air.

No human habitation could be seen, but in the fields groups of women tended broad-beans and millet. As Cugel jogged past, they raised from their work to stare. Cugel found their attention offensive, and ran proudly past, looking neither right nor left.

Clouds sliding over the hills from the west cooled the air and seemed to presage rain. Cugel searched ahead for the village Tustvold, without success. The clouds drifted across the sun, darkening the already wan light, and the landscape took on the semblance of an ancient sepia painting, with flat perspectives and the pungko trees superimposed like scratchings of black ink.

A shaft of sunlight struck through the clouds, to play upon a cluster of white columns, at a distance of something over a mile.

Cugel stopped short to stare at the odd array. A temple? A mausoleum? The ruins of an enormous palace? Cugel continued along the road, and presently stopped again. The columns varied in height, from almost nothing to over a hundred feet, and seemed about ten feet in girth.

Once more Cugel proceeded. As he drew near he saw that the tops of the columns were occupied by men, reclining and basking in what remained of the sunlight.

The rent in the clouds sealed shut and the sunlight faded with finality. The men sat up and called back and forth, and at last descended the columns by ladders attached to the stone. Once on the ground, they trooped off toward a village half-hidden under a grove of shrack-trees. This village, about a mile from the columns, Cugel assumed to be Tustvold.

At the back of the columns a quarry cut into one of the steep-sided knolls Cugel had noted before. From this quarry emerged a white-haired old man with stooping shoulders, sinewy arms and the slow gait of one who precisely gauges each movement. He wore a white smock, loose gray trousers and well-used boots of strong leather. From a braided leather cord around his neck hung an amulet of five facets. Spying Cugel he halted, and waited as Cugel approached.

Cugel used his most cultivated voice: "Sir, jump to no conclusions! I am neither a vagabond nor a mendicant, but rather a seafarer who arrived on shore by way of the mud-flats."

"That is not the ordinary route," said the old man. "Practised men of the sea most often use the docks at Port Perdusz."

"Quite so. The village yonder is Tustvold?"

"Properly speaking, Tustvold is that mound of ruins yonder which I quarry for white-stone. The local folk use the name for the village as well, and no great harm is done. What do you seek from Tustvold?"

"Food and shelter for the night. However, I cannot pay a groat, since my belongings remain aboard the ship."

The old man gave his head a disparaging shake. "In Tustvold you will get only what you pay for. They are a parsimonious lot, and spend only for advancement. If you will be satisfied with a pallet and a bowl of soup for your supper, I can gratify your needs, and you may dismiss all thought of payment."

''That is a generous offer,'' said Cugel. ''I accept with pleasure. May I introduce myself? I am Cugel.''

The old man bowed. ''I am Nisbet, the son of Nisvangel, who quarried here before me and the grandson of Rounce, who was also a quarry-man. But come! Why stand here shivering when a warm fire awaits inside?''

The two walked toward Nisbet's abode: a huddle of ramshackle sheds leaning one on the other, built of planks and stone: the accretion of many years, perhaps centuries. Conditions within, while comfortable, were no less undisciplined. Each chamber was cluttered with curios and antiques collected by Nisbet and his predecessors while quarrying the ruins of Old Tustvold and elsewhere.

Nisbet poured a bath for Cugel and provided a musty old gown which Cugel might wear until his own clothes were clean. ''That is a task better left to the women of the village,'' said Nisbet.

''If you recall, I lack all funds,'' said Cugel. ''I accept your hospitality with pleasure but I refuse to impose a financial burden upon you.''

''No burden whatever,'' said Nisbet. ''The women are anxious to do me favors, so that I will give them priorities in the work.''

''In that case, I accept the favor with thanks.''

Cugel gratefully bathed and wrapped himself in the old gown, then sat down to a hearty meal of candle-fish soup, bread and pickled ramp, which Nisbet recommmended as a specialty of the region. They ate from antique dishes of many sorts and used utensils no two alike, even to the material from which they were fabricated: silver, glossold, black iron, gold, a green alloy of copper, arsenic and other substances. Nisbet identified these objects in an off-hand manner. ''Each of the mounds you see rising from the plain represents an ancient city, now in ruins and covered over with the sift of time. When I am allowed an hour or two of leisure, I often go out to mine another of the mounds, and often I find objects of interest. That salver, for instance, was taken from the eleventh phase of the city Chelopsik, and is fashioned from corfume inlaid with petrified fire-flies. The characters are beyond my skill to read, but would seem to recite a children's song. This knife is even older; I found it in the crypts below the city I call Arad, though its real name is no longer known.''

''Interesting!'' said Cugel. ''Do you ever find treasure or valuable gems?''

Nisbet shrugged. ''Each of these articles is priceless: a unique memorial. But now, with the sun about to go dark, who would pay good terces to buy them? More useful is a bottle of good wine. In this connection, I suggest that, like grandees of high degree, we repair to the parlor where I will broach a bottle of well-aged wine, and we will warm our shins before the fire.''

''A sound notion!'' declared Cugel. He followed Nisbet into a chamber furnished with an over-sufficiency of chairs, settees, tables, and cushions of many kinds, together with a hundred curios.

Nisbet poured wine from a stoneware bottle of great age, to judge from the iridescent oxides which encrusted the surface. Cugel tasted the wine with caution, to find a liquor heavy and strong, and redolent of strange fragrances.

''A noble vintage,'' pronounced Cugel.

''Your taste is sound,'' said Nisbet. ''I took it from the store-room of a wine-merchant on the fourth level of Xei Cambael. Drink heartily; a thousand bottles still moulder in the dark.''

''My best regards!'' Cugel tilted his goblet. ''Your work lacks nothing for perquisites; this is clear. You have no sons to carry on the traditions?''

''None. My spouse died long years ago by the sting of a blue fanticule, and I lacked all taste for someone new.'' With a grunt Nisbet heaved himself to his feet and fed wood to the fire. He lurched back into his chair and gazed into the flames. ''Yet often I sit here of nights, thinking of how it will be when I am gone.''

''Perhaps you should take an apprentice.''

Nisbet uttered a short hollow laugh. ''It is not all so easy. Boys of the town think of tall columns even before they learn to spit properly. I would prefer the company of a man who knows something of the world. What, by the way, is your own trade?''

Cugel made a deprecatory gesture. ''I am not yet settled upon a career. I have worked as worminger and recently I commanded a sea-going vessel.''

''That is a post of high prestige!''

''True enough, but the the malice of subordinates forced me to vacate the position.''

''By way of the mud-flats?''

''Precisely so.''

''Such are the ways of the world,'' said Nisbet. ''Still, you have much of your life ahead, with many great deeds to do, while I look back on life with my deeds already done, and none of them greatly significant.''

Cugel said: ''When the sun goes out, all deeds, significant or not, will be forgotten together.''

Nisbet rose to his feet and broached another jug of wine. He refilled the goblets, then returned to his chair. "Two hours of loose philosophizing will never tilt the scale against the worth of one sound belch. For the nonce I am Nisbet the quarryman, with far too many columns to raise and far too much work on order. Sometimes I wish that I too might climb a column and bask away the hours."

The two sat in silence, looking into the flames. Nisbet finally said: "I see that you are tired. No doubt you have had a tedious day." He pulled himself to his feet and pointed. "You may sleep on yonder couch."

In the morning Nisbet and Cugel breakfasted upon griddle-cakes with a conserve of fruits prepared by women of the village; then Nisbet took Cugel out to the quarry. He pointed to his excavation which had opened a great cleft in the side of the mound.

"Old Tustvold was a city of thirteen phases, as you can see with your own eyes. The people of the fourth level built a temple to Miamatta, their Ultimate God of Gods. These ruins supply white-stone to my needs. . . . The sun is aloft. Soon the men from the village will be coming out to use their columns; indeed, here they come now."

The men arrived, by the twos and threes. Cugel watched as they climbed their columns and composed themselves in the sunlight.

In puzzlement Cugel turned to Nisbet. "Why do they sit so diligently on their columns?"

"They absorb a healthful flux from the sunlight," said Nisbet. "The higher the column the more pure and rich is the flux, as well as the prestige of place. The women, especially, are consumed with ambition for the altitude of their husbands. When they bring in the terces for a new segment, they want it at once, and hector me unmercifully until I achieve the work, and if I must put off one of their rivals, so much the better."

"Odd that you have no competitors, in what must be a profitable business."

"It is not so odd when you consider the work involved. The stone must be brought down from the temple, sized, polished, cleaned of old inscriptions, given a new number and lifted to the top of a column. This entails considerable work, which would be impossible without this." Nisbet touched the five-faceted amulet that he wore around his neck. "A touch of this object negates the suction of gravity, and the heaviest object rises into the air."

"Amazing!" said Cugel. "The amulet is a valuable adjunct to your trade."

" 'Indispensable' is the word. . . . Ha! Here comes Dame Croulsx to chide me for my lack of diligence."

A portly middle-aged woman with the flat round face and russet hair typical of the village folk approached. Nisbet greeted her with all courtesy, which she dismissed with a curt gesture. "Nisbet, again I must protest! Since I paid my terces, you have raised first a segment to Tobersc and another to Cillincx. Now my husband sits in their shadow, and their wives gloat together at my discomfiture. What is wrong with my money? Have you forgotten the gifts of bread and cheese I sent out by my daughter Turgola? What is your answer?"

"Dame Croulsx, give me only a moment to speak! Your 'Twenty' is ready for the raising and I was so about to inform your husband."

"Ah! That is good news! You will understand my concern."

"Certainly, but to avoid future misunderstanding, I must inform you that both Dame Tobersc and Dame Cillincx have placed orders for their 'Twenty-ones'."

Dame Croulsx's jaw dropped. "So soon, the andelwipes? In that case I too will have my 'Twenty-one', and you must start on it first."

Nisbet gave a piteous groan and clawed at his white beard. "Dame Croulsx, be reasonable! I can work only to the limit of these old hands, and my legs no longer propel me at nimble speed. I will do all possible; I can promise no more."

Dame Croulsx argued another five minutes, then started to march away in a huff, but Nisbet called her back. "Dame Croulsx, a small service you can do for me. My friend Cugel needs his garments expertly washed, cleaned, mended and returned to prime condition. Can I impose this task upon you?"

"Of course! You need only ask! Where are the garments?"

Cugel brought out the soiled clothes and Dame Croulsx returned to the village. "That is the way it goes," said Nisbet with a sad smile. "Strong new hands are needed to carry on the trade. What is your opinion in the matter?"

"The trade has much in its favor," said Cugel. "Let me ask this: Dame Croulsx mentioned her daughter Turgola; is she appreciably more comely than Dame Croulsx? And also: are daughters as anxious to oblige the quarryman as their mothers?"

Nisbet replied in a ponderous voice: "As to your first question: the folk of the village are Keramian stock, fugitives from the Rhab Faag and none are notable for a splendid appearance. Turgola, for instance, is squat, underslung, and shows protruding teeth. As for your second question, perhaps I have misread the signs. Dame Petishko has often offered to massage my back, though I have never complained of pain. Dame Gezx is at times strangely over-familiar. . . . Ha hm. Well, no matter. If, as I hope, you become 'associate quarryman,' you must make your own interpretation of these little cordialities, though I trust that you will not bring scandal to an enterprise which, to now, has been based upon probity."

Cugel laughingly dismissed the possibility of scandal. "I am favorably inclined to your offer; for a fact I lack the means to travel onward. I will therefore undertake at least a temporary commitment, at whatever wage you consider proper."

"Excellent!" said Nisbet. "We will arrange such details later. Now to work! We must raise the Croulsx 'Twenty'."

Nisbet led the way to the work-shop on the quarry floor, where the 'Twenty' stood ready on a pallet: a dolomite cylinder five feet tall and ten feet in diameter.

Nisbet tied several long ropes to the segment. After looking here and there, Cugel put a perplexed question: "I see neither rollers nor hoists nor cranes; how do you, one man alone, move such great masses of stone?"

"Have you forgotten my amulet? Observe! I touch the stone with the amulet and the stone becomes charged with revulsion for its native stuff. If I kick it lightly—so! no more than a tap!—the magic is fugitive and will last only long enough to bring the segment to its place. If I were to kick with force, the stone might stay repulsive to the land for a month, or even longer."

Cugel examined the amulet with respect. "How did you gain such sleight?"

Nisbet took Cugel outside and pointed to a bluff overlooking the plain. "See where the trees hang past the cliff? At that place a great magician named Makke the Maugifer built a manse and ruled the land with his mauging magic. He mauged east and he mauged west, north and south; persons could lift their eyes to his face once, or with effort twice, but never three times, so strong was his maugery.

"Makke planted a square garden with magic trees at the four corners; the ossip tree survives to this day, and there is no better boot-dressing than wax of the ossip berries. I dress my boots with ossip wax and they are proof against the rocks of the quarry: so I was taught by my father, who learned from his father, and so back through time to a certain Nisvaunt, who first went to Makke's garden for ossip berries. There he discovered the amulet and its strength.

"Nisvaunt first established himself in the porterage trade and moved goods great distances with ease. He became weary of the dust and dangers of travel and settled on this spot to become a quarryman, and I am the last of the line."

The two men returned to the work-shed. Under Nisbet's direction, Cugel took up the ropes and pulled at the 'Twenty', so that it slid slowly though the air and out toward the columns.

Nisbet halted at the base of a column marked with a plaque reading:

THE LOFTY MONUMENT OF
CROULSX
"WE EXULT ONLY IN THE UPPER ALTITUDES!"

Nisbet raised his head and called: "Croulsx! Come down from your column! Your segment is ready to mount."

Croulsx's head, as he peered over the side of the column, was silhouetted against the sky. Satisfied that the calls were intended for himself, he descended to the ground. "Your work has not been swift," he told Nisbet gruffly. "Too long have I been forced to use an inferior flux."

Nisbet made light of the complaints. " 'Now' is 'now', and at that instant known as 'now' your segment is ready and 'now' you can enjoy the upper radiances."

"All very well with your 'nows'!" grumbled Croulsx. "You ignore the deterioration of my health."

"I can only work to my best speed," said Nisbet. "In this regard, allow me to introduce my new associate, Cugel. I fancy that work will now go with a fling, owing to Cugel's experience and energy."

"If such is the case I will now place my order for five new segments. Dame Croulsx will validate the order with a deposit."

"I cannot acknowledge your order at this moment," said Nisbet. "However, I will keep your needs in mind. Cugel, are you ready? Then climb, if you will, to the top of Xippin's column and haul the segment gently on high. Croulsx and I will guide it from below."

The segment was efficiently set in place and Croulsx immediately climbed to the top, and arranged himself to best advantage in the red sunlight. Nisbet and Cugel returned to the shed and Cugel was instructed in the techniques of shaping, rounding and smoothing the white-stone.

Cugel soon understood why Nisbet was delinquent in his deliveries. First, age had slowed his movements to a degree for which his efficiency could not compensate. Secondly, Nisbet was almost hourly interrupted by visitors: women of the village with orders, demands, complaints, gifts and persuasions.

On Cugel's third day of employment, a group of merchant traders stopped by Nisbet's abode. They were members of a dark-skinned race notable for amber eyes, aquiline features and proudly erect posture. Their garments were no less distinctive: pantaloons bound with sashes, shirts with wing collars, underjackets and cut-away tabards, in the colors of black, tan, fusk and umber. They wore wide-brimmed black hats with slouch crowns, which Cugel considered of excellent address. They had brought with them a great high-wheeled wagon loaded with objects concealed under a tarpaulin. As the elder of the group conferred with Nisbet, the others removed the cloth, to reveal what appeared to be a large number of stacked corpses.

Nisbet and the elder came to an agreement and the four Maots—so Nisbet identified them to Cugel—began to unload the wagon. Nisbet took Cugel somewhat aside and pointed to a far mound. "That is Old QaHr which once held sway from the Falling Wall to the Silkal Strakes. During their high age the folk of QaHr practiced a unique religion, which, I suppose, is no more preposterous than any other. They believed that a man or woman upon dying entered afterlife using that bodily condition in which he or she had died, thereupon to pass eternity amid feasting, revelry and other pleasures regarding which propriety forbids mention. Hence it became the better part of wisdom to die in the full flower of life, since, for example, a rachitic old man, toothless, short-winded and dyspeptic, could never fully enjoy the banquets, songs and nymphs of paradise. The folk of QaHr therefore arranged to die at an early age, and they were embalmed with such skill that their corpses even today seem fresh with life. The Maots quarry the QaHr mausoleum for these corpses and convey them across the Wild Waste to the Thuniac Conservatory at Noval, where, as I understand it, they are put to some sort of ceremonial use."

While he spoke the Maot traders had unloaded the corpses, laid them in a row, and roped them together. The elder signaled Nisbet who walked along the line of corpses, touching each with his amulet. He then walked back along the line and delivered to each corpse the activating kick. The Maot elder paid Nisbet his fee; there was an interchange of gracious small talk and then the Maots set off to the northeast, the corpses drifting behind at an altitude of fifty feet.

Such interludes, while entertaining and instructive, tended to delay the orders whose delivery was ever more urgently demanded, both by the men, who were invigorated by the upper-air radiance, and by the women, who funded the raising of a column both in the interests of their husbands' health and also to enhance the prestige of the family.

To speed the work, Cugel initiated several labor-saving short-cuts, thereby arousing Nisbet's high approval. "Cugel, you will go far in this business! These are clever innovations!"

"I am pondering others even more novel," said Cugel. "Clearly, we must keep abreast of demand if only to maximize our own profits."

"No doubt, but how?"

"I will give the matter my best attention."

"Excellent! The problem is as good as solved." So declared Nisbet who then went off to prepare a gala supper, which included three bottles of sumptuous green wine from the stores of the Xei Cambael wine-seller. Nisbet indulged himself to such an extent that he fell asleep on a couch in the parlour.

Cugel seized the opportunity to conduct an experiment. From the chain around Nisbet's neck he unclasped the five-sided amulet and rubbed it along the arms of a heavy chair. Then, as he had seen Nisbet do, he gave the chair an activating kick.

The chair remained as heavy as before.

Cugel stood back in perplexity. In some manner he had misapplied the power of the amulet. Or might the magic be immanent in Nisbet and no other?

Unlikely. An amulet was an amulet.

Where then did Nisbet's act differ from his own?

Nisbet, the better to warm his feet before the fire, had removed his boots. Cugel removed his own shoes, which were worn almost to shreds, and slipped his feet into Nisbet's boots.

He rubbed the chair with the five-sided amulet and kicked it with Nisbet's boots. The chair instantly rebuffed gravity, to float in the air.

Most interesting, thought Cugel. He returned the amulet to Nisbet's neck and the boots to where he had found them.

On the morrow Cugel told Nisbet: "I discover that I need boots of strong leather, like yours, proof against the rocks of the quarry. Where can I obtain such boots?"

"Such items are included among our perquisites," said Nisbet. "Today I will send a messenger into the village and call for Dame Tadouc the cobbler-woman." Nisbet laid his finger alongside his crooked old nose and turned Cugel a mischievous leer. "I have learned how to control the women of Tustvold Village, or, for that matter, women in general! Never give them all they want! That is the secret of my success! In this present case, Dame Tadouc's husband sits on a column of only fourteen segments, making do with shadows and low-quality flux, while Dame Tadouc endures the condescension of her peers. For this reason, there is no harder-working woman in the village, save possibly Dame Kylas, who fells trees and shapes the natural wood into timber of specified size. In any event, you will be fitted for boots within the hour and I daresay that you will be wearing them tomorrow."

As Nisbet had predicted, Dame Tadouc came out from the village on the run and asked of Nisbet his requirements. "Meanwhile, Sir Nisbet, I trust that you will give earnest attention to my order for three new segments. Poor Tadouc has developed a cough and needs more intense radiation for his health."

"Dame Tadouc, the boots are needed by my associate Cugel, whose present shoes are all shreds and holes, so that his toes scratch the ground."

"A pity, a pity!"

"In regard to your segments, I believe that the first of the three is scheduled for delivery in perhaps a week, and the others soon after."

"That is good news indeed! Now, Sir Cugel, as to your boots?"

"I have long admired those worn by Nisbet. Please make me exact duplicates."

Dame Tadouc looked at him in bafflement. "But Sir Nisbet's feet are two inches longer than yours, and somewhat more narrow, and as flat as halibuts!"

Cugel paused to think. The dilemma was real. If the magic resided in Nisbet's boots, then only exact replicas would seem to serve the purpose.

Nisbet dissolved the quandary. "Naturally, Dame Tadouc, cobble the boots to fit! Why would Cugel place an order specifically for ill-fitting boots?"

"For a moment I was perplexed," said Dame Tadouc. "Now I must run home to cut leather. I have a hide taken from the back of an old bull bauk and I will make you boots to last your life's span or until the sun goes out, whichever is the sooner. In either case, you will lack all further need for boots. Well then, to work."

On the following day the boots were delivered, and, in response to Cugel's specifications, they matched Nisbet's boots in every particular save size.

Nisbet examined the boots with approval. "Dame Tadouc has applied a dressing which is good enough for common folk, but as soon as it wears off and the leather acquires a thirst, we shall apply ossip wax and your boots will then be as strong as my own."

Cugel enthusiastically clapped his hands together. "To celebrate the arrival of these boots I suggest another gala evening!"

"Why not? A fine pair of boots is something to celebrate!"

The two dined on broad-beans and bacon, marsh-hens stuffed with mushrooms, sour-grass and olives and a hunch of cheese. With these dishes they consumed three bottles of that Xei Cambael wine known as 'Silver Hyssop'. Such was the information supplied by Nisbet, who, as an antiquarian, had studied many of the ancient scripts. As they drank, they toasted not only Dame Tadouc, but also that long-dead wine-merchant whose bounty they now enjoyed, though indeed the wine seemed perhaps a trifle past its prime.

As before, Nisbet became fuddled and lay down on the couch for a nap. Cugel unclasped the five-sided amulet and returned to his experiments.

His new boots, despite their similarity to those of Nisbet, lacked all useful effect, save that for which they were intended, while Nisbet's boots, alone or in conjunction with the amulet, defeated gravity with ease.

Most peculiar! thought Cugel, as he replaced the amulet on Nisbet's chain. The only difference between the two pairs of boots was the dressing of ossip wax—from berries gathered in the garden of Makke the Maugifer.

To ransack the clutter of generations in search of a pot of boot-dressing was not a task to be undertaken lightly. Cugel went off to his own couch.

In the morning Cugel told Nisbet: "We have been working hard, and it is time for a little holiday. I suggest that we stroll over to yonder bluff and there survey the gardens of Makke the Maugifer. We can also pick ossip berries for boot-dressing, and—who knows?—we might come upon another amulet."

"A sound idea," said Nisbet. "Today I too lack zest for work."

The two set off across the plain toward the bluff: a distance of a mile. Cugel towed a sack containing their needs which Nisbet had touched with his amulet and kicked, in order to negate the weight.

By an easy route they climbed the bluff and approached Makke's garden.

"Nothing is left," said Nisbet sadly. "Save only the ossip tree, which seems to flourish despite neglect. That heap of rubble is all that remains of Makke's manse, which was built five-sided like the amulet."

Cugel approached the heap of stones, and thought to notice a wisp of vapor rising through the cracks. He went close and dropping to his knees moved several of the stones. To his ears came the sound of a voice, and then another, engaged in what seemed an excited dialogue. So faint and elusive were the voices that words could not be distinguished and Nisbet, when Cugel summoned him to the crevice, could hear no sounds whatever.

Cugel drew back from the mound. To move the rocks might yield magical treasures, or, more likely, some unimaginable woe. Nisbet was of a like mind and the two moved somewhat back from the ruined manse. Sitting on a slab of mouldering stone, they ate a lunch of bread, cheese, spiced sausage and onions, washed down with pots of village-brewed beer.

A few yards away the ossip tree extended heavy branches from a gnarled silver-gray trunk five feet in diameter. Silver-green berries hung in clusters from the end of every twig, each berry a waxy sphere half an inch in diameter.

After Cugel and Nisbet had finished their lunch, they plucked berries sufficient to fill four sacks, which Nisbet caused to float in the air. Trailing their harvest behind them, the two returned to the quarry.

Nisbet brought out a great cauldron and set water to boiling, then added berries. Presently a scum formed on the surface. "There is the wax," said Nisbet, and skimmed it off into a basin. Four times the process was repeated, until all the berries had been boiled and the basin was filled with wax.

"We have done a good days work," announced Nisbet. "I see no reason why we should not dine accordingly. There are a pair of excellent fillets in the larder, provided by Dame Petish who is butcher to the town. If you will kindly lay a fire I will look through the closet for appropriate wine."

Once again Cugel and Nisbet sat down to a repast of heartening proportions, but as Nisbet worked to open a second flask of wine, the sound of slamming doors and the thud of heavy footsteps reached their ears.

An instant later a woman tall and portly, massive in arm and leg, with a bony jaw, a broken nose and coarse red hair, entered the room.

Nisbet laboriously heaved himself to his feet. "Dame Sequorce! I am surprised to see you here this time of night."

Dame Sequorce surveyed the table with disapproval. "Why are you not out shaping my segments which are long overdue?"

Nisbet spoke with cool hauteur: "Today Cugel and I attended to important business, and now, as is our habit, we dine. You may return in the morning."

Dame Sequorce paid no heed. "You take your morning meal far

too late and your evening meal far too early, and you drink overmuch wine. Meanwhile my husband huddles well below the husbands of Dame Petish, Dame Haxel, Dame Croulsx and others. Since kindliness has no effect, I have decided to try a new tactic, for which I use the term 'fear'. In three words: if you do not gratify my needs in short order, I will bring my sisters here and perform a serious mischief."

Nisbet employed the gentle voice of pure reason: "If I acceded to your request—" "Not a request; a threat!" "—the other women of the town might also try to intimidate me, to the detriment of orderly business."

"I care nothing for your problems! Provide my segments, at once!"

Cugel rose to his feet. "Dame Sequorce, your conduct is singularly gross. Once and for all, Nisbet will not be coerced! He will provide you your segments in his own good time. He now demands that you leave the premises, and on quiet feet!"

"Nisbet now makes demands, does he?" Striding forward, Dame Sequorce seized Nisbet's beard. "I did not come to listen to your braggadocio!" She gave the beard a sharp tweak, then stepped back. "I am going, but only because I have delivered my message, which I hope you will take seriously!"

Dame Sequorce departed, leaving behind a heavy silence. At last Nisbet spoke in falsely hearty tones: "A dramatic incursion, to be sure! I must have Dame Wyxsco look to the locks. Come, Cugel! Return to your supper!"

The two continued with their meal, but the festive mood could not be recaptured. Cugel at last said: "What we need is a stock, or repository, of segments ready for raising, so that we can gratify these prideful women on demand."

"No doubt," said Nisbet. "But how is this to be done?"

Cugel tilted his head cautiously sidewise. "Are you ready for unorthodox procedures?"

With a bravado conferred partly by wine and partly by Dame Sequorce's rude handling of his beard, Nisbet declared: "I am a man to stop at nothing when circumstances cry out for deeds!"

"In that case, let us get to work," said Cugel. "The whole night lies before us! We shall demolish our problems once and for all! Bring lamps."

Despite his brave words Nisbet followed Cugel with hesitant steps. "Exactly what do you have in mind?"

Cugel refused to discuss his plan until they reached the columns.

Here he signaled the laggard Nisbet to greater speed. "Time is of the essence! Bring the lamp to this first column."

"That is the column of Fidix."

"No matter. Put down the lamp, then touch the column with your amulet and kick it very gently: no more than a good brush. First, let me secure the column with this rope. . . . Good. Now, apply amulet and kick!"

Nisbet obeyed; the column momentarily became weightless, during which interval Cugel extricated the 'One' segment and pushed it aside. After a few seconds the magic dissipated and the column returned to its former position.

"Observe!" cried Cugel. "A segment which we shall renumber and sell to Dame Sequorce, and a fig for her nuisances!"

Nisbet uttered a protest: "Fidix will surely notice the deduction!"

Cugel smilingly shook his head. "Improbable. I have watched the men climbing their columns. They come out blinking and half asleep. They trouble to look at nothing but the state of the weather and the rungs of their ladders."

Nisbet pulled dubiously at his beard. "Tomorrow, when Fidix climbs his column, he will find himself unaccountably lower by a segment."

"That is why we must remove the 'One' from every column. So now to work! There are many segments to move."

With dawn lightening the sky Cugel and Nisbet towed the last of the segments to a hiding place behind a pile of rocks on the floor of the quarry. Nisbet now affected a tremulous joy. "For the first time a sufficiency of segments is conveniently to hand. Our lives shall now flow more smoothly. Cugel, you have a fine and resourceful mind!"

"Today we must work as usual. Then, in the unlikely event that the subtractions are noticed, we shall merely disclaim all knowledge of the affair, or blame it on the Maots."

"Or we could claim that the weight of the columns had pushed the 'Ones' into the ground."

"True. Nisbet, we have done a good night's work!"

The sun moved into the sky, and the first contingent of men straggled out from the village. As Cugel had predicted, each climbed to the top of his column and arranged himself without any display of doubt or perplexity, and Nisbet uttered a hollow laugh of relief.

Over the next few weeks Cugel and Nisbet satisfied a large number of orders, though never in such profusion as to arouse comment. Dame Sequorce was allowed two segments, rather than the three she had demanded, but she was not displeased. "I knew I could get what I wanted! To gain the satisfaction of one's wishes one needs only to propose unpleasant alternatives. I will order two more segments shortly when I can afford your exorbitant prices; in fact, you may begin work on them now, so that I need not wait. Eh, Nisbet? Do you remember how I pulled your beard?"

Nisbet responded with formal politeness. "I will make a note of your order, and it will be fulfilled in its proper sequence."

Dame Sequorce responded only with a coarse laugh and went her way.

Nisbet gave a despondent sigh. "I had hoped that a flow of segments would glut our customers, but, if anything, we seem to have stimulated demand. Dame Petish, for instance, is annoyed that Dame Gillincx's husband now sits on the same level as Petish himself. Dame Viberl fancies herself the leader of society, and insists that two segments separate Viberl from his social inferiors."

Cugel shrugged. "We can only do what is possible."

In unexpectedly short order the segments of the stockpile were distributed, and the women of the town once again became importunate. Cugel and Nisbet discussed the situation at length, and decided to meet excessive demands with absolute obduracy.

Certain of the women, however, taking note of Dame Sequorce's success, began to make ever more categorical threats. Cugel and Nisbet at last accepted the inevitable and one night went out to the columns and removed all the 'Twos'. As before, the men noticed nothing. Cugel and Nisbet attempted to fill the backlog of orders, and the antique urn in which Nisbet stored his terces filled to overflowing.

One day a young woman came to confer with Nisbet. "I am Dame Mupo; I have been wed only a week, but it is time to start a column for Mupo, who is somewhat delicate and in need of upper level flux. I have inspected the area and selected a site, but as I walked among the columns I noted an odd circumstance. The bottom segments are numbered 'Three' rather than 'One', which would seem to be more usual. What is the reason for this?"

Nisbet started to stammer, and Cugel quickly entered the conversation. "This is an innovation designed to help young families such as your own. For instance, Viberl enjoys pure and undiluted radiance on his 'Twenty four'. By starting you off with a 'Three' instead of a 'One', you are only twenty one blocks below him, rather than twenty three."

Dame Mupo nodded her comprehension. "That is helpful indeed!"

Cugel went on to say: "We do not publicize the matter, since we cannot be all things to all people. Just regard this service as Nisbet's kindly assistance to you personally, and since poor Mupo is not in the best of health, we will provide you not only your 'Three' but your 'Four' as well. But you must say nothing of this to anyone, not even Mupo, as we cannot extend these favors everywhere."

"I understand completely! No one shall know!"

On the next day Dame Petish appeared at the quarry. "Nisbet, my niece has just married Mupo and brings me a peculiar and garbled story about 'Threes' and 'Fours' which, frankly, I cannot understand. She claims that your man Cugel promised her a segment at no charge, as a service to young families. I am interested because next week another niece is marrying, and if you are giving two segments for the price of one it is only fair that you deal in the same manner with an old and valued customer such as myself."

Cugel said smoothly: "My explanation confused Dame Mupo. Recently we have noticed vagrants and vagabonds among the columns. We warned them off, and then, to confuse would-be thieves, we altered our numerative system. In practice, nothing is changed; you need not concern yourself."

Dame Petish departed, dubiously shaking her head. She paused by the columns and looked them up and down for several minutes, then returned to the village.

Nisbet said nervously: "I hope no one else comes asking questions. Your answers are remarkable and confuse even me, but others may be more incisive."

"I imagine that we have heard the last of the matter," said Cugel, and the two returned to work.

During the early afternoon Dame Sequorce came out from the village with several of her sisters. They paused several minutes by the columns, then continued to the quarry.

Nisbet said in a quavering voice: "Cugel, I appoint you spokesman for the concern. Be good enough to mollify these ladies."

"I will do my best," said Cugel. He went out to confront Dame Sequorce. "Your segments are not yet ready. You may return in a week."

Dame Sequorce seemed not to hear. She turned her pale blue eyes around the quarry. "Where is Nisbet?"

"Nisbet is indisposed. Our delivery time is once again a month or more, since we must quarry more white-stone. I am sorry, but we cannot oblige you any sooner."

Dame Sequorce fixed her gaze full upon Cugel. "Where are the

'Ones' and 'Twos'? Why are they gone so that the 'Threes' rest on the ground?''

Cugel feigned surprise. ''Is this really the case? Very odd. Still, nothing is permanent and the 'Ones' and 'Twos' may have crumbled into dust.''

''There is no evidence of such dust around the base of the columns.''

Cugel shrugged. ''Since the columns remain at their relative elevations, no great damage has been done.''

From the back of the quarry one of Dame Sequorce's sisters came running. ''We have found a pile of segments hidden behind some rocks, and all are 'Twos'!''

Dame Sequorce gave Cugel a brief side-glance, then turned and strode back to the village, followed by her sisters.

Cugel went glumly into Nisbet's abode. Nisbet had been listening from behind the door. ''All things change,'' said Cugel. ''It is now time to leave.''

Nisbet jumped back in shock. '' 'Leave'? My wonderful house? My antiques and famous bibelots? That is unthinkable!''

''I fear that Dame Sequorce will not stop with simple criticism. Remember her dealings with your beard?''

''I do indeed, and this time I will defend myself!'' Nisbet went to a cabinet and selected a sword. ''Here is the finest steel of Old Kharai! Here, Cugel! Another blade of equal worth in a splendid harness! Wear it with pride!''

Cugel buckled the ancient sword about his waist. ''Defiance is all very well but a whole skin is better. I suggest that we prepare for all eventualities.''

''Never!'' cried Nisbet in a passion. ''I will stand in the doorway of my house and the first to attack shall feel the edge of my sword!''

''They will stand back and throw rocks,'' said Cugel.

Nisbet paid no heed and went to the doorway. Cugel reflected a moment, then carried various goods to the wagon left by the Maot traders: food, wine, rugs, garments. In his pouch he placed a pot of ossip boot-dressing, after first anointing his boots, and two handfuls of terces from Nisbet's urn. A second pot of boot dressing he tossed upon the wagon.

Cugel was interrupted in his work by an excited call from Nisbet. ''Cugel! They are coming, at speed! They are like an army of raging beasts!''

Cugel went to the door and surveyed the oncoming women. ''You and your valiant sword may deter this horde from the front door, but they will merely enter from the back. I suggest withdrawal. The wagon is ready."

Reluctantly Nisbet went to the wagon. He looked over Cugel's preparations. "Where are my terces? You load boot dressing but no terces! Is that sensible?"

"The boot dressing, and not your amulet, defies gravity. The urn was too heavy to carry."

Nisbet nevertheless ran inside and staggered out with his urn, spilling terces behind him.

The women were now close at hand. Observing the wagon they emitted a great roar of wrath. "Villains, halt!" cried Dame Sequorce. Neither Cugel nor Nisbet heeded her command.

Nisbet brought his urn to the wagon and loaded it with the other goods but when he tried to climb to the seat he fell, and Cugel had to lift him aboard. Cugel kicked the wagon and gave it a great push so that it floated away into the air, but when Cugel tried to jump upon the wagon, he lost his footing and fell to the ground.

There was no time for a second attempt; the women were upon him. Holding sword and pouch so that they did not impede his running, Cugel took to his heels, with the fastest of the women in pursuit.

After half a mile the women gave up the chase and Cugel paused to catch his breath. Already smoke was rising from Nisbet's abode, as the mob wreaked vicarious vengeance on Nisbet. On top of their columns the men stood up, the better to observe events. High in the sky the wagon drifted eastward on the wind, with Nisbet peering over the side.

Cugel heaved a sigh. Slinging the pouch over his shoulder, he set off to the south toward Port Perdusz.

2

Faucelme

Setting his course by the bloated red sun, Cugel journeyed south across an arid wasteland. Small boulders cast black shadows; an occasional stand-back bush, with leaves like fleshy pink ear-lobes, thrust thorns toward Cugel as he passed.

The horizons were blurred behind haze the color of watered carmine. No human artifact could be seen, nor any living creature, except on a single occasion when, far to the south, Cugel noted a pelgrane of impressive wingspan flying lazily from west to east. Cugel flung himself flat and lay motionless until the creature had disappeared into the eastern haze. Cugel then picked himself up, dusted off his garments and proceeded south.

The pallid soil reflected heat. Cugel paused to fan his face with his hat. In so doing he brushed his wrist lightly across 'Spatterlight', the sky-breaker scale which Cugel now used as a hat ornament. The contact caused an instant searing pain and a sucking sensation as if 'Spatterlight' were anxious to engulf the whole of Cugel's arm and perhaps more. Cugel looked askance at the ornament: his wrist had barely made contact! 'Spatterlight' was not an object to be dealt with casually.

Cugel gingerly replaced the hat on his head and continued south at speed, hoping to come upon shelter before nightfall. He moved at so hasty a gait that he almost blundered over the brink of a sink-hole fifty yards wide. He stopped short with one leg poised over the abyss, with a black tarn a hundred feet below. For a few breathless seconds Cugel tottered in a state of disequilibrium, then lurched back to safety.

After catching his breath, Cugel proceeded with greater caution. The sink-hole, he soon discovered, was not an isolated case. Over the next few miles he came upon others of greater or less dimension and few gave warning of their presence; there was only an instant brink and a far drop into dark water.

At larger sink-holes dark blue weeping-willow trees hung over the edge, half-concealing rows of peculiar habitations. These were narrow and tall, like boxes piled one on the other. There seemed no concern for precision and parts of the structures rested on the branches of the weeping-willows.

The folk who had built the tree-towers were difficult to see among the shadows of the foliage; Cugel glimpsed them as they darted across their queer little windows, and several times he thought to see them slipping into the sink-hole on slides polished from the native limestone. Their stature was that of a small human being or a boy, though their countenances suggested a peculiar hybridization of reptile, stalking bang-nose beetle and miniature gid. To cover their gray-green pelts they wore flounced belly-guards of pale fiber, and caps with black ear-flaps, apparently fabricated from human skulls.

The aspect of these folk gave Cugel little hope of obtaining hospitality, and indeed prompted him to slip away before they decided to pursue him.

As the sun sank low, Cugel became ever more nervous. If he tried to travel by night, he would certainly blunder into a sink-hole. If he thought to wrap himself in his cloak and sleep in the open, he thereupon became prey for visps, which stood nine feet tall and looked across the night through luminous pink eyes, and traced the scent of flesh by means of two flexible proboscises growing from each side of their scalp-crest.

The lower limb of the sun touched the horizon. In desperation Cugel tore up branches of brittlebush, whose wood made excellent torches. He approached a sink-hole fringed with weeping-willows and selected a tree-tower somewhat isolated from the others. As he drew near, he glimpsed weasel-like shapes darting back and forth in front of the windows.

Cugel drew his sword and pounded on the planked wall. ''It is I, Cugel!'' he roared. ''I am king of this wretched wasteland! How is it that none of you have paid your fees?''

From within came a chorus of howling high-pitched invective, and filth was flung from the windows. Cugel drew back and set one of the branches afire. From the windows came piercing cries of outrage, and certain residents of the tree-tower ran out into the branches of the weeping-willow and slid down into the water of the sink-hole.

Cugel kept a wary eye to the rear, so that none of the tree-tower folk should creep up from behind to jump on his back. He pounded again on the walls. "Enough of your slops and filth! Pay over a thousand terces at once, or vacate the premises!"

From within nothing could be heard but hisses and whispers. Watching in all directions, Cugel circled the structure. He found a door and thrust in the torch, to discover a work-room, with a polished limestone bench across one wall, on which rested several alabaster ewers, cups and trenchers. There was neither hearth nor stove; evidently the tree-tower folk shunned the use of fire; nor was there communication with the upper levels, by means of ladders, traps or stairs.

Cugel left his branches of brittlebush and his burning torch on the dirt floor and went to gather more fuel. In the plum-colored afterglow he collected four armloads of branches and brought them to the tree-tower; during the final load he heard at frighteningly close hand the melancholy call of a visp.

Cugel hurriedly returned to the tree-tower. Once again the residents issued furious protests, and strident screams echoed back and forth across the sink-hole.

"Vermin, settle down!" called Cugel. "I am about to take my rest."

His commands went unheeded. Cugel brought his torch from the work-room and flourished it in all directions. The tumult instantly died.

Cugel returned into the work-room and blocked the door with the limestone slab, which he propped into place with a pole. He laid his fire so that it would burn slowly, one brand at a time. Wrapping himself in his cloak, he composed himself to sleep.

During the night he awoke at intervals to tend his fire, to listen and to peer through a crack out across the sink-hole, but all was quiet save for the calls of wandering visps.

In the morning Cugel aroused himself with the coming of sunlight. Through cracks he scrutinized the area outside the tree-tower, but nothing seemed amiss, and no sound could be heard.

Cugel pursed his lips in dubious reflection. He would have been reassured by some more or less overt demonstration of hostility. The quiet was over-innocent.

Cugel asked himself: "How, in similar case, would I punish an interloper as bold as myself?"

And next: "Why risk fire or sword?"

Then: "I would plan a horrid surprise."

Finally: "Logic leads to the concept of a snare. So then: let us see what there is to be seen." Cugel removed the limestone slab from the door. All was quiet: even more quiet than before. The entire sink-hole held its breath. Cugel studied the ground before the tree-tower. He looked right and left, to discover cords dangling from the branches of the tree. The ground before the door had been sprinkled with a suspicious amount of soil, which failed to conceal altogether the outlines of a net.

Cugel picked up the limestone slab and thrust it at the back wall. The planks, secured with pegs and withes, broke loose; Cugel jumped through the hole and was away, with cries of outrage and disappointment ringing after him.

Cugel continued to march south, toward far hills which showed as shadows behind the haze. At noon he came upon an abandoned farmstead beside a small river, where he gratefully sated his thirst. In an old orchard he found an ancient crab-apple tree heavy with fruit. He ate to satiation and filled his pouch.

As Cugel set off on his way he noticed a stone tablet with a weathered inscription:

EVIL DEEDS WERE DONE AT THIS PLACE

***

MAY FAUCELME KNOW PAIN UNTIL THE SUN GOES OUT

***

AND AFTER

A cold draught seemed to touch the back of Cugel's neck, and he looked uneasily over his shoulder. "Here is a place to be avoided," he told himself, and set off at full stride of his long legs.

An hour later Cugel passed beside a forest where he discovered a small octagonal chapel with the roof collapsed. Cugel cautiously peered within, to find the air heavy with the reek of visp. As he backed away, a bronze plaque, green with the corrosion of centuries, caught his eye. The characters read:

MAY THE GODS OF GNIENNE WORK BESIDE

—*—

THE DEVILS OF GNARRE TO WARD US

—*—

FROM THE FURY OF FAUCELME

Cugel suspired a quiet breath, and backed away from the chapel. Both past and present oppressed the region; with the utmost relief would Cugel arrive at Port Perdusz!

Cugel set off to the south at a pace even faster than before.

As the afternoon waned, the land began to swell in hillocks and swales: precursors to the first rise of the hills which now bulked high to the south. Trees straggled down from the upper-level forests: mylax with black bark and broad pink leaves; barrel-cypress, dense and impenetrable; pale gray parments, dangling strings of spherical black nuts; graveyard oak, thick and gnarled with crooked sprawling branches.

As on the previous evening, Cugel saw the day grow old with foreboding. As the sun dropped upon the far hills he broke out into a road running roughly parallel to the hills, which presumably must connect by one means or another with Port Perdusz.

Stepping out upon the road, Cugel looked right and left, and to his great interest saw a farmer's wain halted about half a mile to the east, with three men standing by the back end.

To avoid projecting an impression of urgency, Cugel composed his stride to an easy saunter, in the manner of a casual traveler, but at the wain no one seemed either to notice or to care.

As Cugel drew near, he saw that the wain, which was drawn by four mermelants, had suffered a breakdown at one of its tall rear wheels. The mermelants feigned disinterest in the matter and averted their eyes from the three farmers whom the mermelants liked to consider their servants. The wain was loaded high with faggots from the forest, and at each corner thrust high a three-pronged harpoon intended as a deterrent to the sudden swoop of a pelgrane.

As Cugel approached, the farmers, who seemed to be brothers, glanced over their shoulders, then returned unsmilingly to their contemplation of the broken wheel.

Cugel strolled up to the wagon. The farmers watched him sidelong, with such disinterest that Cugel's affability congealed on his face.

Cugel cleared his throat. "What seems to be wrong with your wheel?"

The oldest of the brothers responded in a series of surly grunts: "Nothing 'seems' to be wrong with the wheel. Do you take us for fools? Something is definitely and factually wrong. The retainer ring has been lost; the bearings have dropped out. It is a serious matter, so go your way and do not disturb our thinking." Cugel held up a finger in arch reproach. "One should never be too cock-sure! Perhaps I can help you."

"Bah! What do you know of such things?"

The second brother said: "Where did you get that odd hat?"

The youngest of the three attempted a thrust of heavy humor. "If you can carry the load on the axle while we roll the wheel, then you can be of help. Otherwise, be off with you."

"You may joke, but perhaps I can indeed do something along these lines," said Cugel. He appraised the wain, which weighed far less than one of Nisbet's columns. His boots had been anointed with ossip wax and all was in order. He stepped forward and gave the wheel a kick. "You will now discover both wheel and wagon to be weightless. Lift, and discover for yourselves."

The youngest of the brothers seized the wheel and lifted, exerting such strength that the weightless wheel slipped from his grasp and rose high into the air, where it was caught in the wind and blown away to the east. The wagon, with a block under the axle, had taken no effect from the magic and remained as before.

The wheel rolled away down the sky. From nowhere, or so it seemed, a pelgrane swung down and, seizing the wheel, carried it off.

Cugel and the three farmers watched the pelgrane and the wheel disappear over the mountains.

"Well then," said the oldest. "What now?"

Cugel gave his head a rueful shake. "I hesitate to make further suggestions."

"Ten terces is the value of a new wheel," said the oldest brother. "Pay over that sum at once. Since I never threaten I will not mention the alternatives."

Cugel drew himself up. "I am not one to be impressed by bluster!"

"What of cudgels and pitchforks?"

Cugel took a step back and dropped a hand to his sword. "If blood runs along the road, it will be yours, not mine!"

The farmers stood back, collecting their wits. Cugel moderated his voice. "A wheel such as yours, damaged, broken, and worn almost through to the spokes, might fairly be valued at two terces. To demand more is unrealistic."

The oldest brother declared in grandiose tones: "We will compromise! I mentioned ten terces, you spoke of two. Subtracting two from ten leaves eight; therefore pay us eight terces and everyone will be satisfied."

Cugel still hesitated. "Somewhere I sense a fallacy. Eight terces is still too much! Remember, I acted from altruism! Must I pay for good deeds?''

''Is it a good deed to send our wheel whirling through the air? If this is your kindness, spare us anything worse.''

''Let us approach the matter from a new direction,'' said Cugel. ''I need lodging for the night. How far is your farmstead?''

''Four miles, but we shall not sleep in our beds tonight; we must stay to guard our property.''

''There is another way,'' said Cugel. ''I can make the whole wagon weightless—''

''What?'' cried the first brother. ''So that we lose wagon as well as wheel?''

''We are not the dunderheads you take us for!'' exclaimed the second brother.

''Give us our money and go your way!'' cried the youngest. ''If you need lodging, apply to the manse of Faucelme a mile along the road.''

''Excellent notion!'' declared the first brother with a broad grin. ''Why did not I think of it? But first: our ten terces.''

''Ten terces? Your jokes are lame. Before I part with a single groat I want to learn where I can securely pass the night.''

''Did we not tell you? Apply to Faucelme! Like you he is an altruist and welcomes passing vagabonds to his manse.''

''Remarkable hats or none,'' chuckled the youngest.

''During the olden times a 'Faucelme' seems to have despoiled the region,'' said Cugel. ''Is the 'Faucelme' yonder a namesake? Does he follow in the footsteps of the original?''

''I know nothing of Faucelme nor his forbears,'' said the oldest brother.

''His manse is large,'' said the second brother. ''He never turns anyone from his door.''

''You can see the smoke from his chimney even now,'' said the youngest. ''Give us our money and be off with you. Night is coming on and we must prepare against the visps.''

Cugel rummaged among the crab-apples and brought out five terces. ''I give up this money not to please you but to punish myself for trying to improve a group of primitive peasants.''

There was another spate of bitter words, but at last the five terces were accepted, and Cugel departed. As soon as he had passed around the wagon he heard the brothers give vent to guffaws of coarse laughter.

The mermelants lay sprawled untidily in the dirt, probing the road-side weeds for sweet-grass with their long tongues. As Cugel passed, the lead animal spoke in a voice barely comprehensible through a mouthful of fodder. "Why are the lumpkins laughing?"

Cugel shrugged. "I helped them with magic and their wheel flew away, so I gave them five terces to stifle their outcries."

"Tricks, full and bold!" said the mermelant. "An hour ago they sent the boy to the farm for a new wheel. They were ready to roll the old wheel into the ditch when they saw you."

"I ignore such paltriness," said Cugel. "They recommended that I lodge tonight at the manse of Faucelme. Again I doubt their good faith."

"Ah, those treacherous grooms!* They think they can trick anyone! So they send you to a sorcerer of questionable repute."

Cugel anxiously searched the landscape ahead. "Is no other shelter at hand?"

"Our grooms formerly took in wayfarers and murdered them in their beds, but no one wanted to bury the corpses so they gave up the trade. The next lodging is twenty miles."

"That is bad news," said Cugel. "How does one deal with Faucelme?"

The mermelants munched at the sweet-grass. One said: "Do you carry beer? We are beer-drinkers of noble repute and show our bellies to all."

"I have only crab-apples, to which you are welcome."

"Yes, those are good," said the mermelant, and Cugel distributed what fruit he carried.

"If you go to Faucelme, be wary of his tricks! A fat merchant survived by singing lewd songs the whole night long and never turning his back on Faucelme."

One of the farmers came around the wagon, to halt in annoyance at the sight of Cugel. "What are you doing here? Be off with you and stop annoying the mermelants."

Deigning no reply, Cugel set off along the road. With the sun scraping along the forested sky-line, he came to Faucelme's manse: a rambling timber structure of several levels, with a profusion of bays, low square towers with windows all around, balconies, decks, high gables and a dozen tall thin chimneys.

*The mermelants, to sustain vanity, refer to their masters as 'grooms' and 'tenders'. Ordinarily amiable, they are fond of beer, and when drunk rear high on their splayed rear legs to show their ribbed white bellies. At this juncture any slight provocation sends them into paroxysms of rage, and they exercise their great strength for destruction.

Concealing himself behind a tree, Cugel studied the house. Several of the windows glowed with light, but Cugel noted no movement within. It was, he thought, a house of pleasant aspect, where one would not expect to find a monster of trickery in residence.

Crouching, keeping to the cover of trees and shrubbery, Cugel approached the manse. With cat-like stealth he sidled to a window and peered within.

At a table, reading from a yellow-leafed book, sat a man of indeterminate age, stoop-shouldered and bald except for a fringe of brown-gray hair. A long nose hooked from his rather squat head, with protuberant milky golden eyes close-set to either side. His arms and legs were long and angular; he wore a black velvet suit and rings on every finger, save the forefingers where he wore three. In repose his face seemed calm and easy, and Cugel looked in vain for what he considered the signals of depravity.

Cugel surveyed the room and its contents. On a sideboard rested a miscellany of curios and oddments: a pyramid of black stone, a coil of rope, glass bottles, small masks hanging on a board, stacked books, a zither, a brass instrument of many arcs and beams, a bouquet of flowers carved from stone.

Cugel ran light-footed to the front door, where he discovered a heavy brass knocker in the form of a tongue dangling from the mouth of a gargoyle. He let the knocker drop and called out: "Open within! An honest wayfarer needs lodging and will pay a fee!"

Cugel ran back to the window. He watched Faucelme rise to his feet, stand a moment with head cocked sidewise, then walk from the room. Cugel instantly opened the window and climbed within. He closed the window, took the rope from the sideboard and went to stand in the shadows.

Faucelme returned, shaking his head in puzzlement. He seated himself in his chair and resumed his reading. Cugel came up behind him, looped the rope around his chest, again and again, and it seemed as if the rope would never exhaust the coil. Faucelme was presently trussed up in a cocoon of rope.

At last Cugel revealed himself. Faucelme looked him up and down, in curiosity rather than rancor, then asked: "May I inquire the reason for this visit?"

"It is simple stark fear," said Cugel. "I dare not pass the night out of doors, so I have come to your house for shelter."

"And the ropes?" Faucelme looked down at the web of strands which bound him into the chair.

"I would not care to offend you with the explanation," said Cugel.

''Would the explanation offend me more than the ropes?''

Cugel frowned and tapped his chin. ''Your question is more profound than it might seem, and verges into the ancient analyses of the Ideal versus the Real.''

Faucelme sighed. ''Tonight I have no zest for philosophy. You may answer my question in terms which proximate the Real.''

''In all candour, I have forgotten the question,'' said Cugel.

''I will re-phrase it in words of simple structure. Why have you tied me to my chair, rather than entering by the door?''

''At your urging then, I will reveal an unpleasant truth. Your reputation is that of a sly and unpredictable villain with a penchant for morbid tricks.''

Faucelme gave a sad grimace. ''In such a case my bare denial carries no great weight. Who are my detractors?''

Cugel smilingly shook his head. ''As a gentleman of honour I must reserve this information.''

''Aha indeed!'' said Faucelme, and became reflectively silent.

Cugel, with half an eye always for Faucelme, took occasion to inspect the room. In addition to the side-board, the furnishings included a rug woven in tones of dark red, blue and black, an open cabinet of books and librams, and a tabouret.

A small insect which had been flying around the room alighted on Faucelme's forehead. Faucelme reached up a hand through the bonds and brushed away the insect, then returned his arm into the coil of ropes.

Cugel turned to look in slack-jawed wonder. Had he tied the ropes improperly? Faucelme seemed bound as tightly as a fly in a spider-web.

Cugel's attention was attracted by a stuffed bird, standing four feet high, with a woman's face under a coarse mop of black hair. A two-inch crest of transparent film rose at the back of the forehead. A voice sounded over his shoulder. ''That is a harpy from the Xardoon Sea. Very few remain. They are partial to the flesh of drowned sailors, and when a ship is doomed they come to keep vigil. Notice the ears—'' Faucelme's finger reached over Cugel's shoulder and lifted aside the hair ''—which are similar to those of a mermaid. Be careful with the crest!'' The finger tapped the base of the prongs. ''The points are barbed.''

Cugel looked around in amazement, to see the finger retreating, pausing to scratch Faucelme's nose before disappearing into the ropes.

Cugel quickly crossed the room and tested the bonds, which

seemed at adequate tension. Faucelme at close range took note of Cugel's hat ornament and made a faint hissing sound between his teeth.

"Your hat is a most elaborate confection," said Faucelme. "The style is striking, though in regions such as this you might as effectively wear a leather stocking over your head." So saying, he glanced down at his book.

"It well may be," replied Cugel. "And when the sun goes out a single loose smock will fulfill every demand of modesty."

"Ha ha! Fashions will then be meaningless! That is a droll notion!" Faucelme stole a glance at his book. "And that handsome bauble: where did you secure so showy a piece?" Again Faucelme swept his eyes across the pages of his book.

"It is a bit of brummagem I picked up along the way," said Cugel carelessly. "What are you reading with such avidity?" He picked up the book. "Hm. . . . 'Madame Milgrim's Dainty Recipes'."

"Indeed, and I am reminded that the carrot pudding wants a stir. Perhaps you will join me for a meal?" He spoke over his shoulder: *"Tzat!"* The ropes fell away to a small loose coil and Faucelme rose to his feet. "I was not expecting guests, so tonight we will dine in the kitchen. But I must hurry, before the pudding scorches."

He stalked on long knob-kneed legs into the kitchen with Cugel coming doubtfully after. Faucelme motioned to a chair. "Sit down and I will find us a nice little morsel or two: nothing high nor heavy, mind you, no meats nor wines as they inflame the blood and according to Madame Milgrim give rise to flactomies. Here is some splendid gingleberry juice which I recommend heartily. Then we shall have a nice stew of herbs and our carrot pudding."

Cugel seated himself at the table and watched with single-minded vigilance as Faucelme moved here and there, collecting small dishes of cakes, preserves, compotes and vegetable pastes. "We shall have a veritable feast! Seldom do I indulge myself, but tonight, with a distinguished guest, all discipline goes by the boards!" He paused in his work. "Have you told me your name? As the years advance, I find myself ever more absent-minded."

"I am Cugel, and originally of Almery, where I am now returning."

"Almery! A far way to go, with curious sights at every step, and many a danger as well. I envy you your confidence! Shall we dine?"

Cugel ate only from the dishes which Faucelme himself ate, and thought to feel no ill effects. Faucelme spoke discursively as he ate from this or that plate with prim little nips: ". . . name has unfortunate antecedents in the region. Apparently the nineteenth aeon knew a 'Faucelme' of violent habit indeed, and there may have been another 'Faucelme' a hundred years later, though at that distance in time lifetimes blur together. I shudder to think of their deeds. . . . Our local villains now are a clan of farmers: angels of mercy by comparison, nevertheless with certain nasty habits. They give their mermelants beer to drink, then send them out to intimidate travellers. They dared to come up here one day, stamping up and down the porch and showing their bellies. 'Beer!' they shouted. 'Give us good beer!' Naturally I keep no such stuff on hand. I took pity on them and explained at length the vulgar qualities of inebriation, but they refused to listen, and used offensive language. Can you believe it? 'You double-tongued old wowser, we have listened long enough to your cackle and now we want beer in return!' These were their very words! So I said: 'Very well; you shall have beer.' I prepared a tea of bitter belch-wort and nuxium; I chilled it and caused it to fume, in the manner of beer. I called out: 'Here is my only beer!' and served it in ewers. They slapped down their noses and sucked it up in a trice. Immediately they curled up like sow-bugs and lay as if dead for a day and a half. Finally they uncoiled, rose to their feet, befouled the yard in a most lavish manner, and skulked away. They have never returned, and perhaps my little homily has brought them to sobriety."

Cugel tilted his head sidewise and pursed his lips. "An interesting story."

"Thank you." Faucelme nodded and smiled as if musing over pleasant memories. "Cugel, you are a good listener; also you do not swill down your food with chin in plate, then look hungrily here and there for more. I appreciate delicacy and a sense of style. In fact, Cugel, I have taken a fancy to you. Let us see what we can do to help you along the road of life. We shall take our tea in the parlour: the finest Amber Moth-wing for an honoured guest! Will you go ahead?"

"I will wait and keep you company," said Cugel. "It would be rude to do otherwise."

Faucelme spoke heartily: "Your manners are those of an earlier generation. One does not see their like among the young folk of today, who think of nothing but self-indulgence."

Under Cugel's watchful eye Faucelme prepared tea and poured it into cups of egg-shell porcelain. He bowed and gestured to Cugel. "Now to the parlour."

"Lead the way, if you will."

Faucelme showed a face of whimsical surprise, then shrugged and preceded Cugel into the parlour. "Seat yourself, Cugel. The green velour chair is most comfortable."

"I am restless," said Cugel. "I prefer to stand."

"Then at least take off your hat," said Faucelme with a trace of petulance.

"Certainly," said Cugel.

Faucelme watched him with bird-like curiosity. "What are you doing?"

"I am removing the ornament." Protecting his hands with a folded kerchief, Cugel slipped the object into his pouch. "It is hard and sharp and I fear that it might mar your fine furniture."

"You are most considerate and deserve a little gift. This rope for instance: it was walked by Lazhnascenthe the Lemurian, and is imbued with magical properties. For instance, it responds to commands; it is extensible and stretches without loss of strength as far as you require. I see that you carry a fine antique sword. The filigree of the pommel suggests Kharay of the eighteenth aeon. The steel should be of excellent quality, but is it sharp?"

"Naturally," said Cugel. "I could shave with the edge, were I of a mind to do so."

"Then cut yourself a convenient length of the rope: let us say ten feet. It will tuck neatly into your pouch, yet it will stretch ten miles at your command."

"This is true generosity!" declared Cugel, and measured off the stipulated length. Flourishing his sword, he cut at the rope, without effect. "Most peculiar," said Cugel.

"Tut, and all the time you thought your sword to be sharp!" Faucelme touched two fingers to a mischievous grin. "Perhaps we can repair the deficiency." From a cabinet he brought a long box, which, when opened, proved to contain a shining silver powder.

"Thrust your blade into the glimmister," said Faucelme. "Let none touch your fingers, or they will become rigid silver bars."

Cugel followed the instructions. When he withdrew the sword, it trailed a fine sift of spangling glimmister. "Shake it well," said Faucelme. "An excess only mars the scabbard."

Cugel shook the blade clean. The edge of the sword twinkled with small coruscations, and the blade itself seemed luminous.

"Now!" said Faucelme. "Cut the rope."

The sword cut through the rope as if it were a strand of kelp.

Cugel gingerly coiled the rope. "And what are the commands?"

Faucelme picked up the loose rope. "Should I wish to seize upon something, I toss it high and use the cantrap '*Tzip*!', in this fashion—"

"Halt!" cried Cugel, raising his sword. "I want no demonstrations!"

Faucelme chuckled. "Cugel, you are as brisk as a tittle-bird. Still, I think none the less of you. In this sickly world, the rash die young. Do not be frightened of the rope; I will be mild. Observe, if you will! To disengage the rope, call the order '*Tzat*', and the rope returns to hand. So then!" Faucelme stood back and held up his hands in the manner of one who dissembles nothing. "Is this the conduct of a 'sly and unpredictable villain'?"

"Decidedly so, if the villain, for the purposes of his joke, thinks to simulate the altruist."

"Then how will you know villain from altruist?"

Cugel shrugged. "It is not an important distinction."

Faucelme seemed to pay no heed; his mercurial intellect was already exploring a new topic. "I was trained in the old tradition! We found our strength in the basic verities, to which you, as a patrician, must surely subscribe. Am I right in this?"

"Absolutely, and in all respects!" declared Cugel. "Recognizing, of course, that these fundamentental verities vary from region to region, and even from person to person."

"Still, certain truths are universal," argued Faucelme. "For instance, the ancient rite of gift exchange between host and guest. As an altruist I have given you a fine and nutritious meal, a length of magic rope and perduration of the sword. You will demand with full vigor what you may give me in return, and I will ask only for your good regard—"

Cugel said with generous spontaneity: "It is yours, freely and without stint, and the basic verities have been fulfulled. Now, Faucelme, I find myself somewhat fatigued and so—"

"Cugel, you are generous! Occasionally, as we toil along our lonely path through life we encounter one who instantly, or so it seems, becomes a dear and trusted friend. I shall be sorry to see you depart! You must leave me some little memento, and in fact I will refuse to take anything other than that bit of tinsel you wear on your hat. A trifle, a token, no more, but it will keep your memory green, until the happy day of your return! You may now give over the ornament."

"With pleasure," said Cugel. Using great care he reached into his pouch and withdrew the ornament which had originally clasped his hat. "With my warmest regards, I present you with my hat ornament."

Faucelme studied the ornament a moment, then looked up and turned the full gaze of his milky golden eyes upon Cugel. He pushed back the ornament. "Cugel, you have given me too much! This is an article of value—no, do not protest!—and I want only that rather vulgar object with the spurious red gem at the center which I noticed before. Come, I insist! It will hang always in a place of honour here in my parlour!''

Cugel showed a sour smile. ''In Almery lives Iucounu the Laughing Magician.''

Faucelme gave a small involuntary grimace.

Cugel continued. ''When I see him he will ask: 'Cugel, where is my 'Pectoral Sky-break Spatterlight' which was entrusted into your care?' What can I tell him? That a certain Faucelme in the Land of the Falling Wall would not be denied?''

''This matter bears looking into,'' muttered Faucelme. ''One solution suggests itself. If, for instance, you decided not to return to Almery, then Iucounu would not learn the news. Or if, for instance—'' Faucelme became suddenly silent.

A moment passed. Faucelme spoke in a voice of affability: ''You must be fatigued and ready for your rest. First then: a taste of my aromatic bitters, which calm the stomach and refresh the nerves!''

Cugel tried to decline but Faucelme refused to listen. He brought out a small black bottle and two crystal cups. Into Cugel's cup he poured a half-inch of pale liquid. ''This is my own distillation,'' said Faucelme, ''See if it is to your taste.''

A small moth fluttered close to Cugel's cup and instantly fell dead to the table.

Cugel rose to his feet. ''I need no such tonic tonight,'' said Cugel. ''Where shall I sleep?''

''Come.'' Faucelme led Cugel up the stairs and opened the door into a room. ''A fine cozy little nook, where you will rest well indeed.''

Cugel drew back. ''There are no windows! I should feel stifled.''

''Oh? Very well, let us look into another chamber. . . . What of this? The bed is soft and fine.''

Cugel voiced a question: ''What is the reason for the massive iron gridwork above the bed? What if it fell during the night?''

''Cugel, this is sheer pessimism! You must always look for the glad things of life! Have you noticed, for instance, the vase of flowers beside the bed!''

''Charming! Let us look at another room.''

''Sleep is sleep!'' said Faucelme peevishly. ''Are you always so captious? . . . Well then, what of this fine chamber? The bed is good; the windows are wide. I can only hope that the height does not affect you with vertigo.''

''This will suit me well,'' said Cugel. ''Faucelme, I bid you good night.''

Faucelme stalked off down the hall. Cugel closed the door and opened wide the window. Against the stars he could see tall thin chimneys and a single cypress rearing above the house.

Cugel tied an end of his rope to the bed-post, then kicked the bed, which at once knew revulsion for the suction of gravity and lifted into the air. Cugel guided it to the window, pushed it through and out into the night. He darkened the lamp, climbed aboard the bed and thrust away from the manse toward the cypress tree, to which he tied the other end of the rope. He gave a command: "Rope, stretch long."

The rope stretched and Cugel floated up into the night. The manse showed as an irregular bulk below, blacker than black, with yellow quadrangles to mark the illuminated rooms.

Cugel let the rope stretch a hundred yards. "Rope, stretch no more!"

The bed stopped with a soft jerk. Cugel made himself comfortable and watched the manse.

Half an hour passed. The bed swayed to the vagrant airs of the night and under the eiderdown Cugel became drowsy. His eyelids became heavy. . . . An effulgence burst soundlessly from the window of the room to which he had been assigned. Cugel blinked and sat upright, and watched a bubble of luminous pale gas billow from the window.

The room went dark, as before. A moment later the window flickered to the light of a lamp, and Faucelme's angular figure, with elbows akimbo, showed black upon the yellow rectangle. The head jerked this way and that as Faucelme looked out into the night.

At last he withdrew and the window went dark.

Cugel became uneasy with his proximity to the manse. He took hold of the rope and said: *"Tzat!"*

The rope came loose in his hand.

Cugel said: "Rope, shrink!"

The rope became once more ten feet long.

Cugel looked back toward the manse. "Faucelme, whatever your deeds or misdeeds, I am grateful to you for this rope, and also your bed, even though, through fear, I must sleep in the open."

He looked over the side of the bed and by starlight saw the glimmer of the road. The night was dead calm. He drifted, if at all, to the west.

Cugel hung his hat on the bed-post. He lay back, pulled the eiderdown over his head and went to sleep.

The night passed. Stars moved across the sky. From the waste came the melancholy call of the visp: once, twice, then silence.

* * *

Cugel awoke to the rising of the sun, and for an appreciable interval could not define his whereabouts. He started to throw a leg over the side of the bed, then pulled it back with a startled jerk.

A black shadow fluttered across the sun; a heavy black object swooped down to alight at the foot of Cugel's bed: a pelgrane of middle years, to judge by the silky gray hair of its globular abdomen. Its head, two feet long, was carved of black horn, like that of a stag-beetle, and white fangs curled up past its snout. Perching on the bedstead it regarded Cugel with both avidity and amusement.

"Today I shall breakfast in bed," said the pelgrane. "Not often do I so indulge myself."

It reached out and seized Cugel's ankle, but Cugel jerked back. He groped for his sword but could not draw it from the scabbard. In his frantic effort he caught his hat with the tip of his scabbard; the pelgrane, attracted by the red glint, reached for the hat. Cugel thrust 'Spatterlight' into its face.

The wide brim and Cugel's own terror confused the flow of events. The bed bounded as if relieved of weight; the pelgrane was gone.

Cugel looked to all sides in puzzlement.

The pelgrane had disappeared.

Cugel looked at 'Spatterlight', which seemed to shine with perhaps a somewhat more vivacious glow.

With great caution Cugel arranged the hat upon his head. He looked over the side and noticed approaching in the road a small two-wheeled cart pushed by a fat boy of twelve or thirteen years.

Cugel threw down his rope to fix upon a stump and drew himself to the surface. When the boy rolled the push-cart past, Cugel sprang out upon the road. "Hold up! What have we here?"

The boy jumped back in fright. "It is a new wheel for the wain and breakfast for my brothers: a pot of good stew, a round of bread and a jug of wine. If you are a robber there is nothing here for you."

"I will be the judge of that," said Cugel. He kicked the wheel to render it weightless, and heaved it spinning away through the sky while the boy watched in open-mouthed wonder. Cugel then took the pot of stew, the bread and the wine from the cart. "You now may proceed," he told the boy. "If your brothers inquire for the wheel and the breakfast, you may mention the name 'Cugel' and the sum 'five terces'."

The boy trundled the cart away at a run. Cugel took the pot, bread and wine to his bed and, loosing the rope, drifted high into the air.

Along the road at a run came the three farmers, followed by the boy. They halted and shouted: "Cugel! Where are you? We want a word or two with you.'' And one added ingenuously: ''We wish to return your five terces!''

Cugel deigned no response. The boy, searching around the sky for the wheel, noticed the bed and pointed, and the farmers, red-faced with fury, shook their fists and bawled curses.

Cugel listened with impassive amusement for a few minutes, until the breeze, freshening, swept him off toward the hills and Port Perdusz.

Chapter IV

FROM PORT PERDUSZ TO KASPARA VITATUS

1

On the Docks

A favorable wind blew Cugel and his bed over the hills in comfort and convenience. As he drifted over the last ridge, the landscape dissolved into far distances, and before him, from east to west, spread the estuary of the River Chaing, in a great sweep of liquid gunmetal.

Westward along the shore Cugel noticed a scatter of mouldering gray structures: Port Perdusz. A half-dozen vessels were tied up at the docks; at so great a distance Cugel could not distinguish one from the other.

Cugel caused the bed to descend by dangling his sword and boots over either side, so that they were seized by the forces of gravity. Driven by capricious gusts of wind, the bed dropped in directions beyond Cugel's control and eventually fell into a thicket of tulsifer reeds only a few yards inland from the river.

Reluctantly abandoning the bed, Cugel picked his way toward the river road, across soggy turf rampant with a dozen species of more or less noxious plants: russet and black burdock, blister-bush, brown-flowered horse, sensitive vine which jumped back in distaste as Cugel approached. Blue lizards hissed angrily and Cugel, already in poor humour owing to contact with the blister-bush, reviled them in return: "Hiss away, vermin! I expect nothing better from such low-caste beasts!"

The lizards, divining the gist of Cugel's rebuke, ran at him by jerks and bounds, hissing and spitting, until Cugel picked up a dead branch, and by beating at the ground kept them at bay.

Cugel finally gained the road. He brushed off his clothes, slapped his hat against his leg, taking care to avoid contact with 'Spatterlight'.

Then, shifting his sword so that it swung at its most jaunty angle, he set off toward Port Perdusz.

The time was middle afternoon. A line of tall deodars bordered the road; Cugel walked in and out of black shadow and red sunlight. He noticed an occasional hut halfway up the hillside and decaying barges along the river-bank. The road passed an ancient cemetery shaded under straggling rows of cypress, then swung toward the river to avoid a bluff on which perched a ruined palace.

Entering the town proper, the road swung around the back of a central plaza, where it passed in front of a large semicircular building, at one time a theater or concert hall, but now an inn. The road then returned to the waterfront and led past those vessels which Cugel had noticed from the air. A question hung heavy in Cugel's mind: might the *Galante* still lie in port?

Unlikely, but not impossible.

Cugel would find most embarrassing a chance confrontation with Captain Baunt, or Drofo, or Madame Soldinck, or even Soldinck himself.

Halting in the roadway, Cugel rehearsed a number of conversational gambits which might be used to ease the tensions. At length he admitted to himself that, realistically, none could be expected to succeed, and that a formal bow, or a simple and noncommittal nod of the head, would serve equally well.

Maintaining a watch in all directions, Cugel sauntered out on the decaying old wharf. He discovered three ships and two small coastwise vessels, as well as a ferry to the opposite shore.

None was the *Galante*, to Cugel's great relief.

The first vessel, and farthest downstream from the plaza, was a heavy and nameless barge, evidently intended for the river trade. The second, a large carrack named *Leucidion* had been discharged of cargo and now appeared to be undergoing repairs. The third, and closest to the plaza, was the *Avventura*, a trim little ship, somewhat smaller than the others, and now in the process of taking on cargo and provisions for a voyage.

The docks were comparatively animated, with the passage of drays, the shouting and cursing of porters, the gay music of concertinas from aboard the barge.

A small man, portly and florid, wearing the uniform of a minor official, paused to inspect Cugel with a calculating eye, then turned away and entered one of the nearby warehouses.

Over the rail of the *Leucidion* leaned a burly man wearing a striped shirt of indigo blue and white, a conical black hat with a golden chain dangling beside his right ear, and a spigoted golden boss in his left cheek: the costume of the Castillion Shorelanders.*

Cugel confidently approached the *Leucidion* and, assuming a jovial expression, waved his hand in greeting.

The ship-master watched impassively, making no response.

Cugel called out: "A fine ship! I see that she has been somewhat disabled."

The ship-master at last responded: "I already have been notified in this regard."

"Where will you sail when the damage is repaired?"

"Our usual run."

"Which is?"

"To Latticut and The Three Sisters, or to Woy if cargo offers."

"I am looking for passage to Almery," said Cugel.

"You will not find it here," said the ship-master with a grim smile. "I am brave but not rash."

In a somewhat peevish voice Cugel protested: "Surely someone must sail south out of Port Perdusz! It is only logical!"

The ship-master shrugged and looked toward the sky. "If this is your reasoned opinion, then no doubt it is so."

Cugel pushed impatiently down at the pommel of his sword. "How do you suggest that I make my journey south?"

"By sea?" The ship-master jerked his thumb toward the *Avventura*. "Talk to Wiskich; he is a Dilk and a madman, with the seamanship of a Blue Mountain sheep. Pay him terces enough and he will sail to Jehane itself."

"This I know for a fact," said Cugel. "Certain cargoes of value arrive at Port Perdusz from Saskervoy, and are then trans-shipped to Almery."

The ship-master listened with little interest. "Most likely they move by caravan, such as Yadcomo's or Varmous'. Or, for all I know, Wiskich sails them south in the *Avventura*. All Dilks are mad. They think they will live forever and ignore danger. Their ships carry mast-head lamps so that, when the sun goes out, they can light their way back across the sea to Dilclusa."

*At Castillion banquets a cask is placed on a balcony over the refection hall. Flexible pipes lead down to each place. The diner seats himself, fixes a pipe to the spigot in his cheek, so that he may drink continously as he dines, so avoiding the drudgery of opening flasks, pouring out mugs or goblets, raising, tilting and setting down the mug or goblet, with the consequent danger of breakage or waste. By this process he both eats and drinks more efficiently, and thus gains time for song.

Cugel started to put another question, but the ship-master had retreated into his cabin.

During the conversation, the small portly man in the uniform had emerged from the warehouse. He listened a moment to the conversation, then went at a brisk pace to the *Avventura*. He ran up the gangplank and disappeared into the cabin. Almost at once he returned down the gangplank where he halted a moment, then, ignoring Cugel, he returned at a placid and dignified gait into the warehouse.

Cugel proceeded to the *Avventura*, hoping at least to learn the itinerary proposed by Wiskich for his ship. At the foot of the gangplank a sign had been posted which Cugel read with great interest:

PASSENGERS FOR THE VOYAGE
SOUTH, TAKE NOTE!
PORTS OF CALL ARE NOW DEFINITE. THEY ARE:
MAHAZE AND THE MISTY ISLES
LAVRRAKI REAL, OCTORUS, KAIIN
VARIOUS PORTS OF ALMERY.
DO NOT BOARD SHIP WITHOUT TICKET!
SECURE TICKET FROM TICKET AGENT
IN GRAY WAREHOUSE ACROSS WHARF

With long strides Cugel crossed the wharf and entered the warehouse. An office to the side was identified by an old sign

OFFICE OF TICKET AGENT

Cugel stepped into the office where, sitting behind a disreputable desk, he discovered the small portly man in the dark uniform, now making entries into a ledger.

The official looked up from his work. ''Sir, your orders?''

''I wish to take passage aboard the *Avventura* for Almery. You may prepare me a ticket.''

The agent turned a page in the ledger and squinted dubiously at a set of entries. ''I am sorry to say that the voyage is fully booked. A pity. . . . Just a moment! There may be a cancellation! If so, you are in luck, as there will be no other voyage this year. . . . Let me see. Yes! The Hierarch Hopple has taken ill.''

''Excellent! What is the fare?''

''The available billet is for first class accommodation and victualling, at two hundred terces.''

"What?" cried Cugel in anguish. "That is an outrageous fee! I have but forty-five terces to my pouch, and not a groat more!"

The agent nodded placidly. "Again you are in luck. The Hierarch placed a deposit of one hundred and fifty terces upon the ticket, which sum has been forfeited. I see no reason why we should not add your forty-five terces to this amount and even though it totals to only one hundred and ninety-five, you shall have your ticket, and I will make certain book-keeping adjustments."

"That is most kind of you!" said Cugel. He brought the terces from his pouch, and paid them over to the agent, who returned him a slip of paper marked with characters strange to Cugel. "And here is your ticket."

Cugel reverently folded the ticket and placed it in his pouch. He said: "I hope that I may go aboard the ship at once, as now I lack the means to pay for either food or shelter elsewhere."

"I am sure that there will be no problem," said the ticket agent. "But if you will wait here a moment I will run over to the ship and say a word to the captain."

"That is good of you," said Cugel, and composed himself in a chair. The agent departed the office.

Ten minutes passed, then twenty minutes, and half an hour. Cugel became restless and, going to the door, looked up and down the wharf, but the ticket agent was nowhere to be seen.

"Odd," said Cugel. He noticed that the sign which had hung by the *Avventura*'s gangplank had disappeared. "Naturally!" Cugel told himself. "There is now a full complement of passengers, and no need for further advertisement."

As Cugel watched, a tall red-haired man with muscular arms and legs came unsteadily along the dock, apparently having taken a drop too many at the inn. He lurched up the *Avventura*'s gang-plank and stumbled into the cabin.

"Ah!" said Cugel. "The explanation is clear. That is Captain Wiskich, and the agent has been awaiting his return. He will be coming down the gang-plank any moment now."

Another ten minutes passed. The sun was now sinking low into the estuary and a dark pink gloom had descended upon Port Perdusz.

The captain appeared on the deck to supervise the loading of supplies from a dray. Cugel decided to wait no longer. He adjusted his hat to a proper angle, strode across the avenue, up the gangplank and presented himself to Captain Wiskich. "Sir, I am Cugel, one of your first-class passengers."

"All my passengers are first-class!" declared Captain Wiskich. "You will find no pettifoggery aboard the *Avventura*!"

Cugel opened his mouth to stipulate the terms of his ticket, then closed it again; to remonstrate would seem an argument in favor of pettifoggery. He observed the provisions now being loaded aboard, which seemed of excellent quality. Cugel spoke approvingly: "The viands appear more than adequate. It would seem that you set a good table for your passengers!"

Captain Wiskich uttered a yelp of coarse laughter. "First things come first aboard the *Avventura*! The viands are choice indeed; they are for the table of myself and the crew. Passengers eat flat beans and semola, unless they pay a surcharge, for which they are allowed a supplement of kangol."

Cugel heaved a deep sigh. "May I ask the length of the passage between here and Almery?"

Captain Wiskich looked at Cugel in drunken wonder. "Almery? Why should anyone sail to Almery? First one mires his ship in a morass of foul-smelling weeds a hundred miles across. The weeds grow over the ship and multitudes of insects crawl aboard. Beyond is the Gulf of Swirls, then the Serene Sea, now bedeviled by pirates of the Jhardine Coast. Then, unless one detours far west around the Isles of Cloud, he must pass through the Seleune and a whole carnival of dangers."

Cugel became outraged. "Am I to understand that you are not sailing south to Almery?"

Captain Wiskich slapped his chest with a huge red hand. "I am a Dilk and know nothing of fear. Still, when Death enters the room by the door, I leave through the window. My ship will sail a placid course to Latticut, thence to Al-Halambar, thence to Witches Nose and The Three Sisters, and so back to Port Perdusz. If you wish to make the passage, pay me your fare and find a hammock in the hold." "I have already bought my ticket!" stormed Cugel. "For the passage south to Almery, by way of Mahaze!"

"That pest-hole? Never. Let me see your ticket."

Cugel presented that document afforded him by the purported ticket-agent. Captain Wiskich looked at it first from one angle, then another. "I know nothing of this. I cannot even read it. Can you?"

"That is inconsequential. You must take me to Almery or return my money, to the sum of forty-five terces."

Captain Wiskich shook his head in wonder. "Port Perdusz is full of touts and swindlers; still, yours is a most imaginative and original scheme! But it falls short. Get off my ship at once."

"Not until you pay me my forty-five terces!" And Cugel laid his hand suggestively on the pommel of his sword.

Captain Wiskich seized Cugel by the collar and seat of the trousers, frog-marched him along the deck, and heaved him down the gang-plank. "Don't come back aboard; I am a busy man. Ahoy, dray-master! You still must bring me another load! I am in haste to make sail!"

"All in good time. I still must despatch a load to Varmous for his caravan. Now pay me for the present consignment; that is how I do business, on a cash basis only."

"Then bring up your invoice and we will check off the items."

"That is not necessary. The items are all on board."

"The items are on board when I say they are on board. You will take none of my terces until that moment."

"You only delay your last consignment, and I have Varmous' delivery to make."

"Then I will make my own tally and pay by this reckoning."

"Never!" Grumbling for the delay, the dray-master went aboard the *Avventura*.

Cugel went across the wharf and accosted a porter. "A moment of your time, if you please! This afternoon I had dealings with a small fat man in a dark uniform. Where can I find him at this moment?"

"You would seem to speak of poor old Master Sabbas, whose case is tragic. At one time owned and managed the draying business. But he went senile and now he calls himself 'Sab the Swindler' to every one's amusement. That is his son Master Yoder aboard the *Avventura* with Captain Wiskich. If you were foolish enough to give him your terces, you must now think of the act as a kindly charity, for you have brightened the day of poor feeble-minded old Master Sabbas."

"Perhaps so, but I gave over the terces in jest, and now I want them back."

The porter shook his head. "They are gone with the moons of ancient Earth."

"But surely Master Yoder reimburses the victims of his father's delusions!"

The porter merely laughed and went off about his duties.

Yoder presently descended the gang-plank. Cugel stepped forward. "Sir, I must complain of your father's actions. He sold me passage for a fictitious voyage aboard the *Avventura* and now—"

"Aboard the *Avventura*, you say?" asked Yoder.

"Precisely so, and therefore—"

"In that case, Captain Wiskich is your man!" So saying, Yoder went off about his business.

Cugel glumly walked back to the central plaza. In a yard beside the inn Varmous prepared his caravan for its journey. Cugel noticed three carriages, each seating a dozen passengers, and four wagons loaded with cargo, equipment and supplies. Varmous was immediately evident: a large man, bulky of shoulder, arm, leg and thigh, with ringlets of yellow hair, mild blue eyes and an expression of earnest determination.

Cugel watched Varmous for a few moments, then stepped forward and introduced himself. "Sir, I am Cugel. You would seem to be Varmous, director of the caravan."

"That is correct, sir."

"When, may I ask, does your caravan leave Port Perdusz?"

"Tomorrow, in the event that I receive all my stores from the indolent dray-master."

"May I ask your itinerary?"

"Certainly. Our destination is Torqual, where we will arrive in time for the Festival of Ennoblements. We travel by way of Kaspara Vitatus, which is a junction point for travel in several directions. However, I am obliged to notify you that our roster is complete. We can accept no more applications for travel."

"Perhaps you wish to employ another driver, or attendant, or guard?"

"I have ample personnel," said Varmous. "Still, I thank you for your interest."

Cugel disconsolately entered the inn, which, so he found, had been converted from a theater. The stage now served as a first-class dining hall for persons of fastidious taste, while the pit served as a common room. Sleeping chambers had been built along the balcony and sojourners could overlook both the first-class dining hall and the common room below merely by glancing from their doors.

Cugel presented himself to the office beside the entrance, where a stout woman sat behind a wicket.

"I have just arrived in town," said Cugel in a formal voice. "Important business will occupy me for the better part of a week. I will require food and lodging of excellent quality for the duration of my visit."

"Very good, sir! We will be happy to oblige. Your name?"

"I am Cugel."

"You may now pay over a deposit of fifty terces against charges."

Cugel spoke stiffly: "I prefer to pay at the end of my visit, when I can examine the bill in detail."

"Sir, this is our invariable rule. You would be astonished to learn of the scurrilous vagabonds who try every conceivable trick upon us."

"Then I must go find my servant, who carries the money."

Cugel departed the inn. Thinking that by chance he might come upon Master Sabbas, Cugel returned to the wharves.

The sun had set; Port Perdusz was bathed in wine-colored gloom. Activity had diminished somewhat, but drays still carried goods here and there among the warehouses.

Sab the Swindler was nowhere to be seen, but Cugel had already put him aside in favor of a new and more positive concept. He went to that warehouse where Yoder stored his victuals and stood waiting in the shadows.

From the warehouse came a dray driven not by Yoder but by a man with a ruff of ginger-colored hair and long bristling mustaches with waxed points. He was a person of style who wore a wide-brimmed hat with a tall green plume, double-toed boots and a mauve knee-length coat embroidered with yellow birds. Cugel removed his own hat, the most notable element of his costume, and tucked it into his waist-band.

As soon as the dray had moved a few yards along the wharf Cugel ran forward and accosted the driver. He spoke briskly: "Is this last load for the *Avventura*? If so, Captain Wiskich does not appreciate so much unnecessary delay."

The driver spoke with unexpected spirit: "I am indeed loaded for the *Avventura*. As for delay, I know of none! These are choice viands and careful selection is of the essence."

"True enough; no need to belabor the point. You have the invoice?"

"I do indeed! Captain Wiskich must pay to the last terce before I unload so much as an anchovy. Those are my strict instructions."

Cugel held up his hand. "Be easy! All will go smoothly. Captain Wiskich is conducting business over here in the warehouse. Come; bring your invoice."

Cugel led the way into the old gray warehouse, now dim with dusk, and signaled the driver into the office marked *Ticket Agent*.

The driver peered into the office. "Captain Wiskich? Why do you sit in the dark?"

Cugel threw his cloak over the driver's head and tied him well with the wonderful extensible rope, then gagged him with his own kerchief.

Cugel took the invoice and the fine wide-brimmed hat. "I will be back shortly; in the meantime, enjoy your rest."

Cugel drove the dray to the *Avventura* and drew up to a halt. He heard Captain Wiskich bawling to someone in the forecastle. Cugel shook his head regretfully. The risks were disproportionate to the gain; let Captain Wiskich wait.

Cugel continued along the wharf, and across the plaza to where Varmous worked among the wagons of his caravan.

Cugel pulled the driver's wide-brimmed hat low over his face and hid the sword under his cloak. With the invoice in hand he sought out Varmous. "Sir, I have delivered your load of victual, and this is the invoice, now due and payable."

Varmous, taking the invoice, read down the billing. "Three hundred and thirty terces? These are high-quality viands! My order was far more modest, and was quoted to me at two hundred terces!"

Cugel made a debonair gesture. "In that case, you need only pay two hundred terces," he said grandly. "We are interested only in the satisfaction of our customers."

Varmous glanced once more at the invoice. "It is a rare bargain! But why should I argue with you?" He handed Cugel a purse. "Count it, if you like, but I assure you that it contains the proper amount."

"That is adequate assurance," said Cugel. "I will leave the dray here and you may unload it at your convenience." He bowed and departed.

Returning to the warehouse Cugel found the driver as he had left him. Cugel said: *"Tzat!"* to loosen the bonds and placed the wide-brimmed hat upon the driver's head. "Do not stir for five minutes! I will be waiting just outside the door and if you stick out your head I will lop it off with my sword. Is that clear?"

"Quite clear," muttered the driver.

"In that case, farewell." Cugel departed and returned to the inn where he placed down a deposit and was assigned a chamber on the balcony.

Cugel dined upon bread and sausages, then strolled out to the front of the inn. His attention was attracted by an altercation near Varmous' caravan. Looking more closely, Cugel found Varmous in angry confrontation with Captain Wiskich and Yoder. Varmous refused to surrender his victuals until Captain Wiskich paid him two hundred terces plus a handling charge of fifty terces. Captain Wiskich, in a rage, aimed a blow at Varmous, who stepped aside, then struck Captain Wiskich with such force that he tumbled over backwards. The crew of the *Avventura* was on hand and rushed forward, only to be met by Varmous' caravan personnel carrying staves, and the seamen were soundly thrashed.

Captain Wiskich, with his crew, retired into the inn to plan new strategies, but instead they drank great quantities of wine and committed such nuisances that they were taken by the town constables and immured in an old fortress half-way up the hill, where they were sentenced to three days of confinement.

When Captain Wiskich and his crew were dragged away, Cugel thought long and carefully, then went out and once more conferred with Varmous.

"Earlier today, if you recall, I requested a place in your caravan."

"Conditions have not changed," said Varmous shortly. "Every place is taken."

"Let us suppose," said Cugel, "that you commanded another large and luxurious carriage, capable of carrying twelve in comfort—could you find enough custom to fill these places?"

"Without doubt! They now must wait for the next caravan and so will miss the Festival. But I leave in the morning and there would be no time to secure the supplies."

"That too can be effected, if we are able to arrive at a compact."

"What do you suggest?"

"I provide the carriage and the supplies. You recruit twelve more travelers and charge them premium prices. I pay nothing. We divide the net profits."

Varmous pursed his lips. "I see nothing wrong with this. Where is your carriage?"

"Come; we shall get it now."

Without enthusiasm Varmous followed Cugel out along the dock where finally all was quiet. Cugel boarded the *Avventura* and tied his rope to a ring under the bow and threw the end to Varmous. He kicked the hull with his ossip-charged boots and the vessel at once became revulsive of gravity. Debarking, Cugel untied the mooring lines and the vessel drifted up into the air, to the amazement of Varmous.

"Stretch, line, stretch!" called Cugel and the *Avventura* rose up into the darkness.

Together Varmous and Cugel towed the ship along the road and somewhat out of town and concealed it behind the cypress trees of the graveyard; the two then returned to the inn.

Cugel clapped Varmous on the shoulder. "We have done a good night's work, to our mutual profit!"

"I am not apt for magic," muttered Varmous. "Weirdness makes me eery."

Cugel waved aside his apprehensions. "Now: for a final goblet of wine to seal our compact, then a good night's sleep, and tomorrow, we set off on our journey!"

2

The Caravan

During the pre-dawn stillness Varmous marshaled his caravan, ordering wagons and carriages, guiding passengers to their allotted places, quieting complaints with mild comments and an ingenuous gaze. He seemed to be everywhere at once: a massive figure in black boots, a peasant's blouse and baggy pantaloons, his blond curls confined under a flat wide-brimmed hat.

Occasionally he brought one of his passengers over to Cugel, saying: "Another person for the 'premier' class!"

One by one these passengers accumulated until there were six, including two women, Ermaulde and Nissifer, both of middle years, or apparently so, since Nissifer shrouded herself from head to toe in a gown of rusty brown satin and wore a clump hat with a heavy veil. Where Nissifer was dry and taciturn, and seemed to creak as she walked, Ermaulde was plump and voluble, with large moist features and a thousand copper-colored ringlets.

In addition to Nissifer and Ermaulde, four men had decided to enjoy the privileges of the 'premier' class: a varied group ranging from Gaulph Rabi, an ecclesiarch and pantologist, through Clissum and Perruquil, to Ivanello, a handsome young man who wore his rich garments with enviable flair and whose manner ranged that somewhat limited gamut between easy condescension and amused disdain.

Last to join the group was Clissum, a portly gentleman of good stature and the ineffable airs of a trained aesthete. Cugel acknowledged the introduction, then took Varmous aside.

"We now have assigned six passengers to the 'premier' category," said Cugel. "Cabins 1, 2, 3, and 4 are those designated for passenger use. We can also take over that double cabin formerly shared by the cook and the steward, which means that our own cook and steward must go to the forecastle. I, as captain of the vessel, will naturally use the after cabin. In short, we are now booked to capacity."

Varmous scratched his cheek and showed Cugel a face of bovine incomprehension. "Surely not yet! The vessel is larger than three carriages together!"

"Possibly true, but the cargo hold claims much of the space."

Varmous gave a dubious grunt. "We must manage better."

"I see no flaws in the existing situation," said Cugel. "If you yourself wish to ride aboard, you can arrange a berth in the forepeak."

Varmous shook his head. "That is not the problem. We must make room for more passengers. Indeed, I intended the after cabin, not for the use of either you or me—after all, we are veterans of the trail and demand no languid comforts—"

Cugel held up his hand. "Not so! It is because I have known hardship that I now so greatly enjoy comfort. The *Avventura* is full. We can offer no further 'premier' accommodation."

Varmous showed a streak of mulish obstinacy. "In the first place, I cannot spare a cook and a steward for the delectation of six passengers and yourself. I counted upon you to fulfill this duty."

"What!" cried Cugel. "Review, if you will, the terms of our compact! I am captain, and no more!"

Varmous heaved a sigh. "Further, I have already sold four other 'premiers'—aha! Here they are now! Doctor Lalanke and his party."

Turning about, Cugel observed a tall gentleman, somewhat sallow and saturnine of countenance, with dense black hair, quizzically arched black eyebrows and a pointed black beard.

Varmous performed the introductions. "Cugel, here is Doctor Lalanke, a savant of remark and renown."

"Tush," said Lalanke. "You are positively effusive!"

Behind, walking in a row with long slow steps and arms hanging straight down to narrow hips, like mechanical dolls, or persons sleepwalking, came three maidens even paler than Doctor Lalanke, with short hair loose and intensely black.

Cugel looked from one to the other; they were much alike, if not identical, with the same large gray eyes, high cheekbones and flat cheeks slanting down to small pointed chins. White trousers fitted snugly to their legs and hips, which were only just perceptibly feminine; soft pale green jackets were belted to their waists. They halted behind Doctor Lalanke and stood looking toward the river, neither speaking nor displaying interest in the folk around them.

Fascinating creatures, thought Cugel.

Doctor Lalanke spoke to Varmous. "These are the component members of my little tableaux: mimes, if you will. They are Sush, Skasja and Rlys, though which name applies to which I do not know and they do not seem to care. I look upon them as my wards. They are shy and sensitive, and will be happy in the privacy of the large cabin you have mentioned."

Cugel instantly stepped forward. "One moment! The after cabin aboard the *Avventura* is occupied by the captain, which is to say myself. There is accomodation for six in the 'premier' category. Ten persons are present. Varmous, you must repair your mistake and at once!"

Varmous rubbed his chin and looked up into the sky. "The day is well underway and we must arrive at Fierkle's Fountain before dark. I suppose we had better inspect the 'premier' categories and see what can be done."

The group walked to the grove of cypress trees which concealed the *Avventura*. Along the way, Varmous spoke persuasively to Cugel: "In a business such as ours, one must occasionally make a small sacrifice for the general advantage. Hence—"

Cugel spoke with emphasis: "No more wheedling! I am adamant!"

Varmous shook his head sadly. "Cugel, I am disappointed in you. Do not forget that I helped acquire the vessel, at some risk to my reputation!"

"My planning and my magic were decisive! You only pulled on a rope. Remember also that at Kaspara Vitatus we part company. You will continue to Torqual while I fare south in my vessel."

Varmous shrugged. "I expect no difficulties except those of the next few minutes. We must discover which among our 'premier' passengers are truly strident and which can be induced to ride the carriages."

"That is reasonable," said Cugel. "I see that there are tricks to the trade, which I will be at pains to learn."

"Just so. Now, as to tactics, we must always seem of the same mind; otherwise the passengers will play us one against the other, and all control is lost. Since we cannot confer on each case, let us signal our opinions in this fashion: a cough for the boat and a sniff for the carriage."

"Agreed!"

Arriving at the boat the passengers stood back in skepticism. Perruquil, who was small, thin, hot-eyed, and seemed to be constructed only of nerves knotted around bones, went so far as to suggest duplicity. "Varmous, what is your plot? You take our terces, put us in the cabins of this ruined vessel, then go quietly off with your caravan: is that the way of it? Be warned: I was not born yesterday!"

"Boats do not ordinarily sail on the dry land," murmured the aesthete Clissum.

"Quite true," said Varmous. "By Cugel's magic, this vessel will fly safely and smoothly through the air."

Cugel spoke in a serious voice: "Because of a regrettable oversight, too many passengers have been booked aboard the *Avventura*, and four persons will be required to ride in our 'premier' carriage, at the head of the column where they can enjoy an intimate view of the nearby landscape. In this connection let me ask: who among you suffers either vertigo or an obsessive fear of heights?"

Perruquil fairly danced to the spasmodic forces of his emotion. "I shall not change to inferior accomodations! I was first to pay over my terces and Varmous guaranteed me a top priority! If necessary, I can bring the constable, who witnessed the transaction; he will support my case."

Varmous coughed significantly and Cugel coughed as well.

Ermaulde took Varmous aside and spoke a few urgent words in his ear, whereopon Varmous raised his hands to the sides of his head and pulled at his golden curls. He looked at Cugel and coughed sharply.

Clissum said: "For me there is no choice, only stark necessity! I cannot tolerate the road-side dust; I would wheeze and gasp and go into asthmatic convulsions."

Perruquil seemed to find Clissum's sonorous diction and epicurean mannerisms offensive. He snapped: "If indeed you are so asthenic, are you not rash to venture so far out along the caravan trails?"

Clissum, rolling his eyes to the sky, spoke in his richest tones: "As I spend the seconds of my life on this dying world, I am never dismal nor sodden with woe! There is too much glory, too much wonder! I am a pilgrim on a life-long quest; I search here, there, everywhere, for that elusive quality—"

Perruquil said impatiently: "How does this bear upon your asthma?"

"The connection is both implicit and explicit. I vowed that, come what may, I would sing my odes at the Festival, even if contorted in the face from an asthmatic fit. When I found that I might journey in the clean upper air, my rapture knew no bounds!"

"Bah," muttered Perruquil. "Perhaps we all are asthmatic; Varmous has never troubled to ask."

During the discussion, Varmous whispered into Cugel's ear. "Ermaulde reveals that she is pregnant with child! She fears that, if subjected to the jolts and jars of the carriage, an untoward event might occur. There is no help for it: she must ride in cushioned ease aboard the *Avventura*."

"I agree, in all respects," said Cugel.

Their attention was attracted by Ivanello's merry laugh. "I have full faith in Varmous! Why? Because I paid double-fare for the best possible accommodation which, so he assured me, I could choose myself. I therefore select the after cabin. Cugel can bed himself down with the other teamsters."

Cugel gave a distinct sniff, and spoke sharply: "In this case, Varmous referred only to the carriages. A lad like you will enjoy jumping on and off and gathering berries along the way. The *Avventura* has been reserved for persons of taste and breeding, such as Clissum and Ermaulde."

"What of me?" cried the ecclesiarch Gaulph Rabi. "I am studied in four infinities and I sit as a full member of the Collegium. I am accustomed to special treatment. In order to perform my meditations I need a quiet place, such as the cabin."

Nissifer, with a rustling and a sour smell, took two steps forward. She spoke in a curious husky whisper. "I will ride the ship. Whoever interferes will be tainted."

Ivanello threw his head back and looked at the woman through half-closed lids. " 'Tainted'? How do you mean 'tainted'?"

"Do you truly care to learn?" came the husky whisper.

Cugel, suddenly alert, looked around the group. Where were Doctor Lalanke and his wards? In sudden apprehension he ran around to the gangplank and bounded aboard.

His fears were well realized. The three mimes had secluded themselves in the after cabin. Doctor Lalanke stood in the doorway making signals. At the sight of Cugel he cried out in vexation: "Irritating little creatures! Once they decide upon a whim they are beyond control. Sometimes I am beside myself with frustration; I admit it freely!"

"Nevertheless, they must leave my cabin!"

Lalanke showed a wan smile. "I can do nothing. Persuade them to leave however you like."

Cugel went into the cabin. The three maidens sat on the bunk watching him through large gray eyes. Cugel pointed to the door. "Out with you! This is the captain's cabin, and I am the captain."

The maidens with one accord drew up their legs and folded their arms around their knees. "Yes, yes, charming indeed," said Cugel. "I am not sure whether or not I have the taste for such epicene little creatures. Under proper circumstances I am willing to experiment, but not in a group of three which would be distracting. So come now: remove your fragile little bodies, or I must eject you."

The maidens sat still as owls.

Cugel heaved a sigh. "So it must be." He started toward the bed but was interrupted by the impatient voice of Varmous. "Cugel? Where are you? We need to make decisions."

Cugel went out on deck to find that all the 'premier' passengers had climbed the gangplank and were disputing possession of the cabins. Varmous told Cugel: "We can delay no longer! I will bring up the caravan and we will tow the boat behind the first carriage."

Cugel cried out in fury: "There are too many passengers aboard! Four must take to the carriages! Meanwhile Doctor Lalanke and his troupe have taken my cabin!"

Varmous shrugged his ponderous shoulders. "Since you are captain, you need only issue the appropriate order. Meanwhile, remove the mooring lines all but one and prepare your magic."

Varmous descended to the ground. "Wait!" cried Cugel. "Where is the steward to cook and serve our meals?"

"All in good time," said Varmous. "You will prepare the noon lunch, as you have nothing better to do. Now pull up your gangplank! Make ready for departure!"

Seething with annoyance, Cugel tied his rope from the stem—head ring to the trunk of a cypress, then drew aboard the other lines. With the help of Doctor Lalanke and Clissum he pulled aboard the gangplank.

The caravan came along the road. Varmous loosened the rope from the cypress and the boat floated into the air. Varmous tied the rope to the back of the first carriage which was pulled by two farlocks of the bulky Black Ganghorn breed. Without further ado Varmous climbed aboard the carriage and the caravan set off along the river road.

Cugel looked about the deck. The passengers lined the rails, looking out over the countryside and congratulating themselves upon their mode of transport. A semblance of cameraderie had already come into being, affecting all save Nissifer who sat huddled in a rather peculiar posture beside the hold. Doctor Lalanke also stood somewhat apart. Cugel joined him by the rail. "Have you removed your wards from my cabin?"

Doctor Lalanke gravely shook his head. "They are curious little creatures, innocent and without guile, motivated only by the force of their own needs."

"Surely they must obey your commands!"

Through some extraordinary flexibility of feature, Doctor Lalanke managed to seem both apologetic and amused. "So one would think. I often wonder how they regard me: certainly not as their master."

"Most singular! How did they come into your custody?"

"I must inform you that I am a man of great wealth. I live beside the Szonglei River not far from Old Romarth. My manse is built of rare woods: tirrinch, gauze difono, skeel, purple trank, camfer and a dozen others. My life might well be one of ease and splendor, but, to validate the fact of my existence, I annotate the lives and works of the great magicians. My collection of memorabilia and curious adjuncts is remarkable." As he spoke his eyes rested upon the scale 'Spatterlight', which Cugel used for a hat ornament.

Cugel asked cautiously: "And you yourself are a magician?"

"Alas! I lack the strength. I can grasp a trifling spell against stinging insects, and another to quiet howling dogs, but magic like yours, which wafts a ship through the air, is beyond my capacity. And while we are on the subject, what of the object you wear on your hat: it exhales an unmistakable flux!"

"The object has a curious history, which I will relate at a more convenient time," said Cugel. "At this moment—"

"Of course! You are more interested in the 'mimes', as I call them, and this may well be the function for which they were contrived."

"I am mostly interested in ejecting them from my cabin."

"I will be brief, though I must revert to Grand Motholam of the late eighteenth aeon. The arch-magician Moel Lel Laio lived in a palace cut from a single moonstone. Even today, if you walk the Plain of Gray Shades, you may find a shard or two. When I excavated the old crypts I found a cambent box containing three figurines, of cracked and discolored ivory, each no larger than my finger. I took these objects to my manse and thought to wash away the grime, but they absorbed water as fast as I applied it, and I finally put them into basins to soak overnight. In the morning I found the three as you see them now. I used the names Sush, Skasja and Rlys after the Tracynthian Graces and tried to give them speech. Never have they uttered a sound, not even one to the other.

"They are strange creatures, oddly sweet, and I could detail their conduct for hours. I call them 'mimes' because when the mood comes on them they will posture and preen and simulate a hundred situations, none of which I understand. I have learned to let them to do as they will; in return they allow me to care for them."

"All very well," said Cugel. "Now the mimes of the late eighteenth aeon must discover the reality of today, as embodied in the person of Cugel. I warn you, I may be forced to eject them bodily!"

Doctor Lalanke shrugged sadly. "I am sure that you will be as gentle as possible. What are your plans?"

"The time for planning is over!" Cugel marched to the door of the cabin and flung it wide. The three sat as before, staring at Cugel with wondering eyes.

Cugel stood to the side and pointed to the door. "Out! Go! Depart! Be off with you! I am ready to lie down on my bunk and take my rest."

None of the three twitched so much as a muscle. Cugel stepped forward and took the arm of the maiden facing him on his right. Instantly the room fluttered with motion and before Cugel understood what was happening he was propelled from the cabin.

Cugel angrily ran back within and tried to seize the nearest of the mimes. She slipped sober-faced from his grasp, and again the room seemed full of fluttering figures: up, down, and around like moths. Finally Cugel managed to seize one from behind and, carrying her to the door, thrust her out on deck. At the same time he was thrust forward and instantly the ejected maiden returned into the cabin.

The other passengers had come to watch. All laughed and called out jocular remarks, save only Nissifer who paid no heed. Doctor Lalanke spoke as if in vindication: "You see how it goes? The more abrupt your conduct, the more determined their response."

Cugel said through gritted teeth: "They will come out to eat; then we shall see."

Doctor Lalanke shook his head. "That is an unreliable hope. Their appetites are slight; now and then they will take a bit of fruit, or a sweet-cake, or a sip of wine."

"Shame, Cugel!" said Ermaulde. "Would you starve three poor girls already so pale and peaked?"

"If they dislike starvation they can leave my cabin!"

The ecclesiarch lifted high a remarkably long white forefinger, with knobbed knuckles and a yellow fingernail. "Cugel, you cultivate your senses as if they were hot-house plants. Why not, once and for all, break the tyranny of your internal organs? I will give you a tract to study."

Clissum spoke: "In the last analysis the comfort of your passengers must supersede your own. Another matter! Varmous guaranteed a gracious cuisine of five or six courses. The sun has risen high and it is time that you set about your preparations for lunch."

Cugel said at last: "If Varmous made this guarantee, let Varmous do the cooking."

Perruquil set up an outcry, but Cugel would not relent. "My own problems are paramount!"

"Then what is our recourse?" demanded Perruquil.

Cugel pointed to the gunwale. "Slide down the rope and complain to Varmous! In any case, do not trouble me."

Perruquil marched to the gunwhale and raised a great shout.

Varmous turned up his broad face. "What is the difficulty?"

"It lies with Cugel. You must attend to the matter at once."

Varmous patiently halted the caravan, pulled down the boat and climbed aboard. "Well then, what now?"

Perruquil, Clissum and Cugel spoke together, until Varmous held up his hands. "One at a time, if you please. Perruquil, what is your complaint?"

Perruquil pointed a trembling finger at Cugel. "He is like a stone! He shrugs off our demands for food and will not relinquish accommodations to those who paid dearly for them!"

With a sigh Varmous said: "Well then, Cugel? How do you account for your conduct?"

"In no way whatever. Evict those insane maidens from my cabin, or the *Avventura* no longer follows the caravan, but sails to best advantage on the wind."

Varmous turned to Doctor Lalanke. "There is no help for it. We must submit to Cugel's demand. Call them out."

"But where then will we sleep?"

"There are three bunks in the crew's forecastle for the maidens. There is another bunk in the forepeak carpenter shop, which is quiet and which will suit His Reverence Gaulph Rabi very well. We will put Ermaulde and Nissifer in the port cabins, Perruquil and Ivanello in the starboard cabins, while you and Clissum will share the double cabin. All problems are thereby solved, so let the maidens come forth."

Doctor Lalanke said dubiously: "That is the nub of the matter! They will not come! Cugel tried twice to put them out; twice they ejected him instead."

Ivanello, lounging to the side, said: "And a most entertaining spectacle it was! Cugel came flying out as if he were trying to leap a wide ditch."

Doctor Lalanke said: "They probably misunderstood Cugel's intentions. I suggest that the three of us enter together. Varmous, you may go first, then I will follow and Cugel can bring up the rear. Allow me to make the signs.''

The three entered the cabin to find the maidens seated demurely on the bunk. Doctor Lalanke made a series of signs; with every show of docility the three filed from the cabin.

Varmous shook his head in bewilderment. ''I cannot understand the furore! Cugel, is this the extent of your complaint?''

''I will say this: the *Avventura* will continue to sail with the caravan.''

Clissum pulled at his plump chin. ''Since Cugel refuses to cook, where and how do we partake of the fine cuisine you advertised?''

In a spiteful voice Perruquil said: ''Cugel suggested that you yourself should do the cooking.''

''I have more serious responsibilities, as Cugel well knows,'' said Varmous stiffly. ''It seems that I must assign a steward to the ship.'' Leaning over the gunwhale he called: ''Send Porraig aboard!''

The three maidens suddenly performed a giddy gyration, then á leaping, crouching ballet of postures, which they accented with mocking glances and flippant gestures toward Cugel. Doctor Lalanke interpreted the movements. ''They are expressing an emotion or, better, an attitude. I would not dare attempt a translation.''

Cugel turned away indignantly, in time to glimpse a flutter of fusty brown satin and the closing of the door to his cabin.

In a fury Cugel called out to Varmous: ''Now the woman Nissifer has taken over my cabin!''

''This fol-de-rol must stop!'' said Varmous. He knocked on the door. ''Madame Nissifer, you must remove to your own quarters!''

From within came a husky whisper, barely audible. ''I will stay here, since I must have the dark.''

''That is impossible! We have already allotted this cabin to Cugel!''

''Cugel must go elsewhere.''

''Madame, I regret that Cugel and I must enter the cabin and conduct you to your proper berth.''

''I will place a taint.''

Varmous looked toward Cugel with puzzled blue eyes. ''What does she mean by that?''

''I am not quite clear,'' said Cugel. ''But no matter! Caravan regulations must be enforced. This is our first concern.''

''Quite so! Otherwise we invite chaos.''

''Here, at least, we are agreed! Enter the cabin; I stand resolutely at your back!''

Varmous settled his blouse, squared the hat upon his golden curls, pushed the door ajar and stepped into the cabin, with Cugel on his heels. . . . Varmous uttered a strangled cry and lurched back into Cugel, but not before Cugel discovered an acrid stench so vile and incisive that his teeth felt tender in their sockets.

Varmous stumbled to the rail, leaned back on his elbows and looked blearily across the deck. Then, with an air of great fatigue, he climbed over the gunwhale and lowered himself to the ground. He spoke a few words to Porraig the steward, who thereupon boarded the vessel. Varmous slackened the rope and the *Avventura* once more floated high.

Cugel, after a moment's reflection, approached Doctor Lalanke. "I am impressed by your gentility and in turn I will be generous. You and your wards are now assigned to the captain's cabin."

Doctor Lalanke became more saturnine than ever. "My wards would be confused. For all their frivolity, they are deeply sensitive and easily disturbed. The forecastle, as it turns out, is quite comfortable."

"Just as you like." Cugel sauntered forward, to find that the cabin formerly allotted to Nissifer had been taken by the ecclesiarch Gaulph Rabi, while Porraig the steward had settled into the carpenter shop.

Cugel made a hissing sound between his teeth. Finding an old cushion and a ragged tarpaulin, he contrived a tent on the foredeck, and there took up residence.

The river Chaing meandered down a wide valley demarcated into fields and folds by ancient stone walls, with groups of stone farmsteads huddling under black feather trees and indigo oaks. At the side, weather-worn hills basking in the red sunlight trapped lunes of black shadow in their hollow places.

All day the caravan followed the banks of the river, passing through the villages Goulyard, Trunash and Sklieve. At sundown camp was made in a meadow beside the river.

When the sun lurched low behind the hills, a great fire was built and the travelers gathered in a circle to warm themselves against the evening chill.

The 'premier' passengers dined together on coarse but hearty fare which even Clissum found acceptable—all except Nissifer, who kept to her cabin, and the mimes, who sat cross-legged beside the hull of the *Avventura* staring fascinated into the flames, Ivanello appeared in a costume of the richest quality: loose breeches of a gold, amber and black corduroy twill, fitted black boots, a loose fusk-ivory shirt embroidered with gold floriations. From his right ear, on three inches of chain, dangled a milk-opal sphere almost an inch in diameter: a gem which fascinated the three mimes to the edge of entrancement.

Varmous poured wine with a generous hand and the company became convivial. One of the ordinary passengers, a certain Ansk-Daveska called out: "Here we sit, strangers cast willy-nilly into each other's company! I suggest that each of us in turn introduces himself and tells his story, of whom he is and something of his achievements."

Varmous clapped his hands together. "Why not? I will start off. Madlick, serve more wine. . . . My story is essentially simple. My father kept a fowl-run at Waterwan across the estuary and produced fine fowl for the tables of the locality. I thought to follow in his footsteps, until he took a new spouse who could not abide the odor of burning feathers. To please this woman my father gave up the fowl and thought to cultivate lirkfish in shallow ponds, which I excavated from the ground. But owls gathered in the trees and so annoyed the spouse that she went off with a dealer in rare incenses. We then operated a ferry service from Waterwan to Port Perdusz, until my father took too much wine and, falling asleep in the ferry, drifted out to sea. I then became involved in the caravan trade and you know all the rest."

Gaulph Rabi spoke: "I hope that my life, in contrast to that of Varmous, will prove inspiring, especially to the younger persons present, or even to such marginal personalities as Cugel and Ivanello."

Ivanello had gone to sit beside the mimes. He called out: "Now then! Insult me as you will, but do not pair me off with Cugel!"

Cugel refused to dignify the comment with his attention.

Gaulph Rabi showed only a faint cold smile. "I have lived a life of rigid discipline, and the benefits of my regimen must be clear to all. While still a catechumen at the Obtrank Normalcy I made a mark with the purity of my logic. As First Fellow of the Collegium, I composed a tract demonstrating that succulent gluttony sickens the spirit like dry rot in wood. Even now, when I drink wine I mix therein three drops of aspergantium which brings about a bitter taste. I now sit on the Council and I am a Pantologist of the Final Revelation."

"An enviable achievement!" declared Varmous. "I drink to your continued success, and here is a goblet of wine without aspergantium, that you may join us in the toast without distraction from the vile flavors."

"Thank you," said Gaulph Rabi. "This is a legitimate usage."

Cugel now addressed the group: "I am a grandee of Almery, where I am heir to an ancient estate. While striving against injustice I ran afoul of an evil magician who sent me north to die. Little did he realize that submission is foreign to my nature—" Cugel looked around the group. Ivanello tickled the mimes with a long straw. Clissum and Gaulph Rabi argued Vodel's Doctrine of Isoptogenesis in a quiet undertone. Doctor Lalanke and Perruquil discussed the hostelries of Torqual.

Somewhat sulkily Cugel returned to his seat. Varmous, who had been planning the route with Ansk-Daveska, finally noticed and called out: "Well done, Cugel! Most interesting indeed! Madlick, I believe that two more jugs of the economy-grade wine are in order. It is not often that we celebrate such festivals along the trail! Lalanke, do you plan to present one of your tableaus?"

Doctor Lalanke made signals; the maidens, preoccupied with Ivanello's nonsense, at last noticed the gesticulations. They leapt to their feet and for a few moments performed a set of dizzying saltations.

Ivanello came over to Doctor Lalanke and whispered a question into his ear.

Doctor Lalanke frowned. "The question is indelicate, or at least over-explicit, but the answer is 'yes'."

Ivanello put another discreet question, to which Doctor Lalanke's response was definitely frosty. "I doubt if such ideas even enter their heads." He turned away and resumed his conversation with Perruquil.

Ansk-Daveska brought out his concertina and played a merry tune. Ermaulde, despite Varmous' horrified expostulations, jumped to her feet and danced a spirited jig.

When Ermaulde had finished dancing, she took Varmous aside; "My symptoms were gas pains only; I should have reassured you but the matter slipped my mind."

"I am much relieved," said Varmous. "Cugel will also be pleased, since, as captain of the *Avventura*, he would have been forced to serve as obstetrician."

The evening proceeded. Each of the group had a story to tell or a concept to impart, and all sat while the fire burned down to embers.

Clissum, so it developed, had composed several odes and upon urging from Ermaulde recited six stanzas from an extended work entitled: *O Time, Be Thou the Sorry Dastard?* in dramatic fashion, with vocal cadenzas between each stanza.

Cugel brought out his packet of cards and offered to teach Varmous and Ansk-Daveska Skax, which Cugel defined as a game of pure chance. Both preferred to listen as Gaulph Rabi responded to the indolent questions of Ivanello: ". . . no confusion whatever! The Collegium is often known as 'the Convergence', or even as 'the Hub', in a jocular sense, of course. But the essence is identical."

"I fear that you have the better of me," said Ivanello. "I am lost in a jungle of terminology."

"Aha! There speaks the voice of the layman! I will simplify!"

"Please do."

"Think of a set of imaginary spokes, representing between twenty and thirty infinities—the exact number is still uncertain. They converge in a focus of pure sentience; they intermingle then diverge in the opposite direction. The location of this 'Hub' is precisely known; it is within the precincts of the Collegium."

Varmous called out a question: "What does it look like?"

Gaulph Rabi gazed a long moment into the dying fire. "I think that I will not answer that question," he said at last. "I would create as many false images as there were ears to hear me."

"Half as many," Clissum pointed out delicately.

Ivanello smiled lazily up toward the night sky, where Alphard the Lonely stood in the ascendant. "It would seem that a single infinity would suffice for your studies. Is it not grandiose to preempt so many?"

Gaulph Rabi thrust forward his great narrow face. "Why not study for a term or two at the Collegium and discover for yourself?"

"I will give thought to the matter."

The second day was much like the first. The farlocks ambled steadily along the road and a breeze from the west pushed the *Avventura* slightly ahead of the foremost carriage.

Porraig the steward prepared an ample breakfast of poached oysters, sugar-glazed kumquats and scones sprinkled with the scarlet roe of land-crabs.

Nissifer remained immured in her cabin. Porraig brought a tray to the door and knocked. "Your breakfast, Madame Nissifer!"

"Take it away," came a hoarse whisper from within. "I want no breakfast."

Porraig shrugged and removed both the tray and himself as rapidly as possible, since the fetor of Nissifer's 'taint' had not yet departed the area.

At lunch matters went in the same style and Cugel instructed Porraig to serve Nissifer no more meals until she appeared in the dining saloon.

During the afternoon Ivanello brought out a long-necked lute tied with a pale blue ribbon, and sang sentimental ballads to gentle chords from the lute. The mimes came to watch in wonder, and it became a topic of general discussion as to whether or not they heard the music, or even grasped the meaning of Ivanello's activities. In any event, they lay on their bellies, chins resting on their folded fingers, watching Ivanello with grave gray eyes and, so it might seem, dumb adoration. Ivanello was emboldened to stroke Skasja's short black hair. Instantly Sush and Rlys crowded close and Ivanello had to caress them as well.

Smiling and pleased with his success, Ivanello played and sang another ballad, while Cugel watched sourly from the foredeck.

Today the caravan passed only a single village, Port Titus, and the landscape seemed perceptibly wilder. Ahead rose a massive stone scrap through which the river had carved a narrow gorge, with the road running close alongside.

Halfway through the afternoon the caravan came upon a crew of timber-cutters, loading their timber aboard a barge. Varmous brought the caravan to a halt. Jumping down from the carriage he went to make inquiries and received unsettling news: a section of mountain had collapsed into the gorge, rendering the river road impassable.

The timber-cutters came out into the road and pointed north toward the hills. "A mile ahead you will come upon a side-road. It leads up through Tuner's Gap and off across Ildish Waste. After two miles the road forks and you must veer to the right, around the gorge and in due course down to Lake Zaol and Kaspara Vitatus."

Varmous turned to look up toward the gap. "And the road: is it safe or dangerous?"

The oldest timber-cutter said: "We have no exact knowledge, since no one has recently come down through Tuner's Gap. This in itself may be a negative sign."

Another timber-cutter spoke. "At the Waterman's Inn I have heard rumors of a nomad band down from the Karst. They are said to be stealthy and savage, but since they fear the dark they will not attack by night. You are a strong company and should be safe unless they take you from ambush. An alert watch should be maintained."

The youngest of the timber-cutters said: "What of the rock goblins? Are they not a serious menace?"

"Bah!" said the old man. "Such things are boogerboos, on the order of wind-stick devils, by which to frighten saucy children."

"Still, they exist!" declared the young timber-cutter. "That, at least, is my best information."

"Bah!" said the old cutter a scond time. "At the Waterman's Inn they drink beer by the gallon, and on their way home they see goblins and devils behind every bush."

The second cutter said thoughtfully: "I will reveal my philosophy. It is better to keep watch for rock-goblins and wind-stick devils and never see them, than not to keep watch so that they leap upon you unawares.''

The old cutter made a peremptory sign. ''Return to work! Your gossip is delaying this important caravan!'' And to Varmous: ''Proceed by Tuner's Gap. A week and a day should bring you into Kaspara Vitatus.''

Varmous returned to the carriage. The caravan moved forward. After a mile a side-road turned off toward Tuner's Gap, and Varmous reluctantly departed the river-road.

The side-road wound back and forth up over the hills to Tuner's Gap, then turned out across a flat plain.

The time was now almost sunset. Varmous elected to halt for the night where a stream issued from a copse of black deodars. He arranged the wagons and carriages with care, and set out a guard-fence of metal strands which, when activated, would discharge streamers of purple lightning toward hostile intruders, thus securing the caravan against night-wandering hoons, erbs and grues.

Once again a great fire was built, with wood broken from the deodars. The 'premier' passengers partook of three preliminary courses served by Porraig aboard the *Avventura*, then joined the 'ordinaries' for bread, stew and sour greens around the fire.

Varmous served wine, but with a hand less lavish than on the previous evening.

After supper Varmous addressed the group. ''As everyone knows, we have made a detour, which should cause us neither inconvenience nor, so I trust, delay. However, we now travel the Ildish Waste, a land which is strange to me. I feel compelled to take special safeguards. You will notice the guard-fence, which is intended to deter intruders.''

Ivanello lounging to the side, could not restrain a facetious remark: ''What if intruders leap the fence?''

Varmous paid him no heed. ''The fence is dangerous! Do not approach it. Doctor Lalanke, you must instruct your wards as best you can of this danger.''

''I will do so.''

''The Ildish Waste is a wild territory. We may encounter nomads down from the Karst or even the Great Erm itself. These folk, either men or half-men, are unpredictable. Therefore I am setting up a system of vigilant look-outs. Cugel, who rides the *Avventura* and makes his headquarters at the bow, shall be our chief look-out. He is keen, sharp-eyed and suspicious; also he has nothing better to do. I will watch from my place on the forward carriage, and Slavoy, who rides the last wagon, shall be the rear-guard. But it is Cugel, with his commanding view across the landscape, to whom we shall look for protection. That is all I wish to say. Let the festivities proceed."

Clissum cleared his throat and stepped forward, but before he could recite so much as a syllable, Ivanello took up his lute and, banging lustily at the strings, sang a rather vulgar ballad. Clissum stood with a pained smile frozen on his face, then turned away and resumed his seat.

A wind blew down from the north, causing the flames to leap and the smoke to billow. Ivanello cried out a light-hearted curse. He put down his lute and began to toy with the mimes, whom, as before, he had hypnotized with his music. Tonight he became bolder in his caresses, and encountered no protest so long as he evenly shared his attentions.

Cugel watched with disapproval. He muttered to Doctor Lalanke: "Ivanello is persuading your wards to laxity."

"That may well be his intent," agreed Doctor Lalanke.

"And you are not concerned?"

"Not in the least."

Clissum once again came forward, and holding high a scroll of manuscript, looked smilingly around the group.

Ivanello, leaning back into the arms of Sush, with Rlys pressed against him on one side and Skasja on the other, bent his head over his lute and drew forth a series of plangent chords.

Clissum seemed on the verge of calling out a quizzical complaint when the wind rolled a cloud of smoke into his face and he retreated coughing. Ivanello, head bent so that his chestnut curls glinted in the firelight, smiled and played glissandos on his lute.

Ermaulde indignantly marched around the fire, to stand looking down at Ivanello. In a brittle voice she said: "Clissum is about to chant one of his odes. I suggest that you put aside your lute and listen."

"I will do so with pleasure," said Ivanello.

Ermaulde turned and marched back the way she had come. The three mimes jumped to their feet and strutted behind her, cheeks puffed out, elbows outspread, bellies thrust forward and knees jerking high. Ermaulde, becoming aware of the activity, turned, and the mimes capered away, to dance for five seconds with furious energy, like maenads, before they once again flung themselves down beside Ivanello.

Ermaulde, smiling a fixed smile, went off to converse with Clissum, and both sent scathing glances toward Ivanello, who, putting aside his lute, now gave free rein to his fondling of the mimes. Far from resenting his touch, they pressed ever more closely upon him.

Ivanello bent his head and kissed Rlys full on the mouth; instantly both Sush and Skasja thrust forward their faces for like treatment.

Cugel gave a croak of disgust. "The man is insufferable!"

Doctor Lalanke shook his head. "Candidly, I am surprised by their complaisance. They have never allowed me to touch them. Ah well, I see that Varmous has become restless; the evening draws to a close."

Varmous, who had risen to his feet, stood listening to the sounds of night. He went to inspect the guard fence, then addressed the travellers. "Do not become absent-minded! Do not walk in your sleep! Make no rendezvous in the forest! I am now going to my bed and I suggest the same for all of you, since tomorrow we travel long and far across the Ildish Waste."

Clissum would not be denied. Summoning all his dignity, he stepped forward. "I have heard several requests for another of my pieces, to which I shall now respond."

Ermaulde clapped her hands, but many of the others had gone off to their beds.

Clissum pursed his mouth against vexation. "I will now recite my Thirteenth Ode, subtitled: *Gaunt Are the Towers of My Mind.*" He arranged himself in a suitable posture, but the wind came in a great gust, causing the fire to wallow and flare. Clouds of smoke roiled around the area and those still present hurried away. Clissum threw his hands high in despair and retired from the scene.

Cugel spent a restless night. Several times he heard a distant cry expressing dejection, and once he heard a chuckling hooting conversation from the direction of the forest.

Varmous aroused the caravan at an early hour, while the pre-dawn sky still glowed purple. Porraig the steward served a breakfast of tea, scones and a savory mince of clams, barley, kangol and pennywort. As usual, Nissifer failed to make an appearance and this morning Ivanello was missing as well.

Porraig called down to Varmous, suggesting that he send Ivanello aboard for his breakfast, but a survey of the camp yielded nothing. Ivanello's possessions occupied their ordinary places; nothing seemed to be missing except Ivanello himself.

Varmous, sitting at a table, made a ponderous investigation, but no one could supply any information whatever. Varmous examined the ground near the guard fence, but discovered no signs of disturbance. He finally made an announcement. "Ivanello for all practical purposes has vanished into thin air. I discover no hint of foul play; still I cannot believe that he disappeared voluntarily. The only explanation would seem to be baneful magic. In truth, I am at a loss for any better explanation. Should anyone entertain theories, or even suspicions, please communicate them to me. Meanwhile, there is no point remaining here. We must keep to our schedule, and the caravan will now get under way. Drivers, bring up your farlocks! Cugel, to your post at the bow!''

The caravan moved out upon Ildish Waste, and the fate of Ivanello remained obscure.

The road, now little more than a track, led north to a fork; here the caravan veered eastward and proceeded beside the hills which rolled away as far as the eye could reach. The landscape was bleak and dry, supporting only a few stunted gong-trees, an occasional tumble of cactus, an isolated dendron, black or purple or red.

Halfway through the morning Varmous called up to the ship: ''Cugel, are you keeping a sharp watch?''

Cugel looked down over the gunwale. ''I could watch with more purpose if I knew what I was watching for.''

''You are looking for hostile nomads, especially those hidden in ambush.''

Cugel scanned the countryside. ''I see nothing answering to this description: only hills and waste, although far ahead I notice the dark line of a forest, or maybe it is only a river fringed with trees.''

''Very good, Cugel. Maintain your look-out.''

The day passed and the line of dark trees seemed to recede before them, and at sundown camp was made on a sandy area open to the sky.

As usual, a fire was built, but the disappearance of Ivanello weighed heavy, and though Varmous served out wine, no one drank with cheer, and conversation was pitched in low tones.

As before Varmous arranged his guard-fence. He spoke again to the company. ''The mystery remains profound! Since we are without a clue, I recommend everyone to extreme caution. Certainly, do not so much as approach the guard-fence!''

The night passed without incident. In the morning the caravan got under way in good time, with Cugel once more serving as look-out.

As the day went by, the countryside became somewhat less arid. The line of trees now could be seen to mark the course of a river wandering down from the hills and out across the waste.

Arriving at the riverbank the road turned abruptly south and followed the river to a stone bridge of five arches, where Varmous called a halt to allow the teamsters to water their farlocks. Cugel ordered the rope to shorten itself and so drew the *Avventura* down to the road. The 'premier' passengers alighted and wandered here and there to stretch their legs.

At the entrance to the bridge stood a monument ten feet tall, holding a bronze plaque to the attention of those who passed. The characters were illegible to Cugel. Gaulph Rabi thrust close his long nose, then shrugged and turned away. Doctor Lalanke, however, declared the script to be a version of Sarsounian, an influential dialect of the nineteenth acon, in common use for more than four thousand years.

"The text is purely ceremonial," said Doctor Lalanke. "It reads:

TRAVELERS! AS DRY SHOD YOU CROSS
THE THUNDERING TURMOIL OF THE RIVER SYK,
BE ADVISED THAT YOU HAVE BEEN ASSISTED
BY THE BENEFICENCE OF
KHAIVE, LORD-RULER OF KHARAD
AND
GUARDIAN OF THE UNIVERSE

As we can see, the River Syk no longer thunders a turmoil, but we can still acknowledge the generosity of King Khaive; indeed, it is wise to do so." And Doctor Lalanke performed a polite genuflection the monument.

"Superstition!" scoffed Gaulph Rabi. "At the Collegium we turn down our ears in reverence only to the Nameless Syncresis at the core of the Hub."

"So it may be," said Doctor Lalanke indifferently and moved away. Cugel looked from Gaulph Rabi to Doctor Lalanke, then quickly performed a genuflection before the monument.

"What?" cried the gaunt ecclesiarch. "You too, Cugel? I took you for a man of judgment!"

"That is precisely why I gave honor to the monument. I judged that the rite could do no harm and cost very little."

Varmous dubiously rubbed his nose, then made a ponderous salute of his own, to the patent disgust of Gaulph Rabi.

The farlocks were brought back to their traces; Cugel caused the *Avventura* to rise high in the air and the caravan proceeded across the bridge.

During the middle afternoon Cugel became drowsy and dropping his head upon his arms, dozed off into a light slumber. . . . Time passed and Cugel became uncomfortable. Blinking and yawning, he surveyed the countryside, and his attention was caught by stealthy movements behind a thicket of smoke-berry bushes which lined the road. Cugel leaned forward and perceived several dozen short swarthy men wearing baggy pantaloons, dirty vests of various colors and black kerchiefs tied around their heads. They carried spears and battle-hooks, and clearly intended harm upon the caravan.

Cugel shouted down to Varmous: "Halt! Prepare your weapons! Bandits hide in ambush behind yonder thicket!"

Varmous pulled up the caravan and blew a blast on his signal horn. The teamsters took up weapons as did many of the passengers and prepared to face an onslaught. Cugel brought the boat down so that the 'premier' passengers might also join the fight.

Varmous came over to the boat. "Exactly where is the ambush? How many lie in wait?"

Cugel pointed toward the ticket. "They crouch behind the smokeberry bushes, to the number of about twenty-three. They carry spears and snaffle-irons."

"Well done, Cugel! You have saved the caravan!" Varmous studied the terrain, then, taking ten men armed with swords, dart-guns and poison go-thithers, went out to reconnoiter.

Half an hour passed. Varmous, hot, dusty and irritated, returned with his squad. He spoke to Cugel: "Again, where did you think to observe this ambush?"

"As I told you: behind the thicket yonder."

"We combed the area and found neither bandits nor any sign of their presence."

Cugel looked frowningly toward the thicket. "They slipped away when they saw that we were forewarned."

"Leaving no traces? Are you sure of what you saw? Or were you having hallucinations?"

"Naturally I am sure of what I saw!" declared Cugel indignantly. "Do you take me for a fool?"

"Of course not," said Varmous soothingly. "Keep up the good work! Even if your savages were but phantasms, it is better to be safe than sorry. But next time look twice and verify before you cry out the alarm."

Cugel had no choice but to agree, and returned aboard the *Avventura*.

The caravan proceeded, past the now-tranquil thicket and Cugel once again kept an alert look-out.

The night passed without incident, but in the morning, when breakfast was served, Ermaulde failed to make an appearance.

As before Varmous searched the ship and the area enclosed by the guard-fence, but, like Ivanello, Ermaulde had disappeared as if into thin air. Varmous went so far as to knock on the door of Nissifer's cabin, to assure himself that she was still aboard.

"Who is it?" came the husky whisper.

"It is Varmous. Are you well?"

"I am well. I need nothing."

Varmous turned to Cugel, his broad face creased with worry. "I have never known such dreadful events! What is happening?"

Cugel spoke thoughtfully: "Neither Ivanello nor Ermaulde went off by choice: this is clear. They both rode the *Avventura*, which seems to indicate that the bane also resides aboard the ship."

"What! In the 'premier' class?"

"Such are the probabilities."

Varmous clenched his massive fist. "This harm must be learned and nailed to the counter!"

"Agreed! But how?"

"Through vigilance and care! At night no one must venture from his quarters, except to answer the call of nature."

"To find the evil-doer waiting in the privy? That is not the answer."

"Meanwhile, we cannot delay the caravan," muttered Varmous. "Cugel, to your post! Watch with care and discrimination."

The caravan once again set off to the east. The road skirted close under the hills, which now showed harsh outcrops of rock and occasional growths of gnarled acacia.

Doctor Lalanke sauntered forward and joined Cugel at the bow, and their conversation turned to the strange disappearances. Doctor Lalanke declared himself as mystified as everyone else. "There are endless possibilities, though none carry conviction. For instance, I could suggest that the ship itself is a harmful entity which during the night opens up its hold and ingests a careless passenger."

"We have searched the hold," said Cugel. "We found only stores, baggage and cockroaches."

"I hardly intended that you take the theory seriously. Still, if we contrived ten thousand theories, all apparently absurd, one among them almost certainly would be correct."

The three mimes came up to the bow and amused themselves by strutting back and forth with long loping bent-kneed strides. Cugel looked at them with disfavor. "What nonsense are they up to now?"

The three mimes wrinkled their noses, crossed their eyes and rounded their mouths into pursy circles, as if in soundless chortling, and looked toward Cugel sidelong as they pranced back and forth.

Doctor Lalanke chuckled. "It is their little joke; they think that they are imitating you, or so I believe."

Cugel turned coldly away, and the three mimes ran back down the deck. Doctor Lalanke pointed ahead to a billow of clouds hanging above the horizon. "They rise from Lake Zaol, beside Kaspara Vitatus, where the road turns north to Torqual."

"It is not my road! I journey south to Almery."

"Just so." Doctor Lalanke turned away and Cugel was left alone at his vigil. He looked around for the mimes, half-wishing that they would return and enliven the tedium, but they were engaged in a new and amusing game, tossing small objects down at the farlocks, which, when so struck, whisked high their tails.

Cugel resumed his watch. To the south, the rocky hillside, ever more steep. To the north, the Ildish Waste, an expanse streaked in subtle colors: dark pink, hazy black-gray, maroon, touched here and there with the faintest possible bloom of dark blue and green.

Time passed. The mimes continued their game, which the teamsters and even the passengers also seemed to enjoy; as the mimes tossed down bits of stuff, the teamsters and passengers jumped down to retrieve the objects.

Odd, thought Cugel. Why was every one so enthusiastic over a game so trifling? . . . One of the objects glinted of metal as it fell. It was, thought Cugel, about the size and shape of a terce. Surely the mimes would not be tossing terces to the teamsters? Where would they have obtained such wealth?

The mimes finished their game. The teamsters called up from below: "More! Continue the game! Why stop now?" The mimes performed a crazy gesticulation and tossed down an empty pouch, then went off to rest.

Peculiar! thought Cugel. The pouch in some respects resembled his own, which of course was safely tucked away in his tent. He glanced down casually, then looked once again more sharply.

The pouch was nowhere to be seen.

Cugel ran raging to Doctor Lalanke, where he sat on the hold conversing with Clissum. Cugel cried out: "Your wards made off with my pouch! They threw my terces down to the teamsters, and my other adjuncts as well, including a valuable pot of boot dressing, and finally the pouch itself!"

Doctor Lalanke raised his black eyebrows. "Indeed? The rascals! I wondered what could hold their attention so long."

"Please take this matter seriously! I hold you personally responsible! You must redress my losses."

Doctor Lalanke smilingly shook his head. "I regret your misfortune, Cugel, but I cannot repair all the wrongs of the world."

"Are they not your wards?"

"In a casual sense only. They are listed on the caravan manifest in their own names, which puts the onus for their acts upon Varmous. You may discuss the matter with him, or even the mimes themselves. If they took the pouch, let them repay the terces."

"These are not practical ideas!"

"Here is one which is most practical: return forward before we plunge headlong into danger!" Doctor Lalanke turned away and resumed his conversation with Clissum.

Cugel returned to the bow. He stared ahead, across the dismal landscape, considering how best to recover his losses. . . . A sinister flurry of movement caught his eye. Cugel jerked forward and focussed his gaze on the hillside, where a number of squat gray beings worked to pile heavy boulders where the hillside beetled over the road.

Cugel looked with care for several seconds. The creatures were plain in his vision: distorted half-human amloids with peaking scalps and neckless heads, so that their mouths opened directly into their upper torsos.

Cugel made a final inspection and at last called down the alarm: "Varmous! Rock-goblins on the hillside! Grave danger! Halt the caravan and sound the horn!"

Varmous pulled up his carriage and returned the hail. "What do you see? Where is the danger?"

Cugel waved his arms and pointed. "On that high bluff I see mountain goblins! They are piling rocks to tumble down upon the caravan!"

Varmous craned his neck and looked where Cugel had pointed. "I can see nothing."

"They are gray, like the rocks! They sidle askew and run crouching this way and that!"

Varmous rose in his seat and gave emergency signals to his teamsters. He pulled the ship down to the road. "We will give them a great surprise," he told Cugel, and called to the passengers. "Alight, if you please! I intend to attack the goblins from the air."

Varmous brought ten men armed with arrow-guns and fire-darts aboard the *Avventura*. He tied the mooring-line to a strong farlock. "Now, Cugel, let the rope extend so that we rise above the bluff and we will send down our compliments from above."

Cugel obeyed the order; the ship with its complement of armed men rose high into the air and drifted over the bluff.

Varmous stood in the bow. "Now: to the exact site of the ambush."

Cugel pointed. "Precisely there, in that tumble of rocks!"

Varmous inspected the hillside. "At the moment I see no goblins."

Cugel scanned the bluff with care, but the goblins had disappeared. "All to the good! They saw our preparations and abandoned their plans."

Varmous gave a surly grunt. "Are you certain of your facts? You are sure that you saw rock goblins?"

"Of course! I am not given to hysterics."

"Perhaps you were deceived by shadows among the rocks."

"Absolutely not! I saw them as clearly as I see you!"

Varmous looked at Cugel with thoughtful blue eyes. "Do not feel that I am chiding you. You apprehended danger and, quite properly, cried out the alarm, though apparently in error. I will not belabor the matter, except to point out that this lack of judiciousness wastes valuable time."

Cugel could find no answer to the imputations. Varmous went to the gunwhale and called down to the driver of the lead carriage. "Bring the caravan forward and past the bluff! We will mount guard to ensure absolute security."

The caravan moved past the bluff without untoward circumstance, whereupon the *Avventura* was lowered so that the 'premier' passengers might re-embark.

Varmous took Cugel aside. "Your work is beyond reproach; still, I have decided to augment the watch. Shilko, whom you see yonder, is a man of seasoned judgment. He will stand by your side, and each will validate the findings of the other. Shilko, step over here, if you please. You and Cugel must now work in tandem."

"That will be my pleasure," said Shilko, a round-faced stocky man with sand-colored hair and a fringe of curling whiskers. "I look forward to the association."

Cugel glumly took him aboard the ship, and, as the caravan moved ahead, the two went forward to the bow and took up their posts. Shilko, a man of affable volubility, spoke of everything imaginable in definitive detail. Cugel's responses were curt, which puzzled Shilko. In an aggrieved voice he explained: "When I am engaged in this kind of work, I like a bit of conversation to while away the time. Otherwise it is a bore to stand here looking out at nothing in particular. After awhile, one begins to observe mental figments and regard them as reality." He winked and grinned. "Eh, Cugel?"

Cugel thought Shilko's joke in poor taste and looked away.

"Ah well," said Shilko. "So goes the world."

At noon, Shilko went off to the mess-hall to take his lunch. He over-indulged himself both in food and wine, so that during the afternoon he became drowsy. He surveyed the landscape and told Cugel: "There is nothing out there but a lizard or two: this is my considered judgement, and now I propose to take a short nap. If you see anything, be sure to arouse me." He crawled into Cugel's tent and made himself comfortable, and Cugel was left to think bitter thoughts of his lost terces and discarded boot-dressing.

When the caravan halted for the night, Cugel went directly to Varmous. He cited the frivolous conduct of the mimes and complained of the losses he had suffered.

Varmous listened with a mild but somewhat detached interest. "Surely Doctor Lalanke intends a settlement?"

"This is the point at issue! He disclaims responsibility in part and in sum! He declares that you, as master of the caravan, must discharge all damages."

Varmous, whose attention had been wandering, became instantly alert. "He called on me to pay the losses?"

"Exactly so. I now present to you this bill of accounting."

Varmous folded his arms and took a quick step backward. "Doctor Lalanke's thinking is inept."

Cugel indignantly shook the accounting under Varmous' nose. "Are you telling me that you refuse to settle this obligation?"

"It has nothing to do with me! The deed occurred aboard your vessel the *Avventura*."

Cugel again thrust the bill upon Varmous. "Then at least you must serve this accounting upon Doctor Lalanke and levy the payment."

Varmous pulled at his chin. "That is not the correct procedure. You are master of the *Avventura*. Hence, in your official capacity, you must summon Doctor Lalanke to a hearing and there levy whatever charges you think proper."

Cugel looked dubiously toward Doctor Lalanke, where he stood in conversation with Clissum. "I suggest that we approach Doctor Lalanke together, and join our mutual authorities the better to compel justice."

Varmous backed away another step. "Do not involve me! I am only Varmous the wagoneer, who rolls innocently along the ground."

Cugel proposed further arguments, but Varmous put on a face of crafty obstinacy and would not be moved. Cugel finally went to a table where he drank wine and stared glumly into the fire.

The evening passed slowly. A somber mood oppressed the entire camp; tonight there were neither recitations, songs nor jokes, and the company sat around the fire, conversing in desultory undertones. An unspoken question occupied all minds: "Who will be the next to disappear?"

The fire burned low, and the company reluctantly went off to their beds, with many a glance over their shoulders and an exchange of nervous comments.

So the night passed. The star Achernar moved up the eastern quadrant and declined into the west. The farlocks grunted and snuffled as they slept. Far out on the waste a blue light flickered into existence for a few seconds, then died and was seen no more. The rim of the east flushed first purple, then the red of dark blood. After several vain attempts, the sun broke free of the horizon and floated into the sky.

With the rebuilding of the fire the caravan came to life. Breakfast was set out; farlocks were brought to their traces and preparations were made for departure.

Aboard the *Avventura* the passengers made their appearance. Each in turn looked from face to face as if half-expecting another disappearance. Porraig the steward served breakfast to all hands, and carried a tray to the aft cabin. He knocked. "Madame Nissifer, I have brought your breakfast. We are worried as to your health."

"I am well," came the whisper. "I wish nothing. You may go away."

After breakfast Cugel took Doctor Lalanke aside. "I have taken counsel with Varmous," said Cugel. "He assures me that, as master of the *Avventura*, I may make a demand on you for damages suffered as a result of your negligence. Here is the bill of account. You must pay over this sum at once."

Doctor Lalanke gave the bill a brief inspection. His black eyebrows peaked even higher than ever. "This item: amazing! 'Boot dressing, one pot. Value: one thousand terces.' Are you serious?"

"Naturally! The boot dressing contained a rare wax."

Doctor Lalanke returned the bill. "You must present this bill to the persons at fault: namely, Sush, Skasja and Rlys."

"What good will that do?"

Doctor Lalanke shrugged. "I could not hazard a guess. Still, I disassociate myself from the entire affair." He bowed and strolled off to join Clissum, in whom he found qualities compatible with his own.

Cugel went forward to the bow, where Shilko was already on duty. Shilko again showed a voluble tendency; Cugel, as before, replied in terse terms, and Shilko at last fell silent. The caravan meanwhile had moved into a region where hills rose to either side, with the road following the course of the valley between.

Shilko looked along the barren hillsides. "I see nothing in these parts to worry us. What of you, Cugel?"

"At the moment, I see nothing."

Shilko took a last look around the landscape. "Excuse me a moment; I have a message for Porraig." He departed and soon, from the galley. Cugel heard sounds of conviviality.

Somewhat later, Shilko returned, lurching to the wine he had consumed. He called out in a hearty voice: "Ahoy there, Captain Cugel! How go the hallucinations?"

"I do not understand your allusion," said Cugel frigidly.

"No matter! Such things can happen to anyone." Shilko scanned the hillsides. "Have you anything to report?"

"Nothing."

"Very good! That's the way to handle this job! A quick look here and a sharp glance there, then down to the galley for a taste of wine."

Cugel made no comment and Shilko, from boredom, took to cracking his knuckles.

At the noon meal Shilko again consumed more than was perhaps advisable, and during the afternoon became drowsy. "I will just catch forty winks to calm my nerves," he told Cugel. "Keep a close watch on the lizards and call me if anything more important appears." He crawled into Cugel's tent and presently began to snore.

Cugel leaned on the gunwale, formulating schemes to repair his fortunes. None seemed feasible, especially since Doctor Lalanke knew a few spells of elementary magic. . . . Peculiar, those dark shapes along the ridge! What could cause them to jerk and jump in such a fashion? As if tall black shadows were thrusting quickly high to peer down at the caravan, then dodging back down out of sight.

Cugel reached down and pulled at Shilko's leg. "Rouse yourself!"

Shilko emerged from the tent blinking and scratching his head. "What now? Has Porraig brought my afternoon wine?"

Cugel indicated the ridge. "What do you see?"

Shilko looked with red-rimmed eyes along the sky-line, but the shadows were now crouched behind the hills. He turned a quizzical gaze upon Cugel. "What do you perceive? Goblins disguised as pink rats? Or centipedes dancing the kazatska?"

"Neither," said Cugel shortly. "I saw what I believe be a band of wind-stick devils. They are now in hiding on the far side of the hill."

Shilko peered cautiously at Cugel and moved a step away. "Most interesting! How many did you see?"

"I could make no count, but we had best call out the alarm to Varmous."

Shilko looked again along the sky-line. "I see nothing. Might your nerves once more be playing you tricks?"

"Absolutely not!"

"Well, please make certain before you call me again." Shilko dropped to his hands and knees and crawled into the tent. Cugel looked down to Varmous, riding placidly on the lead carriage. He opened his mouth to call down the alarm, then gloomily thought better of it and resumed his vigil.

Minutes passed, and Cugel himself began to doubt the sightings.

The road passed beside a long narrow pond of alkali-green water which nourished several thickets of bristling salt-bush. Cugel leaned forward and focused his gaze upon the bushes, but their spindly stalks provided no cover. What of the lake itself? It seemed too shallow to hide any consequential danger.

Cugel straightened himself with a sense of work well done. He glanced up to the ridge, to discover that the wind-stick devils had reappeared in greater number than before, craning high to peer down at the caravan, then ducking quickly from view.

Cugel pulled at Shilko's leg. "The wind-stick devils have returned in force!"

Shilko backed from the tent and heaved himself erect. "What is it this time?"

Cugel indicated the ridge. "Look for yourself!"

The wind-stick devils, however, had completed their survey, and Shilko saw nothing. This time he merely shrugged wearily and prepared to resume his rest. Cugel however went to the gunwale and shouted down to Varmous: "Wind-stick devils, by the dozen! They gather on the other side of the ridge!"

Varmous halted his carriage. "Wind-stick devils? Where is Shilko?"

"I am here, naturally, keeping a keen look-out."

"What of these 'wind-stick devils'? Have you noticed them?"

"In all candour, and with due respect to Cugel, I must say that I have not seen them."

Varmous chose his words carefully. "Cugel, I am obliged to you for your alert warning, but this time I think that we will go forward. Shilko, continue the good work!"

The caravan proceeded along the road. Shilko yawned and prepared to resume his rest. "Wait!" cried Cugel in frustration. "Notice that gap in the hills yonder? If the devils choose to follow us, they must jump across the gap, and you will be sure to see them."

Shilko grudgingly resigned himself to the wait. "These fancies, Cugel, are a most unhealthy sign. Consider to what sorry extremes they may lead! For your own sake, you must curb the affliction. . . . Now: there is the gap! We are coming abreast. Look with great attention and tell me when you see devils jumping across."

The caravan drew abreast of the gap. In a flurry of great smoky shapes, the wind-stick devils leapt over the hill and down upon the caravan.

"Now!" said Cugel.

For a frozen instant Shilko stood with a trembling jaw, then he bawled down to Varmous: "Beware! Wind-stick devils are on the attack!"

Varmous failed to hear properly and looked up toward the boat. He discovered a blur of hurtling dark shapes, but now defense was impossible. The devils tramped back and forth among the wagons while teamsters and passengers fled into the chilly waters of the pond.

The devils wreaked all convenient damage upon the caravan, overturning wagons and carriages, kicking off wheels, scattering stores and baggage. Next, they turned their attention to the *Avventura*, but Cugel caused the rope to lengthen and the vessel floated high. The devils jumped up and clawed at the hull, but fell short by fifty feet. Giving up the attack, they seized all the farlocks, tucking them one under each arm, then jumped over the hill and were gone.

Cugel lowered the boat, while teamsters and passengers emerged from the pond. Varmous had been trapped under his overturned carriage and all hands were required to extricate him.

With difficulty Varmous raised himself to stand upon his bruised legs. He surveyed the damage and gave a despondent groan. "This is beyond understanding! Why are we so cursed?" He looked around the bedraggled company. "Where are the look-outs? . . . Cugel? Shilko? Be good enough to stand forward!"

Cugel and Shilko diffidently showed themselves. Shilko licked his lips and spoke earnestly: "I called out the alarm; all can testify to this! Otherwise the disaster might have been far worse!"

"You were dilatory; the devils were already upon us! What is your explanation?"

Shilko looked all around the sky. "It may sound strange but Cugel wanted to wait until the devils jumped across the gap."

Varmous turned to Cugel. "I am absolutely bewildered! Why would you not warn us of the danger?".

"I did so, if you will recall! When I first saw the devils, I considered calling the alarm, but—"

"This is most confusing," said Varmous. "You saw the devils previous to the occasion of your warning?"

"Certainly, but—"

Varmous, grimacing in pain, held up his hand. "I have heard enough. Cugel, your conduct has been unwise, to say the very least."

"That is not a sound judgment!" cried Cugel hotly.

Varmous made a weary gesture. "Is it not immaterial? The caravan is destroyed! We are left helpless out on the Ildish Waste! In another month the wind will blow sand over our bones."

Cugel looked down to his boots. They were scuffed and dull, but magic might still reside in them. He pitched his voice in tones of dignity. "The caravan can still proceed, through the courtesy of the excoriated and savagely denounced Cugel."

Varmous spoke sharply: "Please convey your exact meaning!"

"It is possible that magic still remains in my boots. Make ready your wagons and carriages. I will raise them into the air and we will continue as before."

Varmous at once became energetic. He instructed his teamsters, who brought as much order as possible to their wagons and carriages. Ropes were tied to each and the passengers took their places. Cugel, walking from vehicle to vehicle, kicked to apply that levitational force still clinging to his boots. The wagons and carriages drifted into the air; the teamsters took the ropes and waited for the signal. Varmous, whose bruised muscles and sprained joints prevented him from walking, elected to ride aboard the *Avventura*. Cugel started to follow, but Varmous stopped him.

"We need only a single look-out, a man of proved judgment, who will be Shilko. If I were not crippled, I would gladly tow the ship, but that duty must now devolve upon you. Take up the rope, Cugel, and lead the caravan along the road at your best speed."

Recognizing the futility of protest, Cugel seized the rope and marched off down the road, towing the *Avventura* behind him.

At sunset, the wagons and carriages were brought down and camp was made for the night. Slavoy, the chief teamster, under the supervision of Varmous, set out the guard-fence; a fire was built and wine was served to defeat the gloom of the company.

Varmous made a terse address. "We have suffered a serious setback and much damage has been done. Still, it serves no purpose to point the finger of blame. I have made calculations and taken advice from Doctor Lalanke, and I believe that four days of travel will bring us to Kaspara Vitatus, where repairs can be made. Until then, I hope that no one suffers undue inconvenience. A final remark! The events of today are now in the past, but two mysteries still oppress us: the disappearances of Ivanello and Ermaulde. Until these matters are clarified, all must be careful! Wander nowhere alone! At any suspicious circumstance, be sure to notify me."

The evening meal was served and a mood of almost frenetic gaiety overcame the company. Sush, Skasja and Rlys performed a set of bounding, hopping exercises and presently it became clear that they were mimicking the wind-stick devils.

Clissum became elevated by wine. "Is it not wonderful?" he cried out. "This excellent vintage has stimulated all three segments of my mind, so that while one observes this fire and the Ildish Waste beyond, another composes exquisitely beautiful odes, while the third weaves festoons of imaginary flowers to cover the nudity of passing nymphs, also imaginary!"

The ecclesiarch Gaulph Rabi listened to Clissum with disapproval and put four drops of aspergantium, rather than the customary three, into his own wine. "Is it necessary to go to such inordinate extremes?"

Clissum raised a wavering finger. "For the freshest flowers and the most supple nymphs, the answer is: emphatically yes!"

Gaulph Rabi spoke severely: "At the Collegium we feel that contemplation of even a few infinities is stimulation enough, at least for persons of taste and culture." He turned away to continue a conversation with Perruquil. Clissum mischievously sprinkled the back of Gaulph Rabi's gown with a pervasively odorous sachet, which caused the the austere ecclesiarch great perplexity to the end of the evening.

With the dying of the embers, the mood of the company again became subdued, and only reluctantly did they go off to their beds.

Aboard the *Avventura* Varmous and Shilko now occupied the berths which had been those of Ivanello and Ermaulde, while Cugel kept to his tent on the bow.

The night was quiet. Cugel, for all his fatigue, was unable to sleep. Midnight was marked by a muffled chime of the ship's clock.

Cugel dozed. An unknown period of time went by.

A small sound aroused Cugel to full alertness. For a moment he lay staring up into the dark; then, groping for his sword, he crawled to the opening of the tent.

The mast-head light cast a pale illumination along the deck. Cugel saw nothing unusual. No sound could be heard. What had aroused him?

For ten minutes Cugel crouched by the opening, then slowly returned to his cushion.

Cugel lay awake. . . . The faintest of sounds reached his ears: a click, a creak, a scrape. . . . Cugel again crawled to the opening of his tent.

The mast-head lamp cast as many shadows as puddles of light. One of the shadows moved and sidled out across the deck. It seemed to carry a parcel.

Cugel watched with an eery prickling at the back of his neck. The shadow jerked to the rail and with a most peculiar motion tossed its burden over the side. Cugel groped back into his tent for his sword, then crawled out upon the fore-deck.

He heard a scrape. The shadow had merged with other shadows, and could no longer be seen.

Cugel crouched in the dark and presently thought to hear a faint squealing sound, abruptly stilled.

The sound was not repeated.

After a time Cugel hunched back into the tent, and there kept vigil, cramped and cold. . . . With eyes open, he slept. A maroon beam from the rising sun glinted into his open eyes, startling him into full awareness.

With groans for twinges and aches, Cugel hauled himself erect. He donned his cloak and hat, buckled the sword around his waist and limped down to the main deck.

Varmous was only just emerging from his berth when Cugel peered in through the doorway. "What do you want?" growled Varmous. "Am I not even allowed time to adjust my garments?"

Cugel said: "Last night I saw sights and I heard sounds. I fear that we may discover another disappearance."

Varmous uttered a groan and a curse. "Who?"

"I do not know."

Varmous pulled on his boots. "What did you see and what did you hear?"

"I saw a shadow. It threw a parcel into the thicket. I heard a clicking sound, and then the scrape of a door. Later I heard a cry."

Varmous donned his rough cape, then pulled the flat broad-brimmed hat down over his golden curls. He limped out on deck. "I suppose that first of all we should count noses."

"All in good time," said Cugel. "First let us look into the parcel, which may tell us much or nothing."

"As you wish." The two descended to the ground. "Now then: where is the thicket?"

"Over here, behind the hull. If I had not been witness, we would never have known."

They circled the ship and Cugel clambered into the black fronds of the thicket. Almost at once he discovered the parcel and gingerly pulled it out into the open. The two stood looking down at the object, which was wrapped in soft blue fabric. Cugel touched it with his toe. "Do you recognize the stuff?"

"Yes. It is the cloak favored by Perruquil."

They looked down at the parcel in silence. Cugel said: "We now can guess the identity of the missing person."

Varmous grunted. "Open the parcel."

"You may do so if you like," said Cugel.

"Come now, Cugel!" protested Varmous. "You know that my legs cause me pain when I stoop!"

Cugel grimaced. Crouching, he twitched at the binding. The folds of the cloak fell back, to reveal two bundles of human bones, cleverly interlocked to occupy a minimum volume. "Amazing!" whispered Varmous. "Here is either magic or sheer paradox! How else can skull and pelvis be interlocked in such intricate fashion?"

Cugel was somewhat more critical. "The arrangement is not altogether elegant. Notice: Ivanello's skull is nested into Ermaulde's pelvis; similarly with Ermaulde's skull and Ivanello's pelvis. Ivanello especially would be annoyed by the carelessness."

Varmous muttered: "Now we know the worst. We must take action."

With one accord the two looked up to the hull of the ship. At the port-hole giving into the aft cabin there was movement as the hanging was drawn aside, and for an instant a luminous eye looked down at them. Then the curtain dropped and all was as before.

Varmous and Cugel returned around the ship. Varmous spoke in a heavy voice. "You, as master of the *Avventura*, will wish to lead the decisive action. I will of course cooperate in every respect."

Cugel pondered. "First we must remove the passengers from the ship. Then you must bring up a squad of armed men and lead them to the door, where you will issue an ultimatum. I will stand steadfast nearby, and—"

Varmous held up his hand. "By reason of sore legs I cannot issue such an ultimatum."

"Well then, what do you suggest?"

Varmous considered a moment or two, then proposed a plan which required, in essence, that Cugel, using the full authority of his rank, should advance upon the door and, if need be, force an entrance—a plan which Cugel rejected for technical reasons.

At last the two formulated a program which both considered feasible. Cugel went to order the ship's passengers to the ground. As he had expected, Perruquil was not among their number.

Varmous assembled and instructed his crew. Shilko, armed with a sword, was posted as guard before the door, while Cugel mounted to the after-deck. A pair of trained carpenters climbed upon tables and boarded over the portholes, while others nailed planks across the door, barring egress.

From the lake buckets of water were transferred along a human chain and passed up to the afterdeck, where the water was poured into the cabin through a vent.

From within the cabin an angry silence prevailed. Then presently, as water continued to pour in through the vent, a soft hissing and clicking began to be heard, and then a furious whisper: "I declare a nuisance! Let the water abate!"

Shilko, before mounting guard, had stepped into the galley for a few swallows of wine to warm his blood. Posturing and waving his sword before the door, he cried out: "Black hag, your time has come! You shall drown like a rat in a sack!"

For a period the sounds within were stilled, and nothing could be heard but the splash of water into water. Then once again: a hissing and clicking, at an ominous pitch, and a set of rasping vocables.

Shilko, emboldened both by wine and the planks across the door, called out: "Odorous witch! Drown more quietly, or I, Shilko, will cut out both your tongues!" He flourished his sword and cut a caper, and all the while the buckets were busy.

From within the cabin something pressed at the door, but the planks held secure. Again from within came a heavy thrust; the planks groaned and water spurted through cracks. Then a third impact, and the planks burst apart. Foul-smelling water washed out upon the deck; behind came Nissifer. Clothed in neither gown, hat nor veil, she stood revealed as a burly black creature of hybrid character, half sime and half bazil, with a bristle of black fur between the eyes. From a rusty black thorax depended the segmented abdomen of a wasp; down the back hung sheaths of black chitin-like wing-cases. Four thin black arms ended in long thin human hands; thin shanks of black chitin and peculiar padded feet supported the thorax with the abdomen hanging between.

The creature took a step forward. Shilko emitted a strangled yell and, stumbling backwards, fell to the deck. The creature jumped forward to stand on his arms, then, squatting, drove its sting into his chest. Shilko uttered a shrill cry, rolled clear, turned several frantic somersaults, fell to the ground, bounded blindly to the lake and thrashed here and there in the water, and at last became still. Almost at once the corpse began to bloat.

Aboard the *Avventura*, the creature named Nissifer turned and started to re-enter the cabin, as if satisfied that it had rebuffed its enemies. Cugel, on the afterdeck, slashed down with his sword and the blade, trailing a thousand sparkling motes, cut through Nissifer's left eye and into the thorax. Nissifer whistled in pain and surprise, and stood back the better to identify its assailant. It croaked: "Ah Cugel! You have hurt me; you shall die by a stench."

With a great pounding flutter of wing-cases, Nissifer sprang up to the afterdeck. In a panic Cugel retreated behind the binnacle. Nissifer advanced, the segmented abdomen squirming up and forward between the thin black legs, revealing the long yellow sting.

Cugel picked up one of the empty buckets and flung it into Nissifer's face; then, while Nissifer fought away the bucket, Cugel jumped forward and with a great sweep, cut the vincus, so as to separate abdomen from thorax.

The abdomen, falling to the deck, writhed and worked and presently rolled down the companion-way to the deck.

Nissifer ignored the mutilation and came forward, dripping a thick yellow liquid from its vincus. It lurched toward the binnacle and thrust out its long black arms. Cugel backed away, hacking at the arms. Nissifer shrieked and lunging forward, swept the sword from Cugel's grasp.

Nissifer stepped forward with clicking wing-cases, and seizing Cugel, drew him close. "Now, Cugel, you will learn the meaning of fetor."

Cugel bent his head and thrust 'Spatterlight' against Nissifer's thorax.

When Varmous, sword in hand, climbed the companionway, he found Cugel leaning limp-legged against the taff-rail.

Varmous looked around the afterdeck. "Where is Nissifer?"

"Nissifer is gone."

Four days later the caravan came down from the hills to the shores of Lake Zaol. Across the glimmering water eight white towers half-hidden in pink haze marked the site of Kaspara Vitatus, sometimes known as 'The City of Monuments.'

The caravan circled the lake and approached the city by the Avenue of the Dynasties. After passing under a hundred or more of the famous monuments, the caravan arrived at the center of town. Varmous led the way to his usual resort, the Kanbaw Inn, and the weary travelers prepared to refresh themselves.

While ordering the cabin occupied by Nissifer, Cugel had come upon a leather sack containing over a hundred terces, which he took into his private possession. Varmous, however, insisted upon helping Cugel explore the effects of Ivanello, Ermaulde, and Perruquil. They discovered another three hundred terces which they shared in equal parts. Varmous took possession of Ivanello's wardrobe, while Cugel was allowed to keep the milk-opal ear-bangle, which he had coveted from the first.

Cugel also offered Varmous full title to the *Avventura* for five hundred terces. "The price is an absolute bargain! Where else will you find a sound vessel, fully outfitted and well-found, for such a price?"

Varmous only chuckled. "If you offered to provide me a goiter of superlative size for ten terces, would I buy, bargain or not?"

"We have here a distinctly different proposition," Cugel pointed out.

"Bah! The magic is failing. Every day the ship sags more heavily to the ground. In the middle of the wilderness what good is a ship which will neither float in the air nor sail in the sand? In a foolhardy spirit, I will offer you a hundred terces, no more."

"Absurd!" scoffed Cugel, and there the matter rested.

Varmous went out to see to the repair of his wagons and discovered a pair of lake fishermen inspecting the *Avventura* with interest. In due course Varmous succeeded in obtaining a firm offer for the vessel, to the amount of six hundred and twenty-five terces.

Cugel, meanwhile, drank beer at the Kanbaw Inn. As he sat musing, into the common room strode a band of seven men with harsh features and rough voices. Cugel looked twice at the leader, then a third time, and finally recognized Captain Wiskich, one-time owner of the *Avventura*. Captain Wiskich evidently had picked up the trail of the vessel and had come in hot pursuit to recover his property.

Cugel quietly departed the common room and went in search of Varmous, who, as it happened, was also on the lookout for Cugel. They met in front of the inn. Varmous wanted to drink beer in the common room, but Cugel led him across the avenue to a bench from which they could watch the sun set into Lake Zaol.

Presently the *Avventura* was mentioned and with surprising ease agreement was reached. Varmous paid over two hundred and fifty terces for full title to the vessel.

The two parted on the best of terms. Varmous went off to locate the fishermen, while Cugel, disguising himself in a hooded cloak and a false beard, took lodging at the Green Star Inn, using the identity Tichenor, a purveyor of antique grave-markers.

During the evening a great tumult was heard, first from the neighborhood of the docks and then at the Kanbaw Inn, and persons coming into the Green Star common room identified the rioters as a group of local fishermen in conflict with a band of newly arrived travelers, with the eventual involvement of Varmous and his teamsters.

Order was restored at last. Not long after, two men looked into the Green Star common room. One called out in a rough voice: "Is there anyone here named Cugel?"

The other spoke with more restraint: "Cugel is urgently needed. If he is here, let him step forward."

When no one responded the two men departed and Cugel retired to his room.

In the morning Cugel went to a nearby hostlery where he purchased a steed for his journey south. The ostler's boy then conducted him to a shop where Cugel bought a new pouch, a pair of saddle-bags into which he packed necessities for his journey. His hat had become shabby and also carried a stench where it had pressed against Nissifer. Cugel removed 'Spatterlight', wrapped it in heavy cloth and tucked it into his new pouch. He bought a short-billed cap of dark green velvet, which, while far from ostentatious, pleased Cugel with its air of restrained elegance.

Cugel paid his account from the terces in the leather sack from Nissifer's cabin; it also exhaled a stench. Cugel started to buy a new sack but was dissuaded by the ostler's boy. "Why waste your terces? I have a sack much like this one which you may have free of charge."

"That is generous of you," said Cugel, and the two returned to the hostlery, where Cugel transferred his terces into the new sack.

The steed was brought forth. Cugel mounted and the boy adjusted the saddle-bags in place. At this moment two men of harsh appearance entered the hostlery, and approached with quick strides. "Is your name Cugel?"

"Definitely not!" declared Cugel. "By no means! I am Tichenor! What do you want with this Cugel?"

"None of your affair. Come along with us; you have an unconvincing manner."

"I have no time for pranks," said Cugel. "Boy, you may hand me up my leather sack." The boy obeyed and Cugel secured the sack to his saddle. He started to ride away but the men interfered. "You must come with us."

"Impossible," said Cugel. "I am on my way to Torqual." He kicked one in the nose and the other in the belly and rode at speed down the Avenue of the Dynasties and so departed Kaspara Vitatus.

After a period he halted, to learn what pursuit, if any, had been offered.

An unpleasant odor reached his nostrils, emanating from the leather sack. To his perplexity, it proved to be the same sack he had taken from Nissifer's cabin.

Cugel anxiously looked within, to find, not terces, but small objects of corroded metal.

Cugel uttered a groan of dismay and, turning his steed, started to return to Kaspara Vitatus, but now he noticed a dozen men crouched low in their saddles coming after him in hot pursuit.

Cugel uttered another wild cry of fury and frustration. He cast the leather sack into the ditch and turning his steed once more rode south at full speed.

Chapter V

FROM KASPARA VITATUS TO CUIRNIF

1

The Seventeen Virgins

The chase went far and long, and led into that dismal tract of bone-colored hills known as the Pale Rugates. Cugel finally used a clever trick to baffle pursuit, sliding from his steed and hiding among the rocks while his enemies pounded past in chase of the riderless mount.

Cugel lay in hiding until the angry band returned toward Kaspara Vitatus, bickering among themselves. He emerged into the open; then, after shaking his fist and shouting curses after the now distant figures, he turned and continued south through the Pale Rugates.

The region was as stark and grim as the surface of a dead sun, and thus avoided by such creatures as sindics, shambs, erbs and visps, for Cugel a single and melancholy source of satisfaction.

Step after step marched Cugel, one leg in front of the other: up slope to overlook an endless succession of barren swells, down again into the hollow where at rare intervals a seep of water nourished a sickly vegetation. Here Cugel found ramp, burdock, squallix and an occasional newt, which sufficed against starvation.

Day followed day. The sun rising cool and dim swam up into the dark-blue sky, from time to time seeming to flicker with a film of blue-black luster, finally to settle like an enormous purple pearl into the west. When dark made further progress impractical, Cugel wrapped himself in his cloak and slept as best he could.

On the afternoon of the seventh day Cugel limped down a slope into an ancient orchard. Cugel found and devoured a few withered hag-apples, then set off along the trace of an old road.

The track proceeded a mile, to lead out upon a bluff over-looking a broad plain. Directly below a river skirted a small town, curved away to the southwest and finally disappeared into the haze.

Cugel surveyed the landscape with keen attention. Out upon the plain he saw carefully tended garden plots, each precisely square and of identical size; along the river drifted a fisherman's punt. A placid scene, thought Cugel. On the other hand, the town was built to a strange and archaic architecture, and the scrupulous precision with which the houses surrounded the square suggested a like inflexibility in the inhabitants. The houses themselves were no less uniform, each a construction of two, or three, or even four squat bulbs of diminishing size, one on the other, the lowest always painted blue, the second dark red, the third and fourth respectively a dull mustard ocher and black; and each house terminated in a spire of fancifully twisted iron rods, of greater or lesser height. An inn on the riverbank showed a style somewhat looser and easier, with a pleasant garden surrounding. Along the river road to the east Cugel now noticed the approach of a caravan of six high-wheeled wagons, and his uncertainty dissolved; the town was evidently tolerant of strangers, and Cugel confidently set off down the hill.

At the outskirts to town he halted and drew forth his old purse, which he yet retained though it hung loose and limp. Cugel examined the contents: five terces, a sum hardly adequate to his needs. Cugel reflected a moment, then collected a handful of pebbles which he dropped into the purse, to create a reassuring rotundity. He dusted his breeches, adjusted his green hunter's cap, and proceeded.

He entered the town without challenge or even attention. Crossing the square, he halted to inspect a contrivance even more peculiar than the quaint architecture: a stone fire-pit in which several logs blazed high, rimmed by five lamps on iron stands, each with five wicks, and above an intricate linkage of mirrors and lenses, the purpose of which surpassed Cugel's comprehension. Two young men tended the device with diligence, trimming the twenty-five wicks, prodding the fire, adjusting screws and levers which in turn controlled the mirrors and lenses. They wore what appeared to be the local costume: voluminous blue knee-length breeches, red shirts, brass-buttoned black vests and broad-brimmed hats; after disinterested glances they paid Cugel no heed, and he continued to the inn.

In the adjacent garden two dozen folk of the town sat at tables, eating and drinking with great gusto. Cugel watched them a moment or two; their punctilio and elegant gestures suggested the manners of an age far past. Like their houses, they were a sort unique to Cugel's experience, pale and thin, with egg-shaped heads, long noses, dark expressive eyes and ears cropped in various styles. The men were uniformly bald and their pates glistened in the red sunlight. The women parted their black hair in the middle, then cut it abruptly short a half-inch above the ears: a style which Cugel considered unbecoming. Watching the folk eat and drink, Cugel was unfavorably reminded of the fare which had sustained him across the Pale Rugatès, and he gave no further thought to his terces. He strode into the garden and seated himself at a table. A portly man in a blue apron approached, frowning somewhat at Cugel's disheveled appearance. Cugel immediately brought forth two terces which he handed to the man. "This is for yourself, my good fellow, to insure expeditious service. I have just completed an arduous journey; I am famished with hunger. You may bring me a platter identical to that which the gentleman yonder is enjoying, together with a selection of side-dishes and a bottle of wine. Then be so good as to ask the innkeeper to prepare me a comfortable chamber." Cugel carelessly brought forth his purse and dropped it upon the table where its weight produced an impressive implication. "I will also require a bath, fresh linen and a barber."

"I myself am Maier the innkeeper," said the portly man in a gracious voice. "I will see to your wishes immediately."

"Excellent," said Cugel. "I am favorably impressed with your establishment, and perhaps will remain several days."

The innkeeper bowed in gratification and hurried off to supervise the preparation of Cugel's dinner.

Cugel made an excellent meal, though the second course, a dish of crayfish stuffed with mince and slivers of scarlet mangoneel, he found a trifle too rich. The roast fowl however could not be faulted and the wine pleased Cugel to such an extent that he ordered a second flask. Maier the innkeeper served the bottle himself and accepted Cugel's compliments with a trace of complacency. "There is no better wine in Gundar! It is admittedly expensive, but you are a person who appreciates the best."

"Precisely true," said Cugel. "Sit down and take a glass with me. I confess to curiosity in regard to this remarkable town."

The innkeeper willingly followed Cugel's suggestion. "I am puzzled that you find Gundar remarkable. I have lived here all my life and it seems ordinary enough to me."

"I will cite three circumstances which I consider worthy of note," said Cugel, now somewhat expansive by reason of the wine. "First: the bulbous construction of your buildings. Secondly: the contrivance of lenses above the fire, which at the very least must stimulate a stranger's interest. Thirdly: the fact that the men of Gundar are all stark bald."

The innkeeper nodded thoughtfully. "The architecture at least is quickly explained. The ancient Gunds lived in enormous gourds. When a section of the wall became weak it was replaced with a board, until in due course the folk found themselves living in houses fashioned completely of wood, and the style has persisted. As for the fire and the projectors, do you not know the world-wide Order of Solar Emosynaries? We stimulate the vitality of the sun; so long as our beam of sympathetic vibration regulates solar combustion, it will never expire. Similar stations exist at other locations: at Blue Azor; on the Isle of Brazel; at the walled city Munt; and in the observatory of the Grand Starkeeper at Vir Vassilis."

Cugel shook his head sadly. "I hear that conditions have changed. Brazel has long since sunk beneath the waves. Munt was destroyed a thousand years ago by Dystropes. I have never heard of either Blue Azor or Vir Vassilis, though I am widely traveled. Possibly, here at Gundar, you are the solitary Solar Emosynaries yet in existence."

"This is dismal news," declared Maier. "The noticeable enfeeblement of the sun is hereby explained. Perhaps we had best double the fire under our regulator."

Cugel poured more wine. "A question leaps to mind. If, as I suspect, this is the single Solar Emosynary station yet in operation, who or what regulates the sun when it has passed below the horizon?"

The innkeeper shook his head. "I can offer no explanation. It may be that during the hours of night the sun itself relaxes and, as it were, sleeps, although this is of course sheerest speculation."

"Allow me to offer another hypothesis," said Cugel. "Conceivably the waning of the sun has advanced beyond all possibility of regulation, so that your efforts, though formerly useful, are now ineffective."

Maier threw up his hands in perplexity. "These complications surpass my scope, but yonder stands the Nolde Huruska." He directed Cugel's attention to a large man with a deep chest and bristling black beard, who stood at the entrance. "Excuse me a moment." He rose to his feet and approaching the Nolde spoke for several minutes, indicating Cugel from time to time. The Nolde finally made a brusque gesture and marched across the garden to confront Cugel. He spoke in a heavy voice: "I understand you to assert that no Emosynaries exist other than ourselves?"

"I stated nothing so definitely," said Cugel, somewhat on the defensive. "I remarked that I had traveled widely and that no other such 'Emosynary' agency has come to my attention; and I innocently speculated that possibly none now operate."

''At Gundar we conceive 'innocence' as a positive quality, not merely an insipid absence of guilt,'' stated the Nolde. ''We are not the fools that certain untidy ruffians might suppose.''

Cugel suppressed the hot remark which rose to his lips, and contented himself with a shrug. Maier walked away with the Nolde and for several minutes the two men conferred, with frequent glances in Cugel's direction. Then the Nolde departed and the innkeeper returned to Cugel's table. ''A somewhat brusque man, the Nolde of Gundar,'' he told Cugel, ''but very competent withal.''

''It would be presumptuous of me to comment,'' said Cugel. ''What, precisely, is his function?''

''At Gundar we place great store upon precision and methodicity,'' explained Maier. ''We feel that the absence of order encourages disorder; and the official responsible for the inhibition of caprice and abnormality is the Nolde . . . What was our previous conversation? Ah yes, you mentioned our notorious baldness. I can offer no definite explanation. According to our savants, the condition signifies the final perfection of the human race. Other folk give credence to an ancient legend. A pair of magicians, Astherlin and Mauldred, vied for the favor of the Gunds. Astherlin promised the boon of extreme hairiness, so that the folk of Gundar need never wear garments. Mauldred, to the contrary, offered the Gunds baldness, with all the consequent advantages, and easily won the contest; in fact Mauldred became the first Nolde of Gundar, the post now filled, as you know, by Huruska.'' Maier the innkeeper pursed his lips and looked off across the garden. ''Huruska, a distrustful sort, has reminded me of my fixed rule to ask all transient guests to settle their accounts on a daily basis. I naturally assured him of your complete reliability, but simply in order to appease Huruska, I will tender the reckoning in the morning.''

''This is tantamount to an insult,'' declared Cugel haughtily. ''Must we truckle to the whims of Huruska? Not I, you may be assured! I will settle my account in the usual manner.''

The innkeeper blinked. ''May I ask how long you intend to stay at Gundar?''

''My journey takes me south, by the most expeditious transport available, which I assume to be riverboat.''

''The town Lumarth lies ten days by caravan across the Lirrh Aing. The Isk river also flows past Lumarth, but is judged inconvenient by virtue of three intervening localities. The Lallo Marsh is infested with stinging insects; the tree-dwarfs of the Santalba Forest pelt passing boats with refuse; and the Desperate Rapids shatter both bones and boats.''

"In this case I will travel by caravan," said Cugel. "Meanwhile I will remain here, unless the persecutions of Huruska become intolerable."

Maier licked his lips and looked over his shoulder. "I assured Huruska that I would adhere to the strict letter of my rule. He will surely make a great issue of the matter unless—"

Cugel made a gracious gesture. "Bring me seals. I will close up my purse which contains a fortune in opals and alumes. We will deposit the purse in the strong-box and you may hold it for surety. Even Huruska cannot now protest!"

Maier held up his hands in awe. "I could not undertake so large a responsibility!"

"Dismiss all fear," said Cugel. "I have protected the purse with a spell; the instant a criminal breaks the seal the jewels are transformed into pebbles."

Maier dubiously accepted Cugel's purse on these terms. They jointly saw the scales applied and the purse deposited into Maier's strong-box.

Cugel now repaired to his chamber, where he bathed, commanded the services of a barber and dressed in fresh garments. Setting his cap at an appropriate angle, he strolled out upon the square.

His steps led him to the Solar Emosynary station. As before, two young men worked diligently, one stoking the blaze and adjusting the five lamps, while the other held the regulatory beam fixed upon the low sun.

Cugel inspected the contrivance from all angles, and presently the person who fed the blaze called out: "Are you not that notable traveler who today expressed doubts as to the efficacy of the Emosynary System?"

Cugel spoke carefully: "I told Maier and Huruska this: that Brazel is sunk below the Melantine Gulf and almost gone from memory; that the walled city Munt was long ago laid waste; that I am acquainted with neither Blue Azor, nor Vir Vassilis. These were my only positive statements."

The young fire-stoker petulantly threw an arm-load of logs into the fire-pit. "Still we are told that you consider our efforts impractical."

"I would not go so far," said Cugel politely. "Even if the other Emosynary agencies are abandoned, it is possible that the Gundar regulator suffices; who knows?"

"I will tell you this," declared the stoker. "We work without recompense, and in our spare time we must cut and transport fuel. The process is tedious.''

The operator of the aiming device amplified his friend's complaint. ''Huruska and the elders do none of the work; they merely ordain that we toil, which of course is the easiest part of the project. Janred and I are of a sophisticated new generation; on principle we reject all dogmatic doctrines. I for one consider the Solar Emosynary system a waste of time and effort.''

''If the other agencies are abandoned,'' argued Janred the stoker, ''who or what regulates the sun when it has passed beyond the horizon? The system is pure balderdash.''

The operator of the lenses declared: ''I will now demonstrate as much, and free us all from this thankless toil!'' He worked a lever. ''Notice I direct the regulatory beam away from the sun. Look! It shines as before, without the slightest attention on our part!''

Cugel inspected the sun, and for a fact it seemed to glow as before, flickering from time to time, and shivering like an old man with the ague. The two young men watched with similar interest, and as minutes passed, they began to murmur in satisfaction. ''We are vindicated! The sun has not gone out!''

Even as they watched, the sun, perhaps fortuitously, underwent a cachectic spasm, and lurched alarmingly toward the horizon. Behind them sounded a bellow of outrage and the Nolde Huruska ran forward. ''What is the meaning of this irresponsibility? Direct the regulator aright and instantly! Would you have us groping for the rest of our lives in the dark?''

The stoker resentfully jerked his thumb toward Cugel. ''He convinced us that the system was unnecessary, and that our work was futile.''

''What!'' Huruska swung his formidable body about and confronted Cugel. ''Only hours ago you set foot in Gundar, and already you are disrupting the fabric of our existence! I warn you, our patience is not illimitable! Be off with you and do not approach the Emosynary agency a second time!''

Choking with fury, Cugel swung on his heel and marched off across the square.

At the caravan terminal he inquired as to transport southward, but the caravan which had arrived at noon would on the morrow depart eastward the way it had come.

Cugel returned to the inn and stepped into the tavern. He noticed three men playing a card game and posted himself as an observer. The game proved to be a simple version of Zampolio, and presently Cugel asked if he might join the play. "But only if the stakes are not too high," he protested. "I am not particularly skillful and I dislike losing more than a terce or two."

"Bah," exclaimed one of the players. "What is money? Who will spend it when we are dead?"

"If we take all your gold, then you need not carry it further," another remarked jocularly.

"All of us must learn," the third player assured Cugel. "You are fortunate to have the three premier experts of Gundar as instructors."

Cugel drew back in alarm. "I refuse to lose more than a single terce!"

"Come now! Don't be a prig!"

"Very well," said Cugel. "I will risk it. But these cards are tattered and dirty. By chance I have a fresh set in my pouch."

"Excellent! The game proceeds!"

Two hours later the three Gunds threw down their cards, gave Cugel long hard looks, then as if with a single mind rose to their feet and departed the tavern. Inspecting his gains, Cugel counted thirty-two terces and a few odd coppers. In a cheerful frame of mind he retired to his chamber for the night.

In the morning, as he consumed his breakfast, he noticed the arrival of the Nolde Huruska, who immediately engaged Maier the innkeeper in conversation. A few minutes later Huruska approached Cugel's table and stared down at Cugel with a somewhat menacing grin, while Maier stood anxiously a few paces to the rear.

Cugel spoke in a voice of strained politeness: "Well, what is it this time? The sun has risen; my innocence in the matter of the regulatory beam has been established."

"I am now concerned with another matter. Are you acquainted with the penalties for fraud?"

Cugel shrugged. "The matter is of no interest to me."

"They are severe and I will revert to them in a moment. First, let me inquire: did you entrust to Maier a purse purportedly containing valuable jewels?"

"I did indeed. The propery is protected by a spell, I may add; if the seal is broken the gems become ordinary pebbles."

Huruska exhibited the purse. "Notice, the seal is intact. I cut a slit in the leather and looked within. The contents were then and are now—" with a flourish Huruska turned the purse out upon the table "—pebbles identical to those in the road yonder."

Cugel exclaimed in outrage: "The jewels are now worthless rubble! I hold you responsible and you must make recompense!"

Huruska uttered an offensive laugh. "If you can change gems to pebbles, you can change pebbles to gems. Maier will now tender the bill. If you refuse to pay, I intend to have you nailed into the enclosure under the gallows until such time as you change your mind."

"Your insinuations are both disgusting and absurd," declared Cugel. "Innkeeper, present your account! Let us finish with this farrago once and for all."

Maier came forward with a slip of paper. "I make the total to be eleven terces, plus whatever gratuities might seem in order."

"There will be no gratuities," said Cugel. "Do you harass all your guests in this fashion?" He flung eleven terces down upon the table. "Take your money and leave me in peace."

Maier sheepishly gathered up the coins; Huruska made an inarticulate sound and turned away. Cugel, upon finishing his breakfast, went out once more to stroll across the square. Here he met an individual whom he recognized to be the pot-boy in the tavern, and Cugel signaled him to a halt. "You seem an alert and knowledgeable fellow," said Cugel. "May I inquire your name?"

"I am generally known as 'Zeller'."

"I would guess you to be well-acquainted with the folk of Gundar."

"I consider myself well-informed. Why do you ask?"

"First," said Cugel, "let me ask if you care to turn your knowledge to profit?"

"Certainly, so long as I evade the attention of the Nolde."

"Very good. I notice a disused booth yonder which should serve our purpose. In one hour we shall put our enterprise into operation."

Cugel returned to the inn where at his request Maier brought a board, brush and paint. Cugel composed a sign:

THE EMINENT SEER CUGEL
COUNSELS, INTERPRETS, PROGNOSTICATES
ASK! YOU WILL BE ANSWERED!
CONSULTATIONS: THREE TERCES.

Cugel hung the sign above the booth, arranged curtains and waited for customers. The pot-boy, meanwhile, had inconspicuously secreted himself at the back.

Almost immediately folk crossing the square halted to read the sign. A woman of early middle-age presently came forward.

"Three terces is a large sum. What results can you guarantee?"

"None whatever, by the very nature of things. I am a skilled voyant, I have acquaintance with the arts of magic, but knowledge comes to me from unknown and uncontrollable sources."

The woman paid over her money. "Three terces is cheap if you can resolve my worries. My daughter all her life has enjoyed the best of health but now she ails, and suffers a morose condition. All my remedies are to no avail. What must I do?"

"A moment, madam, while I meditate." Cugel drew the curtain and leaned back to where he could hear the pot-boy's whispered remarks, then once again drew aside the curtains.

"I have made myself one with the cosmos! Knowledge has entered my mind! Your daughter Dilian is pregnant. For an additional three terces I will supply the father's name."

"This is a fee I pay with pleasure," declared the woman grimly. She paid, received the information and marched purposefully away.

Another woman approached, paid three terces, and Cugel addressed himself to her problem: "My husband assured me that he had put by a canister of gold coins against the future, but upon his death I could find not so much as a copper. Where has he hidden the gold?"

Cugel closed the curtains, took counsel with the pot-boy, and again appeared to the woman. "I have discouraging news for you. Your husband Finister spent much of his hoarded gold at the tavern. With the rest he purchased an amethyst brooch for a woman named Varletta."

The news of Cugel's remarkable abilities spread rapidly and trade was brisk. Shortly before noon, a large woman, muffled and veiled, approached the booth, paid three terces, and asked in a high-pitched, if husky, voice: "Read me my fortune!"

Cugel drew the curtains and consulted the pot-boy, who was at a loss. "It is no one I know. I can tell you nothing."

"No matter," said Cugel. "My suspicions are verified." He drew aside the curtain. "The portents are unclear and I refuse to take your money." Cugel returned the fee. "I can tell you this much: you are an individual of domineering character and no great intelligence. Ahead lies what? Honors? A long voyage by water? Revenge on your enemies? Wealth? The image is distorted; I may be reading my own future."

The woman tore away her veils and stood revealed as the Nolde Huruska. "Master Cugel, you are lucky indeed that you returned my money, otherwise I would have taken you up for deceptive practices. In any event, I deem your activities mischievous, and contrary to the public interest. Gundar is in an uproar because of your revelations; there will be no more of them. Take down your sign, and be happily thankful that you have escaped so easily."

"I will be glad to terminate my enterprise," said Cugel with dignity. "The work is taxing."

Huruska stalked away in a huff. Cugel divided his earnings with the pot-boy, and in a spirit of mutual satisfaction they departed the booth.

Cugel dined on the best that the inn afforded, but later when he went into the tavern he discovered a noticeable lack of amiability among the patrons and presently went off to his chamber.

The next morning as he took breakfast a caravan of ten wagons arrived in town. The principal cargo appeared to be a bevy of seventeen beautiful maidens, who rode upon two of the wagons. Three other wagons served as dormitories, while the remaining five were loaded with stores, trunks, bales and cases. The caravan master, a portly mild-seeming man with flowing brown hair and a silky beard, assisted his delightful charges to the ground and led them all to the inn, where Maier served up an ample breakfast of spiced porridge, preserved quince, and tea.

Cugel watched the group as they made their meal and reflected that a journey to almost any destination in such company would be a pleasant journey indeed.

The Nolde Huruska appeared, and went to pay his respects to the caravan-leader. The two conversed amiably at some length, while Cugel waited impatiently.

Huruska at last departed. The maidens, having finished their meal, went off to stroll about the square. Cugel crossed to the table where the caravan-leader sat. "Sir, my name is Cugel, and I would appreciate a few words with you."

"By all means! Please be seated. Will you take a glass of this excellent tea?"

"Thank you. First, may I inquire the destination of your caravan?"

The caravan-leader showed surprise at Cugel's ignorance. "We are bound for Lumarth; these are the 'Seventeen Virgins of Symnathis' who traditionally grace the Grand Pageant."

"I am a stranger to this region," Cugel explained. "Hence I know nothing of the local customs. In any event, I myself am bound for Lumarth and would be pleased to travel with your caravan."

The caravan-leader gave an affable assent. "I would be delighted to have you with us."

"Excellent!" said Cugel. "Then all is arranged."

The caravan-leader stroked his silky brown beard. ''I must warn you that my fees are somewhat higher than usual, owing to the expensive amenities I am obliged to provide these seventeen fastidious maidens.''

''Indeed,'' said Cugel. ''How much do you require?''

''The journey occupies the better part of ten days, and my minimum charge is twenty terces per diem, for a total of two hundred terces, plus a twenty terce supplement for wine.''

''This is far more than I can afford,'' said Cugel in a bleak voice. ''At the moment I command only a third of this sum. Is there some means by which I might earn my passage?''

''Unfortunately not,'' said the caravan-leader. ''Only this morning the position of armed guard was open, which even paid a small stipend, but Huruska the Nolde, who wishes to visit Lumarth, has agreed to serve in this capacity and the post is now filled.''

Cugel made a sound of disappointment and raised his eyes to the sky. When at last he could bring himself to speak he asked: ''When do you plan to depart?''

''Tomorrow at dawn, with absolute punctuality. I am sorry that we will not have the pleasure of your company.''

''I share the sorrow,'' said Cugel. He returned to his own table and sat brooding. Presently he went into the tavern, where various card games were in progress. Cugel attempted to join the play, but in every case his request was denied. In a surly mood he went to the counter where Maier the innkeeper unpacked a crate of earthenware goblets. Cugel tried to initiate a conversation but for once Maier could take no time from his labors. ''The Nolde Huruska goes off on a journey and tonight his friends mark the occasion with a farewell party, for which I must make careful preparations.''

Cugel took a mug of beer to a side table and gave himself to reflection. After a few moments he went out the back exit and surveyed the prospect, which here overlooked the Isk River. Cugel sauntered down to the water's edge and discovered a dock at which the fishermen moored their punts and dried their nets. Cugel looked up and down the river, then returned up the path to the inn, to spend the rest of the day watching the seventeen maidens as they strolled about the square, or sipped sweet lime tea in the garden of the inn.

The sun set; twilight the color of old wine darkened into night. Cugel set about his preparations, which were quickly achieved, inasmuch as the essence of his plan lay in its simplicity.

The caravan-leader, whose name, so Cugel learned, was Shimilko, assembled his exquisite company for their evening meal, then herded them carefully to the dormitory wagons, despite the pouts and protests of those who wished to remain at the inn and enjoy the festivities of the evening.

In the tavern the farewell party in honor of Huruska had already commenced. Cugel seated himself in a dark corner and presently attracted the attention of the perspiring Maier. Cugel produced ten terces. "I admit that I harbored ungrateful thoughts toward Huruska," he said. "Now I wish to express my good wishes—in absolute anonymity, however! Whenever Huruska starts upon a mug of ale, I want you to place a full mug before him, so that his evening will be incessantly merry. If he asks who has bought the drink you are only to reply: 'One of your friends wishes to pay you a compliment.' Is this clear?"

"Absolutely, and I will do as you command. It is a large-hearted gesture, which Huruska will appreciate."

The evening progressed. Huruska's friends sang jovial songs and proposed a dozen toasts, in all of which Huruska joined. As Cugel had required, whenever Huruska so much as started to drink from a mug, another was placed at his elbow, and Cugel marveled at the scope of Huruska's internal reservoirs.

At last Huruska was prompted to excuse himself from the company. He staggered out the back exit and made his way to that stone wall with a trough below, which had been placed for the convenience of the tavern's patrons.

As Huruska faced the wall Cugel stepped behind him and flung a fisherman's net over Huruska's head, then expertly dropped a noose around Huruska's burly shoulders, followed by other turns and ties. Huruska's bellows were drowned by the song at this moment being sung in his honor.

Cugel dragged the cursing hulk down the path to the dock, and rolled him over and into a punt. Untying the mooring line, Cugel pushed the punt out into the current of the river. "At the very least," Cugel told himself, "two parts of my prophecy are accurate; Huruska has been honored in the tavern and now is about to enjoy a voyage by water."

He returned to the tavern where Huruska's absence had at last been noticed. Maier expressed the opinion that, with an early departure in the offing, Huruska had prudently retired to bed, and all conceded that this was no doubt the case.

The next morning Cugel arose an hour before dawn. He took a quick breakfast, paid Maier his score, then went to where Shimilko ordered his caravan.

"I bring news from Huruska," said Cugel. "Owing to an unfortunate set of personal circumstances, he finds himself unable to make the journey, and has commended me to that post for which you had engaged him.''

Shimilko shook his head in wonder. ''A pity! Yesterday he seemed so enthusiastic! Well, we all must be flexible, and since Huruska cannot join us, I am pleased to accept you in his stead. As soon as we start, I will instruct you in your duties, which are straightforward. You must stand guard by night and take your rest by day, although in the case of danger I naturally expect you to join in the defense of the caravan.''

''These duties are well within my competence,'' said Cugel. ''I am ready to depart at your convenience.''

''Yonder rises the sun,'' declared Shimilko. ''Let us be off and away for Lumarth.''

Ten days later Shimilko's caravan passed through the Methune Gap, and the great Vale of Coram opened before them. The brimming Isk wound back and forth, reflecting a sultry sheen; in the distance loomed the long dark mass of the Draven Forest. Closer at hand five domes of shimmering nacreous gloss marked the site of Lumarth.

Shimilko addressed himself to the company. ''Below lies what remains of the old city Lumarth. Do not be deceived by the domes; they indicate temples at one time sacred to the five demons Yaunt, Jastenave, Phampoun, Adelmar and Suul, and hence were preserved during the Sampathissic Wars.

''The folk of Lumarth are unlike any of your experience. Many are small sorcerers, though Chaladet the Grand Thearch has proscribed magic within the city precincts. You may conceive these people to be languid and wan, and dazed by excess sensation, and you will be correct. All are obsessively rigid in regard to ritual, and all subscribe to a Doctrine of Absolute Altruism, which compels them to virtue and benevolence. For this reason they are known as the 'Kind Folk'. A final word in regard to our journey, which luckily has gone without untoward incident. The wagoneers have driven with skill; Cugel has vigilantly guarded us by night, and I am well pleased. So then: onward to Lumarth, and let meticulous discretion be the slogan!''

The caravan traversed a narrow track down into the valley, then proceeded along an avenue of rutted stone under an arch of enormous black mimosa trees.

At a mouldering portal opening upon the plaza the caravan was met by five tall men in gowns of embroidered silks, the splendid double-crowned headgear of the Coramese Thurists lending them an impressive dignity. The five men were much alike, with pale transparent skins, thin high-bridged noses, slender limbs and pensive gray eyes. One who wore a gorgeous gown of mustard-yellow, crimson and black raised two fingers in a calm salute. ''My friend Shimilko, you have arrived securely with all your blessed cargo. We are well-served and very pleased.''

''The Lirrh-Aing was so placid as almost to be dull,'' said Shimilko. ''To be sure, I was fortunate in securing the services of Cugel, who guarded us so well by night that never were our slumbers interrupted.''

''Well done, Cugel!'' said the head Thurist. ''We will at this time take custody of the precious maidens. Tomorrow you may render your account to the bursar. The Wayfarer's Inn lies yonder, and I counsel you to its comforts.''

''Just so! We will all be the better for a few days rest!''

However, Cugel chose not to so indulge himself. At the door to the inn he told Shimilko: ''Here we part company, for I must continue along the way. Affairs press on me and Almery lies far to the west.''

''But your stipend, Cugel! You must wait at least until tomorrow, when I can collect certain monies from the bursar. Until then, I am without funds.''

Cugel hesitated, but at last was prevailed upon to stay.

An hour later a messenger strode into the inn. ''Master Shimilko, you and your company are required to appear instantly before the Grand Thearch on a matter of utmost importance.''

Shimilko looked up in alarm. ''Whatever is the matter?''

''I am obliged to tell you nothing more.''

With a long face Shimilko led his company across the plaza to the loggia before the old palace, where Chaladet sat on a massive chair. To either side stood the College of Thurists and all regarded Shimilko with somber expressions.

''What is the meaning of this summons?'' inquired Shimilko. ''Why do you regard me with such gravity?''

The Grand Thearch spoke in a deep voice: ''Shimilko, the seventeen maidens conveyed by you from Symnathis to Lumarth have been examined, and I regret to say that of the seventeen, only two can be classified as virgins. The remaining fifteen have been sexually deflorated.''

Shimilko could hardly speak for consternation. ''Impossible!'' he sputtered. ''At Symnathis I undertook the most elaborate precautions. I can display three separate documents certifying the purity of each. There can be no doubt! You are in error!''

"We are not in error, Master Shimilko. Conditions are as we describe, and may easily be verified."

" 'Impossible' and 'incredible' are the only two words which come to mind," cried Shimilko. "Have you questioned the girls themselves?"

"Of course. They merely raise their eyes to the ceiling and whistle between their teeth. Shimilko, how do you explain this heinous outrage?"

"I am perplexed to the point of confusion! The girls embarked upon the journey as pure as the day they were born. This is fact! During each waking instant they never left my area of perception. This is also fact."

"And when you slept?"

"The implausibility is no less extreme. The teamsters invariably retired together in a group. I shared my wagon with the chief teamster and each of us will vouch for the other. Cugel meanwhile kept watch over the entire camp."

"Alone?"

"A single guard suffices, even though the nocturnal hours are slow and dismal. Cugel, however, never complained."

"Cugel is evidently the culprit!"

Shimilko smilingly shook his head. "Cugel's duties left him no time for illicit activity."

"What if Cugel scamped his duties?"

Shimilko responded patiently: "Remember, each girl rested secure in her private cubicle with a door between herself and Cugel."

"Well then—what if Cugel opened this door and quietly entered the cubicle?"

Shimilko considered a dubious moment, and pulled at his silky beard. "In such a case, I suppose the matter might be possible."

The Grand Thearch turned his gaze upon Cugel. "I insist that you make an exact statement upon this sorry affair."

Cugel cried out indignantly: "The investigation is a travesty! My honor has been assailed!"

Chaladet fixed Cugel with a benign, if somewhat chilly, stare. "You will be allowed redemption. Thurists, I place this person in your custody. See to it that he has every opportunity to regain his dignity and self-esteem!"

Cugel roared out a protest which the Grand Thearch ignored. From his great dais he looked thoughtfully off across the square. "Is it the third or fourth month?"

''The chronolog has only just left the month of Yaunt, to enter the time of Phampoun.''

''So be it. By diligence, this licentious rogue may yet earn our love and respect.''

A pair of Thurists grasped Cugel's arms and led him across the square. Cugel jerked this way and that to no avail. ''Where are you taking me? What is this nonsense?''

One of the Thurists replied in a kindly voice: ''We are taking you to the temple of Phampoun, and it is far from nonsense.''

''I do not care for any of this,'' said Cugel. ''Take your hands off of me; I intend to leave Lumarth at once.''

''You shall be so assisted.''

The group marched up worn marble steps, through an enormous arched portal, into an echoing hall, distinguished only by the high dome and an adytum or altar at the far end. Cugel was led into a side-chamber, illuminated by high circular windows and paneled with dark blue wood. An old man in a white gown entered the room and asked: ''What have we here? A person suffering affliction?''

''Yes; Cugel has committed a series of abominable crimes, of which he wishes to purge himself.''

''A total mis-statement!'' cried Cugel. ''No proof has been adduced and in any event I was inveigled against my better judgment.''

The Thurists, paying no heed, departed, and Cugel was left with the old man, who hobbled to a bench and seated himself. Cugel started to speak but the old man held up his hand. ''Calm yourself! You must remember that we are a benevolent people, lacking all spite or malice. We exist only to help other sentient beings! If a person commits a crime, we are racked with sorrow for the criminal, whom we believe to be the true victim, and we work without compromise that he may renew himself.''

''An enlightened viewpoint!'' declared Cugel. ''Already I feel regeneration!''

''Excellent! Your remarks validate our philosophy; certainly you have negotiated what I will refer to as Phase One of the program.''

Cugel frowned. ''There are other phases? Are they really necessary?''

''Absolutely; these are Phases Two and Three. I should explain that Lumarth has not always adhered to such a policy. During the high years of the Great Magics the city fell under the sway of Yasbane the Obviator, who breached openings into five demon-realms and constructed the five temples of Lumarth. You stand now in the Temple of Phampoun.''

"Odd," said Cugel, "that a folk so benevolent are such fervent demonists."

"Nothing could be farther from the truth. The Kind Folk of Lumarth expelled Yasbane, to establish the Era of Love, which must now persist until the final waning of the sun. Our love extends to all, even Yasbane's five demons, whom we hope to rescue from their malevolent evil. You will be the latest in a long line of noble individuals who have worked to this end, and such is Phase Two of the program."

Cugel stood limp in consternation. "Such work far exceeds my competence!"

"Everyone feels the same sensation," said the old man. "Nevertheless Phampoun must be instructed in kindness, consideration and decency; by making this effort, you will know a surge of happy redemption."

"And Phase Three?" croaked Cugel. "What of that?"

"When you achieve your mission, then you shall be gloriously accepted into our brotherhood!" The old man ignored Cugel's groan of dismay. "Let me see now: the month of Yaunt is just ending, and we enter the month of Phampoun, who is perhaps the most irascible of the five by reason of his sensitive eyes. He becomes enraged by so much as a single glimmer, and you must attempt your persuasions in absolute darkness. Do you have any further questions?"

"Yes indeed! Suppose Phampoun refuses to mend his ways?"

"This is 'negativistic thinking' which we Kind Folk refuse to recognize. Ignore everything you may have heard in regard to Phampoun's macabre habits! Go forth in confidence!"

Cugel cried out in anguish: "How will I return to enjoy my honors and rewards?"

"No doubt Phampoun, when contrite, will send you aloft by a means at his disposal," said the old man. "Now I bid you farewell."

"One moment! Where is my food and drink? How will I survive?"

"Again we will leave these matters to the discretion of Phampoun." The old man touched a button; the floor opened under Cugel's feet; he slid down a spiral chute at dizzying velocity. The air gradually became syrupy; Cugel struck a film of invisible constriction which burst with a sound like a cork leaving a bottle, and Cugel emerged into a chamber of medium size, illuminated by the glow of a single lamp.

Cugel stood stiff and rigid, hardly daring to breathe. On a dais across the chamber Phampoun sat sleeping in a massive chair, two black hemispheres shuttering his enormous eyes against the light.

The grey torso wallowed almost the length of the dais; the massive splayed legs were planted flat to the floor. Arms, as large around as Cugel himself, terminated in fingers three feet long, each bedecked with a hundred jeweled rings. Phampoun's head was as large as a wheelbarrow, with a huge snout and an enormous loose-wattled mouth. The two eyes, each the size of a dishpan, could not be seen for the protective hemispheres.

Cugel, holding his breath in fear and also against the stench which hung in the air, looked cautiously about the room. A cord ran from the lamp, across the ceiling, to dangle beside Phampoun's fingers; almost as a reflex Cugel detached the cord from the lamp. He saw a single egress from the chamber: a low iron door directly behind Phampoun's chair. The chute by which he had entered was now invisible.

The flaps beside Phampoun's mouth twitched and lifted; a homunculus growing from the end of Phampoun's tongue peered forth. It stared at Cugel with beady black eyes. "Ha, has time gone by so swiftly?" The creature, leaning forward, consulted a mark on the wall. "It has indeed; I have overslept and Phampoun will be cross. What is your name and what are your crimes? These details are of interest to Phampoun—which is to say myself, though from whimsy I usually call myself Pulsifer, as if I were a separate entity."

Cugel spoke in a voice of brave conviction: I am Cugel, inspector for the new regime which now holds sway in Lumarth. I decended to verify Phampoun's comfort, and since all is well, I will now return aloft. Where is the exit?"

Pulsifer asked plaintively: "You have no crimes to relate? This is harsh news. Both Phampoun and I enjoy great evils. Not long ago a certain sea-trader, whose name evades me, held us enthralled for over an hour."

"And then what occurred?"

"Best not to ask." Pulsifer busied himself polishing one of Phampoun's tusks with a small brush. He thrust his head forth and inspected the mottled visage above him. "Phampoun still sleeps soundly; he ingested a prodigous meal before retiring. Excuse me while I check the progress of Phampoun's digestion." Pulsifer ducked back behind Phampoun's wattles and revealed himself only by a vibration in the corded grey neck. Presently he returned to view. "He is quite famished, or so it would appear. I had best wake him; he will wish to converse with you before. . . ."

"Before what?"

"No matter."

"A moment," said Cugel. "I am interested in conversing with you rather than Phampoun."

"Indeed?" asked Pulsifer, and polished Phampoun's fang with great vigor. "This is pleasant to hear; I receive few compliments."

"Strange! I see much in you to commend. Necessarily your career goes hand in hand with that of Phampoun, but perhaps you have goals and ambitions of your own?"

Pulsifer propped up Phampoun's lip with his cleaning brush and relaxed upon the ledge so created. "Sometimes I feel that I would enjoy seeing something of the outer world. We have ascended several times to the surface, but always by night when heavy clouds obscure the stars, and even then Phampoun complains of the excessive glare, and he quickly returns below."

"A pity," said Cugel. "By day there is much to see. The scenery surrounding Lumarth is pleasant. The Kind Folk are about to present their Grand Pageant of Ultimate Contrasts, which is said to be most picturesque."

Pulsifer gave his head a wistful shake. "I doubt if ever I will see such events. Have you witnessed many horrid crimes?"

"Indeed I have. For instance I recall a dwarf of the Batvar Forest who rode a pelgrane—"

Pulsifer interrupted him with a gesture. "A moment. Phampoun will want to hear this." He leaned precariously from the cavernous mouth to peer up toward the shuttered eyeballs. "Is he, or more accurately, am I awake? I thought I noticed a twitch. In any event, though I have enjoyed our conversation, we must get on with our duties. Hm, the light cord is disarranged. Perhaps you will be good enough to extinguish the light."

"There is no hurry," said Cugel. Phampoun sleeps peacefully; let him enjoy his rest. I have something to show you, a game of chance. Are you acquainted with 'Zambolio'?"

Pulsifer signified in the negative, and Cugel produced his cards. "Notice carefully! I deal you four cards and I take four cards, which we conceal from each other." Cugel explained the rules of the game. "Necessarily we play for coins of gold or some such commodity, to make the game interesting. I therefore wager five terces, which you must match."

"Yonder in two sacks is Phampoun's gold, or with equal propriety, my gold, since I am an integral adjunct to this vast hulk. Take forth gold sufficient to equal your terces."

The game proceeded. Pulsifer won the first sally, to his delight, then lost the next, which prompted him to fill the air with dismal complaints; then he won again and again until Cugel declared himself lacking further funds. "You are a clever and skillful player; it is a joy to match wits with you! Still, I feel I could beat you if I had the terces I left above in the temple."

Pulsifer, somewhat puffed and vainglorious, scoffed at Cugel's boast. "I fear that I am too clever for you! Here, take back your terces and we will play the game once again."

"No; this is not the way sportsmen behave; I am too proud to accept your money. Let me suggest a solution to the problem. In the temple above is my sack of terces and a sack of sweetmeats which you might wish to consume as we continue the game. Let us go fetch these articles, then I defy you to win as before!"

Pulsifer leaned far out to inspect Phampoun's visage. "He appears quite comfortable, though his organs are roiling with hunger."

"He sleeps as soundly as ever," declared Cugel. "Let us hurry. If he wakes our game will be spoiled."

Pulsifer hesitated. "What of Phampoun's gold? We dare not leave it unguarded!"

"We will take it with us, and it will never be outside the range of our vigilance."

"Very well; place it here on the dais."

"So, and now I am ready. How do we go aloft?"

"Merely press the leaden bulb beside the arm of the chair, but please make no untoward disturbance. Phampoun might well be exasperated should he awake in unfamiliar surroundings."

"He has never rested easier! We go aloft!" He pressed the button; the dais shivered and creaked and floated up a dark shaft which opened above them. Presently they burst through the valve of the constrictive essence which Cugel had penetrated on his way down the chute. At once a glimmer of scarlet light seeped into the shaft and a moment later the dais glided to a halt level with the altar in the Temple of Phampoun.

"Now then, my sack of terces," said Cugel. "Exactly where did I leave it? Just over yonder, I believe. Notice! Through the great arches you may overlook the main plaza of Lumarth, and those are the Kind Folk going about their ordinary affairs. What is your opinion of all this?"

"Most interesting, although I am unfamiliar with such extensive vistas. In fact, I feel almost a sense of vertigo. What is the source of the savage red glare?"

"That is the light of our ancient sun, now westering toward sunset."

"It does not appeal to me. Please be quick about your business; I have suddenly become most uneasy."

"I will make haste," said Cugel.

The sun, sinking low, sent a shaft of light through the portal, to play full upon the altar. Cugel, stepping behind the massive chair, twitched away the two shutters which guarded Phampoun's eyes, and the milky orbs glistened in the sunlight.

For an instant Phampoun lay quiet. His muscles knotted, his legs jerked, his mouth gaped wide, and he emitted an explosion of sound: a grinding scream which propelled Pulsifer forth to vibrate like a flag in the wind. Phampoun lunged from the altar to fall sprawling and rolling across the floor of the temple, all the while maintaining his cataclysmic outcries. He pulled himself erect, and pounding the tiled floor with his great feet, he sprang here and there and at last burst through the stone walls as if they were paper, while the Kind Folk in the square stood petrified.

Cugel, taking the two sacks of gold, departed the temple by a side entrance. For a moment he watched Phampoun careering around the square, screaming and flailing at the sun. Pulsifer, desperately gripping a pair of tusks, attempted to steer the maddened demon, who, ignoring all restraint, plunged eastward through the city, trampling down trees, bursting through houses as if they failed to exist.

Cugel walked briskly down to the Isk and made his way out upon a dock. He selected a skiff of good proportions, equipped with mast, sail and oars, and prepared to clamber aboard. A punt approached the dock from upriver, poled vigorously by a large man in tattered garments. Cugel turned away, pretending no more than a casual interest in the view, until he might board the skiff without attracting attention.

The punt touched the dock; the boatman climbed up a ladder.

Cugel continued to gaze across the water, affecting indifference to all except the river vistas.

The man, panting and grunting, came to a sudden halt. Cugel felt his intent inspection, and finally turning, looked into the congested face of Huruska, the Nolde of Gundar, though his face was barely recognizable for the bites Huruska had suffered from the insects of the Lallo Marsh.

Huruska stared long and hard at Cugel. "This is a most gratifying occasion!" he said huskily. "I feared that we would never meet again. And what do you carry in those leather bags?" He wrested a bag from Cugel. "Gold from the weight. Your prophecy has been totally vindicated! First honors and a voyage by water, now wealth and revenge! Prepare to die!"

"One moment!" cried Cugel. "You have neglected properly to moor the punt! This is disorderly conduct!"

Huruska turned to look, and Cugel thrust him off the dock into the water.

Cursing and raving, Huruska struggled for the shore while Cugel fumbled with the knots in the mooring-line of the skiff. The line at last came loose; Cugel pulled the skiff close as Huruska came charging down the dock like a bull. Cugel had no choice but to abandon his gold, jump into the skiff, push off and ply the oars while Huruska stood waving his arms in rage.

Cugel pensively hoisted the sail; the wind carried him down the river and around a bend. Cugel's last view of Lumarth, in the dying light of afternoon, included the low lustrous domes of the demon temples and the dark outline of Huruska standing on the dock. From afar the screams of Phampoun were still to be heard and occasionally the thud of toppling masonry.

2

The Bagful of Dreams

The River Isk, departing Lumarth, wandered in wide curves across the Plain of Red Flowers, bearing generally south. For six halcyon days Cugel sailed his skiff down the brimming river, stopping by night at one or another of the river-bank inns.

On the seventh day the river swung to the west, and passed by erratic sweeps and reaches through that land of rock spires and forested hillocks known as the Chaim Purpure. The wind blew, if at all, in unpredictable gusts, and Cugel, dropping the sail, was content to drift with the current, guiding the craft with an occasional stroke of the oars.

The villages of the plain were left behind; the region was uninhabited. In view of the crumbled tombs along the shore, the groves of cypress and yew, the quiet conversations to be overheard by night, Cugel was pleased to be afloat rather than afoot, and drifted out of the Chaim Purpure with great relief.

At the village Troon, the river emptied into the Tsombol Marsh, and Cugel sold the skiff for ten terces. To repair his fortunes he took employment with the town butcher, performing the more distasteful tasks attendant upon the trade. However, the pay was adequate and Cugel steeled himself to his undignified duties. He worked to such good effect that he was called upon to prepare the feast served at an important religious festival.

Through oversight, or stress of circumstance, Cugel used two sacred beasts in the preparation of his special ragout. Half-way through the banquet the mistake was discovered and once again Cugel left town under a cloud.

After hiding all night behind the abattoir to evade the hysterical mobs, Cugel set off at best speed across the Tsombol Marsh.

The road went by an indirect route, swinging around bogs and stagnant ponds, veering to follow the bed of an ancient highway, in effect doubling the length of the journey. A wind from the north blew the sky clear of all obscurity, so that the landscape showed in remarkable clarity. Cugel took no pleasure in the view, especially when, looking ahead, he spied a far pelgrane cruising down the wind.

As the afternoon advanced the wind abated, leaving an unnatural stillness across the marsh. From behind tussocks water-wefkins called out to Cugel, using the sweet voices of unhappy maidens: "Cugel, oh Cugel! Why do you travel in haste? Come to my bower and comb my beautiful hair!"

And: "Cugel, oh Cugel! Where do you go? Take me with you, to share your joyous adventures!"

And: "Cugel, beloved Cugel! The day is dying; the year is at an end! Come visit me behind the tussock, and we will console each other without constraint!"

Cugel only walked the faster, anxious to discover shelter for the night.

As the sun trembled at the edge of Tsombol Marsh Cugel came upon a small inn, secluded under five dire oaks. He gratefully took lodging for the night, and the innkeeper served a fair supper of stewed herbs, spitted reed-birds, seed-cake and thick burdock beer.

As Cugel ate, the innkeeper stood by with hands on hips. "I see by your conduct that you are a gentleman of high place; still you hop across Tsombol Marsh on foot like a bumpkin. I am puzzled by the incongruity."

"It is easily explained," said Cugel. "I consider myself the single honest man in a world of rogues and blackguards, present company excepted. In these conditions it is hard to accumulate wealth."

The innkeeper pulled at his chin, and turned away. When he came to serve Cugel a dessert of currant cake, he paused long enough to say: "Your difficulties have aroused my sympathy. Tonight I will reflect on the matter."

The innkeeper was as good as his word. In the morning, after Cugel had finished his breakfast, the innkeeper took him into the stable-yard and displayed a large dun-colored beast with powerful hind legs and a tufted tail, already bridled and saddled for riding.

"This is the least I can do for you," said the innkeeper. "I will sell this beast at a nominal figure. Agreed, it lacks elegance, and in fact is a hybrid of dounge and felukhary. Still, it moves with an easy stride; it feeds upon inexpensive wastes, and is notorious for its stubborn loyalty.''

Cugel moved politely away. ''I appreciate your altruism, but for such a creature any price whatever is excessive. Notice the sores at the base of its tail, the eczema along its back, and, unless I am mistaken, it lacks an eye. Also, its odor is not all it might be.''

''Trifles!'' declared the innkeeper. ''Do you want a dependable steed to carry you across the Plain of Standing Stones, or an adjunct to your vanity? The beast becomes your property for a mere thirty terces.''

Cugel jumped back in shock. ''When a fine Cambalese wheriot sells for twenty? My dear fellow, your generosity outreaches my ability to pay!''

The innkeeper's face expressed only patience. ''Here, in the middle of Tsombol Marsh, you will buy not even the smell of a dead wheriot.''

''Let us discard euphemism,'' said Cugel. ''Your price is an outrage.''

For an instant the innkeeper's face lost its genial cast and he spoke in a grumbling voice: ''Every person to whom I sell this steed takes the same advantage of my kindliness.''

Cugel was puzzled by the remark. Nevertheless, sensing irresolution, he pressed his advantage. ''In spite of a dozen misgivings, I offer a generous twelve terces!''

''Done!'' cried the innkeeper almost before Cugel had finished speaking. ''I repeat, you will discover this beast to be totally loyal, even beyond your expectations.''

Cugel paid over twelve terces and gingerly mounted the creature. The landlord gave him a benign farewell. ''May you enjoy a safe and comfortable journey!''

Cugel replied in like fashion. ''May your enterprises prosper!''

In order to make a brave departure, Cugel tried to rein the beast up and around in a caracole, but it merely squatted low to the ground, then padded out upon the road.

Cugel rode a mile in comfort, and another, and taking all with all, was favorably impressed with his acquisition. ''No question but what the beast walks on soft feet; now let us discover if it will canter at speed.''

He shook out the reins; the beast set off down the road, its gait a unique prancing strut, with tail arched and head held high.

Cugel kicked his heels into the creature's heaving flanks. ''Faster then! Let us test your mettle!''

The beast sprang forward with great energy, and the breeze blew Cugel's cloak flapping behind his shoulders.

A massive dire oak stood beside a bend in the road: an object which the beast seemed to identify as a landmark. It increased its pace, only to stop short and elevate its hind-quarters, thus projecting Cugel into the ditch. When he managed to stagger back up on the road, he discovered the beast cavorting across the marsh, in the general direction of the inn.

"A loyal creature indeed!" grumbled Cugel. "It is unswervingly faithful to the comfort of its barn." He found his green velvet cap, clapped it back upon his head and once more trudged south along the road.

During the late afternoon Cugel came to a village of a dozen mud huts populated by a squat long-armed folk, distinguished by great shocks of whitewashed hair.

Cugel gauged the height of the sun, then examined the terrain ahead, which extended in a dreary succession of tussock and pond to the edge of vision. Putting aside all qualms he approached the largest and most pretentious of the huts.

The master of the house sat on a bench to the side, whitewashing the hair of one of his children into radiating tufts like the petals of a white chrysanthemum, while other urchins played nearby in the mud.

"Good afternoon," said Cugel. "Are you able to provide me food and lodging for the night? I naturally intend adequate payment."

"I will feel privileged to do so," replied the householder. "This is the most commodious hut of Samsetiska, and I am known for my fund of anecdotes. Do you care to inspect the premises?"

"I would be pleased to rest an hour in my chamber before indulging myself in a hot bath."

His host blew out his cheeks, and wiping the whitewash from his hands beckoned Cugel into the hut. He pointed to a heap of reeds at the side of the room. "There is your bed; recline for as long as you like. As for a bath, the ponds of the swamp are infested with threlkoids and wire-worms, and cannot be recommended."

"In that case I must do without," said Cugel. "However, I have not eaten since breakfast, and I am willing to take my evening meal as soon as possible."

"My spouse has gone trapping in the swamp," said his host. "It is premature to discuss supper until we learn what she has gleaned from her toil."

In due course the woman returned carrying a sack and a wicker basket. She built up a fire and prepared the evening meal, while Erwig the householder brought forth a two-string guitar and entertained Cugel with ballads of the region.

At last the woman called Cugel and Erwig into the hut, where she served bowls of gruel, dishes of fried moss and ganions, with slices of coarse black bread.

After the meal Erwig thrust his spouse and children out into the night, explaining: "What we have to say is unsuitable for unsophisticated ears. Cugel is an important traveler and does not wish to measure his every word."

Bringing out an earthenware jug, Erwig poured two tots of arrak, one of which he placed before Cugel, then disposed himself for conversation. "Whence came you and where are you bound?"

Cugel tasted the arrak, which scorched the entire interior of his glottal cavity. "I am native to Almery, to which I now return."

Erwig scratched his head in perplexity. "I cannot divine why you go so far afield, only to retrace your steps."

"Certain enemies worked mischief upon me," said Cugel. "Upon my return, I intend an appropriate revenge."

"Such acts soothe the spirit like no others," agreed Erwig. "An immediate obstacle is the Plain of Standing Stones, by reason of asms which haunt the area. I might add that pelgrane are also common."

Cugel gave his sword a nervous twitch. "What is the distance to the Plain of Standing Stones?"

"Four miles south the ground rises and the Plain begins. The track proceeds from sarsen to sarsen for a distance of fifteen miles. A stout-hearted traveler will cross the plain in four to five hours, assuming that he is not delayed or devoured. The town Cuirnif lies another two hours beyond."

"An inch of foreknowledge is worth ten miles of after-thought—"

"Well spoken!" cried Erwig, swallowing a gulp of arrak. "My own opinion, to an exactitude! Cugel, you are astute!"

"—and in this regard, may I inquire your opinion of Cuirnif?"

"The folk are peculiar in many ways," said Erwig. "They preen themselves upon the gentility of their habits, yet they refuse to white-wash their hair, and they are slack in their religious observances. For instance, they make obeisance to Divine Wiulio with the right hand, not on the buttock, but on the abdomen, which we here consider a slipshod practice. What are your own views?"

"The rite should be conducted as you describe," said Cugel. "No other method carries weight."

Erwig refilled Cugel's glass. "I consider this an important endorsement of our views!"

The door opened and Erwig's spouse looked into the hut. "The night is dark. A bitter wind blows from the north, and a black beast prowls at the edge of the marsh."

"Stand among the shadows; divine Wiulio protects his own. It is unthinkable that you and your brats should annoy our guest."

The woman grudgingly closed the door and returned into the night. Erwig pulled himself forward on his stool and swallowed a quantity of arrak. "The folk of Cuirnif, as I say, are strange enough, but their ruler, Duke Orbal, surpasses them in every category. He devotes himself to the study of marvels and prodigies, and every jack-leg magician with two spells in his head is feted and celebrated and treated to the best of the city."

"Most odd!" declared Cugel.

Again the door opened and the woman looked into the hut. Erwig put down his glass and frowned over his shoulder. "What is it this time?"

"The beast is now moving among the huts. For all we know it may also worship Wiulio."

Erwig attempted argument, but the woman's face became obdurate. "Your guest might as well forego his niceties now as later, since we all, in any event, must sleep on the same heap of reeds." She opened wide the door and commanded her urchins into the hut. Erwig, assured that no further conversation was possible, threw himself down upon the reeds, and Cugel followed soon after.

In the morning Cugel breakfasted on ash-cake and herb tea, and prepared to take his departure. Erwig accompanied him to the road. "You have made a favorable impression upon me, and I will assist you across the Plain of Standing Stones. At the first opportunity take up a pebble the size of your fist and make the trigrammatic sign upon it. If you are attacked, hold high the pebble and cry out: 'Stand aside! I carry a sacred object!' At the first sarsen, deposit the stone and select another from the pile, again make the sign and carry it to the second sarsen, and so across the plain."

"So much is clear," said Cugel. "But perhaps you should show me the most powerful version of the sign, and thus refresh my memory."

Erwig scratched a mark in the dirt. "Simple, precise, correct! The folk of Cuirnif omit this loop and scrawl in every which direction."

"Slackness, once again!" said Cugel.

"So then, Cugel: farewell! The next time you pass be certain to halt at my hut! My crock of arrak has a loose stopper!"

"I would not forego the pleasure for a thousand terces. And now; as to my indebtedness—"

Erwig held up his hand. "I accept no terces from my guests!" He jerked and his eyes bulged as his spouse came up and prodded him in the ribs. "Ah well," said Erwig. "Give the woman a terce or two; it will cheer her as she performs her tasks."

Cugel paid over five terces, to the woman's enormous satisfaction, and so departed the village.

After four miles the road angled up to a gray plain studded at intervals with twelve-foot pillars of gray stone. Cugel found a large pebble, and placing his right hand on his buttock made a profound salute to the object. He scratched upon it a sign somewhat similar to that drawn for him by Erwig and intoned: "I commend this pebble to the attention of Wiulio! I request that it protect me across this dismal plain!"

He scrutinized the landscape, but aside from the sarsens and the long black shadows laid by the red morning sun, he discovered nothing worthy of attention, and thankfully set off along the track.

He had traveled no more than a hundred yards when he felt a presence and whirling about discovered an asm of eight fangs almost on his heels. Cugel held high the pebble and cried out: "Away with you! I carry a sacred object and I do not care to be molested!"

The asm spoke in a soft blurred voice: "Wrong! You carry an ordinary pebble. I watched and you scamped the rite. Flee if you wish! I need the exercise."

The asm advanced. Cugel threw the stone with all his force. It struck the black forehead between the bristling antennae, and the asm fell flat; before it could rise Cugel had severed its head.

He started to proceed, then turned back and took up the stone. "Who knows who guided the throw so accurately? Wiulio deserves the benefit of the doubt."

At the first Sarsen he exchanged stones as Erwig had recommended, and this time he made the trigrammatic sign with care and precision.

Without interference he crossed to the next sarsen and so continued across the plain.

The sun made its way to the zenith, rested a period, then descended into the west. Cugel marched unmolested from sarsen to sarsen. On several occasions he noted pelgrane sliding across the sky, and each time flung himself flat to avoid attention.

The Plain of Standing Stones ended at the brink of a scarp overlooking a wide valley. With safety close at hand Cugel relaxed his vigilance, only to be startled by a scream of triumph from the sky. He darted a horrified glance over his shoulder, then plunged over the edge of the scarp into a ravine, where he dodged among rocks and pressed himself into the shadows. Down swooped the pelgrane, past and beyond Cugel's hiding place. Warbling in joy, it alighted at the base of the scarp, to evoke instant outcries and curses from a human throat.

Keeping to concealment Cugel descended the slope, to discover that the pelgrane now pursued a portly black-haired man in a suit of black and white diaper. This person at last took nimble refuge behind a thick-boled olophar tree, and the pelgrane chased him first one way, then another, clashing its fangs and snatching with its clawed hands.

For all his rotundity, the man showed remarkable deftness of foot and the pelgrane began to scream in frustration. It halted to glare through the crotch of the tree and snap out with its long maw.

On a whimsical impulse Cugel stole out upon a shelf of rock; then, selecting an appropriate moment, he jumped to land with both feet on the creature's head, forcing the neck down into the crotch of the olophar tree. He called out to the startled man: "Quick! Fetch a stout cord! We will bind this winged horror in place!"

The man in the black and white diaper cried out: "Why show mercy? It must be killed and instantly! Move your foot, so that I may hack away its head."

"Not so fast," said Cugel. "For all its faults, it is a valuable specimen by which I hope to profit."

"Profit?" The idea had not occurred to the portly gentleman. "I must assert my prior claim! I was just about to stun the beast when you interfered."

Cugel said: "In that case I will take my weight off the creature's neck and go my way."

The man in the black-and-white suit made an irritable gesture. "Certain persons will go to any extreme merely to score a rhetorical point. Hold fast then! I have a suitable cord over yonder."

The two men dropped a branch over the pelgrane's head and bound it securely in place. The portly gentleman, who had introduced himself as Iolo the Dream-taker, asked: "Exactly what value do you place upon this horrid creature, and why?"

Cugel said: "It has come to my attention that Orbal, Duke of

Ombalique, is an amateur of oddities. Surely he would pay well for such a monster, perhaps as much as a hundred terces."

"Your theories are sound," Iolo admitted. "Are you sure that the bonds are secure?"

As Cugel tested the ropes he noticed an ornament consisting of a blue glass egg on a golden chain attached to the creature's crest. As he removed the object, Iolo's hand darted out, but Cugel shouldered him aside. He disengaged the amulet, but Iolo caught hold of the chain and the two glared eye to eye.

"Release your grip upon my property," said Cugel in an icy voice.

Iolo protested vigorously. "The object is mine since I saw it first."

"Nonsense! I took it from the crest and you tried to snatch it from my hand."

Iolo stamped his foot. "I will not be domineered!" He sought to wrest the blue egg from Cugel's grasp. Cugel lost his grip and the object was thrown against the hillside where it broke in a bright blue explosion to create a hole into the hillside. Instantly a golden-gray tentacle thrust forth and seized Cugel's leg.

Iolo sprang back and from a safe distance watched Cugel's efforts to avoid being drawn into the hole. Cugel saved himself at the last moment by clinging to a stump. He called out: "Iolo, make haste! Fetch a cord and tie the tentacle to this stump; otherwise it will drag me into the hill!"

Iolo folded his arms and spoke in a measured voice: "Avarice has brought this plight upon you. It may be a divine judgment and I am reluctant to interfere."

"What? When you fought tooth and nail to wrench the object from my hand?"

Iolo frowned and pursed his lips. "In any case I own a single rope: that which ties my pelgrane."

"Kill the pelgrane!" panted Cugel. "Put the cord to its most urgent use!"

"You yourself valued this pelgrane at a hundred terces. The worth of the rope is ten terces."

"Very well," said Cugel through gritted teeth. "Ten terces for the rope, but I cannot pay a hundred terces for a dead pelgrane, since I carry only forty-five."

"So be it. Pay over the forty-five terces. What surety can you offer for the remainder?"

Cugel managed to toss over his purse of terces. He displayed the opal ear-bangle which Iolo promptly demanded, but which Cugel refused to relinquish until the tentacle had been tied to the stump.

With poor grace Iolo hacked the head off the pelgrane, then brought over the rope and secured the tentacle to the stump, thus easing the strain upon Cugel's leg.

"The ear-bangle, if you please!" said Iolo, and he poised his knife significantly near the rope.

Cugel tossed over the jewel. "There you have it: all my wealth. Now, please free me from this tentacle."

"I am a cautious man," said Iolo. "I must consider the matter from several perspectives." He set about making camp for the night.

Cugel called out a plaintive appeal: "Do you remember how I rescued you from the pelgrane?"

"Indeed I do! An important philosophical question has thereby been raised. You disturbed a stasis and now a tentacle grips your leg, which is, in a sense, the new stasis. I will reflect carefully upon the matter."

Cugel argued to no avail. Iolo built up a campfire over which he cooked a stew of herbs and grasses, which he ate with half a cold fowl and draughts of wine from a leather bottle.

Leaning back against a tree he gave his attention to Cugel. "No doubt you are on your way to Duke Orbal's Grand Exposition of Marvels?"

"I am a traveler, no more," said Cugel. "What is this 'Grand Exposition'?"

Iolo gave Cugel a pitying glance for his stupidity. "Each year Duke Orbal presides over a competition of wonder-workers. This year the prize is one thousand terces, which I intend to win with my 'Bagful of Dreams'."

"Your 'Bagful of Dreams' I assume to be a jocularity, or something on the order of a romantic metaphor?"

"Nothing of the sort!" declared Iolo in scorn.

"A kaleidoscopic projection? A program of impersonations? A hallucinatory gas?"

"None of these. I carry with me a number of pure unadulterated dreams, coalesced and crystallized."

From his satchel Iolo brought a sack of soft brown leather, from which he took an object resembling a pale blue snowflake an inch in diameter. He held it up into the firelight where Cugel could admire its fleeting lusters. "I will ply Duke Orbal with my dreams, and how can I fail to win over all other contestants?"

"Your chances would seem to be good. How do you gather these dreams?"

"The process is secret; still I can describe the general procedure.

I live beside Lake Lelt in the Land of Dai-Passant. On calm nights the surface of the water thickens to a film which reflects the stars as small globules of shine. By using a suitable cantrap, I am able to lift up impalpable threads composed of pure starlight and water-skein. I weave this thread into nets and then I go forth in search of dreams. I hide under valances and in the leaves of outdoor bowers; I crouch on roofs; I wander through sleeping houses. Always I am ready to net the dreams as they drift past. Each morning I carry these wonderful wisps to my laboratory and there I sort them out and work my processes. In due course I achieve a crystal of a hundred dreams, and with these confections I hope to enthrall Duke Orbal.''

''I would offer congratulations were it not for this tentacle gripping my leg,'' said Cugel.

''That is a generous emotion,'' said Iolo. He fed several logs into the fire, chanted a spell of protection against creatures of the night, and composed himself for sleep.

An hour passed. Cugel tried by various means to ease the grip of the tentacle, without success, nor could he draw his sword or bring 'Spatterlight' from his pouch.

At last he sat back and considered new approaches to the solution of his problem.

By dint of stretching and straining he obtained a twig, with which he dragged close a long dead branch, which allowed him to reach another of equal length. Tying the two together with a string from his pouch, he contrived a pole exactly long enough to reach Iolo's recumbent form.

Working with care Cugel drew Iolo's satchel across the ground, finally to within reach of his fingers. First he brought out Iolo's wallet, to find two hundred terces, which he transfered to his own purse; next the opal ear-bangle, which he dropped into the pocket of his shirt; then the bagful of dreams.

The satchel contained nothing more of value, save that portion of cold fowl which Iolo had reserved for his breakfast and the leather bottle of wine, both of which Cugel put aside for his own use. He returned the satchel to where he had found it, then separated the branches and tossed them aside. Lacking a better hiding place for the bagful of dreams, Cugel tied the string to the bag and lowered it into the mysterious hole. He ate the fowl and drank the wine, then made himself as comfortable as possible.

The night wore on. Cugel heard the plaintive call of a night-jar and also the moan of a six-legged shamb, at some distance.

In due course the sky glowed purple and the sun appeared. Iolo roused himself, yawned, ran his fingers through his tousled hair, blew up the fire and gave Cugel a civil greeting. "And how passed the night?"

"As well as could be expected. It is useless, after all, to complain against inexorable reality."

"Exactly so. I have given considerable thought to your case, and I have arrived at a decision which will please you. This is my plan. I shall proceed into Cuirnif and there drive a hard bargain for the ear-bangle. After satisfying your account, I will return and pay over to you whatever sums may be in excess."

Cugel suggested an alternative scheme. "Let us go into Cuirnif together; then you will be spared the inconvenience of a return trip."

Iolo shook his head. "My plan must prevail." He went to the satchel for his breakfast and so discovered the loss of his property. He uttered a plangent cry and stared at Cugel. "My terces, my dreams! They are gone, all gone! How do you account for this?"

"Very simply. At approximately four minutes after midnight a robber came from the forest and made off with the contents of your satchel."

Iolo tore at his beard with the fingers of both hands. "My precious dreams! Why did you not cry out an alarm?"

Cugel scratched his head. "In all candor I did not dare disturb the stasis."

Iolo jumped to his feet and looked through the forest in all directions. He turned back to Cugel. "What sort of man was this robber?"

"In certain respects he seemed a kindly man; after taking possession of your belongings, he presented me with half a cold fowl and a bottle of wine, which I consumed with gratitude."

"You consumed my breakfast!"

Cugel shrugged. "I could not be sure of this, and in fact I did not inquire. We held a brief conversation and I learned that like ourselves he is bound for Cuirnif and the Exposition of Marvels."

"Ah, ah ha! Would you recognize this person were you to see him again?"

"Without a doubt."

Iolo became instantly energetic. "Let us see as to this tentacle. Perhaps we can pry it loose." He seized the tip of the golden-gray member and bracing himself worked to lift it from Cugel's leg. For several minutes he toiled, kicking and prying, paying no heed to Cugel's cries of pain. Finally the tentacle relaxed and Cugel crawled to safety.

With great caution Iolo approached the hole and peered down into the depths. "I see only a glimmer of far lights. The hole is mysterious! . . . What is this bit of string which leads into the hole?"

"I tied a rock to the string and tried to plumb the bottom of the hole," Cugel explained. "It amounts to nothing."

Iolo tugged at the string, which first yielded, then resisted, then broke, and Iolo was left looking at the frayed end. "Odd! The string is corroded, as if through contact with some acrid substance."

"Most peculiar!" said Cugel.

Iolo threw the string back into the hole. "Come, we can waste no more time! Let us hasten into Cuirnif and seek out the scoundrel who stole my valuables."

The road left the forest and passed through a district of fields and orchards. Peasants looked up in wonder as the two passed by: the portly Iolo dressed in black and white diaper and the lank Cugel with a black cloak hanging from his spare shoulders and a fine dark green cap gracing his saturnine visage.

Along the way Iolo put ever more searching questions in regard to the robber. Cugel had lost interest in the subject and gave back ambiguous, even contradictory, answers, and Iolo's questions became ever more searching.

Upon entering Cuirnif, Cugel noticed an inn which seemed to offer comfortable accommodation. He told Iolo: "Here our paths diverge, since I plan to stop at the inn yonder."

"The Five Owls? It is the dearest inn of Cuirnif! How will you pay your account?"

Cugel made a confident gesture. "Is not a thousand terces the grand prize at the Exposition?"

"Certainly, but what marvel do you plan to display? I warn you, the Duke has no patience with charlatans."

"I am not a man who tells all he knows," said Cugel. "I will disclose none of my plans at this moment."

"But what of the robber?" cried Iolo. "Were we not to search Cuirnif high and low?"

"The Five Owls is as good a vantage as any, since the robber will surely visit the common room to boast of his exploits and squander your terces on drink. Meanwhile, I wish you easy roofs and convenient dreams." Cugel bowed politely and took his leave of Iolo.

At the Five Owls Cugel selected a suitable chamber, where he refreshed himself and ordered his attire. Then, repairing to the common room, he made a leisurely meal upon the best the house could provide.

The innkeeper stopped by to make sure that all was in order and Cugel complimented him upon his table. "In fact, all taken with all, Cuirnif must be considered a place favored by the elements. The prospect is pleasant, the air is bracing, and Duke Orbal would seem to be an indulgent ruler."

The innkeeper gave a somewhat noncommital assent. "As you indicate, Duke Orbal is never exasperated, truculent, suspicious, nor harsh unless in his wisdom he feels so inclined, whereupon all mildness is put aside in the interests of justice. Glance up to the crest of the hill; what do you see?"

"Four tubes, or stand-pipes, approximately thirty yards tall and one yard in diameter."

"Your eye is accurate. Into these tubes are dropped insubordinate members of society, without regard for who stands below or who may be coming after. Hence, while you may converse with Duke Orbal or even venture a modest pleasantry, never ignore his commands. Criminals, of course, are given short shrift."

Cugel, from habit, looked uneasily over his shoulder. "Such strictures will hardly apply to me, a stranger in town."

The innkeeper gave a skeptical grunt. "I assume that you came to witness the Exposition of Marvels?"

"Quite so! I may even try for the grand prize. In this regard, can you recommend a dependable hostler?"

"Certainly." The innkeeper provided explicit directions.

"I also wish to hire a gang of strong and willing workers," said Cugel. "Where may these be recruited?"

The innkeeper pointed across the square to a dingy tavern. "In the yard of the 'Howling Dog' all the riffraff in town take counsel together. Here you will find workers sufficient to your purposes."

"While I visit the hostler, be good enough to send a boy across to hire twelve of these sturdy fellows."

"As you wish."

At the hostler's Cugel rented a large six-wheeled wagon and a team of strong farlocks. When he returned with the wagon to the Five Owls, he found waiting a work-force of twelve individuals of miscellaneous sort, including a man not only senile but also lacking a leg. Another, in the throes of intoxication, fought away imaginary insects. Cugel discharged these two on the spot. The group also included Iolo the Dream-taker, who scrutinized Cugel with the liveliest suspicion.

Cugel asked: "My dear fellow, what do you do in such sordid company?"

"I take employment so that I may eat," said Iolo. "May I ask how you came by the funds to pay for so much skilled labor? Also, I notice that from your ear hangs that gem which only last night was my property!''

''It is the second of a pair,'' said Cugel. ''As you know, the robber took the first along with your other valuables.''

Iolo curled his lips. ''I am more than ever anxious to meet this quixotic robber who takes my gem but leaves you in possession of yours.''

''He was indeed a remarkable person. I believe that I glimpsed him not an hour ago, riding hard out of town.''

Iolo again curled his lip. ''What do you propose to do with this wagon?''

''If you care to earn a wage, you will soon find out for yourself.''

Cugel drove the wagon and the gang of workers out of Cuirnif along the road to the mysterious hole, where he found all as before. He ordered trenches dug into the hillside; crating was installed, after which that block of soil surrounding and including the hole, the stump and the tentacle, was dragged up on the bed of the wagon.

During the middle stages of the project Iolo's manner changed. He began calling orders to the workmen and addressed Cugel with cordiality. ''A noble idea, Cugel! We shall profit greatly!''

Cugel raised his eyebrows. ''I hope indeed to win the grand prize. Your wage, however, will be relatively modest, even scant, unless you work more briskly.''

''What!'' stormed Iolo. ''Surely you agree that this hole is half my property!''

''I agree to nothing of the sort. Say no more of the matter, or you will be discharged on the spot.''

Grumbling and fuming Iolo returned to work. In due course Cugel conveyed the block of soil, with the hole, stump and tentacle, back to Cuirnif. Along the way he purchased an old tarpaulin with which he concealed the hole, the better to magnify the eventual effect of his display.

At the site of the Grand Exposition Cugel slid his exhibit off the wagon and into the shelter of a pavilion, after which he paid off his men, to the dissatisfaction of those who had cultivated extravagant hopes.

Cugel refused to listen to complaints. ''The pay is sufficient! If it were ten times as much, every last terce would still end up in the till at the 'Howling Dog'.''

''One moment!'' cried Iolo. You and I must arrive at an understanding!''

Cugel merely jumped up on the wagon and drove it back to the hostelry. Some of the men pursued him a few steps; others threw stones, without effect.

On the following day trumpets and gongs announced the formal opening of the exposition. Duke Orbal arrived at the plaza wearing a splendid robe of magenta plush trimmed with white feathers, and a hat of pale blue velvet three feet in diameter, with silver tassels around the brim and a cockade of silver puff.

Mounting a rostrum, Duke Orbal addressed the crowd. ''As all know, I am considered an eccentric, what with my enthusiasm for marvels and prodigies, but, after all, when the preoccupation is analyzed, is it all so absurd? Think back across the aeons to the times of the Vapurials, the Green and Purple College, the mighty magicians among whose number we include Amberlin, the second Chidule of Porphyrhyncos, Morreion, Calanctus the Calm, and of course the Great Phandaal. These were the days of power, and they are not likely to return except in nostalgic recollection. Hence this, my Grand Exposition of Marvels, and withal, a pale recollection of the way things were.

''Still, all taken with all, I see by my schedule that we have a stimulating program, and no doubt I will find difficulty in awarding the grand prize.''

Duke Orbal glanced at a paper. ''We will inspect Zaraflam's 'Nimble Squadrons', Bazzard's 'Unlikely Musicians', Xallops and his 'Compendium of Universal Knowledge'. Iolo will offer his 'Bagful of Dreams', and, finally, Cugel will present for our amazement that to which he gives the tantalizing title: 'Nowhere'. A most provocative program! And now without further ado we will proceed to evaluate Zaraflam's 'Nimble Squadrons'.''

The crowd surged around the first pavilion and Zaraflam brought forth his 'Nimble Squadrons': a parade of cockroaches smartly turned out in red, white, and black uniforms. The sergeants brandished cutlasses; the foot soldiers carried muskets; the squadrons marched and countermarched in intricate evolutions.

''Halt!'' bawled Zaraflam.

The cockroaches stopped short.

''Present arms!''

The cockroaches obeyed.

''Fire a salute in honor of Duke Orbal!''

The sergeants raised their cutlasses; the footmen elevated their muskets. Down came the cutlasses; the muskets exploded, emitting little puffs of white smoke.

"Excellent!" declared Duke Orbal. "Zaraflam, I commend your painstaking accuracy!"

"A thousand thanks, your Grace! Have I won the grand prize?"

"It is still too early to predict. Now, to Bazzard and his 'Unlikely Musicians'!"

The spectators moved on to the second pavilion where Bazzard presently appeared, his face woebegone. "Your Grace and noble citizens of Cuirnif! My 'Unlikely Musicians' were fish from the Cantic Sea and I felt sure of the grand prize when I brought them to Cuirnif. However, during the night a leak drained the tank dry. The fish are dead and their music is lost forever! I still wish to remain in contention for the prize; hence I will simulate the songs of my former troupe. Please adjudicate the music on this basis."

Duke Orbal made an austere sign. "Impossible. Bazzard's exhibit is hereby declared invalid. We now move on to Xallops and his remarkable 'Compendium'."

Xallops stepped forward from his pavilion. "Your Grace, ladies and gentlemen of Cuirnif! My entry at this exposition is truly remarkable; however, unlike Zaraflam and Bazzard, I can take no personal credit for its existence. By trade I am a ransacker of ancient tombs, where the risks are great and rewards few. By great good luck I chanced upon that crypt where several aeons ago the sorcerer Zinqzin was laid to rest. From this dungeon I rescued the volume which I now display to your astounded eyes."

Xallops whisked away cloth to reveal a great book bound in black leather. "On command this volume must reveal information of any and every sort; it knows each trivial detail, from the time the stars first caught fire to the present date. Ask; you shall be answered!"

"Remarkable!" declared Duke Orbal. "Present before us the Lost Ode of Psyrme!"

"Certainly," said the book in a rasping voice. It threw back its covers to reveal a page covered with crabbed and interlocked characters.

Duke Orbal put a perplexed question: "This is beyond my comprehension; you may furnish a translation."

"The request is denied," said the book. "Such poetry is too sweet for ordinary ears."

Duke Orbal glanced at Xallops, who spoke quickly to the book: "Show us scenes from aeons past."

"As you like. Reverting to the Nineteenth Aeon of the Fifty-second Cycle, I display a view across Linxfade Valley, toward Kolghut's Tower of Frozen Blood."

"The detail is both notable and exact!" declared Duke Orbal. "I am curious to gaze upon the semblance of Kolghut himself."

"Nothing could be easier. Here is the terrace of the Temple at Tanutra. Kolghut stands beside the flowering wail-bush. In the chair sits the Empress Noxon, now in her hundred and fortieth year. She has tasted no water in her entire lifetime, and eats only bitter blossom, with occasionally a morsel of boiled eel."

"Bah!" said Duke Orbal. "A most hideous old creature! Who are those gentlemen ranked behind her?"

"They constitute her retinue of lovers. Every month one of their number is executed and a new stalwart is recruited to take his place. Competition is keen to win the affectionate regard of the Empress."

"Bah!" muttered Duke Orbal. "Show us rather a beautiful court lady of the Yellow Age."

The book spoke a petulant syllable in an unknown language. The page turned to reveal a travertine promenade beside a slow river.

"This view reveals to good advantage the topiary of the time. Notice here, and here!" With a luminous arrow the book indicated a row of massive trees clipped into globular shapes. "Those are irix, the sap of which may be used as an effective vermifuge. The species is now extinct. Along the concourse you will observe a multitude of persons. Those with black stockings and long white beards are Alulian slaves, whose ancestors arrived from far Canopus. They are also extinct. In the middle distance stands a beautiful woman named Jiao Jaro. She is indicated by a red dot over her head, although her face is turned toward the river."

"This is hardly satisfactory," grumbled Duke Orbal. "Xallops, can you not control the perversity of your exhibit?"

"I fear not, your Grace."

Duke Orbal gave a sniff of displeasure. "A final question! Who among the folk now residing in Cuirnif presents the greatest threat to the welfare of my realm?"

"I am a repository of information, not an oracle," stated the book. "However, I will remark that among those present stands a fox-faced vagabond with a crafty expression, whose habits would bring a blush to the cheeks of the Empress Noxon herself. His name—"

Cugel leapt forward and pointed across the plaza. "The robber! There he goes now! Summon the constables! Sound the gong!"

While everyone turned to look, Cugel slammed shut the book and dug his knuckles into the cover. The book grunted in annoyance.

Duke Orbal turned back with a frown of perplexity. "I saw no robber."

"In that case, I was surely mistaken. But yonder waits Iolo with his famous 'Bagful of Dreams'!"

The Duke moved on to Iolo's pavilion, followed by the enthralled onlookers. Duke Orbal said: "Iolo the Dream-taker, your fame has preceded you all the distance from Dai-Passant! I hereby tender you an official welcome!"

Iolo answered in an anguished voice: "Your Grace, I have sorry news to relate. For the whole of one year I prepared for this day, hoping to win the grand prize. The blast of midnight winds, the outrage of householders, the terrifying attentions of ghosts, shrees, roof-runners and fermins: all of these have caused me discomfort! I have roamed the dark hours in pursuit of my dreams! I have lurked beside dormers, crawled through attics, hovered over couches; I have suffered scratches and contusions; but never have I counted the cost if through my enterprise I were able to capture some particularly choice specimen.

"Each dream trapped in my net I carefully examined; for every dream cherished and saved I released a dozen, and finally from my store of superlatives I fashioned my wonderful crystals, and these I brought down the long road from Dai-Passant. Then, only last night, under the most mysterious circumstances, my precious goods were stolen by a robber only Cugel claims to have seen.

"I now point out that the dreams, whether near or far, represent marvels of truly superlative quality, and I feel that a careful description of the items—"

Duke Orbal held up his hand. "I must reiterate the judgment rendered upon Bazzard. A stringent rule stipulates that neither imaginary nor purported marvels qualify for the competition. Perhaps we will have the opportunity to adjudicate your dreams on another occasion. Now we must pass on to Cugel's pavilion and investigate his provocative 'Nowhere'."

Cugel stepped up on the dais before his exhibit. "Your Grace, I present for your inspection a legitimate marvel: not a straggle of insects, not a pedantic almanac, but an authentic miracle." Cugel whisked away the cloth. "Behold!"

The Duke made a puzzled sound. "A pile of dirt? A stump? What is that odd-looking member emerging from the hole?"

"Your Grace, I have here an opening into an unknown space, with the arm of one of its denizens. Inspect this tentacle! It pulses with the life of another cosmos! Notice the golden luster of the dorsal surface, the green and lavender of these encrustations. On the underside you will discover three colors of a sort never before seen!"

With a nonplussed expression Duke Orbal pulled at his chin. "This is all very well, but where is the rest of the creature? You present not a marvel, but the fraction of a marvel! I can make no judgment on the basis of a tail, or a hindquarters, or a proboscis, whatever the member may be. Additionally, you claim that the hole enters a far cosmos; still I see only a hole, resembling nothing so much as the den of a wysen-imp."

Iolo thrust himself forward. "May I venture an opinion? As I reflect upon events, I have become convinced that Cugel himself stole my Dreams!" "Your remarks interest no one," said Cugel. "Kindly hold your tongue while I continue my demonstration."

Iolo was not to be subdued so easily. He turned to Duke Orbal and cried in a poignant voice: "Hear me out, if you will! I am convinced that the 'robber' is no more than a figment of Cugel's imagination! He took my dreams and hid them, and where else but in the hole itself? For evidence I cite that length of string which leads into the hole."

Duke Orbal inspected Cugel with a frown. "Are these charges true? Answer exactly, since all can be verified."

Cugel chose his words with care. "I can only affirm what I myself know. Conceivably the robber hid Iolo's dreams in the hole while I was otherwise occupied. For what purpose? Who can say?"

Duke Orbal asked in a gentle voice: "Has anyone thought to search the hole for this elusive 'bag of dreams'?"

Cugel gave an indifferent shrug. "Iolo may enter now and search to his heart's content."

"You claim this hole!" retorted Iolo. "It therefore becomes your duty to protect the public!"

For several minutes an animated argument took place, until Duke Orbal intervened. "Both parties have raised persuasive points; I feel, however, that I must rule against Cugel. I therefore decree that he search his premises for the missing dreams and recover them if possible."

Cugel disputed the decision with such vigor that Duke Orbal turned to glance along the skyline, whereupon Cugel moderated his position. "The judgment of your Grace of course must prevail, and if I must, I will cast about for Iolo's lost dreams, although his theories are clearly absurd."

"Please do so, at once."

Cugel obtained a long pole, to which he attached a grapple. Gingerly thrusting his contrivance into the hole, he raked back and forth, but succeeded only in stimulating the tentacle, which thrashed from side to side.

Iolo suddenly cried out in excitement. "I notice a remarkable fact! The block of earth is at most six feet in breadth, yet Cugel plunged into the hole a pole twelve feet in length! What trickery does he practice now?"

Cugel replied in even tones: "I promised Duke Orbal a marvel and a wonderment, and I believe that I have done so."

Duke Orbal nodded gravely. "Well said, Cugel! Your exhibit is provocative! Still, you offer us only a tantalizing glimpse: a bottomless hole, a length of tentacle, a strange color, a far-off light—to the effect that your exhibit seems somewhat makeshift and impromptu. Contrast, if you will, the precision of Zaraflam's cockroaches!" He held up his hand as Cugel started to protest. "You display a hole: admitted, and a fine hole it is. But how does this hole differ from any other? Can I in justice award the prize on such a basis?"

"The matter may be resolved in a manner to satisfy us all," said Cugel. "Let Iolo enter the hole, to assure himself that his dreams are indeed elsewhere. Then, on his return, he will bear witness to the truly marvelous nature of my exhibit."

Iolo made an instant protest. "Cugel claims the exhibit; let him make the exploration!"

Duke Orbal raised his hand for silence. "I pronounce a decree to the effect that Cugel must immediately enter his exhibit in search of Iolo's properties, and likewise make a careful study of the environment, for the benefit of us all."

"Your Grace!" protested Cugel. "This is no simple matter! The tentacle almost fills the hole!"

"I see sufficient room for an agile man to slide past."

"Your Grace, to be candid, I do not care to enter the hole, by reason of extreme fear."

Duke Orbal again glanced up at the tubes which stood in a row along the skyline. He spoke over his shoulder to a burly man in a maroon and black uniform. "Which of the tubes is most suitable for use at this time?"

"The second tube from the right, your Grace, is only one-quarter occupied."

Cugel declared in a trembling voice: "I fear, but I have conquered my fear! I will seek Iolo's lost dreams!"

"Excellent," said Duke Orbal with a tight-lipped grin. "Please do not delay; my patience wears thin."

Cugel tentatively thrust a leg into the hole, but the motion of the tentacle caused him to snatch it out again. Duke Orbal muttered a few words to his constable, who brought up a winch. The tentacle was hauled forth from the hole a good five yards.

Duke Orbal instructed Cugel: "Straddle the tentacle, seize it with hands and legs and it will draw you back through the hole."

In desperation Cugel clambered upon the tentacle. The tension of the winch was relaxed and Cugel was pulled into the hole.

The light of Earth curled away from the opening and made no entrance; Cugel was plunged into a condition of near-total darkness, where, however, by some paradoxical condition he was able to sense the scope of his new environment in detail.

He stood on a surface at once flat, yet rough, with rises and dips and hummocks like the face of a windy sea. The black spongy stuff underfoot showed small cavities and tunnels in which Cugel sensed the motion of innumerable near-invisible points of light. Where the sponge rose high, the crest curled over like breaking surf, or stood ragged and crusty; in either case, the fringes glowed red, pale blue and several colors Cugel had never before observed. No horizon could be detected and the local concepts of distance, proportion, and size were not germane to Cugel's understanding.

Overhead hung dead Nothingness. The single feature of note, a large disk the color of rain, floated at the zenith, an object so dim as to be almost invisible. At an indeterminate distance—a mile? ten miles? a hundred yards?—a hummock of some bulk overlooked the entire panorama. On closer inspection Cugel saw this hummock to be a prodigious mound of gelatinous flesh, inside which floated a globular organ apparently analogous to an eye. From the base of this creature a hundred tentacles extended far and wide across the black sponge. One of these tentacles passed near Cugel's feet, through the intra-cosmic gap, and out upon the soil of Earth.

Cugel discovered Iolo's sack of dreams, not three feet distant. The black sponge, bruised by the impact, had welled a liquid which had dissolved a hole in the leather, allowing the star-shaped dreams to spill out upon the sponge. In groping with the pole, Cugel had damaged a growth of brown palps. The resulting exudation had dripped upon the dreams and when Cugel picked up one of the fragile flakes, he saw that its edges glowed with eery fringes of color. The combination of oozes which had permeated the object caused his fingers to itch and tingle.

A score of small luminous nodes swarmed around his head, and a soft voice addressed him by name. "Cugel, what a pleasure that you have come to visit us! What is your opinion of our pleasant land?''

Cugel looked about in wonder; how could a denizen of this place know his name? At a distance of ten yards he noticed a small hummock of plasm not unlike the monstrous bulk with the floating eye.

Luminous nodes circled his head and the voice sounded in his ears: ''You are perplexed, but remember, here we do things differently. We transfer our thoughts in small modules; if you look closely you will see them speeding through the fluxion: dainty little animalcules eager to unload their weight of enlightenment. There! Notice! Directly before your eyes hovers an excellent example. It is a thought of your own regarding which you are dubious; hence it hesitates, and awaits your decision.''

''What if I speak?'' asked Cugel. ''Will this not facilitate matters?''

''To the contrary! Sound is considered offensive and everyone deplores the slightest murmur.''

''This is all very well,'' grumbled Cugel, ''but—''

''Silence, please! Send forth animalcules only!''

Cugel dispatched a whole host of luminous purports: ''I will do my best. Perhaps you can inform me how far this land extends?''

''Not with certainty. At times I send forth animalcules to explore the far places; they report an infinite landscape similar to that which you see.''

''Duke Orbal of Ombalique has commanded me to gather information and he will be interested in your remarks. Are valuable substances to be found here?''

''To a certain extent. There is proscedel and diphany and an occasional coruscation of zamanders.''

''My first concern, of course, is to collect information for Duke Orbal, and I must also rescue Iolo's dreams; still I would be pleased to acquire a valuable trinket or two, if only to remind myself of our pleasant association.''

''Understandable! I sympathize with your objectives.''

''In that case, how may I obtain a quantity of such substances?''

''Easily. Simply send off animalcules to gather up your requirements.'' The creature emitted a whole host of pale plasms which darted away in all directions and presently returned with several dozen small spheres sparkling with a frosty blue light. ''Here are zamanders of the first water,'' said the creature. ''Accept them with my compliments.''

Cugel placed the gems in his pouch. ''This is a most convenient system for gaining wealth. I also wish to obtain a certain amount of diphany."

"Send forth animalcules! Why exert yourself needlessly?"

"We think along similar lines." Cugel dispatched several hundred animalcules which presently returned with twenty small ingots of the precious metal.

Cugel examined his pouch. "I still have room for a quantity of proscedel. With your permission I will send out the requisite animalcules."

"I would not dream of interfering," asserted the creature.

The animalcules sped forth, and before long returned with sufficient proscedel to fill Cugel's pouch. The creature said thoughtfully: "This is at least half of Uthaw's treasure; however, he appears not to have noticed its absence."

" 'Uthaw'?" inquired Cugel. "Do you refer to yonder monstrous hulk?"

"Yes, that is Uthaw, who sometimes is both coarse and irascible."

Uthaw's eyes rolled toward Cugel and bulged through the outer membrane. A tide of animalcules arrived pulsing with significance. "I notice that Cugel has stolen my treasure, which I denounce as a breach of hospitality! In retribution, he must dig twenty-two zamanders from below the Shivering Trillows. He must then sift eight pounds of prime proscedel from the Dust of Time. Finally he must scrape eight acres of diphany bloom from the face of the High Disk."

Cugel sent forth animalcules. "Lord Uthaw, the penalty is harsh but just. A moment while I go to fetch the necessary tools!" He gathered up the dreams and sprang to the aperture. Seizing the tentacle he cried through the hole: "Pull the tentacle, work the winch! I have rescued the dreams!"

The tentacle convulsed and thrashed, effectively blocking the opening. Cugel turned and putting his fingers to his mouth emitted a piercing whistle. Uthaw's eye rolled upward and the tentacle fell limp.

The winch heaved at the tentacle and Cugel was drawn back through the hole. Uthaw, recovering his senses, jerked his tentacle so violently that the rope snapped; the winch was sent flying; and several persons were swept from their feet. Uthaw jerked back his tentacle and the hole immediately closed.

Cugel cast the sack of dream-flakes contemptuously at the feet of Iolo. "There you are, ingrate! Take your vapid hallucinations and go your way! Let us hear no more of you!"

Cugel turned to Duke Orbal. "I am now able to render a report upon the other cosmos. The ground is composed of a black sponge-like substance and flickers with a trillion infinitesimal glimmers. My research discovered no limits to the extent of the land. A pale disk, barely visible, covers a quarter of the sky. The denizens are, first and foremost, an ill-natured hulk named Uthaw, and others more or less similar. No sound is allowed and meaning is conveyed by animalcules, which also procure the necessities of life. In essence, these are my discoveries, and now, with utmost respect, I claim the grand prize of one thousand terces.''

From behind his back Cugel heard Iolo's mocking laughter. Duke Orbal shook his head. ''My dear Cugel, what you suggest is impossible. To what exhibit do you refer? The boxful of dirt yonder? It lacks all pretensions to singularity.''

''But you saw the hole! With your winch you pulled the tentacle! In accordance with your orders, I entered the hole and explored the region!''

''True enough, but hole and tentacle are both vanished. I do not for a moment suggest mendacity, but your report is not easily verified. I can hardly award honors to an entity so fugitive as the memory of a non-existent hole! I fear that on this occasion I must pass you by. The prize will be awarded to Zaraflam and his remarkable cockroaches.''

''A moment, your Grace!'' Iolo called out. ''Remember, I am entered in the competition! At last I am able to display my products! Here is a particularly choice item, distilled from a hundred dreams captured early in the morning from a bevy of beautiful maidens asleep in a bower of fragrant vines.''

''Very well,'' said Duke Orbal. ''I will delay the award until I test the quality of your visions. What is the procedure? Must I compose myself for slumber?''

''Not at all! The ingestion of the dream during waking hours produces not a hallucination, but a mood: a sensibility fresh, new and sweet: an allurement of the faculties, an indescribable exhilaration. Still, why should you not be comfortable as you test my dreams? You there! Fetch a couch! And you, a cushion for his Grace's noble head. You! Be good enough to take his Grace's hat.''

Cugel saw no profit in remaining. He moved to the outskirts of the throng.

Iolo brought forth his dream and for a moment seemed puzzled by the ooze still adhering to the object, then decided to ignore the matter, and paid no further heed, except to rub his fingers as if after contact with some viscid substance.

Making a series of grand gestures, Iolo approached the great chair where Duke Orbal sat at his ease. ''I will arrange the dream for its most convenient ingestion,'' said Iolo. ''I place a quantity into each ear; I insert a trifle up each nostril; I arrange the balance under your Grace's illustrious tongue. Now, if your Grace will relax, in half a minute the quintessence of a hundred exquisite dreams will be made known.''

Duke Orbal became rigid. His fingers clenched the arms of the chair. His back arched and his eyes bulged from their sockets. He turned over backward, then rolled, jerked, jumped and bounded about the plaza before the amazed eyes of his subjects.

Iolo called out in a brassy voice: ''Where is Cugel? Fetch that scoundrel Cugel!''

But Cugel had already departed Cuirnif and was nowhere to be found.

Chapter VI

FROM CUIRNIF TO PERGOLO

1

The Four Wizards

Cugel's visit to Cuirnif was marred by several disagreeable incidents, and he left town with more haste than dignity. At last he pushed through an alder thicket, jumped a ditch and scrambled up on the Old Ferghaz High-road. Pausing to look and listen, and discovering that pursuit apparently had been abandoned, he set off at best speed to the west.

The road lay across a wide blue moor patched here and there with small forests. The region was eerily silent; scanning the moor, Cugel found only distance; a wide sky and solitude, with no sign of hut or house.

From the direction of Cuirnif came a trap drawn by a one-horned wheriot. The driver was Bazzard, who, like Cugel, had exhibited at the Exposition of Marvels. Bazzard's entry, like Cugel's 'Nowhere', had been disqualified for technical reasons.

Bazzard halted the trap. "So, Cugel, I see that you decided to leave your exhibit at Cuirnif."

"I had no real choice," said Cugel. "With the hole gone, 'Nowhere' became a massive boxful of dirt, which I was happy to leave in the custody of Duke Orbal."

"I did the same with my dead fish," said Bazzard. He looked around the moor. "This is a sinister district, with robber asms watching from every forest. Where are you bound?"

"Ultimately, to Azenomei in Almery. As of now, I would be happy to find shelter for the night."

"In that case, why not ride with me? I will be grateful for your company. Tonight we will stop at the Iron Man Inn, and tomorrow should bring us to Llaio where I live with my four fathers."

"Your offer is welcome," said Cugel. He climbed to the seat; Bazzard touched up the wheriot and the trap moved along the road at good speed.

After a period Bazzard said: "If I am not mistaken, Iucounu the Laughing Magician, as he is known, makes his resort at Pergolo, which is near Azenomei. Perhaps you and he are acquainted?"

"We are indeed," said Cugel. "He has enjoyed several choice jokes at my expense."

"Aha then! I gather that he is not one of your most trusted comrades."

Cugel looked over his shoulder and spoke in a distinct voice. "Should any casual ears be listening, let it be known that my regard for Iucounu is of a high order."

Bazzard made a sign of comprehension. "Whatever the case, why are you returning to Azenomei?"

Again Cugel looked in all directions. "Still in reference to Iucounu: his many friends often report overheard messages, but sometimes in garbled form; hence I am careful to avoid loose talk."

"That is correct conduct!" said Bazzard. "At Llaio, my four fathers are equally prudent." After a moment Cugel asked: "Many times I have known a father with four sons, but never before a son with four fathers. What is the explanation?"

Bazzard scratched his head in puzzlement. "I have never thought to ask," he said. "I will do so at the earliest opportunity."

The journey proceeded without incident and late in the afternoon of the second day, the two arrived at Llaio, a large manse of sixteen gables.

A groom took the trap into charge; Bazzard conducted Cugel through a tall iron-bound door, across a reception hall and into a parlour. High windows, each of twelve violet panes, dimmed the afternoon sunlight; fusty magenta beams, slanting down across the room, warmed the dark oak wainscoting. A long table rested on dark green carpeting. Close together, with their backs to the fire, sat four men of unusual aspect, in that they shared between them a single eye, a single ear, a single arm and a single leg. In other respects the four were much alike: small and slight, with round serious faces and black hair cut short.

Bazzard performed the introductions. As he spoke the four men deftly passed arm, eye and ear back and forth, so that each was able to appraise the quality of their visitor.

"This gentleman is Cugel," said Bazzard. "He is a minor grandee of the Twish River Valley, who has suffered the jokes of someone who shall remain nameless. Cugel, allow me to present my four fathers! They are Disserl, Vasker, Pelasias and Archimbaust: at one time wizards of repute until they too ran afoul of a certain prankster magician.''

Pelasias, who at this moment wore both the eye and ear, spoke: ''Be assured of our welcome! Guests at Llaio are all too rare. How did you chance to meet our son Bazzard?''

''We occupied close pavilions at the Exposition,'' said Cugel. ''With due respect for Duke Orbal, I feel that his rulings were arbitrary, and neither Bazzard nor I won the prize.''

''Cugel's remarks are not exaggerated,'' said Bazzard. ''I was not even allowed to simulate the songs of my unfortunate fish.''

''A pity!'' said Pelasias. ''Still, the Exposition no doubt provided memorable experiences for you both, so the time was not wasted. Am I right in this, Bazzard?''

''Quite right, sir, and while the subject is fresh in my mind, I would like you to resolve a perplexity. A single father often boasts four sons, but how does a single son boast four fathers?''

Disserl, Vasker and Archimbaust rapidly tapped the table; the eye, ear and arm were interchanged. At last Vasker made a curt gesture. ''The question is nuncupatory.''

Archimbaust, providing himself with eye and ear, examined Cugel with care. He seemed especially interested in Cugel's cap, to which Cugel had again attached 'Spatterlight'. ''That is a remarkable ornament,'' said Archimbaust.

Cugel bowed politely. ''I consider it very fine.''

''As to the origin of this object: do you care to provide us any information?''

Cugel smilingly shook his head. ''Let us change the subject to more interesting topics. Bazzard tells me that we have a number of friends in common, including the noble and popular Iucounu.''

Archimbaust blinked his eye in puzzlement. ''Are we speaking of that yellow, immoral and repulsive Iucounu, sometimes known as the 'Laughing Magician'?''

Cugel winced and shuddered. ''I would never make such insulting references to dear Iucounu, especially if I thought that he or one of his loyal spies might overhear.''

''Aha!'' said Archimbaust. ''Now I understand your diffidence! You need not worry! We are protected by a warning device. You may speak freely.''

''In that case I will admit that my friendship with Iucounu is not deep and abiding. Recently, at his command, a leather-winged demon carried me across the Ocean of Sighs and dropped me sprawling upon a dreary beach known as Shânglestone Strand.''

''If that is a joke, it is in poor taste!'' declared Bazzard.

''That is my opinion,'' said Cugel. ''In regard to this ornament, it is actually a scale known as the 'Pectoral Sky-break Spatterlight', from the prow of the demiurge Sadlark. It exhibits power which, frankly, I do not understand, and is dangerous to the touch unless your hands are wet.''

''All very well,'' said Bazzard, ''but why did you not wish to discuss it before?''

''By reason of a most interesting fact: Iucounu owns all the rest of Sadlark's scales! He will therefore covet 'Spatterlight' with all of that intense and excitable yearning which we associate with Iucounu.''

''Most interesting!'' said Archimbaust. He and his brothers tapped a flurry of messages back and forth, interchanging their single eye, ear and arm with swift precision. Cugel, watching, at last was able to hazard a guess as to how four fathers might sire a single son.

Vasker presently asked: ''What are your plans in connection with Iucounu and this extraordinary scale?''

''I am both uncertain and uneasy,'' said Cugel. ''Iucounu covets 'Spatterlight': true! He will approach me and say: 'Ah, dear Cugel, how nice that you bring me 'Spatterlight'! Hand it over, or prepare for a joke!' So then: where is my recourse? My advantage is lost. When one deals with Iucounu, he must be prepared to jump nimbly from side to side. I have quick wits and agile feet, but are these enough?''

''Evidently not,'' said Vasker. ''Still—''

A hissing noise made itself heard. Vasker at once imposed upon his voice the tremolo of fond recollection: ''Yes, dear Iucounu! How strange, Cugel, that you should also number him among your friends!''

Noting Bazzard's secret sign, Cugel spoke in tones equally melodious. ''He is known far and wide as an excellent fellow!''

''Just so! We have had our little differences, but is this not sometimes the way? Now, all is forgotten, on both sides, I am sure.''

Bazzard spoke: ''If you should chance to see him in Almery, please convey our very warmest regards!''

''I will not be seeing Iucounu,'' said Cugel. ''I plan to retire to a snug little cabin beside the River Sune and perhaps learn a useful trade.'

''On the whole, this seems a sensible plan,'' said Archimbaust. ''But come now, Bazzard, tell us more of the Exposition!''

''It was grandly conceived,'' said Bazzard. ''No doubt as to that! Cugel displayed a remarkable hole, but Duke Orbal disallowed it on grounds of fugacity. Xallops showed a 'Compendium of Universal Knowledge' which impressed everyone. The cover depicted the Gnostic Emblem, in this fashion. . . .''

Taking up stylus and paper, Bazzard scribbled: *Do not look now, but Iucounu's spy hangs above, in a wisp of smoke.* ''There, Cugel! Am I not correct?''

''Yes, in the main, although you have omitted several significant flourishes.''

''My memory is not the best,'' said Bazzard. He crumpled the paper and threw it into the fire.

Vasker spoke. ''Friend Cugel, perhaps you would enjoy a sip of dyssac, or might you prefer wine?''

''I will be happy with either,'' said Cugel.

''In that case, I will suggest the dyssac. We distill it ourselves from local herbs. Bazzard, if you will.''

While Bazzard served the liquor, Cugel glanced as if casually around the chamber. High in the shadows he noticed a wisp of smoke from which peered a pair of small red eyes.

In a droning voice Vasker spoke of the Llaio fowl-run and the high price of feed. The spy at last became bored; the smoke slipped down the wall, into the chimney and was gone.

Pelasias looked through the eye to Bazzard. ''The alarm again is set?''

''Quite so.''

''Then once again we can speak freely. Cugel, I will be explicit. At one time we were wizards of reputation, but Iucounu played us a joke which still rankles. Our magic for the most part is forgotten; nothing remains but a few tendrils of hope and, of course, our abiding detestation of Iucounu.''

''Clarity itself! What do you propose to do?''

''More to the point: what are your plans? Iucounu will take your scale without remorse, laughing and joking all the while. How will you prevent him?''

Cugel pulled uneasily at his chin. ''I have given some attention to the matter.''

''To what effect?''

''I had thought perhaps to hide the scale, and confuse Iucounu with hints and lures. Already I am troubled by doubts. Iucounu might simply ignore my conundrums in favor of Panguire's Triumphant Displasms. No doubt I would be quick to say: 'Iucounu, your jokes are superb and you shall have your scale.' My best hope may be to present the scale to Iucounu face to face, as a purported act of generosity.''

''In this case, how are your goals advanced?'' asked Pelasias.

* * *

Cugel looked around the room. "We are secure?"

"Definitely so."

"Then I will reveal an important fact. The scale consumes whomever it touches, save in the presence of water, which dulls its voracity."

Pelasias regarded Cugel with new respect. "I must say that you wear this lethal trinket with aplomb."

"I am always aware of its presence. It has already absorbed a pelgrane and a female hybrid of bazil and grue.

"Aha!" said Pelasias. "Let us put this scale to the test. At the fowl run we trapped a weasel who now awaits execution: why not by the power of your ornament?"

Cugel assented. "As you like."

Bazzard fetched the captive predator, which snarled and hissed in defiance. Wetting his hands, Cugel tied the scale to a stick and thrust it down upon the weasel, which was instantly absorbed. The node showed new coruscations of red, vibrating to such vivid fervor that Cugel was reluctant to pin it again to his cap. He wrapped it in several layers of heavy cloth and tucked it into his pouch.

Disserl now wore eye and ear. "Your scale has shown its power. Nonetheless, it lacks projective scope. You need our help, sickly though it may be. Then, if you are successful, perhaps you will restore our orphan members."

"They may no longer be in useful condition," said Cugel dubiously.

"We need not worry on this score," replied Disserl. "The organs, fully sound and competent, reside in Iucounu's vault."

"That is good news," said Cugel. "I agree to your terms, and I am anxious to hear how you can help me."

"First and most urgently, we must ensure that Iucounu cannot take the scale either through force or intimidation, or by means of Arnhoult's Sequestrous Digitalia, or by a time stoppage, such as the Interminable Interim. If he is so thwarted, then he must play the game by your rules, and victory is at your command."

Vasker took the organs. "Already I am cheered! In Cugel we have a man who can confront Iucounu nose to nose and never flinch!"

Cugel jumped to his feet and paced nervously back and forth. "A truculent posture may not be the best approach. Iucounu, after all, knows a thousand tricks. How will we prevent him from using his magic? Here is the nub of the matter."

"I will take counsel with my brothers," said Vasker. "Bazzard, you and Cugel may dine in the Hall of Trophies. Be mindful of spies."

After a dinner of fair quality, Bazzard and Cugel returned to the parlour, where the four wizards sipped in turn from a great mug of tea. Pelasias, now wearing eye, arm and ear, spoke: "We have consulted Boberg's *Pandaemonium* and also the Vapurial Index. We now are convinced that you carry something more than just a handsome scale. Rather, it is Sadlark's cerebral nexus itself. It has ingested several creatures of strong personality, including our own good weasel, and now displays signs of vitality, as if recovering from an estivation. No more strength may be allowed Sadlark at this time."

Archimbaust took the organs. "We think in terms of pure logic: Proposition One: in order to achieve our goals, Cugel must confront Iucounu. Proposition Two: Iucounu must be deterred from seizing the scale out of hand."

Cugel frowned. "Your propositions are orderly, but I envision a program somewhat more subtle. The scale will bait a trap; Iucounu will run eagerly forward and be rendered helpless."

"Inept, on three counts! First: you will be watched by spies, or by Iucounu himself. Second: Iucounu recognizes bait from afar and will send either a casual passer-by or you yourself into the trap. Third: in preference to negotiation, Iucounu uses Tinkler's Old-fashioned Froust, and you would find yourself running from Pergolo on thirty-foot strides to retrieve the scale for Iucounu."

Cugel held up his hand. "Let us return to the propositions of pure logic. As I recall, Iucounu must not be allowed to seize the scale out of hand. What follows?"

"We have several dependent corollaries. To slow the quick grasp of his avarice, you must feign the submission of a cowed dog, a pose which Iucounu in his vanity will readily accept. Next we will need an article of confusion, to give us a range of options from which to choose. Tomorrow, therefore, Bazzard will duplicate the scale in fine gold, with a good red hypolite for the node. He will then cement the false scale to your cap in a bed of explosive diambroid."

"And I am to wear the cap?" asked Cugel.

"Of course! You will then have three strings to your bow. All will be destroyed if Iucounu tries even the least of his tricks. Or you can give Iucounu the cap itself, then go somewhat apart and wait for the blast. Or, if Iucounu discovers the diambroid, other avenues appear. For instance, you can temporize, then make play with the authentic scale."

Cugel rubbed his chin. "Propositions and corollaries to the side,

I am not anxious to wear a charge of high explosive attached to my cap."

Archimbaust argued the program, but Cugel remained dubious. Somewhat sulkily Archimbaust relinquished the organs to Vasker who said: "I propose a somewhat similar plan. As before, Cugel, you will enter Almery in an unobtrusive manner. You will stroll quietly by the side of the road with the cloak pulled across your face, using any name but your own. Iucounu will be intrigued, and come out in search of you. At this point your policy will be restrained courtesy. You will politely decline all offers and go your own way. This conduct will surely prompt Iucounu to unwise excess! Then you will act!"

"Just so," said Cugel. "What if he simply seizes cap and scale, false or real, and preempts it to his own use?"

"That is the virtue of Archimbaust's scheme," Vasker pointed out.

Cugel gnawed at his lower lip. "Each plan seems to lack a certain full elegance."

Archimbaust, taking the organs, spoke with emphasis: "My plan is best! Do you prefer Forlorn Encystment at a depth of forty-five miles to an ounce or two of diambroid?"

Bazzard, who had spoken little, put forward an idea: "We need only use a small quantity of diambroid, and thus allay the worst of Cugel's fears. Three minims is enough to destroy Iucounu's hand, arm and shoulder, in the case of improper conduct."

Vasker said: "This is an excellent compromise! Bazzard, you have a good head on your shoulders! The diambroid, after all, need not come into use. I am sure that Cugel will deal with Iucounu as a cat plays with a mouse."

Disserl spoke to the same effect: "Show only diffidence! His vanity will then become your ally!"

Pelasias said: "Above all, accept no favors! Or you will find yourself in his obligation, which is like a bottomless pit. At one time—"

A sudden hiss, as the alarm web detected a spy.

"—packet of dried fruits and raisins for your pouch," droned Pelasias. "The way is long and tiring, especially if you use the Old Ferghaz Way which traces every swing and meander of the River Sune. Why not make for Taun Tassel on the Waters-gleam?"

"A good plan! The way is long and Forest Da is dark, but I hope to evade even the whisper of notoriety, and all my old friends as well."

"And your ultimate plans?"

Cugel gave a wistful laugh. "I will build a little hut beside the river and there live out my days. Perhaps I will do a small trade in nuts and wild honey."

"There is always a market for home-baked loaves," Bazzard pointed out.

"A good thought! Again, I might search out scraps of old calligraphy, or just give myself to meditation and watch the flow of the river. Such, at least, is my modest hope."

"It is a pleasant ambition! If only we could help you along your way! But our magic is small; we know a single useful spell: Brassman's Twelve-fold Bounty, by which a single terce becomes a dozen. We have taught it to Bazzard, that he may never want; perhaps he will share the sleight with you."

"With pleasure," said Bazzard. "You will find it a great comfort!"

"That is most kind," said Cugel. "What with the packet of fruit and nuts, I am well-provided for my journey."

"Just so! Perhaps you will leave us your cap ornament as a keepsake, so that when we see it we will think of you."

Cugel shook his head in distress. "Anything else is yours! But I could never part with my lucky talisman!"

"No matter! We will remember you in any case. Bazzard, foster the fire! Tonight is unseasonably cold."

So went the conversation until the spy departed, whereupon, at Cugel's request, Bazzard instructed him in that cantrap controlling the Twelve-fold Bounty. Then, upon sudden thought, Bazzard addressed Vasker, now wearing eye, ear and arm. "Another of our small magics which might help Cugel on his way: the Spell of the Tireless Legs."

Vasker chuckled. "What a thought! Cugel will not care to be visited with a spell customarily reserved for our wheriots! Such a spell does not accord with his dignity."

"I give dignity second place to expedience," said Cugel. "What is this spell?"

Bazzard said half-apologetically: "It guards the legs from the fatigue of a long day's march, and as Vasker indicates, we use it mainly to encourage our wheriots."

"I will consider the matter," said Cugel, and there the subject rested.

In the morning Bazzard took Cugel to his work-shop, where, after donning wet gloves, he duplicated the scale in fine gold, with a central node of flaming red hypolite. "Now then," said Bazzard. "Three minims of diambroid, or perhaps four, and Iucounu's fate is as good as sealed."

Cugel watched glumly as Bazzard cemented diambroid to the ornament and attached it to his cap by a secret clasp. "You will find this a great comfort," said Bazzard.

Cugel gingerly donned the cap. "I see no obvious advantage to this false, if explosive, scale, save for the fact that duplicity is valuable for its own sake." He folded 'Spatterlight' into the flap of a special glove provided by the four wizards.

"I will provide you with a packet of nuts and fruit, and then you will be ready for the road," said Bazzard. "If you move at a good pace, you should arrive at Taun Tassel on Water's-gleam before nightfall."

Cugel said thoughtfully: "As I consider the way ahead, I become ever more favorably inclined to the Spell of the Untiring Legs."

"It is the work of a few minutes only," said Bazzard. "Let us consult my fathers."

The two repaired to the parlour, where Archimbaust consulted an index of spells. Encompassing the syllables with effort, he released the salutary force toward Cugel.

To the amazement of all, the spell struck Cugel's legs, rebounded, struck again without effect, then clattered away, reverberated from wall to wall, and finally lapsed in a series of small grinding sounds.

The four wizards consulted together at length. Finally Disserl turned to Cugel: "This is a most extraordinary happening! It can only be explained by the fact that you carry 'Spatterlight', whose alien force acts as a crust against earthly magic!"

Bazzard cried out in excitement: "Try the Spell of Internal Effervescence upon Cugel; if it proves fruitless, then we shall know the truth!"

"And if the spell is efficacious?" asked Disserl coldly. "Is this your concept of hospitality?"

"My apologies!" said Bazzard in confusion. "I failed to think the matter through."

"It seems that I must forego the 'Untiring Legs'," said Cugel. "But no matter: I am accustomed to the road, and now I will take my leave."

"Our hopes go with you!" said Vasker. "Boldness and caution: let them work hand in hand!"

"I am grateful for your wise counsel," said Cugel. "Everything now depends upon Iucounu. If avarice dominates his prudence, you shall soon know the enjoyment of your missing organs. Bazzard, our chance acquaintance has yielded profit, so I hope, for all concerned." Cugel departed Llaio.

2

Spatterlight

Where a bridge of black glass crossed the River Sune, Cugel found a marker announcing that he had once again come into the Land of Almery.

The road forked. Old Ferghaz Way followed the Sune, while the Kang Kingdom Marchway, swinging south, crossed the Hanging Hills and so descended into the valley of the River Twish.

Cugel held to the right and so fared west through a countryside of small farmsteads, demarcated one from the other by lines of tall mulgoon trees.

A stream flowed down from the Forest Da to join the Sune; the road crossed over by a bridge of three arches. At the far side, leaning against a damson tree and chewing a straw stood Iucounu.

Cugel halted to stare, and at last decided that he saw, not an apparition nor a yellow-faced hallucination with pendulous jowls, but Iucounu himself. A tawny coat contained the pear-shaped torso; the thin legs were encased in tight pink-and black-striped trousers.

Cugel had not expected to see Iucounu so soon. He leaned forward and peered, as if in doubt. "Am I correct in recognizing Iucounu?"

"Quite correct," said Iucounu, rolling his yellow eyes in every direction except toward Cugel.

"This is a true surprise!"

Iucounu put his hand to his mouth to conceal a smile. "A pleasant surprise, I hope?"

"Needless to say! I never expected to find you loitering along the wayside, and you quite startled me! Have you been fishing from the bridge? But I see that you carry neither tackle nor bait."

Iucounu slowly turned his head and surveyed Cugel from under drooping eyelids. "I too am surprised to see you back from your travels. Why do you walk so far afield? Your former depredations took place along the Twish."

"I am purposely avoiding my old haunts, and my old habits as well," said Cugel. "Neither have brought me profit."

"In every life comes a time for change," said Iucounu. "I too consider metamorphosis, to an extent which might surprise you." He discarded the straw from his mouth and spoke with energy. "Cugel, you are looking well! Your garments become you, as does that cap! Where did you find so handsome an ornament?"

Cugel reached up and touched the duplicated scale. "This little piece? It is my lucky talisman. I found it in a mire near Shanglestone Strand."

"I hope that you brought me another of the same sort, as a memento?"

Cugel shook his head as if in regret. "I found but a single specimen of this quality."

"Tsk. I am disappointed. What are your plans?"

"I intend a simple life: a cabin on the banks of the Sune, with a porch overhanging the water, and there I will devote myself to calligraphy and meditation. Perhps I will read Stafdyke's *Comprehensive Survey of All the Aeons*, a treatise to which everyone alludes, but which no one has read, with the probable exception of yourself."

"Yes, I know it well. Your travels, then, have brought you the means to gratify your desires."

Cugel smilingly shook his head. "My wealth is scant. I plan a life of simplicity."

"The ornament in your cap is very showy. Is it not valuable? The nexus, or node, gleams as brightly as a good hypolite."

Cugel once more shook his head. "It is only glass refracting the red rays of sunlight."

Iucounu gave a noncommittal grunt. "Footpads are common along this road. Their first objective would be this famous ornament of yours."

Cugel chuckled. "So much the worse for them."

Iucounu became attentive. "How so?"

Cugel fondled the gem. "Whoever tried to take the jewel by force would be blown to bits, along with the jewel."

"Rash but effective," said Iucounu. "I must be off about my business."

Iucounu, or his apparition, vanished. Cugel, assured that spies watched his every move, gave a shrug and went his own way.

An hour before sundown Cugel arrived at the village Flath Foiry, where he took lodging at the Inn of Five Flags. Dining in the common room, he became acquainted with Lorgan, a dealer in fancy embroideries. Lorgan enjoyed both large talk and generous quantities of drink. Cugel was in no mood for either and pleading fatigue retired early to his chamber. Lorgan remained in bibulous conversation with several merchants of the town.

Upon entering his chamber, Cugel locked the door, then made a thorough inspection by lamp-light. The couch was clean; the windows overlooked a kitchen garden; songs and shouts from the common room were muted. With a sigh of satisfaction, Cugel dimmed the lamp and went to his couch.

As Cugel composed himself for slumber, he thought to hear an odd sound. He raised his head to listen, but the sound was not repeated. Cugel once again relaxed. The odd sound came again, somewhat louder, and a dozen large whispering bat-like creatures flew out of the shadows. They darted into Cugel's face and climbed on his neck with their claws, hoping to distract his attention while a black eel with long trembling hands worked to steal Cugel's cap.

Cugel tore aside the bat-things, touched the eel with 'Spatterlight', causing its instant dissolution, and the bat-things flew crying and whispering from the room.

Cugel brought light to the lamp. All seemed in order. He reflected a moment, then, stepping out into the hall, he investigated the chamber next to his own. It proved to be vacant, and he took immediate possession.

An hour later his rest was again disturbed, this time by Lorgan, now thoroughly in his cups. Upon seeing Cugel he blinked in surprise. "Cugel, why are you sleeping in my chamber?"

"You have made a mistake," said Cugel. "Your chamber is next door over."

"Ah! All is explained! My profuse apologies!"

"It is nothing," said Cugel. "Sleep well."

"Thank you." Lorgan staggered off to bed. Cugel, locking the door, once more threw himself down on the couch and passed a restful night, ignoring the sounds and outcries from the room next door.

In the morning, as Cugel took his breakfast, Lorgan limped downstairs and described to Cugel the events of the night: "As I lay in a pleasantly drowsy state, two large madlocks with heavy arms, staring green eyes and no necks entered by the window. They dealt me any number of heavy blows despite my appeals for mercy. Then they stole my hat and made for the window as if to leave, only to turn back and strike further blows. 'That is for causing so much trouble,' they said, and finally they were gone. Have you ever heard the like?"

"Never!" said Cugel. "It is an outrage."

"Strange things happen in life," mused Lorgan. "Still, I will not stop at this inn again."

"A sensible decision," said Cugel. "Now, if you will excuse me, I must be on my way."

Cugel paid his score and set off along the high-road, and the morning passed uneventfully.

At noon Cugel came upon a pavilion of pink silk, erected upon a grassy place beside the road. At a table laden with fine food and drink sat Iucounu, who, at the sight of Cugel, jumped up in surprise. "Cugel! What a happy occasion! You must join me at my meal!"

Cugel measured the distance between Iucounu and the spot where he would be obliged to sit; the distance would not allow him to reach across the space holding 'Spatterlight' in his gloved hand.

Cugel shook his head. "I have already taken a nutritious lunch of nuts and raisins. You have chosen a lovely spot for your picnic. I wish you a happy appetite, and good day."

"Wait, Cugel! One moment, if you please! Taste a goblet of this fine Fazola! It will put spring in your steps!"

"It will, more likely, put me to sleep in the ditch. And now—"

Iucounu's ropy mouth twitched in a grimace. But at once he renewed his affability. "Cugel, I hereby invite you to visit me at Pergolo; surely you have not forgotten the amenities? Every night we will host a grand banquet, and I have discovered a new phase of magic, by which I recall remarkable persons from across the aeons. The entertainments are splendid at Pergolo!"

Cugel made a rueful gesture. "You sing siren songs of inducement! One taste of such glamour might shatter my resolve! I am not the rakehelly Cugel of old!"

Iucounu strove to keep his voice even. "This is becoming all too clear." Throwing himself back in his chair, he glowered morosely at Cugel's cap. Making a sudden impatient gesture, he muttered a spell of eleven syllables, so that the air between himself and Cugel twisted and thickened. The forces veered out toward Cugel and past, to rattle away in all directions, cutting russet and black streaks through the grass.

Iucounu stared with yellow eyes bulging, but Cugel paid no heed to the incident. He bade Iucounu a civil farewell and continued along the way.

For an hour Cugel walked, using that loping bent-kneed gait which had propelled him so many long leagues. Down from the fells on the right hand came the Forest Da, softer and sweeter than the Great Erm to the far north. River and road plunged into the shade, and all sound was hushed. Long-stemmed flowers grew in the mold: delice, bluebell, rosace, cany-flake. Coral fungus clung to dead stumps like cloths of fairy lace. Maroon sunlight slanted across the forest spaces, creating a gloom saturated with a dozen dark colors. Nothing moved and no sound could be heard but the trill of a far bird.

Despite the apparent solitude, Cugel loosened the sword in its scabbard and walked with soft feet; the forests often revealed awful secrets to the innocent.

After some miles the forest thinned and retreated to the north. Cugel came upon a cross-roads; here waited a fine double-sprung carriage drawn by four white wheriots. High on the coachman's bench sat a pair of maidens with long orange hair, complexions of dusky tan and eyes of emerald green. They wore a livery of umber and oyster-white and, after quick side-glances toward Cugel, stared haughtily ahead.

Iucounu threw open the door. "Hola, Cugel! By chance I came this route and behold! I perceive my friend Cugel striding along at a great rate! I had not expected to find you so far along the way!"

"I enjoy the open road," said Cugel. "I march at quick-step because I intend to arrive at Taun Tassel before dark. Forgive me if, once again, I cut our conversation short."

"Unnecessary! Taun Tassel is on my way. Step into the carriage; we will talk as we ride."

Cugel hesitated, looking first one way, then another, and Iucounu became impatient. "Well then?" he barked. "What now?"

Cugel attempted an apologetic smile. "I never take without giving in return. This policy averts misunderstandings."

Iucounu's eyelids drooped at the corners in moist reproach. "Must we quibble over minor points? Into the carriage with you, Cugel; you may enlarge upon your qualms as we ride."

"Very well," said Cugel. "I will ride with you to Taun Tassel, but you must accept these three terces in full, exact, final, comprehensive and complete compensation for the ride and every other aspect, adjunct, by-product and consequence, either direct or indirect, of the said ride, renouncing every other claim, now, and forever, including all times of the past and future, without exception, and absolving me, in part and in whole, from any and all further obligations."

Iucounu held up small balled fists and gritted his teeth toward the sky. "I repudiate your entire paltry philosophy! I find zest in giving!

I now offer you in title full and clear this excellent carriage, inclusive of wheels, springs and upholstery, the four wheriots with twenty-six ells of gold chain and a pair of matched maidens. The totality is yours! Ride where you will!''

''I am dumbfounded by your generosity!'' said Cugel. ''What, may I ask, do you want in return?''

''Bah! Some trifle, perhaps, to symbolize the exchange. The kick-shaw that you wear in your hat will suffice.''

Cugel made a sign of regret. ''You ask the one thing I hold dear. That is the talisman I found near Shanglestone Strand. I have carried it through thick and thin, and now I could never give it up. It may even exert a magical influence.''

''Nonsense!'' snorted Iucounu. ''I have a sensitive nose for magic. The ornament is as dull as stale beer.''

''Its spark has cheered me through dreary hours; I could never give it up.''

Iucounu's mouth drooped almost past his chin. ''You have become over-sentimental!'' Glancing past Cugel's shoulder, Iucounu uttered a shrill cry of alarm. ''Take care! A plague of tasps is upon us!''

Turning, Cugel discovered a leaping horde of green scorpion-things the size of weasels close upon the carriage.

''Quick!'' cried Iucounu. ''Into the carriage! Drivers, away!''

Hesitating only an instant Cugel scrambled into the carriage. Iucounu uttered a great sigh of relief. ''A very near thing! Cugel, I believe that I saved your life!''

Cugel looked through the back window. ''The tasps have disappeared into thin air! How is that possible?''

''No matter; we are safely away, and that is the main point. Give thanks that I was on hand with my carriage! Are you not appreciative? Perhaps now you will concede me my whim, which is the ornament on your hat.''

Cugel considered the situation. From where he sat he could not easily apply the authentic scale to Iucounu's face. He thought to temporize. ''Why would you want such a trifle?''

''Truth to tell, I collect such objects. Yours will make a famous centerpiece for my display. Be so good as to hand it over, if only for my inspection.''

''That is not easily done. If you look closely you will see that it is fixed to my cap on a matrix of diambroid.''

Iucounu clicked his tongue in vexation. ''Why would you go to such lengths?''

''To deter the hands of thieves; why else?''

"Surely you can detach the article in safety?"

"While we bump and sway in a speeding carriage? I would not dare make the attempt."

Iucounu turned Cugel a lemon-yellow side-glance. "Cugel, are you trying to 'twiddle my whiskers', as the saying goes?"

"Naturally not."

"Just so." The two sat in silence while the landscape flashed past. All in all, thought Cugel, a precarious situation, even though his plans called for just such a progression of events. Above all, he must not allow Iucounu the close scrutiny of the scale; Iucounu's lumpy nose indeed could smell out magic, or its lack.

Cugel became aware that the carriage traversed, not forest, but open countryside. He turned toward Iucounu. "This is not the way to Taun Tassel! Where are we going?"

"To Pergolo," said Iucounu. "I insist upon extending you my best hospitality."

"Your invitation is hard to resist," said Cugel.

The carriage plunged over a line of hills and descended into a valley well-remembered by Cugel. Ahead he glimpsed the flow of the Twish River, with a momentary flash of red sunlight on the water, then Iucounu's manse Pergolo appeared on the brow of a hill, and a moment later the carriage drew up under the portico.

"We have arrived," said Iucounu. "Cugel, I welcome you once again to Pergolo! Will you alight?"

"With pleasure," said Cugel.

Iucounu ushered Cugel into the reception hall. "First, Cugel, let us take a glass of wine to freshen our throats after the dust of the journey. Then we will tie up the loose strands of our business, which extend somewhat further into the past than you may care to remember." Here Iucounu referred to a period during which Cugel had held him at a disadvantage.

"Those days are lost in the mists of time," said Cugel. "All is now forgotten."

Iucounu smiled behind pursed lips. "Later in your visit we will reminisce, to our mutual amusement! As for now, why not remove your cap, cloak and gloves?"

"I am quite comfortable," said Cugel, gauging the distance between himself and Iucounu. One long step, a swing of the arm, and the deed would be done.

Iucounu seemed to divine the quality of Cugel's thoughts and moved back a pace. "First, our wine! Let us step into the small refectory."

Iucounu led the way into a hall panelled in fine dark mahogany, where he was greeted effusively by a small round animal with long fur, short legs and black button eyes. The creature bounded up and down and voiced a series of shrill barks. Iucounu patted the beast. "Well then, Ettis, how goes your world? Have they been feeding you enough suet? Good! I am glad to hear such happy tidings, since, other than Cugel, you are my only friend. Now then! To order! I must confer with Cugel."

Iucounu signaled Cugel to a chair at the table, and seated himself opposite. The animal ran back and forth barking, pausing only long enough to gnaw at Cugel's ankles.

A pair of young sylphs floated into the room with trays of silver which they set before Cugel and Iucounu, then drifted once more back the way they had come.

Iucounu rubbed his hands together. "As you know, Cugel, I serve only the best. The wine is Angelius from Quantique, and the biscuits are formed from the pollen of red clover blossom."

"Your judgment has always been exquisite," said Cugel.

"I am content only with the subtle and the refined," said Iucounu. He tasted the wine. "Matchless!" He drank again. "Heady, tart, with a hint of arrogance." He looked across the table at Cugel. "What is your opinion?"

Cugel shook his head in sad abnegation. "One taste of this elixir and I never again could tolerate ordinary drink." He dipped a biscuit into the wine and tendered it to Ettis, who again had paused to gnaw at his leg. "Ettis of course has a wider discrimination than I."

Iucounu jumped to his feet with a protest, but Ettis had already gulped down the morsel, thereupon to perform a curious contortion and fall down on its back, with feet raised stiffly into the air.

Cugel looked questioningly at Iucounu. "You have trained Ettis well in the 'dead dog' trick. He is a clever beast."

Iucounu slowly subsided into his chair. Two sylphs entered the chamber and carried Ettis away on a silver tray.

Iucounu spoke through tight lips. "Let us get down to business. While strolling Shanglestone Strand, did you meet a certain Twango?"

"I did indeed," said Cugel. "An extraordinary individual! He became perturbed when I would not sell him my little trinket."

Iucounu fixed Cugel with the keenest of scrutinies. "Did he explain why?"

"He spoke of the demiurge Sadlark, but in such an incoherent fashion that I lost interest."

Iucounu rose to his feet. "I will show you Sadlark. Come! To the work-room, which of course is dear to your memory."

" 'Work-room'? These episodes are lost in the past."

"I remember them distinctly," said Iucounu in an easy voice. "All of them."

As they walked toward the work-room, Cugel tried to sidle close to Iucounu, but without success; Iucounu seemed always a yard or so beyond the reach of Cugel's gloved hand, in which he held 'Spatterlight' at the ready.

They entered the work-room. "Now you shall see my collection," said Iucounu. "You will wonder no longer as to my interest in your talisman." He jerked up his hand; a dark red cloth was whisked away, to reveal the scales of Sadlark, arranged upon an armature of fine silver wire. From the evidence of the restoration, Sadlark would have been a creature of moderate size, standing on two squat motilators, with two pairs of jointed arms ending each in ten clasping fingers. The head, if the term were at all appropriate, was no more than a turret surmounting the keen and taut torso. The belly scales were white-green, with a dark green keel tinged with vermilion swinging up to end at the frontal turret in a blank and eye-catching vacancy.

Iucounu made a grand gesture. "There you see Sadlark, the noble over-world being, whose every contour suggests power and velocity. His semblance fires the imagination. Cugel, do you agree?"

"Not altogether," said Cugel. "Still, by and large, you have recreated a remarkably fine specimen, and I congratulate you." He walked around the structure as if in admiration, all the while hoping to come within arm's-length of Iucounu, but as Cugel moved, so did the Laughing Magician, and Cugel was thwarted in his intent.

"Sadlark is more than a mere specimen," said Iucounu in a voice almost devout. "Now notice the scales, each fixed in its proper place, except at the thrust of the keel where a staring vacancy assaults the eye. A single scale is missing, the most important of all: the protonastic centrum, or, as it is called, the 'Pectoral Sky-break Spatterlight'. For long years I thought it lost, to my unutterable anguish. Cugel, can you imagine my surge of gladsomeness, the singing of songs in my heart, the crepitations of pure joy along the appropriate passages, when I looked at you, and discovered there in your cap the missing scale? I rejoiced as if the sun had been conceded another hundred years of life! I could have leapt in the air from sheer exhilaration. Cugel, can you understand my emotion?"

"To the extent that you have described it—yes. As to the source of this emotion, I am puzzled." And Cugel approached the armature, hoping that Iucounu in his enthusiasm would step within reach of his arm.

Iucounu, moving in the other direction, touched the armature to set the scales jingling. ''Cugel, in some respects you are dense and dull; your brain is like luke-warm porridge, and I say this without heat. You understand only what you see, and this is the smallest part.'' Iucounu emitted a whinny of laughter, so that Cugel sent him a questioning look. ''Observe Sadlark!'' said Iucounu. ''What do you see?''

''An armature of wires and a number of scales, in the purported shape of Sadlark.''

''And what if the wires were removed?''

''The scales would fall into a heap.''

''Quite so. You are right. The protonastic centrum is the node which binds the other scales with lines of force. This node is the soul and force of Sadlark. With the node in place, Sadlark lives once again; indeed Sadlark was never dead, but merely disassociated.''

''What of, let us say, his inner organs?''

''In the overworld, such parts are considered unnecessary and even somewhat vulgar. In short, there are no inner parts.

Have you any other questions or observations?''

''I might politely venture to point out that the day is waning and that I wish to arrive at Taun Tassel before dark.''

Iucounu said heartily: ''And so you shall! First, be good enough to place upon the work-table the 'Pectoral Sky-break Spatterlight', with all traces of diambroid detached. No other option is open to you.''

''Only one,'' said Cugel. ''I prefer to keep the scale. It brings me luck and wards off acrid magic, as you have already learned.''

Yellow lights flickered behind Iucounu's eyes. ''Cugel, your obstinacy is embarrassing. The scale indeed holds a proud crust between you and enemy magic of the casual sort. It is indifferent to overworld magic, some of which I command. Meanwhile, please desist from this constant skulking forward in the attempt to bring me within range of your sword. I am tired of jumping backward every time you sidle in my direction.''

Cugel spoke haughtily: ''Such an ungracious act never so much as crossed my mind.'' He drew his sword and laid it on the work-bench. ''There! See for yourself how you have misjudged me!''

Iucounu blinked at the sword. ''Still, keep your distance! I am not a man who welcomes intimacies.''

''You may expect my full cooperation,'' said Cugel with dignity.

''I will be frank! Your deeds have long cried out for retribution, and as a man of conscience I am forced to act. Still, you need not aggravate my task.''

''This is harsh language!'' said Cugel. ''You offered me a ride to Taun Tassel. I did not expect treachery.''

Iucounu paid no heed. ''I will now make my final request: give me the scale at once!''

''I can not oblige you,'' said Cugel. ''Since that was your final request, we can now leave for Taun Tassel.''

''The scale, if you please!''

''Take it from my cap, if you must. I will not assist you.''

''And the diambroid?''

''Sadlark will protect me. You must take your chances.''

Iucounu uttered a cry of laughter. ''Sadlark also protects me, as you will see!'' He threw aside his garments and with a quick movement inserted himself into the center of the matrix, so that his legs fitted into Sadlark's motilators and his face showed behind the gap in the turret. The wires and scales contracted around his pudgy body; the scales fit him as if they were his own skin.

Iucounu's voice rang like a choir of brass horns: ''Well then, Cugel: what do you think now?''

Cugel stood gaping in wonder. At last he said: ''Sadlark's scales fit you remarkably well.''

''It is no accident, of this I am certain!''

''And why not?''

''I am Sadlark's avatar; I partake of his personal essence! This is my destiny, but before I can enjoy my full force, I must be whole! Without further quibbling you may fit 'Spatterlight' into place. Remember, Sadlark will no longer protect you against my magic, since it is his magic, as well.''

A crawling sensation in Cugel's glove indicated that Sadlark's protonastic centrum 'Spatterlight' endorsed the remark. ''So it must be,'' said Cugel. He carefully detached the ornament from his cap and removed the diambroid. He held it in his hand a moment, then placed it against his forehead.

Iucounu cried out: ''What are you doing?''

''For the last time I am renewing my vitality. Often this scale has helped me through my trials.''

''Stop at once! I will be needing every iota of force for my own purposes. Hand it over!''

Cugel let the true scale slip into his gloved palm and concealed the false ornament. He spoke in a melancholy voice: ''With pain I give up my treasure. May I for a final few moments hold it to my brow?''

"By no means!" declared Iucounu. "I plan to put it to my own brow. Lay the scale on the work-bench, then stand back!"

"As you wish," sighed Cugel. He placed 'Spatterlight' on the work-bench, then, taking his sword, walked mournfully from the room.

With a grunt of satisfaction, Iucounu applied the scale to his brow.

Cugel went to stand by the fountain in the foyer, with one foot raised to the lip of the basin. In this position he listened gravely to the awful noises rising from Iucounu's throat.

Silence returned to the work-room.

Several moments passed.

A thudding clashing sound reached Cugel's ears.

Sadlark propelled himself by clumsy hops and jumps into the foyer, using his motilators in the manner of feet, with only fair success, so that he fell heavily from time to time, to wallow and roll with a great rattling of scales.

Late afternoon light streamed through the door; Cugel made no move, hoping that Sadlark would blunder out into the open and return to the overworld.

Sadlark came to a halt and spoke in a gasping voice. "Cugel! Where is Cugel? Each of the forces I have consumed, including eel and weasel, requests that they be joined by Cugel! Where are you? Cugel, announce yourself! I cannot see by this peculiar Earth-light, which explains why I plunged into the mire."

Cugel remained silent, scarcely daring to breathe. Sadlark slowly turned the red node of his sky-breaker around the foyer. "Ah, Cugel, there you are! Stand without motion!"

Sadlark lurched forward. Disobeying the order, Cugel ran to the far side of the fountain. Angry at Cugel's insubordination, Sadlark gave a great bound through the air. Cugel seized a basin, scooped up water and flung it upon Sadlark, who thereby misjudged his distance and fell flat into the fountain.

The water hissed and bubbled as Sadlark's force was spent. The scales fell apart and swirled idly about the bottom of the fountain.

Cugel stirred among the scales until he found 'Spatterlight'. He wrapped the scale in several thicknesses of damp cloth and taking it into the work-room placed it into a jar of water, which he sealed and stored away.

Pergolo was silent, but Cugel could not rest easy; Iucounu's presence hung in the air. Could the Laughing Magician be watching from some secret place, stifling his merriment with great effort while he planned a set of humorous pranks?

Cugel searched Pergolo with care but discovered no significant clues except Iucounu's black opal thumb-ring, which he found in the fountain among the scales, and at last Cugel felt assured that Iucounu was no more.

At one end of the table sat Cugel; at the other, Bazzard. Disserl, Pelasias, Archimbaust and Vasker ranged at either side. The missing parts had been recovered from the vaults, sorted and restored to their owners, to the general satisfaction.

Six sylphs served the banquet, which, while lacking the bizarre condiments and improbable juxtapositions of Iucounu's 'novel cuisine', was nevertheless enjoyed by the company.

Various toasts were proposed: to Bazzard's ingenuity, to the fortitude of the four wizards, to Cugel's brave deceits and duplicities. Cugel was asked, not once but several times, as to where his ambitions might now take him; on each occasion he responded with a glum shake of the head. "With Iucounu gone, there is no whip to drive me. I look in no direction and I have no plans."

After draining his goblet, Vasker voiced a generalization: "Without urgent goals, life is insipid!"

Disserl also tilted his goblet high, then responded to his brother: "I believe that this thought has been enunciated before. A surly critic might even use the word 'banality'."

Vasker replied in even tones: "These are the ideas which true originality rediscovers and renews, for the benefit of mankind. I stand by my remark! Cugel, do you concur?"

Cugel signalled the sylphs to the better use of their decanters. "The intellectual interplay leaves me bewildered; I am quite at a loss. Both viewpoints carry conviction."

Vasker said: "Perhaps you will return with us to Llaio and we will explain our philosophies in full detail."

"I will keep your invitation in mind. For the next few months I will be busy at Pergolo, sorting through Iucounu's affairs. Already, a number of his spies have submitted claims and invoices which almost certainly are falsified. I have dismissed them out of hand."

"And when all is in order?" asked Bazzard. "What then? Is it to be the rustic hut by the river?"

"Such a cabin, with nothing to do but watch sunlight moving on the water, exerts an attraction. But I fear that I might become restless."

Bazzard ventured a suggestion. "There are far parts of the world to be seen. The floating city Jehaz is said to be splendid. There is also the Land of the Pale Ladies, which you might care to explore. Or will you pass your days in Almery?"

"The future is blurred as if in a fog."

"The same is true for all of us," declared Pelasias. "Why make plans? The sun might well go out tomorrow."

Cugel peformed an extravagant gesture. "That thought must be banished from our minds! Tonight we sit here drinking purple wine! Let tonight last forever!"

"This is my own sentiment!" said Archimbaust. "Now is now! There is never more to experience than this single 'now', which recurs at an interval exactly one second in length."

Bazzard knit his brows. "What of the first 'now', and the last 'now'? Are these to be regarded as the same entity?"

Archimbaust spoke somewhat severely: "Bazzard, your questions are too profound for the occasion. The songs of your musical fish would be more appropriate."

"Their progress is slow," said Bazzard. "I have appointed a cantor and a contralto choir, but the harmony is not yet steady."

"No matter," said Cugel. "Tonight we will do without. Iucounu, wherever you are, in underworld, overworld or no world whatever: we drink to your memory in your own wine! This is the final joke, and, feeble though it may be, it is at your expense, and hence, enjoyed by the company! Sylphs, make play with the decanters! Once again to the goblets! Bazzard, have you tried this excellent cheese? Vasker: another anchovy? Let the feast proceed!"

Rhialto
The
Marvellous

Contents

Foreword

These are tales of the 21st Aeon, when Earth is old and the sun is about to go out. In Ascolais and Almery, lands to the west of the Falling Wall, live a group of magicians who have formed an association the better to protect their interests. Their number fluctuates, but at this time they are:

Ildefonse, the Preceptor.

Rhialto the Marvellous.

Hurtiancz, short and burly, notorious for his truculent disposition.

Herark the Harbinger, precise and somewhat severe.

Shrue, a diabolist, whose witticisms mystify his associates, and sometimes disturb their sleep of nights.

Gilgad, a small man with large gray eyes in a round gray face, always attired in rose-red garments. His hands are clammy, cold and damp; his touch is avoided by all.

Vermoulian the Dream-walker, a person peculiarly tall and thin, with a stately stride.

Mune the Mage, who speaks minimally and manages a household of four spouses.

Zilifant, robust of body with long brown hair and a flowing beard.

Darvilk the Miaanther, who, for inscrutable purposes, affects a black domino.

Perdustin, a slight blond person without intimates, who enjoys secrecy and mystery, and refuses to reveal his place of abode.

Ao of the Opals, saturnine, with a pointed black beard and a caustic manner.

Eshmiel, who, with a delight almost childish in its purity, uses a bizarre semblance half-white and half-black.

Barbanikos, who is short and squat with a great puff of white hair.

Haze of Wheary Water, a hot-eyed wisp with green skin and orange willow-leaves for hair.

Panderleou, a collector of rare and wonderful artifacts from all the accessible dimensions.

Byzant the Necrope.

Dulce-Lolo, whose semblance is that of a portly epicure.

Tchamast, morose of mood, an avowed ascetic, whose distrust of the female race runs so deep that he will allow only male insects into the precincts of his manse.

Teutch, who seldom speaks with his mouth but uses an unusual sleight to flick words from his finger-tips. As an Elder of the Hub, he has been allowed the control of his private infinity.

Zahoulik-Khuntze, whose iron fingernails and toenails are engraved with curious signs.

Nahourezzin, a savant of Old Romarth.

Zanzel Melancthones.

Hache-Moncour, whose vanities and airs surpass even those of Rhialto.

Magic is a practical science, or, more properly, a craft, since emphasis is placed primarily upon utility, rather than basic understanding.

This is only a general statement, since in a field of such profound scope, every practitioner will have his individual, style, and during the glorious times of Grand Motholam, many of the magician-philosophers tried to grasp the principles which governed the field.

In the end, these investigators, who included the greatest names in sorcery, learned only enough to realize that full and comprehensive knowledge was impossible. In the first place, a desired effect might be achieved through any number of modes, any of which represented a life-time of study, each deriving its force from a different coercive environment.

The great magicians of Grand Motholam were sufficiently supple that they perceived the limits of human understanding, and spent most of their efforts dealing with practical problems, searching for abstract principles only when all else failed. For this reason, magic retains its distinctly human flavor, even though the activating agents are never human. A casual glance into one of the basic catalogues emphasizes this human orientation; the nomenclature has a quaint and archaic flavor. Looking into (for instance) Chapter Four of Killiclaw's Primer of Practical Magic, Interpersonal Effectuations, one notices, indited in bright purple ink, such terminology as:

Xarfaggio's Physical Malepsy
Arnhoult's Sequestrious Digitalia
Lutar Brassnose's Twelve-fold Bounty
The Spell of Forlorn Encystment
Tinkler's Old-fashioned Froust
Clambard's Rein of Long Nerves
The Green and Purple Postponement of Joy
Panguire's Triumphs of Discomfort
Lugwiler's Dismal Itch
Khulip's Nasal Enhancement
Radl's Pervasion of the Incorrect Chord

A spell in essence corresponds to a code, or set of instructions, inserted into the sensorium of an entity which is able and not unwilling to alter the environment in accordance with the message conveyed by the spell. These entities are not necessarily 'intelligent,' nor even 'sentient,' and their conduct, from the tyro's point of view, is unpredictable, capricious and dangerous.

The most pliable and cooperative of these creatures range from the lowly and frail elementals, through the sandestins. More fractious entities are known by the Temuchin as 'daihak,' which include 'demons' and 'gods.' A magician's power derives from the abilities of the entities he is able to control. Every magician of consequence employs one or more sandestins. A few arch-magicians of Grand Motholam dared to employ the force of the lesser daihaks. To recite or even to list the names of these magicians is to evoke wonder and awe. Their names tingle with power. Some of Grand Motholam's most notable and dramatic were:

Phandaal the Great
Amberlin I
Amberlin II
Dibarcas Maior (who studied under *Phandaal*)
Arch-Mage Mael Lel Laio (he lived in a palace carved from a single moon-stone)
The Vapurials
The Green and Purple College
Zinqzin the Encyclopaedist
Kyrol of Porphyrhyncos
Calanctus the Calm
Llorio the Sorceress

The magicians of the 21st Aeon were, in comparison, a disparate and uncertain group, lacking both grandeur and consistency.

1

The Murthe

1

One cool morning toward the middle of the 21st Aeon, Rhialto sat at breakfast in the east cupola of his manse Falu. On this particular morning the old sun rose behind a curtain of frosty haze, to cast a wan and poignant light across Low Meadow.

For reasons Rhialto could not define, he lacked appetite for his breakfast and gave only desultory attention to a dish of watercress, stewed persimmon and sausage in favor of strong tea and a rusk. Then, despite a dozen tasks awaiting him in his work-room, he sat back in his chair, to gaze absently across the meadow toward Were Woods.

In this mood of abstraction, his perceptions remained strangely sensitive. An insect settled upon the leaf of a nearby aspen tree; Rhialto took careful note of the angle at which it crooked its legs and the myriad red glints in its bulging eyes. Interesting and significant, thought Rhialto.

After absorbing the insect's full import, Rhialto extended his attention to the landscape at large. He contemplated the slope of the meadow as it dropped toward the Ts and the distribution of its herbs. He studied the crooked boles at the edge of the forest, the red rays slanting through the foliage, the indigo and dark green of the shadows. His vision was remarkable for its absolute clarity; his hearing was no less acute. . . . He leaned forward, straining to hear—what? Sighs of inaudible music?

Nothing. Rhialto relaxed, smiling at his own odd fancies, and poured out a final cup of tea. . . . He let it cool untasted. On impulse he rose to his feet and went into the parlour, where he donned a cloak, a hunter's cap, and took up that baton known as 'Malfezar's Woe.' He then summoned Ladanque, his chamberlain and general factotum.

"Ladanque, I will be strolling the forest for a period. Take care that Vat Five retains its roil. If you wish, you may distill the contents of the large blue alembic into a stoppered flask. Use a low heat and avoid breathing the vapor; it will bring a purulent rash to your face."

"Very well, sir. What of the clevenger?"

"Pay it no heed. Do not approach the cage. Remember, its talk of both virgins and wealth is illusory; I doubt if it knows the meaning of either term."

"Just so, sir."

Rhialto departed the manse. He set off across the meadow by a trail which took him to the Ts, over a stone bridge, and into the forest.

The trail, which had been traced by night-creatures from the forest on their way across the meadow, presently disappeared. Rhialto went on, following where the forest aisles led: through glades where candole, red meadow-sweet and white dymphne splotched the grass with colour; past stands of white birches and black aspens; beside ledges of old stone, springs and small streams.

If other creatures walked the woods, none were evident. Entering a little clearing with a single white birch at the center, Rhialto paused to listen. . . . He heard only silence.

A minute passed. Rhialto stood motionless.

Silence. Had it been absolute?

The music, if such it had been, assuredly had evolved in his own brain.

Curious, thought Rhialto.

He came to an open place, where a white birch stood frail against a background of dense black deodars. As he turned away, again he thought to hear music.

Soundless music? An inherent contradiction!

Odd, thought Rhialto, especially since the music seemed to come from outside himself. . . . He thought to hear it again: a flutter of abstract chords, imparting an emotion at once sweet, melancholy, triumphant: definite yet uncertain.

Rhialto gazed in all directions. The music, or whatever it might be, seemed to come from a source near at hand. Prudence urged that he turn in his tracks and hurry back to Falu, never looking over his shoulder. . . . He went forward, and came upon a still pool, dark and deep, reflecting the far bank with the exactness of a mirror. Standing motionless, Rhialto saw reflected the image of a woman, strangely pale, with silver hair bound by a black fillet. She wore a knee-length white kirtle, and went bare-armed and bare-legged.

Rhialto looked up to the far bank. He discovered neither woman, nor man, nor creature of any kind. He dropped his eyes to the surface of the pool, where, as before, the woman stood reflected.

For a long moment Rhialto studied the image. The woman appeared tall, with small breasts and narrow flanks; she seemed fresh and clean-limbed as a girl. Her face, while lacking neither delicacy nor classic proportion, showed a stillness from which all frivolity was absent. Rhialto, whose expertise in the field of calligynics had earned him his cognomen, found her beautiful but severe, and probably unapproachable, especially if she refused to show herself except as a reflection . . . And perhaps also for other reasons, thought Rhialto, who had conceived an inkling as to the identity of the woman.

Rhialto spoke: "Madame, did you call me here with your music? If so, explain how I can help you, though I promise no definite undertaking."

The woman showed a cool smile not altogether to Rhialto's liking. He bowed stiffly. "If you have nothing to say to me, I will intrude no longer upon your privacy." He performed another curt bow, and as he did so, something thrust him forward so that he plunged into the pool.

The water was extremely cold. Rhialto floundered to the bank and pulled himself ashore. Whoever or whatever had thrust him into the water could not be seen.

Gradually the surface of the pool became smooth. The image of the woman was no longer visible.

Rhialto trudged glumly back to Falu, where he indulged himself in a hot bath and drank verbena tea.

For a period he sat in his work-room, studying various books from the 18th Aeon. The adventure in the forest had not agreed with him. He felt feverish and ringing noises sounded in his ears.

Rhialto at last prepared himself a prophylactic tonic which caused him even greater discomfort. He took to his bed, swallowed a soporific tablet, and at last fell into a troubled sleep.

The indisposition persisted for three days. On the morning of the fourth day Rhialto communicated with the magician Ildefonse, at his manse Boumergarth beside the River Scaum.

Ildefonse felt sufficient concern that he flew at speed to Falu in the smallest of his whirlaways.

In full detail Rhialto described the events which had culminated at the still pool in the forest. "So there you have it. I am anxious to learn your opinion."

Ildefonse looked frowning off toward the forest. Today he used his ordinary semblance: that of a portly middle-aged gentleman with thin blond whiskers, a balding pate, and a manner of jovial innocence. The two magicians sat under the purple plumanthia arbor to the side of Falu. On a nearby table, Ladanque had arranged a service of fancy pastries, three varieties of tea and a decanter of soft white wine. "Extraordinary, certainly," said Ildefonse, "especially when taken with a recent experience of my own."

Rhialto glanced sharply sidelong toward Ildefonse. "You were played a similar trick?"

Ildefonse responded in measured tones: "The answer is both 'yes' and 'no.' "

"Interesting," said Rhialto.

Ildefonse selected his words with care. "Before I elaborate, let me ask this: have you ever before heard this, let us say, 'shadow music'?"

"Never."

"And its purport was—?"

"Indescribable. Neither tragic nor gay; sweet, yet wry and bitter."

"Did you perceive a melody, or theme, or even a progression, which might give us a clue?"

"Only a hint. If you will allow me a trifle of preciosity, it filled me with a yearning for the lost and unattainable."

"Aha!" said Ildefonse. "And the woman? Something must have identified her as the Murthe?"

Rhialto considered. "Her pallor and silver hair might have been that of a forest wefkin, in the guise of an antique nymph. Her beauty was real, but I felt no urge to embrace her. I daresay all might have changed upon better acquaintance."

"Hmmf. Your elegant airs, so I suspect, will carry small weight with the Murthe. . . . When did her identity occur to you?"

"I became certain as I slogged home, water squelching in my boots. My mood was glum; perhaps the squalm was starting its work. In any case, woman and music came together in my mind and the name evolved. Once home I instantly read Calanctus and took advice. The squalm apparently was real. Today I was finally able to call on you."

"You should have called before, though I have had similar problems. . . . What is that irksome noise?"

Rhialto looked along the road. "Someone is approaching in a vehicle. . . . It appears to be Zanzel Melancthones."

''And what is that strange bounding thing behind him?''

Rhialto craned his neck. ''It is unclear. . . . We shall soon find out.''

Along the road, rolling at speed on four tall wheels, came a luxurious double-divan of fifteen golden-ocher cushions. A man-like creature attached by a chain ran behind in the dust.

Rising to his feet, Ildefonse held up his hand. ''Halloa, Zanzel! It is I, Ildefonse! Where do you go in such haste? Who is that curious creature coursing so fleetly behind?''

Zanzel brought the vehicle to a halt. ''Ildefonse, and dear Rhialto: how good to see you both! I had quite forgotten that this old road passes by Falu, and I discover it now to my pleasure.''

''It is our joint good fortune!'' declared Ildefonse. ''And your captive?''

Zanzel glanced over his shoulder. ''We have here an insidiator: that is my reasoned opinion. I am taking him to be executed where his ghost will bring me no bad luck. What of yonder meadow? It is safely clear of my domain.''

''And hard on my own,'' growled Rhialto. ''You must find a spot convenient to us both.''

''What of me?'' cried the captive. ''Have I nothing to say in the matter?''

''Well then, convenient to the three of us.''

''Just a moment, before you prosecute your duties,'' said Ildefonse. ''Tell me more of this creature.''

''There is little to tell. I discovered him by chance when he opened an egg from the wrong end. If you notice, he has six toes, a crested scalp and tufts of feathers growing from his shoulders, all of which puts his origin in the 18th or even the late 17th Aeon. His name, so he avers, is Lehuster.''

''Interesting!'' declared lldefonse. ''He is, in a sense, a living fossil. Lehuster, are you aware of your distinction?''

Zanzel permitted Lehuster no response. ''Good day to you both! Rhialto, you appear somewhat peaked! You must dose yourself with a good posset and rest: that is my prescription.''

''Thank you,'' said Rhialto. ''Come past again when your leisure allows and meanwhile remember that my domain extends to yonder ridge. You must execute Lehuster well beyond this point.''

''One moment!'' cried Lehuster. ''Are there no reasonable minds in the 21st Aeon? Have you no interest why I have come forward to these dismal times? I hereby offer to trade my life for important information!''

"Indeed!" said Ildefonse. "What sort of information?"

"I will make my revelations only at a conclave of high magicians, where pledges are a matter of public record and must be honoured."

The short-tempered Zanzel jerked around in his seat. "What! Do you now blacken my reputation as well?"

Ildefonse held up his hand. "Zanzel, I implore your patience! Who knows what this six-fingered rascal has to tell us? Lehuster, what is the thrust of your news?"

"The Murthe is at large among you, with squalms and ensqualmations. I will say no more until my safety is assured."

"Bah!" snorted Zanzel. "You cannot fuddle us with such fol-derol. Gentlemen, I bid you good-day; I must be off about my business."

Ildefonse demurred. "This is an extraordinary case! Zanzel, you are well-meaning but unaware of certain facts. As Preceptor, I now must order you to bring Lehuster alive and well to an immediate conclave at Boumergarth, where we will explore all phases of this matter. Rhialto, I trust that you are well enough to be on hand?"

"Absolutely and by all means! The topic is of importance."

"Very well then: all to Boumergarth, in haste!"

Lehuster ventured an objection. "Must I run all the way? I will arrive too fatigued to testify."

Ildefonse said: "To regularize matters, I will assume custody of Lehuster. Zanzel, be good enough to loosen the chain."

"Folly and nonsense!" grumbled Zanzel. "This scoundrel should be executed before he confuses all of us!"

Rhialto, somewhat surprised by Zanzel's vehemence, spoke with decision: "Ildefonse is correct! We must learn what we can."

2

The conclave at Boumergarth, assembled to hear the revelations of Lehuster, attracted only fifteen of the association's membership, which at this time numbered approximately twenty-five. On hand today were Ildefonse, Rhialto, Zanzel, the diabolist Shrue, Hurtiancz, Byzant the Necrope, Teutch who directed the intricacies of a private infinity, Mune the Mage, the cool and clever Perdustin, Tchamast who claimed to know the source of all IOUN stones, Barbanikos, Haze of Wheary Water, Ao of the Opals, Panderleou, whose collection of ultra-world artifacts was envied by all, and Gilgad.

Without ceremony Ildefonse called the conclave to order. "I am disappointed that our full roster has not appeared, since we must consider a matter of extraordinary importance.

"Let me first describe the recent experience of our colleague Rhialto. In barest outline, he was lured into Were Woods by the hint of an imaginary song. After wandering for a period, he met a woman who pushed him into a pool of extremely cold water. . . . Gentlemen, please! I see no occasion for levity! This is a most important affair, and Rhialto's misfortunes are not to be taken lightly! Indeed, for various reasons our speculations lead us to the Murthe." Ildefonse looked from face to face. "Yes, you heard me correctly."

When the mutter of comment had dwindled away, Ildefonse continued his remarks. "In an apparently unrelated circumstance, Zanzel recently made the acquaintance of a certain Lehuster, a denizen of the 18th Aeon. Lehuster, who stands yonder, indicates that he has important news to bring us, and again he mentions the Murthe. He has kindly agreed to share his information with us, and I now call upon Lehuster to step forward and report those facts of which he is cognizant. Lehuster, if you will!"

Lehuster made no move. "I must withhold my testimony until I am guaranteed fairly my life, a bargain which should cause no pain, since I have committed no crime."

Zanzel called out angrily: "You forget that I myself witnessed your conduct!"

"Merely a solecism. Ildefonse, do you then promise to hold my life in security?"

"You have my guaranty! Speak on!"

Zanzel sprang to his feet. "This is preposterous! Must we welcome each scoundrel of time into our midst, to satiate himself on our good things, meanwhile perverting our customs?"

The burly and irascible Hurtiancz spoke. "I endorse the progressive views of Zanzel! Lehuster may be only the first of a horde of deviates, morons, and incorrect thinkers sluiced into our placid region!"

Ildefonse spoke in soothing tones: "If Lehuster's news is truly valuable, we must reluctantly concede him his due. Lehuster, speak! We will overlook your flawed conduct as well as your offensive feathers. I, for one, am anxious to hear your news."

Lehuster advanced to the podium. "I must place my remarks in historical perspective. My personal time is the late First Epoch of the 18th Aeon, at a time well before Grand Motholam, but when the Master Magicians and the Great Witches rivalled each other in power: a case similar to the Eleventh Epoch of the 17th Aeon, when the magicians and the sorceresses each strove to outdo the other, and eventually precipitated the War of the Wizards and Witches.

"The witches won this great war. Many of the wizards became archveults; many others were destroyed and the witches, led by the White Witch Llorio, dominated all.

"For an epoch they lived in glory. Llorio became the Murthe and took up residence in a temple. There, as a living idol, comprised both of organic woman and abstract female force, she was joyfully worshipped by every woman of the human race.

"Three magicians survived the war: Teus Treviolus, Schliman Shabat and Phunurus the Orfo. They joined in a cabal and after deeds of daring, craft and cunning to tax credibility, they seized the Murthe, compressed her to a poincture, and took her from the temple. The women became distraught; their power waned while that of the magicians revived. For epochs they lived in a taut accommodation; and these were adventurous times!

"Finally the Murthe won free and rallied her witches. But Calanctus the Calm, under whom I served, rose to the challenge. He broke the witches and chased them north to the back of the Great Erm, where to this day a few still crouch in crevices dreading every sound lest it be the foot-fall of Calanctus.

"As for the Murthe, Calanctus dealt nobly with her and allowed her exile to a far star, then went into seclusion, after first charging me to keep the Murthe under surveillance.

"His orders came too late; she arrived neither at Naos nor at Sadal Suud. I never abandoned the search and recently discovered a trail of time-light* leading to the 21st Aeon; in fact, the terminus is now.

"I am therefore convinced that the Murthe is extant today, and so must be considered a danger of immediacy; indeed, she has already ensqualmed among this present group.

"As for myself, Lehuster the Benefer, I am here for a single purpose: to marshal the magicians into a faithful cabal that they may control the resurgent female force and so maintain placidity. The urgency is great!"

Lehuster went to the side and stood with arms folded: a posture which caused the red feathers growing along his shoulders to project like epaulettes.

Ildefonse cleared his throat. "Lehuster has rendered us a circumstantial account. Zanzel, are you satisfied that Lehuster has fairly won his life and liberty, provided that he agrees to mend his ways?"

*time-light: an untranslatable and even incomprehensible concept. In this context, the term implies a track across the chronic continuum, perceptible to an appropriate sensory apparatus.

''Bah!'' muttered Zanzel. ''He has produced only hearsay and old scandal. I am not so easily hoodwinked.''

Ildefonse frowned and pulled at his yellow beard. He turned to Lehuster. ''You have heard Zanzel's comment. Can you sustain your remarks?''

''Ensqualmation will prove me out, as you will see, but by then it will be too late.''

Vermoulian the Dream-walker chose to address the group. Rising to his feet, he spoke with transparent sincerity. ''As I go about my work, I walk through dreams of many sorts. Recently—indeed, only two nights since—I came upon a dream of the type we call the 'intractive' or 'inoptative' in which the walker exerts little control, and even may encounter danger. Oddly enough, the Murthe was a participant in this dream, and so it may well be relevant to the present discussion.''

Hurtiancz jumped to his feet and made a gesture of annoyance. ''We came here at great inconvenience, to sentence and execute this archveult Lehuster; we do not care to ramble through one of your interminable dreams.''

''Hurtiancz, be silent!'' snapped Vermoulian with peevish vigor. ''I now have the floor, and I shall regale everyone with my account, including as many particulars as I deem necessary.''

''I call upon the Preceptor for a ruling!'' cried Hurtiancz.

Ildefonse said: ''Vermoulian, if your dream is truly germane to the issues, continue, but please speak to the point.''

''That goes without saying!'' said Vermoulian with dignity. ''For the sake of brevity, I will merely state that in attempting to walk that dream identified as AXR-11 GG7, Volume Seven of the Index, I entered a hitherto unclassified dream of the inoptative series. I found myself in a landscape of great charm, where I encountered a group of men, all cultured, artistic and exquisitely refined of manner. Some wore soft silky beards of a chestnut color, while others dressed their hair in tasteful curls, and all were most cordial.

''I will allude only to the salient points of what they told me. All possessions are in common, and greed is unknown. In order that time should be adequate for the enrichment of the personality, toil is kept to a minimum, and shared equally among all. 'Peace' is the watchword; blows are never struck, nor are voices raised in strident anger, nor to call out chiding criticism. Weapons? The concept is a cause for shuddering and shock.

''One of the men became my special friend, and told me much. 'We dine upon nutritious nuts and seeds and ripe juicy fruit; we drink only the purest and most natural water from the springs. At night we sit around the campfire and sing merry little ballads. On special occasions we make a punch called *opo*, from pure fruits, natural honey, and sweet sessamy, and everyone is allowed a good sip.'

" 'Still, we too know moments of melancholy. Look! Yonder sits noble young Pulmer, who leaps and dances with wonderful grace. Yesterday he tried to leap the brook but fell short into the water; we all rushed to console him, and soon he was happy once more.'

"I asked: 'And the women: where do they keep themselves?'

" 'Ah, the women, whom we revere for their kindness, strength, wisdom and patience, as well as for the delicacy of their judgments! Sometimes they even join us at the campfire and then we have some fine romps and games. The women always make sure that no one becomes outrageously foolish, and propriety is never exceeded.'

" 'A gracious life! And how do you procreate?'

" 'Oh ho ho! We have discovered that if we make ourselves very agreeable, the women sometimes allow us little indulgences. . . . Ah! Now! Be at your best! Here is the Great Lady herself!'

"Across the meadow came Llorio the Murthe: a woman pure and strong; and all the men jumped to their feet and waved their hands and smiled their greetings. She spoke to me: 'Vermoulian, have you come to help us? Splendid! Skills like yours will be needed in our effort! I welcome you into our group!'

"Entranced by her stately grace, I stepped forward to embrace her, in friendship and joy, but as I extended my arms she blew a bubble into my face. Before I could question her, I awoke, anxious and bewildered."

Lehuster said: "I can resolve your bewilderment. You were ensqualmed."

"During a dream?" demanded Vermoulian. "I cannot credit such nonsense."

Ildefonse spoke in a troubled voice: "Lehuster, be good enough to instruct us as to the signs by which ensqualmation may be recognized?"

"Gladly. In the final stages the evidence is obvious: the victim becomes a woman. An early mannerism is the habit of darting the tongue rapidly in and out of the mouth. Have you not noticed this signal among your comrades?"

"Only in Zanzel himself, but he is one of our most reputable associates. The concept is unthinkable."

"When one deals with the Murthe, the unthinkable becomes the ordinary, and Zanzel's repute carries no more weight than last year's mouse-dropping—if that much.''

Zanzel pounded the table. ''I am infuriated by the allegation! May I not so much as moisten my lips without incurring a storm of recrimination?''

Again Ildefonse spoke sternly to Lehuster: ''It must be said that Zanzel's complaints carry weight. You must either utter an unequivocal accusation, presenting documents and proofs, or else hold your tongue.''

Lehuster performed a polite bow. ''I will make a terse statement. In essence, the Murthe must be thwarted if we are not to witness the final triumph of the female race. We must form a strong and defiant cabal! The Murthe is not invincible; it is three aeons since she was defeated by Calanctus, and the past is barred to her.''

Ildefonse said ponderously: ''If your analysis is correct, we must undertake to secure the future against this pangynic nightmare.''

''Most urgent is the present! Already the Murthe has been at work!''

''Balderdash, flagrant and wild!'' cried Zanzel. ''Has Lehuster no conscience whatever?''

''I admit to puzzlement,'' said Ildefonse. ''Why should the Murthe select this time and place for her operations?''

Lehuster said: ''Here and now her opposition is negligible. I look around this room; I see fifteen seals dozing on a rock. Pedants like Tchamast; mystics like Ao; buffoons like Hurtiancz and Zanzel. Vermoulian explores unregistered dreams with notepad, calipers and specimen-bottles. Teutch arranges the details of his private infinity. Rhialto exerts his marvels only in the pursuit of pubescent maidens. Still, by ensqualming this group, the Murthe creates a useful company of witches, and so she must be thwarted.''

Ildefonse asked: ''Lehuster, is this your concept of a 'terse statement' in response to my question? First rumor, then speculation, then scandal and bias?''

''For the sake of clarity perhaps I overshot the mark,'' said Lehuster. ''Also—in all candour—I have forgotten your question.''

''You were asked to supply proof in the matter of a certain ensqualmation.''

Lehuster looked from face to face. Everywhere tongues darted in and out of mouths. ''Alas,'' said Lehuster. ''I fear that I must wait for another occasion to finish my statement.''

The room exploded into a confusion of bursting lights and howling sound. When quiet returned, Lehuster was gone.

3

Black night had come to both High and Low Meadows. In the workroom at Falu Ildefonse accepted a half-gill of aquavit from Rhialto, and settled into a slung-leather chair.

For a space the two magicians warily inspected each other; then Ildefonse heaved a deep sigh. "A sad case when old comrades must prove themselves before they sit at ease!"

"First things first," said Rhialto. "I will fling a web around the room, that no one knows our doings. . . . It is done. Now then! I have avoided the squalm; it only remains to prove that you are a whole man."

"Not so fast!" said Ildefonse. "Both must undergo the test; otherwise credibility walks on one leg."

Rhialto gave a sour shrug. "As you wish, though the test lacks dignity."

"No matter; it must be done."

The tests were accomplished; mutual reassurance was achieved. Ildefonse said: "Truth to tell, I felt little concern when I noticed *Calanctus: His Dogma and Dicta* out upon the table."

Rhialto spoke in a confidential manner: "When I met Llorio in the forest, she tried most earnestly to beguile me with her beauty. Gallantry forbids my recitation of details. But I recognized her at once and even the vanity of a Rhialto could not credit her in the role of a heart-sick amourette, and only by thrusting me into the pond and distracting my attention was she able to apply her squalm. I returned to Falu and followed the full therapy as prescribed by Calanctus and the squalm was broken."

Raising his goblet, Ildefonse swallowed the contents at a gulp. "She also appeared before me, though on an elevated level. I encountered her in a waking dream on a wide plain, marked out in a gridwork of distorted and abstract perspectives. She stood at an apparent distance of fifty yards, truly effulgent in her silver-pale beauty, arranged obviously for my benefit. She seemed tall in stature, and towered over me as if I were a child. A psychological ploy, of course, which caused me to smile.

"I called out in a forthright voice: 'Llorio the Murthe, I can see you easily; you need not soar so high.'

"She responded gently enough: 'Ildefonse, my stature need not concern you; my words carry the same import, spoken high or low.'

" 'All very well, but why incur the risk of a vertigo? Your natural proportions are certainly more pleasing to the eye. I can see every pore in your skin. Still, no matter; it is all one with me. Why do you wander into my musing?'

" 'Ildefonse, of all men alive, you are the wisest. The time now is late, but not too late! The female race may still reshape the universe! First, I will lead a sortie to Sadal Suud; among the Seventeen Moons we will renew the human destiny. Your kindly strength, your virtue and grandeur are rich endowments for the role which now you must play.'

"The flavor of these words was not to my liking. I said: 'Llorio, you are a woman of surpassing beauty, though you would seem to lack that provocative warmth which draws man to woman, and adds dimension to the character.'

"The Murthe responded curtly: 'The quality you describe is a kind of lewd obsequiousness which, happily, has now become obsolete. As for the 'surpassing beauty,' it is an apotheotic quality generated by the surging music of the female soul, which you, in your crassness, perceive only as a set of pleasing contours.'

"I replied with my usual gusto: 'Crass or not, I am content with what I see, and as for sorties to far places, let us first march in triumph to the bed-chamber at Boumergarth which is close at hand and there test each other's mettle. Come then, diminish your stature so that I may take your hand; you stand at an inconvenient altitude and the bed would collapse under your weight—in fact, under present conditions, our coupling would hardly be noticed by either of us.'

"Llorio said with scorn: 'Ildefonse, you are a disgusting old satyr, and I see that I was mistaken in my appraisal of your worth. Nevertheless, you must serve our cause with full force.'

"In a stately manner she walked away, into the eccentric angles of the perspective, and with every step she seemed to dwindle, either in the distance or in stature. She walked pensively, in a manner which almost might be construed as invitational. I succumbed to impulse and set out after her—first at a dignified saunter, then faster and faster until I galloped on pounding legs and finally dropped in exhaustion to the ground. Llorio turned and spoke: 'See how the grossness of your character has caused you a foolish indignity!'

"She flicked her hand to throw down a squalm which struck me on the forehead. 'I now give you leave to return to your manse.' And with that she was gone."

"I awoke on the couch in my work-room. Instantly I sought out my *Calanctus* and applied his recommended prophylactics in full measure."

"Most odd!" said Rhialto. "I wonder how Calanctus dealt with her."

"Just as we must do, by forming a strong and relentless cabal."

"Just so, but where and how? Zanzel has been ensqualmed, and certainly he is not alone."

"Bring out your farvoyer; let us learn the worst. Some may still be saved."

Rhialto rolled out an ornate old tabouret, waxed so many times as to appear almost black. "Who will you see first?"

"Try the staunch if mysterious Gilgad. He is a man of discrimination and not easily fooled."

"We may still be disappointed," said Rhialto. "When last I looked, a nervous snake might have envied the deft motion of his tongue." He touched one of the scallops which adorned the edge of the tabouret and spoke a cantrap, to evoke the miniature of Gilgad in a construct of his near surroundings.

Gilgad stood in the kitchen of his manse Thrume, berating the cook. Rather than his customary plum-red suit, the new Gilgad wore wide rose-red pantaloons tied at waist and ankle with coquettish black ribbons. Gilgad's black blouse displayed in tasteful embroidery a dozen red and green birds. Gilgad also used a smart new hair-style, with opulent rolls of hair over each ear, a pair of fine ruby hair-pins to hold the coiffure in place, and a costly white plume surmounting all.

Rhialto told Ildefonse: "Gilgad has been quick to accept the dictates of high fashion."

Ildefonse held up his hand. "Listen!"

From the display came Gilgad's thin voice, now raised in anger: "—grime and grit in profusion; it may have served during my previous half-human condition, but now many things have altered and I see the world, including this sordid kitchen, in a new light. Hence forth, I demand full punctilio! All areas and surfaces must be scoured; extreme neatness will prevail! Further! My metamorphosis will seem peculiar to certain among you, and I suppose that you will crack your little jokes. But I have keen ears and have little jokes of my own! Need I mention Kuniy, who hops about his duties on little soft feet with a mouse-tail trailing behind him, squeaking at the sight of a cat?"

Rhialto touched a scallop to remove the image of Gilgad. "Sad. Gilgad was always something of a dandy and, if you recall, his temper was often uncertain, or even acrid. Ensqualmation evidently fails to ennoble its victim. Ah well, so it goes. Who next?"

''Let us investigate Eshmiel, whose loyalty surely remains staunch.''

Rhialto touched a scallop and on the tabouret appeared Eshmiel in the dressing room of his manse Sil Soum. Eshmiel's previous guise had been notable for its stark and absolute chiaroscuro, with the right side of his body white and the left side black. His garments had followed a similar scheme, though their cut was often bizarre or even frivolous.*

In squalmation, Eshmiel had not discarded his taste for striking contrast, but now he seemed to be wavering between such themes as blue and purple, yellow and orange, pink and umber: these being the colours adorning the mannequins ranged around the room. As Rhialto and Ildefonse watched, Eshmiel marched back and forth, inspecting first one, then another, but finding nothing suitable to his needs, which caused him an obvious vexation.

Ildefonse sighed heavily. ''Eshmiel is clearly gone. Let us grit our teeth and investigate the cases first of Hurtiancz and then Dulce-Lolo.''

Magician after magician appeared on the tabouret, and in the end no doubt remained but that ensqualmation had infected all.

Rhialto spoke gloomily: ''Not one of the group showed so much as a twitch of distress! All wallowed in the squalming as if it were a boon! Would you and I react in the same way?''

Ildefonse winced and pulled at his blond beard. ''It makes the blood to run cold.''

''So now we are alone,'' said Rhialto. ''The decisions are ours to make.''

''They are not simple,'' said Ildefonse after reflection. ''We have come under attack: do we retaliate? If so: how? Or even: why? The world is moribund.''

''But I am not! I am Rhialto, and such treatment offends me!''

Ildefonse nodded thoughtfully. ''That is an important point. I, with equal vehemence, am Ildefonse!''

''More, you are Ildefonse the Preceptor! And now you must use your legitimate powers.''

Ildefonse inspected Rhialto through blue eyes blandly half-closed. ''Agreed! I nominate you to enforce my edicts!''

Rhialto ignored the pleasantry. ''I am thinking of IOUN stones.''

*Eshmiel's more thoughtful associates often speculated that Eshmiel used this means to symbolize the Grand Polarities permeating the universe, while at the same time asserting the infinite variety to be derived from the apparent simplicity. These persons considered Eshmiel's message profound but optimistic, though Eshmiel himself refused to issue an analysis.

Ildefonse sat up in his chair. "What is your exact meaning?"

"You must decree confiscation from the ensqualmated witches of all IOUN stones, on grounds of policy. Then we will work a time-stasis and send sandestins out to gather the stones."

"All very well, but our comrades often conceal their treasures with ingenious care."

"I must confess to a whimsical little recreation—a kind of intellectual game, as it were. Over the years I have ascertained the hiding-place of every IOUN stone current among the association. You keep yours, for instance, in the water reservoir of the convenience at the back of your work-room."

"That, Rhialto, is an ignoble body of knowledge. Still, at this point, we cannot gag at trifles. I hereby confiscate all IOUN stones in the custody of our bewitched former comrades. Now, if you will impact the continuum with a spell, I will call in my sandestins Osherl, Ssisk and Walfing."

"My creatures Topo and Bellume are also available for duty."

The confiscation went with an almost excessive facility. Ildefonse declared: "We have struck an important blow. Our position is now clear; our challenge is bold and direct!"

Rhialto frowningly considered the stones. "We have struck a blow; we have issued a challenge: what now?"

Ildefonse blew out his cheeks. "The prudent course is to hide until the Murthe goes away."

Rhialto gave a sour grunt. "Should she find us and pull us squeaking from our holes, all dignity is lost. Surely this is not the way of Calanctus."

"Let us then discover the way of Calanctus," said Ildefonse. "Bring out Poggiore's *Absolutes*; he devotes an entire chapter to the Murthe. Fetch also *The Decretals* of Calanctus, and, if you have it, *Calanctus: His Means and Modes*."

4

Dawn was still to come. The sky over Wilda Water showed a flush of plum, aquamarine and dark rose. Rhialto slammed shut the iron covers of the *Decretals*. "I find no help. Calanctus describes the persistent female genius, but he is not explicit in his remedies."

Ildefonse, looking through the *The Doctrines of Calanctus*, said: "I find here an interesting passage. Calanctus likens a woman to the Ciaeic Ocean which absorbs the long and full thrust of the Antipodal

Current as it sweeps around Cape Spang, but only while the weather holds fair. If the wind shifts but a trifle, this apparently placid ocean hurls an abrupt flood ten or even twenty feet high back around the cape, engulfing all before it. When stasis is restored and the pressure relieved, the Ciaeic is as before, placidly accepting the current. Do you concur with this interpretation of the female geist?''

''Not on all counts,'' said Rhialto. ''At times Calanctus verges upon the hyperbolic. This might be regarded as a typical case, especially since he provides no program for holding off or even diverting the Ciaeic flood.''

''He seems to suggest that one does not strive, ordinarily, to control this surge but, rather, rides over it in a staunch ship of high freeboard.''

Rhialto shrugged. ''Perhaps so. As always, I am impatient with obscure symbolism. The analogy assists us not at all.''

Ildefonse ruminated. ''It suggests that rather than meeting the Murthe power against power, we must slide across and over the gush of her hoarded energy, until at last she has spent herself and we, like stout ships, float secure and dry.''

''Again, a pretty image, but limited. The Murthe displays a protean power.''

Ildefonse stroked his beard and looked pensively off into space. ''Indeed, one inevitably starts to wonder whether this fervor, cleverness and durability might also govern her—or, so to speak, might tend to influence her conduct in, let us say, the realm of—''

''I understand the gist of your speculation,'' said Rhialto. ''It is most likely nuncupatory.''

Ildefonse gave his head a wistful shake. ''Sometimes one's thoughts go where they will.''

A golden insect darted out of the shadows, circled the lamp and flew back into the darkness. Rhialto instantly became alert. ''Someone has entered Falu, and now waits in the parlour.'' He went to the door and called out sharply: ''Who is there? Speak, or dance the tarantella on feet of fire.''

''Hold hard your spell!'' spoke a voice. ''It is I, Lehuster!''

''In that case, come forward.''

Into the work-room came Lehuster, soiled and limping, his shoulder feathers bedraggled, in a state of obvious fatigue. He carried a sack which he gratefully dropped upon the leather-slung couch under the window.

Ildefonse surveyed him with frowning disfavor. ''Well then, Lehuster, you are here at last! A dozen times during the night we might have used your counsel, but you were nowhere to be found. What, then, is your report?"

Rhialto handed Lehuster a tot of aquavit. "This will alleviate your fatigue; drink and then speak freely."

Lehuster consumed the liquid at a gulp. "Aha! A tipple of rare quality! . . . Well then, I have little enough to tell you, though I have spent a most toilsome night, performing necessary tasks. All are ensqualmed, save only yourselves. The Murthe, however, believes that she controls the entire association."

"What?" cried Rhialto. "Does she take us so lightly?"

"No great matter." Lehuster held out the empty goblet. "If you please! A bird flies erratically on one wing. . . . Further, the Murthe appropriated all IOUN stones to her personal use—"

"Not so!" said Ildefonse with a chuckle. "We cleverly took them first."

"You seized a clutch of glass baubles. The Murthe took the true stones, including those owned by you and Rhialto, and left brummagem in their place."

Rhialto ran to the basket where the presumptive IOUN stones reposed. He groaned. "The mischievous vixen has robbed us in cold blood!"

Lehuster gestured to the sack he had tossed upon the couch. "On this occasion, we have bested her. Yonder are the stones! I seized them while she bathed. I suggest that you send a sandestin to replace them with the false stones. If you hurry, there is still time; the Murthe dallies at her toilette. Meanwhile hide the true stones in some extradimensional cubby-hole, so that they may not be taken from you again."

Rhialto summoned his sandestin Bellume and issued an appropriate instruction.

Ildefonse turned to Lehuster: "By what means did Calanctus confound this dire and frightening female?"

"Mystery still shrouds the occasion," said Lehuster. "Calanctus apparently used an intense personal force and so kept Llorio at bay."

"Hmmf. We must learn more of Calanctus. The chronicles make no mention of his death; he may still be extant, perhaps in the Land of Cutz!"

"Such questions also trouble the Murthe," said Lehuster. "We may well be able to confuse her and induce her retreat."

"How so?"

"There is no time to lose. You and Rhialto must create an ideal semblance in the shape of Calanctus, and here, at least, I can be of assistance. The creation need not be permanent, but it must be sufficiently vital so that Llorio is persuaded that once again she pits herself against Calanctus."

Ildefonse pulled doubtfully at his beard. "That is a major undertaking."

"With scant time for its execution! Remember, by winning the IOUN stones you have defied the Murthe with a challenge which she cannot ignore!"

Rhialto jumped to his feet. "Quickly then! Let us do as Lehuster suggests! Time is short."

"Hmmf," growled Ildefonse. "I do not fear this misguided harridan. Is there no easier way?"

"Yes! Flight to a far dimension!"

"You know me better than that!" declared Ildefonse. "To work! We will send this witch squealing and leaping with skirts held high as she bounds over the brambles!"

"That shall be our slogan," declared Lehuster. "To work!"

The semblance of Calanctus took form on the work table: first an armature of silver and tantalum wires built upon an articulated spinal truss, then a shadowy sheathing of tentative concepts, then the skull and sensorium, into which were inserted all the works of Calanctus, and a hundred other tracts, including catalogues, compendia, pantologies and universal syntheses, until Lehuster counselled a stop. "Already he knows twenty times as much as the first Calanctus! I wonder if he can organize such a mass?"

The muscles were stretched and drawn taut; the skin was applied, along with a thick pelt of dark short hair over the scalp and down the forehead. Lehuster worked long and hard at the features, adjusting the jut of the jaw, the thrust of the short straight nose, the breadth of the forehead, the exact shape and curve of eyebrows and hair-line.

The ears were affixed and the auditory channels adjusted. Lehuster spoke in an even voice: "You are Calanctus, first hero of the 18th Aeon."

The eyes opened and gazed thoughtfully at Lehuster.

"I am your friend," said Lehuster. "Calanctus, arise! Go sit in yonder chair."

The Calanctus-form rose from the table with only a trifling effort, swung his strong legs to the floor and went to sit in the chair.

Lehuster turned to Rhialto and Ildefonse. "It would be better if now you stepped into the parlour for a few minutes. I must instill memories and associations into this mind; he must be vivid with life."

"A full lifetime of memories in so short a time?" demanded Ildefonse. "Impossible!"

"Not so, in a time-compression! I will also teach him music and poetry; he must be passionate as well as vivid. My instrument is this bit of dry flower-petal; its perfume works magic."

Somewhat reluctantly Ildefonse and Rhialto went to the parlour, where they watched morning come full to Low Meadow.

Lehuster called them to the work-room. "There sits Calanctus. His mind is rich with knowledge; he is perhaps even broader in his concepts than his namesake. Calanctus, this is Rhialto and this is Ildefonse; they are your friends."

Calanctus looked from one to the other with mild blue eyes. "I am glad to hear that! From what I have learned, the world is sorely in need of amity."

Lehuster said aside: "He is Calanctus, but with a difference, or even a certain lack. I have given him a quart of my blood, but perhaps it is not enough. . . . Still, we shall see."

Ildefonse asked: "What of power? Can he enforce his commands?"

Lehuster looked toward the neo-Calanctus. "I have loaded his sensorium with IOUN stones. Since he has never known harm he is easy and gentle despite his innate force."

"What does he know of the Murthe?"

"All there is to be known. He shows no emotion."

Rhialto and Ildefonse regarded their creation with skepticism. "So far Calanctus seems still an abstraction, without over-much volition," said Rhialto. "Can we not give him a more visceral identification with the real Calanctus?"

Lehuster hesitated. "Yes. It is a scarab which Calanctus always wore on his wrist. Dress him now in apparel, then I will give him the scarab."

Ten minutes later Rhialto and Ildefonse entered the parlour with Calanctus, who now wore a black helmet, a breast-plate of polished black metal, a black cape, black breeches and black boots, with silver buckles and accoutrements.

Lehuster nodded. "He is as he should be. Calanctus, hold out your arm! I will give you a scarab worn by the first Calanctus, whose identity you must assume. This bracelet is yours. Wear it always around your right wrist."

Calanctus said: "I feel the surge of power. I am strong! I am Calanctus!"

Rhialto asked: "Are you strong enough to accept the sleight of magic? The ordinary man must study forty years even to become an apprentice.''

''I have the power to accept magic.''

''Come then! You shall ingest the *Encyclopedia*, then the Three Books of Phandaal, and if then you are neither dead nor mad I will pronounce you a man strong beyond any of my experience. Come! Back to the work-room.''

Ildefonse remained in the parlour. . . . Minutes passed. He heard a queer choking outcry, quickly quelled.

Calanctus returned to the parlour with firm steps. Rhialto, coming after, walked on sagging knees with a green pallor on his face.

Calanctus spoke somberly to Ildefonse: ''I have accepted magic. My mind reels with spells; they are wild, but still I control their veering forces. The scarab gave me the strength.''

Lehuster spoke. ''The time is near. Witches gather on the meadow: Zanzel, Ao of the Opals, Barbanikos, and others. They are fretful and agitated. . . . In fact, Zanzel approaches.''

Rhialto looked to Ildefonse. ''Shall we use the opportunity?''

''We would be fools if we did not!''

''My thoughts precisely. If you will take yourself to the side arbor. . . .''

Rhialto went out on the front terrace, where he met Zanzel, who lodged an emphatic protest in the matter of the missing IOUN stones.

''Quite right!'' said Rhialto. ''It was a dastardly act, done at the behest of Ildefonse. Come to the side arbor and I will redress the wrong.''

Zanzel walked to the side arbor where Ildefonse desensitized her with the Spell of Internal Solitude. Ladanque, Rhialto's chamberlain, lifted Zanzel to a barrow and wheeled her to the gardener's shed.

Rhialto, emboldened by his success, stepped to the front terrace and signaled to Barbanikos, who, following Rhialto into the side arbor, met a similar disposition.

So it went with Ao of the Opals, Dulce-Lolo, Hurtiancz and others, until the only witches remaining upon the meadow were the absent-minded Vermoulian and Tchamast the Didactor, both of whom ignored Rhialto's signal.

Llorio the Murthe dropped down upon the meadow in a whirl of white cloud-spume. . . . She wore an ankle-length white gown, silver sandals, a silver belt and a black fillet to confine her hair. She put a question to Vermoulian, who pointed toward Rhialto, at the front of Falu.

Llorio slowly approached. Ildefonse, stepping from the arbor, bravely directed a double spell of Internal Solitude against her; it bounced back and, striking Ildefonse, sent him sprawling.

Llorio the Murthe halted. ''Rhialto! You have mistreated my coterie! You have stolen my magic stones, and so now you must come to Sadal Suud not as a witch, but as a servant of menial sort, and this shall be your punishment. Ildefonse will fare no better.''

From Falu came Calanctus. He halted. Llorio's taut jaw sagged; her mouth fell open.

Llorio spoke in a gasping voice: ''How are you here? How did you evade the triangle? How . . .'' The voice seemed to catch in her throat; in consternation she stared into the face of Calanctus. She found her voice. ''Why do you look at me like that? Faithless I have not been; I now depart for Sadal Suud! Here I do only what must be done and it is you who are faithless!''

''I also did what must be done, and so it must be done again, for you have ensqualmated men to be your witches; so you have broken the Great Law, which ordains that man shall be man and woman shall be woman.''

''When Necessity meets Law, then Law gives way: so you spoke in your Decretals!''

''No matter. Go you shall to Sadal Suud! Go now, go alone, without the ensqualmations.''

Llorio said: ''It is all one; a sorry band they are, either as wizards or witches, and in candour I wanted them only for entourage.''

''Go then, Murthe!''

Llorio instead looked at Calanctus with a peculiar expression mingled of puzzlement and dissatisfaction on her face. She made no move to depart, which would seem to be both a taunt and a provocation. ''The aeons have not dealt kindly with you; now you stand like a man of dough! Remember how you threatened to deal with me should we meet again?'' She took another step forward, and showed a cool smile. ''Are you afraid of my strength? So it must be! Where now are your erotic boasts and predictions?''

''I am a man of peace. I carry concord in my soul rather than attack and subjugation. I threaten naught; I promise hope.''

Llorio came a step closer and peered into his face. ''Ah!'' she cried softly. ''You are an empty facade, no more, and not Calanctus! Are you then so ready to taste death's sweetness?''

''I am Calanctus.''

Llorio spoke a spell of twisting and torsion, but Calanctus fended it away with a gesture, and called a spell in turn of compressions from seven directions, which caught the Murthe unready and sent her reeling to her knees. Calanctus bent in compassion to lift her erect; she flared into blue flame and Calanctus held her around the waist with charred arms.

Llorio pushed him back, her face contorted. ''You are not Calanctus; you are milk where he is blood!''

Even as she spoke the scarab in the bracelet brushed her face; she screamed and from her throat erupted a great spell—an explosion of power too strong for the tissues of her body, so that blood spurted from her mouth and nose. She reeled back to support herself against a tree, while Calanctus toppled slowly to lie broken and torn on his back.

Panting in emotion, Llorio stood looking down at the toppled hulk. From the nostrils issued a lazy filament of black smoke, coiling and swirling above the corpse.

Moving like a man entranced, Lehuster stepped slowly into the smoke. The air shook to a rumble of sound; a sultry yellow glare flashed like lightning; in the place of Lehuster stood a man of massive body, his skin glowing with internal light. He wore short black pantaloons and sandals, with legs and chest bare; his hair was black, his face square, with a stern nose and jutting jaw. He bent over the corpse and taking the scarab clasped it to his own wrist.

The new Calanctus spoke to Llorio: ''My trouble has gone for nought! I came to this time as Lehuster, thus to leave sleeping old pains and old rages; now these hopes are forlorn, and all is as before. I am I, and once more we stand at odds!''

Llorio stood silent, her chest heaving.

Calanctus spoke on: ''What of your other spells, to batter and break, or to beguile men's dreams and soften resolve? If so, try them on me, since I am not the poor mild Calanctus who carried the hopes of all of us, and who met so rude a destiny.''

''Hope?'' cried Llorio. ''When the world is done and I have been thwarted? What remains? Nothing. Neither hope nor honour nor anguish nor pain! All is gone! Ashes blow across the desert. All has been lost, or forgotten; the best and the dearest are gone. Who are these creatures who stand here so foolishly? Ildefonse? Rhialto? Vapid ghosts, mowing with round mouths! Hope! Nothing remains. All is gone, all is done; even death is in the past.''

So cried out Llorio, from the passion of despair, the blood still dripping from her nose. Calanctus stood quietly, waiting till her passion spent itself.

''To Sadal Suud I will go. I have failed; I stand at bay, surrounded by the enemies of my race.''

Calanctus, reaching forward, touched her face. "Call me enemy as you like! Still, I love your dear features; I treasure your virtues and your peculiar faults; and I would not have them changed save in the direction of kindliness."

Llorio took a step backward. "I concede nothing; I will change nothing."

"Ah well, it was only an idle thought. What is this blood?"

"My brain is bleeding; I used all my power to destroy this poor futile corpse. I too am dying; I taste the savor of death. Calanctus, you have won your victory at last!"

"As usual, you overshoot the mark. I have won no victory; you are not dying nor need you go off to Sadal Suud, which is a steaming quagmire infested by owls, gnats and rodents: quite unsuitable for one of your delicacy. Who would do the laundry?"

"You will allow me neither death, nor yet refuge on a new world! Is this not defeat piled on defeat?"

"Words only. Come now; take my hand and we will call a truce."

"Never!" cried Llorio. "This symbolizes the ultimate conquest, to which I will never surrender!"

"I will gladly put by the symbol for the reality. Then you shall see whether or not I am able to make good my boasts."

"Never! I submit my person to no man's pleasure."

"Then will you not at least come away with me, so that we may drink wine on the terrace of my air-castle, and look across the panorama, and speak as the words idly come to mind?"

"Never!"

"One moment!" called Ildefonse. "Before you go, be good enough to desqualmate this coterie of witches, and so spare us the effort!"

"Bah, it is no great task," said Calanctus. "Evoke the Second Retrotropic, followed by a stabilizing fixture: a matter of minutes."

"Precisely so," said Ildefonse. "This, essentially, was my plan."

Rhialto turned to Ladanque. "Bring out the witches. Rank them on the meadow."

"And the corpse?"

Rhialto spoke a spell of dissolution; the dead thing collapsed into dust.

Llorio hesitated, looking first north, then south, as if in indecision; then, turning, she walked pensively across the meadow. Calanctus followed; the two halted and stood facing each other. First Llorio spoke, then Calanctus, then Llorio; then they both looked together toward the east, and then they were gone.

2

Fader's Waft

1

By day the sun cast a wan maroon gloom across the land; by night all was dark and still, with only a few pale stars to post the old constellations. Time went at a languid pace, without purpose or urgency, and folk made few long-range plans.

Grand Motholam was three aeons gone; the great masters of magic were extinct, each having suffered a more or less undignified demise: through the treachery of a trusted confidante; or during an amorous befuddlement; or by the machinations of a secret cabal; or through some unexpected and horrifying disaster.

The magicians of this, the 21st Aeon, for the most part resided in the quiet river valleys of Almery and Ascolais, though a few recluses kept to the Land of Cutz in the north, or the Land of the Falling Wall, or even the Steppes of Shwang in the distant east.

By reason of special factors (which lie beyond the scope of this present exposition) the magicians of the day were a various lot; gathered in colloquy, they seemed an assembly of rare and wonderful birds, each most mindful of his own plumage. While, on the whole, lacking the flamboyant magnificence of Grand Motholam, they were no less capricious and self-willed, and only after a number of unhappy incidents were they persuaded to regulate themselves by a code of conduct. This code, known as 'the Monstrament,' or, less formally, 'the Blue Principles,' was engraved upon a blue prism, which was housed in a secret place. The association included the most notable magicians of the region. By unanimous acclaim, Ildefonse was proclaimed Preceptor, and invested with large powers.

Ildefonse resided at Boumergarth, an ancient castle of four towers on the banks of the River Scaum. He had been chosen Preceptor not only for his dedication to the Blue Principles, but also for his equable temperament, which at times seemed almost bland. His tolerance was proverbial; at one turn he might be found chuckling to the lewd jokes of Dulce-Lolo; the next might find him engrossed in the opinions of the ascetic Tchamast, whose suspicions of the female sex ran deep.

Ildefonse ordinarily appeared as a jovial sage with twinkling blue eyes, a bald pate and a straggling blond beard: a semblance which tended to engender trust, frequently to private advantage, and the use of the word 'ingenuous,' when applied to Ildefonse, was probably incorrect.

At this juncture the magicians subscribing to the Blue Principles numbered twenty-two.* Despite the clear advantages of orderly conduct, certain agile intelligences could not resist the thrill of the illicit and played mischievous tricks, on one occasion performing a most serious transgression against the Blue Principles.

The case involved Rhialto, sometimes known as 'the Marvellous.' He resided at Falu, not far from Wilda Water, in a district of low hills and dim forests at the eastern verge of Ascolais.

Among his fellows Rhialto, for whatever justification, was considered somewhat supercilious and enjoyed no wide popularity. His natural semblance was that of a proud and distinguished grandee, with short black hair, austere features, and a manner of careless ease. Rhialto was not without vanity, which, when taken with his aloof manner, often exasperated his fellows. And certain among them pointedly turned away when Rhialto appeared at a gathering, to Rhialto's sublime indifference.

Hache-Moncour was one of the few who cultivated Rhialto. He had contrived for himself the semblance of a Ctharion nature-god, with bronze curls and exquisite features, flawed (in the opinion of some) by a fulsome richness of mouth and eyes perhaps a trifle too round and limpid. Motivated, perhaps, by envy, at times he seemed almost to emulate Rhialto's mannerisms.

In Hache-Moncour's original condition, he had formed a number of fidgeting habits. When absorbed in thought, he squinted and pulled at his ears; when perplexed, he scratched vigorously under his arms. Such habits, which he found hard to abandon, marred the careless aplomb toward which he so earnestly worked. He suspected Rhialto of smiling at his lapses, which honed the edge of his envy, and so the mischiefs began.

*See Foreword.

After a banquet at the hall of Mune the Mage, the magicians prepared to depart. Making their way into the foyer, they took up their cloaks and hats. Rhialto, always punctilious in his courtesies, extended to Hurtiancz first his cloak, then his hat. Hurtiancz, whose heavy-featured head rested directly upon his squat shoulders, acknowledged the service with a grunt. Hache-Moncour, standing nearby, saw his opportunity and cast a spell which enlarged Hurtiancz's hat by several sizes, so that when the irascible magician clapped the hat on his head, it dropped in back almost to his shoulders, while in front only the bulbous tip of his nose remained visible.

Hurtiancz tore the hat from his head and studied it from all angles, but Hache-Moncour had removed the spell and nothing seemed out of order. Once again Hurtiancz tried the hat on his head, and now it fit properly.

Even then all might have been ignored had not Hache-Moncour made a pictorial imprint of the scene, which he subsequently circulated among the magicians and other persons of the local nobility whose good opinion Hurtiancz wished to cultivate. The picture showed Hurtiancz with only the red lump of his nose in sight and Rhialto in the background wearing a smile of cool amusement.

Only Rhialto failed to receive a copy of the picture and no one thought to mention it to him, least of all Hurtiancz, whose outrage knew no bounds, and who now could hardly speak calmly when Rhialto's name was mentioned.

Hache-Moncour was delighted by the success of his prank. Any tarnishing of Rhialto's repute could only serve to enhance his own; additionally, he discovered a malicious pleasure in Rhialto's discomfiture.

Hache-Moncour thereupon initiated a whole series of intrigues, which at last became for Hache-Moncour something of an obsession, and his goal became the full and utter humiliation of the proud Rhialto.

Hache-Moncour worked with consummate subtlety, so that Rhialto at first noticed nothing. The plots were for the most part paltry, but always carried a sting.

Upon learning that Rhialto was refurbishing the guestrooms at Falu, Hache-Moncour purloined a prized gem from Ao of the Opals and arranged that it should hang from the drop-chain of the commode in the new lavatory at Falu.

In due course, Ao learned of the use to which his magnificent two-inch tear-drop opal had been put, and his rancor, like that of Hurtiancz, approached the violence of a shivering fit. Despite all, Ao was constrained by Article Four of the Blue Principles, and so kept his resentment within check.

On another occasion, during Rhialto's experiments with bubbles of luminous plasm, Hache-Moncour caused such a bubble to settle into a unique harquisade tree which Zilifant had imported from Canopus and thereupon had nurtured by day and by night with intense solicitude. Once within the tree, the plasm exploded, pulverizing the brittle glass foliage and permeating Zilifant's premises with a vile and persistent odor.

Zilifant instantly complained to Rhialto in a voice croaking and creaking under the weight of anger. Rhialto responded with cool logic, citing six definite reasons why none of his plasms were responsible for the damage, and, while expressing regret, refused to make restitution of any sort. Zilifant's convictions were quietly reinforced by Hache-Moncour, who stated that Rhialto had boastfully announced his intention of using the harquisade tree as a target. "Further," said Hache-Moncour, "Rhialto went on to say, and here I quote, 'Zilifant constantly exudes such a personal chife into the air that the stench of the plasm may well be redundant.' "

And so it went. Gilgad owned a pet simiode, of which he was inordinately fond. At twilight Hache-Moncour, wearing a black domino, a black cloak and a black hat identical to the garments worn by Rhialto, captured the beast and dragged it away at the end of a chain to Falu. Here Hache-Moncour beat the beast well and tied it on a short scope between a pair of chastity-plants, which caused the beast an additional affliction.

Gilgad, taking information from peasants, followed the trail to Falu. He released the simiode, listened to its howling complaints, then confronted Rhialto with the evidence of his guilt.

Rhialto crisply denied all knowledge of the deed, but Gilgad, waxing passionate, would not be convinced. He cried out: "Boodis identifies you explicitly! He claims that you made terrifying threats; that you declared: 'I am Rhialto, and if you think you have been beaten soundly, wait only until I refresh myself!' Is that not an attitude of merciless cruelty?"

Rhialto said: "You must decide whom you will believe: me or that repulsive beast." He gave a disdainful bow, and returning into Falu, closed the door. Gilgad cried out a final complaint, then wheeled Boodis home in a barrow padded with silken cushions. Thereafter, among his detractors, Rhialto could confidently include Gilgad.

On another occasion, Rhialto, acting in all innocence, was played false by the ordinary fluxions of circumstance, and once again became the target of recrimination. Initially, Hache-Moncour played no part in the affair, but later made large of it, to compound its effect.

The episode began on a level of pleasant anticipation. The ranking nobleman of the region was Duke Tambasco, a person of impeccable dignity and ancient lineage. Each year, to celebrate the sun's gallant efforts to survive, Duke Tambasco sponsored a Grand Ball at his palace Quanorq. The guest-list was most select, and on this occasion included Ildefonse, Rhialto and Byzant the Necrope.

Ildefonse and Byzant met at Boumergarth, and over tots of Ildefonse's best hyperglossom each congratulated the other on his splendid appearance, and made lewd wagers as to who would score the most notable triumphs among the beauties at the ball.

For the occasion Ildefonse chose to appear as a stalwart young bravo with golden curls falling past his ears, a fine golden mustache, and a manner both hearty and large. To complement the thrust of the image, he wore a suit of green velvet, a dark green and gold sash, and a dashing wide-brimmed hat with a white plume.

Byzant, planning with equal care, chose the semblance of a graceful young aesthete, sensitive to nuance and vulnerable to the most fugitive breath of beauty. He joined emerald-green eyes, copper-red ringlets and a marmoreal complexion into a juxtaposition calculated to excite the ardor of the most beautiful women at the ball. "I will seek out the most ravishing of all!" he told Ildefonse. "I will fascinate her with my appearance and captivate her with my soul; she will fall into an amorous swoon which I will shamelessly exploit."

"I see but a single flaw in your argument," chuckled Ildefonse. "When you discover this creature of superb attraction, she will already be on my arm and oblivious to all else."

"Ildefonse, you have always been a braggart in connection with your conquests!" cried Byzant. "At Quanorq we shall judge by performance alone, and then we shall see who is the true adept!"

"So it shall be!"

After a final tot of the hyperglossom, the two gallants set off to Falu, where to their astonishment they found that Rhialto had totally forgotten the occasion.

Ildefonse and Byzant were impatient, and would allow Rhialto no time to make preparations, so Rhialto merely pulled a tasseled cap over his black hair and declared himself ready to depart.

Byzant stood back in surprise. "But you have made no preparations! You are not arrayed in splendid garments! You have neither laved your feet nor scented your hair!"

"No matter," said Rhialto. "I will seclude myself in the shadows and envy you your successes. At least I shall enjoy the music and the spectacle."

Byzant chuckled complacently. "No matter, Rhialto; it is time that you had some wind taken from your sails. Tonight Ildefonse and I are primed and ready; you will be entitled to watch our superb talents used to absolutely compelling effect!"

"Byzant speaks with exact accuracy," declared Ildefonse. "You have had your share of triumphs; tonight you are fated to stand aside and watch while a pair of experts do what is needful to bring the loveliest of the lovely to their knees!"

"If it must be, so it must be," said Rhialto. "My concern now is for the heart-sick victims of your craft. Have you no pity?"

"None whatever!" declared Ildefonse. "We wage our amorous campaigns with full force; we give no quarter and accept no paroles!"

Rhialto gave his head a rueful shake. "A tragedy that I was not reminded of the ball in time!"

"Come now, Rhialto!" chuckled Byzant. "You must take the bad with the good; whimpering avails nothing."

Ildefonse cried out. "Meanwhile, time advances! Shall we depart?"

Arriving at Quanorq the three paid their respects to Duke Tambasco and congratulated him upon the magnificence of his arrangements: compliments which the duke acknowledged with a formal bow, and the three magicians made way for others.

For a period the three wandered here and there, and indeed on this occasion Duke Tambasco had outdone himself. Grandees and their charming ladies crowded the halls and galleries, and at four buffets choice viands and fine liquors were deployed in profusion.

The three magicians at last repaired to the foyer of the great ballroom where, stationing themselves to the side, they took note of the beautiful ladies as they passed and discussed the merits and distinguishing characteristics of each. In due course they decided that, while many comely maidens were in evidence, none could match the agonizingly exquisite beauty of the Lady Shaunica of Lake Island.

Ildefonse presently puffed out his fine blond mustaches and went his way. Byzant also took his leave of Rhialto, who went to sit in a shadowed alcove to the side.

Ildefonse found the first opportunity to exert his expertise. Advancing upon the Lady Shaunica he performed a sweeping salute and offered to escort her through the measures of a pavane. "I am profoundly skillful in the execution of this particular dance," he assured her. "I with my bold flourishes and you with your gracious beauty make a notable pair; we shall be the focus of all eyes! Then, after the dance, I will escort you to the buffet. We will take a goblet or two of wine and you will discover that I am a person of remarkable parts!

More than this, I now declare that I am prepared to offer you my fullest esteem!''

''That is most gracious of you,'' said the Lady Shaunica. ''I am profoundly moved. However, at this juncture, I have no taste for dancing, and I dare drink no more wine for fear of becoming coarse, which would certainly arouse your disapproval.''

Ildefonse performed a punctilious bow and prepared to assert his charm even more explicitly, but when he looked up, Lady Shaunica already had made her departure.

Ildefonse gave a grunt of annoyance, pulled at his mustaches, and strode off to seek a maiden of more malleable tendency.

By chance, the Lady Shaunica almost immediately encountered Byzant. To attract her attention and possibly win her admiration, Byzant addressed her with a quatrain in an archaic language known as Old Naotic, but the Lady Shaunica was only startled and bewildered.

Byzant smilingly translated the lyric and explained certain irregularities of the Naotic philology. ''But after all,'' said Byzant, ''these concepts need not intrude into the rapport between us. I sense that you feel its warm languor as strongly as I!''

''Perhaps not quite so strongly,'' said the Lady Shaunica. ''But then I am insensitive to such influences, and in fact I feel no rapport whatever.''

''It will come, it will come!'' Byzant assured her. ''I own a rare perception in that I can see souls in all their shimmering colour. Yours and mine waver in the same noble radiances! Come, let us stroll out on the terrace! I will impart to you a secret.'' He reached to take her hand.

The Lady Shaunica, somewhat puzzled by Byzant's effusiveness, drew back. ''Truly, I do not care to hear secrets upon such short acquaintance.''

''It is not so much a secret as an impartment! And what, after all is duration? I have known you no more than half an hour, but already I have composed two lyrics and an ode to your beauty! Come! Out on the terrace! Away and beyond! Into the star-light, under the trees; we shall discard our garments and stride with the wild innocence of sylvan divinities!''

Lady Shaunica drew back still another step. ''Thank you, but I am somewhat self-conscious. Suppose we ran so briskly that we could not find our way back to the palace, and in the morning the peasants found us running naked along the road? What could we tell them? Your proposal lacks appeal.''

Byzant threw high his arms and, rolling back his eyes, clutched at his red curls, hoping that the Lady Shaunica would recognize his agony of spirit and take pity, but she had already slipped away. Byzant went angrily to the buffet, where he drank several goblets of strong wine.

A few moments later the Lady Shaunica, passing through the foyer, chanced upon one of her acquaintances, the Lady Dualtimetta. During their conversation the Lady Shaunica chanced to glance into a nearby alcove, where Rhialto sat alone on a couch of maroon brocade. She whispered to the Lady Dualtimetta: "Look yonder into the alcove: who is that who sits so quietly alone?"

The Lady Dualtimetta turned her head to look. "I have heard his name; it is Rhialto, and sometimes 'Rhialto the Marvellous.' Do you think him elegant? I myself find him austere and even daunting!"

"Truly? Surely not daunting; is he not a man?"

"Naturally! But why does he sit apart as if he disdained everyone at Quanorq?"

"Everyone?" mused the Lady Shaunica as if to herself.

The Lady Dualtimetta moved away. "My dear, excuse me; now I must hurry; I have an important part in the pageant." She went her way.

The Lady Shaunica hesitated, then, smiling as if at some private amusement, went slowly to the alcove. "Sir, may I join you here in the shadows?"

Rhialto rose to his feet. "Lady Shaunica, you are well aware that you may join me wherever you wish."

"Thank you." She seated herself on the couch and Rhialto resumed his own place. Still smiling her secret half-smile she asked: "Do you wonder why I come to sit with you?"

"The question had not occurred to me." Rhialto considered a moment. "I might guess that you intend to meet a friend in the foyer, and here is a convenient place to wait."

"That is a genteel reply," said the Lady Shaunica. "In sheer truth, I wonder why a person such as yourself sits aloof in the shadows. Have you been dazed by tragic news? Are you disdainful of all others at Quanorq, and their pitiful attempts to put forward an appealing image?"

Rhialto smiled his own wry half-smile. "I have suffered no tragic shocks. As for the appealing image of the Lady Shaunica, it is enhanced by a luminous intelligence of equal charm."

"Then you have arranged a rendezvous of your own?"

"None whatever."

"Still, you sit alone and speak to no one."

"My motives are complex. What of yours? You sit here in the shadows as well."

The Lady Shaunica laughed. "I ride like a feather on wafts of caprice. Perhaps I am piqued by your restraint, or distance, or indifference, or whatever it may be. Every other gallant has dropped upon me like a vulture on a corpse." She turned him a sidelong glance. "Your conduct therefore becomes provocative, and now you have the truth."

Rhialto was silent a moment, then said: "There are many exchanges to be made between us—if our acquaintance is to persist."

The Lady Shaunica made a flippant gesture. "I have no strong objections."

Rhialto looked across the foyer. "I might then suggest that we discover a place where we can converse with greater privacy. We sit here like birds on a fence."

"A solution is at hand," said the Lady Shaunica. "The duke has allowed me a suite of apartments for the duration of my visit. I will order in a collation and a bottle or two of Maynesse, and we will continue our talk in dignity and seclusion."

"The proposal is flawless," said Rhialto. He rose and, taking the Lady Shaunica's hands, drew her to her feet. "Do I still seem as if dazed by tragic news?"

"No, but let me ask you this: why are you known as 'Rhialto the Marvellous'?"

"It seems to be an old joke," said Rhialto. "I have never been able to trace the source."

As the two walked arm in arm along the main gallery they passed Ildefonse and Byzant standing disconsolately under a marble statue. Rhialto accorded them a polite nod, and made a secret sign of more complicated significance, to the effect that they might feel free to return home without him.

The Lady Shaunica, pressing close to his side, giggled. "What a pair of unlikely comrades! The first a roisterer with mustaches a foot long, the second a poet with the eyes of a sick lizard. Do you know them?"

"Only slightly. In any case it is you who interests me and all your warm sensitivities which to my delight you are allowing me to share."

The Lady Shaunica pressed even more closely against him. "I begin to suspect the source of your soubriquet."

Ildefonse and Byzant, biting their lips in vexation, returned to the foyer, where Ildefonse finally made the acquaintance of a portly matron wearing a lace cap and smelling strongly of musk. She took Ildefonse off to the ball-room, where they danced three galops, a triple-polka and a kind of a strutting cake-walk where Ildefonse, in order to dance correctly, was obliged to raise one leg high in the air, jerk his elbows, throw back his head, then repeat the evolution with all briskness, using the other leg.

As for Byzant, Duke Tambasco introduced him to a tall poetess with coarse yellow hair worn in loose lank strands. Thinking to recognize a temperament similar to her own, she took him into the garden where, behind a clump of hydrangeas, she recited an ode of twenty-nine stanzas.

Eventually both Ildefonse and Byzant won free, but now the night was waning and the ball was at an end. In sour spirits they returned to their domiciles, and each, through some illogical transfer of emotion, blamed Rhialto for his lack of success.

2

Rhialto at last became impatient with the plague of ill feeling directed his way for no very clear reason, and kept to himself at Falu.

After a period, solitude began to pall. Rhialto summoned his major-domo. "Frole, I will be absent from Falu for a time, and you will be left in charge. Here—" he handed Frole a paper "—is a list of instructions. See that you follow them in precise detail. Upon my return I wish to find everything in exact and meticulous order. I specifically forbid that you entertain parties of guests or relatives on, in or near the premises. Also, I warn that if you meddle with the objects in the work-rooms, you do so at risk of your life, or worse. Am I clear?"

"Absolutely and in all respects," said Frole. "How long will you be gone, and how many persons constitute a party?"

"To the first question: an indefinite period. To the second, I will only rephrase my instruction: entertain no persons whatever at Falu during my absence. I expect to find meticulous order upon my return. You may now be off about your duties. I will leave in due course."

Rhialto took himself to the Sousanese Coast, in the remote far corner of South Almery, where the air was mild and the vegetation grew in a profusion of muted colors, and in the case of certain forest trees, to prodigious heights. The local folk, a small pale people with dark hair and long still eyes, used the word 'Sxyzyskzyiks'—"The Civilized People"—to describe themselves, and in fact took the sense of the word seriously. Their culture comprised a staggering set of precepts, the mastery of which served as an index to status, so that ambitious persons spent vast energies learning finger-gestures, ear-decoration, the proper knots by which one tied his turban, his sash, his shoe-ribbons; the manner in which one tied the same knots for one's grandfather; the proper and distinctive placement of pickles on plates of winkles, snails, chestnut stew, fried meats and other foods; the curses specifically appropriate after stepping on a thorn, meeting a ghost, falling from a low ladder, falling from a tree, or any of a hundred other circumstances.

Rhialto took lodging at a tranquil hostelry, and was housed in a pair of airy rooms built on stilts out over the sea. The chairs, bed, table and chest were constructed of varnished black camphor-wood; the floor was muffled from the wash of the sea among the stilts by a rug of pale green matting. Rhialto took meals of ten courses in an arbor beside the water, illuminated at night by the glow of candlewood sticks.

Slow days passed, ending in sunsets of tragic glory; at night the few stars still extant reflected from the surface of the sea, and the music of curve-necked lutes could be heard from up and down the beach. Rhialto's tensions eased and the exasperations of the Scaum Valley seemed far away. Dressed native-style in a white kirtle, sandals and a loose turban with dangling tassels, Rhialto strolled the beaches, looked through the village bazaars for rare sea-shells, sat under the arbor drinking fruit toddy, watching the slender maidens pass by.

One day at idle whim Rhialto built a sand-castle on the beach. In order to amaze the local children he first made it proof against the assaults of wind and wave, then gave the structure a population of minuscules, accoutered as Zahariots of the 14th Aeon. Each day a force of knights and soldiers marched out to drill upon the beach, then for a period engaged in mock-combat amid shrill yells and cries. Foraging parties hunted crab, gathered sea-grapes and mussels from the rocks, and meanwhile the children watched in delighted wonder.

One day a band of young hooligans came down the beach with terriers, which they set upon the castle troops.

Rhialto, watching from a distance, worked a charm and up from a court-yard flew a squadron of elite warriors mounted on hummingbirds. They projected volley after volley of fire-darts to send the curs howling down the beach. The warriors then wheeled back upon the youths who, with buttocks aflame, were likewise persuaded to retreat.

When the cringing group returned somewhat later with persons of authority, they found only a wind-blown heap of sand and Rhialto lounging somnolently in the shade of the nearby arbor.

The episode aroused a flurry of wonder and Rhialto for a time became the object of doubt, but along the Sousanese Coast sensation quickly became flat, and before long all was as before.

Meanwhile, in the Valley of the Scaum, Hache-Moncour made capital of Rhialto's absence. At his suggestion, Ildefonse convened a 'Conclave of Reverence,' to honor the achievements of the Great Phandaal, the intrepid genius of Grand Motholam who had systematized the control of sandestins. After the group assembled, Hache-Moncour diverted the discussion and guided it by subtle means to the subject of Rhialto and his purported misdeeds.

Hache-Moncour spoke out with vehemence: "Personally, I count Rhialto among my intimates, and I would not think of mentioning his name, except, where possible, for the sake of vindication, and, where impossible, to plead the mitigating circumstances when the inevitable penalties are assessed."

"That is most generous of you," said Ildefonse. "Am I then to take it that Rhialto and his conduct is to become a formal topic of discussion?"

"I fail to see why not," growled Gilgad. "His deeds have been meretricious."

"Come, come!" cried Hache-Moncour. "Do not skulk and whimper; either make your charges or I, speaking as Rhialto's defender, will demand a vote of approbation for Rhialto the Marvellous!"

Gilgad leapt to his feet. "What? You accuse me of skulking? Me, Gilgad, who worked ten spells against Keino the Sea-demon?"

"It is only a matter of form," said Hache-Moncour. "In defending Rhialto, I am obliged to use extravagant terms. If I hurl unforgivable insults or reveal secret disgraces, you must regard them as the words of Rhialto, not those of your comrade Hache-Moncour, who only hopes to exert a moderating influence. Well then: since Gilgad is too cowardly to place a formal complaint, who chooses to do so?"

"Bah!" cried Gilgad furiously. "Even in the role of Rhialto's spokesman, you use slurs and insults with a certain lewd gusto. To set the record straight, I formally accuse Rhialto of impropriety and the beating of a simiode, and I move that he be called to account."

Ildefonse suggested: "In the interest of both brevity and elegance, let us allow 'impropriety' to include the 'beating.' Are you agreed?"

Gilgad grudgingly acquiesced to the change.

Ildefonse called out: "Are there seconds to the motion?"

Hache-Moncour looked around the circle of faces. "What a group of pusillanimous nail-biters! If necessary, as Rhialto's surrogate, I will second the motion myself, if only to defeat with finality this example of childish spite!"

"Silence!" thundered Zilifant. "I second the motion!"

"Very good," said Ildefonse. "The floor is open for discussion."

"I move that we dismiss the motion out of hand as a pack of nonsense," said Hache-Moncour. "Even though Rhialto boasts of his success at the Grand Ball, and laughingly describes Ildefonse's antics with a fat matron and Byzant's comic efforts to seduce a raw-boned poetess in a blonde wig."

"Your motion is denied," said Ildefonse through gritted teeth. "Let the charges be heard, in full detail!"

"I see that my intercession is useless," said Hache-Moncour. "I therefore will step aside from my post and voice my own complaints, so that when the final fines and confiscations are levied, I will receive my fair share of the booty."

Here was a new thought, which occupied the assemblage for several minutes, and some went so far as to inscribe lists of items now owned by Rhialto which might better serve their own needs.

Ao of the Opals spoke ponderously: "Rhialto's offenses unfortunately are many! They include deeds and attitudes which, while hard to define, are nonetheless as poignant as a knife in the ribs. I include in this category such attributes as avarice, arrogance, and ostentatious vulgarity."

"The charges would seem to be impalpable," intoned Ildefonse. "Nevertheless, in justice, they must be reckoned into the final account."

Zilifant raised his finger dramatically high: "With brutal malice Rhialto destroyed my prized harquisade from Canopus, the last to be found on this moribund world! When I explained as much to Rhialto, first, with mendacity dripping from his tongue, he denied the deed, then declared: 'Look yonder to Were Wood and its darkling oaks! When the sun goes out they will fare no better and no worse than your alien dendron.' Is that not a travesty upon ordinary decency?"

Hache-Moncour gave his head a sad shake. "I am at a loss for words. I would render an apology in Rhialto's name, were I not convinced that Rhialto would make a flippant mockery of my efforts. Still, can you not extend mercy to this misguided man?"

"Certainly," said Zilifant. "To the precise measure in which he befriended my harquisade. I declare Rhialto guilty of a felony!"

Again Hache-Moncour shook his head. "I find it hard to credit."

Zilifant swung about in a passion. "Have a care! Even in your quixotic advocacy of this scoundrel, I will not have my veracity assailed!"

"You misunderstood me!" stated Hache-Moncour. "I then spoke for myself, in wonder at Rhialto's callous acts."

"Ah, then! We are agreed."

Others of the group cited grievances which Ildefonse noted upon a bill of particulars. At last all had declared themselves, and Ildefonse, in looking down the list, frowned in perplexity. "Amazing how one like Rhialto could live so long among us and never be exposed! Hache-Moncour, do you have anything more to say?"

"Merely a *pro forma* appeal for mercy."

"The appeal has been heard," said Ildefonse. "We shall now vote. Those who endorse Rhialto's conduct and find him blameless, raise their hands."

Not a hand could be seen.

"Those convinced of Rhialto's guilt?"

All hands were raised.

Ildefonse cleared his throat. "It now becomes my duty to assess the penalty. I must say that Rhialto's absence makes our sad task somewhat easier. Are there any suggestions?"

Byzant said: "I feel that each of us, in the order that we sit at the table, starting with myself, shall be numerated. We will then go to Falu and there, in order of number, select among Rhialto's goods until no one wishes to make a further choice."

Ao of the Opals concurred. "The idea is essentially sound. But the numeration must be made by lot, with a monitor against all spells of temporal stasis."

The system suggested by Ao was eventually put into effect, and all repaired to Falu. Frole the major-domo stepped forward and in an authoritative voice inquired what might be the business of so large a company. "You must know that Rhialto is absent! Come again when he can receive you with suitable ceremony."

Ildefonse began a legalistic declamation but Gilgad, impatient with words, cast a spell of inanition upon Frole, and the magicians, entering Falu, set about enforcing the penalties which had been levied at the conclave.

The irascible Hurtiancz was especially anxious to find Rhialto's IOUN stones, and sought everywhere, to no avail. A document indited in blue ink on blue paper and cased in a frame of blue gold hung on the wall; certain that he had discovered Rhialto's secret hiding place, Hurtiancz impatiently tore the document from the wall and threw it aside, to reveal only the vacant wall, and it was Ildefonse himself who discovered the IOUN stones where they hung among the crystals of a chandelier.

The fine at last was levied in total degree, though not to the satisfaction of those who had been allotted high numbers, nor those who had been slow in pre-empting goods without reference to the numbers. Ildefonse used all his influence to dampen the claims and accusations, meanwhile defending his own retention of the IOUN stones, by reason of service and selfless rectitude.

At last the magicians went their ways, satisfied that justice had been done.

3

In due season Rhialto returned to Falu. His first intimation that all was not as it should be was the sight of Frole standing stiff before the doorway, frozen in a posture of admonition; then, entering the manse, Rhialto took wrathful note of the depredation.

Returning to the doorway, Rhialto dissolved the spell which had held Frole immobile through night and day, rain and shine.

Frole took a cup of tea and a slice of currant cake, after which he was able to report to Rhialto those circumstances which had come under his purview.

Rhialto grimly restored order to the premises, then made an inventory of his losses and damages. They reduced his powers to a low level.

For a period Rhialto paced back and forth beside Wilda Water. At last, with no better program suggesting itself, he donned a pair of old air-boots which had been left behind and made his way to Boumergarth.

Pryffwyd, Ildefonse's chamberlain, met him at the door.

''Your wishes, sir?''

''You may inform Ildefonse that Rhialto is here to consult with him.''

''Sir, Lord Ildefonse is preoccupied with matters of importance and will be unable to receive visitors today or at any time in the near future.''

Rhialto brought forth a small red disk and, clasping it between his hands, began to chant a set of rhythmic syllables. In sudden concern Pryffwyd asked: ''What are you doing?''

''Pryffwyd, your vision is dim; you do not recognize me for Rhialto. I am working to place your eyeballs at the end of foot-long stalks. You will soon be able to see in all directions at once.''

Pryffwyd's voice instantly changed. ''Ah! The noble Lord Rhialto!

I now see you perfectly in every phase! This way, if you will! Lord Ildefonse is meditating in the herb-garden.''

Rhialto found Ildefonse dozing in the slanting red rays of the afternoon sunlight. Rhialto clapped his hands together. ''Ildefonse, rouse from your torpor! Vile deeds have been done at Falu; I am anxious to hear your explanation.''

Ildefonse turned a glance of reproach upon Pryffwyd, who merely bowed and asked: ''Will there be anything else, sir?''

Ildefonse sighed. ''You may serve refreshments, of a light nature, as Rhialto's business will not take us long and he will very shortly be leaving.''

''To the contrary!'' said Rhialto. ''I will be here for an indefinite period. Pryffwyd, serve the best your pantry affords!''

Ildefonse heaved himself up in his chair. ''Rhialto, you are taking a high-handed line with my chamberlain and, since we have gone so far, with my refreshments as well!''

''No matter. Explain why you robbed me of my goods. My man Frole tells me that you marched in the forefront of the thieves.''

Ildefonse pounded the table with his fist. ''Specious and egregious! Frole has misrepresented the facts!''

''How do you explain these remarkable events, which of course I intend to place before the Adjudicator?''*

Ildefonse blinked and blew out his cheeks. ''That of course is at your option. Still, you should be aware that legality was observed in every bound and degree. You were charged with certain offenses, the evidence was closely examined and your guilt was ascertained only after diligent deliberation. Through the efforts of myself and Hache-Moncour, the penalty became a small and largely symbolic levy upon your goods.''

'' 'Symbolic'?'' cried Rhialto. ''You picked me clean!''

Ildefonse pursed his lips. ''I concede that at times I noticed a certain lack of restraint, at which I personally protested.''

Rhialto, leaning back in his chair, drew a deep sigh of dumb-

*The Monstrament, placed in a crypt at Fader's Waft, drew its coercive force from the 'Adjudicator,' ensconced in his 'Blue Egg': a shell opaque to distracting influences. The Adjudicator was Sarsem, a sandestin trained in the interpretation of the Monstrament. Sarsem's judgments were swift and stern, and enforced by the Wiih, a mindless creature from the ninth dimension.

When applying to the Adjudicator for justice, the plaintiff was well advised to come with a clear conscience. Sarsem felt an almost human impatience with his cramped seclusion inside the egg; at times he refused to limit his verdict to the issue at hand, and examined the conduct both of plaintiff and defendant for offenses against the Monstrament, and distributed his penalties with even-handed liberality.

founded wonder. He considered Ildefonse down the length of his aristocratic nose. In a gentle voice he asked: "The charges were brought by whom?"

Ildefonse frowned thoughtfully. "By many. Gilgad declared that you had beaten his pet simiode."

"Aha. Continue."

"Zilifant charged that your reckless deployment of plasms had destroyed his fine hardquisade tree."

"And further?"

"The complaints are too numerous to mention. Almost everyone—save myself and the loyal Hache-Moncour—preferred charges. Then, the conclave of your peers with near-unanimity adjudged you guilty on all counts."

"And who robbed me of my IOUN stones?"

"As a matter of fact, I myself took them into protective custody."

"This trial was conducted by exact legal process?"

Ildefonse took occasion to drink down a goblet of the wine which Pryffwyd had served. "Ah yes, your question! It pertained, I believe, to legality. In response, I will say that the trial, while somewhat informal, was conducted by appropriate and practical means."

"In full accordance with the terms of the Monstrament?"

"Yes, of course. Is that not the proper way? Now then—"

"Why was I not notified and allowed an opportunity for rebuttal?"

"I believe that the subject might well have been discussed," said Ildefonse. "As I recall, no one wished to disturb you on your holiday, especially since your guilt was generally conceded."

Rhialto rose to his feet. "Shall we now visit Fader's Waft?"

Ildefonse raised his hand in a bluff gesture. "Seat yourself, Rhialto! Here comes Pryffwyd with further refreshment; let us drink wine and consider this matter dispassionately; is not that the better way, after all?"

"When I have been vilified, slandered and robbed, by those who had previously shone upon me the sweetest rays of their undying friendship? I had never—"

Ildefonse broke into the flow of Rhialto's remarks. "Yes, yes; perhaps there were procedural errors, but never forget, the findings might have gone worse but for the efforts of myself and Hache-Moncour."

"Indeed?" asked Rhialto coldly. "You are familiar with the Blue Principles?"

"I am generally aware of the important passages," declared Ildefonse bluffly. "As for the more abstruse sections, I may be a trifle dim, but these in any event do not apply."

"Indeed?" Rhialto brought out a torn blue document. "I will read from Paragraph C, of the 'Precursive Manifesto':

> " 'The Monstrament, like a perdurable edifice, depends on integrated blocks of wisdom, each supporting others with bonds of equal strength. He who maximizes the solemnity of certain passages and demeans another as trivial or paltry for the sake of his special pleading is guilty of subversion and submulgery, and shall be punished as directed by Schedule B, Section 3.' "

Ildefonse blinked. "My present remarks are truly no more than badinage."

"In that case, why did you not testify that at the time Gilgad's beast was abused, you and I were walking beside the River Scaum?"

"That is a good question. In sheer point of fact, I acted on grounds of procedural effect."

"How so?"

"Simple enough! The question: 'Did you walk with Rhialto by the River Scaum at the exact time Gilgad's simiode was beaten?' was never asked. By the rules of jurisprudence I could not properly introduce such evidence. Secondly, you already had been convicted on a number of other counts, and my remarks would only have caused confusion."

"Should not truth be known? Did you not ask yourself who in fact had beaten the beast, and why he identified himself as 'Rhialto'?"

Ildefonse cleared his throat. "Under the circumstances, as I have explained them, such questions are nuncupatory."

Rhialto consulted the torn copy of the Blue Principles. "Paragraph K of Section 2 would seem to describe your act as 'enhanced dereliction.' A harsh penalty—possibly too harsh—is specified, but the Adjudicator will read justice as it is written and apply the strictures to calm and thorough effect."

Ildefonse held up his hands. "Will you take so trivial an affair to Fader's Waft? The consequences are beyond calculation!"

"I will cite a third offense. In the looting of Falu, my copy of the Blue Principles was seized, torn and hurled to the ground. In this deed, which is precisely proscribed under Paragraph A: 'Treasonable Acts,' all conspirators share the guilt, and all must pay the penalty. This is far from a 'trivial affair'! I thought that you might share my indignation, and work for restitution and punishment of the guilty, but—"

"Your hopes have been validated!" cried Ildefonse. "I was on the verge of convoking a new conclave, to review the findings of the last session, which now seem to have been guided by emotion. Have patience! The Adjudicator need not be distracted from his passivity."

"Convene the conclave as of this instant! Declare at the outset that I am innocent of all charges, that I have suffered inexcusable wrongs, that I demand not only restitution but multiple damages—"

Ildefonse cried out in shock. "That is an irrational penalty!"

Rhialto said stonily: "As Preceptor this is your decision to make. Otherwise the Adjudicator must assess the penalties."

Ildefonse sighed. "I will call the conclave."

"Announce that only two issues will be considered: first, restitution and the imposition of fines, ranging from three-fold to five-fold, and I will hear neither bluster nor obfuscation; and secondly, identification of the malefactor."

Ildefonse grumbled something under his breath, but Rhialto paid no heed. "Convoke the conclave! Accept no excuses! All must be present, as I am an exasperated man!"

Ildefonse put on an air of forlorn good cheer. "All may yet be well. First I will communicate with your only true ally, other than myself."

"You refer to whom?"

"Hache-Moncour, naturally! We will take his advice at once."

Ildefonse went to a table, where he placed the semblance of Hache-Moncour's face over a pair of orifices shaped to represent an ear and a mouth. "Hache-Moncour, Ildefonse speaks into your ear! I bring significant news! Speak with your mouth!"

"Ildefonse, I speak! What is your news?"

"Rhialto the Marvellous has come to Boumergarth! His mood is one of doubt and malaise. He feels that the conclave made several legalistic mistakes which tend to vitiate its findings; indeed, he demands triple damages from all parties concerned. Otherwise he threatens to take his case to the Adjudicator."

"A great mistake," said the mouth. "An act of reckless despair."

"So I have advised him, but Rhialto is an obstinate man."

The mouth spoke: "Can you not reason with him? Is he quite inflexible?"

"He yields by not so much as the twitch of an eyelash, and only speaks in tedious repetition of the Monstrament and the imposition of penalties. He seems obsessively convinced that a malefactor—"

Rhialto called out: "Speak more tersely, if you will; my time is valuable! Merely convene the conclave; you need not describe my troubled spirit in such sardonic detail."

Ildefonse angrily threw nineteen semblances down upon his communication device. He put a clamp upon the mouth to impede protests and questions, then, speaking out into nineteen ears at once, he ordered an immediate conclave at Boumergarth.

4

The magicians one by one took their places in the Grand Saloon. Hache-Moncour was the last to arrive. Before seating himself he spoke a few quiet words to Herark the Harbinger, with whom he was on good terms.

Rhialto, leaning against a wood-paneled wall to the side, somberly watched the arrival of his erstwhile colleagues. None save Hache-Moncour, who gave him a polite bow, so much as looked in his direction.

Ildefonse convened the meeting in his usual manner, then glanced sidelong toward Rhialto, who maintained his silence. Ildefonse coughed and cleared his throat. "I will come directly to the point. Rhialto claims an unjust confiscation of his property. He demands restitution and punitive damages; failing satisfaction, he states that he will take his case to the Adjudicator. There, in a nut-shell, is the gist of our business today."

Gilgad sprang to his feet, face purple with rage. "Rhialto's posture is grotesque! How can he deny his crime? He beat poor Boodis and tethered him among nettles: a vile and heartless act! I declared as much before; I do so now, and will never revoke the charge!"

"I did not beat your beast," said Rhialto.

"Ha ha! Easy for you to say! Can you prove as much?"

"Certainly. I was walking with Ildefonse beside the River Scaum at the time of the incident."

Gilgad whirled upon Ildefonse. "Is this true?"

Ildefonse made a sour face. "It is true, in every particular."

"Then why did you not say so before?"

"I did not want to confuse a case already turbulent with emotion."

"Most peculiar." With a set face Gilgad resumed his seat, but Zilifant immediately sprang erect. "Nonetheless and undeniably, Rhialto destroyed my harquisade tree with his floating plasm and left a horrid stench about the premises; further, so the rumor goes, he boasted of his accuracy, and imputed the source of the odor to me, Zilifant!''

''I did nothing of the sort,'' said Rhialto.

''Bah! The evidence is clear, straightforward and unambiguous!''

''Is it, indeed? Mune the Mage and Perdustin were both present at Falu during the experiment. They saw me create four lumes of plasm. One drifted through my delicate silvanissa tendrils, doing no harm. Mune walked through another and failed to complain of odor. We watched all four lumes dwindle to sparks and die. None escaped; none departed the area adjacent to Falu.''

Zilifant looked uncertainly from Mune the Mage to Perdustin. ''Are these allegations accurate?''

''In a word: yes,'' said Mune the Mage.

''Why did you not so inform me?''

''Since Rhialto was guilty of other offenses, it seemed unimportant.''

''Not to me,'' said Rhialto.

''Possibly not to you.''

''Who informed you of my boasts and insults?''

Zilifant glanced uncertainly toward Hache-Moncour. ''I am not sure that I remember properly.''

Rhialto turned back to Ildefonse. ''What are these other crimes of which I am guilty?''

Hurtiancz responded to the challenge. ''You cast a spell upon my hat! You sent out mocking pictures!''

''I did nothing of the sort.''

I suppose you can prove otherwise.''

''What does the pattern of events suggest? Clearly, the act was performed by the same person who beat Gilgad's beast and vandalized Zilifant's tree. That person was not I.''

Hurtiancz uttered a sour grunt. ''So much seems to the point. I retract the charge.''

Rhialto stepped forward. ''Now then: what other crimes have I committed?''

No one spoke.

''In that case, I must now place counter-charges. I accuse the members of this association, singly and jointly, with the exception of myself, of several felonies.''

Rhialto presented a tablet to Ildefonse. ''Thereon I detail the charges. Preceptor, be good enough to read them off.''

With a grimace of distaste Ildefonse took the tablet.

''Rhialto, are you sure that you wish to go so far? Mistakes have been made; so much we acknowledge! Let us all, yourself included, make a virtue of humility, and proceed with renewed faith into the future! Each of your comrades will advise and assist you in every convenient way, and soon your situation will repair itself! Rhialto, is not this the better way?''

Rhialto enthusiastically clapped his hands together. ''Ildefonse, as always, your wisdom is profound! Why, indeed, should we undergo the sordid excesses of a full-blown legal action? Each member of this group need only tender his apology, restore my goods along with triple damages, and we will return to the old footing. Hache-Moncour, why do you not set the example?''

''Gladly,'' declared Hache-Moncour. ''However, I would thereby compromise the others of the group. Whatever my personal concepts, I must await a vote.''

Rhialto asked: ''Hurtiancz, what of you? Do you care to come forward and apologize?''

Hurtiancz shouted something incomprehensible.

Rhialto turned to Ildefonse: ''What of yourself?''

Ildefonse cleared his throat. ''I will now read the bill of accusations brought by Rhialto against this association. In detail the charges occupy eighteen pages. I will first read the 'Topic Headings':

''Title One: Trespass.
''Title Two: Larceny, Grand.
''Title Three: Larceny, Petty.
''Title Four: Vandalism.
''Title Five: Assault, upon the person of Frole.
''Title Six: Slander.
''Title Seven: Dishonour to the Monstrament, including wilful mutilation and casting down of a certified copy thereof.
''Title Eight: Conspiracy to commit the above crimes.
''Title Nine: Wilful Retention of stolen property.
''Title Ten: Failure to abide by the Blue Principles, as propounded in the Monstrament.''

Ildefonse put the tablet down upon his desk. ''I will read the full charges presently, but at this moment, let me ask this: your topics and titles—are they not excessive to the case?''

Rhialto shrugged. ''They decribe most of the crimes involved, but not all.''

''How so? The list seems all-inclusive.''

"Have you forgotten the basic mystery? Who sent the pictures which mocked Hurtiancz? Who hung the opal on the drop-chain and thereby offended Ao? Who beat Gilgad's beast? Who destroyed Zilifant's tree? Do not these mysteries cry out for a solution?"

"They are cryptic indeed," admitted Ildefonse. "Of course sheer coincidence might be at work—no? You reject this theory? Well, perhaps so. Still, the questions are not included on your bill of accusations, and so lack immediate relevance."

"As you like," said Rhialto. "I suggest that you appoint a committee composed of Hurtiancz, Ao, Gilgad and Zilifant to pursue the matter."

"All in good time. I will now read the 'Bill of Accusations' in full."

"There is no need to do so," said Rhialto. "The association is well aware of the charges. I myself am not inflexible; three avenues, at least, are open. First, the group by acclamation may yield the damages I seek; secondly, the Preceptor, using his executive powers, may impose the specified levies; or thirdly, we will present the bill to the Adjudicator, for his judgment by the exact schedules of the Monstrament. Ildefonse, will you kindly ascertain which avenue is most congenial to this group?"

Ildefonse gave a guttural grunt. "What must be, must be. I move that we accept Rhialto's demands, even though a few minor hardships may be encountered. Is there a second?"

"Hold!" Barbanikos leapt to his feet, his great plume of white hair waving like a flame. "I must point out that the penalties invoked against Rhialto were partly in censure of his odious personality, so that in no way can he demand full restitution, let alone damages!"

"Hear, hear!" cried Haze of Wheary Water and others.

Thus encouraged, Barbanikos continued: "Any sensitive person would have recognized the reprimand for what it was; he would have returned meekly to the group, anxious only to vindicate himself. Instead, what do we have? A surly visage, a hectoring manner, slurs and threats! Is this appropriate conduct for a person who has just been decisively chastised by his peers?"

Barbanikos paused to refresh himself with a sip of tonic, then proceeded.

"Rhialto has learned nothing! He shows the same impudence as before! Therefore I earnestly recommend that Rhialto's tantrums be ignored. If they proceed, I suggest that he be turned out of doors by the footmen. Rhialto, I say this to you and no more: take care! Be ruled by prudence! You will be the happier man for it! That is my first remark. Now, as for my second—''

Ildefonse interrupted. ''Yes, most interesting! Barbanikos, thank you for your incisive opinions.''

Barbanikos reluctantly resumed his seat. Ildefonse asked: ''Once again: is there a second to my motion?''

''I second the motion,'' said Rhialto. ''Let us now see who votes for and who votes against the Blue Principles.''

Hache-Moncour stepped forward. ''There is still another point to be considered. In our discussion we have made frequent reference to the Monstrament. May I ask as to who can furnish the group a full, undamaged and authentic text? Ildefonse, you naturally include such a document among your references?''

Ildefonse groaned toward the ceiling. ''I would not know where to look. Rhialto, however, has brought here, as an exhibit, such a document.''

''Unfortunately, Rhialto's exhibit, whatever it purports to be, is torn and no longer valuable. We must insist upon absolute authenticity: in this case, the Perciplex itself. Put Rhialto's damaged scrap out of mind. We will study the Monstrament at Fader's Waft; then and only then will we be able to vote with conviction.''

Ildefonse said: ''Do you put that in the form of a motion?''

''I do.''

Herark the Harbinger called out: ''I second the motion!''

The vote was carried almost unanimously, the only silent voices being those of Ildefonse and Rhialto.

Herark rose to his feet. ''The hour is late; our time is short! Each of us must resolve to visit Fader's Waft and study the Perciplex at his earliest convenience. Then, when Ildefonse ascertains that all have done their duty, he shall reconvene the conclave and we will once more consider this affair, in a more conciliatory atmosphere, or so I trust.''

Rhialto uttered a grim laugh and stepped up on the dais beside Ildefonse. ''Any who wish may go to Fader's Waft and test Hache-Moncour's didactic theories at their leisure. I am going now to consult the Adjudicator. Let no one think to test his magic against me! I did not leave all my spells at Falu, and I am protected in dimension.''

Byzant the Necrope took exception to the remark. ''Rhialto, you are contentious! Must the Adjudicator be troubled by every trifling snit and swivet? Be large, Rhialto!''

''Good advice!'' declared Rhialto. ''I shall solicit mercy for you at Fader's Waft. Ildefonse, the 'Bill of Accusations,' if you please! The Adjudicator will also need this list of names.''

Hache-Moncour spoke politely: ''Since Rhialto is determined, I must warn him of the dangers he will incur at Fader's Waft. They are large indeed!''

''How so?'' asked Ildefonse. ''Where and how does Rhialto face danger?''

''Is it not clear? The Monstrament states that any person who presents an altered or damaged copy of the Blue Principles in the effort to prove a case at law is guilty of a Schedule H crime and must be expunged. Rhialto, I reluctantly must declare, has today committed such a crime which vitiates his entire case. He will go before the Adjudicator at peril to his life.''

Rhialto frowned down at his copy of the Monstrament. ''I see no such interdict here. Please indicate the passage which you are citing.''

Hache-Moncour took a quick step backward. ''If I did so, I would then become guilty of the identical crime we are now discussing. The passage perhaps has been elided by the damage.''

''Most peculiar,'' said Rhialto.

Herark spoke out. ''Rhialto, your accusations have been voided by this new crime, and your claims must now be abandoned. Ildefonse, I move that the meeting be adjourned.''

''Not so fast,'' said Ildefonse. ''We are suddenly faced with a most complex matter. I suggest that, in view of Hache-Moncour's exposition, we send a committee to Fader's Waft, consisting, let us say, of myself, Eshmiel, Barbanikos, and perhaps Hache-Moncour, there to study the Monstrament quietly and carefully, without reference to our little troubles.''

''I will meet you there,'' said Rhialto. ''Even if Hache-Moncour's recollection is correct, which I doubt, I have not quoted from the damaged Monstrament and so am innocent.''

''Not so!'' declared Hache-Moncour. ''You just now examined your spurious document and used it to dispute my statement. Your crime takes precedence and you will be expunged before uttering the first of your charges, which thereupon become moot. Return at this instant to Falu! We will ascribe your conduct to mental disorder.''

Ildefonse spoke wearily: ''This advice, no matter how well-meant, clearly lacks persuasion. Therefore, as Preceptor, I rule that all present shall go now to Fader's Waft, there to inspect the Monstrament. Our purposes are informational only; we will not disturb the Adjudicator. Come, then! All to Fader's Waft! We will ride in my commodious whirl-away.''

5

Ildefonse's majestic whirlaway flew southward, into a region of low rolling hills at the southern edge of Ascolais. Certain of the magicians strolled the upper promenade, intent upon the far vistas of air and cloud; others kept to the lower deck that they might overlook the lands below; still others preferred the leather-cushioned comfort of the saloon.

The time was close upon evening; the near-horizontal light spread odd patterns of red and black shadow across the landscape; Fader's Waft, a hillock somewhat higher and more massive than its fellows, loomed ahead.

The whirlaway settled upon the summit, which, exposed to the draughts of Fader the west wind, was bare and stony. Alighting from the vehicle, the magicians marched across a circular terrace to a six-sided structure roofed with tiles of blue gold.

Rhialto had visited Fader's Waft on a single other occasion, for reasons of simple curiosity. The west wind Fader flapped his cloak as he approached the fane; entering the vestibule he waited for his eyes to adapt to the gloom, then stepped forward into the central chamber.

A pedestal supported the Egg: a spheroid three feet across the widest diameter. A window at one end displayed the Perciplex, a blue prism four inches tall, inwardly engraved with the text of the Monstrament. Through the window the Perciplex projected an image of the Monstrament in legible characters upon a vertical dolomite slab, and so charged with magic was the Perciplex that should an earthquake or other shock cause it to topple, it must right itself immediately, so that it should never present a faulty image, or one which might be misconstrued, to the viewer.

So it had been; so it was now.

Ildefonse led the way across the terrace, with Hache-Moncour, erect and controlled in his movements on one side, and on the other Hurtiancz in full gesticulation. Behind came the others in a hurrying clot, with Rhialto sauntering disdainfully alone at the rear.

Into the vestibule marched the group, and into the central chamber. Rhialto at the rear heard Hache-Moncour's voice raised in sudden shock and dismay, followed by a mingling of other astonished voices.

Pressing forward, Rhialto saw all as he remembered from his previous visit: pedestal supporting Judicial Egg, Perciplex glowing blue, and the projection of the Monstrament upon the dolomite slab. Today, however, there was a note-worthy difference: the text of the Monstrament appeared in reverse or mirror-image, upon the dolomite slab.

Rhialto felt a sudden flicker across his consciousness, and almost instantly he heard Ildefonse's roar of protest. "Impropriety, bad faith! The monitor shows a hiatus!* Who would so dare to work a spell on us?"

"This is an outrage!" declared Hache-Moncour. "Whoever is the guilty party, let him step forward and explain his conduct!"

No one replied to the challenge, but Mune the Mage cried out in wonder: "The Monstrament! Was it not in reverse? It now seems in correct condition!"

"Odd!" said Ildefonse. "Most odd!"

Hache-Moncour looked angrily around the company. "These sly tricks are intolerable! They besmirch the dignity of us all! In due course I will personally investigate the case, but as of now our business is the tragic determination of Rhialto's guilt. Let us study the Monstrament."

Rhialto spoke in a voice of icy politeness: "Are you not ignoring a most remarkable fact? The Monstrament was projected in reverse."

Hache-Moncour looked back and forth between Rhialto and the Monstrament in puzzled inquiry. "It seems now as steadfast as ever! I suspect that your eyes played you false; entering darkness from the daylight is often confusing. Now then! With true sorrow I call attention to this passage in Section 3, Paragraph D, which reads—"

"One moment," said Ildefonse. "I too saw the reverse projection. Am I also confused?"

Hache-Moncour gave a light laugh. "Such little errors betoken neither degeneracy nor turpitude; perhaps for your lunch you enjoyed a surfeit of plum-pickle, or took a mug too many of your excellent sub-cellar ale! Ha ho! Dyspepsia is the plight of many strong men! Shall we proceed with our business?"

"By no means!" declared Ildefonse in brusque tones. "We shall return to Boumergarth for a fuller investigation of what at every turn becomes a more mystifying situation."

Amid a subdued murmur of conversation, the magicians departed the fane. Rhialto, who had paused to inspect the Egg, held Ildefonse back until they were alone. "You may be interested to learn that this is not even the authentic Perciplex. It is a forgery."

*hiatus: The Spell of Temporal Stasis, affecting all save he who works the spell. All others are frozen into immotility. Magicians bitterly resent being placed in hiatus by other magicians; too many untoward events take place under these conditions and many carry monitors to warn when a hiatus has occurred.

"What!" cried Ildefonse. "Surely you are mistaken!"

"Look for yourself. This prism is too small for the housing. The workmanship is crude. Most significant of all, the true Perciplex could never project in reverse. Watch now! I will shake the Egg and topple the prism. The true Perciplex will right itself."

Rhialto jarred the Egg with such effect that the Perciplex fell to its side, in which position it remained.

Ildefonse faced the Egg. "Adjudicator! Speak! It is Ildefonse the Preceptor who commands!"

No reply was audible.

Once again Ildefonse called out: "Adjudicator! Sarsem! I charge you: speak!"

Again, silence.

Ildefonse turned away. "Back to Boumergarth. The mystery is compounded. It is no longer trivial."

"Never was it trivial," said Rhialto.

"No matter," said Ildefonse curtly. "The affair, now that it concerns me, has taken on a new and large dimension. To Boumergarth!"

6

Assembling again in the grand hall, the magicians set up a colloquy of many voices. Ildefonse for a time listened to the somewhat formless interchanges without comment, darting his pale blue eyes from face to face and giving an occasional tug to his untidy beard.

The discussions began to grow heated. Vehement in his wrath was Haze of Wheary Water: a hot-eyed little wefkin who affected a green pelt and a thatch of yellow will-leaves in the place of hair. Moving with irregular starts and jerks, he asserted his opinions with ever-increasing agitation. "Willy-nilly, backwards, forwards, the Blue is the Blue! As Hache-Moncour averred, the text condemns Rhialto's conduct out of hand, and that is all we care about. I will gladly stand on my head to read such news, or look through a mirror, or peek from behind my handkerchief!" And Haze spoke on, ever more fervently, until the company began to fear that he might injure himself in a paroxysm, or even blurt out some terrible all-inclusive curse to disable everyone. Ildefonse finally invoked the Spell of Soft Silence, so that while Haze ranted as before, his voice no longer could be heard, not even by himself, and presently he returned to his place.

The corpulent and loose-featured Dulce-Lolo analyzed the peculiar reversal of the projection. "I suspect that Sarsem the Adjudicator became careless and allowed the Perciplex to project in reverse, then, observing our consternation, he brought a hiatus upon us and turned the Perciplex to its proper position."

Ildefonse stepped ponderously up on the dais. "I must make an important announcement. The prism you saw tonight is false: a fraud, a forgery. The question of reversal is irrelevant."

Darvilk the Miaanther, normally taciturn, emitted an angry cry. "Then why did you, in full and pompous authority, dragoon us and march us lock-step to Fader's Waft, if only to inspect what you claim to be a falsity?"

Shrue spoke out. "The Miaanther's question strikes the nail! Ildefonse, your conduct merits a reproach."

Ildefonse held his arms high. "The group is not addressing itself to the issue! I repeat again: the Monstrament, the basis of our association, is missing from the Judicial Egg! We are left without law; we are naked as the Egg itself to that faceless shape which walks among us! We cannot dare the duration of a day without undertaking strategies of protection."

Hache-Moncour said with a gentle smile: "Ildefonse, dear friend! Must you cry cataclysm in such wild despair? Our association is based on the wisdom of its members!"

Vermoulian the Dream-walker said: "I predict a simple explanation to the apparent mystery. Sarsem may have removed the Perciplex for cleaning and left a simulacrum temporarily in place."

"This must indeed be the explanation," said Hache-Moncour. "Meanwhile, the simulacrum can be used at need."

"Precisely so!" cried Hurtiancz. "And never forget that, in making use of this version, simulacrum though it may be, we shackle the animal ferocity of Rhialto, and quell his insensate demands."

Ildefonse struck his gavel upon the podium. "Hurtiancz, your remarks are out of order. If you recall, Rhialto staunchly defended his conduct, and where this was impossible, he simply denied it."

Hurtiancz muttered: "I only give tongue to the consensus."

"Your remarks are not appropriate at this time. Rhialto, you have spoken no word: what is your opinion?"

"I am not yet ready to speak."

"Shrue, what of you?"

"Only this: lacking the true Monstrament, all issues of legality must be held in abeyance. Practically, the 'status quo' must be considered as definite and final."

"Nahourezzin: what are your thoughts?"

Nahourezzin, known in Old Romarth as "the Striped Sadwan,"

already was pondering the possible courses of the future. ''If the Perciplex is indeed gone, then, using the simulacrum as a basis, we must create a new Monstrament, to be known as the Orange Principles.''

''Or the Lime-green,'' suggested Dulce-Lolo. ''Or even the Rose-purple, to suggest both splendour and pomp.''

''The suggestion lacks merit,'' said Ildefonse. ''Why create a new document of some unfamiliar colour, when the Blue Principle has served us staunchly and well? Rhialto's document, though slightly torn, will suffice for the nonce.''

Hurtiancz again bounded out to claim the floor. ''If we accept Rhialto's document, then his charges prevail! With a new Perciplex based upon the simulacrum, all previous claims, including Rhialto's demand for triple damages, are repudiated, and Rhialto willy-nilly must pay the penalty for his mischiefs.''

''An important point!'' cried Tchamast. ''Hurtiancz has slashed a clear avenue through this jungle of verbiage; he has clamped his admirable teeth deep into the very gist of the matter.'' Here Tchamast made reference to the exquisitely shaped rubies which replaced Hurtiancz's original complement of teeth; and Hurtiancz bowed in acknowledgment of the compliment.

Vermoulian the Dream-walker, a person tall and thin as a wand, with a high crest of glossy black hair like the dorsal fin of a sail-fish, was not known for his loquacity. His prominent eyes tended to gaze unfocused past the bony jut of his nose, and were often obscured by a nictitating membrane which conceivably served a useful purpose during his dream-walking. In the punitive phase of the proceedings against Rhialto, he had acquired a very fine glossolary, which, translating as it did the most corrupt gibberish into clear common speech, served him well in the course of his vocation. In any event, and for whatever reason, Vermoulian now thrust himself erect and spoke in a voice dry and precise: ''I put the thesis of Hurtiancz into the form of a motion!''

''That is not regular procedure,'' declared Ildefonse. ''Our task at hand is to learn the whereabouts of the Blue Perciplex! We must not be diverted!''

Hache-Moncour stepped forward. ''I endorse the views of Ildefonse! I now undertake to make a full, thorough and exhaustive investigation into this deplorable matter, and let the chips fall where they may! In the meantime, our normal business may well proceed, and I suggest to the Preceptor that, in view of my undertaking, Vermoulian's motion now be ruled in order.''

Rhialto glanced toward Ildefonse. He raised his hand to his mouth as if to stifle a yawn, making a secret sign in the process. Ildefonse gave a wince of distaste, but nevertheless invoked the Spell of Temporal Stasis.

7

Rhialto and Ildefonse inspected the chamber where their associates sat or stood poised in frozen postures.

"This is a nuisance," grumbled Ildefonse. "Everyone in the group carries a monitor, that he may not be swindled by his friends. Now each of these monitors must be searched out and justified if the deception is to succeed."

"No great matter. I have evolved a new technique which easily befuddles the monitors. I need only a pair of quampics and a red-eyed bifaulgulate sandestin."

Ildefonse brought forth an object of eccentric shape derived from a fulgurite. From the opening peered a small face with eyes as red as currants. "This is Osherl," said Ildefonse. "He is not altogether bifaulgulate, but he is clever and swift, if sometimes a trifle moody. His indenture runs to five points."

"The count is far too high," said Osherl. "Somewhere a mistake has been made."

"I believe the count to be valid and just," said Ildefonse, "Still, in due course I will check my records."

Rhialto spoke to Osherl: "You are anxious to reduce your indenture?"

"Naturally."

"A simple 'yes' or 'no' will suffice."

"Whatever you like; it is all one with me."

Rhialto went on: "Today Ildefonse and I are in a lenient mood. For a few trifling tasks we will mark you down a full point—"

"What?" roared Ildefonse. "Rhialto, you distribute points among my sandestins with a lavish hand!"

"In a good cause," said Rhialto. "Remember, I intend to impose triple damages, with total confiscation in at least one case. I will here and now stipulate that your seizure of my IOUN stones was in the nature of a safeguard, and not subject to the punitive provisions which otherwise might be applied."

Ildefonse spoke more equably: "That is taken for granted. Deal with Osherl as you will."

Osherl said persuasively: "A single point is of no great account—"

Rhialto turned to Ildefonse. "Osherl seems tired and languid. Let us use a more zestful sandestin."

"Perhaps I spoke in haste," said Osherl. "What are your requirements?"

"First, visit each of the persons caught in the stasis, and use these quampics to adjust each monitor so that it will fail to register this particular stasis."

"That is no great work." A gray shadow flitted about the room. "It is done, and I have won an entire point."

"Not so," said Rhialto. "The point is yours after all the tasks have been accomplished."

Osherl gave a sour grunt. "I suspected something of the sort."

"Nevertheless, you have made a good start," said Ildefonse. "Do you see how nicely things go when one is amiable?"

"They only go nicely when you are generous with your points," said Osherl. "What now?"

"Now you will go to each magician in turn," said Rhialto. "With great care remove the dust, chaff and small bits of detritus from the boots of each person present including Ildefonse and myself. Place the yield from each pair of boots in a separate bottle, identified properly with the name of the magician."

"I know none of your names," grumbled Osherl. "You all look alike to me."

"Place the yield in a series of labeled bottles. I will name off the names. First is Herark the Harbinger . . . Ao of the Opals . . . Perdustin . . . Dulce-Lolo . . . Shrue . . ." Rhialto named off each of the magicians, and instantly a glass bottle containing dust and trash in greater or lesser quantity appeared on the table.

"Again, no great matter," said Osherl. "What now?"

"The next task may or may not take you afield," said Rhialto. "In any case, do not dally nor loiter along the way, as important consequences rest upon our findings."

"To a dung-beetle, a pile of brontotaubus droppings is a matter of prime significance," said Osherl.

Rhialto knit his brows. "Ildefonse and I are both perplexed by the allusion. Do you care to explain?"

"The concept is abstract," said Osherl. "What is the task?"

"The Adjudicator at Fader's Waft, whom we know as Sarsem, is absent from his post. Bring him here for consultation."

"For a single point? The balance becomes uneven."

"How so? I ask you to locate only one sandestin."

"The process is tedious. I must go first to La, there pull on what might be called the tails of ten thousand sandestins, then listen for the characteristic exclamations of Sarsem."

"No matter," said Ildefonse. "An entire point is an item to be cherished; you will have earned it well and honestly."

Rhialto added: "I will say this: if our business goes well, you will not have cause to complain. Mind, I promise nothing!"

"Very well. But you must dissolve the Stasis; I ride the flux of time as a sailor sails on the wind."

"A final word! Time is of the essence! For you, a second differs little from a century; we are more sensitive in this regard. Be quick!"

Rhialto cried: "Wait! We must hide the bottles of dust. Hurtiancz has the eyes of a hawk, and he might wonder to find a bottle of dust labeled with his name. Under the shelf with the lot! . . . Good. Ildefonse, remember! We must terminate this colloquy with dispatch!"

"Just so! Are you ready?"

"Not quite! There is one last bit of business!" Rhialto repossessed the glossolary which Vermoulian had obtained at Falu; then Rhialto and Ildefonse, working together and chuckling like schoolboys, fashioned a simulation of the glossolary, changing the vocabulary so that it yielded not clear and precise language but absurdities, insults and sheer nonsense. This new and faulty glossolary was then restored into Vermoulian's keeping. "Now I am ready!" said Rhialto.

Ildefonse lifted the spell and the conference proceeded as if it had never been interrupted.

Hache-Moncour's words hung in the air: "—of my undertaking, Vermoulian's motion may now be ruled in order."

Rhialto jumped up. "I move that the meeting be adjourned until such time as Hache-Moncour completes his investigation. Then we will have full information on which to base our findings."

Vermoulian gave a croak of protest; Ildefonse quickly declared: "Vermoulian seconds the motion; are all in favor? No one seems opposed; the motion is carried and the meeting is adjourned until Hache-Moncour reports his findings. The lights are about to go out and I am off to take my rest. To all: good night."

Casting dark looks toward Rhialto, the magicians departed Boumergarth and went their various ways.

8

Rhialto and Ildefonse repaired to the small study. Ildefonse set out double spy-guards and for a period the two sat drinking wine with their feet raised to the flicker of the fire.

"A dreary business," said Ildefonse at last. "It leaves an evil savor worthy of an archveult! Let us hope we can find guidance in the dust of your bottles or from the testimony of Sarsem. If not, we have no basis for action."

Rhialto gripped the arms of his chair. "Shall we study the bottles? Or would you prefer to take your rest?"

Ildefonse heaved himself to his feet. "I know no fatigue! To the work-room! We shall study each grain of dust under the pantavist: up, down, back, forth—until finally it cries out its tale! Then we drive home the nail with Sarsem's testimony!"

The two went to the work-room. "Now!" declared Ildefonse. "Let us look to your famous bottles!" He examined the contents of several. "From such nondescript sifts I expect nothing of value."

"That remains to be seen," said Rhialto. "We shall need your best macrotic enlarging pantavist, and then your latest edition of *Characteristic Stuffs: Dusts and Microvies of the Latter Aeons.*"

"I have anticipated you," said Ildefonse. "All is here to hand. I will also order up a classificator, to make our work less tedious."

"Excellent."

The inquiry proceeded with easy efficiency. One at a time the bottles were emptied and their contents examined, identified, graded, and classified. By middle morning the work was through, and the two tired magicians went out upon the terrace to take rest and nourishment.

In the opinion of Ildefonse, the work had yielded little of significance, and his mood was glum. He said at last: "In the main, we are faced with ambiguities. We neither prove nor disprove; the 'Extraordinarys' are too many: specifically, the dusts of Vermoulian, Hurtiancz, Hache-Moncour, Dulce-Lolo and Byzant. Additionally, the 'Extraordinarys' may simply be special cases of the 'Ordinarys,' while the 'Ordinarys' may be associated with cryptic deeds beyond our detection."

Rhialto nodded. "Your indications are accurate! Still I do not share your pessimism. Each 'Extraordinary' tells its own tale, except in one case."

"Aha! You are referring to Vermoulian, since the dust from his boots is unique in shape, colour and complexity, and different from everything classified in the catalogue."

Rhialto, smiling, shook his head. "I am not referring to Vermoulian. In his case we would seem to be investigating dream-dust, scuffed up from one or another of his dream-landscapes. The catalogues are understandably noncommittal. As for Hurtiancz, he uses medicinal powder to relieve a fungoid infection of the toes, and we can confidently place him on the 'Ordinary' list. Byzant's dust is in the main a powder of phosphatic calcars, evidently deriving from his field of interest, which again the catalogue prefers to ignore. In regard to Dulce-Lolo's amazing many-coloured particles, I recall that his part in a recent 'Charade of Folly' required that he paint each of his feet to represent a grotesque face.''

Ildefonse stared at Rhialto in wonder. ''What purpose could possibly be served by this conduct?''

''I gather that Dulce-Lolo's role in the Pageant was thereby enhanced. Reclining on his back, he kicked his feet on high, meanwhile reciting a dialogue in two voices, falsetto and bass. Particles of the pigment evidently were trapped in his boots, and I must consider him, at least from our immediate perspective, as an 'Ordinary.' ''

''And what of Hache-Moncour?''

''His dust, while 'Extraordinary,' may or may not be instructive. We lack a critical item of information, to this effect: is Hache-Moncour an amateur of caverns and underground chambers?''

Ildefonse tugged at his beard. ''Not to my knowledge, but this means little. I did not realize until last week, for instance, that Zahoulik-Khuntze is an Elder at the Hub and Controller of his own distinct infinity.''

''Odd but interesting! Back to Hache-Moncour, his boots were rife with a singular dust, discovered only in a few underground places of the world.''

''Ha hm. The fact might mean much or nothing.''

''Nevertheless, my suspicions incline toward Hache-Moncour.''

Ildefonse gave a noncommittal grunt. ''For proof we must await Sarsem, and hear his story.''

''That goes without saying. Osherl will report at the earliest possible instant?''

''So I would expect.'' Ildefonse glanced thoughtfully toward the work-room. ''Excuse me a moment.''

Ildefonse left the terrace and almost immediately sounds of contention came from the direction of the work-room. Ildefonse presently returned to the terrace, followed by Osherl and a second sandestin using the guise of a gaunt blue bird-like creature, some six feet in height.

Ildefonse spoke in scathing tones: ''Behold these two creatures! They can roam the chronoplex as easily as you or I can walk around the table; yet neither has the wit to announce his presence upon arrival. I found Osherl asleep in his fulgurite and Sarsem perched in the rafters.''

''You demean our intellects,'' snapped Osherl. ''Persons of your ilk are unpredictable; they must be dealt with on the basis of exactitude. I have learned never to act without explicit instructions. If I were to do otherwise, your complaints would rasp even more stridently upon my attention. You sent me on a mission from the work-room; with mission accomplished I returned to the work-room. If you wished me to disturb you at your vulgar ingestions you should have made this clear.''

Ildefonse puffed out his cheeks. ''I detect more than a trace of insolence in these rejoinders!''

''No matter,'' said Rhialto. ''He has brought Sarsem, and this was the requirement. In the main, Osherl, you have done well!''

''And my indenture point?''

''Much depends upon Sarsem's testimony. Sarsem, will you sit?''

''In this guise, I find it more convenient to stand.''

''Then why not alter to human form and join us in comfort at the table?''

''That is a good idea.'' Sarsem became a naked young epicene in an integument of lavender scales with puffs of purple hair like pompoms growing down his back. He seated himself at the table but declined refreshment. ''This human semblance, though typical, is after all, only a guise. If I were to put such things inside myself, I might well become uneasy.''

''As you like. Now to business. Where is the Blue Perciplex which you were required to guard?''

Sarsem asked cautiously: ''You refer to the blue prism reposing on the pedestal? You will find such an object as sage as ever in its accustomed place.''

''And why have you deserted your post?''

''Simplicity itself! One of your ilk delivered a new and official Perciplex to replace the obsolete version, which had lost its effect.''

Rhialto gave a hollow laugh. ''And how do you know this for a fact?''

''Through the assertion of your representative.'' Sarsem sprawled back in the chair. ''As I now reflect on the matter, what with the sun's death only a jerk and a tinkle away, a new Perciplex seems a pointless refinement.''

''So then: what next?''

''I pointed out the burden of guarding two sacred objects, rather than one. The new, so I was told, would occupy the place of the old, and your representative would take the old to a place of reverent safety. Meanwhile, my services were no longer required.''

Rhialto leaned forward. "No doubt indenture points were discussed?"

"I recall some such discussion."

"To what number and to what degree?"

"An appreciable proportion: in fact, all."

"How is this possible when your chug* resides in my workroom?"

Sarsem scowled. "That is as may be."

Upon sudden thought Ildefonse lurched to his feet and departed the terrace. A moment later he returned, and threw himself down in his chair. With a bleak expression he said to Rhialto: "Sarsem's chug is gone. Have you ever heard the like?"

Rhialto reflected. "When might this event have taken place?"

"Evidently during the temporal stasis: when else?" Ildefonse turned upon Sarsem. "We have been victimized together! The reduction of your indenture points was unauthorized! You are the victim of a cruel joke! The reduction is null and void, and we have lost the Perciplex! Sarsem, I cannot commend your performance."

"Ha ha!" cried Sarsem, waving a pale lavender forefinger upon which glinted a silver fingernail. "There is more to come! I am not quite the fool you take me for!"

"How so, and in what regard?"

"I am that rare individual who can instantly scrutinize all sides of a situation! Without reference to my motives, I decided to retain the old Perciplex within the scope of my vigilance."

"Ha, ha, hah! Bravo, Sarsem!"

"Thereupon, your representative—"

"Speak less loosely, Sarsem. The person was not my representative."

"While this person was temporarily distracted, I laid the old prism safely aside. This person, whose good faith you decry, still cannot be deemed irresponsible."

"Why do you say that?"

"Because, like myself, he worried about the safety of the old Perciplex and would not rest until he learned where I had placed it."

Rhialto groaned. "Within the confines of a cavern?"

"Yes; how did you know?"

*chug: a semi-intelligent sub-type of sandestin, which by a system too intricate to be presently detailed, works to control the sandestins. Even use of the word 'chug' is repellent to the sandestin.

''We are not without resources. In effect you yielded up the Perciplex to the criminal!''

''Not at all. I placed the prism in a place well-known to me, accessible only by a small and narrow fissure. For double security I reverted the object to the 16th Aeon.'' ''And how do you know that the criminal himself has not reverted to this era and taken the Perciplex for his own?''

''Can he walk the length of a fissure into which you cannot even thrust your hand? Especially while I keep the opening under survey from then till now, as you might scan the surface of the table? Nothing has come or gone. Ergo, by the rotes of rationality, the Perciplex reposes in its subterranean place, as secure as ever.''

Rhialto rose to his feet. ''Come: once more back to Fader's Waft! You shall grope down the fissure into the 16th Aeon and reclaim the Perciplex. Ildefonse, are you ready? Summon your small air-carriage.''

9

Rhialto, Ildefonse and Sarsem stood disconsolate on the summit of Fader's Waft. Sarsem spoke in a troubled voice. ''A most confusing dilemma! I searched the fissure without success; I guarantee that the Perciplex did not leave by this route. I admit to perplexity.''

Rhialto suggested: ''There may be another route into the cavern; what of that?''

''The idea is plausible,'' admitted Sarsem. ''I will make a survey across the Aeons.''

Sarsem presently returned to make his report. ''The cave opened to the valley for a brief period during the 16th Aeon. The entrance is not evident now. This is good news, since if I am a trifle nonplussed, our antagonist must be crazy with bafflement.''

''Not necessarily true,'' intoned Rhialto.

Sarsem peered here and there. ''In the 16th Aeon, so I recall, three black crags rose yonder, and a river swung into the valley from the east . . . Fader's Waft at that time was a tall peak defying the storms. . . . Now I am straight. We must drop down into yonder valley.''

Sarsem led the way down a barren slope into a gulch choked with tumbled stones.

''Much has changed,'' said Sarsem. ''A crag the shape of a skatler horn rose yonder and another there, and another there, where you now see rounded hummocks. Perhaps among these rocks. . . . Here is the place, though the entrance is tumbled over with detritus. Stand aside; I will skew the latifers, so as to allow access.''

Sarsem caused a pulse to shiver along the hillside, whisking away the overburden and revealing an aperture leading into the mountain.

The three marched forward. Ildefonse sent a flux of light into the passage, and started forward, but Rhialto held him back. "One moment!" He indicated a double line of foot-prints in the fine sand which covered the floor of the cavern.

"Sarsem, did you leave these marks?"

"Not I! When I left the cavern, the sand showed a smooth surface."

"Then I deduce that someone has entered the cave after you departed. This person might well have been Hache-Moncour, to judge by the evidence of his boots."

Sarsem drifted into the cavern, making no marks upon the sand. He returned almost at once. "The Perciplex is not where I placed it."

Rhialto and Ildefonse stood stiff with disappointment. "This is dismal news," said Ildefonse. "You have not dealt well with your assigned duty."

"More to the point," said Rhialto, "where now is the Perciplex? In the past, or in the present, or has it been destroyed?"

"Who could be reckless enough to destroy the Blue?" muttered Ildefonse. "Not even an archveult. I believe that the Perciplex is somewhere extant."

"I am inclined to agree," said Rhialto. "Sarsem, in regard to these footprints: from their direction it seems that they were formed before the cavern's mouth was covered—which is to say, the 16th Aeon."

"True. I can also say this: if they were made by someone hoping to find the Perciplex, he failed. The tracks enter the cave, pass the niche where I concealed the prism, continue into the central cavern, wander this way and that in a random pattern, then depart with long strides denoting angry failure. The Perciplex was taken from the cavern prior to the footprints."

Rhialto turned to Ildefonse. "If you recall, Hache-Moncour came to Boumergarth with the subterranean dust still clinging to his boots. Unless he found the Perciplex immediately upon leaving the cave, he failed in his mission."

"Convincing!" said Ildefonse. "Who then took the Perciplex?"

Rhialto said sternly: "Sarsem, your conduct has been less than wise. Need I remind you of this?"

"You need say nothing! In sheer disgust, discharge me from my indenture! The humiliation will be an overwhelming punishment."

"We are not so cruel," said Ildefonse. "We prefer that you make amends by retrieving the Perciplex for us."

Sarsem's lavender face fell. ''I must fail you still a second time. I cannot return to the 16th Aeon, because, in effect, I am already there.''

''What?'' Ildefonse raised high his bristling yellow eyebrows. ''I cannot understand.''

''No matter,'' said Sarsem. ''The restraints are definite.''

''Hmmf,'' grunted Ildefonse. ''We are faced with a problem.''

''I observe the single solution,'' stated Rhialto. ''The Preceptor must step back into the 16th Aeon to recover the Perciplex. Ildefonse, prepare yourself! And then—''

''Hold!'' cried Ildefonse. ''Have you put aside that rationality which once marked your thinking? I cannot possibly leave while turmoil threatens the association! With your keen eyes and rare intelligence, you are the man to recover what is lost! Sarsem, do you not support this point of view?''

''At the moment my thoughts run shallow,'' said Sarsem. ''However, this much is clear: whoever most anxiously wants to restore the old Perciplex to its place will be he who retrieves it from the past.''

Rhialto sighed. ''Poor Sarsem is by almost any standard feebleminded; still in this case he has deftly stripped the issue to its naked essentials. If I must go, I must.''

The three returned to Boumergarth. Rhialto made careful preparations, packing in his wallet the glossolary, proliferant coins, a catalogue of simple spells, and Osherl enclosed in a walnut shell.

Ildefonse extended his unqualified assurances. ''It is, after all, a simple and pleasant adventure,'' he told Rhialto. ''You will find yourself in the Land of Shir-Shan, which at this time is considered the center of the universe. The Grand Gazetteer lists only six magicians currently active, the nearest far to the north, in the present Land of Cutz. A flying creature known as the 'dyvolt' rules the skies; it resembles a pelgrane with a long nasal horn and uses the common language. You should recognize three rules of genteel conduct: the sash is tied to the left; only acrobats, actors and sausage-makers wear yellow; grapes are eaten with a knife and fork.''

Rhialto drew back in annoyance. ''I do not plan so much as a single meal in Shir-Shan. Perhaps, after all, it would be better if you went.''

''Impossible! You are the man for the job! You need only step back, secure the Perciplex, then return to the present. So then, Rhialto! Are you ready?''

''Not quite! How, in fact, do I return to the present?''

''A good question!'' Ildefonse turned to Sarsem. ''What, exactly, is the procedure?''

''That is out of my province,'' said Sarsem. ''I can project Rhialto any number of aeons into the past, but thereafter he must make his own arrangements.''

''Rhialto, do not be impatient!'' said Ildefonse. ''Sarsem, answer! How then does Rhialto make his return?''

''I suppose that he must rely upon Osherl.''

''Good enough!'' said Ildefonse. ''Osherl can be trusted in this regard, or I am much mistaken.''

So went the preparations. Rhialto made himself ready, not neglecting to change his yellow sash tied on the right for a black sash of good quality tied on the left. Osherl disposed himself within the walnut shell, and the two were reverted into the past.

10

Rhialto stood in warm sunlight of a complicated colour: a peach-pink orange suffused with rose and white-rose. He found himself in a valley surrounded by sharp peaks rising a mile into the air. That peak which he would later know as Fader's Waft stood highest of all, with the summit hidden in a tuft of white cloud.

The prospect was at once grand and serene. The valley seemed empty of habitation, although Rhialto noted plantations of melon and blue vines heavy with purple grapes along the valley and up the mountain-side.

To Rhialto's satisfaction, the landmarks cited by Sarsem, an outcrop of glistening black stone flanked by three cypress saplings, were plainly visible, although 'sapling' seemed an inexact description of the gnarled and massive trees in question. Still, Rhialto confidently set off toward the site of the cave.

By Sarsem's best calculations, the time was immediately subsequent to his own visit. Ildefonse had tried to elicit the exact measure of this interval: ''A second? A minute? An hour?''

Rhialto's attention had been distracted by Osherl in the matter of indenture points, and he had heard only a phrase or two of Sarsem's response: ''—accuracy of high degree!'' and ''—occasionally a curious kinking and backlash in the inter-aeon sutures—''

Ildefonse had put another inquiry and again Osherl's attempts to secure advantage had diverted Rhialto's attention, and he had only heard Sarsem discussing what seemed to be mathematical theory with

Ildefonse: "—often closer than the thousandth part of one percent, plus or minus, which must be reckoned excellent."

Rhialto turned to join the conversation, but the avaricious Osherl placed a new demand, and Rhialto only heard Ildefonse's reference to "—five aeons: an unwieldy period!" Sarsem's response had only been that peculiarly supple shrug characteristic of his sort.

The entrance to the cave was now close at hand. Sarsem had been inexact in his instructions; rather than a barely perceptible crevice behind the first of the gabbro crags, Rhialto found a square opening five feet wide and taller than himself decorated with a careful pattern of pink shells, and a path of crushed white marl.

Rhialto uttered a hiss of vexation. Something was clearly amiss. He advanced up the path to the opening and looked into the cave. Here, at least, Sarsem had spoken accurately: to the right, immediately within the opening and something above the height of his head, a small pocket opened into the stone, and into this pocket Sarsem had placed the Perciplex.

The pocket was now empty, not altogether to Rhialto's surprise. An indefinable odor suggesting organic processes hung in the air; the cave seemed to be inhabited.

Rhialto retreated from the cave entrance and went to sit on a ledge of rock. Across the valley an old man came down the mountainside: a person small and slight, with a great ruff of white hair and a narrow blue face which seemed mostly nose. He wore a garment of black and white stripes and sandals with toes of exaggerated length, with a black sash about his waist tied on the left, in a manner which Rhialto considered absurd and unbecoming, but which evidently found favor with the pace-setters of the day.

Jumping down from the fence, Rhialto approached the old man, and a touch of the finger was enough to activate the glossolary.

The old man noticed Rhialto's approach, but paid no heed and continued on his way, skipping and trotting with lightfooted agility. Rhialto called out: "Sir, stop to rest a moment! You move at speed! At your age a man should be kind to himself!"

The old man paused. "No danger there! If all were equally kind I should live the life of a magnate!"

"That is the usual concept. Still, we must do as best we can! What brings you out here among these lonely mountain crags?"

"Simply put, I would rather be here than out on the plain, where confusion reigns supreme. And yourself? From a distant land, so I perceive, from the rather awkward knot by which you tie your sash."

"Fashions differ," said Rhialto. "I am in fact a scholar, sent here to retrieve an important historical object."

The old man looked suspiciously sidewise at Rhialto. "Are you in earnest? I know of nothing within a hundred miles which answers that description—save perhaps the skeleton of my double-headed goat."

"I refer to a blue prism which was left in yonder cave for safe-keeping, but which is not there now."

The old man made a negative sign. "My knowledge of prisms, historical or otherwise, is small. For a fact, I recall the cave before the twastics took up residence, when nothing could be seen but a crevice into the rocks."

"How long ago might this be?"

The old man pulled at his nose. "Let me calculate . . . It was while Nedde still supplied my barley . . . Garler had not yet taken his third wife. Still, he had already built his new barn. . . . I would estimate a period of thirty-one years."

Rhialto gritted his teeth. "These twastics: what of them?"

"Most have returned to Canopus; the climate suits them better. Still, the two yonder are decent in their habits and settle their debts in good time, which is more than I can say of my own son-in-law, though to be sure I would not choose a twastic as spouse to my daughter. . . . I hear them now; they are returning from a function at their social club."

A tinkling sound reached Rhialto's ears, as if from the vibration of many small bells. Up the valley road came a pair of twenty-legged creatures eight feet long and four feet high, with large round heads studded with stalks, knobs and tufts, fulfilling functions not immediately apparent. Their caudal segments rose and curled forward in an elegant spiral, and each boasted an iron gong dangling from the tip. Smaller bells and vibrilators hung in gala style from the elbows of each leg. The first wore a robe of dark green velvet; the second a similar robe of cherry-rose plush.

"Yonder go the twastics," said the old man. "As for the contents of the cavern, they can answer your questions better than I."

Rhialto watched the tinkling creatures askance. "All very well, but how should I address them?"

"They are easy in this regard; a simple 'Sir' or 'Your Honor' suffices."

Returning across the valley, Rhialto was able to intercept the twastics before they entered the cavern. He called out: "Sirs! May I put a question? I am here on an important historical mission!"

The twastic wearing the dark green robe responded in a somewhat sibilant voice, using sounds created by a rapid clicking of the mandibles. "This is not our customary time for business. If you wish to order any of our service gungeons, be advised that the minimum shipment is one gross."

"I am interested in another matter. You have inhabited this cavern for about thirty years, so I understand."

"You have been gossiping with Tiffet, who is more garrulous than he should be. Still, your figures are correct."

"When you first arrived, did you find a blue crystal placed in a niche above the entrance? I would appreciate candour in this regard."

"There is no reason why you should not have it. I myself discovered the blue crystal, and cast it away immediately. On Canopus, blue is considered an unfavorable colour."

Rhialto clapped a hand to his forehead. "And then: what next?"

"You must ask Tiffet. He found the trinket in the rubbish." The twastics entered the cavern and disappeared into the darkness.

Rhialto hastened back across the valley and managed to overtake Tiffet.

"Wait, sir!" called Rhialto. "Another historical question or two!"

Tiffet halted. "What now?"

"As you know, I have come far in search of an important blue prism. The twastics threw it from the cave and it seems that you rescued it from the rubbish heap. Where is it now? Produce it and I will make you a rich man."

Tiffet blinked and pulled at his nose. "A blue prism? True. I had quite forgotten it. Quite so! I took it from the rubbish heap and put it on my mantle-piece. Not a week later the taxers came from the King of all Kings, and they took the blue jewel in payment of my taxes and even rescinded the standard beating with staves, for which I was grateful."

"And the blue prism?"

"It was taken to the Royal Treasury at Vasques Tohor, or so I suppose. And now, sir, I must be on my way. Tonight we eat squash soup with cheese and I must be nimble if I am to get my share."

Rhialto once more went to sit on the stone fence and watched as Tiffet hobbled briskly around the mountain. Reaching into his pouch, Rhialto brought out the walnut shell from which stepped Osherl, now, by reason of some obscure whim, wearing a fox's mask.

The pink mouth spoke: "Well then, Rhialto! You are ready to return with the Perciplex?"

Rhialto thought to perceive a subtly mocking flavor to the question. He said coldly: ''May I ask the source of your amusement?''

''It is nothing, Rhialto; I am naturally light-hearted.''

''Try as I may, I find nothing amusing in this present situation, and in fact I wish to speak with Sarsem.''

''As you wish.''

Sarsem appeared across the road, still using the guise of an epicene youth clad in lavender scales. ''Rhialto, you wish to confer with me?''

''I am displeased with your work,'' said Rhialto. ''You missed the target date by something over thirty years.''

''Only thirty years in five aeons? Such accuracy is far better than adequate.''

''Not for my purposes. The Perciplex is not in the cave. Certain merchandisers from Canopus threw it aside. You were required to guard the Perciplex and it is now lost.''

Sarsem thought a moment, then said: ''I failed in my duty. No more need be said.''

''Except this: by reason of your failure, you now must help me find the Perciplex.''

Sarsem became argumentative. ''Rhialto, you are illogical! I failed in my duty, true. Still, there is no linkage between this idea and the unrelated concept of my attempting to find the missing article. I hope you perceive your mistake, which is of a fundamental nature.''

''The linkage is indirect, but real. By failing in your duty, you have incurred a severe penalty. This penalty may be partially expiated by your help in recovering the prism.''

Sarsem reflected a moment then said: ''I am unconvinced; somewhere I smell sophistry at work. For instance, who will apply the penalty? You are five aeons gone and no longer even real.''

''Ildefonse is my stout ally; he will protect my interests.''

Sarsem gave that curious croak which, among creatures of his ilk, indicated amusement. ''Rhialto, your innocence is droll. Have you not recognized that Ildefonse is the leader of the cabal against you?''

''Not so!'' declared Rhialto. ''You refer to an occasion when he jocularly availed himself of my IOUN stones.''

Sarsem looked at Osherl. ''What is the truth of this?''

Osherl considered. ''As of now, Ildefonse breathes fire against Hache-Moncour.''

Sarsem scratched his violet nose with a silver fingernail. ''Ah well, on the slight chance that Rhialto is correct, I would not have him accusing me of falsity. Rhialto, take this pleurmalion; it will show a blue spot in the sky directly above the Perciplex. Remember, in case of any inquiry—for instance, from Hache-Moncour-it came through Osherl, and not through me. Am I clear on this?''

''Certainly. Hache-Moncour has filled your mind with foolishness. If you decide to share his destiny in the hope of gaining indenture points, you will have the Wiih to deal with.''

Sarsem gave a small squeak of consternation, then cried out with somewhat hollow bravado: ''You have over-spoken yourself! Trouble me no further; I am bored with the Perciplex; the present version will serve until the sun goes out. As for you, Ildefonse will never notice when you fail to return. Already Hache-Moncour eclipses him in power.''

''And when in fact I return with the Perciplex, what then of Hache-Moncour?''

Sarsem chuckled. ''Rhialto, have I not made myself clear? Find the Perciplex as you like, glory in your achievement, then settle yourself to enjoy the radiance of the 16th Aeon, even though you will never revenge yourself against your enemies.''

''What of Osherl?'' asked Rhialto idly. ''Will he not take me back to Boumergarth?''

''Ask him yourself.''

''Well, Osherl? Are you too defiant and treasonable?''

''Rhialto, I believe that you will enjoy your life in this halcyon aeon. And so that you may start your new life free of fretful oddments and petty details, you may now finalize my indenture.''

Rhialto smiled that aloof, almost sinister, smile which so often had annoyed his adversaries. From his wallet darted a black- and red-striped object like a long thin snake. ''Chug!'' screamed Sarsem in horror. The chug wound itself around Osherl, darted its head into one of the fox-ears, emerged from the other and tied itself in a knot across Osherl's head. Osherl was then dragged to a nearby tree and suspended by the rope through the ears to dangle three feet off the ground.

Rhialto turned to Sarsem: ''Eventually I will deal with Osherl as he deserves. Meanwhile, he will assist me to his best abilities. Osherl, am I right in this? Or shall we take further steps?''

Osherl's fox-mask licked its chops nervously. ''Rhialto, this is a poor response to my light-hearted badinage, and unworthy threats now hang in the air.''

''I never make threats,'' said Rhialto. ''In all candour, I am dumbfounded by Sarsem's recklessness. He totally misjudges the wrath of Ildefonse and myself. His treachery will cost him an awful price. That is not a threat; it is a statement of certainty.''

Sarsem, smiling a glazed and insincere smile, faded from sight.

Osherl kicked and thrashed his legs to set himself swinging. He cried out: "Your allegations have been too much for poor Sarsem! It would have been far more graceful if—"

"Silence!" Rhialto took up the pleurmalion. "I am interested only in the Perciplex!" He searched around the sky through the tube, but the surrounding mountain-sides blocked most of the view.

Rhialto affected his boots with the Spell of Lightsome Striding, which allowed him to walk through the air, high or low, at his pleasure. Osherl looked on with growing disquiet. At last he called out: "What of me? How long must I dangle here for birds to roost upon?"

Rhialto feigned surprise. "I had already forgotten you. . . . I will say this. It is not pleasant to be betrayed by one's associates."

"Naturally not!" cried Osherl with enthusiasm. "How could you so mistake my little joke?"

"Very well, Osherl, I accept your explanation. Perhaps you can be of some slight assistance, after all, such as facilitating our return to Boumergarth."

"Naturally! It goes without saying!"

"Then we will resume as before." The chug dropped Osherl to the ground and returned to Rhialto's wallet. Osherl grimaced, but without further words returned to the walnut shell.

Rhialto jumped into the air; climbing to a height of twenty feet, he set off down the valley on long stately bounds, and Fader's Waft was left behind.

11

The valley opened upon a plain of far distances, distinguished principally by clouds of dust and smoke lowering over the northern horizon. Closer at hand, where the hills first began to swell up from the plain, Rhialto saw a number of small farmsteads each with its small white silo, round white barn, and orchard of globular blue trees. A mile or so to the west, a village of round pink houses enjoyed the shade of a hundred tall parasol palms. Details of the landscape beyond were blurs of delicate colour, until, at the horizon, curtains of dust and smoke rose ominously high.

Rhialto alighted upon a ledge of rock and bringing out the pleurmalion scrutinized the sky. To his gratification, he discovered a dark blue spot on the sapphire vault of the northern sky, in the general direction of the smoke and dust.

Rhialto replaced the tube in his pouch, and now, a hundred yards down the slope, he noticed three young girls picking berries from a thicket. They wore black vests over striped blouses, black pantaloons tied at the knee with black ribbons, black stockings and black shoes tied with white puffs at the ankles. Their faces were round; straight black hair was cut square across their foreheads. Rhialto thought them not ill-favored, somewhat in the manner of odd little dolls.

Rhialto approached at a dignified pace, and halted at a distance of ten yards. Always disposed to create a favorable impression before members of the female sex, so long as they were of an age and degree of vitality to notice, Rhialto leaned an arm against a stump, disposed his cloak so that it hung in a casual yet dramatic style.

The girls, preoccupied with their chatter, failed to notice his presence. Rhialto spoke in melodious tones: "Young creatures, allow me to intrude upon your attention, at least for a moment. I am surprised to find so much fresh young beauty wasted upon work so dull, and among brambles so sharp."

The girls looked up slack-jawed, then uttered small squeaks of terror, and stood paralyzed, too frightened to run.

Rhialto frowned. "Why do you tremble? Do I seem such a monster of evil?"

One of the girls managed to quaver: "Sir Ghoul, your ugliness is inspiring! Pray give us our lives so that we may appall others with the tale!"

Rhialto spoke coldly. "I am neither ghoul nor demon, and your horror is not at all flattering."

The girl was emboldened to ask: "In that case, what manner of strange thing might you be?"

A second girl spoke in an awed voice: "He is a Pooner, or perhaps a Bohul, and we are as good as dead!"

Rhialto controlled his irritation. "What foolish talk is this? I am only a traveler from a far land, neither Pooner nor Bohul, and I intend you no harm. Have you never seen a stranger before?"

"Certainly, but never one so dour, meanwhile wearing so comical a hat."

Rhialto nodded crisply. "I do not care to modify my face, but I will gladly hear your advice as to a more fashionable hat."

The first girl said: "This year everyone is wearing a clever felt 'soup-pot'—so are they called—and magenta is the only suitable colour. A single blue ear-flap suffices for modesty, and a caste-sign of glazed faience is considered somewhat dashing."

Rhialto squeezed the walnut shell. "Osherl, procure me a hat of this description. You may also set out a table with a collation of foods tempting to the ordinary tastes of today."

The hat appeared. Rhialto tossed his old hat behind a bush and donned the faddish new article, and the girls clapped their hands in approval.

Meanwhile Osherl had arranged a table laden with dainties on a nearby area.

Rhialto waved the girls forward. ''Even the most brittle personalities relax at the sight of viands such as these, and pretty little courtesies and signs of favor, otherwise unthinkable, are sometimes rendered almost automatically—especially in the presence of these fine pastries, piled high with creams and sweet jellies. My dear young ladies, I invite you to partake.''

The most cautious of the girls said: ''And then, what will you demand of us?''

Another said chidingly: ''Tish Tush! The gentleman has freely invited us to share his repast; we should respond with equal freedom!''

The third gave a merry laugh. ''Dine first and worry later! After all, he can enforce his wishes upon us as he chooses, without the formality of feeding us first, so that worry leads nowhere.''

''Perhaps you are right,'' said the first girl. ''For a fact, in his new hat he is less ugly than before, and indeed I am most partial to this thrasher pâté, come what may.''

Rhialto said with dignity: ''You may enjoy your meal without qualms.''

The girls advanced upon the table and, discovering no peculiar conduct on the part of Rhialto, devoured the viands with zest.

Rhialto pointed across the plain. ''What are those curious clouds in the sky?''

The girls turned to look as if they had not previously noticed. ''That is the direction of Vasques Tohor. The dust doubtless results from the war now being fought.''

Rhialto frowned across the plain. ''What war is this?''

The girls laughed at Rhialto's ignorance. ''It was launched by the Bohulic Dukes of East Attuck; they brought their battle-gangs down in great numbers and threw them without remorse against Vasques Tohor, but they can never prevail against the King of all Kings and his Thousand Knights.''

''Very likely not,'' said Rhialto. ''Still, from curiosity I will wander northward and see for myself. I now bid you farewell.''

The girls slowly returned to the thicket, but their enthusiasm for berry-picking was gone, and they worked with laggard fingers, watching over their shoulders at the tall form of Rhialto as he sauntered off to the north.

Rhialto proceeded half a mile, then climbed into the air and ran through the sky toward Vasques Tohor.

By the time he arrived on the scene, the battle had been decided. The Bohul battle-gangs, with their memrils and rumbling war-wagons, had done the unthinkable; on the Finneian Plain east of Vasques Tohor the Twenty Potences of the Last Kingdom had been destroyed; Vasques Tohor could no longer be denied to the Bohul Dukes.

The tragic peach-rose light of late afternoon illuminated a clutter of smoke, dust, toppled machines and broken corpses. Legions of long pedigree and many honours had been smashed; their standards and uniforms bedizened the field with colour. The Thousand Knights, riding half-living, half-metal flyers from Canopus, had thrown themselves against the Bohul war-wagons, but for the most part had been destroyed by fire-rays before they could do damage in return.

The war-wagons now commanded the plain: grim, dismal vehicles rearing sixty feet into the air, armed with both Red Ruin and barb-drivers. On the first tier and wherever they could cling rode assault troops from East Attuck. These were not pretty troops; they were neither handsome, nor clean-limbed nor even dauntless. Rather they were surly veterans of many types and conditions, with only dirt, sweat and foul language in common. At first glance they seemed no more than a rabble, lacking both discipline and morale. Some were old, bearded and pallid; others were bald and fat, or bandy-legged, or thin as weasels. All were unkempt, with faces more petulant than ferocious. Their uniforms were improvised; some wore skull-caps, others leather battle-caps with ear-flaps, others tufted barb-catchers adorned with scalps cut from the blond young heads of the Thousand Knights. Such were the troops which had defeated the Twenty Legions, skulking, hiding, striking, feigning death, striking again, screaming in pain but never fear; the Iron Dukes had long before sated them full with fright.

To the side of the war-wagons stalked rows of memrils: gracile creatures apparently all legs and arms of brown chitin, with small triangular heads raised twenty feet above the ground; it was said that the magician Pikarkas, himself reportedly half-insect, had contrived the memrils from ever more prodigious versions of the executioner beetle.

Tam Tol, King of the Final Kingdom, had stood all day on the parapets of Vasques Tohor, overlooking the Finneian Plain. He watched his elite Knights on their flyers darting down upon the war-wagons; he saw them consumed by Red Ruin. His Twenty Legions, led by the Indomitables, deployed under their ancient standards. They were guarded from above by squadrons of black air-lions, each twenty feet long, armed with fire, gas-jet and fearful sounds.

Tam Tol stood immobile as the Bohul battle-gangs, cursing and sweating, cut down his brave noblemen, and stood long after all hope was gone, heedless of calls and urgencies. His courtiers one by one moved away, to leave Tam Tol at last standing alone, either too numb or too proud to flee.

Behind the parapets mobs ranged the city, gathering all portable wealth, then, departing by the Sunset Gates, made for the sacred city Luid Shug, fifty miles to the west across the Joheim Valley.

Rhialto, running through the sky, halted and surveyed the sky through the pleurmalion. The dark blue spot hung over the western sector of the city; Rhialto proceeded slowly in this direction, at a loss for a means to locate the Perciplex quickly and deftly among so much confusion. He became aware of Tam Tol standing alone on the parapets: even as he watched, a barb from the turret of a war-wagon struck up through the afternoon sunlight and Tam Tol, struck in the forehead, fell slowly and soundlessly down the face of the parapets to the ground.

The noise from the Finneian Plain dwindled to a whispering murmur. All flyers had departed the air and Rhialto ran on soft plunging steps a mile closer to the dying city. Halting, he used the pleurmalion once more, and discovered, somewhat to his relief, that the blue sky-spot no longer hovered over the city, but out over the Joheim Valley, where the Perciplex was now evidently included in the loot of someone in the column of refugees.

Rhialto ran through the air to station himself directly below the blue spot, merely to discover a new frustration: the individual with the Perciplex could not be isolated in the crowds of trudging bodies and pale faces.

The sun sank into a flux of colour, and the blue spot no longer could be seen on the night sky. Rhialto turned away in vexation. He ran south through the twilight, beyond the Joheim Valley and across a wide meandering river. He descended at the outskirts of a town: Vils of the Ten Steeples, and took lodging for the night at a small inn at the back of a garden of rose-trees.

In the common room the conversation dealt with the war and the power of the Bohul battle-gangs. Speculation and rumor were rife, and all marvelled, with gloomy shakes of the head, at the fateful passing of the Last Kingdom.

Rhialto sat at the back of the room, listening but contributing nothing to the conversation, and presently he went quietly off to his chamber.

12

Rhialto breakfasted upon melon and fried clam dumplings in rose syrup. He settled his account and, departing the town, returned to the north.

A human river still flowed across the Joheim Valley. Multitudes had already arrived before the holy city, only to be denied entry, and their encampment spread like a crust away from the city walls. Above hung the blue spot.

Luid Shug had been ordained a holy place during an early era of the aeon by the legendary Goulkoud the God-friend. Coming upon the crater of a small dead volcano, Goulkoud had been seized by twenty paroxysms of enlightenment, during which he stipulated the form and placement of twenty temples in symmetry around the central volcanic neck. Prebendary structures, baths, fountains and hostels for pilgrims occupied the floor of the crater; a narrow boulevard encircled the rim. Around the outside periphery stood twenty enormous god-effigies in twenty niches cut into the crater walls, each corresponding to one of the temples within the city.

Rhialto descended to the ground. Somewhere among the host huddled before the city was the Perciplex, but the sky-spot seemed to wander, despite Rhialto's best efforts to bring it directly overhead, in which effort he was sorely hampered by the crowds.

At the center of the city, atop the old volcanic neck, stood a rose-quartz and silver finial. The Arch-priest stepped out upon the highest platform and, holding his arms high, he spoke to the refugees in a voice amplified by six great spiral shells.

"To victims and unfortunates, we extend twenty profound solaces! However, if your hopes include entry into this sacred place, they must be abandoned. We have neither food to feed hunger nor drink to slake thirst!

"Furthermore, I can extend no fair portents! The glory of the world is gone; it will never return until a hundred dreary centuries have run their course! Then hope and splendour will revivify the land, in a culmination of all that is good! This era will then persist until the earth finally rolls beyond Gwennart the Soft Curtain.

"To prepare for the ultimate age we will now select a quota of the choicest and the best, to the number of five thousand, six hundred and forty-two, which is a Holy and Mysterious Number heavy with secrets.

"Half of this company will be the noble 'Best of the Best': heroes of ancient lineage! Half will be chosen from 'Nephryne's Foam': maidens of virtue and beauty no less brave and gallant than their masculine counterparts. Together they are the 'Paragons': the highest excellence of the kingdom, and the flower of the race!

"By the Spell of a Hundred Centuries we will bind them, and they shall sleep through the Dark Epoch which lies ahead. Then, when the Spell is done and the Age of Glory has come, the Paragons will march forth to institute the Kingdom of Light!

"To all others I give this instruction: continue on your way. Go south to the Lands of Cabanola and Eio, or—should you find there no respite—onward to the Land of Farwan, or—should you so elect—across the Lutic Ocean to the Scanduc Isles.

"Time presses upon us! We must take our Paragons. Let the King's Companions and their families come forward, and the surviving Knights, and the maidens from the Institute of Gleyen and the Flower Songs, as well as Nephryne's Foam, and all others who in pride and dignity must be considered Paragons!

"To expedite matters, all those of the lowest castes: the twittlers, public entertainers and buffoons; the stupid and ill-bred; the criminals and night-runners; those with short ears and long toenails: let them continue on their journey.

"The same suggestion applies to the somewhat more worthy castes, who, despite their rectitude, will not be included among the 'Paragons.'

"All aspiring to the Golden Age: let them step forward! We will choose with all possible facility."

Rhialto again tried to position himself directly below the sky-spot, hoping by some means to identify that person who carried the Perciplex, but found no success.

Either through vanity or desperate hope, few indeed heeded the strictures of the Arch-priest, so that those who pressed forward declaring themselves 'Paragons' included not only the noble and well-formed, but also the toothless and corpulent; the hydrocephalics, victims of chronic hiccup, notorious criminals, singers of popular songs and several persons on their death-beds.

The confusion tended to impede the process of selection, and so the day passed. Toward the end of the afternoon, some of the more realistic individuals gave up hope of finding sanctuary in Luid Shug and began to trudge off across the plain. Rhialto watched the sky-spot attentively, but it hung in the sky as before, until at last it faded into the murk of evening. Rhialto somberly returned to the inn at Vils of the Ten Steeples, and passed another restless night.

In the morning he again coursed north to Luid Shug, to discover that the selectors had worked the whole night through, so that all of the 'Paragons' had been selected and taken into the city. The gates were now sealed.

A pair of Bohul armies, moving slowly across the Joheim Valley, converged upon Luid Shug, and all those refugees still encamped near the crater departed in haste.

The dark blue sky-spot now hung over Luid Shug. Rhialto, descending to the ground, approached a postern beside the west gate. He was denied admittance. A voice from the shadows said: "Go your way, stranger; a hundred centuries will pass before Luid Shug again opens its gates. The Spell of Distended Time is on us; go, therefore, and do not bother to look back, since you will see only dreaming gods."

The Bohul armies were close at hand. Rhialto took to the air and climbed to the tumble of a low white cumulus cloud."

A strange silence muffled the valley. The city showed no movement. With a deliberation more menacing than haste the war-wagons rolled toward the eastern gates of Luid Shug. The Bohul veterans, grumbling and walking as if their feet hurt, came behind.

From the spiral voice-horns above the city came amplified words: "Warriors, turn away! Make no molestation upon us. Luid Shug is now lost to your control."

Paying no heed, the commanders prepared to strike down the gates with blast-bolts. Five of the stone effigies moved in their niches and raised their arms. The air quivered; the war-wagons shriveled to small tumbles of char. The peevish veterans became like the husks of dead insects. The Joheim Valley was once again quiet.

Rhialto turned away, and strode thoughtfully from cloud to cloud into the south. Where the hills began to rise, some twenty or thirty miles west of Fader's Waft, he stepped down upon a hummock covered with dry grass and, seeking the shade of a solitary tree, sat leaning against the bole.

The time was close on noon. The fragrance of dry grass came pleasantly on puffs of warm wind. Far to the northeast a coil of smoke rose above the corpse of Vasques Tohor.

Chewing a straw, Rhialto sat reflecting upon his condition. Circumstances were not at the optimum, even though the Perciplex had been more or less precisely located. Osherl must be considered a weak reed, sullen and indifferent. Ildefonse? His interests comported more with those of Rhialto them those of the treacherous Hache-Moncour. Still, Ildefonse was known for his tendencies toward flexibility and expedience. As Preceptor, Ildefonse, even lacking the chug, might be able to compel Sarsem to correct conduct; in the main, however, and all taken with all, Sarsem must be reckoned even less dependable than Osherl.

Rhialto put the pleurmalion to his eye, and as before took note of the dark blue sky-spot over Luid Shug. Rhialto put aside the pleurmalion and caged Osherl out from his walnut shell.

Osherl showed himself as a wefkin four feet high with blue skin and green hair. He spoke in a voice meticulously polite. ''My best regards, Rhialto! As I look about, I discover a fine warm day of the 16th Aeon! The air tingles at one's skin with characteristic zest. You are chewing grass like an idle farm-boy; I am happy to perceive your enjoyment of time and place.''

Rhialto ignored the pleasantries. ''I still lack the Perciplex, and for this failure, you and Sarsem share the blame.''

The wefkin, laughing soundlessly, combed its green silk hair between blue fingers. ''My dear fellow! This style of expression becomes you not at all!''

''No matter,'' said Rhialto. ''Go now to yonder city, and bring me back the Perciplex.''

The wefkin uttered a gay laugh. ''Dear Rhialto, your witticisms are superb! The concept of poor Osherl trapped, dragged, pounded, stamped upon, dissected and maltreated by twenty vicious gods is a masterpiece of absurd imagery!''

''I intended no joke,'' said Rhialto. ''Yonder lies the Perciplex; the Perciplex I must have.''

Osherl himself plucked a blade of grass and waved it in the air to emphasize his remarks. ''Perhaps you should recast your goals. In many ways the 16th Aeon is more kindly than the 21st. You chew grass like one born to it. This time is yours, Rhialto! So it has been ordained by stronger voices than either yours or mine!''

''My voice is adequately strong,'' said Rhialto. ''Also I am friend to the chug and I distribute indenture points with lavish prodigality.''

''Such humor is mordant,'' growled Osherl.

''You refuse to enter Luid Shug for the Perciplex?''

''Impossible while the gods stand guard.''

''Then you must take us forward exactly a hundred centuries, so that when Luid Shug awakens to the Age of Gold, we will be on hand to claim our property.''

Osherl wished to discuss the onerous quality of his indenture, but Rhialto would not listen. "All in good time, when we are once more in Boumergarth, Perciplex in hand!"

"The Perciplex? Is that all you want?" asked Osherl with patently false heartiness. "Why did you not say so in the first place? Are you prepared?"

"I am indeed. Work with accuracy."

13

The hillock and the solitary tree were gone. Rhialto stood on the slope of a stony valley, with a river wandering sluggishly below.

The time seemed to be morning, although a heavy overcast concealed the sky. The air felt raw and damp against his skin; to the east dark wisps of rain drifted down into a black forest.

Rhialto looked about the landscape, but found no evidences of human habitancy: neither fence, farm-house, road, track or path. Rhialto seemed to be alone. Where was Osherl? Rhialto looked here and there in annoyance, then called out: "Osherl! Make yourself known!"

Osherl stepped forward, still the blue-skinned wefkin. "I am here."

Rhialto indicated the dour landscape. "This does not seem the Age of Gold. Have we come exactly one hundred centuries? Where is Luid Shug?"

Osherl pointed to the north. "Luid Shug is yonder, at the edge of the forest."

Rhialto brought out the pleurmalion, but the dark blue sky-spot could not be seen for the overcast. "Let us make a closer approach."

The two coursed north to the site of the sacred city, to discover only a tumble of ruins. Rhialto spoke in perplexity: "This is a most dreary prospect! Where have the gods gone?"

"I will go to Gray Dene and there make inquiry," said Osherl. "Wait here; in due course I will return with all information."

"Stop! Hold up!" cried Rhialto. "My question was casual. First find the Perciplex; then you can seek after the gods as long as you like."

Osherl grumbled under his breath: "You have dawdled away a hundred centuries, yet if I spent a single year in Gray Dene I would still hear threats and abuse on my return. It dulls the edge of one's initiative."

"Enough!" said Rhialto. "I am interested only in the Perciplex."

The two approached the ruins. Wind and weather had worked at the old crater walls so that only traces remained. The temples were rubble; the twenty gods, carved from marble, had likewise eroded to a few toppled fragments, with all their force seeped into the mire.

Rhialto and Osherl walked slowly around the edge of the old city, testing the pleurmalion from time to time, without result.

To the north the forest grew close to the old parapets, and at this point they caught the scent of wood smoke on the wind. Looking here and there, they discovered a crude village of twenty huts just inside the edge of the forest.

"We will make inquiries," said Rhialto. "I suggest that you change your appearance; otherwise they will think us a queer pair indeed."

"You should also make alterations. Your hat, for instance, is the shape of an inverted soup-pot, and purple to boot. I doubt if this is the current fashion."

"There is something in what you say," admitted Rhialto.

Using the semblance of Lavrentine Redoubtables in glistening armor, barbed and spiked, and with helmets crested with tongues of blue fire, Rhialto and Osherl approached the village, which lacked all charm and smelled poorly.

Rhialto reinforced himself with his glossolary and called out: "Villagers, attention! Two Lavrentine grandees stand nearby; come perform the proper ceremonies of welcome."

One by one the villagers appeared from their huts, yawning and scratching: folk of a squat, long-armed race with liver-coloured skins and long lank hair. Their garments were fashioned from bird-skins and the village showed few civilized amenities; still they seemed sleekly well-fed. At the sight of Rhialto and Osherl, certain of the men called out in pleasure, and taking up long-handled nets advanced upon the two with sinister purpose.

Rhialto called out: "Stand back! We are magicians! Your first sneer of menace will bring down a spell of great distress; be warned!"

The men refused to heed and raised high their nets. Rhialto made a sign to Osherl. The nets folded over backwards to enclose and clench into tight balls those who had thought to use them. Osherl jerked his thumb to whisk these balls way, into the northern sky, through the overcast and out of sight.

Rhialto looked around the group and spoke to a flat-faced woman: "Who is the chieftain of this repulsive group?"

The woman pointed. "There is Doulka who is butcher and trundleman. We need no chieftain; such folk eat more than their share."

A big-bellied old man with gray wattles sidled a few steps forward. He spoke in a wheedling nasal voice: ''Must your disgust be so blatant? True: we are anthropophages. True: we put strangers to succulent use. Is this truly good cause for hostility? The world is as it is and each of us must hope in some fashion to be of service to his fellows, even if only in the form of a soup.''

''Our talents lie elsewhere,'' said Rhialto. ''If I see any more nets, you will be first to fly the sky.''

''No fear, now that we know your preferences,'' declared Doulka. ''What are your needs? Are you hungry?''

''We are curious in regard to Luid Shug, which at this time should be awakening to the Age of Gold. Instead we find only rubble, slime and the stink from your village. Why have events gone in this unhappy fashion?''

Doulka had recovered his confidence and blinked at his visitors with torpid complacence. Idly, as if through the force of habit, he began to twist and interweave his fingers with a dexterity which Rhialto found interesting, even fascinating. He spoke in a droning nasal monotone: ''The mystery surrounding the ruins is more apparent than real.'' As Doulka spoke, he wove his fingers slowly back and forth. ''Centuries passed by, one upon the other, and the gods stood steadfast, by day and by night. At last they succumbed to the grind of wind and rain. They became dust and their power was gone.

Doulka worked his fingers in and out. ''The land was empty and the ruins lay quiet. The 'Paragons' slept their long sleep in alabaster eggs. Youths and maidens of prime quality ripened on their silken couches, unknown to all!''

Doulka's fingers created odd patterns. Rhialto began to feel a pleasant lassitude, which he ascribed to his efforts of the day.

''My dear fellow, I see that you are weary!'' said Doulka. ''I reproach myself!'' Three ceremonial chairs of woven withe were brought out, their backs carved to represent contorted human faces.

''Sit,'' said Doulka in a soothing voice. ''Rest yourself.''

Doulka ponderously placed his own fat buttocks upon the creaking withe of a chair. Rhialto also seated himself, to ease his tired limbs. He turned to Osherl and spoke in the language of the 21st Aeon: ''What is this sly old devil doing to me, that I feel such torpor?''

Osherl responded in an offhand manner: ''He commands four sandestins of an inferior sort: the type we call 'madlings.' They are building patterns of lassitude in and out of your eyes, which are now somewhat skewed. Doulka has already given orders to prepare for a feast.''

Rhialto spoke indignantly: "Why did you not prevent this trickery? Where is your loyalty?"

Osherl merely coughed in discomfiture.

Rhialto told Osherl: "Order the madlings to pull Doulka's nose out to a length of two feet, to impose an ulcerous cyst at the tip, and also a large painful carbuncle on each buttock."

"As you wish."

The work was done to his satisfaction. "Now," he told Osherl, "and this should go without saying, order the madlings to desist from all further nuisances upon my person."

"Yes, true. We would not want Doulka to retaliate in kind."

"Then you will accord the madlings their freedom, and send them on their way, with instructions never again to serve Doulka."

"A generous thought!" declared Osherl. "Does the same instruction apply to me?"

"Osherl, do not distract me. I must question Doulka, despite his new preoccupations." Rhialto turned back to the agitated trundleman and spoke in the language of the village: "You have learned the penalty of bad faith. All in all, I consider myself merciful, so be grateful and rejoice in this fact! Now then: shall we continue our conversation?"

Doulka said sulkily: "You are an irritable man! I intended no great harm! What more can I tell you?"

"You have explored the ruins thoroughly?"

"We are not interested in the ruins, except as they yield alabaster eggs for our delectation."

"I see. How many eggs have you devoured?"

"Over the years they number five thousand, six hundred and forty-one. Few remain."

Rhialto said: " 'Few'? Unless you have miscounted, a single Paragon remains to institute the Age of Gold. You have eaten all the others."

Doulka momentarily forgot his nose and buttocks. "Only one remaining? This is bad news! Our feasts are at an end!"

"What of treasure?" asked Rhialto. "Have you taken gems and crystals from the vaults of the city?"

"We have indeed, since we take pleasure in fine things: notably all red, pink and yellow gems. Those which are blue and green induce bad luck and we use them for our amusement."

"How so?"

"We tie them to the tails of bogadils, or ursial lopers or even manks, which prompts them to absolutely comical acts of worry and shame, so that they run pell-mell through the forest.''

''Hmmf. And what of a luminous blue crystal in the form of a prism, thus and so? Has such an object come to your attention?''

Doulka ruefully felt the length of his nose. ''I seem to recall such an item, in the not too distant past.''

Rhialto, all kindliness, asked: ''Does your nose truly cause you such distress?''

''Oh indeed, indeed!''

''And your buttocks?''

''They are exquisitely painful.''

''When you bring me the blue crystal I seek, your sores will be healed.''

Doulka gave a surly grunt. ''That is no easy task.''

Rhialto had no more to say and with Osherl moved somewhat away from the village, where Osherl established a comfortable pavilion of dark blue silk. On a heavy red and blue rug of intricate pattern Osherl arranged a massive table of carved dark timber surrounded by four low chairs with dark red velvet cushions. Outside the structure he laid down a similar rug and a second table, for occasions when the day was fine. Above he arranged a canopy and at each corner placed a tall black iron pedestal with a lamp of many facets.

Leaving Osherl sitting at the interior table, Rhialto climbed into the sky, up through the overcast and out into a glare of vermilion sunlight charged with an acrid blue overtone.

The time was middle afternoon; the sun hung half-way down the sky. The cloud-cover extended without break for as far as Rhialto could see in all directions. He looked through the pleurmalion, and to his pleasure discovered the dark spot hanging in the sky somewhat to the north and east of where he stood.

Rhialto ran at speed above the clouds and ranged himself immediately below the spot, then dropped down through the overcast and toward the forest below. Finally he reached the forest floor, where he made a quick and superficial search, finding nothing.

Returning to the pavilion, Rhialto found Osherl sitting as before. Rhialto described his activities. ''My search definitely lacked accuracy. Tomorrow you shall mount as high as possible with the pleurmalion and post yourself precisely under the spot. From this point you will lower a weighted cord until it dangles close to the forest, where we can hope to find the Perciplex. . . . What is that savage hooting and yelping sound?''

Osherl looked out through the silken flap at the front of the pavilion. ''The villagers are excited; they are calling out in enthusiam.''

''Curious,'' said Rhialto. ''Perhaps Doulka, rather than cooperate, has seen fit to cut off his nose. . . . Otherwise they would seem to have little reason to rejoice. Now then, another thought has occurred to me: why does the blue spot fly so high in the air?''

''No mystery there: for reasons of far visibility.''

''All very well, but surely another signal could have served more efficiently: for instance, a rod of blue light, conspicuous from afar, but also accurate at its lower end.''

''In candour, I do not understand Sarsem's motives, unless he truly took Hache-Moncour's injunctions to heart.''

''Oh? What injunctions were these?''

''Just idle badinage, or so I suppose. Hache-Moncour ordered that the sky-spot be made to perform so rudely that you would never truly strike home to the crystal, but would forever be chasing it back and forth like some mad fool chasing the will o' the wisp.''

''I see. And why did you not tell me this before? No matter; the day will come when you learn who controls your indenture points: me or Hache-Moncour. . . . That howling and whooping is incessant! Doulka must be cutting off his nose an inch at a time. Osherl, order them to quiet.''

''It seems a harmless jollity; they are merely preparing a feast.''

Rhialto looked up alertly. ''A feast? Of what sort?''

''The last of the Paragons: a maiden who has only just emerged from the alabaster egg. After ingestion is under way, the noise no doubt will abate.''

Rhialto leapt to his feet. ''Osherl, words fail me. Come along, on the double-quick.''

Striding back to the village, Rhialto found Doulka sitting before his hut on a pair of enormous down pillows, his nose tied in a poultice. Preparations for a feast were under way, with women of the village cutting and slicing roots, vegetables and seasonings to the specifications of their recipe. In a pen to the side stood the last of the Paragons: a maiden whom a butcher might classify in the 'slightly smaller than medium' range, of 'choice quality,' 'tender if lacking in excessive fat.' Her garments had disintegrated during her long sleep; she wore nothing but a necklace of copper and turquoise. Haggard with fear, she looked through the bars of the pen as a pair of hulking apprentice butchers arranged a work table and began to sharpen their implements.

Doulka the Trundleman saw the approach of Rhialto and Osherl with a scowl. ''What is it this time? We are preparing to indulge ourselves in a last feast of quality. Your business must wait, unless you have come to relieve me of my pain.''

Rhialto said: ''There will be no feast, unless you yourself wish to climb into the pot. Osherl, bring the lady from the pen and provide her suitable garments.''

Osherl split the pen into a million motes, and draped the girl's body in a pale blue robe. Doulka cried out in grief and the villagers went so far as to take up weapons. For distraction, Osherl evoked four blue goblins eight feet tall. Hopping forward and gnashing their fangs, they sent the villagers fleeing with high heels into the forest.

Rhialto, Osherl and the dazed maiden returned to the pavilion, where Rhialto served her a cordial, and explained the circumstances in a gentle voice. She listened with a blank gaze and perhaps understood something of what Rhialto told her, for presently she wept tears of grief. Rhialto had mixed an anodyne into the cordial, and her grief became a languid dream-state in which the disasters of her life were without emotive force, and she was content to sit close beside Rhialto and take comfort from his presence.

Osherl looked on with cynicism. ''Rhialto, you are a curious creature, one of an obstinate and enigmatic race.''

''How so?''

''Poor Doulka is desolate; his folk creep through the forest, afraid to go home for fear of goblins; meanwhile you console and flatter this mindless female.''

Rhialto responded with quiet dignity: ''I am motivated by gallantry, which is a sentiment beyond your understanding.''

''Bah!'' said Osherl. ''You are as vain as a jay-cock and already you are planning fine postures to strike in front of this pubescent little creature, with whom you will presently attempt a set of amorous pastimes. Meanwhile Doulka goes hungry and my indenture is as irksome as ever.''

Rhialto reflected a moment. ''Osherl, you are clever but not clever enough. I am not so easily distracted as you would hope. Therefore, let us now resume our conversation. What else have you concealed from me in connection with Sarsem and Hache-Moncour?''

''I gave little attention to their strategies. You should have specified the topics in which you were interested.''

''Before the fact? I can not know whether I am interested or not until the plans are made.''

''In truth, I know little more than you. Hache-Moncour hopes to advance his own cause, with Sarsem's help, but this is no surprise.''

''Sarsem is playing a dangerous game. Ultimately he will suffer the penalties of duplicity! Let all others learn from Sarsem's despicable example!''

''Ah well, who knows how the game will go?'' said Osherl airily.

''And what do you mean by that?''

Osherl would say no more, and Rhialto with pointed displeasure sent him out into the night to guard the pavilion. Osherl eased his task by setting up four large goblin's heads glowing with a ghastly blue luminosity, which startled Rhialto himself when he stepped out to see how went the night.

Returning within, Rhialto arranged a couch for the maiden, where she presently slept the sleep of emotional exhaustion. A short time later Rhialto also took his repose.

In the morning the maiden awoke composed but listless. Rhialto arranged a bath of perfumed water in the lavatory, while Osherl, using the guise of a serving woman, laid out for her use a crisp outfit of white duck trousers, a scarlet coat trimmed with golden buttons and black frogging, and black ankle-boots trimmed with red floss. She bathed, dressed, ordered her ear-length black hair, and came tentatively out into the main chamber where Rhialto joined her at breakfast.

Through the power of the glossolary, he spoke to her in her own tongue: ''You have suffered a terrible tragedy, and I offer you my sympathy. My name is Rhialto; like yourself I am not native to this dreary epoch. May I inquire your name?''

At first the maiden seemed indisposed to respond, then said in a resigned voice: ''My secrets are no longer of consequence. In my personal thought-language I have named myself 'Furud Dawn-stuff' or 'Exquisite Dawn-thing.' At my school I won a credential as 'Shalukhe' or 'Expert Water-Swimmer' and this was used as my friend-name.''

''That seems a good name, and it is the name I will use, unless you prefer otherwise.''

The maiden showed him a dreary smile. ''I no longer have the status to command the luxury of preference.''

Rhialto found the concept complex but comprehensible. ''It is true that 'innate quality' and 'merit derived from bold assertion' must be the source of your self-esteem. You shall be known as Shalukhe the Survivor; is not that a prideful condition?''

''Not particularly, since your help alone saved my life.''

Osherl, overhearing the remark, ventured a comment: ''Nevertheless, your tactics are instinctively correct. To deal with Rhialto the Marvellous, and here I allude to your host and the conservator of my indenture, you must fuel the fires of his bloated vanity. Exclaim upon his handsome countenance; feign awe at his wisdom; he will be putty in your hands."

Rhialto said in a measured voice: "Osherl's mood is often acerb; despite his sarcasm, I will be happy to earn your good opinion."

Shalukhe the Swimmer could not restrain her amusement. "You have already gained it, Sir Rhialto! I am also grateful to Osherl for his assistance."

"Bah!" said Rhialto. "He felt greater concern for the hunger of poor Doulka."

"Not so!" cried Osherl. "That was just my little joke!"

"In any event, and if you will forgive me the presumption of asking: what is to become of me now?"

"When our business here is done, we shall return to Almery, and talk further of the matter. As for now, you may regard yourself as my subaltern, and you are assigned to the supervision of Osherl. See that he is at all times neat, alert and courteous!"

Again half-smiling, Shalukhe appraised Osherl. "How can I supervise someone so clever?"

"Simplicity itself! If he shirks, speak only two words: 'indenture points.' "

Osherl uttered a hollow laugh. "Already Rhialto the Marvellous works his supple wiles."

Rhialto paid no heed. He reached down, took her hands and pulled her erect. "And now: to work! Are you less distraught than before?"

"Very much so! Rhialto, I thank you for your kindness."

"Shalukhe the Swimmer, or Dawn-thing, or however you will be called: a shadow still hangs over you, but it is a pleasure to see you smile."

Osherl spoke in the language of the 21st Aeon: "Physical contact has been made, and the program now enters its second phase. . . . Such a poor torn little wretch, how could she resist Rhialto?"

"Your experience is limited," said Rhialto. "It is more a case of 'How could Rhialto resist such a poor torn little wretch?' "

The girl looked from one to the other, hoping to divine the sense of the interchange. Rhialto spoke out: "Now, to our business! Osherl, take the pleurmalion—" he handed the object to Osherl "—then climb above the clouds to locate the sky-spot. From a point directly below, lower a heavy flashing red lantern on a long cord until it hangs close above the Perciplex. The day is windless and accuracy should be fine."

Osherl, for reasons of caprice, now took upon himself the guise of a middle-aged Walvoon shopkeeper dressed in baggy black breeches, a mustard-ocher vest and a wide-brimmed black hat. He took the pleurmalion in a pudgy hand, mounted the sky on three lunging strides.

"With any luck," Rhialto told Shalukhe, "my irksome task is close to its end, whereupon we will return to the relative calm of the 21st Aeon. . . . What's this? Osherl back so soon?"

Osherl jumped down from the sky to the rug before the pavilion. He made a negative signal and Rhialto uttered a poignant cry. "Why have you not located the Perciplex?"

Osherl gave his fat shop-keeper's face a doleful shake. "The sky-spot is absorbed in the mists and cannot be seen. The pleurmalion is useless."

Rhialto snatched the device and sprang high through the air, into the clouds and out, to stand in the acrid vermilion radiance. He put the pleurmalion to his eye, but, as Osherl had asserted, the sky-spot no longer could be seen.

For a period Rhialto stood on the white expanse, casting a long pale blue shadow. With frowning attention he examined the pleurmalion, then again looked around the sky, to no avail.

Something was amiss. Staring thoughtfully off across the white cloud-waste, Rhialto pondered the conceivable cases. Had the Perciplex been moved? Perhaps the pleurmalion had lost its force? . . . Rhialto returned to the pavilion.

Osherl stood to the side, gazing vacantly toward the mouldering ruins. Rhialto called out: "Osherl! A moment of your time, if you please."

Osherl approached without haste, to stand with hands thrust into the pockets of his striped pantaloons. Rhialto stood waiting, tossing the pleurmalion from one hand to the other, and watching Osherl with a pensive gaze.

"Well then, Rhialto: what now?" asked Osherl, with an attempt at ease of manner.

"Osherl, who suggested to you that the projection of the Perciplex might be captured by the overcast?"

Osherl waved one of his hands in a debonair flourish. "To an astute intellect, so much is apparent."

"But you lack an astute intellect. Who provided this insight?"

"I learn from a multitude of sources," muttered Osherl. "I cannot annotate or codify each iota of information which comes my way."

"Let me imagine a sequence of events," said Rhialto. "Osherl, are you paying close attention?"

Osherl, standing disconsolate with hanging jowls and moist gaze, muttered: "Where is my choice?"

"Then consider these imagined events. You climb above the overcast where Sarsem greets you. A conversation ensues, in this fashion:

"Sarsem: 'What now, Osherl? What is your task?'
"Osherl: 'That stone-hearted Rhialto wants me to search about the sky for signs of the Perciplex, using this pleurmalion.'
"Sarsem: 'Indeed? Let me look. . . . I see nothing.'
"Osherl: 'No? Most singular! What shall I tell Rhialto?'
"Sarsem: 'He is easily confused. Tell him that the image is trapped in the clouds. This pleurmalion is now worthless. Take it back.'
"Osherl: 'But this is a different pleurmalion from the one I gave you! It is only a trifle of ordinary glass!'
"Sarsem: 'What then? Both are now equally useless. Take it back and give it to that mooncalf Rhialto; he will never know the difference.'
"Osherl: 'Hm. Rhialto is a mooncalf, but a cunning mooncalf.'
"Sarsem: 'He is very troublesome to our friend Hache-Moncour, who has promised us so many indulgences. . . . My advice is this: by some subterfuge induce him to cancel your indenture; then leave him to cool his heels here in this dank and tiresome epoch.'
"Osherl: 'The concept has much to recommend it.'

"So saying, the two of you chuckled together, then you took leave of your crony and descended with the false pleurmalion and the news that the sky showed no projection, owing to the overcast."

Osherl cried out with quivering jowls: "Is this not plausible? You have no reason to believe either that the new pleurmalion is false, or that Sarsem's views are incorrect!"

"First of all: why did you not report your conversation with Sarsem?"

Osherl shrugged. "You failed to ask."

"Explain, if you will, why the sky-spot was clear and evident last night, through this self-same overcast?"

"I am mystified."

"Would you not say that either the Perciplex was moved or that the true pleurmalion was exchanged for a falsity?"

"I suppose that a case could be made along these lines."

"Precisely so. Osherl, the game is up! I here and now fine you three indenture points for faulty and faithless conduct."

Osherl uttered a wild cry of emotion. Rhialto raised his hand to induce quiet. "Further, I will now put to you a most earnest question, which you must answer with truth and any elaboration necessary to provide me a practical and accurate picture of the situation. Sarsem took from you the pleurmalion. Did he also take, touch, hide, move, alter, destroy, make temporal transfer of, or any other sort of transfer, or in any other way disturb or influence the condition of the Perciplex? Here I refer to that true Perciplex he guarded at Fader's Waft. I dislike verbosity, but it must be used in dealing with you."

"No."

" 'No'? No what? I myself have become confused."

"Sarsem, despite the urgings of Hache-Moncour, does not dare to touch the Perciplex."

"Bring Sarsem here."

After another interchange of acrimony Sarsem, as usual in the form of the lavender-scaled youth, appeared before the pavilion.

"Sarsem, return to me the pleurmalion," said Rhialto evenly.

"Impossible! By order of the new Preceptor I destroyed it."

"Who is the new Preceptor?"

"Hache-Moncour, of course."

"And how do you know this for a fact?"

"He so assured me from his own mouth, or at least implied that this would shortly be the case."

"He told you incorrectly. You should have ascertained the facts from Ildefonse. I fine you three indenture points!"

Like Osherl, Sarsem set up an outcry. "You have no such authority!"

"Hache-Moncour's lack of authority worried you not at all."

"That is different."

"I now order you and Osherl to search the forest and find the Perciplex, and then immediately bring it here to me."

"I cannot do so. I am working to other orders. Let Osherl search. He has been assigned to your service."

"Sarsem, listen carefully! Osherl, you must be my witness! I hesitate to call out that Great Name on such small affairs, but I am becoming ever more annoyed by your tricks. If you interfere once again in my recovery of the Perciplex, I will call upon—"

Both Osherl and Sarsem set up a fearful outcry. "Do not so much as mention the Name; he might hear!"

"Sarsem, is my meaning clear?"

"Most clear," muttered the youth.

"And how will you guide your conduct now?"

"Hmmf . . . I must use evasive tactics in the service of Hache-Moncour so as to satisfy both him and you."

"I warn you that I am henceforth highly sensitive. Your three points have been justly earned; already you have caused me far too much travail."

Sarsem made an inarticulate sound and was gone.

14

Rhialto turned his attention to Osherl. "Yesterday I thought to locate the Perciplex near that tall button-top. Now there is work to be done!"

"By me, no doubt," gloomed Osherl.

"Had you been faithful, the work would have been done, we would be at Boumergarth arranging Hache-Moncour's well-earned penalties; you would have earned probably two points, instead of being fined three: a difference of five indenture points!"

"It is a tragedy over which I, alas! have little control!"

Rhialto ignored the implicit insolence. "So then: shoulders to the wheel! A scrupulous search must be made!"

"And I must work alone? The task is large."

"Exactly so. Range around the forest and assemble here, in order and discipline, all bogadils, ursial lopers, manks and flantics, and any other creatures of sentience."

Osherl licked the ropy lips of his shop-keeper face. "Do you include the anthropophages?"

"Why not? Let tolerance rule our conduct! But first, elevate the pavilion upon a pedestal twenty feet high so that we need not be subjected to the crush. Instruct all these creatures to civil conduct."

In due course Osherl assembled the specified creatures before the pavilion. Stepping forward, Rhialto addressed the group: remarks which his glossolary, working at speed, rendered into terms of general comprehension.

"Creatures, men, half-men and things! I extend to you my good wishes, and my deep sympathy that you are forced to live so intimately in the company of each other.

"Since your intellects are, in the main, of no great complexity, I will be terse. Somewhere in the forest, not too far from yonder tall button-top, is a blue crystal, thus and so, which I wish to possess. All of you are now ordered to search for this crystal. He who finds it and brings it here will be greatly rewarded. To stimulate zeal and expedite the search, I now visit upon each of you a burning sensation, which will be repeated at ever shorter intervals until the blue crystal is in my possession. Search everywhere: in the rubbish, among the forest detritus, in the branches and foliage. The anthropophages originally tied this crystal to the person of someone present, so let that be a clue. Each should search his memory and go to the spot where he might have discarded or scraped off the object. Go now to the button-top tree, which will be the center of your effort. Search well, since the pangs will only intensify until I hold the blue crystal in my hand. Osherl, inflict the first pang, if you will.''

The creatures cried out in pain and departed on the run.

Only moments passed before an ursial loper returned with a fragment of blue porcelain, and demanded the reward. Rhialto bestowed upon him a collar woven of red feathers and sent him out once again.

During the morning a variety of blue objects were laid hopefully before Rhialto, who rejected all and increased both the frequency and force of the stimulating pangs.

Somewhat before noon Rhialto noticed unusual conduct on the part of Osherl, and instantly made inquiry: ''Well then, Osherl: what now?''

Osherl said stiffly: ''It is actually none of my affair, but if I kept my own counsel, you would never let me hear the end of it. There might even be spiteful talk of indenture points—''

Rhialto cried: ''What do you have to tell me?''

''It is in connection with the Perciplex, and since you have made certain efforts to secure this crystal—''

''Osherl, I command you! Get to the point! What of the Perciplex?''

''To make a long story short, I tend to believe that it has been discovered by a flantic,* who at first thought to bring it to you, and then was diverted by a counter-offer from someone who shall go nameless, but the flantic now swoops here and there in indecision. . . . There! See him now! He is coming in this direction. The Perciplex is clutched in his dextral claw. . . . No! He wavers. . . . He has changed his mind; no doubt he has heard more persuasive terms.''

''Quick then! After him! Strike him with pervulsions! Turn him back, or wrest away the Perciplex! Osherl, will you make haste?''

Osherl stood back. ''This is a matter between you and Hache-Moncour; I am not allowed to enter such contests, and here Ildefonse will support me.''

*flantic: winged creature with grotesque man-like head; precursor of the pelgrane.

Rhialto roared furious curses. "Then come; I will chase down the creature! He will learn more of sorrow than even he cares to know! Put a full charge of speed into my air-boots!"

Rhialto sprang into the air and ran on great lunging strides after the flapping black flantic, which, swinging its gray head about and observing Rhialto, only flew the faster.

The chase led to the south and west: over a range of mountains and a forest of ocher and gray palmatics, then across a swamp of slime-puddles, trickling watercourses and tufts of black rushes. In the distance the Santune Sea reflected a leaden gleam from the overcast.

The flantic began to tire; its wings beat down with ever less force, and Rhialto, leaping across chasms of air, began to overtake the creature.

With the sea below and no haven in sight, the flantic turned suddenly to attack Rhialto with claws and battering wings, and Rhialto was almost taken unawares. He dodged the furious lunge, but by so close a margin that the wingedge struck his shoulder. He reeled and toppled; the flantic dived upon him, but Rhialto desperately twisted away. Osherl, standing to the side, uttered a compliment: "You are more agile than I expected. That was a deft contortion."

Rhialto jerked aside a third time, and the flantic's claws tore his cloak and sent Rhialto whirling away. He managed to scream a spell of effectiveness and threw a handful of Blue Havoc toward the swooping hulk, and the dazzling slivers penetrated the torso and slashed holes in the wings. The flantic threw back its head and vented a scream of fear and agony. "Manling, you have killed me; you have taken my one precious life, and I have no other! I curse you and I take your blue crystal with me where you can never recover it: to the Kingdom of Death!"

The flantic became a limp tangle of arms, wings, torso and long awkward neck, and toppled into the sea, where it sank quickly from sight.

Rhialto cried out in vexation. "Osherl! Down with you; into the sea! Recover the Perciplex!"

Osherl descended to look diffidently into the water. "Where did the creature fall?"

"Precisely where you stand. Dive deep, Osherl; it is by your negligence that we are here today."

Osherl hissed between his teeth and lowered a special member into the water. Presently he said: "There is nothing to be found. The bottom is deep and dark. I discover only slime."

"I will hear no excuses!" cried Rhialto. "Dive and grope, and do not show yourself until you have found the Perciplex!"

Osherl uttered a hollow moan and disappeared below the surface. At last he returned.

Rhialto cried: "You have retrieved it? Give it to me, at once!"

"All is not so simple," stated Osherl. "The gem is lost in slime. It shows no radiance, and it has no resonance. In short, the Perciplex must be considered lost."

"I am more sanguine than you," said Rhialto. "Anchor yourself on this site, and on no account allow either Hache-Moncour or Sarsem to interfere. I will consult with you shortly."

"Make haste," called Osherl. "The water is deep, dark and cold, and unknown creatures toy with my member."

"Be patient! Most important: do not shift your position by so much as an inch; since you are now like a buoy marking the location of the Perciplex."

Rhialto returned to the pavilion beside the ruins of Luid Shug. He terminated the search and allowed the stimulations to lapse, to the relief of the company.

Rhialto flung himself wearily into a chair and gave his attention to Shalukhe, the Paragon of Vasques Tohor, where she sat pensively on the couch. She had recovered much of her self-possession, and watched Rhialto with eyes dark and brooding. Rhialto thought: "She has had time to reflect on her plight. She sees nothing optimistic in her future."

Rhialto spoke aloud: "Our first concern is to leave this dismal place forever. And then—"

"And then?"

"We will study the options open to you. They are not entirely cheerless, as you will presently learn."

Shalukhe gave her head a shake of perplexity. "Why do you trouble yourself for me? I have no wealth; my status is now gone. I have few skills and no great diligence. I can climb hyllas trees for pods and squeeze hyssop; I can recite the Naughty Girls' Dream of Impropriety; these are skills of specialized value. Still—" she shrugged and smiled "—we are strangers and you owe me not even caste-duty."

Rhialto, happy in the absence of Osherl's cynical gaze, went to sit beside her. He took her hands in his. "Would you not rescue a helpless civilized person from a cannibal's cutting-table if you were able?"

"Yes, naturally."

"I did the same. Then, with so much accomplished, I became aware of you as a person, or rather, a combination of persons: first a lost and forlorn waif; then as Shalukhe the Swimmer, a maiden of remarkable charm and urgent physical attributes. This combination, for a vain and pompous person like myself, exerts an irresistible appeal. Still, as a man of perhaps inordinate self-esteem, I would not think it proper to intrude unwelcome intimacies upon you; so, whatever your fears in this regard, you may put them aside. I am first and last a gentleman of honour."

Shalukhe the Swimmer's mouth twitched at the corners. "And also a master of extravagant sentiments, some of which perhaps I should not take seriously."

Rhialto rose to his feet. "My dear young lady, here you must trust to the accuracy of your instincts. Still, you may look to me for both comfort and protection, and whatever may be your other needs."

Shalukhe laughed. "At the very least, Rhialto, you are able to amuse me."

Rhialto sighed and turned away. "Now we must go off to deal with Osherl. I suspect that he is acting in concert with my enemies, if only passively. This of course is intolerable. We will now fly this pavilion south, across the Mag Mountains, over the Santune Sea, to where Osherl has stationed himself. There we will make further plans."

Rhialto uttered a cantrap of material transfer, to convey the pavilion across the land and over the sea to where the flantic had sunk beneath the waves. Osherl, for the sake of convenience, had assumed the form of a buoy, painted red and black to conform with maritime regulations. A human head wrought in iron protruded from the top, with a navigation light above.

"Rhialto, you have returned!" cried Osherl in a metallic voice. "Not a moment too soon! I have no taste for a life at sea."

"No more have I! As soon as we recover the Perciplex, our work is done."

Osherl gave a harsh melancholy cry, in the tones of a sea-bird. "Have I not explained that the Perciplex is lost in the depths? You must give up this obsession and accept the inevitable!"

"It is you who must accept the inevitable," said Rhialto. "Until the Perciplex is in my hands, you must remain here to mark and certify this spot."

Osherl tolled his warning bell in agitation. "Why not exercise your magic and move the sea aside? Then we may search in convenience!"

"I no longer command such magic; my best power was stolen by Hache-Moncour and others. Still, you have supplied me with the germ of an idea. . . . What is the name of this particular sea?"

"That is an irrelevant item of trivia!"

"Not at all! I am never irrelevant, nor yet trivial."

Osherl produced a heavy moaning curse. "During this epoch, it is an inland arm of the Accic Ocean: the Santune Sea. During the 17th Aeon, a land-bridge rises across the Straits of Garch; the sea slowly dries and becomes extinct. During the last epoch of the 17th Aeon the old sea-bed is known as the Tchaxmatar Steppe. In the second epoch of the 18th Aeon, Baltanque of the Tall Towers rises five miles to the north of our present station, and persists until its capture by Isil Skilte the archveult. Later in the 18th Aeon the sea returns. I hope that your sudden fascination with Middle-Earth geography has been satiated?"

"Quite so," said Rhialto. "I now issue the following orders, which must be implemented in most minute detail. Without stirring from your position, you will transfer me and my subaltern, Shalukhe the Swimmer, to a convenient moment during the latter 17th Aeon when the bed of the erstwhile Santune Sea is dry and ready to be searched for the Perciplex.

"Meanwhile you are explicitly ordered not to move from your present anchorage by so much as one inch, nor may you appoint substitute guardians, specifically and particularly Sarsem, to maintain the vigil while you deal with other business."

Osherl set up a weird moaning sound, which Rhialto ignored. "The Perciplex is under your foot at this moment; if it is not there when we return in the 17th Aeon, there can be only one party at fault: yourself. Therefore, guard well, with all obduracy. Allow neither Sarsem nor Hache-Moncour, nor any other, to hoodwink you and seduce you from your duty!

"We are now disposed to the transfer. Let there be no errors! The recovery of the true and original Perciplex, and its delivery to me, has become your responsibility! Many, many indenture points ride on the outcome of your work! So then: to the 17th Aeon!"

15

The pavilion now stood in the blaze of geranium-red sunlight. The sky was clear of clouds and overcast; the air felt warm, dry and carried a smoky-tart odor exhaled by a low-growing black bush. To the west the gleam of the retreating Santune Sea was yet visible, with a village of white cottages among low trees a half-mile away. In other directions the steppe spread away over the horizon.

At a distance of a hundred feet stood a small white cottage, with a massive black shairo tree rising high to each side. On the porch sat

Osherl, in the guise of a low-caste vagabond, or lack-wit with blinking eyes, sandy hair and upper teeth hanging foolishly over a receding chin. Osherl wore a soiled grown of coarse white cloth and a low flap-brimmed hat.

Taking note of Rhialto, Osherl waved a limp-fingered hand. "Ah Rhialto! After so long a vigil, even your face is welcome!"

Rhialto responded in a manner somewhat more cool. He surveyed the cottage. "You seem to have made yourself thoroughly comfortable. I hope that, in your ease, you have not neglected the security of the Perciplex?"

Osherl responded evenly: "My 'comfort,' as you put it, is primordial, and is basically designed to protect me from night-prowling beasts. I lack both silken couches and attentive subalterns."

"And the Perciplex?"

Osherl jerked his thumb toward a rusty iron post fifty yards away. "Directly under that post, at some unknown depth, lies the Perciplex."

Rhialto, surveying the area, noticed racks of empty flagons to the side of the cottage. "Mind you, I intend neither criticism nor scorn, but is it possible that you have taken to drink?"

"And if so, what then?" grumbled Osherl. "The vigil has been long. To vary the tedium, I compound tonics of various flavors which I sell to the villagers."

"Why did you not start an exploratory tunnel toward the Perciplex?"

"Need I explain? I feared that if I did so and found nothing, I would be forced to endure your reproaches, I decided to take no initiatives."

"What of, let us say, competing entities?"

"I have not been molested."

Rhialto's keen ear detected an almost imperceptible nicety of phrasing. He asked sharply: "Have either Sarsem or Hache-Moncour made their presence known?"

"To no significant degree, if any. They understand the importance of our work, and would not think to interfere."

"Just so. Might they have sunk a shaft at a distance, let us say, of ten miles, and driven a tunnel so that they came upon the Perciplex in a manner beyond your knowledge?"

"Impossible. I am not easily fooled. I arranged devices to signal all illicit incursions, either temporal, torsional, squalmaceous, or dimensional. The Perciplex is as before."

"Excellent. You may commence your excavation at once."

Osherl only made himself more comfortable in his chair. "First things first! This acreage is owned by a certain Um-Foad, resident at the village Az-Khaf, which you see yonder. He must be consulted before a single shovelful of dirt is turned. I suggest that you visit him at his home and make the arrangements. But first! Dress in garments like my own, to avoid ridicule.''

Dressed in accordance with Osherl's recommendations, Rhialto and Shalukhe sauntered off to Az-Khaf.

They discovered a neat village of stark white houses in gardens of enormous red sun-flowers.

Rhialto made inquiries and the two were directed to a house with windows of blue glass and a roof of blue tile. Standing in the street Rhialto called across the garden, until Um-Foad at last came out upon his porch: a man small and white-haired with a shrewd darting gaze and a fine mustache with sharply upturned points. He called out sharply: ''Who calls the name 'Um-Foad' and for what purpose? He may or may not be at home.''

''I am Rhialto, a student of antiquities. This is my assistant Shalukhe the Swimmer. Will you come here, or shall we go there, so that we need not shout?''

''Shout as loud as you like. I am only here to listen.''

Rhialto spoke in a quiet voice: ''I wish to speak of money.''

Um-Foad came bounding forward, mustache a-bristle. ''Speak up, sir! Did you mention money?''

''Perhaps you mis-heard me. We want to dig a hole on your land.''

''For what purpose, and how much will you pay?''

''More to the point: what will you pay us?'' demanded Rhialto. ''We are enhancing the value of your land.''

Um-Foad laughed scornfully. ''So that when I walk out by night, I fall in the hole and break my head? If you dig, you must pay! And you must pay once again for the refill! That is the first stipulation.''

''And the second?''

Um-Foad chuckled wisely and tapped the side of his nose. ''Do you take me for a fool? I know full well that valuable objects are buried on my land. If treasure is found, all belongs to me. If you dig, you acquire rights only in the hole.''

''Unreasonable! Is there a third stipulation?''

''There is indeed! The excavation contract must be tendered to my brother Um-Zuic. I will personally act as project supervisor. Further, all payments must be made in gold zikkos of recent mintage.''

Rhialto tried to argue, but Um-Foad proved to be a negotiator of great skill and in every important essential had his way with Rhialto.

As Rhialto and Shalukhe returned to the pavilion, she said: ''You are most generous in your dealings, or so it seems to me. Um-Foad is obsessively avaricious."

Rhialto agreed. "In the presence of money, Um-Foad is like a hunger-maddened shark. Still, why not allow the fellow his hour of pleasure? It is as easy to promise two hundred gold zikkos as a hundred."

"Rhialto, you are a kindly man!" said Shalukhe.

Um-Foad and his brother Um-Zuic brought a gang of labourers to Osherl's hut and commenced to dig a hole fifty feet in diameter at the spot designated by Osherl. The dirt excavated was sifted through a screen before the attentive scrutiny of Osherl, Rhialto, and Um-Foad.

Inch by inch, foot by foot, the hole sank into the old seabed, but not at a rate to suit Rhialto. At last he complained to Um-Foad: "What is wrong with the work-force? They saunter here and there; they laugh and gossip at the water-barrel; they stare into space for long periods. That old gaffer yonder, he moves so seldom that twice I have feared for his life."

Um-Foad made an easy response: "Come now, Rhialto! Do not forever be carping and chiding! These men are being paid handsomely by the hour. They are in no hurry to see the end of so noble an enterprise. As for the old man, he is my uncle Yaa-Yimpe, who suffers severe back pains, and is also deaf. Must he be penalized on this account? Let him enjoy the same perquisites as the others!"

Rhialto shrugged. "As you wish. Our contract encompasses situations of this sort."

"Eh? How so?"

"I refer to the section: 'Rhialto at his option may pay all charges on the basis of cubic footage removed from the hole. The amount of said payment shall be determined by the speed at which Rhialto, standing beside a pile of soft dirt with a stout shovel, can transfer ten cubic feet of said dirt to a new pile immediately adjacent.' "

Um-Foad cried out in consternation, and consulted the contract. "I do not remember including any such provision!"

"I added it as an afterthought," said Rhialto. "Perhaps you failed to notice."

Um-Foad darted away to exhort the workers. Grudgingly they bent to their shovels, and even old Yaa-Yimpe shifted his position from time to time.

As the hole grew deeper, the soil began to yield articles lost into the ancient sea from passing ships. Each of these items Um-Foad seized upon with quick fingers, then tried to sell them to Rhialto.

"Look now, Rhialto! We have here a true treasure, this earthenware mug, despite its broken handle! It represents the culmination of a free and unself-conscious art no longer practiced in the crass world of today."

Rhialto agreed. "A fine piece! It will grace the mantlepiece of your home and bring you hours of pleasure."

Um-Foad clicked his tongue in vexation. "Then this is not the object you are seeking?"

"Definitely not. Still, put it with the other articles you have salvaged and perhaps someday I will take the lot off your hands."

"Please, then, define for me exactly what you are seeking!" demanded Um-Foad. "If we knew, we could use a keener eye at the sifting table."

"And you could also put an exorbitant value upon this object if and when it comes to light."

Um-Foad showed Rhialto an unpleasantly avaricious grin. "My recourse is clear. I shall set large values on everything discovered."

Rhialto reflected a moment. "In that case, I too must alter my tactics."

During the noon-time rest-period, Rhialto addressed the workers. "I am pleased to see that the hole is sinking apace. The object I seek must now be near at hand. I will now describe it, so that all may work alertly, inasmuch as the man who finds this object will earn a bonus of ten golden zikkos in addition to his pay."

Um-Foad interjected a quick remark. "These gold zikkos, needless to say, are to be paid by Rhialto."

"Just so," said Rhialto. "Listen then! Are all attentive?" He glanced around the group and even deaf old Yaa-Yimpe seemed to sense the importance of the occasion. "We are seeking the Sacred Lantern which at one time graced the bow of the Cloud-king's Pleasure-barge. During a terrible storm, it was dislodged by a dart of blue lightning-ice, and toppled into the sea. So then: to whomever finds the lantern, ten golden zikkos! To whomever finds a fragment, a shatter, or even so much as a small prism of the blue lightning-ice I will pay a bonus of one gold zikko, in true coin; such a fragment will indicate to me that the Sacred Lantern is close at hand. Such a fragment, or shard, or prism, is recognizable by its blue lightning-like colour, and must instantly be brought to me for inspection. So now, to work, and with utmost vigilance for the blue lightning-ice, as this will lead us to our goal!"

Um-Foad gave the signal to return to work. "All hands to the shovels; let the work go at double-quick time! Heed well the words of Rhialto!''

A moment later Um-Foad took Rhialto aside. ''Since the subject has come up, you may now pay me an instalment of ten gold zikkos against my costs to date, along with another five zikkos in settlement of licensing fees. Let us say twenty gold zikkos in all.''

''Five must suffice.''

Um-Foad at last accepted the coins. ''I am puzzled by one of your phrases. You spoke to the workmen of 'one gold zikko, in true coin.' What, precisely, do you imply by use of the word 'true'?''

Rhialto made a negligent gesture. ''Merely a mode of speaking—a touch of hyperbole, if you will—to express our reverence for such a gold coin.''

''An interesting usage.'' said Um-Foad. ''Nevertheless, quite clear and commendable. . . . Now then! Who is this odd fellow, who comes sauntering across my property like Pululias, Friend of the Oak Trees?''

Rhialto looked around to where a tall handsome man with chestnut curls and graceful mannerisms stood casually inspecting the excavation. Rhialto said shortly: ''I know the gentleman slightly; he has probably come to pay his respects. Hache-Moncour! Are you not far from your usual haunts?''

''Yes, in some degree.'' Hache-Moncour turned away from the hole and approached. ''The excellent Sarsem mentioned that you were indulging your fancies in these parts and since I had a trifle of other business along the way, I decided to pay my respects. You have dug a fine hole yonder, though I cannot divine its purpose here in this reprehensible landscape.''

Um-Foad retorted sharply: ''Rhialto is a famous savant and student of antiquities; this landscape, of which you are making salutary use, is a parcel of my private acreage.''

''You must forgive me my trespass. I envy you a property so notable! Rhialto is indeed a scholar of wide fame. . . . I will be moving along. It has been pleasant chatting with you both.''

Hache-Moncour strolled off behind Osherl's cottage and disappeared from view.

''A most curious fellow!'' declared Um-Foad. ''Surely you do not number him among your intimates?''

''An acquaintance, only.''

From behind the shairo trees flanking Osherl's cottage floated an almost invisible bubble. Rhialto watched with a frown as the bubble drifted over the hole and hung motionless.

''Still,'' said Rhialto, ''Hache-Moncour is a man of sensitive perceptions and many extraordinary talents.''

''He was notably fast on his feet when I hinted at a fee for his trespass. Yes, what have we here?'' This to one of the diggers who had approached with an earthenware bowl. ''Rhialto, here is the lantern! I claim your reward.''

Rhialto examined the object. ''This is no lantern; it is a child's porridge bowl, no doubt flung overboard during a tantrum. Notice the quaint scenes depicted in the base of the bowl. Here we have a flantic flying to its lair with a baby gripped in its claws. Here a pouncing langomir devours a somewhat older child, while here, aboard this ship, a small girl is being dragged overboard by a parrot-headed sea-monster. An interesting find, but neither lightning-ice nor lantern.''

Rhialto handed the bowl to Um-Foad, then, glancing casually about, took note that the bubble had drifted directly overhead.

An hour after sunset, with an afterglow the color of persimmon still rimming the sky, Rhialto took Osherl aside. ''Who watches from the floating bubble? Is it Sarsem?''

''It is a madling, no more, with an eye illuminating a section of Hache-Moncour's vision, so that he may watch all that transpires.''

''Catch it in a net and put it into a box, so that Hache-Moncour may enjoy a good night's rest.''

''As you wish. . . . It is done.''

''And who watches us now, and who listens to us?''

''No one. We are alone.''

''Osherl, I wonder why you persist in your deceptions?''

Osherl spoke in a startled tone: ''What is it this time?''

''Today a bowl was brought from the hole. It had been thrown into the Santune Sea an epoch before the Perciplex was lost: so much I infer from the style of the ship and the nature of its rigging, and also from the animal species depicted in the decorations. Therefore, the stratum containing the Perciplex has already been mined. Still I lack the Perciplex! How do you explain this?''

''A curious situation, I readily admit,'' said Osherl in hearty tones. ''Let us examine the pit.''

''Bring light.''

Osherl and Rhialto went to the excavation and peered over the edge, with their lights illuminating the bottom. Osherl said: ''See there?'' With a beam of light he indicated an area to the side, near the circumference, which had been dug two feet deeper than the area at the center. ''That is the spot where the bowl was found: in a deeper section of the hole. Are you now satisfied?''

"Not yet. If that level predated the Perciplex, and all other levels have yielded nothing, then the Perciplex must now reside in that small hummock of dirt at the very center of the hole."

"So it would seem."

"Well then, Osherl, why are you waiting? Descend into the hole, take up shovel and dig, while I hold the light."

A figure came briskly out of the dusk. "Osherl? Rhialto? Why are you shining lights into my hole? Is this act not in default of our contract? Why, tonight of all nights, do you take these steps?"

"One night is much like another," said Rhialto. "Do you begrudge us our evening stroll, that we may breathe the cool fresh air?"

"Certainly not! Still, why do you equip yourselves with strong and vibrant lights?"

"Obviously, to avoid stumbling into holes and excavations! Already, as you have noted, the lights have served us well. Careful there, Osherl! Shine your light behind you! That is a thorn-bush into which you were backing."

"One cannot be too careful," said Osherl. "Rhialto, have you taken enough of the evening air?"

"Quite enough. Good night, Um-Foad."

"One moment! I want another instalment paid on your debt."

"Um-Foad, do you always work to such narrow margins? Here is another five gold zikkos. Be content for a period."

In the morning Rhialto was early at the sifting box, and scrutinized each load of dirt brought from the hole with special care. Um-Foad, taking note of Rhialto's attentiveness became even more officious, often pushing Rhialto aside so that he might be first to inspect the siftings. The workmen, observing Um-Foad's distraction, relaxed their efforts to such an extent that dirt arrived to the screen at ever longer intervals. Um-Foad at last took note of the situation and, running to the edge of the hole, set matters right. The workers, however, had lost the edge of their zeal. Yaa-Yimpe, complaining both of ague and lumbar spasms, refused to work under what he felt to be Rhialto's niggardly dispositions. Climbing from the hole, he returned to the village.

Somewhat later, a young man came running out from the village and accosted Rhialto. "Yaa-Yimpe is somewhat deaf; he did not understand that you had offered gold coins in exchange for blue lightning-ice. He now wishes to inform you that he found a fragment of the stuff today. You may entrust the reward to me, his grandson; Yaa-Yimpe is too tired to come out himself, and also he is planning a feast." The grandson, brisk and eager, with bright round eyes and a toothy grin, extended his hand.

Rhialto spoke crisply. "I must inspect this lightning-ice, to test its quality. Come, take me to Yaa-Yimpe."

The young man scowled. "He does not wish to be irked with details; give me the gold coins now, as well as my gratuity."

"Not another word!" thundered Rhialto. "At once! To the village!"

The young man sulkily led Rhialto to a house where festivities congratulating Yaa-Yimpe on the occasion of his reward were already in progress. Joints of meat turned on the spit and casks of wine had been broached. On a platform to the side six musicians played tankles, jigs and tyreens for the pleasure of the guests.

As Rhialto approached, Yaa-Yimpe himself, wearing only a pair of short loose pantaloons, emerged from the house. The company called out plaudits and the musicians struck up a lively quickstep. Yaa-Yimpe darted forward to dance a high-kicking saltarello, entailing quick rushing lunges back and forth, with thrust-forward belly shaking in double-time.

In his fervor Yaa-Yimpe jumped on the table, to perform a stamping arm-swinging hornpipe. Around his neck the Perciplex swung by a thong tied around its middle.

Yaa-Yimpe suddenly took note of Rhialto and jumped to the ground.

Rhialto spoke politely: "I am happy to find that your sufferings have been eased."

"True! Notice the lightning-ice! You may now give me the twenty gold zikkos."

Rhialto held out his hand. "Immediately, but let me inspect the prism!"

Hache-Moncour jumped forward from the side. "One moment! It is more appropriate that I take custody of this object! Here, sir! Your twenty gold zikkos!" Hache-Moncour flung the coins into Yaa-Yimpe's ready hand, snatched the Perciplex and strode to the side.

Rhialto made a convulsive motion forward but Hache-Moncour cried out: "Stand back, Rhialto! I must study the authenticity of this object!" He held the prism up to the light. "As I expected: a shameless hoax! Rhialto, we have been misled!" Hache-Moncour flung the prism to the ground, pointed his finger; the object broke into a hundred gouts of blue fire and was gone.

Rhialto stared numbly at the scorched ground. Hache-Moncour spoke in a kindly voice: "Seek elsewhere, Rhialto, if you are so minded; your work is truly useful! If you discover another arrant forgery, or even if you suspect as much, call on me again for advice. I bid you good-day.'' Hache-Moncour was gone as quickly as he had come, leaving Yaa-Yimpe and his guests staring open-mouthed.

Rhialto slowly returned to the excavation. Osherl stood in front of his hut, looking pensively off into the sky. Shalukhe the Swimmer sat cross-legged on a rug before the pavilion, eating grapes. Um-Foad came at the run from the excavation. ''Rhialto, what are all these rumors?''

''I have no time for rumors,'' said Rhialto. ''Still, you may now halt the digging.''

''So soon? What of the Cloud-king's lantern?''

''I begin to think it a myth. I must return to study my references.''

''In that case, I demand the full balance of what you owe.''

''Certainly,'' said Rhialto. ''Where is your invoice?''

''I have prepared no formal document. The due amount, however, is fifty-two golden zikkos.''

''Highly exorbitant!'' cried Rhialto. ''Have you not miscalculated?''

''I include the use and enjoyment of my land, by day and by night; labor costs, in both digging and refilling the hole; re-landscaping and re-planting the site; my own fees, both as supervisor and consultant; certain honorariums due the civic functionaries; imposts and—''

Rhialto held up his hand. ''You have already told me more than I care to hear. For my part, I want only the porridge bowl, for a souvenir.''

Um-Foad's mustaches bristled anew. ''Can you be serious? That is a valuable antique, worth at least ten zikkos!''

''Whatever you say.''

Um-Foad found the porridge bowl and tendered it to Rhialto. ''Now then, my money, and let there be no mistakes in the tally.''

Rhialto passed over a satchel. Um-Foad counted the contents with satisfaction. He rose to his feet. ''I take it that you are now vacating the premises?''

''Almost immediately.''

''My fees resume at Midnight.'' Um-Foad gave a crisp signal of farewell, then striding to the pit, called up the workers and the group returned to the village.

The geranium-red sun floated down the western sky. With the cessation of activity the site seemed unnaturally quiet. Rhialto stood in contemplation of the pit. Shalukhe the Swimmer lazed on the rug before the pavilion. Osherl stood in the entrance to his cottage, looking off across the landscape with a somewhat moony expression.

Rhialto heaved a deep sigh and turned to Osherl: "Well then, I am waiting to hear what you have to say."

Osherl's eyes went unfocused. "Ah yes . . . I am happy to hear that Yaa-Yimpe has recovered his health."

"Is that all? You are curiously placed. Have you no word in regard to the Perciplex?"

Osherl scratched his cheek. "Did you not come to agreement with Yaa-Yimpe?"

"Why should I bother, when he held a patently false version of the Perciplex?"

"Indeed? How could even Rhialto make so definite a finding, when he never so much as laid hands on the object?"

Rhialto shook his head sadly. "My dear fellow, you yourself certified the object as brummagem when you allowed it to be found in the same stratum as the porridge bowl."

"Not at all! You yourself saw how the area of the porridge bowl was well below the central knob which yielded the Perciplex."

"Exactly so: the same levels, when they should have been six feet or more apart."

"Hmmf," said Osherl. "Somewhere you have made errors. One cannot judge important matters on the basis of porridge bowls."

"In sheer point of fact, you and Sarsem were careless, though I am sure you enjoyed your trick, chuckling and nudging each other in the ribs as you envisioned poor Rhialto's distress."

Osherl, stung, cried out: "Error once again! The arrangements were made in all dignity! Also, your theories lack proof. The bowl may imitate the early style, or it might have been preserved exactly one epoch and then thrown into the sea!"

"Osherl, you walk the very brink of absurdity. My so-called theories stand on two legs: first, logical deduction; and second, simple observation. The object which you allowed Yaa-Yimpe to find admittedly resembled the Perciplex—in fact enough to deceive Hache-Moncour. But not me."

Osherl blinked in puzzlement. "How are your eyes so keen and Hache-Moncour's so dull?"

"I am not only wise and just; I am intelligent. Hache-Moncour boasts only a low animal cunning scarcely superior to your own."

"You are still telling me nothing."

"Have you no eyes? The false object dangled on a thong around Yaa-Yimpe's neck—at the horizontal. The true Perciplex holds itself forever upright, so that its sacred text may never be misread. Hache-

Moncour paid no heed, and I am grateful for his vulgar haste. So now, what have you to say?''

''I must give the matter thought.''

''Two questions remain. First: who has the Perciplex, you or Sarsem? Second: how will you and Sarsem be at once rewarded for your services and punished for your faithlessness?''

''The former far outweigh the latter, at least in my case,'' said Osherl. ''As for Sarsem, who was so adroitly gulled by Hache-Moncour, I will make no recommendations.''

''And the Perciplex?''

''Ah! That is a delicate subject, which I am not free to discuss before unauthorized ears.''

''What?'' cried Rhialto in outrage. ''You include me in this category, when Ildefonse specifically placed you under my orders?''

''Subject to the limits of common sense.''

''Very well! We will lay the facts before Ildefonse at Boumergarth, and I hope that I may restrain all prejudice in my report. Still, I must take note of your sullen obduracy, which can only add aeons to your indenture.''

Osherl blinked and winced, ''Is is truly so important? Well then, I can offer a hint. Hache-Moncour and Sarsem devised the plan as a joke. I instantly pointed out the serious nature of this matter, and gave Yaa-Yimpe a false crystal.'' Osherl uttered a nervous laugh. ''Sarsem of course retained possession of the true Perciplex, and his guilt far outweighs mine.''

At the pavilion Shalukhe the Swimmer jumped to her feet. ''I hear a great tumult from the village. . . . It sounds like men shouting in rage, and it seems to be growing louder.''

Rhialto listened. ''I expect that Hache-Moncour's gold zikkos have become bull-frogs or acorns, or perhaps my payments to Um-Foad have altered prematurely. . . . In any event, it is time we were moving on. Osherl, we will now return to Boumergarth, at a time one minute subsequent to our departure.''

16

In response to Ildefonse's urgent summons, the magicians assembled in the Great Hall at Boumergarth. Only Rhialto appeared to be absent from the conclave, but no one mentioned his name.

Ildefonse sat silently in his massive chair behind the podium, head bowed so that his yellow beard rested on his folded arms. The other magicians conversed in subdued voices, glancing from time to time toward Ildefonse and discussing the purported purpose of the meeting.

The moments passed, one by one, and still Ildefonse sat in silence. Other small conversations around the room gradually quieted, and all sat looking toward Ildefonse wondering at his reason for delay. . . . At last Ildefonse, perhaps at the receipt of a signal, stirred himself and spoke, in a voice of gravity.

"Noble magicians: the occasion today is momentous! In full panoply of reason and wisdom we must consider issues of importance.

"Our business is unusual, even unprecedented. To forestall any intrusions, I have arranged a web of impermeability around Boumergarth. There is a consequential inconvenience, to the effect that, while no one can enter to disturb us, neither can anyone depart, neither forward nor backward, nor thither nor yon."

Hurtiancz, with his usual asperity, called out: "Why these unique precautions? I am not one for stays and restrictions; I must inquire the reason why I should be thus pent!"

"I have already explained my motives," said Ildefonse. "In short, I wish neither entries nor exits during our discussions."

"Proceed," said Hurtiancz in clipped tones. "I will restrain my impatience as best I can."

"To establish a basis for my remarks, I advert to the authority of Phandaal, the Grand Master of our art. His admonitions are stern and direct, and form the theoretical background to the protocol by which we rule our conduct. Here, naturally, I refer to the Blue Principles."

Hache-Moncour called out: "Truly, Ildefonse, your periods, while resonant, are somewhat protracted. I suggest that you get on with the business of the day. I believe you mentioned that new discoveries compel a redistribution of Rhialto's properties. May I ask, then, what new articles have appeared, and what may be their quality?"

"You anticipate me!" rumbled Ildefonse. "Still, since the subject has been broached, I trust that everyone has brought with him the full tally of those effects awarded him and distributed after Rhialto's trial? Has everyone done so? No? In all candour, I expected not much else. . . . Well then—where was I? I believe that I had just paid my respects to Phandaal."

"True," said Hache-Moncour. "Now, describe the new findings, if you will. Where, for instance, were they secreted?"

Ildefonse held up his hand. "Patience, Hache-Moncour! Do you recall the chain of events which stemmed from the impulsive conduct of Hurtiancz at Falu? He tore Rhialto's copy of the Blue Principles, thus prompting Rhialto to take legal action."

"I recall the situation perfectly: a tempest in a tea-pot, or so it seems to me."

A tall figure wearing black trousers, a loose black blouse and a loose black cap pulled low, moved forward from the shadows. "It does not seem so to me," said the man in black and moved back into the shadows.

Ildefonse paid him no heed. "If only from a theoretical point of view, this case absorbs our interest. Rhialto was the plaintiff; the group now assembled are the defendants. As Rhialto stated his case, the issues were simple. The Blue, so he claimed, declared that any purposeful alteration or destruction of the Monstrament or obvious and ostensible copy thereof, constituted a crime, punishable at minimum by a fine equal to three times the value of any wrongful losses sustained; at maximum, total confiscation. Such was Rhialto's contention, and he brought forward the torn copy both as evidence of the crime and as his documentation of the law itself.

"The defendants, led by Hache-Moncour, Hurtiancz, Gilgad and others, decried the charges as not only artificial but also a wrongful act in themselves. Rhialto's action, so they claim, formed the substance of a counter-action. To support this position, Hache-Moncour and the others took us to Fader's Waft, and where we examined the Monstrament there projected, and where Hache-Moncour asserted, and now I paraphrase, that any attempt to present a damaged, mutilated or purposefully altered copy of the Monstrament is in itself a crime of major consequence.

"Hache-Moncour and his group argue, therefore, that in presenting the damaged copy of the Blue as evidence, Rhialto committed a crime which must be adjudicated even before his own charges can be considered. They argue that Rhialto is clearly guilty, and that not only are his charges moot, but that the only real issue becomes the degree of Rhialto's punishment."

Ildefonse here paused and looked from face to face. "Have I fairly stated the case?"

"Quite so," said Gilgad. "I doubt if you will find dissent anywhere. Rhialto has long been a thorn in our side."

Vermoulian spoke. "I do not favor Forlorn Encystment* for Rhialto; I say, let him live out his days as a salamander, or a Gangue River lizard."

Ildefonse cleared his throat. "Before passing sentence—or, for

*The spell of Forlorn Encystment operates to bury that luckless individual subject to the spell in a capsule forty-five miles below the surface of the earth.

that matter, before arriving at a judgment—there are certain odd facts to be considered. First of all, let me ask this question: how many here have consulted their own copies of the Blue Principles in connection with this case? . . . What? No one?''

Dulce-Lolo gave a light laugh. ''It is hardly necessary; am I not right? After all, we made that chilly and inconvenient visit to Fader's Waft for that very purpose.''

''Just so,'' said Ildefonse. ''Peculiarly, my recollection of the passage accorded with Rhialto's torn copy, rather than that at Fader's Waft.''

''The mind plays peculiar tricks,'' said Hache-Moncour. ''Now then, Ildefonse, in order to accelerate a possibly tedious—''

''In a moment,'' said Ildefonse. ''First, let me add that I referred to my personal copy of the Blue, and discovered that the text duplicated that placed in evidence by Rhialto.''

The room became silent, with the stillness of bewilderment. Then Hurtiancz made a vehement gesture. ''Bah! Why ensnare ourselves in subtleties? Rhialto irrefutably committed the crime, as defined by the Perciplex. What more is there to be said?''

''Only this! As our esteemed colleague Hache-Moncour has pointed out, the mind plays strange tricks. Is it possible that the other night we were all victims of mass hallucination? If you recall, we found the projection unaccountably turned upside-down, which had a very confusing effect, certainly upon me.''

Once more the figure in black stepped forward from the shadows. ''Most especially when the Perciplex will not allow itself to be altered from the upright position, for fear of just such a consequence.''

The dark shape returned to the shadows, and as before both he and his words were ignored as if non-existent.

Hache-Moncour said weightily: ''Could this entire group, all keen observers, have witnessed the same hallucination? I tend to scout such a possibility.''

''I also!'' cried Hurtiancz. ''I have never hallucinated!''

Ildefonse said: ''Nevertheless, in my capacity as Preceptor, I hereby rule that we now transfer ourselves into my whirl-away, which is also enwebbed to protect us from nuisance, and visit Fader's Waft, so that we may settle the matter once and for all.''

''As you like,'' said Dulce-Lolo peevishly. ''But why this elaborate system of webs and screens? If no one can molest us, neither can any of us go off about his business should, for instance, a sudden emergency develop at his manse.''

"True," said Ildefonse. "Precisely so. This way then, if you please."

Only the man in black who sat in the shadows remained behind.

17

The whirlaway flew high through the red light of afternoon: south across Ascolais to a set of soft swelling hills and at last settled upon Fader's Waft.

From the whirlaway to the six-sided fane extended an arch of web: "—lest archveults seize upon this opportunity to expunge all of us together!" So Ildefonse explained the precaution.

Into the enclosure filed the group, with Ildefonse bringing up the rear. As always, the Perciplex rested upon its cushion of black satin. In a chair to the side sat a man-shaped creature white of skin and white of eye, with a soft fluff of pink feathers for hair.

"Ah Sarsem," said Ildefonse in a hearty voice. "How goes the vigil?"

"All is well," said Sarsem in a glum voice.

"No difficulties? Neither incursions nor excursions since I saw you last? All is in order?"

"The vigil proceeds unmarred by incident."

"Good!" declared Ildefonse. "Now let us examine the projection. Possibly it confused us before, and this time we will all look closely and make no mistakes. Sarsem, the projection!"

Upon the wall flashed the Blue Principles. Ildefonse chortled with delight. "Precisely so! As I declared, we were all confused together—even the redoubtable Hurtiancz, who now reads the Monstrament for a third and decisive time. Hurtiancz! Be kind enough to read the passage aloud!"

Tonelessly Hurtiancz read: " 'Any person who knowingly and purposefully alters, mutilates, destroys or secretes the Blue Principles or any copy thereof is guilty of a crime, and likewise in equal measure his conspirators, punishable by the measures described in Schedule D. If said acts are committed in the progress of an unlawful act, or for unlawful purposes, the penalties shall be those described in Schedule G.' "

Ildefonse turned to Hache-Moncour, who stood with bulging eyes and sagging jaw. "So there you are, Hache-Moncour! I was right after all and now you must acknowledge as much."

Hache-Moncour muttered abstractedly: "Yes, yes; so it seems."

He turned a long frowning glance toward Sarsem, who avoided his gaze.

"So much is now settled!" declared Ildefonse. "Let us return to Boumergarth and proceed with our inquiry."

Hache-Moncour said sulkily: "I am not well. Raise your web so that I may return to my manse."

"Impossible!" said Ildefonse. "All must be present during the deliberations. If you recall, we are trying a case against Rhialto."

"But there is no longer a case against Rhialto!" bleated Byzant the Necrope. "The proceedings are now devoid of interest! We must go home to look to our properties!"

"To Boumergarth, all!" thundered Ildefonse. "I will brook no further reluctance!"

With poor grace the magicians trooped to the whirlaway and sat in silence during the return flight. Three times Hache-Moncour raised a finger as if to address Ildefonse, but each time caught himself and held his tongue.

At Boumergarth the magicians filed glumly into the Great Hall and took their places. In the shadows stood the man in black, as if he had never moved.

Ildefonse spoke: "We now resume consideration of the action brought by Rhialto and its counter-action. Are there any opinions to be heard?"

The chamber was silent.

Ildefonse turned to the man in black. "Rhialto, what have you to say?"

"I have stated my case against Hurtiancz and his conspirators. I now await resolution of the action."

Ildefonse said: "The persons present are divided into two categories: Rhialto, the plaintiff, and the defendants who number all the rest of us. In such a case we can only go for guidance to the Blue, and there can be no question as to the findings. Rhialto, as Preceptor, I declare that you have fairly proved your case. I declare that you are entitled to recover your sequestered goods and a stipulated penalty."

Rhialto came forward to lounge against the lectern. "I have won a sad and profitless victory, against persons whom I deemed my lesser or greater friends."

Rhialto looked around the room. Few returned his gaze. In a flat voice Rhialto continued: "The victory has not been easy. I have known toil, fear, and disappointment. Nevertheless, I do not intend to grind home my advantage. I make the same demand upon each of you, save in one case only: return all my sequestered property to Falu, with the addition of a single IOUN stone from each as penalty.''

Ao of the Opals said: ''Rhialto, your act is both generous and wise. Naturally you have won little popularity with your victory; in fact, I notice both Hurtiancz and Zilifant grinding their teeth. Still, you have incurred no new enmity. I admit my mistake; I accept the penalty and will pay you an IOUN stone with humility. I urge my fellows to do the same.''

Eshmiel cried out: ''Well spoken, Ao! I share your sentiments. Rhialto, who is the one person whom you except from the penalty and why do you do so?''

''I except Hache-Moncour, whose actions cannot be excused. By his attack upon our law he attacked us all; you are his victims no less than I, though your sufferings would be yet to come.

''Hache-Moncour must lose all his magic, and all his capacity for magic. This effect was worked upon him by Ildefonse as I spoke to you. The Hache-Moncour you see yonder is not the same man who stood here an hour ago, and even now Ildefonse is calling his servants. They will take him down to the local tannery, where he will be afforded suitable employment.

''As for me, tomorrow I return to Falu, where my life will continue more or less as before, or so I hope.''

18

Shalukhe the swimmer sat beside the River Ts under the blue aspens which grew along the banks and partly screened Falu from sight. Rhialto, with his household restored to order, came out to join her. She turned her head, took note of his approach, then returned to her contemplation of the river.

Rhialto seated himself nearby and, leaning back, watched the shiver of dark sunlight along the moving water. Presently he turned his head and studied first the delicate profile, then the graceful disposition of her body. Today she wore sand-coloured trousers fitted close at the ankles, loose around the hips, black slippers, a white shirt and a black sash. A red ribbon confined her dark hair. In her own time, reflected Rhialto, she had been a Paragon of Excellence, the Best of the Best, and now who would ever know?

She became aware of his inspection and turned him a questioning glance.

Rhialto spoke. ''Shalukhe the Swimmer, Furud Dawn-thing: what shall be done with you?''

The Paragon returned to her contemplation of the river. ''I too wonder what to do with myself.''

Rhialto raised his eyebrows. ''Admittedly this era, the last to be known on the world Earth, is in many ways dark and disturbing. Still, you want nothing; you are irked by no enemies; you are free to come and go as you wish. What then troubles you?''

Shalukhe the Swimmer shrugged. ''I would seem captious were I to complain. Your conduct has been courteous; you have treated me with both dignity and generosity. But I am alone. I have watched you at your colloquy, and I was minded of a group of crocodiles basking on a Kuyike River mud-bank.''

Rhialto winced. ''I as well?''

Shalukhe, preoccupied with her own musings, ignored the remark. ''At the Court of the East-Rising Moon I was Paragon, the Best of the Best! Gentlemen of rank came eagerly to touch my hand; when I passed, my perfume evoked sighs of wistful passion and sometimes, after I passed, I heard muffled exclamations, which I took to signify admiration. Here I am shunned as if I were the Worst of the Worst; no one cares whether I leave a perfume in my wake or the odor of a pig-sty. I have become gloomy and full of doubts. Am I so bland, dull and tiresome that I instill apathy everywhere I go?''

Rhialto leaned back in his seat and stared toward the sky. ''Absurdity! Mirage! Dream-madness!''

Shalukhe smiled a tremulous bitter-sweet smile. ''If you had treated me shamefully, and ravished me to your desires, at least I would have been left with my pride. Your courteous detachment leaves me with nothing.''

Rhialto at last found his voice. ''You are the most perverse of all maidens! How often my hands have tingled and twitched to seize you; always I have held back so that you might feel secure and easy! And now you accuse me of cold blood and call me a crocodile! My graceful and poetic restraint you choose to regard as senile disability. It is I who should feel the pangs!''

Jumping to his feet, Rhialto went to sit beside her; he took her hands. ''The most beautiful maidens are also the most cruel! Even now you use a subtle means to rack my emotions!''

''Oh? Tell me, so that I may do it again.''

''You are troubled because I seemed to ignore your presence. But, by this reasoning, you would feel equally diminished in your pride had the man been Dulce-Lolo with his expressive feet, or Zilifant, or even Byzant the Necrope. That it was I, Rhialto, who treated you so shabbily seems to be incidental! My own vanity now torments me; am I then so unappealing? Do you feel not the slightest regard for me?''

Shalukhe the Swimmer at last smiled. ''Rhialto, I will say this: were you Dulce-Lolo, or Zilifant, or Byzant, or any other than Rhialto, I would not be sitting here holding your hands so tightly in my own.''

Rhialto sighed in relief. He drew her close; their faces met. ''Confusions and cross-purposes: they are now resolved; perhaps the 21st Aeon now seems a less dismal time.''

Shalukhe looked sidelong toward the sun where it hung low over the River Ts. ''To a certain extent. Still, what if the sun goes out even while we sit here: what then?''

Rhialto rose to his feet and pulled her up after him; he kissed the upturned face. ''Who knows? The sun may totter and lurch still another hundred years!''

The maiden sighed and pointed. ''Ah! Notice how it blinks! It seems tired and troubled! But perhaps it will enjoy a restful night.''

Rhialto whispered a comment into her ear, to the effect that she should not expect the same. She gave his arm a tug, and the two, close together, walked slowly back to Falu.

3

Morreion

1

The archveult Xexamedes, digging gentian roots in Were Woods, became warm with exertion. He doffed his cloak and returned to work, but the glint of blue scales was noticed by Herark the Harbinger and the diabolist Shrue. Approaching by stealth they leapt forth to confront the creature. Then, flinging a pair of nooses about the supple neck, they held him where he could do no mischief.

After great effort, a hundred threats and as many lunges, twists and charges on the part of Xexamedes, the magicians dragged him to the castle of Ildefonse, where other magicians of the region gathered in high excitement.

In times past Ildefonse had served the magicians as preceptor and he now took charge of the proceedings. He first inquired the archveult's name.

"I am Xexamedes, as well you know, old Ildefonse!"

"Yes," said Ildefonse, "I recognize you now, though my last view was your backside, as we sent you fleeting back to Jangk. Do you realize that you have incurred death by returning?"

"Not so, Ildefonse, since I am no longer an archveult of Jangk. I am an immigrant to Earth; I declare myself reverted to the estate of a man. Even my fellows hold me in low esteem."

"Well and good," said Ildefonse. "However, the ban was and is explicit. Where do you now house yourself?" The question was casual, and Xexamedes made an equally bland response.

"I come, I go; I savor the sweet airs of Earth, so different from the chemical vapors of Jangk."

Ildefonse was not to be put off. "What appurtenances did you bring: specifically, how many IOUN stones?"

"Let us talk of other matters," suggested Xexamedes. "I now wish to join your local coterie, and, as a future comrade to all present, I find these nooses humiliating."

The short-tempered Hurtiancz bellowed, "Enough impudence! What of the IOUN stones?"

"I carry a few such trinkets," replied Xexamedes with dignity.

"Where are they?"

Xexamedes addressed himself to Ildefonse. "Before I respond, may I inquire your ultimate intentions?"

Ildefonse pulled at his yellow beard and raised his eyes to the chandelier. "Your fate will hinge upon many factors. I suggest that you produce the IOUN stones."

"They are hidden under the floorboards of my cottage," said Xexamedes in a sulky voice.

"Which is situated where?"

"At the far edge of Were Woods."

Rhialto the Marvellous leapt to his feet. "All wait here! I will verify the truth of the statement!"

The sorcerer Gilgad held up both arms. "Not so fast! I know the region exactly! I will go!"

Ildefonse spoke in a neutral voice. "I hereby appoint a committee to consist of Rhialto, Gilgad, Mune the Mage, Hurtiancz, Kilgas, Ao of the Opals, and Barbanikos. This group will go to the cottage and bring back all contraband. The proceedings are adjourned until your return."

2

The adjuncts of Xexamedes were in due course set forth on a sideboard in Ildefonse's great hall, including thirty-two IOUN stones: spheres, ellipsoids, spindles, each approximately the size of a small plum, each displaying inner curtains of pale fire. A net prevented them from drifting off like dream-bubbles.

"We now have a basis for further investigation," said Ildefonse. "Xexamedes, exactly what is the source of these potent adjuncts?"

Xexamedes jerked his tall black plumes in surprise, either real or simulated. He was yet constrained by the two nooses. Haze of Wheary Water held one rope, Barbanikos the other, to ensure that Xexamedes could touch neither. Xexamedes inquired, "What of the indomitable Morreion? Did he not reveal his knowledge?"

Ildefonse frowned in puzzlement. " 'Morreion?' I had almost forgotten the name . . . What were the circumstances?"

Herark the Harbinger, who knew lore of twenty aeons, stated: "After the archveults were defeated, a contract was made. The archveults were given their lives, and in turn agreed to divulge the source of the IOUN stones. The noble Morreion was ordered forth to learn the secret and was never heard from since."

"He was instructed in all the procedures," declared Xexamedes. "If you wish to learn—seek out Morreion!"

Ildefonse asked, "Why did he not return?"

"I cannot say. Does anyone else wish to learn the source of the stones? I will gladly demonstrate the procedure once again."

For a moment no one spoke. Then Ildefonse suggested, "Gilgad, what of you? Xexamedes has made an interesting proposal."

Gilgad licked his thin brown lips. "First, I wish a verbal description of the process."

"By all means," said Xexamedes. "Allow me to consult a document." He stepped toward the sideboard, drawing Haze and Barbanikos together; then he leaped back. With the slack thus engendered he grasped Barbanikos and exuded a galvanic impulse. Sparks flew from Barbanikos' ears; he jumped into the air and fell down in a faint. Xexamedes snatched the rope from Haze and before anyone could prevent him, he fled from the great hall.

"After him!" bawled Ildefonse. "He must not escape!"

The magicians gave chase to the fleet archveult. Across the Scaum hills, past Were Woods ran Xexamedes; like hounds after a fox came the magicians. Xexamedes entered Were Woods and doubled back, but the magicians suspected a trick and were not deceived.

Leaving the forest Xexamedes approached Rhialto's manse and took cover beside the aviary. The bird-women set up an alarm and old Funk, Rhialto's servitor, hobbled forth to investigate.

Gilgad now spied Xexamedes and exerted his Instantaneous Electric Effort—a tremendous many-pronged dazzle which not only shivered Xexamedes but destroyed Rhialto's aviary, shattered his antique way-post and sent poor old Funk dancing across the sward on stilts of crackling blue light.

3

A linden leaf clung to the front door of Rhialto's manse, pinned by a thorn. A prank of the wind, thought Rhialto, and brushed it aside. His new servant Puiras, however, picked it up and, in a hoarse grumbling voice, read:

NOTHING THREATENS MORREION.

''What is this regarding Morreion?'' demanded Rhialto. Taking the leaf he inspected the minute silver characters. ''A gratuitous reassurance.'' A second time he discarded the leaf and gave Puiras his final instructions. ''At midday prepare a meal for the Minuscules—gruel and tea will suffice. At sunset serve out the thrush pâté. Next, I wish you to scour the tile of the great hall. Use no sand, which grinds at the luster of the glaze. Thereafter, clear the south sward of debris; you may use the aeolus, but take care; blow only down the yellow reed; the black reed summons a gale, and we have had devastation enough. Set about the aviary; salvage all useful material. If you find corpses, deal with them appropriately. Is so much clear?''

Puiras, a man spare and loose-jointed, with a bony face and lank black hair, gave a dour nod. ''Except for a single matter. When I have accomplished all this, what else?''

Rhialto, drawing on his cloth-of-gold gauntlets, glanced sidewise at his servant. Stupidity? Zeal? Churlish sarcasm? Puiras' visage offered no clue. Rhialto spoke in an even voice. ''Upon completion of these tasks, your time is your own. Do not tamper with the magical engines; do not, for your life, consult the portfolios, the librams or the compendiary. In due course, I may instruct you in a few minor dints; until then, be cautious!''

''I will indeed.''

Rhialto adjusted his six-tiered black satin hat, donned his cloak with that flourish which had earned him his soubriquet ''the Marvellous.'' ''I go to visit Ildefonse. When I pass the outer gate impose the boundary curse; under no circumstances lift it until I signal. Expect me at sunset: sooner, if all goes well.''

Making no effort to interpret Puiras' grunt, Rhialto sauntered to the north portal, averting his eyes from the wreckage of his wonderful aviary. Barely had he passed the portal by, when Puiras activated the curse, prompting Rhialto to jump hastily forward. Rhialto adjusted the set of his hat. The ineptitude of Puiras was but one in a series of misfortunes, all attributable to the archveult Xexamedes. His aviary destroyed, the way-post shattered, old Funk dead! From some source compensation must be derived!

4

Idefonse lived in a castle above the River Scaum: a vast and complex structure of a hundred turrets, balconies, elevated pavilions and pleasaunces. During the final ages of the 21st Aeon, when Ildefonse had served as preceptor, the castle had seethed with activity. Now only a single wing of this monstrous edifice was in use, with the rest abandoned to dust, owls and archaic ghosts.

Ildefonse met Rhialto at the bronze portal. "My dear colleague, splendid as usual! Even on an occasion like that of today! You put me to shame!" Ildefonse stood back the better to admire Rhialto's austerely handsome visage, his fine blue cloak and trousers of rose velvet, his glossy boots. Ildefonse himself, for reasons obscure, presented himself in the guise of a jovial sage, with a bald pate, a lined countenance, pale blue eyes, an irregular yellow beard—conceivably a natural condition which vanity would not let him discard.

"Come in, then," cried Ildefonse. "As always, with your sense of drama, you are last to arrive!"

They proceeded to the great hall. On hand were fourteen sorcerers: Zilifant, Perdustin, Herark the Harbinger, Haze of Wheary Water, Ao of the Opals, Eshmiel, Kilgas, Byzant the Necrope, Gilgad, Vermoulian the Dream-walker, Barbanikos, the diabolist Shrue, Mune the Mage, Hurtiancz. Ildefonse called out, "The last of our cabal has arrived: Rhialto the Marvellous, at whose manse the culminating stroke occurred!"

Rhialto doffed his hat to the group. Some returned the salute; others: Gilgad, Byzant the Necrope, Mune the Mage, Kilgas, merely cast cool glances over their shoulders.

Ildefonse took Rhialto by the arm and led him to the buffet. Rhialto accepted a goblet of wine, which he tested with his amulet.

In mock chagrin Ildefonse protested: "The wine is sound; have you yet been poisoned at my board?"

"No. But never have circumstances been as they are today."

Ildefonse made a sign of wonder. "The circumstances are favorable! We have vanquished our enemy; his IOUN stones are under our control!"

"True," said Rhialto. "But remember the damages I have suffered! I claim corresponding benefits, of which my enemies would be pleased to deprive me."

"Tush," scolded Ildefonse. "Let us talk on a more cheerful note. How goes the renewal of your way-post? The Minuscules carve with zest?"

"The work proceeds," Rhialto replied. "Their tastes are by no means coarse. For this single week their steward has required two ounces of honey, a gill of Misericord, a dram and a half of malt spirits, all in addition to biscuit, oil and a daily ration of my best thrush pâté."

Ildefonse shook his head in disapproval. "They become ever more splendid, and who must pay the score? You and I. So the world goes." He turned away to refill the goblet of the burly Hurtiancz.

"I have made investigation," said Hurtiancz ponderously, "and I find that Xexamedes had gone among us for years. He seems to have been a renegade, as unwelcome on Jangk as on Earth."

"He may still be the same," Ildefonse pointed out. "Who found his corpse? No one! Haze here declares that electricity to an archveult is like water to a fish."

"This is the case," declared Haze of Wheary Water, a hot-eyed wisp of a man.

"In that event, the damage done to my property becomes more irresponsible than ever!" cried Rhialto. "I demand compensation before any other general adjustments are made."

Hurtiancz frowned. "I fail to comprehend your meaning."

"It is elegantly simple," said Rhialto. "I suffered serious damage; the balance must be restored. I intend to claim the IOUN stones."

"You will find yourself one among many," said Hurtiancz.

Haze of Wheary Water gave a sardonic snort. "Claim as you please."

Mune the Mage came forward. "The archveult is barely dead; must we bicker so quickly?"

Eshmiel asked, "Is he dead after all? Observe this!" He displayed a linden leaf. "I found it on my blue tile kurtivan. It reads, 'NOTHING THREATENS MORREION.' "

"I also found such a leaf!" declared Haze.

"And I!" said Hurtiancz.

"How the centuries roll, one past the other!" mused Ildefonse. "Those were the days of glory, when we sent the archveults flitting like a band of giant bats! Poor Morreion! I have often puzzled as to his fate."

Eshmiel frowned down at his leaf. " 'NOTHING THREATENS MORREION'—so we are assured. If such is the case, the notice would seem superfluous and over-helpful."

"It is quite clear," Gilgad grumbled. "Morreion went forth to learn the source of the IOUN stones; he did so, and now is threatened by nothing."

"A possible interpretation," said Ildefonse in a pontifical voice. "There is certainly more here than meets the eye."

"It need not trouble us now," said Rhialto. "To the IOUN stones in present custody, however, I now put forward a formal claim, as compensation for the damage I took in the common cause."

"The statement has a specious plausibility," remarked Gilgad. "Essentially, however, each must benefit in proportion to his contribution. I do not say this merely because it was my Instantaneous Electric Effort which blasted the archveult."

Ao of the Opals said sharply, "Another casuistic assumption which must be rejected out-of-hand, especially since the providential energy allowed Xexamedes to escape!"

The argument continued an hour. Finally a formula proposed by Ildefonse was put to vote and approved by a count of fifteen to one. The goods formerly owned by the archveult Xexamedes were to be set out for inspection. Each magician would list the items in order of choice; Ildefonse would collate the lists. Where conflict occurred determination must be made by lot. Rhialto, in recognition of his loss, was granted a free selection after choice five had been determined; Gilgad was accorded the same privilege after choice ten.

Rhialto made a final expostulation: "What value to me is choice five? The archveult owned nothing but the stones, a few banal adjuncts and these roots, herbs and elixirs."

His views carried no weight. Ildefonse distributed sheets of paper; each magician listed the articles he desired; Ildefonse examined each list in turn. "It appears," he said, "that all present declare their first choice to be the IOUN stones."

Everyone glanced toward the stones; they winked and twinkled with pale white fire.

"Such being the case," said Ildefonse, "determination must be made by chance."

He set forth a crockery pot and sixteen ivory disks. "Each will indite his sign upon one of the chips and place it into the pot, in this fashion." Ildefonse marked one of the chips, dropped it into the pot. "When all have done so, I will call in a servant who will bring forth a single chip."

"A moment!" exclaimed Byzant. "I apprehend mischief; it walks somewhere near."

Ildefonse turned the sensitive Necrope a glance of cold inquiry. "To what mischief do you refer?"

"I detect a contradiction, a discord; something strange walks among us; there is someone here who should not be here."

''Someone moves unseen!'' cried Mune the Mage. ''Ildefonse, guard the stones!''

Ildefonse peered here and there through the shadowy old hall. He made a secret signal and pointed to a far corner: ''Ghost! Are you on hand?''

A soft sad whisper said, ''I am here.''

''Respond: who walks unseen among us?''

''Stagnant eddies of the past. I see faces: the less-than-ghosts, the ghosts of dead ghosts. . . . They glimmer and glimpse, they look and go.''

''What of living things?''

''No harsh blood, no pulsing flesh, no strident hearts.''

''Guard and watch.'' Ildefonse returned to Byzant the Necrope. ''What now?''

''I feel a strange flavor.''

Byzant spoke softly, to express the exquisite delicacy of his concepts. ''Among all here, I alone am sufficiently responsive to the subtlety of the IOUN stones. They should be placed in my custody.''

''Let the drawing proceed!'' Hurtiancz called out. ''Byzant's plan will never succeed.''

''Be warned!'' cried Byzant. With a black glance toward Hurtiancz, he moved to the rear of the group.

Ildefonse summoned one of his maidens. ''Do not be alarmed. You must reach into the pot, thoroughly stir the chips, and bring forth one, which you will then lay upon the table. Do you understand?''

''Yes, Lord Magician.''

''Do as I bid.''

The girl went to the pot. She reached forth her hand. At this precise instant Rhialto activated a spell of Temporal Stasis, with which, in anticipation of some such emergency, he had come prepared.

Time stood still for all but Rhialto. He glanced around the chamber, at the magicians in their frozen attitudes, at the servant girl with one hand over the pot, at Ildefonse staring at the girl's elbow.

Rhialto leisurely sauntered over to the IOUN stones. He could now take possession, but such an act would arouse a tremendous outcry and all would league themselves against him. A less provocative system was in order. He was startled by a soft sound from the corner of the room, when there should be no sound in still air.

''Who moves?'' called Rhialto.

''I move,'' came the soft voice of the ghost.

''Time is at a standstill. You must not move, or speak, or watch, or know.''

''Time, no-time—it is all one. I know each instant over and over.''

Rhialto shrugged and turned to the urn. He brought out the chips. To his wonder each was indited ''Ildefonse.''

''Aha!'' exclaimed Rhialto. ''Some crafty rascal selected a previous instant for his mischief! Is it not always the case? At the end of this, he and I will know each other the better!'' Rhialto rubbed out Ildefonse's signs and substituted his own. Then he replaced all in the pot.

Resuming his former position, he revoked the spell.

Noise softly filled the room. The girl reached into the pot. She stirred the chips, brought forth one of them which she placed upon the table. Rhialto leaned over the chip, as did Ildefonse. It gave a small jerk. The sign quivered and changed before their eyes.

Ildefonse lifted it and in a puzzled voice read, ''Gilgad!''

Rhialto glanced furiously at Gilgad, who gave back a bland stare. Gilgad had also halted time, but Gilgad had waited until the chip was actually upon the table.

Ildefonse said in a muffled voice, ''That is all. You may go.'' The girl departed. Ildefonse poured the chips on the table. They were correctly indited; each bore the sign or the signature of one of the magicians present. Ildefonse pulled at his white beard. He said, ''It seems that Gilgad has availed himself of the IOUN stones.''

Gilgad strode to the table. He emitted a terrible cry. ''The stones! What has been done to them?'' He held up the net, which now sagged under the weight of its contents. The brooding translucence was gone; the objects in the net shone with a vulgar vitreous glitter. Gilgad took one and dashed it to the floor, where it shattered into splinters. ''These are not the IOUN stones! Knavery is afoot!''

''Indeed!'' declared Ildefonse. ''So much is clear.''

''I demand my stones!'' raved Gilgad. ''Give them to me at once or I loose a spell of anguish against all present!''

''One moment,'' growled Hurtiancz. ''Delay your spell. Ildefonse, bring forth your ghost; learn what transpired.''

Ildefonse gave his beard a dubious tug, then raised his finger toward the far corner. ''Ghost! Are you at hand?''

''I am.''

''What occurred while we drew chips from the pot?''

''There was motion. Some moved, some stayed. When the chip at last was laid on the table, a strange shape passed into the room. It took the stones and was gone.''

''What manner of strange shape?''

"It wore a skin of blue scales; black plumes rose from its head, still it carried a soul of man."

"Archveult!" muttered Hurtiancz. "I suspect Xexamedes!"

Gilgad cried, "So then, what of my stones, my wonderful stones? How will I regain my property? Must I always be stripped of my valued possessions?"

"Cease your keening!" snapped the diabolist Shrue. "The remaining items must be distributed. Ildefonse, be so good as to consult the lists."

Ildefonse took up the papers. "Since Gilgad won the first draw, his list will now be withdrawn. For second choice—"

He was interrupted by Gilgad's furious complaint. "I protest this intolerable injustice! I won nothing but a handful of glass gewgaws!"

Ildefonse shrugged. "It is the robber-archveult to whom you must complain, especially when the drawing was attended by certain temporal irregularities, to which I need make no further reference."

Gilgad raised his arms in the air; his saturnine face knotted to the surge and counter-surge of his passions. His colleagues watched with dispassionate faces. "Proceed, Ildefonse," said Vermoulian the Dream-walker.

Ildefonse spread out the papers. "It appears that among the group only Rhialto has selected, for second choice, this curiously shaped device, which appears to be one of Houlart's Preterite Recordiums. I therefore make this award and place Rhialto's list with Gilgad's. Perdustin, Barbanikos, Ao of the Opals, and I myself have evinced a desire for this Casque of Sixty Directions, and we must therefore undertake a trial by lot. The jar, four chips—"

"On this occasion," said Perdustin, "let the maid be brought here now. She will put her hand over the mouth of the pot; we will insert the chips between her fingers; thus we ensure against a disruption of the laws of chance."

Ildefonse pulled at his yellow whiskers, but Perdustin had his way. In this fashion all succeeding lots were drawn. Presently it became Rhialto's turn to make a free choice.

"Well then, Rhialto," said Ildefonse. "What do you select?"

Rhialto's resentment boiled up in his throat. "As restitution for my seventeen exquisite birdwomen, my ten-thousand-year-old waypost, I am supposed to be gratified with this packet of Stupefying Dust?"

Ildefonse spoke soothingly. "Human interactions, stimulated as they are by disequilibrium, never achieve balance. In even the most favorable transaction, one party—whether he realizes it or not—must always come out the worse."

"The proposition is not unknown to me," said Rhialto in a more reasonable voice. "However—"

Zilifant uttered a sudden startled cry. "Look!" He pointed to the great mantle-piece; here, camouflaged by the carving, hung a linden leaf. With trembling fingers Ildefonse plucked it down. Silver characters read:

MORREION LIVES A DREAM.
NOTHING IS IMMINENT!

"Ever more confusing," muttered Hurtiancz. "Xexamedes persists in reassuring us that all is well with Morreion: an enigmatic exercise!"

"It must be remembered," the ever cautious Haze pointed out, "that Xexamedes, a renegade, is enemy to all."

Herark the Harbinger held up a black-enameled forefinger. "My habit is to make each problem declare its obverse. The first message, 'NOTHING THREATENS MORREION,' becomes 'SOMETHING DOES NOT THREATEN MORREION'; and again, 'NOTHING DOES THREATEN MORREION.' "

"Verbiage, prolixity!" grumbled the practical Hurtiancz.

"Not so fast!" said Zilifant. "Herark is notorously profound! 'NOTHING' might be intended as a delicate reference to death; a niceness of phrase, so to speak."

"Was Xexamedes famous for his exquisite good taste?" asked Hurtiancz with heavy sarcasm. "I think not. Like myself, when he meant 'death' he said 'death.' "

"My point exactly!" cried Herark. "I ask myself: What is the 'Nothing,' which threatens Morreion? Shrue, what or where is 'Nothing?' "

Shrue hunched his thin shoulders. "It is not to be found among the demon-lands."

"Vermoulian, in your peregrine palace you have traveled far. Where or what is 'Nothing'?"

Vermoulian the Dream-walker declared his perplexity. "I have never discovered such a place."

"Mune the Mage: What or where is 'Nothing'?"

"Somewhere," reflected Mune the Mage, "I have seen a reference to 'Nothing,' but I cannot recall the connection."

"The key word is 'reference,'" stated Herark. "Ildefonse, be so good as to consult the Great Gloss."

Ildefonse selected a volume from a shelf, threw back the broad covers. " 'Nothing.' Various topical references . . . a metaphysical description . . . a place? '*Nothing: the nonregion beyond the end of the cosmos.*' "

Hurtiancz suggested, "For good measure, why not consult the entry 'Morreion?' "

Somewhat reluctantly Ildefonse found the reference. He read: " '*Morreion: A legendary hero of the 21st Aeon, who vanquished the archveults and drove them, aghast, to Jangk. Thereupon they took him as far as the mind can reach, to the shining fields where they win their IOUN stones. His erstwhile comrades, who had vowed their protection, put him out of mind, and thereafter nought can be said.*' A biased and inaccurate statement, but interesting nonetheless."

Vermoulian the Dream-walker rose to his feet. "I have been planning an extended journey in my palace; this being the case I will take it upon myself to seek Morreion."

Gilgad gave a croak of fury and dismay. "You think to explore the 'shining fields'! It is I who has earned the right, not you!"

Vermoulian, a large man, sleek as a seal, with a pallid inscrutable face, declared: "My exclusive purpose is to rescue the hero Morreion; the IOUN stones to me are no more than an idle afterthought."

Ildefonse spoke: "Well said! But you will work more efficaciously with a very few trusted colleagues; perhaps myself alone."

"Precisely correct!" asserted Rhialto. "But a third person of proved resource is necessary in the event of danger. I also will share the hardships; otherwise I would think ill of myself."

Hurtiancz spoke with truculent fervor. "I never have been one to hold back! You may rely upon me."

"The presence of a Necrope is indispensable," stated Byzant. "I must therefore accompany the group."

Vermoulian asserted his preference for traveling alone, but no one would listen. Vermoulian at last capitulated, with a peevish droop to his usually complacent countenance. "I leave at once. If any are not at the palace within the hour I will understand that they have changed their minds."

"Come, come!" chided Ildefonse. "I need three-and-a-half hours simply to instruct my staff! We require more time."

"The message declared, 'Nothing is imminent,'" said Vermoulian. "Haste is of the essence!"

"We must take the word in its context," said Ildefonse. "Morreion has known his present condition several aeons; the word 'imminent' may well designate a period of five hundred years.''

With poor grace Vermoulian agreed to delay his departure until the following morning.

5

The ancient sun sank behind the Scaum hills; thin black clouds hung across the maroon afterlight. Rhialto arrived at the outer portal to his domain. He gave a signal and waited confidently for Puiras to lift the boundary curse.

The manse showed no responsive sign.

Rhialto made another signal, stamping impatiently. From the nearby forest of sprawling kang trees came the moaning of a grue, arousing the hairs at the back of Rhialto's neck. He flashed his finger-beams once more: where was Puiras? The white jade tiles of the roof loomed pale through the twilight. He saw no lights. From the forest the grue moaned again and in a plaintive voice called out for solace. Rhialto tested the boundary with a branch, to discover no curse, no protection whatever.

Flinging down the branch, he strode to the manse. All seemed to be in order, though Puiras was nowhere to be found. If he had scoured the hall the effort was not noticeable. Shaking his head in deprecation, Rhialto went to examine the way-post, which was being repaired by his Minuscules. The superintendent flew up on a mosquito to render his report; it seemed that Puiras had neglected to set out the evening victuals. Rhialto did so now and added half an ounce of jellied eel at his own expense.

With a dram of Blue Ruin at his elbow, Rhialto examined the convoluted tubes of bronze which he had brought from the castle of Ildefonse: the so-called Preterite Recordium. He tried to trace the course of the tubes but they wound in and out in a most confusing fashion. He gingerly pressed one of the valves, to evoke a sibilant whispering from the horn. He touched another, and now he heard a far-off guttural song. The sound came not from the horn, but from the pathway, and a moment later Puiras lurched through the door. He turned a vacuous leer toward Rhialto and staggered off toward his quarters.

Rhialto called sharply: ''Puiras!''

The servitor lurched about, ''What then?''

''You have taken too much to drink; in consequence you are drunk.''

Puiras ventured a knowing smirk. "Your perspicacity is keen, your language is exact. I take no exception to either remark."

Rhialto said, "I have no place for an irresponsible or bibulous servant. You are hereby discharged."

"No, you don't!" cried Puiras in a coarse voice, and emphasized the statement with a belch. "They told me I'd have a good post if I stole no more than old Funk and praised your noble airs. Well then! Tonight I stole only moderately, and from me the lack of insult is high praise. So there's the good post and what's a good post without a walk to the village?"

"Puiras, you are dangerously intoxicated," said Rhialto. "What a disgusting sight you are indeed!"

"No compliments!" roared Puiras. "We can't all be fine magicians with fancy clothes at the snap of a finger."

In outrage Rhialto rose to his feet. "Enough! Be off to your quarters before I inflict a torment upon you!"

"That's where I was going when you called me back," replied Puiras sulkily.

Rhialto conceived a further rejoinder to be beneath his dignity. Puiras stumbled away, muttering under his breath.

6

At rest upon the ground, Vermoulian's wonderful peregrine palace, together with its loggias, formal gardens and entrance pavilion, occupied an octagonal site some three acres in extent. The plan of the palace proper was that of a four-pointed star, with a crystal spire at each apex and a spire, somewhat taller, at the center, in which Vermoulian maintained his private chambers. A marble balustrade enclosed the forward pavilion. At the center a fountain raised a hundred jets of water; to either side grew lime trees with silver blossoms and silver fruit. The quadrangles to the right and left were laid out as formal gardens; the area at the rear was planted with herbs and salads for the palace kitchen.

Vermoulian's guests occupied suites in the wings; under the central spire were the various salons, the morning and afternoon rooms, the library, the music chamber, the formal dining room and the lounge.

An hour after sunrise the magicians began to arrive, with Gilgad first on the scene and Ildefonse the last. Vermoulian, his nonchalance restored, greeted each magician with carefully measured affability. After inspecting their suites the magicians gathered in the grand salon. Vermoulian addressed the group. "It is my great pleasure to entertain so distinguished a company! Our goal: the rescue of the hero Morreion! All present are keen and dedicated—but do all understand that we must wander far regions?'' Vermoulian turned his placid gaze from face to face. ''Are all prepared for tedium, discomfort and danger? Such may well eventuate, and if any have doubts or if any pursue subsidiary goals, such as a search for IOUN stones, now is the time for these persons to return to their respective manses, castles, caves, and eyries. Are any so inclined? No? We depart.''

Vermoulian bowed to his now uneasy guests. He mounted to the control belvedere where he cast a spell of buoyancy upon the palace; it rose to drift on the morning breeze like a pinnacled cloud. Vermoulian consulted his Celestial Almanac and made note of certain symbols; these he inscribed upon the carnelian mandate-wheel, which he set into rotation; the signs were spun off into the interflux, to elucidate a route across the universe. Vermoulian fired a taper and held it to the speed-incense; the palace departed; ancient Earth and the waning sun were left behind.

Beside the marble balustrade stood Rhialto. Ildefonse came to join him; the two watched Earth dwindle to a rosy-pink crescent. Ildefonse spoke in a melancholy voice: ''When one undertakes a journey of this sort, where the event is unknown, long thoughts come of their own accord. I trust that you left your affairs in order?''

''My household is not yet settled,'' said Rhialto. ''Puiras has proved unsatisfactory; when drunk he sings and performs grotesque capers; when sober he is as surly as a leech on a corpse. This morning I demoted him to Minuscule.''

Ildefonse nodded absently. ''I am troubled by what I fear to be cross-purposes among our colleagues, worthy fellows though they may be.''

''You refer to the 'shining fields' of IOUN stones?'' Rhialto put forward delicately.

''I do. As Vermoulian categorically declared, we fare forth to the rescue of Morreion. The IOUN stones can only prove a distraction. Even if a supply were discovered, I suspect that the interests of all might best be served by a highly selective distribution, the venal Gilgad's complaints notwithstanding.''

''There is much to be said for this point of view,'' Rhialto admitted. ''It is just as well to have a prior understanding upon a matter so inherently controversial. Vermoulian of course must be allotted a share.''

''This goes without saying.''

At this moment Vermoulian descended to the pavilion where he was approached by Mune the Mage, Hurtiancz and the others. Mune raised a question regarding their destination. "The question of ultimates becomes important. How, Vermoulian, can you know that this precise direction will take us to Morreion?"

"A question well put," said Vermoulian. "To respond, I must cite an intrinsic condition of the universe. We set forth in any direction which seems convenient; each leads to the same place: the end of the universe."

"Interesting!" declared Zilifant. "In this case, we must inevitably find Morreion; an encouraging prospect!"

Gilgad was not completely satisfied. "What of the 'shining fields' in the reference? Where are these located?"

"A matter of secondary or even tertiary concern," Ildefonse reminded him. "We must think only of the hero Morreion."

"Your solicitude is late by several aeons," said Gilgad waspishly. "Morreion may well have grown impatient."

"Other circumstances intervened," said Ildefonse with a frown of annoyance. "Morreion will certainly understand the situation."

Zilifant remarked, "The conduct of Xexamedes becomes ever more puzzling! As a renegade archveult, he has no ostensible reason to oblige either Morreion, the archveults, or ourselves."

"The mystery in due course will be resolved," said Herark the Harbinger.

7

So went the voyage. The palace drifted through the stars, under and over clouds of flaming gas, across gulfs of deep black space. The magicians meditated in the pergolas, exchanged opinions in the salons over goblets of liquor, lounged upon the marble benches of the pavilion, leaned on the balustrade to look down at the galaxies passing below. Breakfasts were served in the individual suites, luncheons were usually set forth al fresco on the pavilion, the dinners were sumptuous and formal and extended far into the night. To enliven these evenings Vermoulian called forth the most charming, witty and beautiful women of all the past eras, in their quaint and splendid costumes. They found the peregrine palace no less remarkable than the fact of their own presence aboard. Some thought themselves dreaming; others conjectured their own deaths; a few of the more sophisticated made the correct presumption. To facilitate social intercourse Vermoulian gave them command of contemporary language, and the evenings frequently became merry affairs. Rhialto became enamored of a certain Mersei from the land of Mith, long since foundered under the waters of the Shan Ocean. Mersei's charm resided in her slight body, her grave pale face behind which thoughts could be felt but not seen. Rhialto plied her with all gallantry, but she failed to respond, merely looking at him in disinterested silence, until Rhialto wondered if she were slack-witted, or possibly more subtle than himself. Either case made him uncomfortable, and he was not sorry when Vermoulian returned this particular group to oblivion.

Through clouds and constellations they moved, past bursting galaxies and meandering star-streams; through a region where the stars showed a peculiar soft violet and hung in clouds of pale green gas; across a desolation where nothing whatever was seen save a few far luminous clouds. Then presently they came to a new region, where blazing white giants seemed to control whirlpools of pink, blue and white gas, and the magicians lined the balustrade looking out at the spectacle.

At last the stars thinned; the great star-streams were lost in the distance. Space seemed darker and heavier, and finally there came a time when all the stars were behind and nothing lay ahead but darkness. Vermoulian made a grave announcement. "We are now close to the end of the universe! We must go with care. 'Nothing' lies ahead."

"Where then is Morreion?" demanded Hurtiancz. "Surely he is not to be found wandering vacant space."

"Space is not yet vacant," stated Vermoulian. "Here, there and roundabout are dead stars and wandering star-hulks; in a sense, we traverse the refuse-heap of the universe, where the dead stars come to await a final destiny; and notice, yonder, far ahead, a single star, the last in the universe. We must approach with caution; beyond lies 'Nothing.' "

" 'Nothing' is not yet visible," remarked Ao of the Opals.

"Look more closely!" said Vermoulian. "Do you see that dark wall? That is 'Nothing.' "

"Again," said Perdustin, "the question arises: Where is Morreion? Back at Ildefonse's castle, when we formed conjectures, the end of the universe seemed a definite spot. Now that we are here, we find a considerable latitude of choice."

Gilgad muttered, half to himself, "The expedition is a farce. I see no 'fields,' shining or otherwise."

Vermoulian said, "The solitary star would seem an initial object of investigation. We approach at a rash pace; I must slake the speed-incense."

The magicians stood by the balustrade watching as the far star waxed in brightness. Vermoulian called down from the belvedere to announce a lone planet in orbit around the sun.

"A possibility thereby exists," stated Mune the Mage, "that on this very planet we may find Morreion."

8

The palace moved down to the solitary star and the lone planet became a disk the colour of moth-wing. Beyond, clearly visible in the wan sunlight, stood the ominous black wall. Hurtiancz said, "Xexamedes' warning now becomes clear—assuming, of course, that Morreion inhabits this drab and isolated place."

The world gradually expanded, to show a landscape dreary and worn. A few decayed hills rose from the plains; as many ponds gleamed sullenly in the sunlight. The only other features of note were the ruins of once-extensive cities; a very few buildings had defied the ravages of time sufficiently to display a squat and distorted architecture.

The palace settled close above one of the ruins; a band of small weasel-life rodents bounded away into the scrub; no other sign of life was evident. The palace continued west around the planet. Vermoulian presently called down from the belvedere: "Notice the cairn; it marks an ancient thoroughfare."

Other cairns at three-mile intervals appeared, mounds of carefully fitted stones six feet high; they marked a way around the planet.

At the next tumble of ruins Vermoulian, observing a level area, allowed the palace to settle so that the ancient city and its cluster of surviving structures might be explored.

The magicians set off in various directions, the better to pursue their investigations. Gilgad went toward the desolate plaza, Perdustin and Zilifant to the civic amphitheatre, Hurtiancz into a nearby tumble of sandstone blocks. Ildefonse, Rhialto, Mune the Mage and Herark the Harbinger wandered at random, until a raucous chanting brought them up short.

"Peculiar!" exclaimed Herark. "It sounds like the voice of Hurtiancz, the most dignified of men!"

The group entered a cranny through the ruins, which opened into a large chamber, protected from sifting sand by massive blocks of rock. Light filtered through various chinks and apertures; down the middle ran a line of six long slabs. At the far end sat Hurtiancz, watching the entry of the magicians with an imperturbable gaze. On the slab in front of him stood a globe of dark brown glass, or glazed stone. A rack behind him held other similar bottles.

"It appears," said Ildefonse, "that Hurtiancz has stumbled upon the site of the ancient tavern."

"Hurtiancz!" Rhialto called out. "We heard your song and came to investigate. What have you discovered?"

Hurtiancz hawked and spat on the ground. "Hurtiancz!" cried Rhialto. "Do you hear me? Or have you taken too much of this ancient tipple to be sensible?"

Hurtiancz replied in a clear voice, "In one sense I have taken too much: in another, not enough."

Mune the Mage picked up the brown glass bottle and smelled the contents. "Astringent, tart, herbal." He tasted the liquid. "It is quite refreshing."

Ildefonse and Herark the Harbinger each took a brown glass globe from the rack and broke open the bung; they were joined by Rhialto and Mune the Mage.

Ildefonse, as he drank, became garrulous, and presently he fell to speculating in regard to the ancient city: "Just as from one bone the skilled palaeontologist deduces an entire skeleton, so from a single artifact the qualified scholar reconstructs every aspect of the responsible race. As I taste this liquor, as I examine this bottle, I ask myself, What do the dimensions, textures, colours and flavors betoken? No intelligent act is without symbolic significance."

Hurtiancz, upon taking drink, tended to become gruff and surly. Now he stated in an uncompromising voice, "The subject is of small import."

Ildefonse was not to be deterred. "Here the pragmatic Hurtiancz and I, the man of many parts, are at variance. I was about to carry my argument a step farther, and in fact I will do so, stimulated as I am by this elixir of a vanished race. I therefore suggest that in the style of the previous examples, a natural scientist, examining a single atom, might well be able to asseverate the structure and history of the entire universe!"

"Bah!" muttered Hurtiancz. "By the same token, a sensible man need listen to but a single word in order to recognize the whole for egregious nonsense."

Ildefonse, absorbed in his theories, paid no heed. Herark took occasion to state that in his opinion not one, but at least two, even better, three of any class of objects was essential to understanding. "I cite the discipline of mathematics, where a series may not be determined by less than three terms."

"I willingly grant the scientist his three atoms," said Ildefonse, "though in the strictest sense, two of these are supererogatory."

Rhialto, rising from his slab, went to look into a dirt-choked aperture, to discover a passage descending by broad steps into the ground. He caused an illumination to proceed before him and descended the steps. The passage turned once, turned twice, then opened into a large chamber paved with brown stone. The walls held a number of niches, six feet long, two feet high, three feet deep; peering into one of these Rhialto discovered a skeleton of most curious structure, so fragile that the impact of Rhialto's gaze caused it to collapse into dust.

Rhialto rubbed his chin. He looked into a second niche to discover a similar skeleton. He backed away, and stood musing a moment or two. Then he returned up the steps, the drone of Ildefonse's voice growing progressively louder: "—in the same manner to the question: Why does the universe end here and not a mile farther? Of all questions, *why?* is the least pertinent. It begs the question; it assumes the larger part of its own response; to wit, that a sensible response exists." Ildefonse paused to refresh himself, and Rhialto took occasion to relate his discoveries in the chamber below.

"It appears to be a crypt," said Rhialto. "The walls are lined with niches, and each contains the veriest wraith of a dead corpse."

"Indeed, indeed!" muttered Hurtiancz. He lifted the brown glass bottle and at once put it down.

"Perhaps we are mistaken in assuming this place a tavern," Rhialto continued. "The liquid in the bottles, rather than tipple, I believe to be embalming fluid."

Ildefonse was not so easily diverted. "I now propound the basic and elemental verity: What is IS. Here you have heard the basic proposition of magic. What magician asks *Why*? He asks *How? Why* leads to stultification; each response generates at least one other question, in this fashion:

"Question: Why does Rhialto wear a black hat with gold tassels and a scarlet plume?

"Answer: Because he hopes to improve his semblance.

"Question: Why does he want to improve his semblance?

"Answer: Because he craves the admiration and envy of his fellows.

"Question: Why does he crave admiration?

"Answer: Because, as a man, he is a social animal.

"Question: Why is Man a social animal?

''So go the questions and responses, expanding to infinity. Therefore—''

In a passion Hurtiancz leapt to his feet. Raising the brown glass pot above his head he dashed it to the floor. ''Enough of this intolerable inanity! I propose that such loquacity passes beyond the scope of nuisance and over the verge of turpitude.''

''It is a fine point,'' said Herark. ''Ildefonse, what have you to say on this score?''

''I am more inclined to punish Hurtiancz for his crassness,'' said Ildefonse. ''But now he simulates a swinish stupidity to escape my anger.''

''Absolute falsity!'' roared Hurtiancz. ''I simulate nothing!''

Ildefonse shrugged. ''For all his deficiencies as polemicist and magician, Hurtiancz at least is candid.''

Hurtiancz controlled his fury. He said, ''Who could defeat your volubility? As a magician, however, I outmatch your bumbling skills as Rhialto the Marvellous exceeds your rheumy decrepitude.''

Ildefonse in his turn became angry. ''A test!'' He flung up his hand; the massive blocks scattered in all directions; they stood on a vacant floor in the full glare of sunlight. ''What of that?''

''Trivial,'' said Hurtiancz. ''Match this!'' He held up his two hands; from each finger issued a jet of vivid smoke in ten different colours.

''The pretty prank of a charlatan,'' declared Ildefonse. ''Now watch! I utter a word: 'Roof!' '' The word leaving his lips hesitated in the air, in the form of symbol, then moved out in a wide circle, to impinge upon the roof of one of the strangely styled structures still extant. The symbol disappeared; the roof glowed a vivid orange and melted to spawn a thousand symbols like the word Ildefonse had sent forth. These darted high in the sky, stopped short, disappeared. From above, like a great clap of thunder, came Ildefonse's voice: ''ROOF!''

''No great matter,'' stated Hurtiancz. ''Now—''

''Hist!'' said Mune the Mage. ''Cease your drunken quarrel. Look yonder!''

From the structure whose roof Ildefonse had demolished came a man.

9

The man stood in the doorway. He was impressively tall. A long white beard hung down his chest; white hair covered his ears; his eyes glittered black. He wore an elegant caftan woven in patterns of dark red, brown, black and blue. Now he stepped forward, and it could be seen that he trailed a cloud of glowing objects. Gilgad, who had returned from the plaza, instantly set up a shout: "The IOUN stones!"

The man came forward. His face showed an expression of calm inquiry. Ildefonse muttered, "It is Morreion! Of this there can be no doubt. The stature, the stance—they are unmistakable!"

"It is Morreion," Rhialto agreed. "But why is he so calm, as if each week he received visitors who took off his roof, as if 'Nothing' loomed over someone else?"

"His perceptions may have become somewhat dulled," Herark suggested. "Notice: he evinces no signal of human recognition."

Morreion came slowly forward, the IOUN stones swirling in his wake. The magicians gathered before the marble steps of the palace. Vermoulian stepped forth and raised his hand. "Hail, Morreion! We have come to take you from this intolerable isolation!"

Morreion looked from one face to the other. He made a guttural sound, then a rasping croak, as if trying organs whose use he had long forgotten.

Ildefonse now presented himself. "Morreion, my comrade! It is I, Ildefonse; do you not remember the old days at Kammerbrand? Speak then!"

"I hear," croaked Morreion. "I speak, but I do not remember."

Vermoulian indicated the marble stairs. "Step aboard, if you will; we depart this dreary world at once."

Morreion made no move. He examined the palace with a frown of vexation. "You have placed your flying hut upon the area where I dry my skeins."

Ildefonse pointed toward the black wall, which through the haze of the atmosphere showed only as a portentous shadow. " 'Nothing' looms close. It is about to impinge upon this world, whereupon you will be no more; in short, you will be dead."

"I am not clear as to your meaning," said Morreion. "If you will excuse me, I must be away and about my affairs."

"A quick question before you go," spoke Gilgad. "Where does one find IOUN stones?"

Morreion looked at him without comprehension. At last he gave his attention to the stones, which swirled with a swifter motion. In comparison, those of the archveult Xexamedes were listless and dull. These danced and curveted, and sparkled with different colours. Closest to Morreion's head moved the lavender and the pale green stones, as if they thought themselves the most loved and most privileged.

Somewhat more wayward were the stones glowing pink and green together; then came stones of a proud pure pink, then the royal carmine stones, then the red and blue; and finally, at the outer periphery, a number of stones glittering with intense blue lights.

As Morreion cogitated, the magicians noted a peculiar circumstance: certain of the innermost lavender stones lost their glow and became as dull as the stones of Xexamedes.

Morreion gave a slow thoughtful nod. "Curious! So much which I seem to have forgotten. . . . I did not always live here," he said in a voice of surprise. "There was at one time another place. The memory is dim and remote."

Vermoulian said, "That place is Earth! It is where we will take you."

Morreion smilingly shook his head. "I am just about to start on an important journey."

"Is the trip absolutely necessary?" inquired Mune the Mage. "Our time is limited, and even more to the point, we do not care to be engulfed in 'Nothing.' "

"I must see to my cairns," said Morreion in a mild but definite manner.

For a moment there was silence. Then Ildefonse asked, "What is the purpose of these cairns?"

Morreion used the even voice of one speaking to a child. "They indicate the most expeditious route around my world. Without the cairns it is possible to go astray."

"But remember, there is no longer need for such landmarks," said Ao of the Opals. "You will be returning to Earth with us!"

Morreion could not restrain a small laugh at the obtuse persistence of his visitors. "Who would look after my properties? How would I fare if my cairns toppled, if my looms broke, if my kilns crumbled, if my other enterprises dissolved, and all for the lack of methodical care?"

Vermoulian said blandly, "At least come aboard the palace to share our evening banquet."

"It will be my pleasure," replied Morreion. He mounted the marble steps, to gaze with pleasure around the pavilion. "Charming. I must consider something of this nature as a forecourt for my new mansion."

"There will be insufficient time," Rhialto told him.

" 'Time'?" Morreion frowned as if the word were unfamiliar to him. Other of the lavender stones suddenly went pale. "Time indeed! But time is required to do a proper job! This gown for instance." He indicated his gorgeously patterned caftan. ''The weaving required four years. Before that I gathered beast-fur for ten years; then for another two years I bleached and dyed and spun. My cairns were built a stone at a time, each time I wandered around the world. My wanderlust has waned somewhat, but I occasionally make the journey, to rebuild where necessary, and to note the changes of the landscape.''

Rhialto pointed to the sun. ''Do you recognize the nature of that object?''

Morreion frowned. ''I call it 'the sun'—though why I have chosen this particular term escapes me.''

''There are many such suns,'' said Rhialto. ''Around one of them swings that ancient and remarkable world which gave you birth. Do you remember Earth?''

Morreion looked dubiously up into the sky. ''I have seen none of these other suns you describe. At night my sky is quite dark; there is no other light the world over save the glow of my fires. It is a peaceful world indeed. . . . I seem to recall more eventful times.'' The last of the lavender stones and certain of the green stones lost their colour. Morreion's eyes became momentarily intent. He went to inspect the tame water-nymphs which sported in the central fountain. ''And what might be these glossy little creatures? They are most appealing.''

''They are quite fragile, and useful only as show,'' said Vermoulian. ''Come, Morreion, my valet will help you prepare for the banquet.''

''You are most gracious,'' said Morreion.

10

The magicians awaited their guest in the grand salon.

Each had his own opinion of the circumstances. Rhialto said, ''Best that we raise the palace now and so be off and away. Morreion may be agitated for a period, but when all the facts are laid before him he must surely see reason.''

The cautious Perdustin demurred. ''There is power in the man! At one time, his magic was a source of awe and wonder; what if in a fit of pique he wreaks a harm upon all of us?''

Gilgad endorsed Perdustin's view. ''Everyone has noted Morreion's IOUN stones. Where did he acquire them? Can this world be the source?''

''Such a possibility should not automatically be dismissed,'' admitted Ildefonse. ''Tomorrow, when the imminence of 'Nothing' is described, Morreion will surely depart without resentment.''

So the matter rested. The magicians turned their discussion to other aspects of this dismal world.

Herark the Harbinger, who had skill as a cognizancer, attempted to divine the nature of the race which had left ruins across the planet, without notable success. "They have been gone too long; their influence has waned. I seem to discern creatures with thin white legs and large green eyes. . . . I hear a whisper of their music: a jingling, a tinkle, to a rather plaintive obbligato of pipes. . . . I sense no magic. I doubt if they recognized the IOUN stones, if in fact such exist on this planet."

"Where else could they originate?" demanded Gilgad.

"The 'shining fields' are nowhere evident," remarked Haze of Wheary Water.

Morreion entered the hall. His appearance had undergone a dramatic change. The great white beard had been shaved away; his bush of hair had been cropped to a more modish style. In the place of his gorgeous caftan he wore a garment of ivory silk with a blue sash and a pair of scarlet slippers. Morreion now stood revealed as a tall spare man, attentive and alert. Glittering black eyes dominated his face, which was taut, harsh at chin and jaw, massive of forehead, disciplined in the even lines of the mouth. The lethargy and boredom of so many aeons were nowhere evident; he moved with easy command, and behind him, darting and circling, swarmed the IOUN stones.

Morreion greeted the assembled magicians with an inclination of the head, and gave his attention to the appointments of the salon. "Magnificent and luxurious! But I will be forced to use quartz in the place of this splendid marble, and there is little silver to be found; the Sahars plundered all the surface ores. When I need metal I must tunnel deep underground."

"You have led a busy existence," declared Ildefonse. "And who were the Sahars?"

"The race whose ruins mar the landscape. A frivolous and irresponsible folk, though I admit that I find their poetic conundrums amusing."

"The Sahars still exist?"

"Indeed not! They became extinct long ages go. But they left numerous records etched on bronze, which I have taken occasion to translate."

"A tedious job, surely!" exclaimed Zilifant. "How did you achieve so complicated a task?"

"By the process of elimination," Morreion explained. "I tested a succession of imaginary languages against the inscriptions, and in due course I found a correspondence. As you say, the task was time-consuming; still I have had much entertainment from the Sahar chronicles. I want to orchestrate their musical revelries; but this is a task for the future, perhaps after I complete the palace I now intend.''

Ildefonse spoke in a grave voice, ''Morreion, it becomes necessary to impress certain important matters upon you. You state that you have not studied the heavens?''

''Not extensively,'' admitted Morreion. ''There is little to be seen save the sun, and under favorable conditions a great wall of impenetrable blackness.''

''That wall of blackness,'' said Ildefonse, ''is 'Nothing,' toward which your world is inexorably drifting. Any further work here is futile.''

Morreion's black eyes glittered with doubt and suspicion. ''Can you prove this assertion?''

''Certainly. Indeed we came here from Earth to rescue you.''

Morreion frowned. Certain of the green stones abruptly lost their colour. ''Why did you delay so long?''

Ao of the Opals gave a bray of nervous laughter, which he quickly stifled. Ildefonse turned him a furious glare.

''Only recently were we made aware of your plight,'' explained Rhialto. ''Upon that instant we prevailed upon Vermoulian to bring us hither in his peregrine palace.''

Vermoulian's bland face creased in displeasure. '' 'Prevailed' is not correct!'' he stated. ''I was already on my way when the others insisted on coming along. And now, if you will excuse us for a few moments, Morreion and I have certain important matters to discuss.''

''Not so fast,'' Gilgad cried out. ''I am equally anxious to learn the source of the stones.''

Ildefonse said, ''I will put the question in the presence of us all. Morreion, where did you acquire your IOUN stones?''

Morreion looked around at the stones. ''To be candid, the facts are somewhat vague. I seem to recall a vast shining surface. . . . But why do you ask? They have no great usefulness. So many ideas throng upon me. It seems that I had enemies at one time, and false friends. I must try to remember.''

Ildefonse said, ''At the moment you are among your faithful friends, the magicians of Earth. And if I am not mistaken, the noble Vermoulian is about to set before us the noblest repast in any of our memories!''

Morreion said with a sour smile, ''You must think my life that of a savage. Not so! I have studied the Sahar cuisine and improved upon it! The lichen which covers the plain may be prepared in at least one hundred-seventy fashions. The turf beneath is the home of succulent helminths. For all its drab monotony, this world provides a bounty. If what you say is true, I shall be sorry indeed to leave.''

''The facts cannot be ignored,'' said Ildefonse. ''The IOUN stones, so I suppose, derive from the northern part of this world?''

''I believe not.''

''The southern area, then?''

''I rarely visit this section; the lichen is thin; the helminths are all gristle.''

A gong-stroke sounded; Vermoulian ushered the company into the dining room, where the great table glittered with silver and crystal. The magicians seated themselves under the five chandeliers; in deference to his guest who had lived so long in solitude, Vermoulian refrained from calling forth the beautiful women of ancient eras.

Morreion ate with caution, tasting all set before him, comparing the dishes to the various guises of lichen upon which he usually subsisted. ''I had almost forgotten the existence of such food,'' he said at last. ''I am reminded, dimly, of other such feasts—so long ago, so long. . . . Where have the years gone? Which is the dream?'' As he mused, some of the pink and green stones lost their colour. Morreion sighed. ''There is much to be learned, much to be remembered. Certain faces here arouse flickering recollections; have I known them before?''

''You will recall all in due course,'' said the diabolist Shrue. ''And now, if we are certain that the IOUN stones are not to be found on this planet—''

''But we are not sure!'' snapped Gilgad. ''We must seek, we must search; no effort is too arduous!''

''The first to be found necessarily will go to satisfy my claims,'' declared Rhialto. ''This must be a definite understanding.''

Gilgad thrust his vulpine face forward. ''What nonsense is this? Your claims were satisfied by a choice from the effects of the archveult Xexamedes!''

Morreion jerked around. ''The archveult Xexamedes! I know this name. . . . How? Where? Long ago I knew an archveult Xexamedes; he was my foe, or so it seems. . . . Ah, the ideas which roil my mind!'' The pinkand green stones all had lost their colour. Morreion groaned and put his hands to his head. ''Before you came my life was placid; you have brought me doubt and wonder.''

''Doubt and wonder are the lot of all men,'' said Ildefonse.

''Magicians are not excluded. Are you ready to leave Sahar Planet?''

Morreion sat looking into a goblet of wine. ''I must collect my books. They are all I wish to take away.''

11

Morreion conducted the magicians about his premises. The structures which had seemed miraculous survivals had in fact been built by Morreion, after one or another mode of the Sahar architecture. He displayed his three looms: the first for fine weaves, linens and silks; the second where he contrived patterned cloths; the third where his heavy rugs were woven. The same structure housed vats, dyes, bleaches and mordants. Another building contained the glass cauldron, as well as the kilns where Morreion produced earthenware pots, plates, lamps and tiles. His forge in the same building showed little use. ''The Sahars scoured the planet clean of ores. I mine only what I consider indispensable, which is not a great deal.''

Morreion took the group to his library, in which were housed many Sahar originals as well as books Morreion had written and illuminated with his own hand: translations of the Sahar classics, an encyclopedia of natural history, ruminations and speculations, a descriptive geography of the planet with appended maps. Vermoulian ordered his staff to transfer the articles to the palace.

Morreion turned a last look around the landscape he had known so long and had come to love. Then without a word he went to the palace and climbed the marble steps. In a subdued mood the magicians followed. Vermoulian went at once to the control belvedere where he performed rites of buoyancy. The palace floated up from the final planet.

Ildefonse gave an exclamation of shock. '' 'Nothing' is close at hand—more imminent than we had suspected!''

The black wall loomed startlingly near; the last star and its single world drifted at the very brink.

''The perspectives are by no means clear,'' said Ildefonse. ''There is no sure way of judging but it seems that we left not an hour too soon.''

''Let us wait and watch,'' suggested Herark. ''Morreion can learn our good faith for himself.''

So the palace hung in space, with the pallid light of the doomed sun playing upon the five crystal spires, projecting long shadows behind the magicians where they stood by the balustrade.

The Sahar world was first to encounter 'Nothing.' It grazed against the enigmatic nonsubstance, then urged by a component of orbital motion, a quarter of the orginal sphere moved out clear and free: a mound-like object with a precisely flat base, where the hitherto secret strata, zones, folds, intrusions and core were displayed to sight. The sun reached 'Nothing'; it touched, advanced. It became a half-orange on a black mirror, then sank away from reality. Darkness shrouded the palace.

In the belvedere Vermoulian indited symbols on the mandate-wheel. He struck them off, then put double fire to the speed-incense. The palace glided away, back toward the star-clouds.

Morreion turned away from the balustrade and went into the great hall, where he sat deep in thought.

Gilgad presently approached him. "Perhaps you have recalled the source of the IOUN stones?"

Morreion rose to his feet. He turned his level black eyes upon Gilgad, who stepped back a pace. The pink and green stones had long become pallid, and many of the pink as well.

Morreion's face was stern and cold. "I recall much! There was a cabal of enemies who tricked me—but all is as dim as the film of stars which hangs across far space. In some fashion, the stones are part and parcel of the matter. Why do you evince so large an interest in stones? Were you one of my former enemies? Is this the case with all of you? If so, beware! I am a mild man until I encounter antagonism."

The diabolist Shrue spoke soothingly. "We are not your enemies! Had we not lifted you from Sahar Planet, you would now be with 'Nothing.' Is this not proof?"

Morreion gave a grim nod; but he no longer seemed the mild and affable man they had first encountered.

To restore the previous amiability, Vermoulian hastened to the room of faded mirrors where he maintained his vast collection of beautiful women in the form of matrices. These could be activated into corporeality by a simple antinegative incantation; and presently from the room, one after the other, stepped those delightful confections of the past which Vermoulian had seen fit to revivify. On each occasion they came forth fresh, without recollection of previous manifestations; each appearance was new, no matter how affairs had gone before.

Among those whom Vermoulian had called forth was the graceful Mersei. She stepped into the grand salon, blinking in the bewilderment common to those evoked from the past. She stopped short in amazement, then with quick steps ran forward. "Morreion! What do you do here? They told us you had gone against the archveults, that you had been killed! By the Sacred Ray, you are sound and whole!"

Morreion looked down at the young woman in perplexity. The

pink and red stones wheeled around his head. "Somewhere I have seen you; somewhere I have known you."

"I am Mersei! Do you not remember? You brought me a red rose growing in a porcelain vase. Oh, what have I done with it? I always keep it near. . . . But where am I? Where is the rose? No matter. I am here and you are here."

Ildefonse muttered to Vermoulian, "An irresponsible act, in my judgment; why were you not more cautious?"

Vermoulian pursed his lips in vexation. "She stems from the waning of the 21st Aeon but I had not anticipated anything like this!"

"I suggest that you call her back into your room of matrices and there reduce her. Morreion seems to be undergoing a period of instability; he needs peace and quietude; best not to introduce stimulations so unpredictable."

Vermoulian strolled across the room. "Mersei, my dear; would you be good enough to step this way?"

Mersei cast him a dubious look, then beseeched Morreion: "Do you not know me? Something is very strange; I can understand nothing of this—it is like a dream. Morreion, am I dreaming?"

"Come, Mersei," said Vermoulian suavely. "I wish a word with you."

"Stop!" spoke Morreion. "Magician, stand back; this fragrant creature is something which once I loved, at a time far gone."

The girl cried in a poignant voice: "A time far gone? It was no more than yesterday! I tended the sweet red rose, I looked at the sky; they had sent you to Jangk, by the red star Kerkaju, the eye of the Polar Ape. And now you are here, and I am here—what does it mean?"

"Inadvisable, inadvisable," muttered Ildefonse. He called out: "Morreion, this way, if you will. I see a curious concatenation of galaxies. Perhaps here is the new home of the Sahars."

Morreion put his hand to the girl's shoulder. He looked into her face. "The sweet red rose blooms, and forever. We are among magicians and strange events occur." He glanced aside at Vermoulian, then back to Mersei. "At this moment, go with Vermoulian the Dreamwalker, who will show you to your chamber."

"Yes, dear Morreion, but when will I see you again? You look so strange, so strained and old, and you speak so peculiarly—"

"Go now, Mersei. I must confer with Ildefonse."

Vermoulian led Mersei back toward the room of matrices. At the door she hesitated and looked back over her shoulder, but Morreion had already turned away. She followed Vermoulian into the room. The door closed behind them.

Morreion walked out on the pavilion, past the dark lime trees with their silver fruit, and leaned upon the balustrade. The sky was still dark, although ahead and below a few vagrant galaxies could now be seen. Morreion put his hand to his head; the pink stones and certain of the red stones lost their colour.

Morreion swung around toward Ildefonse and those other magicians who had silently come out on the pavilion. He stepped forward, the IOUN stones tumbling one after the other in their hurry to keep up. Some were yet red, some showed shifting glints of blue and red, some burnt a cold incandescent blue. All the others had become the colour of pearl. One of these drifted in front of Morreion's eyes; he caught it, gave it a moment of frowning inspection, then tossed it into the air. Spinning and jerking, with colour momentarily restored, it was quick to rejoin the others, like a child embarrassed.

"Memory comes and goes," mused Morreion. "I am unsettled, in mind and heart. Faces drift before my eyes; they fade once more; other events move into a region of clarity. The archveults, the IOUN stones—I know something of these, though much is dim and murky, so best that I hold my tongue—"

"By no means!" declared Ao of the Opals. "We are interested in your experiences."

"To be sure!" said Gilgad.

Morreion's mouth twisted in a smile that was both sardonic and harsh, and also somewhat melancholy. "Very well, I tell this story, then, as if I were telling a dream.

"It seems that I was sent to Jangk on a mission—perhaps to learn the provenance of the IOUN stones? Perhaps. I hear whispers which tell me so much; it well may be. . . . I arrived at Jangk; I recall the landscape well. I remember a remarkable castle hollowed from an enormous pink pearl. In this castle I confronted the archveults. They feared me and stood back, and when I stated my wishes there was no demur. They would indeed take me to gather stones, and so we set out, flying through space in an equipage whose nature I cannot recall. The archveults were silent and watched me from the side of their eyes; then they became affable and I wondered at their mirth. But I felt no fear. I knew all their magic; I carried counter-spells at my fingernails, and at need could fling them off instantly. So we crossed space, with the archveults laughing and joking in what I considered an insane fashion. I ordered them to stop. They halted instantly and sat staring at me.

"We arrived at the edge of the universe, and came down upon a sad cinder of a world; a dreadful place. Here we waited in a region of burnt-out star-hulks, some still hot, some cold, some cinders like the world on which we stood—perhaps it, too, was a dead star. Occasionally we saw the corpses of dwarf stars, glistening balls of stuff so heavy that a speck outweighs an Earthly mountain. I saw such objects no more than ten miles across, containing the matter of a sun like vast Kerkaju. Inside these dead stars, the archveults told me, were to be found the IOUN stones. And how were they to be won? I asked. Must we drive a tunnel into that gleaming surface? They gave mocking calls of laughter at my ignorance; I uttered a sharp reprimand; instantly they fell silent. The spokesman was Xexamedes. From him I learned that no power known to man or magician could mar stuff so dense! We must wait.

" 'Nothing' loomed across the distance. Often the derelict hulks swung close in their orbits. The archveults kept close watch; they pointed and calculated, they carped and fretted; at last one of the shining balls struck across 'Nothing,' expunging half of itself. When it swung out and away the archveults took their equipage down to the flat surface. All now ventured forth, with most careful precaution; unprotected from gravity a man instantly becomes as no more than an outline upon the surface. With slide-boards immune to gravity we traversed the surface.

"What a wonderful sight! 'Nothing' had wrought a flawless polish; for fifteen miles this mirrored plain extended, marred only at the very center by a number of black pockmarks. Here the IOUN stones were to be found, in nests of black dust.

"To win the stones is no small task. The black dust, like the slide-boards, counters gravity. It is safe to step from the slide-boards to the dust, but a new precaution must be taken. While the dust negates the substance below, other celestial objects suck, so one must use an anchor to hold himself in place. The archveults drive small barbed hooks into the dust, and tie themselves down with a cord, and this I did as well. By means of a special tool the dust is probed—a tedious task! The dust is packed tightly! Nevertheless, with great energy I set to work and in due course won my first IOUN stone. I held it high in exultation, but where were the archveults? They had circled around me; they had returned to the equipage! I sought my slide-boards—in vain! By stealth they had been purloined!

"I staggered, I sagged; I raved a spell at the traitors. They held forward their newly won IOUN stones; the magic was absorbed, as water entering a sponge.

''With no further words, not even signals of triumph—for this is how lightly they regarded me—they entered their equipage and were gone. In this region contiguous with 'Nothing,' my doom was certain—so they were assured.''

As Morreion spoke the red stones went pale; his voice quavered with passion he had not hitherto displayed.

''I stood alone,'' said Morreion hoarsely. ''I could not die, with the Spell of Untiring Nourishment upon me, but I could not move a step, not an inch from the cavity of black dust, or I would instantly have been no more than a print upon the surface of the shining field.

''I stood rigid—how long I cannot say. Years? Decades? I cannot remember. This period seems a time of dull daze. I searched my mind for resources, and I grew bold with despair. I probed for IOUN stones, and I won those which now attend me. They became my friends and gave me solace.

''I embarked then upon a new task, which, had I not been mad with despair, I would never have attempted. I brought up particles of black dust, wet them with blood to make a paste; this paste I molded into a circular plate four feet in diameter.

''It was finished. I stepped aboard; I anchored myself with the barbed pins, and I floated up and away from the half-star.

''I had won free! I stood on my disk in the void! I was free, but I was alone. You cannot know what I felt until you, too, have stood in space, without knowledge of where to go. Far away I saw a single star; a rogue, a wanderer; toward this star I fared.

''How long the voyage required, again I cannot say. When I judged that I had traveled half-way, I turned the disk about and slowed my motion.

''Of this voyage I remember little. I spoke to my stones, I gave them my thoughts. I seemed to become calm from talking, for during the first hundred years of this voyage I felt a prodigious fury that seemed to overwhelm all rational thought; to inflict but a pin prick upon a single one of my adversaries I would have died by torture a hundred times! I plotted delicious vengeance, I became yeasty and exuberant upon the imagined pain I would inflict. Then at times I suffered unutterable melancholy—while others enjoyed the good things of life, the feasts, the comradeship, the caresses of their loved ones, here stood I, alone in the dark. The balance would be restored, I assured myself. My enemies would suffer as I had suffered, and more! But the passion waned, and as my stones grew to know me they assumed their beautiful colours. Each has his name; each is individual; I know each stone by its motion. The archveults consider them the brain-eggs of fire-folk who live within these stars; as to this I cannot say.

"At last I came down upon my world. I had burned away my rage. I was calm and placid, as now you know me. My old lust for revenge I saw to be futility. I turned my mind to a new existence, and over the aeons I built my buildings and my cairns; I lived my new life.

"The Sahars excited my interest. I read their books, I learned their lore. . . . Perhaps I began to live a dream. My old life was far away; a discordant trifle to which I gave ever less importance. I am amazed that the language of Earth returned to me as readily as it has. Perhaps the stones held my knowledge in trust, and extended it as the need came. Ah, my wonderful stones, what would I be without them?

"Now I am back among men. I know how my life has gone. There are still confused areas; in due course I will remember all."

Morreion paused to consider; several of the blue and scarlet stones went quickly dim. Morreion quivered, as if touched by galvanic essence; his cropped white hair seemed to bristle. He took a slow step forward; certain of the magicians made uneasy movements.

Morreion spoke in a new voice, one less reflective and reminiscent, with a harsh grating sound somewhere at its basis. "Now I will confide in you." He turned the glitter of his black eyes upon each face in turn. "I intimated that my rage had waned with the aeons; this is true. The sobs which lacerated my throat, the gnashing which broke my teeth, the fury which caused my brain to shudder and ache: all dwindled; for I had nothing with which to feed my emotions. After bitter reflection came tragic melancholy, then at last peace, which your coming disturbed.

"A new mood has now come upon me! As the past becomes real, so I have returned along the way of the past. There is a difference. I am now a cold cautious man; perhaps I can never experience the extremes of passion which once consumed me. On the other hand, certain periods in my life are still dim." Another of the red and scarlet stones lost its vivid glow; Morreion stiffened, his voice took on a new edge. "The crimes upon my person call out for rebuttal! The archveults of Jangk must pay in the fullest and most onerous measure! Vermoulian the Dream-walker, expunge the present symbols from your mandate-wheel! Our destination now becomes the planet Jangk!"

Vermoulian looked to his colleagues to learn their opinion.

Ildefonse cleared his throat. "I suggest that our host Vermoulian first pause at Earth, to discharge those of us with urgent business.

Those others will continue with Vermoulian and Morreion to Jangk; in this way the convenience of all may be served.''

Morreion said in a voice ominously quiet: ''No business is as urgent as mine, which already has been delayed too long.'' He spoke to Vermoulian: ''Apply more fire to the speed-incense! Proceed directly to Jangk.''

Haze of Wheary Water said diffidently, ''I would be remiss if I failed to remind you that the archveults are powerful magicians; like yourself they wield IOUN stones.''

Morreion made a furious motion; as his hand swept the air, it left a trail of sparks. ''Magic derives from personal force! My passion alone will defeat the archveults! I glory in the forthcoming confrontation. Ah, but they will regret their deeds!''

''Forbearance has been termed the noblest of virtues,'' Ildefonse suggested. ''The archveults have long forgotten your very existence; your vengeance will seem an unjust and unnecessary tribulation.''

Morreion swung around his glittering black gaze. ''I reject the concept. Vermoulian, obey!''

''We fare toward Jangk,'' said Vermoulian.

12

On a marble bench between a pair of silver-fruited lime trees sat Ildefonse. Rhialto stood beside him, one elegant leg raised to the bench; a posture which displayed his rose satin cape with the white lining to dramatic advantage. They drifted through a cluster of a thousand stars; great lights passed above, below, to each side; the crystal spires of the palace gave back millions of scintillations.

Rhialto had already expressed his concern at the direction of events. Now he spoke again, more emphatically. ''It is all very well to point out that the man lacks facility; as he asserts, sheer force can overpower sophistication.''

Ildefonse said bluffly, ''Morreion's force is that of hysteria, diffuse and undirected.''

''Therein lies the danger! What if by some freak his wrath focuses upon us?''

''Bah, what then?'' demanded Ildefonse. ''Do you doubt my ability, or your own?''

''The prudent man anticipates contingencies,'' said Rhialto with dignity. ''Remember, a certain area of Morreion's life remains clouded.''

Ildefonse tugged thoughtfully at his white beard. "The aeons have altered all of us; Morreion not the least of any."

"This is the core of my meaning," said Rhialto. "I might mention that not an hour since I essayed a small experiment. Morreion walked the third balcony, watching the stars pass by. His attention being diverted, I took occasion to project a minor spell of annoyance toward him—Houlart's Visceral Pang—but with no perceptible effect. Next I attempted the diminutive version of Lugwiler's Dismal Itch, again without success. I noted, however, his IOUN stones pulsed bright as they absorbed the magic. I tried my own Green Turmoil; the stones glowed bright and this time Morreion became aware of the attention. By happy chance Byzant the Necrope passed by. Morreion put an accusation upon him, which Byzant denied. I left them engaged in contention. The instruction is this: first, Morreion's stones guard him from hostile magic; second, he is vigilant and suspicious; third, he is not one to shrug aside an offense."

Ildefonse nodded gravely. "We must certainly take these matters into consideration. I now appreciate the scope of Xexamedes' plan: he intended harm to all. But behold in the sky yonder! Is that not the constellation Elektha, seen from obverse? We are in familiar precincts once more. Kerkaju must lie close ahead, and with it that extraordinary planet Jangk."

The two strolled to the forward part of the pavilion. "You are right!" exclaimed Rhialto. He pointed. "There is Kerkaju; I recognize its scarlet empharism!"

The planet Jangk appeared: a world with a curious dull sheen.

At Morreion's direction, Vermoulian directed the palace down to Smokedancers Bluff, at the southern shore of the Quicksilver Ocean. Guarding themselves against the poisonous air, the magicians descended the marble steps and walked out on the bluff, where an inspiring vista spread before them. Monstrous Kerkaju bulged across the green sky, every pore and flocculation distinct, its simulacrum mirrored in the Quicksilver Ocean. Directly below, at the base of the bluff, quicksilver puddled and trickled across flats of black hornblende; here the Jangk 'dragoons'—purple pansy-shaped creatures six feet in diameter—grazed on tufts of moss. Somewhat to the east the town Kaleshe descended in terraces to the shore.

Morreion, standing at the edge of the bluff, inhaled the noxious vapors which blew in from the ocean, as if they were a tonic. "My memory quickens," he called out. "I remember this scene as if it were yesterday. There have been changes, true. Yonder far peak has eroded to half its height; the bluffs on which we stand have been thrust upwards at least a hundred feet. Has it been so long? While I built my cairns and pored over my books the aeons flitted past. Not to mention the unknown period I rode through space on a disk of blood and star-stuff. Let us proceed to Kaleshe; it was formerly the haunt of the archveult Persain."

"When you encounter your enemies, what then?" asked Rhialto. "Are your spells prepared and ready?"

"What need I for spells?" grated Morreion. "Behold!" He pointed his finger; a flicker of emotion spurted forth to shatter a boulder. He clenched his fists; the constricted passion crackled as if he had crumpled stiff parchment. He strode off toward Kaleshe, the magicians trooping behind.

The Kalsh had seen the palace descend; a number had gathered at the top of the bluff. Like the archveults they were sheathed in pale blue scales. Osmium cords constricted the black plumes of the men; the feathery green plumes of the women, however, waved and swayed as they walked. All stood seven feet tall, and were slim as lizards.

Morreion halted. "Persain, stand forth!" he called.

One of the men spoke: "There is no Persain at Kaleshe."

"What? No archveult Persain?"

"None of this name. The local archveult is a certain Evorix, who departed in haste at the sight of your peregrine palace."

"Who keeps the town records?"

Another Kalsh stepped forth. "I am that functionary."

"Are you acquainted with Persain the archveult?"

"I know by repute a Persain who was swallowed by a harpy toward the end of the 21st Aeon."

Morreion uttered a groan. "Has he evaded me? What of Xexamedes?"

"He is gone from Jangk; no one knows where."

"Djorin?"

"He lives, but keeps to a pink pearl castle across the ocean."

"Aha! What of Ospro?"

"Dead."

Morreion gave another abysmal groan. "Vexel?"

"Dead."

Morreion groaned once more. Name by name he ran down the roster of his enemies. Four only survived.

When Morreion turned about his face had become haunted and haggard; he seemed not to see the magicians of Earth. All of his scarlet and blue stones had given up their colour. "Four only," he muttered. "Four only to receive the charge of all my force. . . . Not enough, not enough! So many have won free! Not enough, not enough! The balance must adjust!'' He made a brusque gesture. ''Come! To the castle of Djorin!''

In the palace they drifted across the ocean while the great red globe of Kerkaju kept pace above and below. Cliffs of mottled quartz and cinnabar rose ahead; on a crag jutting over the ocean stood a castle in the shape of a great pink pearl.

The peregrine palace settled upon a level area; Morreion leapt down the steps and advanced toward the castle. A circular door of solid osmium rolled back; an archveult nine feet tall, with black plumes waving three feet over his head, came forth.

Morreion called, ''Send forth Djorin; I have dealings with him.''

''Djorin is within! We have had a presentiment! You are the land-ape Morreion, from the far past. Be warned; we are prepared for you.''

''Djorin!'' called Morreion. ''Come forth!''

''Djorin will not come forth,'' stated the archveult, ''nor will Arvianid, Ifhix, Herclamon, or the other archveults of Jangk who have come to combine their power against yours. If you seek vengeance, turn upon the real culprits; do not annoy us with your peevish complaints.'' The archveult returned within and the osmium door rolled shut.

Morreion stood stock-still. Mune the Mage came forward, and stated: ''I will winkle them out, with Houlart's Blue Extractive.'' He hurled the spell toward the castle, to no effect. Rhialto attempted a spell of brain pullulations, but the magic was absorbed; Gilgad next brought down his Instantaneous Galvanic Thrust, which spattered harmlessly off the glossy pink surface.

''Useless,'' said Ildefonse. ''Their IOUN stones absorb the magic.''

The archveults in their turn became active. Three ports opened; three spells simultaneously issued forth, to be intercepted by Morreion's IOUN stones, which momentarily pulsed the brighter.

Morreion stepped three paces forward. He pointed his finger; force struck at the osmium door. It creaked and rattled, but held firm.

Morreion pointed his finger at the fragile pink nacre; the force slid away and was wasted.

Morreion pointed at the stone posts which supported the castle. They burst apart. The castle lurched, rolled over and down the crags. It bounced from jut to jut, smashing and shattering, and splashed into the Quicksilver Ocean, where a current caught it and carried it out to sea. Through rents in the nacre the archveults crawled forth, to clamber to the top. More followed, until their accumulated weight rolled the pearl over, throwing all on top into the quicksilver sea, where they sank as deep as their thighs. Some tried to walk and leap to the shore, others lay flat on their backs and sculled with their hands. A gust of wind caught the pink bubble and sent it rolling across the sea, tossing off archveults as a turning wheel flings away drops of water. A band of Jangk harpies put out from the shore to envelop and devour the archveults closest at hand; the others allowed themselves to drift on the current and out to sea, where they were lost to view.

Morreion turned slowly toward the magicians of Earth. His face was gray. "A fiasco," he muttered. "It is nothing."

Slowly he walked toward the palace. At the steps he stopped short. "What did they mean: 'The real culprits'?"

"A figure of speech," replied Ildefonse. "Come up on the pavilion; we will refresh ourselves with wine. At last your vengeance is complete. And now . . ." His voice died as Morreion climbed the steps. One of the bright blue stones lost its colour. Morreion stiffened as if at a twinge of pain. He swung around to look from magician to magician. "I remember a certain face: a man with a bald head; black beardlets hung from each of his cheeks. He was a burly man. . . . What was his name?"

"These events are far in the past," said the diabolist Shrue. "Best to put them out of mind."

Other blue stones became dull: Morreion's eyes seemed to assume the light they had lost.

"The archveults came to Earth. We conquered them. They begged for their lives. So much I recall. . . . The chief magician demanded the secret of the IOUN stones. Ah! What was his name? He had a habit of pulling on his black beardlets. . . . A handsome man, a great popinjay—I almost see his face—he made a proposal to the chief magician. Ah! Now it begins to come clear!" The blue stones faded one by one. Morreion's face shone with a white fire. The last of the blue stones went pallid.

Morreion spoke in a soft voice, a delicate voice, as if he savored each word. "The chief magician's name was Ildefonse. The popinjay was Rhialto. I remember each detail. Rhialto proposed that I go to learn the secret; Ildefonse vowed to protect me, as if I were his own life. I trusted them; I trusted all the magicians in the chamber: Gilgad was there, and Hurtiancz and Mune the Mage and Perdustin. All my dear friends, who joined in a solemn vow to make the archveults hostage for my safety. Now I know the culprits. The archveults dealt with me as an enemy. My friends sent me forth and never thought of me again. Ildefonse—what have you to say, before you go to wait out twenty aeons in a certain place of which I know?''

Ildefonse said bluffly, ''Come now, you must not take matters so seriously. All's well that ends well; we are now happily reunited and the secret of the IOUN stones is ours!''

''For each pang I suffered, you shall suffer twenty,'' said Morreion. ''Rhialto as well, and Gilgad, and Mune, and Herark and all the rest. Vermoulian, lift the palace. Return us the way we have come. Put double fire to the incense.''

Rhialto looked at Ildefonse, who shrugged.

''Unavoidable.'' said Rhialto. He evoked the Spell of Temporal Stasis. Silence fell upon the scene. Each person stood like a monument.

Rhialto bound Morreion's arms to his side with swaths of tape. He strapped Morreion's ankles together, and wrapped bandages into Morreion's mouth, to prevent him uttering a sound. He found a net and, capturing the IOUN stones, drew them down about Morreion's head, in close contact with his scalp. As an afterthought he taped a blindfold over Morreion's eyes.

He could do no more. He dissolved the spell. Ildefonse was already walking across the pavilion. Morreion jerked and thrashed in disbelief. Ildefonse and Rhialto lowered him to the marble floor.

''Vermoulian,'' said Ildefonse, ''be so good as to call forth your staff. Have them bring a trundle and convey Morreion to a dark room. He must rest for a spell.''

13

Rhialto found his manse as he had left it, with the exception of the way-post, which was complete. Well satisfied, Rhialto went into one of his back rooms. Here he broke open a hole into subspace and placed therein the netful of IOUN stones which he carried. Some gleamed incandescent blue; others were mingled scarlet and blue; the rest shone deep red, pink, pink and green, pale green and pale lavender.

Rhialto shook his head ruefully and closed the dimension down upon the stones. Returning to his work-room he located Puiras among the Minuscules and restored him to size.

''Once and for all, Puiras, I find that I no longer need your services. You may join the Minuscules, or you may take your pay and go.''

Puiras gave a roar of protest. ''I worked my fingers to the bone; is this all the thanks I get?''

"I do not care to argue with you; in fact, I have already engaged your replacement."

Puiras eyed the tall vague-eyed man who had wandered into the work-room. "Is this the fellow? I wish him luck. Give me my money; and none of your magic gold, which goes to sand!"

Puiras took his money and went his way. Rhialto spoke to the new servitor. "For your first task, you may clear up the wreckage of the aviary. If you find corpses, drag them to the side; I will presently dispose of them. Next, the tile of the great hall. . . ."